D1067430

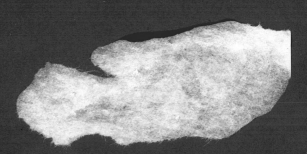

CZAR!

A Novel of Ivan the Terrible

CZAR!
A Novel of Ivan the Terrible

BY

Larry Townsend

L. T. Publications
Los Angeles

With special thanks to:
Jerry Martz,
Victor Terry,
Rick Leathers,
who edited, proofed and advised
And to Fred, who lived with Ivan
for all these years.

Published by L. T. Publications
Los Angeles, CA

This is a first edition, hard cover book.
Cover art by Jame´

For mail order and other information, contact:
L. T. Publications
P. O. Box 302
Beverly Hills, CA 90213
E–mail: ltpub@telcen.com

ISBN: 1–881684–16–4

PREFACE

The story of Prince Dmitri Simeonevitch Marensky is also the story of Ivan IV, or Ivan the Terrible. The fictional relationship between these two men forms the basis for our tale, with legitimate history as the background. Dmitri reflects the barbaric superstitions of his time in the blind loyalty he lays upon the being of his Caesar. Refusing to acknowledge the growing madness of the Czar, he watches it progress through the accelerating phases of manic–depression in the early years, until it acquires the dreadful paranoid overtones resulting in the *Opritchina* and eventually in Ivan's ultimate crime of filicide.

The greatest problem in presenting this story was to provide the reader with the background necessary to understand all that came to pass, without subjecting him to a constant barrage of superfluous historical data. Following the example of the immortal Robert Graves, I have attempted to define the essential background and structure of the royal descent in the early portions of Book One. Because Ivan's reign lasted for fifty–one years, his story is not quickly told. As Ivan the Good he was one of history's greatest conquerors; as *Ivan Grozny* he was one of the most unrestrained tyrants of all time. Although the number of his victims may pale in comparison to other men in other eras – including such villains as Stalin and Mao who had the benefit of more modern methods of mass murder – Ivan performed his rites with a personal élan, and sometimes with his own hands. In this sense, his tally should more properly be compared with our latter–day serial killers than the national leaders who simply ordered the deaths of millions without ever staining their own hands with blood.

Russia was Christian, as the Second Rome of Byzantium was Christian. Men believed in the spirit of Christ and the one God; yet underneath these beliefs there remained an older faith and unnamed dread, the illogical fear of the unknown and reliance on mysticism neither they nor their Church could explain. While claiming the status of being the Third Rome, these Russian Caesars never claimed the divine descent of Augustus or Nero. But much of this mystic power was ascribed to them by their people; they were anointed with holy oil, and became endowed with a certain aura of godliness no other could possess.

Dmitri, in some respects, represents his time – being a man whose feet were rooted in these barbaric and mystic beliefs left over from his cultural past. At the same time, his hands reached upward for the golden apple of wisdom and civilization represented by the knowledge and skills of the West. If we can see some parallel to our own time in this, we may ascribe it to our own failures in achieving an age of absolute civilization and reason. As we look back on Dmitri's time, so future generations will look back on us, evaluating our era as but a short step further than Dmitri's along the path between the beasts from which we evolved and the apex of humanity we have yet to reach.

As to the specifics in our story: Of the main characters, all are interpretations of reality with the following notable exceptions: Dmitri and his mother, Eleanor; the kennelmaster Ivor; Dmitri's wife, Nina and his fictional servant Toby. Several secondary characters are also fictional: Abraham, Jacob, Serge, Lilly, Lotus Flower, Illya. The rest are characterizations of people who really lived, and in most cases these are much as the archives describe them. The greatest liberties I have taken were with Heinrich von Staden, whom history notes as a profligate villain not present in the Russian court prior to the time of Dmitri's last journal, and with Ediger, or Simon of Tver, whose character represents a composite of two real–life men.

In essence, the history is sound, the greatest deviations being errors one might expect of an old man attempting to write his life story from memory. Admittedly, a few historical sequences have been altered to fit the tale; and if Dmitri exaggerates a bit, or seems a little melodramatic in moments of high emotion, what Russian of his period would not? The scenes of death and terror are dramatizations of history's descriptions or implications. In these, Dmitri seems to have been quite accurate, if anything a little reticent. His assessment of his own descent into the abyss of sin and degradation can only be cast into religious terminology, since his age lacked the more profound insights of Freud and his successors.

Another difficulty was to translate the words of a man who wrote in an age long past, and with a culture unknown to the average Western reader. The curse of the classic Russian name form has been largely eliminated, and a good many first names have been Anglicized or Germanized to facilitate the reader's ease. This may offend the purist, the disciples of Dostoyevsky and Tolstoy, but I cannot hope to compete with these idols of the past and thus have foregone the temptation to emulate them. I have presented the story in contemporary idiom – even to the use of temporal and linear measurements which are somewhat anarchic – making the story read as Dmitri would most probably have expressed himself were he to have written today. I have also included a glossary of terms at the end of the book. I hope these efforts have culminated in an enjoyable glimpse of a time long past, and have permitted the contemplation of an age even more brutal than our own.

Larry Townsend, West Hollywood 1996

BOOK ONE

The Orphan

CHAPTER I

They question me, even my own sons, asking how many men have perished at my hands. What tortures did I employ? How long could I keep a man alive, conscious, and in some ultimate agony? Then they submit a liturgy of techniques and methods, asking if I knew of them, if I had ever seen them practiced. In the end, however, it always comes down to some final question regarding the Czar. Was it he, they ask, who designed the machines and the methodology by which so many suffered and perished? Was I present when such–and–such a devise was invisioned? Did Ivan command me to use it? How did it function? Was it as effective in actual use as in its conception?

I wonder now at the perfidity of a man who asks such questions in a tone of condemnation, while his eyes can not quite mask the lust within his soul or prevent the quickening of his pulse, nor the rigid lust from rising in his groin. Even within my hearing, they indict the Czar as a monster, a murderer, a maniac who lived only to torture and to maim, and whose very existence cast a shameful shadow upon mankind. They make only slightly less damning accusations of me when they think I cannot hear them, and are confident that their words will not be repeated back to me. At least where their voices can reach my ears their accusations are less shrill, for even now in the nadir of my physical prowess they fear me. It is as if they sense a hovering spirit of evil still lingering about my head. Perhaps they think of me as some master of witchcraft who has only to shout a protest and a terrible misfortune will befall any who arouse my anger.

So be it. While I enjoy whatever grace these fears bestow, and while my mind is still lucid, I will set down a true account of all that transpired – all that I can remember, for no one else is left alive to help or dispute me. In doing this, I will confess my own sins – even those which no man might otherwise suspect, for this will help confirm my truthfulness. And I will tell the story of the Czar, for his life and mine were inextricably intertwined. Whatever sins may be ascribed to me can only be understood as they relate to the needs and commands of the man who was both my friend and master.

In order that one may understand the tangled threads of our later lives, it is necessary that I explain how it began, for I was ever a servant of the Czar, even in my infancy. I do not seek to ameliorate my own transgressions by hiding behind a facade of duty and obedience. Yet, most of the sins I committed were done in the honest belief that by committing them I also served the Majesty of Russia – the state just slightly less than the Czar, himself. This is a fine distinction that men in the West are only now beginning to make; yet for me I think it matters little. I served, and I sinned. God alone can assign my eventual punishment or reward.

The events of one's childhood must form the framework upon which his soul gradually develops. I think this no less true for kings and emperors than for men of lesser rank. I believe that most of the Czar's anger and suspicion grew out of those youthful years when he was too young and too politically weak to defend himself. When Ivan was left an orphan, he fell prey to the greed of men who were quick to forsake their oaths of fealty. As a man, he never forgot, or forgave.

Ivan was the first to demand his proper titles and to enforce his claim to them. Thus, he was not born as the Son of Caesar. His father was Basil, Grand Duke of Muscovy, who claimed direct descent from Ghengis Khan. His mother was Helena Glinskaya, daughter of an emigre from Lithuania who could also claim royal Mongolian descent – from Khan Mamay of the Golden Horde. The title of Caesar – Czar in our language – should rightfully have devolved on the father, for Moscow had every legal claim to the mantle of Byzantium, last bastion of the Eastern Roman Empire. Only in our realm did the legitimate Orthodox Faith flourish as the state religion, and the imperial blood of this Second Rome flowed through the veins of no other ruling monarch. But Basil never felt himself quite strong enough to assume the rank that was properly his, and only in moments of patriotic passion was he hailed as "Czar" by his subjects.

Basil died when Ivan was three years old, and on his deathbed he entrusted the regency to his widow, Helena. Ancient and outmoded custom would have directed the succession to the Grand Duke's eldest surviving brother; but the oaths to Helena were demanded and received before Basil's soul was claimed by the Angel of Death. On his final passing, his son became Ivan IV, Grand Duke of Muscovy, heir to this and to all the other titles achieved or held by the father.

I cannot testify from first–hand knowledge as to all that happened over the next few years, because I was too young to be aware of them. Nor has my mother, who recounted the tales to me many times, always been as accurate as I might have wished. Still, I must depend on her version for much of the story. She certainly had every opportunity to hear the court gossip and to observe every instance inside Basil's palace. Her vantage point was decidedly intimate.

When the Glinski family fled from Lithuania, my mother Eleanor and her husband Simon von Marienburg came with them. Mother had always been a close friend of Helena's, and in the Muscovite court she assumed a position which would be akin to "lady–in–waiting" in the West. Of course, Russian women are sequestered in the *terem*, and are not permitted to make the vulgar displays that their sisters do in other countries. Despite these restrictions, Helena was able to attract the eye of the Grand Duke during the latter's frequent visits to the Glinski estate. This was a very fine *dacha* in the Sparrow Hills, across the river from the Kremlin, which Basil had given to the family during the secret negotiations prior to their emigration.

Basil, who was considerably older than Helena, had been married for some twenty years to an aging shrew named Salome – a dreadful woman by all reports, and one who had never been able to bear her husband an heir. As sometimes happens, even to those of highest rank and morals, the Grand Duke became so enamored of this Lithuanian beauty that he ignored all the warnings and prophesies in his desire to have her. He placed Salome in a nunnery and declared himself free to marry – this against the sternest injunctions of the Church, but apparently through the connivance of the Metropolitan Daniel. He shaved his beard to make himself appear younger, thereby committing a mortal sin and bringing forth a veritable stream of ascetics who predicted a series of misfortunes, including the birth of an evil son. None of this dissuaded Basil. He married Helena in a grand court ceremony at which the Metropolitan officiated. Ivan was born less than ten months later. This would have been in the Year 7035 by the Russian calendar, or the Year of Our Lord 1526 by western computation.

It is here that the story becomes less certain, and I have had cause to question my mother's account. Two years after Ivan's birth, Helena was *enceinte* for a second time, carrying Yuri. During her confinement, it was only natural for Basil to grow restless and to seek elsewhere for companionship. As my mother's husband Simon had been slain in an encounter with the Tartars a few months earlier, it was rumored that Helena personally saw to Basil's being consoled within the walls of his own *terem*. Whether this was true or not is a matter of conjecture, but a great many people seemed to believe it. Add the fact that by this time the Grand Duchess had acquired a lover, and the possibilities are considerably lengthened. My own birth was said to have resulted from one of these liaisons. But which one? At the appropriate points in my narrative I will tell what I know, and what I have been told, for – in truth – I have never been certain of my father's identity. Fortunately for my family and myself, I was presumed by most people to be the bastard son of Basil, thus Ivan's brother.

According to my mother – and, again, I have only her word for it – Helena conspired with her to have my birth recorded in the Kremlin archives, as if I had been born the son of Simon. But they coined a Russian surname for me. Simon, in his youth, had been adopted by old Prince Pytor Demetrovich Marensky of the Kiev line, although my supposed father Simon had never actually used the name. Still, he would have been entitled to do so, had he wished. While the title of Prince would not have conferred boyar status, due to its being a Lithuanian barony, it would surely have been disputed. However, the old man had no sons of his own, and his death left the princely title vacant. Thus my birth is recorded: Dmitri Simeonevitch Marensky. Beyond this single act of friendship rendered my mother, Helena seemed quite indifferent to the circumstances of my birth. Following Basil's death, she became the most powerful person, male or female, in the entire region east of Poland and north of the Sultan's Turkish Empire. Her official duties, in addition to her personal activities, kept her sufficiently occupied. She had no time to waste on thoughts of me.

Helena's situation was doomed to failure from the start. All other circumstances not withstanding, she was still a woman in a land where women were little more than chattel. She was also a foreigner. Conditions within the palace became very uncomfortable, and in the end a dreadful terror lurked behind every door. A vicious series of encounters took place among the boyars, the barons of the realm. Although Ivan was the rightful heir, and all of these men had sworn a holy oath to protect him, it was impossible for Helena to maintain control without playing one group of nobles against another. As long as two or three of the strongest took her side, none of the others could muster the strength to unseat her. Of all Basil's court, however, the only loyal, devoted support came from the elderly Metropolitan Daniel. He was a determined, uncompromising little man, who strongly condemned any boyar he felt acted contrary to the vows taken at Basil's bedside. All had kissed the sacred cross, he warned them, and all had sworn fealty to Ivan. Those who failed to remember were endangering their very souls.

With Daniel's backing, Helena might have survived her ordeal, as there were several princes and boyars whose advantage lay with her cause. One of these was Prince Feodor Vorontsof, a distant cousin of my mother's. He is one of the few people I can remember with any clarity from this period, although this is probably due to later impressions. The real trouble arose when Helena openly acknowledged her relationship with Basil's former master-of-the-horse, Prince Ivan Ovchina Telepnef Obolenski, of the Nizhni Novgorod line. By reputation, he was accounted the most handsome man ever to grace the Russian court, endowed with every superb physical attribute that nature could bestow. As if some capricious effort had been expended to balance the scales, however, the Creator had denied the prince an equally brilliant mind. Stupidity and pride combined to bring about his end – possibly the end of the regency itself.

I would not dwell long on an account of a man who was dead and gone before I was old enough to remember him, except that his presence has added another facet to the confused circumstances surrounding my own origins. I have been told that in my youth I very much resembled the unfortunate prince. Thus my birth may have been tainted with a greater fraud than simple bastardy. I bear the name of a man who died too soon to have been my sire, and I have lived as the presumed half brother of the Czar. In actuality, I may have been no more than the off spring of a casual affair between two young and passionate sinners. It is a question I can never resolve, for my status as Ivan's brother was too valuable an asset to be denied. I have often wondered, though, how different my life might have been had something happened to alter the Regent's belief that I was the son of Basil. The ties of friendship might have been more greatly strained by jealousy over a captured lover – should such have been the case – than was ever likely concerning the affection of an elderly husband. Fortunately, Helena had long been in her grave before the questionable stamp of Obolenski began to appear upon my features. By then, through a series of careful manipulations, my mother had assured Ivan's acceptance of me as his kinsman.

Obolenski died of starvation in a prison cell, placed there through the manipulations of the two major competing families within the court: the Shuiskys and the Bielskys. Helena died a short while later, some say by poison, although my mother has always insisted it was from eating tainted fish. I know only that there were some who claimed my mother had been responsible for administering a fatal potion, and that for several months we were forced to live in a dreadful hovel in the Arbat, the outer section of Moscow. We might well have died there, had it not been for Feodor, who somehow arranged for us to take up residence in his *dacha*, located among the boyar homes inside the Kremlin walls.

Once installed in the home of Feodor Vorontsof, Mother and I enjoyed a degree of safety, as he was allied to the Bielsky family, and the balance of power placed him in a more or less inviolable position. Gradually, probably through some maneuverings by my mother of which I was never fully aware, I was pushed into an increasingly regular contact with Yuri, Ivan's younger brother. As we were age mates, the association was natural. Also, as Mother surely intended, my visits to one brother placed me in frequent contact with both. At this time, each prince was fairly free to come and go as he would, although restricted to the palace grounds. Neither was old enough to account for anything in the running of the state, and except for those few occasions when Ivan was needed to participate in some ceremony or reception, they were mostly ignored. Mother was on friendly terms with Ivan's nurse, however, for she was the sister of Obolenski. This made it easy for her to insinuate me into association with the two brothers.

Vassily Shuisky acted as regent, with the tacit consent of the other boyars. He was an older, gray–haired man as I remember him, sly and rapacious as a wolf. Those who did not support his faction were afraid of him, or at least not strong enough to unseat him, although Feodor's house was the frequent meeting place for those who wished to do exactly that. I can also remember, during the earliest days of our living with Feodor, that Vassily's younger brother John had visited a number of times. Following a heated dispute between themselves, John and Feodor ceased any association whatever. Mother was somehow involved in this, though again I cannot say how. As a woman, she should have been nothing.

Despite all the political struggles, and even the occasional violence, the functions of the government continued. Beneath the surface, from their various offices within the Kremlin, the many bureaus – or *prikaz* – continued to operate. While the man in power was able to replace the heads of these bureaus, the clerks seldom changed. The usual routine of running the state went on, disregarding the activities of the mighty. There were a great many of these *prikaz*, most of them having been created by Basil or his father, Ivan the Great. They included everything from the Bureau for Entertainment of Ambassadors and the Bureau of Secret Affairs to the the offices that handled palace routine and amusement. These latter were of lesser importance and concerned themselves with running the royal kennels or stables. There was even a Bureau of Hawk Tenders. Typical of such organizations in any government, they would survive regardless of who called himself Règent.

The places where the effects of Shuisky misrule fell most strongly were among the merchants and landlords. These men suddenly found themselves burdened with scores of new taxes. Indirectly, this affected us all, forcing up the prices of fuel, food, and clothing. But no one understood these relationships very well; such lessons were only to be learned in the years to come. The strongest popular objections at this time resulted from the unfair laws the Shuiskys imposed to protect their trading interests at the expense of all the other merchants.

Gradually, a powerful opposing faction developed to confront Vassily and his Novgorod allies. Johannes Bielsky became the recognized leader, although Feodor and his friends were just as active. Another important boyar whom both groups sought was Alexi Basmanov, a great bear of a man, too stupid to comprehend all the intrigue. Still, his family represented enormous wealth, and his voice meant something about the Kremlin. Physically, he was a man to be feared, for his strength was tremendous. Unfortunately, he tended to side with the Shuiskys, simply because Vassily had more patience with him. The old wolf flattered Alexi, and explained everything he wished the other to know. Eventually, even this unimaginative man came into conflict with the Shuiskys, but that was later.

The great pride men take in their families and in the honor attached to the names of ancestors contributed to the bitterness of these continuing struggles. The greatest family, of course, was that of Staritsky. It included Ivan, as well as his cousin Vladimir. They were descendants of Rurik, the ancient Norse ruler of Great Novgorod. Rurik had been asked to come into the Land of Rus during a time of chaos, to organize the state and rule the people. That was at least six hundred years ago, although I do not think anyone knows exactly when.

Mixed with the sacred blood of Rurik was another, which only Vladimir shared with the sons of Basil. This was the imperial inheritance of Byzantium, and Rome itself. Basil was the son of Ivan III, properly called "the Great," who was a Staritsky of the House of Rurik. His Duchess was Sophia Paleologus, the niece of Constantine XI, last Emperor of Byzantium. Although this woman, our grandmother, seems to be remembered for little more than regal blood, it was this regal blood that gave foundation to Ivan's later demand for recognition as the last heir of Rome. The Shuiskys, having none of this proud nobility, cared nothing for such refinements as instituted during the reign of Ivan III. Instead, they allowed the court to drop back into the old ways of our barbaric ancestors.

There were many other powerful families, some of them also descended from Rurik: the Vorotinskys, Mstislavskys, Morozofs – great warrior clans who formerly commanded our armies when we fought the infidels. But most of these men remained away from the politics of the Kremlin, I suppose because of their being afraid of choosing the wrong side. Later, many claimed to have remained alert to protect Ivan's rights, never committing themselves as they believed all who struggled for power to have been evil men. I could never believe this, and neither could Ivan.

Because of this indifference on the part of so many wealthy and powerful boyars, Ivan and Yuri nearly starved. Ivan's nurse was sent home to Nizhni Novgorod, leaving the princes with no proper servants. Vassily soon began restricting them to their own part of the palace, especially when there were foreigners in the capital. Although on these occasions, Ivan would sometimes be dressed in his fine robes and put on display for the visitors, he would always be returned to close custody afterward. Unable to leave their apartments, the two boys were frequently forgotten and left without food for days at a time. There may have been others who knew and were disturbed about this, but none dared show his concern.

Mother and Feodor were the ones who offered help, doing this for a variety of reasons, perhaps. The two of them would pack up large slices of meat and cheese, wrapping these with bread. The parcel would be tied about my waist, beneath my clothing. Because no one paid any attention to me, I could usually pass in and out of the palace, seldom failing to deliver the food to the princes. Naturally, such a messenger was greeted with extreme pleasure by both boys, and it was thus I first found favor in Ivan's heart. He would speak to me, telling me the things he dreamed of doing, comparing himself with the great rulers of the past. He was hungry for more than food.

Even at this age – at this time Ivan must have been ten, possibly eleven years old – his mind was casting about for new knowledge, for answers to the many questions he was able to formulate during the long hours of boredom and inactivity. He read everything he could get, having books smuggled into him by palace servants, sometimes at the expense of the food they might have brought instead. He also played chess, teaching me the game and playing with me for many hours because there was no one else. I seldom won, for I was even younger than Ivan – seven perhaps, or eight. It is difficult now to remember exactly. I know that I eventually developed the skill to give him a fairly good game—better, certainly, than poor Yuri, who never progressed beyond the beginner's stage. A little later, Feodor also began to visit the princes.

Vassily would probably have liked to prevent these visits by a potentially hostile boyar, but there was nothing he could do. There had been questions raised in many quarters, and rumors were circulating to the effect that Ivan was dead. The Shuiskys had to permit men from factions other than their own to see him from time to time. I am certain that Feodor's visits had been contrived as part of a Bielsky plot, as the Vorontsof family was as noble and distinguished as any. Short of open swordplay, there was no way for Shuisky to prevent his coming.

I could see that Ivan had come to admire Feodor greatly, as he indicated to me several times, mentioning the similarities of their family backgrounds. The Vorontsofs were also descended from a Norwegian prince, Shimon Afrikanovich. The clan had branches in Kiev and Yaroslavl, as well as Lithuania. Feodor personally controlled large estates to the northeast, but preferred to leave his brother to manage the land while he spent most of his time in Moscow. If Ivan had been just a little older, he might have rendered Feodor a great service. Shuisky may have been able to look ahead to a time when it would happen. With the predominantly Germanic background of his family, Feodor was strongly supported by The Teutonic Knights of the Hanseatic League, who competed in trade against the Order of Livonian Sword Bearers and the old Knights of the Golden Fleece. Both of these groups sought to absorb traditional trade rights held by the Vorontsof family. Ivan would have set this right, but Vassily refused. His interests lay with the other side.

Most of the discussions between Ivan and Feodor centered around their ideas for getting rid of the Shuiskys, even if it meant replacing Vassily with Johannes Bielsky. Although Ivan had his doubts about Johannes, he believed the man could be more easily manipulated than Vassily, especially as his power would partially depend on Vorontsof support. And Ivan was confident of Feodor's loyalty.

As was true of many political groupings during this time, a regency based on an alliance between the families of Bielsky and Vorontsof would be a strange mating of forces. Previously, they had never been especially friendly. The Bielskys were descended from Grand Prince Ol'gerd of Lithuania, and Johannes was the great great grandson of this legendary hero, through the line of Jagiello. This made him related by blood to the present King of Poland. With the diverse histories of the two families, there had been many times when the respective clans had stood on opposite sides in battle. This type of interfamilial hatred was common among the boyars, although they were often forgotten for political expediency – but only for political expediency, a fact that became deeply embedded in Ivan's mind. The terrible dread he was forced to endure, during these years of his childhood, later gave birth to a bitter, lifelong hatred.

While still a boy at this time, Ivan was on the verge of manhood. His voice broke when he tried to shout, and straggly hairs had started to grow on his chin. He was not exactly handsome, but he already showed promise of the imposing figure he would attain as a man. His blue–gray eyes were penetrating when he spoke with intensity. His nose was beaked, but not overly large for his face. He was lean, his body hard with sinew and strongly corded muscles. His hair was a blaze of red, and he had yet to start shaving his head. By the time he did this, his beard was a great mass of the same color. It was the expression of his eyes, I think, that most characterized him. Like his fingers, they were never still. Living as he did in constant fear, he began forming habits of temperament and ferocity I later saw become his dominant traits. But with all of this, a factor which most people failed to understand, he possessed a driving urge to further the greatness of his realm and to see Orthodox Christianity spread into the far reaches of the world.

When Feodor discussed with him the moves they must make to rid themselves of the Shuisky oppression I could see Ivan tense with anger. It humiliated him to be forced into a position where he must plot and plan to obtain a status that was his by right of birth. I remember one day when we were awaiting Feodor's arrival Ivan had expressed himself with particular vehemence, driving himself into a state of anger before my kinsman arrived with news of additional Shuisky retainers having arrived in the Kremlin. At this Ivan's anger turned to an agitated fear, and the two of them discussed the situation in whispered tones, although there was no one around to overhear them. I was so upset to see Ivan's depression and terror I spoke up, interrupting them.

"As long as you stay alive, Ivashka," I said, "that is the important thing. One day we'll all be men, and your time will come!"

"*I shall live!*" he muttered fiercely. "But I have to gain my birthright before the boyars destroy everything my father and his father have built. I want to start from where they left off, not be forced to retrace the steps of past generations." His eyes blazed with determination, and while I was too young to appreciate all it implied, I was impressed with a sense of destiny.

"We must still tread with care," added Feodor. He spoke softly, with a dignity borne of greater maturity. He was nineteen or twenty at the time.

Ivan nodded sagely. Beneath his strength and determination there must always be caution. "I don't want to live like my great–grandfather," he muttered, "blinded by his treacherous boyars and forced to rule in darkness."

"If we move too soon," said Feodor, "it could find us all in a dungeon."

They talked for some time, planning the actions they must take, discussing which men were to be trusted, which were not. Yuri and I played draughts on the floor, our comments not desired.

Sessions similar to this went on each time Ivan and Feodor came together, and because I was not a participant it is difficult to fit together the pieces of their intrigues. I do know that the Grand Master of the Hanseatic League came to Moscow during the summer, and that Feodor's *dacha* always had a number of these knights in residence. I also knew that Johannes Bielsky was maneuvering himself into a position of greater power, until he eventually became a serious threat to the Shuiskys. Johannes had apparently been in prison during Helena's regency, but had somehow been released. Again I am guessing at the time, but I presume this happened shortly after Helena's death, possibly as a result of some general amnesty proclaimed by Vassily to gain support from a variety of dissidents.

Obviously, in trying to describe these events, I find myself struggling to reconcile the facts as I later learned them, with the distorted impressions I received through my child's eyes. Much of the intrigue, however, was conducted so openly it would be considered less than secret by any but a Russian. It is part of our nature to be boastful, and Johannes's actions were certainly this. His constant bluster was never hidden, not even from myself and the other palace children. I knew, for instance, of his open approach to the Kurbsky family, although it was only later that I could understand the words spoken on each side. The Kurbsky rejection of him was also quite public.

"Although we support the Grand Duke in all he may do," was the reply, "we do not feel justified in disrupting the existing status of the Regency. Doing so could bring on civil war, from which neither the Grand Duke nor any other worthy Christian man could benefit."

While I am uncertain of my own age during some of the various episodes I have described, I know for certain that I was nine when this happened. Feodor had given me a pony for my birthday, and it was shortly afterward that the furor resulting from the Kurbsky statement forced Vassily's hand. Johannes had finally frightened him enough to bring retribution upon himself. He was arrested the same night, and for several days afterward the Kremlin became a scene of chaotic infighting.

The next day dawned very bleak and cold. Snow was piled high about the Kremlin courts, with narrow footpaths cut through the older drifts, now rapidly being refilled by a fresh cascade of white. From our front windows I watched the flakes fall in a distorted pattern as the mica panes made them appear to twist and alter shape. I could barely see the palace in the distance, framed by the walls of two houses standing closer to the imperial residence than ours. I watched a figure emerge from that direction, and as he drew closer I recognized Feodor, who had been out since early that morning. Our kinsman raced across the open courtyards, stumbling in the drifts and kicking up sprays of ice granules. I realized, suddenly, that he was badly frightened, glancing back repeatedly as he ran, and hammering desperately on the door as soon as he reached it.

Because his knock was so urgent, Mother answered herself. It was close to midday, so she had been sitting in the front room with Sonya, one of her young attendants, doing needle work and making idle chatter. It was warmer downstairs than in the *terem* rooms, above, giving Mother the excuse to stay below.

Vorontsof stumbled inside as soon as Mother opened the door. She shoved it closed hastily, as a mass of snow swirled in behind him. "Johannes has been arrested!" he gasped after a moment's struggle to catch his breath. He shook his head and scooped bits of snow from inside his collar. More small tufts of powdery white fell from his beard and hat.

My mother's face turned as pale as the small patches, now melting on the inlaid wooden floor. She helped Feodor shed his heavy coat, which a servant woman came to carry away. Seeming to make one of her usual quick recoveries from shock, Mother led the gasping boyar into the salon as her friend retreated upstairs to the women's quarters. I trailed behind my mother and pulled up an ottoman for Feodor's feet as she settled him into a chair.

"Has anyone else been arrested?" she asked.

"Not that I know of." His voice was calmer, now, and his eyes began to focus again. "Still, I don't know how far it's going."

"And Ivan?" she asked. "Is he under extra guard?"

"I couldn't get in, but I don't think there have been any particular moves to secure him." Vorontsof looked down at me, seemingly aware of my presence for the first time. "Dmitri, do you think you could get into the palace without calling attention to yourself?"

I nodded, although the fright exhibited by my elders was affecting me as well. I went to the palace nearly every day, so regularly in fact that no one ever paid me any mind. At the moment, I experienced a peculiar mixture of emotions, wanting to be near the scene of action, also being fearful of the consequences. I was to endure this many more times in my life, and then as later it was actually curiosity which won. Fortunately, most people perceived it as bravery.

Mother started to say something, probably that she didn't want me to go. But they had to know what was happening, and it was far less dangerous for me than for anyone else. Whenever a purge took place, the younger men always drank more heavily than usual, resulting in a ravaging pack capable of striking down whomever they construed as an enemy. I had been present on more than one occasion when men were seized or beaten, so I knew what they were likely to do. I had never been harmed, myself, although I had been chased a few times, usually a sporting pursuit, with the men laughing loudly and making no real effort to catch me. I was small, of course, and I knew the twists and turns of the palace corridors so well I could escape at a moment's warning.

Mother and Feodor talked a while longer, before definitely deciding I should go. I remember that of the several subjects mentioned, there was reference to Vassily's attempt to rekindle the rumor about Helena's having been poisoned. While there had been no fresh discoveries to bring it to mind, there was an ominous air about the Shuiskys' seeing fit to revive the suspicion. Mother was a possible victim, should the purge be carried to its ultimate conclusion. For this reason, if for no other, it was essential they learn the facts.

Also in the course of this conversation, Mother made a far-reaching decision, although I failed then to grasp its significance. Among the Germanic knights who were frequently in the house, there was one particularly great lion of a man, named Heinrich. He was tall and very blond, wearing his hair clipped short in the style of his homeland. He carried himself like a warrior king. I suppose he was little more than a vagabond adventurer when he first came, but his prowess at arms and his agile mind had already won him a number of followers. Most of the men who stayed in the back part of the house were already a part of his growing retinue.

I can recall Mother's remark: "Heinrich's the best answer," to which Feodor added: "You could do much worse."

A few minutes later I was running quickly through the rapidly filling footpath, hardly able to see the buildings on either side through the heavy curtain of falling snow. It was not as bitterly cold as it had been earlier; the wind had stopped, and the huge feathery clumps drifted straight downward. I could hear my own breathing and the slight, muffled squeaks as my feet squashed into the fresh fall. Otherwise, it was dead silence; the silence one can only experience within a windless snowstorm. I crossed the open court, unseen through the wall of white. I reached the Cathedral of the Assumption – the Uspensky, and seeing a group of men on the side steps of the palace, I turned sharply toward the bell tower, where I took cover between some of the wooden houses clustered about its base. I could see lights glowing dimly yellow through the frosted mica windows. Few houses had glass in those days, and I knew the several panes in Feodor's *dacha* had cost as much as diamonds.

Despite the early hour, no one stirred outside any of the houses. Even the men I had seen were probably inside by now, but I took no chances. I knew I would have to get past the guard at the outside door, regardless which palace entrance I used. There would also be a man stationed at the end of the hall leading to Ivan's and Yuri's chambers. As I knew most of the guardsmen, I anticipated no problem once I got inside. New recruits were sometimes posted on the lower doors, however, and one of them might stop me.

After making a wide circle, I cut back, toward the Cathedral of the Annunciation. This smaller church was built within an enfolding arm of the palace. Keeping a good distance from the arched facade along the front of the royal residence, I ran until I rounded the corner and was in the court between the palace proper and the Kremlin wall. For the first time I stopped to catch my breath, and afterward made my way more slowly to the doorway at the rear of the building. This was below the same wing where Mother and I had lived, and where she had given little gifts to the guards to assure their discretion. Some of these same men now worked for Vassily, so I hoped one might be on duty.

Unfortunately, both men inside the portal were longtime Shuisky retainers. I recognized only one of them from my previous trips, though I had seen the other following behind his master on several occasions. Acting as if I had every right to be there, I walked through the doorway and started past them. They made no attempt to stop me, the one even giving me a toothy grin. "Come to see the excitement, eh, Dmitri?"

I looked at him innocently. "What excitement? Won't I be able to see Yuri?"

"Sure, you can see little Basilevitch," he replied, "but your momma's boy friend better keep his nose out of here."

They both laughed and I shuffled nervously. I wanted to get away from them, but knew better than to appear in a hurry. I would still have the problem of getting out later. "What's Feodor done?" I asked.

"He's just friends with the wrong people," chuckled the other man. He had a big curved scar across one cheek, and was chewing on a piece of beef hide.

"Your mother's got some other strange friends, too," added the first man.

"You know my mother likes everybody," I returned. "She just wishes they'd all stop fighting each other."

"I wager she *would* like that!" shouted scarface. He aimed a kick at my rump. "Run along now, and play with your prince."

I ran, dodging his foot as the laughter of both men echoed behind me. I encountered no other guards until I reached the corridor outside Yuri's rooms. Ivan's chambers lay across the hall, a little farther down the passage. This guard hardly looked up, but he stuck his foot out to trip me as I went by. I kicked his ankle and ran for the safety of Yuri's room as the man jerked back in surprise.

As Feodor told me I should, I always made a point of going to see Yuri first. No one cared anything about him, while direct visits to Ivan might have excited Vassily's suspicions that I was carrying messages for Mother. I found Yuri lying on his back on the floor, playing with some string which he had wound into a hopeless tangle. When I entered, he turned his head to look at me, never lifting it from the rug. He was a pleasant little boy, more gifted in appearance than Ivan. But the older he became, the more obvious was his unfortunate lack of wit.

"Hello, Dmitri," he called. "See the bird net I'm making?"

I pulled the door shut and knelt on the floor beside him. "What's going on down there?" I asked, pointing toward the lower levels.

"Oh, Old Vassily's arresting somebody again," he said offhandedly. "Ivashka was here a few minutes ago, and said he was going to talk to the Shuiskys."

"Do you know who they arrested?"

"I think it was the fat Bielsky," he said, tangling his clumsy fingers deeper into the ball of string. "The skinny one got away."

"Simon?" I asked. That would be Johannes's brother.

"Yes, but Johannes got it good. They whipped him when he wouldn't go quietly, and he was drunk."

"Did anyone bother you or 'Vashka?"

"No, but 'Vashka didn't like it, anyway," he said, pouting at his unsuccessful handiwork. "He told me if he couldn't get to Shuisky he'd go find Vorontsof, 'cause Feodor might be able to help him. Only I don't think the guards let him go downstairs. I think I heard him go back into his rooms." He sat up abruptly. "Uh, did your momma send anything to eat?"

"No," I said. "No, I left in a hurry."

Yuri cocked his head to one side, slyly. "Then you did know that something was happening, didn't you?" he asked triumphantly. As usual, his moments of perception were surprising.

"Yes," I admitted. "Vorontsof is at home."

"Well, you better go back and tell him Ivashka wants to see him," said Yuri firmly.

"I want to see Ivashka first," I told him. "Think the guards would let us get into his room without stopping us?"

Yuri struggled to his feet through the tangles of string and sticks. "I guess so," he said. "Come on." He plucked at my sleeve, leading me to the door. He opened it calmly and, ignoring the guard, we turned toward Ivan's apartment. I glanced back at the man, who was watching us with a surly expression. He frowned and I stuck my tongue out at him, at which he made a move as if to rise and we ran the last few steps to Ivan's door. There was another guard standing there, whom I had not noticed previously. Usually, there was just the one at the end of the corridor. I looked up at him as Yuri knocked, but the man pretended to see through me.

There was no answer from inside, and Yuri called. "Ivashka, can I come in?"

After another moment of silence Ivan's voice called out resignedly. "Come on!"

The room was dark and gloomy, as Ivan always kept the drapes pulled across his windows. He had been reading, I was sure, but must have shoved the book out of sight when he heard Yuri's knock. He seemed surprised and pleased to see me, but said nothing until the door was closed. "Did you have any trouble getting in?" he asked.

I shook my head. "No, but I don't know how easy it's going to be to get out."

"I don't expect they'll bother you," he said, lying back on his couch. "They just don't want me out of sight – want to be sure they know where I am."

"Did they arrest anybody except Johannes?" I asked abruptly.

"Just a few of his servants," Ivan replied, turning on his side to face us. Yuri and I had squatted on the floor near him, speaking in whispers so the guards would not overhear. "Bielsky got drunk last night," Ivan continued, "and he made the old wolf angry. If he hadn't, I don't think they'd have thrown him in prison, even after that mess with Kurbsky."

"Is Vassily in the palace?" I asked.

"No. He left after Bielsky was arrested last night. He's supposed to be here any minute, though."

"Did he send word to you?"

Ivan bristled. "I sent for him!" he growled. "When one of my boyars is arrested, I expect at least to be informed!"

Yuri giggled, and I bowed in exaggerated respect from my sitting position. "And if I may be permitted to speak," I began, using the formal court address of a vassal to his lord, "what does our mighty Prince crave for his dinner tonight?"

Ivan expelled a lungful of air and stared at me, scratching his thigh. "Well, what am I supposed to do?" he bellowed helplessly. "That old bag of gas doesn't even pretend to consult me, anymore!"

"The day will come," I said softly.

"As you have pointed out before," he replied just as softly, "the day will come, *if* I live to see it." The Grand Duke of Muscovy curled his knees up, almost to his chin, making himself as small as he could. He was wearing a threadbare brown tunic which pulled up at his movement, revealing a hole in his hose over the knee.

"How could he harm you?" I asked seriously. "We know he's already afraid of a war with the other boyars."

"He might poison me, and pretend I died of the pox or something."

"If he ever gave you anything to eat," added Yuri.

Ivan cast a disgusted glance at his brother. "What do you think, Dmitri? Has your mother said anything to you?"

I shook my head, patting the exposed kneecap. "If they killed you, they'd have to do something about your cousin Vladimir Andreyevitch," and sensing Yuri's gaze, added hastily, " . . . and Yuri, too. Novgorod might like a Shuisky Duke, but not the Muscovites."

"Did your mother say that?" he asked.

I bit my lip and nodded.

"Then they do talk about it!" Ivan snapped.

"Yes, but only to say it couldn't happen," I assured him.

We heard some movement in the corridor outside a few minutes later, and all turned toward the door as it burst open. I think Ivan had drawn up involuntarily into an even smaller ball at the first sound. Now he came quickly to his feet, uncurling like a cat as Vassily bustled into the room, followed by a group of his sycophants.

"Ivashka, my dear boy," he intoned jovially, extending his arms as if he expected Ivan to leap into them for joy. He maintained the posture as he lumbered across the room. "I only received your message a few moments ago," he lied, "and I made all haste to get here."

I saw Ivan's lip curl as the old man approached him, but he allowed the massive arms to encircle his shoulders and the ceremonial kiss to be placed on either side of his head. I had not seen Vassily Shuisky since the first snow, and even in that short time he seemed to have grown older and grayer. Stepping back from Ivan, he wheezed into a rag he carried in his left hand and lapsed into a violent fit of coughing. There were already brownish stains on the cloth, like dried blood.

The old man seated himself on the couch where Ivan had been lying, and motioned his men out of the room. His glance fell on Yuri and me, but apparently he considered us too young and insignificant to bother asking us to leave. Or perhaps he wanted me to carry the tale of his visit to my mother.

Breathing heavily, and mopping his rheumy eyes with the back of his sleeve, Vassily began speaking to Ivan, sounding like the kindly guardian he was supposed to be. "What troubles you, my son?" he asked. "Are you and your brother being well cared for?"

"Why did you arrest Johannes?" Ivan demanded, ignoring the boyar's question. He looked straight into the watery blue eyes, and in spite of himself the haggard old man looked away. He still wore his huge boyar's hat, and I could see the encrusted snow begin to melt, running down the back of his ratty fur coat.

"But Bielsky was conspiring against you, my Prince," answered Vassily with a surprised intonation. He looked at Ivan in crafty innocence. Gesturing with his free hand, he went on, "You know I seek only to serve your interests."

"Who are you going to arrest next?" demanded Ivan coldly.

"No one, why no one at all." He attempted to chuckle, which ended in another spasm of coughing. This time there was fresh blood on his cloth.

Once the hacking of the elderly boyar had subsided, Ivan questioned him further. "Where is my friend Vorontsof?"

I glanced meaningfully at Yuri, who had started to answer. The younger prince responded to my cue and remained silent. I had not thought to tell Ivan that Feodor was with my mother.

Vassily tried to clear his throat, could not, and answered Ivan in a raspy whisper. "I don't know, my son. I would suppose he is at home." The old wolf flicked his glance at me. "I should imagine Dmitri knows better than I."

"He's in no danger, then?" Ivan insisted, still maintaining his cold tone of command.

"Certainly not!" gasped Shuisky, feigning surprise that Ivan should suspect him of such motives. "He is a loyal friend to us both, isn't he?"

"I am sure he is," said Ivan evenly. "I hope he will remain free to continue displaying that loyalty." Noticing my look of concern, he added, ". . . and Dmitri's mother? You will also leave her alone?"

Vassily hesitated. "You may be sure I would never harm our friends," he said, placing a strong emphasis on the last word. Leaning on the sofa back, he pushed himself heavily to his feet. He patted my shoulder, rather absently, without looking in my direction. Then he stood respectfully before Ivan for another moment, bowed slightly from the waist. "If Your Highness has no other business with me. . . ."

"You may leave Us," said Ivan haughtily, as Vassily had already turned to go. The old man reached the door when he thought to add, "You may also send Us some food!"

Apparently Ivan's last order, at least, was heeded. Almost at once, a large tray of roasted meat, two whole cabbages, bread, cheese, and fish was brought to him. They even included a flagon of vodka, which Ivan insisted I share with him.

"I am worried about the Metropolitan," Ivan told me, about half way through the liquor. "I know he has been seeing Bielsky lately."

I had fallen far behind Ivan in consuming the fiery liquid, as he was quaffing bumper after bumper, completely enjoying it. He was getting very drunk, while my own head was spinning from the smaller quantity I had downed.

"They wouldn't dare do anything to the head of the Church," I answered. I lolled on the floor next to Ivan's couch. Yuri, who did not like any spirits, had abstained from our folly and sat grinning at us.

"I don't really believe they'll touch him, either," said Ivan, "but you had better tell Feodor to have a talk with him. Maybe they can do us some good, too."

I had continued to drink after the effects were quite apparent, and I now lay with my head against the couch, trying to regain my balance and to stop the room from spinning. When I closed my eyes to halt the motion I still felt it, and worse, I could feel a dreadful pull at my stomach. My memory grows foggy beyond this point, but I seem to remember Feodor appearing sometime later and carrying me back to my mother. I do not know whether he had been allowed into Ivan's chambers, or whether the guards had brought me down to him. I awakened long enough to discover how terribly funny my mother thought it was for her nine–year-old son to be carried home drunk from the imperial palace.

"I should have started him a little earlier," she giggled, "but these are the lessons that make a man."

CHAPTER II

A fresh blanket of snow lay like the mantle of God's innocence upon the Kremlin grounds. The previous night's wind had left a sparkling crust of ice, beneath this a depth of powdery white. In some places the snow touched the eaves of the boyars' *dachas*, and almost everywhere it rose to the level of my eyes – aching as they were from my excesses of the previous night. I was on the way to join Ivan in his devotions, as I vaguely remembered his commanding my attendance. It was just after sunrise, but several of our household retainers had been out ahead of me, leaving trails to crisscross those leading from the neighboring houses. With the Shuisky usurpers too involved in their plots and counterplots to concern themselves with the groundskeepers, the lazy wretches had done nothing to clear the courtyards or other areas about the palace.

As I neared the eastern wall of the royal residence I saw Mishurin, a young *voivode* who had recently been more vocal than he should have been in support of the Bielsky faction. He had come out a side door and was starting in my direction, although I did not think he had seen me. He seemed in a hurry, nervously glancing backward over his shoulder as he struggled through the drifts. At first I thought he was drunk and I almost shouted to him, but there was something about his frenzied flight that warned me, held me back despite my liking the man. He had visited our home several times, often bringing sweets for my mother. As she never ate such things they were usually given to me. Impelled by the instincts of the wild – the same which must abide in all of us if we are to survive – I stopped at a place where the snow was deep enough to conceal me.

In his haste to leave the building, Mishurin had neglected to don his heavy clothing. Wearing just a lightweight robe, he must have felt the cold, for I could see how he hugged himself as he continued to blunder through the drifts. Suddenly, there was a rush of bodies from around the corner of the building, and they were on top of Mishurin before he could flounder through to the nearest path. I recognized the attackers, and pressed myself more closely against the snowbank. They were mostly young men in their teens, sons or younger brothers of various boyars. The leader was John Shuisky, the Regent's nephew. While I was to witness some strange and bizarre executions in the years to come, I never saw a more terrifying sight than this fur clad pack, leaping and bounding about in the snow as they subdued their victim.

Right in the open, with no concern for who might see them, the boys ripped every shred of clothing from Mishurin's body, forcing him to stand in quivering, naked humility while half their number ran back around the corner, and returned dragging a sleigh. They must have prepared for their act ahead of time, as the sled had been cleared of its extra parts, leaving only a wooden framework above the runners. Mishurin was thrown down on this, his arms and legs stretched in different directions as they bound him, heedless of his screams and pleas for mercy.

Once he was secured, the young men immediately drew their knives and started to strip the skin from their victim's body – exactly as I had seen huntsmen do with their quarry. But human skin does not come off like an animal's. It adheres to the flesh, and its removal is excruciatingly painful. They also mutilated his face, and cut off his genitals in their frenzy.

Mishurin's screams resounded off the walls of the surrounding houses, echoing through the entire Kremlin until a great many people came to their doors. More than a few remained to watch, although none sought to interfere. As the flaying continued, the cries became more bestial than human. Bloody chunks of skin were tossed onto the frozen crust, while the trampled area around the sleigh grew pink, then red, as Mishurin's blood drained from his writhing body, sinking into the snow to be crushed beneath the young men's feet.

I continued to watch in horrified fascination until my mother came out to get me. She was sobbing, shrieking at me to break my trance, grabbing my arm and dragging me home. Despite the cold, her face was ashen and she had difficulty drawing breath – frightened beyond any previous display of hysteria. As we neared our own front door, Mother began to curse the Shuiskys with every foul word she could think of, some of which I would not have expected her to know. She pushed me into the house and personally barred the door, ordering me not to leave and assigning two retainers to assure that I obeyed. I went to my room, inexplicably affected by all I had seen. For in truth, despite the gruesome, painful death of a young man I had known and liked, I now experienced an unbidden lust to watch it all again. For months afterward I replayed the scene in my mind, experiencing a physical sensation in my nether regions that I could not explain, and about which I dared not ask even Ivan's opinion – although he would have been my most likely confidant.

Whether the death of Mishurin drove Mother into acting more quickly than she intended, I have no way to know. But two days after this, the banns were posted and she informed me that I was soon to have a new father. She had decided to marry Heinrich vonStaden, she said, the golden knight whom I had always considered such a hero. Surprised, I was also very pleased. I was tired of living without a father, being constantly embarrassed by having to ask a woman's permission. If Mother must re–marry, she could not have made a better choice, I thought. At least this was my feeling until the first time Heinrich corrected me. Then I resented it. He was suddenly a foreigner, a German interloper in our home. For a time I hated him. In the end, however, he proved to be the greatest gift my mother ever gave me. Without Heinrich, I would never have been able to serve Ivan as I did. From the very beginning he began training me to use the weapons of a knight.

Once Heinrich became head of our household, we moved out of the Vorontsof *dacha* in the Kremlin, into a nice house of our own in the *Kitaigorod*, or inner city. It was a smaller place than Feodor's, only a short distance from the Savior's Gate. Both Mother and I liked it better than Vorontsof's, for it was our own – and Heinrich's. For the first time I could remember, Mother and I were able to feel secure from the Shuisky bullies. No one was willing to challenge the men who served my stepfather. While his small force could not account for much in the great struggle for power, it was more than sufficient to protect our home. Nor did Heinrich seek more at this time than the establishment of a successful trade.

Neither did it take me long to accept Heinrich in his proper role of father. He was a man, the like of which I had never known before. Powerful in the use of arms and in every way a warrior, he was also a man of knowledge. Mother had already insisted on teaching me to read; in fact, I had read several scrolls from Ivan's collection, although I generally found them boring. Heinrich imposed still heavier demands, requiring that I be able to read and write in any language I could speak. I therefore had to learn the alphabets of both Russian and German, as well as the spelling and structure of the several dialects with which I was conversant. I found the western system of lettering difficult, but Heinrich was as strict in keeping me at this as he was in training me to wield a sword. As I continued to become more proficient in reading, I began to realize how much pleasure one could derive from it. It also gave me a new cotenancy with Ivan, who delighted in providing manuscripts for me to read, later discussing them with me. Mother even contrived to have me included in the regular sessions when the Metropolitan Daniel instructed Ivan and Yuri. My attendance, of course, provided an easy means for transmitting messages.

In looking back on this period, I recognize the terrible elements of fear and desperation which subsequently became impressed on Ivan's mind – twisting the twig, so to speak, into the form the tree would later take. He had always been what the Germans call *unruhig*, possessed of a certain restlessness. He was also dominated by an extremely volatile temper. He tended at times to be cruel, even to Yuri and me, although he never really hurt either of us. He sometimes took advantage of his station, however, and would occasionally administer a whipping to one of the kennel boys whom he had not been able to defeat in a contest of skill or strength. None of them dared fight back, because Shuisky's guards always hovered in the background with orders to assure the safety of both princes. Regardless of these abuses – or perhaps because of them – Ivan developed a loyal following among these and several other groups of palace servants. He had no one else to lead, while they in turn were flattered by his attention and apparent friendship. The Kennelmaster, a fellow named Ivor who had been given his post by Basil as a reward for heroism as a soldier, was the most devoted of all these followers.

There came a time, not too long after my mother's marriage, when a great many foreigners converged on the capital, and it was necessary for Shuisky to use Ivan in receiving them. On these occasions, both princes would be hustled off to the treasury where their fine robes were stored, and dressed as befitted their stations. Ivan would be seated on the imperial throne, with Yuri close by, where both would go through the well–rehearsed rituals under Vassily's watchful eye. After performing these regal duties, Ivan would be stripped of his finery and returned to his usual condition. Again, the princes were frequently left to scavenge what food they could from the palace kitchen. I can remember Ivan screaming one day: "*My* kitchens! *My* kitchens, and I must beg at my own back door!"

This influx of foreigners, of course, took place in the spring and early summer, when it was possible to travel more easily on the roads between major cities. Thus, at a time when the weather turned warm and it would have been enjoyable for the princes to be outside, they were more closely restricted than usual. This was also the season when many Russians came to the capital, ostensibly for the Easter services in the major cathedrals. Among the nobility who came this year were the Kurbskys – the first visit since their refusal to become involved in the Bielsky–Shuisky power struggle. Their son Andrew was a lad about Ivan's age, and surprisingly enough Vassily allowed him to spend quit a bit of time with Ivan.

To me, Andrew was a person to be admired. He had a wonderful bearing and dignified self–control. He always wore beautiful clothes, and already spoke like a cultured gentleman. His father had been trained in some of the disciplines of western philosophy, which Andrew had obviously learned from him. Ivan very much appreciated the attention from both Andrew and his brother Roman, and after they returned to their estates he carried on a correspondence with them. With the departure of the Kurbskys and the other powerful, uninvolved nobles, the ominous tension returned, and Ivan was subjected to a fresh series of indignities. John Shuisky led his pack of rowdies like a mob of marauding wolves. I remember once when they all got drunk and had a tumbling match on the very bed where Basil had died. Ivan's only consolation lay in the knowledge that a number of men were supporting the Shuiskys only for personal gain, while secretly promising the rightful heir that they would assure no harm befell him.

Alexi Basmanov, particularly, started speaking more respectfully, taking time to stand and talk with Ivan if he encountered him in the halls. Alexi was such a huge, heavy man, we took to calling him "the Big Bear." Too dull–witted to know any better, he followed Vassily. But his was one sure hand in Ivan's defense, should the need ever arise. Then, in late summer, Feodor and all foreign residents were barred from the palace. This included Heinrich and my mother, although she had never tried to get in anyway. As I was considered Russian, in addition to being young and insignificant, the ban did not apply to me. I could still come and go as I wished, most of the time. On occasion, though, there would be a guard on duty who refused to let me pass.

Boys being what they are, I soon discovered a way to get in, even when I wasn't supposed to. There was a secret entrance, known only to a few of the kennel boys, who passed the knowledge on to Ivan and myself. Whereas it would not necessarily get me into the palace proper, it did give me access to the Kremlin when the outer gates were closed. Under a paving stone in the courtyard, next to the kennels, was a passage. It had been built many years before, probably by the original settlers of Moscow. It led through a stone tunnel, out into the river, although I think it had originally been entered through an opening along the bank. Over the years the river had changed its course and now obscured the outer end. Thus, one had to swim under water, going out several yards from shore. I would hide my clothes near the river bank and swim naked into the passage. It was then a long, gradual climb through the slimy, pitch black passage to the vault beneath the courtyard, where I kept a second set of clothes. After changing into them, I would knock against the underside of the stones and the kennel boys would help me out. The stone was a little too heavy for me to lift by myself, which meant I could only use the passage when I was sure someone would be about to help me.

I am sure that Heinrich and Feodor remained active in whatever conspiracies were underfoot to oppose the Shuiskys, but I had no direct knowledge of these things. I know that Mother was much happier than I had ever seen her, and regardless what her original motives may have been for marrying Heinrich, I think she sincerely loved him. On his part, Heinrich had severed all loyalties to the Germanic orders, and took up the life of a Russian merchant and sportsman. Before the cold weather set in, he took me hunting a number of times and taught me the art of handling a gyrfalcon – pursuits in which I knew I was envied by Ivan.

Feodor began to play a peculiar game of his own, often drinking with the followers of John Shuisky and pretending, at least, to be friendly with them. By order of the regent, however, he was still banned from Ivan's rooms. In all, the palace atmosphere appeared to be attaining a degree of balance, wherein the princes were safe and fairly well cared for. Then, in the early fall, Vassily died. The immediate result was a power struggle within the Shuisky clan, centering around John and Andrew.

Andrew was Vassily's younger brother, and in many ways the more wicked person of the two. But John was more intelligent, and at this particular time he commanded more wealth. He also had a better organized gang of bullies. Only his age was against him, for he must have been barely twenty. Still, he won out and acted as regent without really daring to assume the title. This galled Ivan more than anything the Shuiskys had done before.

Although I note John's being a little less dull than Andrew, I do not mean to imply he was bright. He certainly was not; he was also a terrible coward. He attempted to conceal this by his loud boasting and by bullying anyone with whom he could get away with it. By another strange twist of his nature, however, he enjoyed encouraging Ivan to commit the same sins he relished himself, even permitting his ward an occasional ride into the city.

John's appearance was in keeping with his personality and behavior. His hair and beard were black, poorly trimmed and greasy from his habit of rubbing fat from his fingers when he ate. His face was white and puffy from too much drink, and he had a huge red beak for a nose. Although he wore clothing of the finest cut, trimmed with exotic furs from the far north, he always looked dirty. Spots cascaded down the front of his robe, a mixture of liquors and meat juices.

John's first act was typical of his stupidity and godlessness. He deposed the Metropolitan Daniel, who, in addition to supporting Ivan's rightful claims, had previously shown favor to the Bielsky faction. Some of Johannes's friends had sought sanctuary with Daniel immediately following the arrest of their leader. John especially hated the Metropolitan because the old man openly condemned the murders and other violence. He had recently delivered a fiery sermon from the pulpit of the Great Cathedral, assailing John and his friends for their drunkenness and immorality.

Daniel was dragged from his home in the middle of the night, barefoot and clad only in his nightshirt. Several servants witnessed this sacrilegious outrage, as the Metropolitan of Moscow was bundled off in a cart and removed from the Kremlin. I do not know exactly what happened to him, as there have been several conflicting stories. I doubt he was murdered, only because Shuisky was superstitious enough to fear having the blood of a partiarch on his hands. In all likelihood, Daniel lived out the rest of his life in some remote monastery, praying for the souls of his oppressors.

Our new Metropolitan was Joseph, Archimandrite of the Sergey-Troitsky Monastery. This was the abbey about forty-five miles northwest of Moscow, built to the memory of Saint Sergey and the Holy Trinity. It was the largest monastery in Russia, perhaps in all the world. There were over a hundred thousand priests, peasants, monks, and serfs assigned to it, and its land holdings were enormous. Its archimandrite was generally considered equal in rank to an archbishop, holding great honor and status. Joseph, considerably younger than Daniel, was also a more worldly man. He brought with him the experience of having managed a huge complex of men and wealth.

I cannot say why Joseph was chosen, except that his prestige within Church circles may have forced him on the Shuiskys, who had overstepped all bounds of reason or judgment by driving Daniel away. While Joseph had yet to speak out in the ongoing controversies, he had always been closely allied with the royal family, having been personally suggested for archimandrite by Basil. From the very beginning he made his new power felt, certainly expressing no apparent gratitude to the Shuiskys. His election, of course, was by the bishops of all the Russian cities, but if John had opposed him he could not have become Metropolitan.

Shortly after the ceremony conferring the See of Moscow on Joseph, Heinrich told us he had to make one final trip to Danzig. He still had property there, he said, and it was necessary to settle some land holdings with the family of his only brother, recently killed while serving the King of France. Because the trip would take several months, he made a sort of pact with Feodor, resulting in some of our cousin's men being assigned to us, replacing those who accompanied my stepfather.

By now, our household had become fairly large. In addition to the servitors who had taken posts with Heinrich, Mother had a number of women living in the *terem* quarters. There were a couple of old servants, one being the woman who had cared for me in the palace before Helena died. The other was an elderly *Frau* called Frieda, who had served my grandmother. There were five or six younger women, two of them girls not much older than I. They had been collected over a period of time, being mostly Germans or Lithuanians who had no place to go after losing a father or husband. It made for a constant cackling and giggling in the upper rear portion of the house, one reason I stayed away as much as I could.

One evening, shortly before Heinrich was due to return, Mother insisted I accompany her to a vesper service in the women's chapel, behind the royal palace. I protested, but she refused to hear me. I was embarrassed to be attending services with my mother, and I was really too old to be seen in the women's chapel. Furthermore, no well bred Russian woman would have considered walking that distance in the open, exposing herself to the eyes of any man who happened to pass. I knew of a few foreign women who did such things, but they were not considered to be people of quality. It was no wonder men laughed at her behind her back, I thought, and made lewd remarks about her past. Before going out the door, I had one final scene of remonstrance, but as usual to no avail.

Like some heretic follower of Luther, Mother set out with me and four of her women, walking toward the Kremlin. In our section of the city there were few people in the streets, for our class traveled mostly on horseback or in carriages. The few souls we did pass were men, who glanced at us in disapproval. We had only a few steps to go, between the front door of our house and the Square of Executions, then through the Savior's Gate into the Kremlin. Because we lived on one of the better streets, it had timbers pounded into the surface as paving. The Square itself had only recently been decked, partly with stone, the rest with wood. In all, it made walking easier and there was little dust unless a high wind came up. Even in a rain storm, one could ride all the way to the palace without bogging down in the mud, as happened in the outer portions of Moscow.

With Mother on my arm, trailed by our flock of pretty girls – the older crones had remained at home – we entered the Kremlin and walked across the courtyard to the chapel. People nodded to me as we passed, but several averted their eyes to spare my mother the humiliation of their gaze. My own face was flushed with shame. I remember wishing for total darkness, as the sky began to lose its sunset colors and a chill wind whistled down from the north. I could feel the icy fingers of night begin to creep toward us from the deepening shadows between the buildings, but we were still several minutes short of the all–concealing veil I desired. A trio of young men walked past us as we neared the chapel, making vulgar noises at which Sonya, who was a hopeless wanton, giggled and whispered to her companions.

The fading rays of sunlight still glinted off the angles and curves of cupolas and rooftops, silhouetting the Kremlin buildings all around us. I was trying to look at these and forget the humiliating circumstances when I became aware of our suddenly being within a fairly sizable group of people. Mother stopped walking, and I felt her arm tighten on mine. At the top of the steps leading into the women's chapel stood John Shuisky, surrounded by his gang of ruffians. The other people who stood below were mostly Kremlin women going to service, and a few loiterers who had drifted up, anticipating some excitement.

"Well, Eleanor," roared John – I'm sure he was drunk – "I see you've brought your entire staff!" His fish–belly face, surrounding the red drunkard's nose, seemed to ooze out between the black fur of his towering boyar's hat, and the equally black, greasy beard. They both seemed to glisten with some obscene moisture.

The noisy, roistering group behind him shifted slightly as Mother attempted to mount the stairs, the rest of us following close behind her. The men rudely blocked our way, one of the besodden louts even giving my mother a slight shove. I started forward, but Sonya grabbed my sleeve. "Be still," she whispered. "Let your mother handle this."

We were almost surrounded by them. The sickly, sweet–sour odors of mead and unclean bodies were stifling, even in the cold open air. Mother, instead of losing her temper, smiled pleasantly at Shuisky, ignoring his vulgar comments. "John, dear boy," she purred. "You've been drinking that horrid beer again, haven't you? I should have thought you'd have outgrown such poor taste."

Her boldness brought another roar of laughter from the men, who now ceased to harass, but stood like a wall between us and the chapel door. They were obviously awaiting John's next move. Dull–witted, he was momentarily at a loss for an answer. A few more women arrived behind us, and were also waiting to enter the church. I do not think they had been close enough to hear what was said before, but one old lady in the crowd shouted angrily at John. She called him a servant of Satan, keeping honest women from their worship.

The noise from those behind us became greater, as the chattering of women always will, and the sound must have carried into the chapel. Unexpectedly, the door behind Shuisky was opened and a priest looked out, possibly wondering where his congregation could be. Seeing Shuisky, he hastily retreated inside, much to the amusement of the louts who took it as a sign of fear, evoked by their awesome might.

Before their laughter could die away, the door opened again, and this time Joseph stood in front of us. Despite his being dressed in a plain black habit and wearing a *tafyi*, or skull cap, the sight of him was impressive. No one expected the Metropolitan to be there, which added to the startling effect of his appearance. The entire group fell silent. In all probability, he had merely been making an inspection tour of the various churches and chapels, instructing the priests in his capacity as Bishop of Moscow. I can think of no other reason, unless it were the Hand of God, placing His curator where he was needed.

It took the Metropolitan but a moment to size up the situation, and level a scathing denunciation against John Shuisky. He did it without mincing words, right there in front of the entire group of people! By morning, it would be told all over the city. John, of course, was furious. He glowered at the priest in impotent rage, but he did not dare strike out against him; there had been enough controversy over his disgraceful mistreatment of Daniel. To touch Joseph this soon might have brought even the neutral boyars into alliance against him.

Finally, John left, turning his back on the Metropolitan without even asking his forgiveness or blessing. Watching him go, Joseph shook his head in wonderment at such poor manners. He then raised his hands above the whole group, making the sign of the cross, and stood aside to let us enter the church.

A few days after this, Heinrich was back.

The incident between John Shuisky and the Metropolitan took place a month or so before Johannes Bielsky managed to secure his release from prison. I am not certain how this happened, but later events would seem to imply that Joseph had a hand in it, as well as Feodor and Heinrich. Other than to use me as a messenger when they wished to contact Ivan, I was not privy to any of the discussions that went on under our roof. By the end of winter, however, Bielsky had succeeded in gathering enough of a force to displace John Shuisky in the Kremlin hierarchy – temporarily. I can remember a number of skirmishes, and several groups of armed men moving in and about the citadel. But in the end, it came to nothing. Johannes was defeated and forced to surrender. The last I ever saw of him was early in the morning, two days after the Shuiskys had regained control of the palace. He was brought from his cell, his clothes in tatters, arms bound behind his back. Shuisky retainers hustled him into a cart and wheeled him into the Square of Executions. As word had been passed by guardsmen throughout the city, a large crowd stood around the *lobonoyo mesto*, apparently expecting a few heads to fall.

For once, John exercised a semblance of good judgment. Instead of risking a full civil war, he rode into the square behind the cart and announced Johannes's sentence of imprisonment instead of execution. Surrounded by his followers, he made a long speech, extolling himself and his virtues, boasting of his victories over the Tartars and over the enemies of the Grand Duke, in general.

I tried to get past the guards, and into the apartments of Ivan and Yuri. But Shuisky had apparently ordered them to keep everyone out. So, I mounted the Kremlin wall, looking down into the square where John was well into his speech. I could hear the carefully timed applause of his lackeys, half of whom were already drunk. There was not much response from the rest of the crowd, until Shuisky announced that he was providing food and drink for their celebration of his glory. His shouting was so loud, all of this was clearly audible inside the walls. I was standing with a couple of the kennel boys, crowded now by the flock of servants who had also climbed the stairs to watch. We poked our heads over the edge, looking down on the mob of milling citizens and soldiers. The Shuisky army was still camped outside the city, and as John spoke I could see a steady stream of men coming in through the various gates. A ragtag bunch of peasants out playing soldier, Heinrich had called them. There was no telling what they would do when drunk and left unsupervised.

As more soldiers arrived, and as the casks were tapped, the men began drinking as fast as they could fill their bumpers. It was a very warm day; well before noon the sun beat down like a furnace. Gradually, many of the townspeople began to slip away as the soldiers grew more boisterous. They were so loud, in fact, it was impossible to hear John Kubensky, a Novgorod boyar who attempted to make a speech after Shuisky had finished. Finally, he gave up and Shuisky signaled for the cart. Johannes was still tied in a standing position as he was wheeled away to Beelozersk, a bitter cold pile of stone in the far north. I could see the cart for a long time, being pulled by two old cobs along the dusty road beside the river. Johannes was looking back at the receding Kremlin walls, and I remember wondering what he thought. This time he would never come back. Although there were rumors of assassins being sent to assure his demise, I was never able to learn whether they killed him, or if he died a natural death. I know only that he was dead two or three years later.

Once the Shuiskys were firmly installed in the Kremlin again, their Novgorod army departed. For the rest of the summer and fall the situation returned to its former state of uneasy tension. There were not many immediate arrests, and no open acts of terrorism on the part of the reinstated regent. He was not secure enough to risk a further open conflict.

In this period of tenuous quiet, Mother took up some of her social activities again, visiting with other ladies of the court. Heinrich took me on several hunting trips, and the daily exercises in the use of arms were resumed. So, too, were the lessons with the Metropolitan. Despite the facade of normalcy, however, I noticed that my stepfather was much more vigilant than he had been before. Even when we hunted wolves, traveling a fair distance into the countryside to get them, we never stayed away overnight. At least half of our household guard was always on duty. It was rare for any member of the family to be outside after dark, unless in a sizable group.

Yet, time alone continued to lessen the tensions, and the precautions became more routine. John consented to allow Ivan's going with us on a few short hawking expeditions, near the end of the summer when the geese were beginning to fly south. I think the Prince surprised Heinrich by his fine horsemanship, given the limited opportunities he had had for practice. He also did very well in handling his falcon, which brought down the largest bird the first time we went out.

Through all of this, I began to feel myself a man among men. There was a genuine bond between my stepfather and myself. He discussed all the family business with me, and even listened when I made suggestions. His men would obey me, although my commands never involved more than routine matters. Still, they addressed me respectfully, and I had bested at least a third of them in the practice yard. My beard was definitely beginning to grow – a few silken, gold colored threads which were hard to see unless the light was exactly right. But I was very proud of them, and of the deeper tones I was able to formulate when I spoke.

My next exposure to the essence of manhood came from my mother's girls, who had not failed to note my physical development. Whenever they had a chance to speak without Mother hearing them, they teased me and sometimes made quite lewd remarks. Sonya was the worst, although she was also the prettiest. At first I blushed, and stood stupidly with my tongue tied in knots, having no idea how to answer them. I discussed the problem with Ivan, fearful that Heinrich would punish the girls if I said anything to him. The Prince thought it amusing, but he was happy to advise me. He had already been brought a number of young virgins by the palace servants, and was fully experienced in the art of making love. (Or so he believed.) He described a great many things to me, and suggested several ways I might handle the girls, leaving the final choice to me. I should note that during the Bielsky tenure, Ivan had contrived to present Heinrich with a Kremlin *dacha*, and we were still living in it. In years past, it had been a boyar home, and while smaller than the Shuiskys' or Mstislavskys', it was laid out in the usual Russian manner. The *terem* occupied one whole wing of the second floor, with the master's bedroom being in the center front, where it gave access to the women's quarters. Other bedrooms, including mine, extended down the hall of the other wing, separated from the *terem* by the master's chambers.

Because Mother had never observed the proper rules of seclusion, she and any of her charges were likely to be found in any part of the house they chose to visit. The only time they restricted themselves was when Heinrich entertained. Loose as the moral codes had become, a man was still expected to maintain proper control within his own home. While I know that Heinrich never beat my mother, as was common practice in most Russian homes, he did insist on this show of propriety. To do less would have depreciated his status among the men with whom he dealt, a fact which Mother recognized and to which she grudgingly acceded.

Both she and Heinrich made jokes about it, as the customs were different in their respective homelands.

Returning from the baths one afternoon, still glowing from the scrubbing and scourging with willow wands, I encountered three of the girls in the downstairs salon. They were seated about the room, demurely picking out designs with their needles, laughing and giggling as they always did. Mother must have just left them, because I saw her own piece of tapestry cloth lying on a table. As soon as I came in, the girls started whispering and the giggling became worse. My immediate predilection was to run away from them and retire to my own room, but Ivan had told me I shouldn't do this. Braving it out, I entered the salon and lolled on a chair opposite the girls. When Sonya made a cute remark to me, I had the answer prepared, making such an obscene suggestion it surprised them all into silence. Even Sonya blushed.

I heard Mother coming back, so I got up to leave. As I went out, I mumbled to Sonya that any time she wanted to test her theories, she would find my bedroom door unlocked. With that I left, just in time to avoid Mother, who came in from the other side. I was proud of myself, then, and felt certain I had put them in their place. I looked forward to our next encounter, curious how my cleverly contrived response would affect them.

Heinrich had visitors that night, and I sat up with them long after the women had retired. Feodor, forced by circumstances to maintain his alliance with Heinrich, remained after the others had left. They were playing draughts, I think, and discussing politics. In any event, it was quite late when I went to bed. I lay awake a long time, because I had been fired by some of the conversation, and by the peculiar twistings of my own thoughts. As I lay there I heard a soft noise at my door and was about to call out a challenge, when I saw Sonya pushing it open. I froze in surprise – or maybe terror. Not knowing what else to do, I pretended to be asleep.

The shutters on my windows were closed because the winter had set in, but I had banked the stove just before getting into bed, and a fairly bright crimson glow showed through the grill. Through half–closed eyelids, I watched as Sonya closed the door and turned to look at me. She stood very still beside the bed, with the redness of the fire behind her making little peaks of light appear along the edge of her ample figure. She wore a heavy robe over her shift, and her light auburn hair had been combed out, fastened by a single ribbon at the back of her neck.

Slowly, almost uncertainly, she shrugged the robe from her shoulders. When it fell to the floor I saw her body twist as one foot pried the other out of their slippers. She now stood barefoot on the heavy carpet, dressed only in her shift. The light from the stove was enough to outline her body through the thin material, and I could feel the strange, surging rush of heat within my loins and I felt a fierce gathering of blood in my manhood. Still I didn't move, and continued my heavy breathing as if I were deep in sleep. Sonya stood beside my bed for a long time, while the compelling fires of my body became almost more than I could bear and I longed for her to hurry. Even beneath the heavy coverlet my desire would have been apparent to her, had there been a bit more light.

Then she reached down and picked up her robe. Shoving her feet back into the slippers, she wrapped the robe about her and glided back out the door – gone before I realized she was going. I sat up in a welter of tumbled emotions. She had been afraid! She had wanted me badly enough to creep down the back stairs, through the servants' quarters, and up the stairway on my side of the house. She had risked my mother's anger and a certain beating from Heinrich. But at this last moment she had been afraid! It was my most poignant lessen to date, in a budding study of the female creature, to discover that her desire could be as great as mine, greater perhaps, but her fears could also be as strong. This knowledge, on top of the lustful fires she had ignited within me – for I was surely as stiff as a board – made it impossible to fall asleep until I had committed the sin of Onan.

The next day, I could hardly wait to visit the women's quarters. I spoke casually with Mother, not telling her about Sonya, of course, just pretending to pass some time as I frequently did. While I was with her, several of the girls came into the room, some to sit with us, others to pass through into another chamber. None of them acted as if they knew. Sonya came in after I had been there a few minutes and sat demurely at the rack where a large, half–completed tapestry was stretched. All of them worked on this from time to time. A couple of other girls joined her, the three of them pecking at the cloth with their needles and chattering like a flock of sparrows.

Heinrich called Mother into the next room, and I was abruptly left alone with them. As soon as my mother was gone, they started their usual giggling, as if I had never made any remarks and as if Sonya had never come into my room. I let them go on, because I was surprised and didn't know exactly what to do. The whole situation was extremely frustrating, but as I sat there tongue–tied I began to sense the truth. Sonya obviously believed I had been asleep, and was thus unaware that I knew of her visit. Secondly, she must not have told the other girls. I stood up to leave, passing close to the rack as I went out. To Sonya I whispered, "Why don't you finish what you start?" In the couple of heartbeats it took me to reach the door I could see her face turn brilliant red, as the other girls looked at her curiously.

She let me wait two more days before she came again. I had started to get circles under my eyes from lack of sleep, lying awake waiting for her. I would become so inflamed I could not drift off. Even after it was too late to reasonably expect her, I did not dare relieve my lust, on the off–chance that she might suddenly appear. But I knew she was affected by the same carnality as I. Her looks had become furtive whenever I passed her, and she had stopped making fun of me. How much the others knew, I could only guess, but my comment must have forced Sonya to compose some story for the others' benefit. I was sure she would never tell them the truth, as one would surely have tattled to Mother.

On the third night she came. Again I lay as if asleep, watching her in the glow from the stove as she slipped off her robe and shoes. She hesitated as she had before, with the reds and oranges of the embers making her body seem to to glow beneath the light material of her shift. At last she pulled it off over her head, standing naked beside the bed. In anticipation of her return, I had been sleeping in the nude, myself, which now heightened my own sensuality until my loins felt ready to burst with desire. One arm lay outstretched under the coverlet on the side nearest her. Silently, I lifted the blankets a foot or so off the mattress, and without a word she slid inside.

She lay with her back to me, curled into a ball, shivering from the cold, or from her own fear. I wanted to press against her, the more so as the heat from her body began to engulf me, but it required several moments to muster the courage. When I finally eased my trembling being into an encircling wall around her, the velvet texture of her skin pulled taut beneath my fingers gave rise to emotions I had never imagined could possess me. I worked one arm beneath her, the other on top, and cupped my hands about her breasts, fondling the nipples with my thumbs as Ivan had told me I should.

I could feel the temperature of her body increase, and soon the trembling stopped. Slowly she straightened and turned to face me, her lips touching my shoulder in the dark as they traced their way upward, seeking my mouth. I could smell the womanly odor of her, the soaps and perfumes used in the *terem* bath, and the cloves she had sucked to sweeten her breath. I kissed her, pressing my lips on hers until her tongue flicked between and her body pushed hard against my own. With a fierce strength, she shoved me onto my back and her hands began to explore the front of my body with a gentle, cloying touch. All sense of strangeness fell away, and I knew only the total bliss of her enveloping acceptance.

Apparently, I did not disappoint her, although I was still very young and had not attained the degree of manhood I would in later years. At length, she drove my face onto her breasts, where again I followed Ivan's instructions, projecting her into a frenzy of passion by working my lips and tongue over the ends of the firm, softly pointed cones, fondling the one with my hand, while working the other with my teeth. Finally, she could not withhold herself, and my own desires were aroused close to explosion. Skillfully, she drew me into her, savoring every movement, forcing me to enter slowly, tantalizing me with the languid twisting of flesh and sinew. At last we formed a union, complete and incapable of further joining. Never had I experienced a feeling of such warmth, nor such a majesty of exotic fires burning and spreading from my loins, through my hips and thighs, and into the lower pit of my belly. I felt a terrible urgency, the need to hurry, to pound my hips against hers, to rush into the final, compelling moment. My whole body throbbed with this ache, the desire to release the pressures that threatened to tear me apart. But her arms were around my shoulders, and her lips pressed hard against mine.Her tongue completed the unity of our bodies, her legs encircling mine, holding us tightly together, slowing my motion, forcing us to rock back and forth in a delirium of floating, pulsating, drifting, misty unreality . . . until at last even her restraints could not suppress me. I arched my back in a flood of sweetly painful swellings. Lights and colors, spasms of warmth and cold, gripping, struggling for a closer unity when there was no way to be any closer. At last, an exhausted shudder, a sigh, an awareness of sweaty dampness between her skin and mine. A final, lingering kiss . . . gradual release, separation, a memory of love's initial awakening, so intense it would require the strength of a true and deeper emotion to exceed. But that was many years in the future.

The following morning, I could hardly wait to tell Ivan that I was no longer a virgin. I arrived so early he was still at his prayers. I had cut mine short to get away, and when I joined him I was trembling with excitement – simply bursting with my news. But Ivan's devotions were extremely important to him, and he would not be hurried. A young priest went through the liturgy, the signs, the rituals, all with a painful slowness.

At last they were finished, and we went into the palace for breakfast. At the table I told Ivan all that had happened the night before, and described how his suggestions had made it such a sublime experience. He listened with great interest, questioning me in a knowing manner on some of the finer points. When I had finished my account, he complimented me and asked if she had bled very much.

"She didn't bleed at all," I said in surprise. I had not thought about it till now, but I was certain there had been no stain upon my sheets.

"Then she was not a virgin," he said sagely.

I looked at him in surprise, a little concerned. Then I shrugged. "Well, I suppose it doesn't much matter," I said, smiling to myself.

But Ivan's face was grim. "If she is not a virgin," he said, "she has been possessed by another man and may have given you the pox."

I felt the blood drain from my face. "Do you think?" I asked. "How can I tell?"

"It takes a few days," he said, his tone wise and knowing. "But it is always a danger. That is why I never have anything but a virgin."

I went about for a week in a dreadful state of terror, not daring to say anything or ask anyone. Sonya came to me again a few nights later, and it took a while to overcome my fear, but my desire was too great. After a few moments I was all over her again, and in her again, savoring the same delicious emotions I had before. I wanted to ask her about it when we finished, but I did not think it right that I should. I did make her swear she would have no others, and she never gave me the pox. Unfortunately, this insistence that she reserve herself for me convinced Sonya that I loved her – which, in a way, perhaps I did.

She now began coming to me regularly, two or three times a week, and our lovemaking extended beyond the original rites of our first few times. After a month or so, when I was sure I had not been infected, my actions were completely unrestrained. When I reported them to Ivan, he always had suggestions for things I should try the next time. Sonya was so uninhibited she would do anything I asked of her, or allow me to do anything I wished. It was a blissful relationship.

Then one night after a particularly heavy snowfall we were nearly caught. We were lying together, drained of passion and close to sleep. (This was our greatest danger, for we had both actually fallen asleep one night and awoke just in time for Sonya to slip back to her own room before the servants came into the kitchen downstairs.) Suddenly, there was a frantic pounding on the side door of the house, directly under my bedroom window.

We both leaped up, struggling into our shifts. I ran to the window, shoving the casement out to look below. The imperial palace across the way was ablaze with light, and I could see a number of running, shouting figures all over the Kremlin grounds. It was Ivan who beat so furiously on our door!

Sonya slipped into the hall, as I shouted to the Prince and turned to run downstairs. Sonya stood huddled in a corner of the passage, but Mother and Heinrich had rushed down the front way, leaving the hall door open into the master's chamber. Sonya ran across and disappeared into the darkness. I went down the back way to the kitchen, where my parents had seated Ivan at the table. Mother had thrown a huge white table cloth about his shoulders, apparently the first thing she could find. He was dressed in just a nightshirt and was quivering from fear and cold, his speech incoherent.

When he finally gained enough control to speak, he stammered out the story. John Shuisky, never completely lacking in informants, had discovered the Metropolitan's complicity in Bielsky's release from prison. How long he had known we could not be sure, but he had certainly given no indication before that night. Without warning, he had sent some of his men to seize Joseph, just as he had done to Daniel. But Joseph was more cautious, and had his own warning system. As Shuisky's men were approaching his front door, the Metropolitan had slipped out the back. Having no better place to go, he had fled into Ivan's bedroom, seeking protection from the Grand Duke. However, Joseph's departure had been observed and the Shuisky men had thrown stones and balls of ice at him, chasing him right up to the doors of the palace. They had made quite a sport of it, certain he could not get away.

Joseph managed to elude them for only a few moments, just long enough to reach Ivan and tell his story. Then the Shuisky henchmen found him. A mob of armed men had invaded Ivan's rooms, where they attacked the Metropolitan inside the royal bedchamber. Joseph had been badly beaten, but between his own efforts and those of Ivan – assisted by two or three servants who had rushed in to protect them – the bullies were driven off. Realizing that Ivan was powerless to shield him, the Metropolitan of Moscow, Head of the entire Orthodox Church, had been forced to flee down a back staircase and into the icy courtyard behind. There he found a *troika*, a large sleigh drawn by three horses, left unattended by its owner. Still clad in his nightclothes, and with one shoe missing, he whipped the animals to life and fled toward the Monastery of Sergey–Troitsky. Most of the attackers had been younger sons of prominent families, Shuisky lackeys, and the usual riffraff raised to power by the ruling thieves. It did not take them long to organize a chase, and it had been this motley, drunken mob I had seen running about when I went to the window. They were now in hot pursuit of Joseph, shouting foul curses and blasphemies as they chased their quarry across the icy fields beyond the capital.

Ivan spent the rest of the night at our house, sitting up with my stepfather and me, because he was too upset to sleep and too frighted to be left alone. He had been certain the armed mob was after him when they first broke in, so his fear was more than understandable. The few remaining roisterers from the night's debacle were still asleep when Heinrich escorted the Prince back to his rooms, just as a gray dawn began to lighten the eastern sky. My stepfather left two men with him, but I do not think anyone had realized Ivan was gone. Our guards were asked to leave before midday, which they did after Shuisky swore no harm would come to either Prince. Yuri, surprisingly, had slept through the entire noisy episode.

As for Joseph, we later learned that he had made good his flight to his former monastery, where he remained in sanctuary for several days. The young men who had chased him did not dare break in, nor were they anxious to have the blood of so holy a man on their hands – not after they had slept off the effects of drink. They returned to Moscow a day or two later, straggling back in groups of two or three.

It was a full week before Shuisky was able to persuade Joseph to leave his refuge in the *larva*, again having to promise not to harm him. The Metropolitan was sent into exile at Beelozersk, where he temporarily shared his banishment with Bielsky. He was allowed to return to Sergey–Troitsky less than a year later, where he lived as a simple monk. Makari, the saintly Bishop of Novgorod, came to Moscow as the new Metropolitan.

Makari arrived to take over his new duties before Christmas. The turmoil of the Shuisky administration caused his installation to be done hurriedly, so I think many people did not even realize he had taken over until he began officiating at services in the Cathedral of Assumption. It was Epiphany (Twelth Night in western terminology, but the true Christmas to us), when he publicly consecrated the river waters, that everyone in Moscow knew the new Metropolitan had arrived.

This insult to such a reverent churchman aggravated the schism between Feodor Vorontsof and John Shuisky. They had several terrible arguments, first over the disgraceful ouster of Joseph, then about the poor reception Makari had received. The Metropolitan of Moscow, after all, was second only to the Grand Duke in rank – a fact that Shuisky would probably have liked to forget. In his outward behavior he did forget it, conducting himself as he had before, as if he were the permanent ruler of Muscovy. What he neglected – what they all neglected – was Ivan's coming into manhood. Already, many of the people looked on him as their Lord and Guardian. Behind much of John's loutish attitude, I suppose, was his having been overruled by the Council of Bishops in the selection of a new Metropolitan. According to Feodor, at least, the Shuiskys had opted for a candidate of their own choosing and had been furious when the bishops acted so quickly to name Makari. John had never been given a chance to make his desires known.

As the new year progressed, a new powerful little clique began to form, comprised of Ivan, Feodor, Heinrich, and Makari. Acting in concert, they forced a lifting of the ban on Vladya, Ivan's cousin. Vladimir Andreyevitch Staritsky was the son of Ivan's uncle Andrew, who had been executed by Helena. Vladya and his mother, Euphrosyne, had first been exiled to the family estates. Later, they were actually imprisoned for a short while, and again banished to Staritsa after their release. For a long while, Ivan had felt it would strengthen him to have his cousin in the capital.

Vladya later became one of my closest friends, but I was not in his company very much during this period. As he was close to my age – about 13 – it was his rank and the circumstances of his presence that made him important, not any actual activities. His mother, however, from the moment of her arrival, was involved in one conspiracy after another. Euphrosyne, unfortunately, was another woman who constantly fought against the rigors of current fashion, loathing the rules of decency imposed upon females. She refused to remain cloistered in the *terem*, and having no husband to enforce a proper discipline she caused a series of minor scandals. She was also extremely snobbish, and jealous of her son's position in the hierarchy of princes. Vladya, of course, was close to the throne and considered by many to be Ivan's most likely heir, since Yuri was regarded as a simpleton. Euphrosyne hated my mother, apparently for no reason other than her having borne me. And I, of course – as Basil's presumed bastard – was beneath her contempt.

Sharp tongued and homely, Euphrosyne's presence could never be ignored, and on more than one occasion she made an almost comic spectacle of herself. I remember her as being very tall and horse faced, with a high, arched forehead of a type said to have been fashionable in Italy a generation ago. In keeping with her equine features, her voice was high pitched, raucous, and very grating on the ears. When she laughed, which wasn't often, she brayed like a nervous stallion about to copulate a mare. After his first glimpse of her, Heinrich dubbed her *Maultasch*, an insulting title used whenever she was mentioned within our family circle. I think the closest translation would be "bag mouth."

With her unfortunate traits, it is understandable that few men were attracted to Euphrosyne's company, other than those who sought to acquire her considerable wealth. After the absolute authority she had wielded in running Vladya's estates, it must have been doubly hard for her to assume the subservient status of a female in Kremlin court society. Regardless of his own disgraceful lack of personal restraint, John Shuisky was very much a prig when it came to the morals of others. While it was true that he encouraged Ivan to commit the same sins and debauchery in which he engaged himself, he was quick to demand a proper behavior in family matters, most especially when this concerned the activities of women.

Euphrosyne responded quickly to the realities of life at court. Realizing the hopelessness of openly confronting the Shuiskys, she quickly retired to the family *dacha* across the river from the Kremlin. From this place of privacy and security, she conducted her manipulations in more or less furtive secrecy. She was extremely ambitious for her son, seeing in Ivan's present weakness an opportunity that might not present itself again. Nothing would have pleased her more than to have Ivan removed, leaving the way open for Vladya to become Grand Duke.

But Vladya was very like his father. He was a stout lad in a fight and in his adherence to the dictates of conscience. Physically, he was slim, sturdy enough to handle a weapon, and also very blond, as I was. Later, when we became friends and went places together, people who did not know us would sometimes take us for brothers. I suppose, of all his father's traits, it was a tendency toward frivolity that appeared most strongly in Vladya's personality. I have never believed that he wished for more than he already possessed, either in material wealth or power. He loved his estates, and would much rather have lived there than in the city. He enjoyed women, and the freedom his high status granted him. He did not desire the notoriety which would have encumbered him, had he been thrust into a higher station.

As to his feelings toward Ivan, it is difficult for me to say. I always fear to be wrong when trying to peer into the depths of another man's heart. But when

Vladya arrived in Moscow at this early age, I doubt he had any feelings other than gratitude. Because his mother hated almost everyone, especially Ivan, it is likely she had already done everything she could to poison her son's mind against his cousin. I can only report my own impressions, based on my intimate association with Vladya, accrued in the years to come. I am convinced that he never harbored any strong hatreds other than toward his proper enemies, and certainly was never a man to loathe someone solely on the basis on another person's opinion. From all outward appearances, at least, Ivan and Vladya seemed to get along extremely well during this period. I have always felt that Andrew Kurbsky was closer to Ivan, however, and enjoyed a less formalized relationship. In fact, there were times when I felt a little jealous of him – left out, when he and Ivan spoke seriously together.

It was Vladya's reaction to these other associations of Ivan's that most clearly defined his attitudes. He was completely unconcerned. His real interests had nothing to do with politics or court intrigues, and Ivan seemed to recognize this. I think he genuinely liked his kinsman and enjoyed his company. It is unfortunate that other men worked so diligently to turn the two of them against one another in the years to come.

It was Euphrosyne who sowed the seeds which were to reap such a bitter harvest for her son, and during the first winter in Moscow she did everything she could to alienate the men who most strongly supported the Grand Duke. She set in motion several poorly conceived conspiracies, none of which developed as she wished, and her attempts to influence several boyars through their wives succeeded only in making her appear ridiculous. When Ivan learned of these manipulations, he thought them very funny. Eventually, so did Vladimir. He had assumed, even in his youth, a rather strange attitude toward his mother. Although she dominated him terribly, he seldom allowed himself to become upset by her peculiar quirks. He never made fun of her, she being his mother, but he did accept some of her tantrums with a smile. I think he was more open with me than with anyone else when it came to expressing his feelings. This was due to our sharing a common dilemma – our respective dams. The two women hated each other from the very beginning, and neither was pleased to see us together. In private, we joked about it and visited several times in Ivan's chambers. When winter ended, and Euphrosyne insisted on returning to the northern estates, I knew it saddened Vladya to be separated from his friends.

CHAPTER III

Before Vladya and Euphrosyne left Moscow, the daily lessons with the Metropolitan resumed, this time with my being included as a matter of course. Through Ivan, Makari heard how pleased Joseph had been with my ability to discuss sacred matters, and to understand the more difficult concepts inherent in our Church dogma. Before I knew it was going to happen, I suddenly found myself not only in the instruction sessions, but "honored" with the post of alter boy. I was devastated! I went to Heinrich in tears for the first time since I had known him, beseeching him to rescue me. But Mother had done it, he told me, and Heinrich advised that I "try it for a while." My only solace was his continuing to instruct me in the use of weapons every afternoon. As long as this went on, there was hope. He also told me some of the knightly legends to convince me that all was not lost, emphasizing that some of the bravest and most famous warrior knights had also served the church.

As to Makari, I can best describe him as a very kindly old man. I suppose he was close to fifty when he assumed this highest post in the Russian Church. His beard was completely white, a long snowy cascade that gave him such a benign air it was difficult to reconcile his appearance with the harsh recriminations of which he was capable. He blasted the Shuiskys periodically from the pulpit, and did it with such well–turned phrases, delving so specifically into their sins, they could never adequately reply.

I soon discovered certain advantages to working within the great Cathedral of the Assumption. The building connected to the royal palace by an underground passage, which gave me access never available before. It was also more difficult for the Shuisky guards to interfere with my movements within the palace, as I could always claim to be on an errand for the Metropolitan. The worst aspect of my duties was having to rise so early, before anyone else was awake. Sometimes, this was from the arms of Sonya, whom I was beginning to think of as "that cursed woman." She took advantage of my early departure to stay with me that extra time, sleeping until I had to leave, then returning to the *terem* before the rest of the household awoke. She shared her room with one other girl, who knew her secret, but who had been sworn to silence. As I was awakened each morning by a palace servant, he also knew – had seen us several times; but he was smaller than I was, and younger. He knew better than to tell.

My feelings are not easy to define, and I look back on this period with some sense of guilt. Sonya was honestly in love with me, while I was still attracted to her physically – much as a drunkard is drawn to his flagon of wine. When I was with her, I could not resist the tender offerings. During the day, I felt contempt both for her and for my weakness in being unable to sever the relationship. I had never explained the reason for my insistence on her faithfulness, and she still assumed that I returned her love. She was so confident of this, in fact, that she began to make demands of me and to question my reticence to discuss my daily activities. I tried to tell her that these were not matters for a woman's ears, regardless of the circumstances, but she – in her innocence – was basing her conceptions of a marital relationship on my mother's. And marriage, of course, was going to be the next problem. So far, I had been able to avoid discussing it, as Sonya's modesty – or sense of womanly pride – had kept her from forcing the issue. Or perhaps she sensed just enough of my feelings to fear it would end our liaison. Still, I knew I could not postpone the decision indefinitely.

I would ponder this dilemma as I made my way across the Kremlin grounds to the Cathedral in the dark, entering the great vault to light the candles and assist the priest – occasionally the Metropolitan – as he prepared for the early matins. I had little else to think about as I stood on one side, hardly hearing the drone of prayers and psalms. I performed my duties without concentrating on them, all the while lost in my own sense of sin and guilt. In truth, I had followed some of Ivan's suggestions and had demanded some extremely disgusting acts of perversion from Sonya, thinking they would so revolt her that she would not want to continue seeing me. Instead, she seemed to accept them fatalistically as her proper role – while it was I who felt guilty about them, especially so when I realized that I had actually enjoyed every one of them!

My new position allowed me to perform a great service to Ivan, and doing this allowed me to excuse some of my own failings. As the years passed, the Prince had amassed a sizeable collection of books, so many that he had difficulty keeping them hidden. He lived in constant dread of the day Shuisky would order a search of his rooms and they would be discovered. We still lived in an age where reading and writing were considered unmanly. With my access to the Cathedral, with all its numerous niches and forgotten recesses, I was able to take Ivan's volumes, one or two at a time, and secrete them all over the building. I never told Makari I was doing this, because some of the works concerned subjects he would not have countenanced. There were tomes of ancient history, particularly of the Greeks and Romans, but also a few of Byzantine lore containing much that dealt with matters considered immoral by the Church. Naturally, there were works concerning all manner of religious matter, but even some of these would have been poorly received, describing as they did the beliefs of the Roman or other heathen churches. I recall homilies of Saint Ambrose, the saints Jerome and Cyril, among others; but I also remember the story of Marcus Antonius and Cleopatra – a very spicy bit of reading, for which Ivan had paid a goodly sum, as he had for two accounts on the exploits of Alexander of Macedon. Some of the material was written in Greek, a language Ivan could read only with some difficulty. The bulk had been translated into one of the Slavic dialects, or into Illyrian, an ancient precursor of our own Russian.

By the utmost of clever maneuvering, Ivan had established an extensive trade to procure these manuscripts. There was a palace servant named Adashev, a skinny, soft-spoken, almost mousy man at this time in his life. He took care of Ivan's rooms, supervising the making of the bed and carrying out the slops – a position he had held almost since the day that Agrafena, Ivan's old nurse, had been banished by the Shuiskys. Adashev came from a family of minor nobility, although some ancestor of his had actually reached *okolnichi* class, this being one of the highest boyar ranks. It comprised those men who were "nearest the throne."

Through Adashev, Ivan made anonymous contact with some of the Moscow–Novgorod traders, buying every book they were able to find and have smuggled to him.

In order to finance these purchases, he stole small items from the palace, or had me do this for him. Once, I was even able to steal a large jade broach off John Shuisky's *shuba* – or fur coat. This brought Ivan two very old scrolls about the history of some Roman emperors. It also started a terrible argument among the Shuisky men, because they were all accusing each other of the theft. As long as Adashev continued to make up the room, or supervise his men in doing it, there was little chance of discovery. Ivan treasured these manuscripts beyond any other possession, and greatly feared losing them. He was most relieved when I had gotten most of them hidden. Many years later, he would openly admit to owning books, and even made some remarks about boyars who were too stupid or too lazy to learn reading. But at this time it would have been Ivan who was thought feeble minded, or soft, had his activities been uncovered.

While I had these books in my possession, I read a number of them. I never understood the Greek script as well as Ivan, but I particularly enjoyed the histories. I could imagine myself doing some of the deeds described on the scrolls, leading armies and conquering new lands for the King. At first, I was afraid to admit having taken these liberties, for several of the things I read had been pieces which Ivan had previously refused to loan me. I finally discussed some of my new knowledge with Heinrich, whom I found to be familiar with most of it. In his youth, he had traveled almost all the way to Rome and was acquainted with men who had actually seen the Holy Land. He told me of the new books being produced in western countries, on presses with removable plates to produce many pages of the same characters.

Makari never discovered the books hidden about his domain, or at least he never indicated he knew of them. However, he was a wise and clever man, so it was possible he did know. He soon began to supply Ivan with reading material from his own collection. These were always things of an ecclestastical nature, like the writings of the monk Nestor, treasured classics copied in the ancient Monastery of the Caves in Kiev. Makari had many old books and scrolls, because he was involved in compiling a single history to describe the activities of all these holy men. To this end, he had brought a large group of priests and monks with him from Novgorod. The work would eventually be called the *Stoglav*, or Book of the Hundred Chapters.

These days of study and more or less peaceful meditation took place within the quiet, sacred walls of the Kremlin cathedrals or in the cells of the Metropolitan and his monks. Between these academic activities and my extensive sessions in Heinrich's practice yard, I had less direct contact with the turmoils in and around the palace. Naturally I knew about them, because either Ivan or Heinrich would tell me – still not exactly the same as observing them. Outside my silent cloister, the endless violence and struggles for power continued, again mounting toward a moment of crisis. John Shuisky was proving such a poor administrator that he was forced more and more to rely on support from the Novgorod nobles. His dependence finally became so obvious, many Muscovites made bitter jokes about our being the subject city.

It all came to a head in late April, maybe early May, after Vladimir and the Kurbskys and several other friendly princes had returned to the country to look after the spring planting. By this time, the insidious Shuiskys had disposed of nearly everyone who had even tacitly supported the Bielsky faction. They had accomplished this by striking down their enemies one by one, having some executed on concocted charges, exiling others, and by doing this frightening the others away. There was only one boyar left who had the wealth and the popular following to threaten their absolute control . . . Feodor Vorontsof.

I think that Ivan looked on Feodor as the only dependably loyal supporter he had among the senior nobility, and consequently was vocal enough in praise of our kinsman that the Shuiskys found it difficult to attack him without openly going against Ivan's wishes. They did this all the time, of course, but always on the pretext of protecting him. Feodor, because of his youth and tendency toward frivolity, did not display a serious enough demeanor to provide the ruling faction with grounds to accuse him. Recently, he had been involved in nothing more sinister than an attempt to reestablish some of his severed trade routes. I suspect that some of these business manipulations were responsible for an underlying hostility between him and Heinrich, but with the coming of spring the two men appeared to have reconciled their differences and were working in concert for their mutual advantage. John Shuisky had hurt both of them by rescinding some of the charters issued while Johannes was regent. Regardless of how it came about, by this point in time it became apparent to everyone that the Shuiskys were anxious to do away with Vorontsof.

Despite the liaison between Feodor and Heinrich, Shuisky never bothered my stepfather, probably because he was afraid of him. But for several weeks, Feodor was openly threatened, called names, and excluded from a number of social functions. Once, he was even spat upon by Andrew Shuisky. He told Ivan each time one of these incidents occurred, and the Prince eventually became concerned for his safety. I do not mean to imply that Feodor went crying to his sovereign, however; he simply recounted the slights and insults as if they meant very little to him, but retold the tales as examples of Shuisky boorishness. With typically Slavic indifference, he answered Ivan's anxious questioning: "What will come will come."

At about this time, Ivan decided to move into larger quarters, selecting a suite of rooms in the same wing of the palace where he had been living for most of his life. He did this without consulting the Shuiskys, but they were apparently too involved in sin and debauchery to care. As a result, those of us who visited regularly were able to meet in comfort, for the salon was spacious and nicely furnished. Feodor and I were with Ivan and Yuri one afternoon – this at Ivan's request, as I would otherwise have been in the practice yard with my stepfather. Makari had sent word that he wished to speak with Ivan on a matter of some importance. Andrei Adashev was moving in and out of the room, taking care of his routine tasks.

We were drinking mead, or rather the others were. I was toying with a mug, not drinking, because I didn't like it. Ivan had just finished a long dialogue, telling of his intention to acquire all the lands to the south and east, outlining his future plans. "The Czar," he said, "should be first among Christian kings." It was a very grandiose destiny he foresaw, but listening to him I was able to dream my own visions of grandeur, planning how I would help him achieve his goals.

Suddenly, Adashev, who had been out of the room for several minutes, burst in and shoved the door shut behind him. He leaned back heavily against the panel, fear showing on his face as he tried to catch his breath. "Shuisky is heading this way!" he announced excitedly. "He has that whole gang of Novgorod rowdies with him!"

"Trouble," sighed Feodor resignedly.

"That must have been what Makari was going to warn us about," I suggested.

Ivan thought first of action. "Go get the Metropolitan," he ordered Adashev. "Get him here as fast as you can!" The servant still hesitated. "Go!" he shouted again.

Adashev vanished out the door, and a few moments later we heard the thunder of heavily booted men approaching outside. "I wish your stepfather were here," whispered Vorontsof. He had no time for more. The door burst open to reveal the mob of nobles, all wearing fine dark robes and many with the tall, flat topped boyar hats. There were no tatters or patches any more, for the royal treasury had served to dress them well. The group included both John and Andrew Shuisky, and their cousin Prince Shopin–Shuisky of Novgorod. The Kubensky brothers were with them, as well as Pronsky, Paletsky, and at the rear of the group – not looking too happy about it – was Alexi Basmanov.

Ivan leaped to his feet as they entered, his face ablaze with anger and indignation. "How dare you come into my rooms without knocking?" he demanded. "Get out of here, all of you!"

"So the little rooster's beginning to grow a comb," said one of the Kubenskys, sarcastically.

"Or a little hair on his chin," one of the others remarked.

"Or on his balls," roared Andrew.

Their mocking laughter rocked against the walls, and I felt my heart swell up in the heat of fear and anger. Ivan had taken a step backward, frightened I am sure by their boldness. They had obviously been drinking – as usual – and it would not have been difficult for one of them to have shoved a sword into his gut. Each of them could then have taken a turn, and like Caesar the rightful ruler would have fallen with no one man his murderer.

Feodor stepped between Ivan and the other boyars. "What are you up to this time, Shuisky?" he demanded, facing John at a distance of no more than a hand's breadth. I noticed Feodor's fingers stroking the hilt of his sword.

"Get your whore's mouth away from me!" shouted John. He shoved both hands against Feodor's shoulders, and he'd grown so heavy he was able to topple the slighter man backward. Ivan jumped quickly out of the way, else they would have landed in a pile on the floor. As it was, Feodor caught himself on a chair and managed to remain standing.

No one said anything for several heartbeats. Each side seemed to await the other's move. Then the Metropolitan arrived, squeezing past the princes who stood at the rear of the group, still blocking the doorway. Yuri was sitting next to me on a bench, and I felt his body begin to tremble.

"John Shuisky," intoned the Metropolitan. "In the name of Holy Church, I demand to know what sin you're about to commit!"

"No sin, Father," snarled Andrew. "We are just going to remove a thorn from the side of the State." The others responded with a menacing growl. Their laughter became bitter, now, as the evil souls of these greedy men seemed bare before the light of God.

"The curse of Heaven will be upon all of you, if you dare harm these boys!" Makari carried a staff with a golden cross on the top. He placed its tip on the floor, between himself and the Shuiskys, forming a holy barrier to keep them from us.

"We mean no harm to the boys," said John, speaking in a softer, nasal whine.

"No!" shouted Basmanov, looking at Ivan. He seemed almost embarrassed. "We will not harm the Duke. We only want the traitor Vorontsof."

A roar of assent went up from the others, and again they surged forward. One of them trod on the edge of the Metropolitan's cassock, and as the priest stepped back to keep from being crushed beneath their bovine mass, the cloth of his holy garb parted. The rich golden mantle fell into a shimmering pile about his feet, leaving him to stand before them in only his bare, white shift. The loss of his fine trappings, however, did nothing to diminish his dignity. The cross–topped staff still held firmly in front of him, he continued to bar their way. I saw a fearful look on a few faces, but none of the Shuiskys seemed moved.

Ivan, recovering his composure now that the invading boyars had indicated they were not intent on harming him, leaped up beside Makari. "Prince Vorontsof is no traitor!" he shouted. "If you harm him, you are the traitors!"

Again the mob surged forward, pushed from the rear by the impatient men in back, who could not see clearly into the room. This time, the Metropolitan was knocked backward, tripping over the folds of his fallen garment. He fell heavily at their feet. Stunned, he said nothing for several minutes.

Andrew shoved Ivan aside roughly, as Feodor attempted to draw his sword. His arms were quickly pinioned at his sides by the others, and one of them produced a length of rope. Feodor's hands were quickly bound behind him, while another length of rope was knotted about his neck. The end of this lead was passed to Andrew, who pulled it taut as Feodor continued to struggle against his captors. By now he was on his belly, with three or four of them sitting on top, striking and kicking at him while they knotted the cords in place.

Makari sat on the floor in a daze through all this. Ivan stood beside him, panting with rage, but helpless to alter the circumstances. Yuri suddenly leaped from his place beside me, and threw himself in front of John and Andrew, encircling a leg of each with his arms.

"Please!" he screamed, his face red and soaked with tears. "Please don't kill him!"

Before I knew what I was doing, I was behind him, trying to drag him away, appalled that he should debase himself before such swine. Between the two of us, we set up a terrible howl.

Some of the men were momentarily confused, I think, by this unexpected outburst. The sounds of struggle had attracted a number of servants and other people from the palace staff, who now crowded the passageway behind the Shuiskys and their henchmen. Those in front were calling out an account of the activity to those who were unable to get close enough to see. This din only added to the confusion, and the tangle of people at the door made it impossible for the group of boyars to move backward. They did manage to kick Yuri and me loose.

It took several pairs of hands, but they were finally able to drag Vorontsof to his feet. With Andrew leaning into it, they began leading Feodor by the rope around his neck, shoving into the crowd. Their exit was halted by a sudden shout from Ivan.

"Wait!" he screamed. This first sound came shrilly, so he paused a moment to get his voice under better control. He was also on the verge of tears. "I order you, here and now, not to harm this man who's been my friend. If you do, I swear the day will come. . . ."

Makari placed his hand on Ivan's shoulder, apparently over the effects of his fall. He continued in a quiet, controlled tone of authority. "Think what it is you do, Noble Princes. To harm this man is to violate a sacred command given by your sovereign, the rightful Prince of Muscovy, the one appointed by God to be your Master!"

Andrew Shuisky snorted contemptuously, and there was a subdued murmur of laughter, in which I could hear "master" mumbled several times. But somehow, the blatant contempt was gone. They moved like a dark thunderhead through the more lightly clad servants, dragging Feodor on the end of his rope. Surrounded by the boyars, he looked back, his eyes turned so deeply in their sockets I could see only the whites. As he tried to cast a last desperate glance at Ivan, his face was almost purple from the pressure of the noose. He was unable to speak, struggling to draw his breath in harsh, wheezing gasps. In another moment they were through the door and gone, the sounds of their progress fading into the distance. The crowd trailed after them, thirsting for the sight of blood.

With the departure of the noble princes, a deadly silence fell upon our group. Yuri and I were still on the floor, where I tried to comfort his sobs. Ivan sat dejectedly on the bench his brother and I had occupied during most of the fray. Makari was absently trying to wrap himself in his torn garments.

"Do you think they'll kill him?" asked Ivan tonelessly, not looking up from his defeated slump.

"They wouldn't dare!" I answered savagely. "The curse of heaven would be upon them."

"And the threat of my sword when I get bigger," added Yuri.

Ivan shook his head, disconsolately. "Nothing will stop them, unless they're convinced I can eventually enforce my demands," he sighed. The Prince looked up expectantly at Makari. "How long, Reverend Father? How much longer must I wait?"

Makari, his robe now more or less in place, settled down beside Ivan. "I think the time is near at hand, My Son." The old priest's voice was calm, and he spoke with the soft assurance of one delivering the message of God. "You must wait only a little longer. To move before the proper moment could spell disaster."

The Metropolitan glanced in my direction. "Dmitri," he said, "it might be a good idea if you went home while they're busy with Vorontsof. Make sure your father knows what has happened." His old man's face was expressionless, but his words were ominous, nonetheless.

"You don't think they –" I started, looking first at Makari, then at Ivan.

"You'd better warn him," said Ivan. "You and Heinrich are about the only friends we have left."

In a final display of emotion, I prostrated myself before him, my hands gripping the hem of his tattered robe. With tears streaming from my eyes, I looked up into his troubled face. "You know I'll serve you with my last breath," I sobbed.

"I know it, Dmitri; I know it," he said softly, absently stroking my head as if I were a favorite pet. "But leave now, while you have the chance. – Adashev!" he called. The servant had reentered the room behind me. "Take Dmitri home, and stay there unless his father wants to send Us a message."

"As you say, my Prince," he answered respectfully, "but I don't think you need fear further trouble today. They've put Vorontsof in a cell, and he wasn't abused after they left your apartments. Now they're celebrating with his wine and liquor."

Ivan nodded acknowledgment, but impatiently waved his hand at us. "Good," he said, "Good. But go now!"

"And God's blessing go with you," added the Metropolitan, as we hurried from the chamber.

We started down the deserted hallway, and Adashev took my hand. Although it was getting dark, no one had lighted the hall tapers. "We'd better leave through the rear," he whispered. He surprised me with the firmness and assurance of his tone, and I followed him without argument. It was my first exposure to the leadership hidden beneath his frail exterior.

We raced down a back staircase, through the servants' rooms off the kitchen, pausing only a moment at the door to make sure we would be unobserved. Then we ran across the central square of the Kremlin. We could hear loud shouts and other sounds of roistering, mingled with drunken laughter. The memory of Mishurin lent an unreasoning terror to my steps. When we reached my house, the front door opened without our having to knock. Heinrich stood there in full armor, with a small semicircle of his armed retainers behind him. "Come in quickly," he commanded, and slammed the door shut as soon as we had obeyed him.

Mother rushed to me as I came through the group of soldiers, and in one of her rare displays of affection she hugged me to her. "Oh, Dmitri, I was so worried about you!"

"I'm fine, Mother," I said, trying to free myself, "but they've arrested Feodor."

"I know," she said, releasing me. She extended her left hand to Adashev, grasping his arm. "Thank you for bringing him home," she whispered emotionally.

"I am ordered to remain with you, unless the *Freiherr* wishes to send a message to the palace," he responded properly.

"Yes, there is a message," growled Heinrich. Adashev turned respectfully to face my stepfather. "Tell the Prince that my men and I stand ready to defend his person, but we do not wish to embarrass him by entering the palace without his request." He paused several times, carefully choosing his words. "I fear our foreign . . . origins. . . might cause. . .misunderstandings."

A murmur of assent echoed his words, as his men compacted more closely behind him.

"I do not believe the Prince is in any immediate danger," said Adashev. "The Metropolitan has remained with him."

"I would suggest, then," said Heinrich, watching the slender servant intently, and speaking slowly, pausing to give full import to each word, "that the Metropolitan take the Prince, without further delay, and they go to the Cathedral. They will attract less attention if they use the passage."

Adashev did not answer immediately, and Heinrich added, "I think a *lengthy* prayer session might be well advised."

The servant nodded. To be in the Cathedral meant to be in sanctuary, where none would dare violate the Holy protection of the Blessed *Bogoroditza*, the Mother of God. Bowing to my parents, Adashev passed quickly out the door, which one of the soldiers held open for him. For the moment that was all, though some young roisterers threw stones at our house during the night and had to be driven off by Heinrich and his men.

The next day dawned drab and gray, with the chill of early spring rains seeping in around the windows and doors. The willow trees along the edge of our property, with their small clusterings of new green leaves, drooped under the heavy accumulation of moisture. As the sun rose the air became humid, almost fetid, with steamy vapors boiling up from the ground. I had been awake for several hours, having gone early to the Cathedral where Ivan and the Metropolitan had spent the night. I doubt if either of them had slept. I found them side by side, before the Icon of Our Lady of Vladimir, repeating the prayer for forgiveness of sins. I waited silently for them to finish.

We spoke together for a few moments, and after cautioning us to be wary, and to return at the first sign of danger, Makari made the sign of the cross over us. Ivan and I slipped out the priests' entrance, into the stone passageway leading to the palace. A few drunken lackeys were sleeping it off, but other than the usual early stirrings in the kitchens there was no one else about. We stopped at Yuri's door to make sure he was all right. Adashev was with him, obviously having spent the night guarding his ward. The four of us went into Ivan's apartment.

About mid–morning, Adashev left to get us some food. After this, we remained inside the rest of the day, and were not disturbed until well after dark. Ivan and I spent most of the time playing chess, although at one point Yuri became bored and we broke off to play a game Andrew Kurbsky had taught us – using dice and round pebbles from the river bank. Because Ivan's rooms faced the west wall, we were unable to observe the happenings in the main courtyard. Thus, we did not see Vorontsof taken from his cell, which must have been about the time Adashev went after our breakfast. We learned later that he was paraded through the Square of Executions, prior to being sent to the prison at Kostroma. The usual furor and speechmaking accompanied this display of Shuisky triumph.

Andrei had gone out in the early afternoon to see what was happening, but guards had been reassigned and would not let him return. For this reason it was several hours before we had any news. The subsequent happenings have been variously attributed to fate, to diabolical conspiracy, to divine intervention – even to the punishment of Heaven. I doubt that anyone will ever be certain. But once poor Feodor was sent off under heavy guard, the roistering boyars reentered his house – the same in which Mother and I had lived after our terrible ordeal in the Arbat. It was located near enough to our present home that our servants could see most of the Shuiskys' disgraceful conduct. Feodor's house was sacked of all its valuables, including the contents of the master's bedchamber. Many of his personal possessions and family keepsakes were plundered, among these a silver vessel containing a quantity of very good German whiskey. My mother had given this to Feodor as a gift several years before; whether she also gave him the liquor later became a point of contention. But the vessel was appropriated by John Shuisky, who consumed the entire contents.

This was around mid–afternoon. By dusk, the Shuisky leader complained of severe stomach cramps, and soon began to vomit blood. Within an hour, he was dead. Because none of the whiskey was left, no one could know for certain that it had been poisoned. However, it was the only thing John had consumed all day not shared by someone else. He had suffered from stomach troubles before, so it may have been a worsening of his previous condition that killed him. No one but Vorontsof could ever know, and when he was questioned about it later he only answered with a knowing smile. The story was given out by the Shuiskys implying John's death as "natural." He was twenty–two or –three at the time.

The report of his cousin's death was brought to us by no less a personage than Andrew Shuisky. Like his cousin, Andrew was large, even heavier than John, and older. He had more the appearance of a statesman, as his hair was gray, cut very short and groomed like a German. Still, his mind was dull, too dull to be completely obscured by his loud, brassy manner. Because his mouth was filled with enormous yellow teeth – like a sheep – we often referred to him as the "ram." He was snarling and insulting when he spoke to Ivan that afternoon, telling him how he must now take up the duties of regent, complaining how hard he would have to work.

A few days later, Andrew grudgingly agreed to Ivan's making a pilgrimage to Sergey–Troitsky.

CHAPTER FOUR

Two days – or rather two nights later, Sonya told me she was pregnant, expressing this in an almost triumphant tone. It had been the first time she was able to come since Feodor's arrest, because Mother had changed the girls' sleeping arrangements. Sonya finished by weeping, and telling me how she loved me and how I would ruin her life if I did not marry her. Naturally, I had no intention of doing that. Not only had I grown to dislike her, but her rank placed no such demand upon me – quite the contrary. She was the daughter of an old retainer who had been in the service of my mother's family for generations. Now an orphan, she would bring neither status, nor dowry, nor any other inducement.

"You have damned my soul!" she wailed.

"There is but one soul in every ten women," I told her, quoting the ancient maxim. I finally asked her to leave my room, and told her not to come back. This was the day before Ivan was to leave for the monastery.

When I returned from seeing him off, I was trying to decide how to handle the situation with Sonya. It bothered me to think of confessing the whole story to my parents, but had more or less made up my mind I would tell one of them. The question was which to choose. Mother would be angry, I thought, although it was difficult to judge for sure. She might think it very humorous. Heinrich could beat me, but if I approached him properly he would be more likely to take me aside in a very manly confidence, planning with me how to settle the matter without further complications or scandal. Of course, scandal need not really become a con-sideration, as Sonya was only a servant in the eyes of anyone outside the family. There was no disgrace in a gentleman's sleeping with a serving wench.

But when I entered the house, I was greeted with an astonishing bit of household gossip. Mother had caught Sonya in a very compromising position with one of the squires! Heinrich had beaten the boy soundly and had been about to start on Sonya, when she sobbingly informed him of her condition. He had then beaten the lad again, and gone off to arrange their marriage. I never knew whether she had been carrying on with the other boy right along, or whether she had contrived the whole affair, possibly including their discovery. It might have been, I reasoned, but I was relieved to be out of it and did not seek to discover more. Nor could I now be sure whether or not the child was mine. Being rid of Sonya was an achievement in itself. I had learned another valuable lesson for my future dealings with women: she must never be allowed to dictate the relationship. She must come when asked; otherwise she must stay away. I swore never to make such a mistake again.

Soon, more serious circumstances diverted the few thoughts I expended on Sonya. Mother was again the victim of vicious rumors. Rumors! Why did my poor mother always have to be their sacrificial lamb? With Ivan away, the court gossips needed another subject, I suppose, and my ever suffering mother became their target. They said there could be no doubt about it; John Shuisky had died of poison supplied by her! Naturally, this rekindled stories of Helena's death, compounded by time into a supposed statement of fact. They then accused her of immorality before she married Heinrich. . .and worse, they went back to the time of my birth and talked about this! It was terribly embarrassing.

Because of the stories, I stayed home most of the time. Without Ivan in the palace there was no reason for me to go, as he had taken Yuri with him. I did take advantage of the situation to put a little plan of my own into operation, however. When I made my next confession, I was careful to select a priest who was close to Makari. I am sure my words got back to him, because I next persuaded Heinrich to ask for my release from duty at the Cathedral, and it was granted! Mother might have objected, but she was too upset over the stories being told about her, and said nothing.

Andrew Kurbsky was in Moscow for a few days, arriving immediately after Vorontsof's arrest. As he had arrived with more than his usual retinue of armed men, I was sure he came to assure Ivan's safety. Vladimir Staritsky and his mother had also come, apparently in answer to a request from Ivan – or possibly from Adashev acting on his own. In any event, they arrived the same day Ivan left for Sergey–Troitsky and reopened their *dacha* in the *Vorobiovo*, or Sparrow Hills, across the river from the Kremlin. During Ivan's absence, I made a number of trips into the city with Vladya, patronizing the taverns and generally getting into mischief. Our meetings were always by arrangement, of course, because our mothers had forbidden us to see one another. Euphrosyne claimed to be disturbed about the stories concerning Mother, and did not want Vladya associating with "Basil's bastard," as she called me. Mother was convinced *Maultasch* was purposely spreading the rumors, if not responsible for having started them.

Then there was some trouble in the Kremlin, a real falling out among thieves. All this furor drowned out the echoes of Euphrosyne's rumors – if they actually were hers. Alexi Basmanov had a violent quarrel with Andrew Shuisky, both of them probably drunk at the time. Neither man had ever liked the other, and there was a tremendous jealousy between their two families. The Basmanovs were the older clan, although their descent was not as noble. They had been extremely wealthy for several generations, but the Shuiskys had now usurped their preeminence among the "guests," or traders. Although Alexi had been a boon companion and drinking partner of Vassily's, and later of John's, his fortunes had continued to decline. Andrew, being less clever in manipulating Basmanov, suddenly found himself confronted by a raging madman. It took seven or eight Shuisky retainers to protect him. Later, Alexi would claim he always detested Andrew, and he was too stupid to make a good liar.

With this break the political pot really came to a boil, with many factions falling into sudden opposition with each other and no clear cut division of power between the usual camps. Euphrosyne began dabbling in court intrigue again, and at one point joined with the Glinskis, Helena's surviving relatives. This strange alliance forced the Kubenskys of Novgorod and the Pronskys to adhere more firmly to the Shuisky group. Many other families became involved, some of them drawn in without their really wanting to be, and making the result a confused tangle of alliances that had no logic or historical justification. As always, the Kurbskys appeared to remain neutral, although Andrew had secretly gone to join Ivan at Sergey–Troitsky. In the end, this was the only alliance which would matter.

In the Basmanov–Shuisky dispute, it would have been in Heinrich's interest to take up with the Basmanovs. His own trade would profit by any harm done the Shuiskys. But Euphrosyne had made some remarks indicating her favor of the Basmanov side, and when Mother heard this she created such a scene Heinrich stayed out of it completely. This frustrated me, and I had an argument with Mother, which ended with her boxing my ears and ordering me to my room in the middle of the afternoon. All summer, the political climate worsened, until the advent of cold weather found us on the verge of another civil war. By remaining away from Moscow for such a long period, Ivan was partially responsible for the situation developing as it had. But I think he planned it that way.

It was November before Ivan returned, attended by a large group of monks who were coming to Moscow for the holy days. He had made his arrangements with Andrew Kurbsky, who arrived in the capital a week before with a veritable army of retainers. Ivan immediately placed himself under their protection. There had been an offer of assistance from Vladya, as well, but Ivan was too suspicious of Euphrosyne to risk placing himself in her power. Now, with the large number of men available on either side, Heinrich's force counted for little.

By maneuvering himself into Kurbsky's guardianship, Ivan had made his person the balance of power. Andrew must have foreseen Ivan's eventual victory, and he knew he would be in highest favor when they succeeded in their current endeavors. Ivan was obviously well informed about all the developments during his absence, as he had been in constant communication with Heinrich, Adashev, and Vladimir. When he returned, his plans were already well formed, needing only the details worked out before they were put into motion.

Ivan sent for me the day after his return, and we met in the courtyard outside the kennels, where there was no chance of our being overheard. A heavy blanket of crusty snow completely covered the paving stones, except for the exercise yard where the dogs had stirred up the surface. A path had been cut from the palace exit to the shack in which Ivor and his boys sat beside the stove. Other than this, the earth's mantle of white lay undisturbed. Ivan was so concerned with secrecy, he led me off the cleared portions. We stood in knee–deep snow, dressed warmly in heavy sables, stamping out a small clearing as we spoke.

After a while we were joined by Yuri, Ivor and Adashev; but by then I was privy to Ivan's plan. With the arrival of the others, we broke off and turned to a more general discussion. Ivan was awaiting word from Andrew Kurbsky before telling the rest as much as they needed to know, and it was not long before a horseman in Kurbsky livery trotted up. Dismounting and bowing respectfully to Ivan, the man handed him a sealed message.

Ivan dismissed the messenger after reading the paper, which he tore into tiny pieces and allowed the wind to scatter. With no further preamble than a cursory glance into each of our faces, he demanded rather than asked: "Are you, each of you, willing to stand loyal to me?"

The question was unexpected, and seemed so needless, all four of us must have stared stupidly for several heartbeats. Then Yuri grinned, and in his innocent way playfully cocked his head to one side. "What kind of trouble are you going to get us into this time, Ivashka?" he asked.

Ivan cut him short with a brisk movement of his gloved hand. "I am not playing!" he growled. "Today I intend to become Grand Duke!"

"But you are Grand Duke," his brother insisted.

"Of course you are," echoed Ivor. He turned to Yuri and me, adding, "Have any of us ever doubted it?"

"I think Ivashka means something more," I told him.

Ivan continued to speak, his tone grating with an almost evil malice. "We have just completed Our plans for Andrew Shuisky," he said, his gaze falling on each of us in turn, and pausing as if to absorb our innermost thoughts before passing to the next. "Will each of you, here and now, swear a life–long fealty to me as your Lord and Prince?"

I was spellbound by his face and his serious attitude. Despite having been told more than the others, I still responded in a rather childish innocence. But then, as in my later years, such a question had only one answer. I fell to my knees in the snow, every fiber of my being aflame with emotion. I swore to be his servant, and to hold his slightest wish above my very life. When I had finished my melo–dramatic dialogue, Ivan placed his hand on my head, replying in tones as solemn as my own: "I accept you, Dmitri, as the first of my followers."

Yuri, Ivor, and Adashev were not far behind in following my lead. They, too, swore their allegiance as I had done—all a very boyish scene, I suppose, played in the cold, slushy snow of the palace kennels. But it was a promise I spent the rest of my days endeavoring to uphold, and our individual promises were only a preamble to the same from all of Muscovy.

Once the oath–taking was completed, we all stood facing Ivan, awaiting his next instructions. Ivor and Andrei stepped back, leaving us three boys by ourselves. I could hear Adashev giving Ivor some instructions, but was unable to make out the words. I looked questioningly at Ivan.

"The kennel keepers are going to make sure Shuisky does not escape," he said. His eyes blazed with a passion I had never seen before, but would learn to know well in the years ahead. "Before many days are past," he continued tightly, "each and every member of the nobility will swear an oath like yours, or they'll find themselves along with the Shuiskys."

From behind us Andrei spoke up, but as he addressed Ivan his tone was no longer that of a guardian to his ward. It bore a subtle difference – a servant speaking to his master. "It still troubles me," he suggested, "that we have not consulted the Metropolitan. His advice. . . ."

"No!" Ivan answered sharply. "Prince Kurbsky will supply the information we need. He is to meet us at Dmitri's house before the dinner hour. If word of my intentions should leak out, we will be protected there." This last he directed to me; then looking back at Adashev, he added, "Go get the things I left on my bed and take them to *Freiherr* von Staden's."

Adashev obeyed immediately, seeming to accept his master's new status without question. As he hurried out of ear shot, Ivan explained: "The Metropolitan is certainly on Our side, but I think it best not to seek his blessing when We do not know how many men We may have to kill."

He said this so offhandedly, and with such seeming lack of concern, it would have been impossible to divine the sinister import from his tone. I wondered, however, if he fully trusted Makari. Although the Metropolitan would surely protect Ivan from harm, and had worked diligently in his interests, he was still the former vicar of Novgorod. I was confident of his loyalty, but at this crucial time Ivan may have had some doubts. In our strange world of human relationships, we are seldom sure of anyone.

As we walked toward my house, I kept thinking of Ivan's words, but more poignantly of his wild expression and blazing eyes. It brought to mind the old prediction of the Patriarch of Jerusalem, given to Basil when he insisted upon marrying Helena after the Church refused its blessing. "You will have a wicked son," the prelate had threatened, "one who will ravage your streets with terror and cause rivers of blood to flow in your lands. The heads of the mighty shall fall. The punishment of hell's fire shall devour your fields and cities."

I had been trudging along, behind Ivan, wallowing in these seditious contemplations, when he turned to look back at me. Seeing I was disturbed, he waited for me to catch up with him. He draped an arm over my shoulders – the first time he had broken his stern bearing all day – and spoke to me in the confidential tone he had used so many times in the past.

"What troubles you, Dmitri?" he asked.

"I don't know," I told him honestly. "Maybe I'm a little scared."

He smiled. "If you are truly frightened, and still don't fail to follow me, you are holding to your vow from the very start."

"I will always be true to my vow," I said firmly, "no matter how afraid I am."

"You are good, Dmitri," Ivan said softly, almost sadly. He had a peculiar, far away look in his eyes. "If I were as good as you, my brother, I would not need to pray the many hours I do." And with these unexpected words his dreamy melancholy dissolved. He clapped me on the back and moved up to Yuri, who still plodded a few feet ahead of us. Even then, poor Ivashka's soul must have been in torment, though it would be years before I fully understood – if, indeed, I or any other man could fully understand him. Many times during my life I have thought back on the words he spoke to me that afternoon, and at various times I have placed different interpretations on what he said. His mind ran too deeply even for me, who knew him better than any. But at that particular moment, our hearts had touched more closely than they ever had before . . . more closely, I suspect, than they ever did again.

I am sure that the real reason for Ivan's calling his "council" in our *dacha* was to assure support by Heinrich and the German knights. Once secure in having this group as his bodyguards if something went wrong, he was willing to take the necessary risks to assume the throne. Kurbsky's men would still attend him, but they seemed more open to Shuisky corruption. If just one man in the force should prove to be untrue, a quick thrust with a dagger could end it all.

I am ashamed to admit the daydreams I conjured up as the men discussed their arrangements and the signals they would use in the event of danger.   I pictured myself beside Ivan, with Heinrich and his warriors striking down clumsy Russian boyars and princes. This, of course, is the problem inherent in employing foreign troops—a problem, incidentally, which Heinrich foresaw and was always at great pains to avoid. One comes to look upon the outanders as the symbols of good and right, whereas one's own people become the enemy. In these final days of Shuisky domination, I confess to a strong identification with my stepfather's people, and for that time my soul was not properly Russian. Perhaps it was my mixed blood, for they say the affinity for one's own kind can draw the spirit like a lodestone attracts iron.

With typical efficiency, my mother had everything ready when we arrived. She had gotten rid of the servants, leaving only Frieda in the kitchen with one of Heinrich's men to help her if she had something heavy to move. The men were all dressed in hunting tunics, but beneath their benign exterior coverings they were protected by sheaths of heavy chain mail. At Ivan's entrance, Heinrich bowed deeply and reverently. My mother kissed his hand. The Grand Duke received these ceremonial greetings gracefully, as if he had been used to such homage all his life. He no longer appeared the frightened boy who had pounded on our door in the dark of night, fleeing for his life from his own palace. Yet today, he was placing himself in a still more dangerous position, and within a few moments would have passed the final milestone from which he could not turn back.

Heinrich conducted Ivan into the larger of our two halls – the room Mother referred to as the "salon." The master's chair had been placed on a board, raised on blocks to make it a few inches higher, all this draped with a dark felt. Yuri and I sat on the side of this dais, at Ivan's feet, while the others seated themselves on chairs facing him. Andrew Kurbsky arrived a few minutes after we did, and although he seemed momentarily surprised to find Ivan enthroned in our living room, he quickly assumed the proper role of vassal. Albeit he was later to criticize the events following this meeting, he was cooperative in organizing the plan, and in fact assured its success.

When Ivor and Adashev came in, quietly taking their places behind the others, the assembly was complete. A strange group for such a glorious task, I thought. We included everything: a Grand Duke and a boyar prince, a German knight, a woman, two boys, a troop of soldiers, and servants who ranked little higher than slaves. It seemed as though we represented the realm, united in our purpose of being together. There was a total, awesome silence as the Grand Duke of Muscovy, Autocrat of Rus, began to speak: "We have decided," he began, using the imperial plural, "the behavior of Our boyars can no longer be tolerated. The people of Muscovy live in a state of confusion, never knowing to whom they will be required to pay taxes, nor to whom they owe allegiance. Our foreign friends, as well as Our enemies, are also confused; this is a dangerous situation if permitted to go uncorrected. We experienced an example of this not too long ago, when the Khan of the Crimean Horde and the forces of Kazan marched into our southern lands, thinking we were too divided to defend ourselves. That time We were fortunate in having dedicated border forces to drive them out. Next time, We many not be so fortunate. For this reason, We have decided there will be no next time. Therefore:

"We have ordered Our boyars to assemble in the Great Hall of the Duma in a little over an hour's time. We shall then make Our decision known to one and all."

"Your Highness may be assured of the full support of every person in this room," said Heinrich, answering whatever question may have hovered in Ivan's mind.

Then Mother, God rest her soul, shattered the decorum by stepping forward, speaking out in an assembly that was properly reserved for men. Using proper court form, she began: "If it may be permitted to speak without harm.. . . ."

Ivan glanced at her in surprise, but he nodded assent and she continued: "In an assembly of Muscovite boyars, the presence of foreign troops might create a situation to be interpreted unfavorably. Did Your Highness intend. . . ?"

Ivan shook his head, and I felt my own face flush with embarrassment. The question was redundant, but I was also relieved, for it indicated that Heinrich had not discussed the entire plan with her. "No, Eleanor," Ivan replied, speaking with exaggerated courtesy, "No, my – Our intention is not to bring anyone who is not of the Duma into the chamber with us, except our brother Yuri and Our. . . friend Dmitri. Prince Kurbsky will escort Us into the room, and will naturally remain. Our servant Adashev will be directly outside the door, where Dmitri can alert him in the event of danger, and he, in turn, can carry word to Our other loyal subjects." He glanced at Ivor as he spoke. "We ask only that the knights and other gentlemen of the *Freiherr's* group remain available on the off chance they should be needed."

"Has the Metropolitan been informed?" asked one of the men.

"His Holiness will be informed when Our announcement has been made," said Ivan dryly. "He favors Our cause, but always advises caution. This is a time for action, gentlemen, for boldness!"

There was a murmur of approval, and as Ivan stood he received a salute from the soldiers. Everyone remained on his feet as Ivan stepped from the dais.

"I must go to the palace now, to assume the proper attire." he announced. "Yuri and Adashev will come with me. Dmitri, you will join Us in Our apartments as soon as you have changed. Prince Kurbsky will come for Us when it's time to leave for the Duma."

Ivan motioned to Adashev, who handed me a large box, obviously the "things" Ivan had left on his bed. I waited until they left before I opened it. Several of the men gathered around to see what I had received, and they gasped in awe at the magnificent robe of gleaming white velvet, trimmed with a thick, ermine collar. It was a very costly garment, far more expensive than Ivan could have provided from the meager sums he was able to come by. It must have been Kurbsky gold, I thought, realizing that this was only one of many items which must have been provided. It somehow impressed me more deeply than anything else Andrew had done, emphasizing his own degree of commitment.

I glanced toward the doorway, where Heinrich was exchanging a few hasty words with Kurbsky. I wanted to say something to him, but knew I shouldn't interrupt them. Nor was I exactly certain of the way to express my feelings. There would be ample time later, I thought. I was pleased to note, however, that my stepfather and the prince seemed friendly, and I could tell that they held each other in respect. They laughed about something, and Andrew turned to leave. "Don't be too long, Dmitri," he called.

Ivan, Yuri, Andrew Kurbsky, and I waited in a nearby antechamber as members of the Boyar Council assembled in the Hall of the Duma. Andrei Adashev was posted in the corridor where he could watch the boyars as they arrived. We were all anxious, and displayed our tensions in characteristic ways. I could feel sweat running down my back, and the insides of my hands were wet and slippery. Ivan paced, rubbing his palms together. Yuri hummed to himself as he sat on a bench with his knees drawn up under his chin. Andrew was quiet and restrained, but the muscles of his jaw were in constant motion as he gritted his teeth, watching the rest of us.

At last Andrei tapped on the door, giving us the signal that all the expected boyars were present, except for Andrew and Ivan, himself.

"It is no longer a matter of saying, 'The time will come,'" Ivan sighed. He stood up, adjusted the drape of his robe, and strode purposefully across the chamber. Yuri and I followed him, as he entered cheek–by–jowl with Kurbsky. We slipped behind the row of boyars nearest the door as soon as we had entered; Ivan had to walk the full length of the room. Andrew went only part way with him, as his seat was against the wall to Ivan's left, about half way along the row. Ivan's step never faltered; he marched the full distance and mounted the dais with its splendid, gilded throne. The room itself was rectangular, without the pillars found in most Kremlin halls. The central floor was sunken, two steps below the wide, surrounding area of parquet. On this higher level stood the cushioned stools of the boyars, each with its back to the wall, so every man faced toward the center of the room. Grilled windows with fine, sheer mica panes allowed brilliant streams of light to enter, making this one of the brightest enclosures in the palace.

At Ivan's entrance, the boyars fell gradually silent, and moved to take their proper seats. When Ivan reached the throne and turned to face them, they were all in place. When he sat, they did likewise, following prescribed custom. Yuri and I sat next to each other, on a pair of tiny stools that had been placed behind the farthest row of boyars. Andrew had done his job well, for all but Shuisky were wearing their finest robes, elegantly embroidered and flecked with gems. The atmosphere was one of expectation.

Ivan was by far the grandest of all. On his head he wore the jeweled crown of a prince – not the Crown of Monomakh, for that would be worn only after his coronation, when he had been annointed with the holy oils. His robe was of heavy white satin, brocaded with pearls and precious stones. When he moved, he glittered like hard crusted snow. He bore himself with the dignity of a true autocrat, and this bearing was as much responsible for the awed silence as the rumors circulated ahead of time by Kurbsky. In his hand, Ivan held the *kisten*, the staff of his father,

Basil. It was a heavy, carved scepter, nearly a foot taller than Ivan, with a polished gold knob at the top, and an equally gleaming sword point at the base.

Resting his left hand easily against the arm of his throne, casually gripping the staff, he allowed his gaze to wander slowly over the assembly. The fire had not left his eyes, and somehow its power seemed to affect the entire group. When the young Grand Duke began to speak, no other sound could be heard. Even the heavy breathing of the older men ceased to be audible.

"We have assembled you here," Ivan began, "to express Our displeasure at the wretched condition of Our court." His voice was mellow, but it carried a stern authority. Even I, who spoke with Ivan almost every day, was surprised at the maturity of his tone. As he continued, it rose in volume and also a little in pitch, yet never lost its princely quality. "Our friends have been struck down," he said, "and some have been taken from Us forever. My brother and I have suffered greatly at your hands; but the time has come for Ivan, son of Basil, his lawful heir, to assume the authority which is rightfully His."

For the first time a hint of concern was whispered by the nobles, but as Ivan went on they fell silent again. "Hear now Our words, Noble Princes and Boyars of Muscovy, and be guided by them. We shall no longer endure insults and neglect within Our Own palace; nor shall We permit decisions affecting the welfare of Our State to be made by others, without proper consultation with Us, the Grand Duke!

"At this particular moment, We do not intend to punish more than one; but this one will be a lesson to you all. Learn it well, and you shall continue as Our vassal lords. Ignore it, and be assured Our wrath shall fall upon you with all the fury of hell!"

Ivan allowed a long pause, that his words might be digested. His eyes again traveled along the rows of boyars, pausing momentarily on each, coming to rest at last upon Andrew Shuisky. There they remained until the boyar began to squirm uncomfortably. Suddenly, Ivan raised his hand and pointed at Shuisky, shouting, "You! You, Andrew Shuisky! I arrest you here and now!"

All heads turned to follow the Grand Duke's accusing finger. Shuisky bolted from his seat. He looked about him, a sly grin on his lips. But that expression lasted only a dubious moment. He glanced toward the other men who had drunk with him and called him friend. But Kurbsky had been thorough, and nowhere did Shuisky see a friendly face, not even an encouraging smirk. Ivan's words had been cleverly phrased, striking fear in a good many hearts. Shuisky stared hard at John Kubensky, who looked only at his own feet. Basmanov watched sightlessly; Vorotinsky frowned in contempt; and Pronsky gazed into space. At length, Shuisky's hauteur melted into stark terror, for he realized he had walked into a trap.

"No!" he screamed. "No!" He stood for a moment in the center of the room, in the recessed area which placed him below the rest of the assemblage. He cast about him like a frightened animal in a pit. Then he broke for the door, running through it before anyone could move to stop him. This brought the audience to an end.

Ivan rose from his throne and raised his hand to silence the flow of words from the astonished group of men. "He will be caught," said Ivan simply. He stepped gracefully down from the platform and, holding his staff before him, walked slowly from the room.

Yuri and I followed him, walking with dignity until we were out of the boyars' sight. Then all three of us broke into a run, racing upstairs to the hall windows overlooking the front of the palace, where a furious struggle was going on. The kennel boys had grabbed Shuisky before he had gone a dozen steps beyond the palace door. Two or three Shuisky retainers had attempted to assist their master, but Ivor's husky young men outnumbered them and quickly dispatched them with heavy sticks. Ivor now had his right arm crooked about Shuisky's neck, as he lifted the struggling boyar off the ground. Some of the boys grabbed Andrew's legs, conveying their terrified captive back toward the kennels.

There were several versions told of how Andrew Shuisky actually died. Some say Ivor strangled him, which certainly did not seem unlikely from the manner in which we saw him carried away. Others say he was thrown to the wolfhounds, who tore his living body to pieces. No one can ever be sure, not even those of us who watched. As the group carrying Shuisky rounded the corner of the palace, we raced to Ivan's apartments, which faced the kennels. We saw Ivor pitch Andrew's body into the compound where he had penned the most vicious hounds, starved for several days to assure their appetites. The dogs tore the body to shreds, but whether Andrew was alive or dead when he was thrown in, even Ivor could not say for sure.

Although Ivan had said he would punish only one, he issued an order that evening for the arrest of Shuisky's entire staff of bullies. However, none of these was among the boyar assembly to whom he had made his statement. This riffraff, collected as they attempted to flee with whatever valuables could be carried from the Shuisky *dacha*, were strung on gallows about the northern entrance to the city, the gate through which the Novgorod caravans entered and left the capital. The bodies were left until the rotting corpses fell in shreds to the dogs that waited below.

Ivan IV, Grand Duke of Muscovy, had started his reign.

BOOK TWO

IVAN THE GOOD

CHAPTER I

The atmosphere within the palace had changed, almost overnight. During the first weeks following Ivan's triumph over the Shuiskys, even the weather seemed to rejoice with us. Although cold winter winds continued to moan through black, starless nights, our days were generally mild, promising an early spring and a warm summer. Most of the paved areas within the Kremlin had been trampled clear of snow by the heavy traffic of men and animals. Long lines of servants formed every day to carry provisions from outside the walls, transferring the heavier goods to small hand carts, because the sleighs carrying materials into Moscow along the frozen river could not be dragged across the intervening patches of dry earth.

Ivan was more relaxed and happy than ever before. Only by the firmest, most constant self control was he able to project a properly dignified image. In public, when he sat before his court or presided at one of the numerous official functions, he never betrayed the wild joy that swelled within his heart. He forced himself to sit stern and stolid, with an attitude befitting the Muscovite Autocrat. Later, when he and Yuri and I were alone, he would cavort about his freshly refurbished apartments, hugging himself with glee and stroking the piles of fine garments jamming his great chests. No more threadbare tunics, nor stockings with holes at the knees! No more need for secrecy, nor for his friends to sneak packets of food past the guards! We ate only the best and were served the finest wines, many from beyond the Polish borders.

A roistering cadre of younger men soon formed about the Grand Duke, mostly fellows who had previously been afraid to approach him. Some were sons or brothers of the very men responsible for the miserable conditions Ivan had just destroyed. But at the moment he did not seek revenge – that would come later, and in terrible severity. Now, he unleashed the pent–up energies he had been forced to suppress during the Shuisky regime.

I deeply resented these new associations, and felt threatened by them. Most were older than I – Ivan's age or more. At first, this seemed to place me at a singular disadvantage, as the years one has lived usually imply a man's degree of experience, define the heightening of his skills and knowledge. But the circumstances were not exactly as I originally perceived them. My own abilities – not only in letters, but in the arts of hunting and horsemanship, and especially in the use of weapons – were the equal of any. The others soon recognized this, and because I was large for my age I was not long in establishing myself within the group. My birth was the one weakness I could not hide, as some tended to look down on my illegitimacy. However, they had to assume I carried the blood of Rurik and of the Roman Emperors in my veins; and Ivan was my friend.

Some of the finest, fastest horses in the country were quartered in the Kremlin stables. Almost every day Ivan led a large retinue through the gates, along the city streets, and into the open country beyond. Woe to anyone in our path! Sometimes a careless peasant would fail to heed the thunder of oncoming hoofs, discovering to his sorrow that no force on earth could halt Ivan's enjoyment of freedom. With the coming of spring there were many organized hunts and racing events. We often traveled into the countryside, toward the swamps of Novgorod, where we might camp out overnight, using gyrfalcons and hawks to bring down swan and geese from the flocks which darkened the skies above marshy meadows.

But all was not play for Ivan. In addition to fulfilling the ceremonial duties at the palace, he never neglected the thanks due our Lord God. He made several trips to different monasteries, traveling farther from Moscow as the weather cleared. By utilizing the services of his Glinski cousins, and the long–tenured clerks of the many Kremlin bureaus, the Grand Duke could be assured his government would continue without his immediate presence.

Before the green of summer burst brilliantly across the land, I noticed cliques beginning to form among Ivan's new followers. For myself, I was usually with Vladimir or Yuri – occasionally with Andrew Kurbsky, although his frequent absences from the city limited our association. Among the young men who eventually became my closest companions, there was one who initially singled me out to be the churl and the butt of his jokes. This fellow was the son of a boyar prince, and his name was Alfansy Buturlin. He was a little older than most of the others, and he prided himself on his knowledge of women. At the time of which I speak, he had already given us a few demonstrations in the finer art of violating the peasant girls who happened across our path.

Alfansy was a good horseman and skilled with both sword and bow. Notwithstanding his stature – for he was big, and he possessed the strength of a big man – he was somewhat soft, his body verging on flabbiness. His face was round and petulant, his lips gathered into a permanent pucker. His eyes were frequently pink from excessive food and drink, and at times seemed to be mired in the rolling flesh of his face. Alfansy`s father had never gotten on well with Heinrich, for the Buturlin family had tacitly supported the Shuiskys. Once, the two men had actually come to blows. Heinrich had pitched the elder Buturlin over a table, seriously injuring his back and leaving him permanently maimed. Ill will over this, combined with Alfansy's being jealous of my close friendship with Ivan, probably motivated his malevolence toward me.

One day, when a group of us were riding at high speed through the city streets, en route to our favorite tavern across the river, Alfansy deliberately shoved his mount against mine. He caused me to careen into a pushcart of vegetables being taken to the bazaar. My horse stumbled, and I would have been badly shaken if I had fallen. Fortunately, I was able to keep upright, and I spurred my mount to rejoin the group. Ivan was farther ahead and had not seen what happened; neither did he hear the derisive laughter of Buturlin and his cronies.

This was the final insult in a long series of petty irritations. I was furious! Racing at top speed, I reached Alfansy's side just as he started across the bridge. Gathering my legs under me on the saddle, I propelled myself against him. The force of my leap carried both of us off the far side of his horse's back, over the bridge railing and into the water. Those who had seen us started shouting, causing the entire group to halt, with those who had been ahead of us circling back to watch. The swift, midstream current swept us quickly away from the bridge, which precluded my revenge being fully observed. Alfansy was wearing heavy wool, despite the sun's warmth. I wore only a light tunic and hose, not nearly as cumbersome in the water. I was the better swimmer, anyway. Long before the current swept us onto a bank, a mile or so below the city, I had thoroughly pummeled him, shoved him under water, and came so close to drowning him that he was hardly able to gasp his pleas for mercy.

The rest of the group had followed our progress along the water's edge, but there were docks and warehouses in the way. It took a few minutes for our friends to find us, at the point where we came ashore. At first, no one knew whether to laugh or take us seriously. But Alfansy finally made a joke of it, bowing to me in clownish apology. Eventually, still dripping wet, we mounted our horses and continued to our destination. I cannot say this experience made Alfansy and myself better friends, but it was enough to convince him to leave me alone – at least for the immediate future. His ultimate revenge came some time later.

As time went on, the reins of government were left more and more in the hands of Ivan's cousins, George and Michael Glinski. While neither bore the title of Regent, I felt they merely pretended to bring major questions to Ivan's attention before rendering a decision. In many ways these Glinski princes were as grasping as the Shuiskys had been; certainly, they were as hated by the common people as any of their predecessors. But they always made sure Ivan was treated with proper respect, and were careful that he lacked nothing for his personal comfort.

One of Ivan's first acts had been to order the release of nearly all political prisoners. These men soon flocked into Moscow from every corner of the realm, and among the returnees was Feodor Vorontsof. But the Feodor who came back that spring was a far different man from the one who had been taken from us in chains. He was gaunt and haggard, wasted almost to skin and bones. His temper was short, and he sought solace in drink as he never had before. His lean appearance bespoke more than merely animal hunger for food and liquor. His long months in prison had also engendered an uncompromising lust for wealth and power – things he must have brooded over the whole time he was gone. Almost immediately, the Glinski spies began bringing reports of his strange, inexplicable activities and associations. After receiving a tremendous reception in our home, he seemed to shun us. In fact, he avoided all of his old friends. Feodor had always been vain, so I tried to excuse his behavior by telling people that I thought his present appearance embarrassed him. In my inner heart, though, I knew his mind had been deranged by his dreadful experiences. Whatever plans he had made and conspiracies he had imagined, these now became a megalomania he could not overcome. For instance, he was overheard discussing plans with John Kubensky, by which the two hoped to assume certain prime positions in the State. Later, he was said to have conferred with Pronsky, and even with Basmanov, who was not clever enough to keep anything to himself. All of these were strange combinations for Feodor, as he had never been friendly with any of them prior to his imprisonment. Kubensky, particularly, had been his enemy.

I was breakfasting with Ivan one morning after having accompanied him to his prayers. Michael Glinski was shown into the dining room and, executing an exaggerated bow, he greeted his cousin with the ceremonial request for permission to speak.

Ivan, full of good spirits, for it was a beautiful day, waved him to a seat at our table. "Our kinsman may not only speak, he may break bread with Us," said

Ivan jovially. "What brings the Royal Seneschal to Our breakfast table?" Michael sat down and nodded a casual greeting to me. "There is a problem," he began, glancing in my direction. He was lean and sly, very gray and pale – like a clerk who seldom sees the sun.

"Dmitri will remain," said Ivan firmly. "Continue."

"The problem concerns one of your . . . nobles." said Michael, toying with the pastry Ivan had poked into his hand, "and I should not wish to take action without first consulting Your Highness to ascertain Your wishes."

Ivan leaned back in his chair, emitting an enormous belch. "Michael, I am going to try out a new mount this morning. The day will be half gone before you say anything. Who is plotting against me this time?" He said this half jokingly, but I saw his left eye twitch. The very mention of betrayal was painful, exciting the dreadful fear that still lingered in his soul.

"It is John Kubensky," said Michael cautiously. "It appears he is trying to involve Vorontsof in a conspiracy to form a new regency."

Ivan's expression hardened at the mention of Feodor's name. "Your spies are efficient," he remarked coolly, "but it sounds as if this conspiracy presents a greater threat to you than to me."

Michael drew himself into a more erect and commanding posture. "Any threat to the government is a threat to both Your Majesty and to his servants," he replied evenly.

As they spoke I remember wondering what my mother might know about this. Feodor had made one of his rare calls on her a few days before, coming when he knew Heinrich wasn't home. I had been present only part of the time, until they asked me to leave. I wondered if Mother would actually work against the Glinskis. While she had never gotten on well with Michael, she seemed very fond of George, who was the opposite of his saturnine brother. George was very fat and jolly – a man who could sit at the table for hours, telling stories to make you laugh until it seemed you were going to expire from lack of breath. Surely she would have more sense, I reasoned. After all we had done to establish Ivan in his rightful position, I could not imagine my mother doing anything to harm him. Still, Feodor had always been able to circumvent her.

"What would my noble advisors recommend?" Ivan was asking, as I returned my attention to their conversation. He seemed less disturbed, now that he knew to whom Michael referred.

"They are both traitors, and they belong in prison," Glinski blurted. Noticing Ivan's frown, he added: "There is enough treachery around us without permitting it to flourish in the open."

Unexpectedly, Ivan dropped his fist against the table with a resounding crash, which brought a servant running to the doorway. Ivan waved him away. "Vorontsof has just been released from prison, after being sent there against my wishes. He was my friend and remained loyal to me when I most needed friends. Without him and his kinsmen, I might not have survived the Shuisky ordeal. I shall not place him back in prison!"

"You are in error, My Prince," said Michael, his black eyes flashing anger.

"You have heard Our decision!" barked Ivan, resuming the formal manner of address. Their eyes locked in silent combat, until Ivan continued in a calmer tone: "You may order the arrest of Kubensky, and I shall personally sign the warrant. You may call Vorontsof before you and speak to him – threaten him, if you wish. But I do not want him harmed, and I do not want him in prison!"

Michael continued to sit at the table, still playing with his pastry, his heavy breathing the only sign of emotion. Ivan terminated the interview by standing up. "You have heard Our decision, Counselor. Dmitri will also speak to Feodor," he added, glancing at me.

Glinski slid from his chair and bowed himself out of the room. "The Grand Duke's word is law," he muttered, but his expression still reflected dissatisfaction.

Once he had withdrawn from sight, Ivan turned to me, the angry fire still flickering in his eyes. "You must see to it that Vorontsof stays away from further involvements," he ordered. "As much as I love him, I shall not permit him – or anyone else – to become another Shuisky."

"He would never do that!" I answered quickly.

"Dmitri, you and I have grown up amidst treachery and deceit of almost unbelievable proportions, yet you still deny the basic evil of men." He shook his head in disbelief. "Can your own soul really be so pure you cannot see the perfidy of others?"

"I just don't think Feodor would ever betray you," I answered honestly.

"The wolf will always devour the lamb," he said sagely.

I laughed. "You have become a rather large lamb."

Ivan responded to my chiding. "Some say a goat!" he chuckled, "with horns!"

"And cloven hoofs?" I asked.

He looked at me slyly, a crooked grin on his lips. "I am not yet the devil," he laughed. Then his expression changed and he went on more seriously. "But Vorontsof will think I am, if he doesn't stay out of trouble!" He tapped his finger against my chest. "You make sure he understands me."

"To hear is to obey," I replied, rendering a Tartar salaam.

Ivan smiled indulgently, but his voice remained firm, almost cold. "I mean it!" he warned.

I decided to go home before beginning my search for Vorontsof. To my surprise, I heard his voice from our smaller reception hall. He was angry and shouting at someone. Entering through the draped doorway, I stood back and listened. Feodor's face was flushed from a combination of drink and rage. He was waving his fist in Heinrich's face, while Mother stood to one side. But I had heard her shouting, too, and knew she was by no means a simple bystander. No one had noticed me.

"I have the whole thing arranged," Feodor insisted. "Even Kubensky has come around, and Alexander Gorbaty has a shipment ready to go the minute we get things settled!"

"You don't know what you're talking about, Feodor," Mother shrilled. "George Glinski has been my friend since I was a little girl."

"And Michael is doing everything he can to help us," added Heinrich. His guttural accent boomed out loudly as the rest, but he retained a calm the others lacked.

"You are both acting like children!" Vorontsof slammed his hand flat against the table, nearly upsetting his stein of mead. "Between Dmitri and me, we can get His Majesty to do anything we want. Think of the money!"

Money! That enchanted word brought a change in Mother's expression. "Well, Heinrich, if they could guarantee the Glinskis wouldn't be harmed. . . ."

"Eleanor!" Now Heinrich was shouting, too. His face became red, and a stream of Germanic oaths followed my mother's name.

She shrank away from her husband. "I only meant –"

"You only meant you would sell your friends for a few pieces of silver," thundered Heinrich.

"And wouldn't you?" sneered Vorontsof, regarding Heinrich crookedly.

"No!" he shouted. "Not that it's the point, anyway. I'm a foreigner, but I want to make my place here. If I get involved in something like this, and it comes out badly, where am I?"

"But if Dmitri could –" Mother broke off in the middle of her sentence, finally noticing me in the doorway.

"If Dmitri could do what?" I asked, coming into the room. They all watched me, looking guilty, like children caught in some minor crime. It did not take much imagination to understand what they were up to. "So Feodor really does want to depose the Glinskis!" I said. I passed up the mead and poured myself a cup of wine.

"You talk as if you knew about the whole thing," said Mother slowly.

I sat in the big chair, hooking my leg over an arm, despite Mother's involuntary move to displace it. "It isn't so much a question of what I know," I said, pausing to let the words achieve their proper effect. "How stupid do you think Ivan is? Don't you imagine he knows what you're doing?"

Feodor blanched. "The boy hasn't any idea –"

"*The boy*," I said, imitating Vorontsof's drunkenness, "has just signed an order placing Kubensky in prison."

"What?" Feodor blanched, sinking slowly into the chair opposite mine. "I can't believe it." He looked so old in that moment, it was hard to reconcile his present appearance with the hardy youth I remembered from my own childhood.

"Not only should you believe it, you had better look to yourself or you're going to be in the cell next to his," I finished.

"Exactly how much does His Majesty know, son?" asked Heinrich.

"He knows there is a plot underfoot between Feodor and Kubensky to usurp the Glinskis," I told them, "only he thinks Kubensky is the instigator."

"Is he going to arrest anyone else?" asked Mother.

"I don't think so," I told her. "He ordered me to have a talk with Feodor. Glinski is going to see him, too."

Mother looked sharply at Vorontsof. "I don't think you handled this very well," she said.

Feodor squirmed uncomfortably, as Mother sat down on the edge of a chair near to his. "I just don't see how we are going to be able to help you," she told Vorontsof. "You've bungled everything very badly."

Feodor spat into the fireplace, this bit of eloquence being followed by some obscenities and a nervous chewing of his lower lip. His gaunt frame seemed actually to tremble. I had been glaring angrily at him, and now shifted my gaze to Mother.

"You don't think I would really have done anything to hurt Ivan, do you?" she asked at length. "After all, you're both my little boys. When Auntie Helena –"

"Stop it, Eleanor!" Heinrich commanded. "When will you realize your son has grown up?"

I looked at Heinrich, feeling a greater affection than ever before. It also struck me that I did not have to tilt my head to look him straight in the eye, when I stood in response to his remark. I was, indeed, growing up. "Thank you, Father," I said.

It was the first time I had used the term without its feeling strange.

Feodor was invited to dine with Ivan that same night, and he was seated close to the Prince, on the side opposite myself. Only once during the meal did Ivan question me. When Feodor was busy telling a story on his side of the table, Ivan leaned toward me and asked, "Did you have a chance to speak with him?"

I nodded assent, and Ivan turned his attention back to Feodor's riotously funny account . . . something about a Pollack lost in a Russian whorehouse. No more was said of the Vorontsof treachery for the time being; nor did Ivan question me further, as he had no reason to expect there was more to be told. I had been ordered to warn my kinsman to desist, and I had done so.

In later years, many stories were told about this part of Ivan's life, and there was some truth to them – though such tales always improve with the telling. Regardless, the blame for these sins should not rest solely on him – or on any one of us. In the callousness of youth we all had some part in the things that happened, and we were encouraged in most of them by the Glinskis. With the Shuiskys gone and the power of the regency in the hands of Ivan's kinsmen, it should have been their concern to offer a better guidance. But the Glinski brothers' principal interest was to keep Ivan occupied, even if this meant injuring his people, or placing them in jeopardy of God's vengeance. With the Grand Duke busy elsewhere, his cousins were free to indulge themselves in the same acts of greed and avarice as their predecessors.

Those of us who rode with Ivan's group did commit a few acts of brigandage: plowing our mounts into stalls at the bazaars, destroying produce or scattering poultry. Andrew Kurbsky was one who later criticized the Czar for this, but I can remember the time he stole a huge white goose from an old peasant woman and rode around all afternoon with the bird squawking from its perch on the front of his saddle.

It was also great sport to shoot stray dogs from horseback, while galloping full speed through the twisting alleyways. The contest was to bring our quarry down with the fewest arrows. I rivaled both Ivan and Andrew Kurbsky in this, for Heinrich had been a good teacher. Ivan's cousin Vladimir could seldom equal us. Shooting was my greatest skill, because there was hardly a day when I didn't practice. Standing on solid ground, I was a better shot than any, and I received several small prizes for my ability.

The one activity I found difficult, and sometimes impossible, was Alfansy Buturlin's favorite sport – capturing a young girl, and making use of her in front of all the others. At times we only teased the maid, laughing at her terrified screams while we rode around her, forming a moving circle so she could not escape, calling obscenities and lewd suggestions to her. Sometimes, if she was attractive, our teasing resulted in a good deal more. It was then I experienced my problems, for I could not always do what was expected of me. As the youngest in the flock, I could not withdraw unnoticed into the group that watched. Alfansy saw to that, and he used his knowledge of my weakness to embarrass me. Afterward, it became increasingly impossible for me, especially when the others noticed and laughed at my failure.

In all fairness to Ivan, I can honestly say that he never participated; he considered such acts undignified. However, he did enjoy observing someone else, and frequently called encouragement to whomever was performing. My own problems finally culminated in one dreadful debacle the day our group captured the daughter of a *guest* who had done business with Heinrich. I had seen the girl before, as she sometimes stayed in the stall with her father. Previously, she had always seemed an innocent child, although this day she displayed all the attributes of flowering womanhood. As usual, Alfansy saw her first and started the chase, leading us out the city gates from the Arbat into an area of small farms. The girl fled like a doe, but she could not outrun our horses. Once in the open she was lost.

Alfansy had her first, nearly tearing her apart in his greedy lust, after which several of the others did the same. I had stayed with Ivan, hoping they would forget about me. Although the girl was no more than a peasant, her pitiful cries and pleas for mercy had disturbed me more than usual. But Alfansy made certain everyone's attention was directed to me. I whispered to Ivan that I did not wish to participate, but he only laughed and shoved me forward, saying it was a task he assigned me.

Because I could not avoid it, I tried. I did everything I could to follow Ivan's orders, but I was helpless. It was worse than it had been in the past, for I actually shriveled when I looked down at her disheveled body and her tear–streaked face. At last I had to give up. I rearranged my clothes and returned to my mount, the derisive laughter of Alfansy and his closest cronies ringing in my ears. However, my reputation was partially saved by Vladya, who called out some vulgar remarks about my expending all my life's fluids by the nightly seduction of my mother's handmaidens.

Little more was said about it, and the others gradually came to accept my abstention from these acts of rapine. Yet for me, the hurt went deeper; the same trouble recurred from time–to–time in other circumstances. Eventually, it passed; but I knew I had suffered a certain loss of manhood, and for this I blamed Alfansy. I think my hatred of him was greater than I had ever held toward anyone else – toward Shuisky, .anyone. It also made me aware of a peculiar, basic component within my soul – one which would remain within me for all of my life. Whereas I might condemn a man to the pain of torture—something I would do many times in the years to come—I could never willingly abuse a woman.

Being as close as I was to the Grand Duke, I suddenly found people approaching me, seeking my help in obtaining positions in the State bureaus, or other concessions such as a reduction of their taxes. I was usually offered gold and other inducements. If the men were strangers I refused, mostly because I thought it a sin to accept their bribes. I did try to help several friends, one of these being Feodor, who approached me in the late summer and asked that I use my influence to obtain John Kubensky's release from prison. I told him I would, but when I mentioned it to Ivan his only comment was, "John is right where he belongs."

Despite his apparent disinterest, my request may have stirred Ivan's memory, reminding him that the boyar was still incarcerated. Without any explanation, Kubensky was released in September. The decision could also have come through the intercession of the Metropolitan, as I knew Feodor had spoken to him as well. Be that as it may, it was not long before the same little group of conspirators began meeting together in supposed secrecy...no one taking them very seriously, as they were usually so drunk they seemed to pose little threat to anyone. Because any plotting that went on after John's release was done outside our house, I am certain my mother had no part in it. She had remained very cold toward me for several weeks following our original argument, but by this time everything had settled back into its usual routine. I had been able to help Heinrich, which may have accelerated my mother's change of attitude. I spoke to Ivan, who in turn made his wishes known to the Glinskis, and some favorable trading concessions were arranged for my stepfather's people. Our caravans were soon bringing in bolts of silk, fine horses, and even precious stones from the south. From Poland and Livonia we procured many items of metal, including the new weapons developed by their craftsmen. In exchange, we shipped them hemp, trane oil, wax and tallow, tar, salt, and hides. Later, we were able to establish a very profitable trade in furs.

Our greatest difficulty became the constant harassment by brigands along the Moscow–Novgorod highway. Heinrich personally led several raids against these robbers, who had grown so strong they threatened to decimate our trade routes. Most of the criminals caught in such forays were hanged from trees bordering the road, but sometimes the leaders' heads were brought back to Moscow. Ivan ordered these impaled on long stakes, and had them set up around the Square of Executions as a warning to those who considered brigandage as a possible occupation. Otherwise, no decisive steps were taken to bring order into the lands beyond our major cities. I think if Makari had been more interested in the secular welfare of his flock, he might have influenced Ivan to do more toward the establishment of civil order, but the Metropolitan had become completely preoccupied with the work on his *stoglav*. While none of us gave it any consideration – simply because it was a condition we had always accepted – it might be noted that at this time there was no such thing as a city watch except in Novgorod, and I believe in Pskov. The *Guba*, or police units established by the Shuiskys to sustain their perfidity had been abandoned. Each man of means kept his own contingent of armed retainers to protect his property. The poor, of course, had nothing worth stealing.

Into October, with the advent of cold weather, many of us who had been friends of Feodor began to be concerned about him. He seemed to have exchanged conspiracy for vodka, and several times he would have frozen to death had he not been discovered by passersby, drunk and unconscious somewhere about the Kremlin grounds. Without Mother to abet his plotting he seemed to have lost interest – or at least we came to believe so. If he did involve himself in any plots at this time they could have been no more than stupid talk. Ivan was abundantly aware of this, and Feodor would undoubtedly have ended in a drunkard's grave except for an unfortunate occurrence a few weeks after Kubensky's release.

Ivan had started taking an active interest in military affairs, and had decided to establish a national army. He had read and talked to foreigners about the mercenary professionals who served as soldiers in most of the states to our west.

Until this time, we had been as bereft of any military establishment as we were of city guardsmen. In Poland and Germany, men were employed for all their lives as uniformed soldiers, serving the king or other national leader, whereas we were still dependent upon the levies supplied by the boyars and wealthy landlords. It was Ivan's intention to appoint certain nobles as permanent military commanders, and to recruit a small number of men to wear his uniform. Thus, in the beginning, our new army wore the white livery of the household guard. Later, they would be assigned proper colors and given the title of *Streltsi* – the ones who shoot. Michael Vorotinsky, a distinguished, graying boyar prince, with great skill as a soldier, was Ivan's choice to command the first contingent.

I was with Ivan and Vorotinsky one day, going through military maneuvers in the open fields beyond Kolomna, a small town southeast of Moscow. Many important men had come to watch, including Alexi Basmanov and George Glinski, whose sweating mount seemed to sag beneath his tremendous weight. His brother Michael had remained at home, claiming that the press of state business forbade his absence from the capital. Andrei Adashev, who had recently been promoted to *postelnik* – gentleman of the bedchamber – was in attendance upon Ivan.

The men had been practicing their drill most of the day, and everyone was drinking mead, as it had turned very warm for this late in the year. The wide, rolling plains had been selected by Vorotinsky because there were few trees to interfere with the horsemen. Everyone was mounted, even the common guardsmen, which allowed us to cover a wide area in a single sweep. Ivan had been in a good mood earlier in the morning, complimenting Vorotinsky several times and remarking on how ideal the area was for military exercises. Gradually, the physical discomforts of his own accouterments – he had come in full armor – began to wear on him, and by midday he was becoming fretful. At this juncture, a group of footsoldiers appeared without warning, coming toward us over the rise of a nearby hill. They were no more than a mile away when we first saw them. Ivan was startled, because they were armed with arquebusks and numbered close to fifty men. They had obviously been looking for us, and when they saw Ivan they threw their hats into the air, charging straight toward him. They shouted wildly, screaming some strange words we could not make out, all of this convincing Ivan that we were being attacked.

Our own force numbered nearly a hundred fifty men, so there was little to fear. But the Grand Duke's life was too important to risk. While the larger part of our troop rode the arquebusiers down and captured them, Ivan retreated in the opposite direction, to a large stone farmhouse. He left me on a hilltop with seven or eight men, where I was to stay and watch the encounter. I would report the outcome to him, after which he would return to the field or flee. As soon as I saw the prisoners being secured, I sent one of the men to inform Ivan and went myself to join the excitement.

The leader of the arquebusiers was kneeling on the ground, his arms tied behind his back. The rest of his men were being similarly restrained, forced to lie face down upon the ground as soon as each was bound. When I drew near I could see the emblem of Great Novgorod stitched onto the leader's tunic. He loudly protested the rude treatment they were receiving.

"We are honorable soldiers of the Czar," he shouted, using the title most flattering to Ivan – the one he had yet to claim officially. "We bear only a petition for His Highness!"

One of the Morozof boyars stood over the captive, leaning on his naked sword. "His Highness will be here in a moment," he sneered, "and we shall see how he reacts to your story."

"But the parchment in my saddlebag," the man whined. "You have only to open it to see for yourselves."

Basmanov came up then, shoving his burly form through the knot of men. He kicked the Novgorodski in the back, forcing him to fall forward on his face. "If all you wanted to do was petition the Prince, we have a perfectly good clerk in the Kremlin who'd have delivered it for you!" He laughed at his wit, and there was a mingling of assent from the other Muscovites as the Novgorod leader struggled to raise his head high enough to speak. "The parchment. . . ." he protested again.

"Even if there is a parchment, it's probably a ruse," muttered Glinski. He spoke seriously and seemed convinced of the man's evil intent. . .much more so than I would have been. George also seemed to be preoccupied with his own thoughts for several moments, which led me to believe that he must have known more than I did about their reason for coming. As yet, there was no cause to suspect his intention to use the situation to his own advantage.

Our entire group was following Glinski's lead, however, and everyone was nodding in agreement with him. "Never trust a Novgorodski," said someone behind me. Then the men made way for Ivan, who rode his horse almost on top of the bound figures. "Did you find out why they attacked us?" he asked, directing his question to George Glinski.

"Not yet, Your Highness," he replied. "They claim to bear a petition."

"Where is it?" Ivan demanded.

"We have not found it yet," said Glinski innocently.

He was so sly, I thought, and I wondered why he didn't admit knowing where the paper might be found. I wanted to speak up, but the fat man's attitude was as intimidating to me as it must have been to anyone else who felt as I did. No one said anything to clarify the previous exchange for Ivan.

The Novgorod leader had managed to wriggle onto his knees again, his voice now squeaky with terror. "If Your Most Gracious Majesty will tell His servants to look in my saddlebags. . . ."

"Silence!" roared Basmanov, kicking out for a second time. "You will address His Highness only when you have permission to speak!"

Ivan watched his boyars without saying any more, but his eyes darted from one group of men to the other. Drawing back close to me he whispered, "What do you think, Dmitri?"

I was flattered he should look to me, but I also noted the hostile glance from George Glinski. "They are very ignorant men," I muttered, my back turned so only Ivan could hear me. "They may be telling the truth, but I wouldn't take a chance on them." I might have expressed my doubts regarding his cousin's excessive severity, but George shoved his bulk into the space between us and the nearest men, having maneuvered his corpulent body down from the saddle.

Ivan turned to him. "Who are the leaders?" he asked.

"This one commands, Highness," said his cousin, pointing to the man abused by Basmanov, "and those other two, whose tunics are less ragged than the rest."

"They should all be hanged," growled Basmanov.

"Time for that later, Old Bear," said Ivan. His fear was gone, and once more his mood seemed lighthearted. He remounted his black stallion, allowing it to prance around the group of prisoners.

"Dmitri," he called. "Take ten men and escort the three ringleaders to Moscow. Turn them over to Zakharof for questioning. Give him the petition, too, if you can find it," he added.

I gave Ivan a proper military salute and motioned some of the men to join me. We took the leader's mount – the only horse the intruders had – and one of our own baggage animals. Binding the prisoners belly–down across their backs, we left immediately for the capital.

The rest of the Novgorodski were treated mercifully. Ivan ordered them stripped and flogged that they might know better how to address their Prince should they ever have occasion to petition him again. They were sent back to Novgorod.

But the leaders did not fare so well. Zakharof was a *dyak*, one of Basil's former clerks, and a man whom Ivan trusted. An older, gray–bearded men, he had always seemed a loyal servant, and had learned much of his present skill from the famous lawyer, Manusurof – the same who had drawn up Basil's final will. Unfortunately, Zakharof's present position placed him in close contact with the Glinskis, who had undoubtedly bought his services. The man was also a thief, selling his influence while pilfering the royal treasury. In this he was probably no worse than many others, except that Zakharof was eventually found out – accused and executed for his crimes. However, this happened a long while later, at a time when I was out of the country. During this early stage of Ivan's reign, he was highly regarded and considered completely trustworthy. While neither Ivan nor I realized it, I am now certain that in the matter of the Novgorod arquebusiers, Zakharof acted solely on instruction from the Glinskis.

Because I had no way to suspect that the investigation of these Novgorodski would have any bearing on myself or my family, I simply turned them over to Zakharof's retainers, along with the parchment from the saddlebag. I then went home. Ivan returned the following afternoon with his troops, and although I knew the *dyak* saw Ivan several times during the next few days, I thought nothing of it. Heinrich was preparing to set out on another expedition, trying to hunt down a particularly vicious band of robbers who had attacked one of his smaller caravans. This time I obtained Ivan's permission and went with him.

My first campaign! I imagined myself leading a mighty army as we traveled the deeply rutted track toward Novgorod, surrounded by the brilliant yellows and reds of autumn. The road wound through forests of heavy, dark green pines, interspersed with the fall colors of birch and sycamore. There were short stretches of cultivated land, where peasants struggled to survive against the encroachment of native shrubs, always seeking to reclaim their fields. Finally, the forests ended and we traveled through mile after mile of endless, open land. There were plains so vast they seemed to stretch toward the very edge of the earth. Later, there were swamps and marshes, where the hoarfrost formed silvery blankets at night, clinging to the patches of reeds and tall grasses. As we rode past an occasional peasant we seemed to attract little attention, for bands of armed men were a common sight. In truth, it was far safer for the local farmers to pretend not to see us. As Heinrich explained, there was an unwritten understanding between these men and the brigands. The robbers left them in peace, because they were too poor to have anything worth stealing. In return, the farmers remained blind to anything done by the highwaymen, and thus knew nothing if questioned by any governmental official. There was little enough of this questioning in any event, since most of the regional governors received tribute from the robbers in exchange for a mutual truce. If an unsubsidized band should enter an area, it was not uncommon for the governor and the local brigands to act in concert to hunt them down.

Heinrich bore a written commission, issued by the Bureau of Trade, demanding that he receive cooperation from all regional officials. This had brought at least a pretense of assistance on his former trips; but this time we were after Boris, a bandit who had been terrorizing the merchants for years. He had all the people, rich and poor alike, so afraid of him we could expect little real help from anyone.

It rained our third night out, and the horses tossed up huge clumps of damp earth as we continued westward in the early hours of the fourth day. Heinrich, relaxed and completely at ease in heavy armor, called me forward to ride next to him. He was almost merry, allowing his horse to prance and rear. Hunting bandits was little different from stalking bears or wolves, in his mind, and he thoroughly enjoyed the excitement.

"All those hours of practice are going to prove their worth," he said happily. "I hope you get a chance to earn your spurs this trip."

"Against a swamp rat?" I asked incredulously.

"If you handle yourself well against this gang of brigands, you"ll be ready for a real opponent next time. He smiled grimly. "But don't think Boris is going to be easy prey. He's destroyed more caravans than a horde of Tartars."

We rode two more days, stopping at several peasant huts to ask questions, but seldom obtaining any information. It was necessary to apply a little more forceful methods a couple of times, else we would have learned nothing. Boris was a clever man, or he would never have survived as long as he had. He had won the respect, or at least an unspoken loyalty, from the poor landholders by honoring his assurances never to harm them. A number of times caravans belonging to ourselves and other merchants had been attacked in full sight of these men who tilled the soil, a fact the few survivors had later verified. But in each instance, the peasants later claimed to have seen nothing. And many times this may have been true, for they would not turn their heads to look. As always, their best protection was ignorance and poverty.

Still, Heinrich was hopeful that we might get some indication of Boris's whereabouts if we could question one man by himself, with none of his companions present to witness his "betrayal" of the brigands. Outside a small village, we rode into a newly planted field and seized the young peasant who was working there. Taking him into a cove of birch trees, Heinrich ordered his men to strip the captive naked and bind him, back against a tree. My stepfather then took a dirk in his gloved hand and ran it down the length of the young man's body, pausing when the point lay against his genitals. "If you wish to remain a man," he said sternly, "perhaps you had better tell us where the criminals are hiding."

The captive was trembling through his whole being, and his eyes were riveted on the gleaming blade; but despite his obvious terror, he could only shake his head and declare that he knew nothing. One of our men produced a knout, with which he proceeded to beat the helpless prisoner, but with tears running down his cheeks, sagging finally in his bonds, the peasant could only repeat his declaration of innocence. Finally, Heinrich shrugged and ordered the men to release him. Grabbing up his discarded clothing, he raced into the underbrush, stumbling as he ran. I watched all of this with a peculiar mixture of emotions. I felt sorry for the youngster, but also experienced a tingling excitement as he struggled against his bonds and responded in obvious pain to the punishment he received. I could not explain all that I felt, but I was almost disappointed when Heinrich decided not to repeat the session with another victim, although we did question a few more peasants without recourse to torture. From all of this we were able to learn only that Boris had last been seen near the swamps, east of Novgorod, where it was assumed he maintained a permanent camp. Because no outsider knew the secret paths, and because even with this knowledge a heavily armored knight could never ride his horse across the marshy bogs, Boris could rest securely within the tall grasses and hidden glades.

We were camped in the open the last night out of Novgorod, when Heinrich explained his plans to me. I was very impressed with them, of course, as this was my first experience in the warrior's guile which must compliment the other skills of a successful officer. "You may be sure that Boris knows we are here, and that we've been asking about him," said my stepfather. "Every quaking, piss–pants peasant along the way has probably passed the word of our coming."

"How will we ever catch him, then?" I asked.

"We can't pursue him into the swamps," said Heinrich. "We must make him come out in the open where we can take him at a disadvantage. We'll press on to Novgorod tomorrow, and make a great show of drunken revelry. Boris is surely in the swamp right now, and he won't come out until he receives word of our being at least a day's ride away."

I feared we would never catch him, and I said so.

Heinrich lifted his finger to silence me. "Fully armored men on heavy war horses like ours would need almost a full day to reach Novgorod from here," he said. "The thickest swamps are also a good distance away, and this is the closest point to them from the road. Now, as you know, there is a caravan coming from Moscow – the one we passed about a day and a half back. It's a very special caravan, carrying nothing of value, but appearing to be heavily laden. Boris undoubtedly knows about it already. He will also know when we reach Novgorod and start our revels. He will feel safe, and I am certain he will attack the caravan when it reaches this point, because it is the only part of the road he'll have time to reach. As soon as we are fairly sure of making a sufficient display in the city, we change into light armor and take the small, fast horses I've arranged to have in Novgorod for our use. We will be back here before Boris's spies can inform him of our coming."

"And take them when they attack the caravan!" I finished.

"But we don't come directly here," he continued. "We can't be sure our timing will be that exact. We'll have to cut across country, placing ourselves between the robbers and the swamps. We'll take them from the rear, either somewhere on the paths between the swamp and the road, or fall upon them as they lay in wait for the caravan."

"And that's why you assigned the men you did to the caravan," I suggested gleefully.

"But we can't be sure they'll arrive in time to help us," Heinrich cautioned. "It will be a hard fight, because we'll be tired from the ride. But if we surprise them as I expect, we can finish Boris once and for all."

We followed Heinrich's plan almost exactly as he outlined it, except that we were delayed by having to pay a social call on Turuntay–Pronsky, who was governor, and who liked to consider himself Heinrich`s friend. My stepfather was reluctant to tell him our plans, because he was known to be a greedy man and might be in loose partnership with the very thieves we sought to destroy. However, in order to get away from him and make our departure from the city as we intended, it was necessary to give an idea of where we were going.

Once out of Novgorod, we fairly flew across the countryside on the light mounts. They were sturdy little animals, hill ponies like those used by the Tartars of the steppes. Fast and sure–footed, they enabled us to race at full speed across the uneven ground. We followed the dark ribbon of roadway for most of the distance back to our campsite of the previous night, cutting off only a few leagues short of it. Almost at once we found ourselves plunging into the squashy turf that borders the marshes. The ground was barely solid enough to sustain our lightened weight, but by dawn we were close enough to stop, having made better time than Heinrich had expected. We were in a heavy clump of birch trees, completely concealed by a dense undergrowth of ferns and marsh grasses.

A broad plain of bright green grass extended beyond the trees, stretching in an almost unbroken mass between the swamps and the forest bordering the highway.

"This is even better than I'd hoped," said Heinrich. "We should be able to wait here and see them as they come across."

"If someone hasn't already spotted us and reported it to Boris," said one of the men.

"We can only wait and watch," said Heinrich.

Two men were set to guard the trail behind us, in the event our quarry tried to reverse the surprise. Everyone else gathered near the edge of our glade, watching the all–but–invisible paths leading from the swamps. Heinrich's decoy caravan should pass our old campsite before midday.

Nearly two hours passed, and no robbers appeared. Then one of the men we had left on guard behind us rode into our midst, leading a horse with its rider tightly bound, his feet secured together beneath the animal's belly. "Caught this one on the way to Boris," said the guard.

Heinrich stepped forward and cut the rope holding the prisoner's feet, dragging the fellow from his saddle and allowing him to fall heavily onto the ground. After a few kicks from our heavy boots the man admitted having been sent to warn the robbers of our departure from Novgorod. I was sure Pronsky had sent him, but the messenger didn't seem to know. If it had been the governor, he had acted through an agent. The man also appeared to be the only one sent. With this much assurance that our presence was not yet known, Heinrich ordered the fellow hanged. He was taken back into the clump of trees where his body would not be seen, and we returned to our vigil.

The sun was nearly at its zenith when our patience was rewarded. First two, then five, and soon several more men began to emerge from the swampy paths. Some were close enough for us to see their facial features. Others were tiny black silhouettes, against the brilliant green hues of marsh plants. I counted better than a score in all. They scurried along on foot, each carrying at least two weapons, heading directly toward the highway. Heinrich gave the signal to mount, cautioning everyone to be quiet. My heart beat like thunder against the inside of my ribs, and I was trembling with excitement as I adjusted my leather armor and tightened the cinch on my saddle. The man who had been sent to recall the guards returned with them, and Heinrich gave the order to charge.

We thundered across the soft earth, traveling at a much slower pace than we would have on the roadbed. No one shouted, and I am sure the brigands didn't see us until we were nearly upon them. By then they had spread out along the side of the road, waiting to ambush the caravan. We rode down upon them, shouting now, and swinging our heavy swords. The men we struck first were close to the center of the enemy group, and we were immediately surrounded by the others who came running from every direction.

The brigands, being on foot, had a greater mobility than we did in such close quarters. They were able to account for seven or eight of our men, losing only about the same themselves. Heinrich rallied the remaining half dozen of us, and though badly outnumbered now, everyone maintained a firm, steady order. We maneuvered our horses into a tight ring, their heads facing outward, and charged at the cluster of robbers as they came at us again. This eliminated a quarter of their remaining force, but Boris was also a competent leader. He was an enormous man, with long red hair, and beard down to his waist. I knew who he was without having him pointed out to me. When he started shouting orders to the others there could no longer be any doubt.

As the fight progressed we might have been in serious trouble, for two more of our men fell before the caravan appeared around the far bend in the highway. Seeing the furious struggle ahead of them, the guards galloped into the melee at full tilt. They sent the robbers tumbling rump–over–head, as their heavier horses crashed against them. I was also knocked down by their charge and fell against a tree, bruising my shoulder. Almost at once, one of the brigands was at my throat, scratching at me with claw–like fingers and swinging a dagger to slit me open.

For a brief instant our eyes were locked as were our bodies, in mortal combat. He was young, very near my own age, perhaps a year or two my senior. His hair and beard were the same color as Boris's, and I have often wondered if it might have been his son. He made two unsuccessful passes with his knife, finally sinking the blade into my hip on the third thrust. However, I was heavily padded by the hard leather shells, and the knife barely scratched my skin. Instead, it caught in the crusty material and refused to come free. Both my hands were occupied, holding strategic points of my opponent's body. I dared not grapple for a better hold, lest I lose the advantage I was beginning to gain from my greater strength.

With a hard lunge, I was able to topple him onto his back, driving a knee hard into his groin as we fell. I held him in place, forcing my arm across his neck until my armored elbow came down against his mouth. I shoved with all my might, until I felt the leather guard slide between his teeth. The rest of my arm was blocking the flow of air into his nostrils.

He struggled violently at first, relaxed for a moment, then shoved and tried to roll his body from under me, using all his remaining strength as he fought desperately for air. I held until his entire form went limp, after which I remained on top of him for another few heartbeats. At length, I disengaged myself and stood up wearily, achingly, to lean against a nearby tree. I looked down at my opponent, expecting he might struggle to this feet. But he made no move, and a fly settled upon a trickle of blood that oozed from the corner of his mouth.

Heinrich came up and patted my back. "Well done!" he said. "You've killed your first criminal."

I looked at him in surprise, then back to the boy lying at my feet. Was he really dead? I kicked at the lifeless form, vaguely wondering why it made no response. I was aware of a sick feeling in the pit of my stomach, a mounting sense of revulsion as I continued to stand over him. But there was something else as well, a sense of pride in what I'd done – also a feeling of mastery, or omnipotence. Later, when my stepfather hailed me as if I were a victorious champion, it awakened an appropriate sense of accomplishment. It had been a hard fight, and a fair one – as if that mattered when dealing with brigands. I had won, I realized. I had killed an enemy of my family's and I had done it single–handedly. That it might have been my body lying there, instead, was another thought to be reserved for later.

There were not many robbers left alive, for they had fought to their last breath. Four of them sat on the ground with their arms bound behind them. Boris was still standing, also with his hands secured in back of him. He had a deep wound in his belly, and blood was still seeping out of it.

"No use prolonging it," Heinrich said. "I'd like to put some distance behind us before nightfall."

With that, our men took ropes from their saddles and tossed the loose ends over the limbs of some nearby trees. With no further ceremony the four robbers were hanged, our men hauling on the ropes until the dangling bodies were far enough above ground not to be reached by wolves or other animals. We left them to kick and wriggle until their souls departed. Boris stood mute through the executions of his followers, defiantly denying us the satisfaction of seeing his fear. His steely eyes were staring blankly ahead, as if he were unable to hear the strangled gasps or leafy rustlings as his companions' death throes shook the boughs.

Heinrich shoved Boris onto his knees, and two men looped a rope about his neck, each of them holding one end of it. They forced the bandit's head down, against the side of a fallen tree. My stepfather severed the neck with a single blow of his heavy sword. Grabbing the head by its flowing beard, he shoved the bloody mass into a game bag, which hung from his saddlebow.

It was late Sunday evening when we trotted briskly onto the Kremlin drawbridge and shouted for the keeper to raise the portcullis. I thought it strange that the gate should have been closed at all. Sullenly, the heavy iron mesh creaked upward, pulled by massive ropes over a wooden windlass. In silence the guards watched us enter, allowing the portcullis to sink into place behind us. There was not the usual gruff friendliness in their demeanor, but being tired and grimy from our travels neither Heinrich nor I paid much attention.

Boris's head was still in Heinrich's game bag, hanging from the pommel of his saddle. He untied the cord and tossed it to me, laughing grimly. "Better give this to His Highness. I don't think your mother would want it around the house."

I caught the leather sack, holding the rancid–smelling trophy at arm's length. I hooked it onto my own saddle, allowing it to hang as far away from my nostrils as possible. Signaling a couple of men to accompany me, I turned toward the palace while Heinrich cantered off in the opposite direction, followed by the rest of our retainers.

Still not realizing that anything was wrong, I reined up in front of the palace, left my horse with the man Erik, and motioned Wolfried to attend me. Handing him my grisly burden, I bounded up the steps. Wolfried followed more slowly. Servitors at the door admitted us without comment, bowing respectfully enough, but showing no expression whatever. It was then I sensed something amiss, for I had known one of the men nearly all my life, and he always had some saucy comment to make when he had not seen me for several days.

Andrei Adashev awaited me at the far side of the atrium, obviously having been informed of my arrival. He hurriedly motioned for me to follow him. We went through several rooms, stopping at last in a small apartment where a servant poured hot water into a washbowl for me. A fresh robe was then laid out on a chair, so I stripped off my dirty clothes and started bathing myself. I resisted the temptation to question Andrei, knowing he would tell me all I needed to know in his own time. Although Wolfried stood at the door and should have assured our privacy, the old maxim of palaces having ears was as true in the Kremlin as anywhere else in the world.

Andrei handed me a towel, and as I dried myself he stood close as if to help. Hardly moving his lips he whispered, "Be careful, my friend. Vorontsof is going to be arrested."

I nearly dropped the towel as I jerked around to face him. "Why?" I asked.

"Not so loud," he cautioned, picking up an end of the cloth and pushing me around to get at my back. He stood behind me, now, and continued. "I don't have time to explain the whole story," he said, "but Zakharof has convinced Ivan of . . . ."

Wolfried, who had remained uncomfortably in the doorway, coughed a warning. Both Andrei and I turned to see a young fellow in wine–colored Glinski livery come into the room.

"His Majesty wants Lord Dmitri to attend him immediately," he commanded curtly.

This boded no good, for my status in court was enough to warrant more respect from a servant. Andrei and I exchanged glances as the retainer began to withdraw, actually turning his back on me! I was too tired to be frightened; instead I lost my temper. "Just a minute, you!" I shouted.

The man stopped short and turned back in surprise. Even standing there naked, I managed a tone of demanding authority. . .and indignation. "You dung scratcher!" I bellowed, using one of Heinrich's favorite epithets. "Who do you think you're talking to?"

Another second of stunned silence, a glance of indecision, and the fellow bowed very low. "Your pardon, My Lord." he groveled. "It was the urgency. . . ."

"Urgency!" I mocked his whining voice. "And since when do Glinski servants bear the Grand Duke's personal orders?" I added sharply.

"I just happened to be nearest at hand when His Majesty heard you had arrived, My Lord."

I watched him narrowly. The fellow was afraid of me – a good sign. Maybe I was not in as much trouble as Andrei seemed to fear; otherwise this churl would have laughed at me. "I take it your master is with His Majesty?" I asked.

"Yes, My Lord."

"And do you serve Prince George, or Prince Michael?" I asked.

"I serve them both, sir," he replied. "But it is Prince Michael who attends upon His Majesty.

Andrei held out the robe and I slipped it over my head. As I struggled to get my arms into the sleeves, I dismissed the servant, who seemed very relieved to go. Once he was out of my sight, I could hear him break into a run down the hallway. I forced a laugh, clapping Andrei on the back and scooping my trophy from Wolfried's hands as we went to see what evil the Glinskis had wrought. Inside, I felt a cold hand of fear about my heart. "Wolfried," I said casually, "you had better go out and tell Erik what just happened. Have him inform the *Freiherr*. You come back, then, and wait upon me outside His Majesty's apartments."

The German departed with a military salute, and Andrei led me to Ivan's rooms. The new apartments of the Grand Duke glowed a warm, deep red, illuminated by tiers of candles along the walls and by oil lamps on the tables. The room was stuffy, despite its size, for the windows were closed and a number of people crowded about. Ivan greeted me indifferently when I entered, hardly acknowledging my formal obeisance. Michael Glinski, looking especially lean and vicious, was seated near Ivan. Basmanov and Vladimir Staritsky were speaking together, a little to one side. Standing over Ivan, and poised as if I had interrupted him in a lecture on immoral behavior, was the Metropolitan. Makari seemed quite agitated, and whatever he had been saying was obviously not pleasing Ivan.

"It appears your hunt was successful," Ivan remarked at length, eyeing Heinrich's game bag.

I handed him the pouch. "Singularly successful, Your Highness." I replied.

Nothing more was said for a moment or two. Ivan opened the pouch and glanced inside, wrinkling his nose in disgust. He passed the container to a servant.

"His Majesty and I have been discussing the problem of Feodor Vorontsof," said Makari evenly. I was sure his glance was intended as a warning.

"Yes, *your kinsman* has seriously overstepped the bounds of His Majesty's pleasure." added Glinski. There was a decided note of malevolence in his tone.

"Perhaps I'm a bit dense this evening," I remarked, "but everyone acts as if I should know something I do not." I was quite honestly confused.

"The results of the *Dyak* Zakharof's investigation would seem to indicate some connection between the Novgorod arquebusiers and your cousin Feodor," explained Makari. He stated the fact simply, still in his level, unemotional tone of voice. I began to understand.

"I find that hard to believe," I said.

"Treachery in one's friends is always hard to believe," replied Glinski.

All three of them were watching me, and from the corner of my vision I noted that Vladimir and Basmanov had also broken off their conversation. Andrei still stood behind me, where I couldn't see him. I knew Makari was aware of my innocence in any plot, and although Glinski seemed to be suggesting I might be implicated, he must have been equally aware of the facts. His motivation, of course, was jealousy over my situation with Ivan. . .Ivan, whose attitude surprised me most. He seemed doubtful!

"You're playing with me, Michael," I said boldly. "Do you dare imply that I was involved in some way?" I made my voice as harsh as I could, and I stared him straight in the eye.

Ivan continued to watch us both coldly until Andrei spoke up from behind me. "If His Majesty's humble servant may be allowed to speak," he began, and waited for Ivan's nod before continuing. "Perhaps a second look at the facts will prove enlightening."

"The facts have already been examined, bed–maker," snorted Glinski.

"Perhaps," said Andrei, undeterred. "But some obvious conclusions seem to have been overlooked."

"You are presumptuous!" snapped Glinski.

"Be still, Michael," Ivan commanded. "Go ahead, Andrei. We are ready to hear you."

"It is very simple," replied the servant. "All the damaging information has come from these captured Novgorodski, all three of whom conveniently expired during the course of their examinations." He cast a meaningful glance at Michael Glinski. "As it was Dmitri who brought these prisoners in from where they were captured, he had every opportunity to silence them. . .either kill then in the course of an alleged escape attempt, or actually have allowed them to flee. I can hardly believe he would have handed them over for interrogation if he knew they could implicate him in treason."

Vladya broke his silence, then, speaking form the other side of the room. He's right, Ivashka. Dmitri may not be as pure as he always seems, but I'm certain he isn't that stupid. Besides, he went blithely on a hunt right after. That doesn't sound like a guilty man. . .with a heavy conscience and a fear of retribution."

Basmanov nodded agreement, and Makari added the final statement in my defense. "Dmitri had already come to me," he said, "prior to his departure, asking that I be wary for Your Majesty's welfare during his absence. I am certain he feared a plot involving the Novgorodski, but I am equally certain he knew nothing of Vorontsof's involvement.

"If, indeed, he is involved," added Vladya.

"Oh, he's involved, all right," Glinski assured us.

"You base this belief on information obtained by Zakharof?" asked Andrei. Glinski nodded.

"But there was no mention ever made of Dmitri, was there?" demanded Ivan, his penetrating stare burning into the avaricious eyes of the Glinski.

"No," admitted Michael reluctantly. "There was never mention of Dmitri."

"Then I think we can safely assume he is as loyal as he has always been," said Makari. "Come here, my son." He held his heavily jeweled hand out to me.

I went to the elderly prelate, experiencing a surge of love and gratitude, not only for him, but for the other friends I had found in this room. Makari placed a hand upon my shoulder and stood beside me, facing Ivan.

"My Prince," he said, "of all your court you have no more faithful servant than this young man. I make my judgment both as a priest who has heard his confessions, and as one who has lived enough years to appreciate the rarity of such devotion."

"I never actually doubted it," Ivan said softly. He spoke in a casual tone, and as if there had never been a question of my loyalty, and as if I had not just endured the hell of suspicion. "Sit down, Dmitri," he said. "We still have the problem of the real conspirators."

"Can there be any doubt?" urged Michael Glinski.

Ivan sighed, and despite the stern expression he strove to maintain I could see he was deeply disturbed. He had loved Vorontsof with the passionate attachment of a young boy for an older brother. Now this favorite boyar— one of the very few for whom Ivan had ever felt any affection—had betrayed him. "Has the guard been dispatched?" he asked Glinski.

Michael went to the door, opening it enough to poke his head outside, where he whispered with one of his men. I could see Wolfried standing against the wall, watching me over Glinski's back. I nodded to him just as Michael closed the door and returned with a triumphant grin on his lips. "Feodor Vorontsof is in prison, along with the other conspirators who were found with him," he said in a loud voice.

Glinski looked at me slyly, his venomous gaze causing my pulse to quicken with fear. Anyone who had been with Feodor this night would surely be included in his web. I prayed my mother had not been present. Surely not, I reasoned to myself; it was after dark and no woman would be out at such an hour – unless she had gotten wind of the arrest and had tried to warn her cousin of his danger. I watched Michael closely, seeking some sign in his expression; but the seneschal had turned back to Ivan, ignoring me as he addressed his Prince. He probably perceived my fear and enjoyed keeping me in suspense for an extra few moments.

"Who are the others?" asked Ivan coldly.

"Prince John Kubensky and Vorontsof's brother, Mikhail," he smirked. "As well as Alexander Gorbaty – all the original group."

He is doing away with his most potent enemies, I thought. Glinski must have waited until his spies reported these three men together – Kubensky, Gorbaty, and Feodor – then made his report to Ivan. Mikhail Vorontsof was surely as innocent as I of any conspiracy, for he had just recently come to Moscow at his brother's request. He had never been interested in anything more serious than hunting or wenching in the countryside. I hardly knew him, which attested to his virtually never having been in the capital. However, if one is to do away with a man it is always best to remove those most likely to seek revenge. In this evil enterprise, Glinski had done his work thoroughly and efficiently. He was a truly dangerous enemy, seeking to destroy anyone who might threaten his influence over Ivan. I shuddered at how nearly successful he had been in removing me.

As I sat listening to them, I was still seeking a flaw in Michael's case. I was certain Feodor had not been involved with the Novgorod arquebusiers, regardless of any other involvements. I was convinced, as well, that those ragged soldiers had been exactly what they claimed – ignorant men who wished to petition their sovereign, as Russian men had been doing for hundreds of years. They simply had not known the proper forms and procedures.

"May I ask a question?" I blurted.

Again a nasty look from Glinski, but Ivan nodded assent.

"I came in late and may have missed the explanation," I apologized, "but what of the petition these men carried? I didn't read it, but. . . ."

"There was no petition," snapped Glinski.

"I handed it to Zakharof's men myself," I insisted.

"But you didn't read it?" asked Glinski with a self–satisfied tone.

I shook my head. "No, I only saw it had writing," I said.

Michael pulled a scroll from the writing table, glancing at Ivan for permission before he handed it to me. I unrolled it and read the most damning evidence there could have been. The thing must have been a forgery. I have always believed that, for it purported to be a letter from an agent of the Polish King to Feodor, offering him governorship of all the lands about Novgorod and Pskov, if he would help overthrow the regime in Moscow. To me, the scheme seemed so clumsy as to be laughable; yet Ivan seemed to believe it. I looked up at him and saw that he had been watching me grimly while I read.

"Is that the parchment you found?" asked Glinski. He looked so intently at me I wanted to shiver; but I didn't. He was threatening me, I realized. He had missed his chance to get rid of me this time, but he was telling me to behave or he would succeed on the next try.

I shrugged. "It may be," I said doubtfully. "It seems the same size."

Glinski spread his hands and returned his attention to Ivan. "Perhaps a trial. . . ." he began, rubbing his palms together.

"They will be executed in the morning." said Ivan evenly.

"No!" I gasped, before I could stop myself. Every head turned toward me.

"Do you wish, then, to see the traitors spared?" asked Glinski, a sly accusation creeping into his tone.

"I don't believe they are traitors!" I answered angrily.

Glinski looked at Ivan, who remained expressionless. Suppressing the pain his words must have caused him, he said simply, "I have made my decision."

Then Makari spoke up. "My son," he said to Ivan, "I ask you to think again of what you do. I ask you to remember the love you bore this man Vorontsof, and the loyalty he has always displayed toward Your Highness. To lay him in his grave, if he is indeed innocent, is to call upon yourself the unending wrath of Heaven. Remember the injunctions placed upon us by Our Most Beloved Savior, how His words were always the words of mercy and forgiveness." He continued in this same vein for several minutes, going into scripture such as I cannot begin to remember. Ivan sat silently, listening to him, allowing him the respectful attention due the Metropolitan of Moscow. But I could see the words were failing to deter him. Glinski saw it, too, for he made no attempt to interrupt or argue. He hovered over Ivan, smirking. Although I thought both Vladimir and Basmanov were unhappy with Ivan's decision, neither of them ventured a comment.

Finally, when Makari seemed to have exhausted his store of words, he stopped abruptly. He could also see how futile his efforts were. I sat frozen in my place, and during Makari's long speech Adashev had slipped down beside me. I whispered to him, "Can't you do something?"

"It would be improper for a servant to speak out against His Majesty's decision," he told me, "but he knows what I think."

Ivan addressed the Metropolitan. "We do not take this action lightly, or without great personal discomfort, Little Father," he said. "Feodor Vorontsof has always been close to Our heart. Nonetheless, We have given him every opportunity to regain Our affection, and he has continued to conspire against Our duly appointed deputies. The decision is made."

Ivan rose, a sign that we were to leave him. He cast a questioning glance at Vladimir and Basmanov, the only important men in the room whose opinions had not been heard.

"The word of the Grand Prince is law," said Vladya, following with the customary words of ceremony.

Basmanov bowed clumsily and echoed the sentiments of Ivan's cousin.

I wanted to say more, but I felt Andrei's restraining hand on my arm. "You can't do any good," he whispered, "and you could hurt yourself."

I left with the others, automatically making the proper genuflections to Ivan. At the first turn in the corridor I met Heinrich, who had come in response to my message. Three of his men were with him, all dressed in fine court costume, but fully armored beneath. My stepfather looked at me quizzically, but I only shook my head and continued toward the main portal. They followed me without further comment, and I walked as fast as I could, away from Ivan's rooms. I did not want any of the people in the palace to see me weep, for angry as I had been with Feodor from time to time, he had still been like an elder brother to me.

I was up the next morning long before dawn, and made my way to the Uspensky Cathedral. I was sure Ivan would be there, as he would certainly wish to speak with God before the executions. Somehow, the atmosphere in this largest house of worship was more satisfying to his needs on difficult occasions than the small, private chapel off his royal suite.

When I entered, Ivan was on his knees before the Icon of the Virgin. His forehead was pressed against the stone floor, and I could hear his groans all the way to the rear of the church. Two men in the white uniforms of the household guard stood inside the door and automatically extended their hands to stop me until they saw who it was.

I went up quickly behind Ivan and knelt beside him, to the left. A brown robed monk was on his right. The Prince glanced at me and smiled grimly for a moment, never breaking the rhythm of his chant, nor the motion of striking his head upon the floor. A bruise was already beginning to show through the sun darkened skin of his brow. Two or three other men were also kneeling, farther back in the church. None dared approach Ivan as I had. No one else of any consequence was there, anyway – certainly not the Glinskis.

My knees and back ached when Ivan finally concluded his prayers and motioned the monk away. When the man stood up, I could hear the rustle of his hair shirt – his *vlasyanitsy*, for he was a penitent whom Ivan must have summoned to help beg for God's understanding and forgiveness. The monk made a reverent sign over Ivan's head before he withdrew. I followed the Prince from the Cathedral, past a small crowd of people waiting to be allowed inside to pray. As we walked through the doors, held open for us by the guards, my plan to make a last effort to dissuade Ivan melted away. The decision had been made, despite the pain it caused. All that remained was to follow through. For this reason, I kept quiet. Nor did Ivan say anything, although I was certain he knew why I had come. We joined the group of officials who awaited us in the courtyard, and mounted up for the ride to the *lobonoyo mesto.*

Dawn had broken while we were at prayer, a chill and dismal day as befitted the occasion of Ivan's first formal execution. (One can hardly count Andrew Shuisky.) Our party exited through the *Spasskaya* – the Savior's Gate, which placed us directly in front of the square. So many people had gathered to watch that at first the guards had trouble making way for us. As the crowd was so noisy, and with the morning mist so heavy, the people did not see us coming.

Gradually, as they realized their Prince was arriving, the mob fell back and Ivan led us through the parted throng. . .much as Moses had led his people through the waters. At least this was the simile which came to mind, the only clear thought I had as I rode between the packed masses of faceless bodies. All other processes within my mind seemed dead and floating, like flotsam on a still pond, or mist above a silent countryside.

Ivan reached the wooden platform, set up for us the previous evening, and took his seat beneath the silken canopy. Others quickly joined him, filling the dais from which our company could command a close view of the raised, stone ring of death. I looked back before dismounting and saw the crowd surge into the open area we had cleared in passing – waters closing on the armies of Pharaoh.

Michael Glinski had arrived ahead of us, his small, unimpressive body draped in shimmering cloth of gold, as if this were a most gala occasion. He stood in the center of the ring of the condemned, extolling the virtues of Grand Duke Ivan IV, against whom these men had sinned. As he stood upon the stones of death, he raised his foot from time to time, thoughtlessly resting it upon the block itself. I could not help visualizing the blood that was soon to flow, and I imagined Glinski's feet immersed in red, sticking to the pavement as the gore of his victims turned to crimson tar. I saw him bound forever to the place of doom, with the headless souls of his victims circling in satanic vengeance about his anguished bones.

But as he continued, my fever seemed to subside. His words had been effective, and they evoked a proper response from the ignorant people who heard him. They murmured in threatening growls when Michael intoned the names of those who were to die; they cheered the mention of their Prince, and in muted tones they also cheered for the Glinski. All this resulted purely from the power of Michael's words, for he was not a popular man. His tax collectors and other henchmen were every bit as hated as those of the Shuiskys had been. But such was the way of mobs. When addressed by one as glib as this, they hung on every syllable, responding as if under the spell of a demon.

Near the end of Michael's ravings I forced the speaker's image from my mind. His voice in its summation became a drone from far away, as did the responses of the mob. Deliberately, I examined the faces of the men around me on the platform. I sat beside Vladimir, who was on Ivan's left. On Ivan's other side was Yuri, and next to him was Andrew Kurbsky, with an empty chair between them. George Glinski had not arrived yet, nor had the Metropolitan. Neither Heinrich nor my mother had showed up either, although I had expected my stepfather to make an appearance. No women of noble birth were on the platform or in the crowd, of course; but it would not have been the first time for my mother to flaunt custom by hiding her face in a shawl and slipping unnoticed into the mass of people.

I glanced at Vladya, who seemed to be staring at the sky until I realized his eyes were turned far in their sockets, allowing him to look toward the high wall of the Kremlin without actually turning his head in that direction. Following his gaze I saw, amidst a fairly sizable group lining the battlements, the tall, imposing figure of his mother. So, Euphrosyne had not been able to pass up the opportunity to savor Feodor's final disgrace! I could not see her face, for it was heavily draped with veils; but the powdered white of her forehead gleamed in contrast to her dark clothing.

Vladimir noticed my interest and shrugged, giving me a brief, wane smile as he returned his attention to the square. Michael, who had paused in his speech, was whispering a few words to one of his men. I looked at Ivan, sitting motionless in his chair, slightly higher than the rest of us. A muscle twitched involuntarily at the base of his jaw, but he displayed no other emotion – certainly nothing that could be seen at any distance. Yuri's eyes were shiny, I noticed, and his jaw definitely trembled as he struggled to hold back the tears. The others reflected a variety of feelings: Kurbsky lolled in his chair, bored by the long speech; Basmanov wriggled uncomfortably on the hard seat that was obviously too small for him. Zakharof was leaning forward, listening intently to every word, like a dog who fawns on his master.

At last the tirade ended and the prisoners were brought out. It required twenty-five or thirty guards to hold back the crowd. Their temper had been cultivated into full-blown fury by Glinski's crafty words, so they now responded with a vicious hatred. Alexander Gorbaty, scheduled as the first to be executed, was led directly onto the platform. The others were forced to stand beside the ring, watching the fate they soon would share.

Little ceremony preceded this first ritual, for Gorbaty was not well known to the people. He was the youngest, except for Mikhail Vorontsof, his silky brown beard free of any gray. But he walked with a stoop, like an old man, and stumbled as he mounted the steps to the platform. With his arms bound behind his back he nearly fell, and had to be assisted by the priest who walked beside him. Reaching the top he seemed to cringe from the axeman, who now stood immobile beside the wooden block, his huge hairy arms resting on the handle of his instrument. There were a few cries of anguish from the crowd – female voices, perhaps some past loves. At least in my mind's eye, this explanation occurred to me.

An old woman reached out her hand, over the edge of the platform, managing to touch the tips of her fingers to the prisoner's boot. She was kicked back by one of the guards—guards, incidentally, in Glinski livery. Once in front of the block, Gorbaty was allowed his final words; but in one this young, death comes especially hard. He turned his face toward Ivan and mumbled only the customary blessing of the condemned, calling upon God and the people to recognize the Majesty of Muscovy. Then seeming to gain some last minute strength, he shrugged off the hands that gripped his shoulders and fell upon his knees before the block. My hands were sweaty and trembling as I watched the priest make a sign of the cross above his head. As the young man stretched his neck, unassisted, upon the pitted wood I felt almost as I had when Heinrich had interrogated the peasant lad – a mixture of excited anticipation and dread – whether for the victim or for my own soul in peril I did not know. By placing his own head on the shelf, Gorbaty had rejected the grace of a blindfold, but I noticed his eyes were tightly clamped.

The headsman looked at Ivan, awaiting permission to carry out the sentence. Ivan nodded, and the executioner raised his ax, its huge blade glinting in a bright streak of sunlight which suddenly burst through the clouds. The ax fell within a dead silence, as each observer seemed to hold his breath. It landed with a resounding thud, and a crunch. But Alexander's head still hung, swinging crazily from the block. Someone laughed in the crowd, and soon a chorus of jeers assaulted the headsman. He had partially missed his stroke, failing to part the neck in a single blow. Undaunted, he raised the ax again. This time, the severed head tumbled onto the stones.

A bucket of water was sloshed over the block, and across the platform surface. Feodor was next. He looked ashen, and very cold—a shivering old man, whose beard had suddenly whitened to scraggle in senile disorder down his chest. His arms were bound with chains, securing him far more tightly than Gorbaty had been. His clothing was tattered, with brown stains showing through the rents, evidence of wounds he must have received when Glinski's men questioned him. Ivan watched Feodor intently, hands gripping the arms of his chair. Again, no expression showed on the Prince's face, although it now seemed pale, completely drained of color, and the pulse along his jaw line had quickened. Yuri displayed his feelings more openly, allowing two long, glistening trails of tears to streak his cheeks. Seeing this made me even more painfully aware of my own uncertain state of mind. I, too, wished to weep for the death of a friend, yet I awaited the final swing of the ax with a sense of undefined expectation—almost excitement—a condition I was helpless to suppress.

Feodor shuffled up the stairs, clinking the length of chain that joined his ankles. He seemed dazed, but shook off the hands that sought to help him as he walked with all the dignity he could muster into the center of the ring. There he paused and turned his face toward Ivan, raising his head for the first and final time.

"I beg the mercy of Heaven for My Prince!" he shouted. "May his reign be long and glorious, and may his throne ever be secure!"

No sound preceded Feodor's end. The axeman took his head in a single stroke. A cheer went up from the street, and it was over. In deference to his rank, Feodor's remains were loaded into a casket and immediately borne away. His head would be buried with the rest of him. I looked up at the wall, as Ivan's personal servants carried his former friend away. Euphrosyne was gone. She had been there when Feodor mounted the stairs, but must have left the moment his head had fallen. She had no interest in the others, I supposed, and their deaths were anticlimactic for me as well. I now felt a dead weight in the pit of my stomach, but I could not look away nor allow my vision to blur as these final executions took place.

Mikhail died as bravely as any. Kubensky, proud and haughty to the last, made a long speech. He expressed his contempt for death and his intention to look after his Prince from heaven, as he had always done on earth. This last came as close as I had ever heard to a condemned man's outright denial of guilt. To make such an insinuation from one's place of execution was improper, and Kubensky's remarks were not well received by the onlookers. What followed, therefore, may have been purposeful, as a result of his insulting suggestion. The headsman took three strokes to behead him, not killing him until the second blow.

Kubensky had been the last, so when his head finally struck the stones, the crowd became a huge, undulating mass. There was a series of disorganized cheers, some for the successful executions, some for the Grand Duke, others being taunts for the headsman, who had butchered his last victim so badly.

Because we were closely hemmed in by the people, Ivan kept his seat. He later admitted that his knees felt a little weak, and he had been glad of the excuse to delay. However, momentarily neglecting protocol, almost all the rest of us stood up. There was just room along the edge of our row for me to slip past Vladya. Ivan looked up expectantly as I came to him, but I knelt down next to his chair and glanced meaningfully across toward Yuri. Ivan had been so involved with his own thoughts, he had not noticed his brother's reactions. Yuri had finally been unable to hold back any longer, and his entire body shook with his sobs. Fortunately, several men seated below and in front of him had gotten up, making it impossible to observe him from the crowd. "It would be better if no one saw him like this," I whispered.

Ivan nodded, and Glinski, who had occupied the empty space saved for him between Yuri and Kurbsky, looked contemptuously at the younger prince. "He should have been left in the palace," he said coldly.

"I shall decide who attends my ceremonies and who does not!" Ivan reproved him.

Glinski sat back in his chair as if slapped, and Ivan tried to comfort his brother. The men in front of them started to move and I reached out, grabbing hold of the nearest man's robe. "Stay put a minute," I told him.

The man turned fully toward us before I realized it had been Alfansy Buturlin I'd touched. I am sure he had been drinking, else he would have had the sense to see what was happening and to keep still. Instead, he opened his mouth at the very worst moment, much to his immediate sorrow.

His lips curled in a nasty sneer when he saw me. "I thought it was you bawling back there," he snarled. "You always were so enamored of Vorontsof!"

The poor fool! He had only tried to bully me for the sake of his companions' adulation. In his own way, he probably intended his remark to be humorous, although it certainly was tinged with the venomous hostility he bore me. His words evoked an immediate and most unexpected response. Yuri stopped crying and looked at the boyar in shocked surprise. Ivan's face flushed a bright crimson. Leaping to his feet, he swung a crashing blow against Buturlin's cheek with the flat of his hand, and his roar brought two guards running from either end of the platform. I had never seen Ivan in such a blind fury before. His blow had staggered Buturlin, and he now howled at the guardsman to seize the man where he had half fallen against the back of a chair.

"Since you are so careless in the way you use your tongue," Ivan shrieked at him, "let's see how you do without one! Perhaps, if you must learn to write your insults, you won't be so quick to make them public!"

Another pair of guards had joined the first, all four men looking up questioningly at the Grand Duke. "Do as I've told you," he shouted, still seething with rage. "Cut out his tongue!"

Realizing that Ivan was dead earnest, Buturlin began to struggle and scream for mercy. The four burly guards had trouble holding him down. Their tussle attracted the attention of almost everyone on the platform, as well as a goodly number of the crowd. A veritable sea of faces was turned our way, and the people began to mutter that Alfansy has tried to attack Ivan. Later, the rumor was modified, and it was said he had only insulted his lord, which was close enough to the truth.

One guard finally forced Alfansy's mouth open, and another grabbed the tongue with his gauntleted left hand pulling it far out of the boyar's mouth. The man looked at Ivan again, to assure himself. The Prince nodded coolly, and the guard quickly sawed off Alfansy's tongue with his dagger.

"Now get out of Our sight!" Ivan shouted.

The guards let go their hold, and Buturlin fell against the men behind him. Clapping his hands over his mouth in a vain attempt to stem the flow of blood, he staggered off the platform, moaning and wailing like a wounded beast. His retainers helped him onto his horse. Not another word passed between any of us. I think we were all too astonished to speak.

A few minutes later, Ivan rose and left the stand, followed by Yuri, Vladimir, Andrew Kurbsky, and myself. We rode back into the Kremlin, where Ivan went immediately to his apartments. Early the next morning he left on a pilgrimage to several monasteries, taking only Yuri and Andrei Adashev with him, along with the usual number of retainers and servants. It was a month before he returned. I was sorry not to be able to speak with either Ivan or Adashev, because my own secret responses to the executions had left me confused and uncertain. I did not feel comfortable discussing this with either Heinrich or Vladya, with whom I would spend much of my time during Ivan's absence. But I was too young then to remain focused indefinitely on such a nebulous conception as this. I comforted myself with the assumption that age would one day bring a greater understanding. And whatever sin might be involved. . .well, it would be a long time before I stood before the final throne of judgment.

CHAPTER II

Except for the brief interval of the executions, it had remained an unusually glorious autumn. Even into November, we enjoyed a few days of second summer – warm afternoons, with nights just crisp and chill enough to foretell the coming of Father Winter. September rains had kept the fields and forest surrounding the city from losing their final flush of green. Grasses and reeds along the river were as tall as I had ever seen them, while the water, itself, remained at a fairly high level.

After Ivan's departure, my anxieties gradually diminished, and I began to find those first few days dull and empty. The palace was silent, devoid of its usual bustling activity. I had none of my customary activities to occupy me, except for the daily practice sessions with my stepfather and his men. Then, to further limit the outlets for my energies, Heinrich became occupied with matters of trade, frequently leaving the city for several days at a time. I was getting on poorly with Mother, partially because Feodor's death had left her in an agitated state – different, of course, from my own – but also for slightly more mundane reasons. She had been suspicious of my activities with the girls for a long time, and had finally obtained a hint regarding my affair with Sonya. At first, she seemed to vacillate between amusement and anger, finally choosing the latter. Among other restrictions, I was forbidden to set foot in the woman's quarters. But at this point, I didn't really care. The thing which was happening within my soul had left me listless and momentarily devoid of passion.

A welcome break came when Vladya sent me a note, asking that I meet him by the main bazaar – the *gostiny dvor*. He had been unable to find sufficient diversion, and together we had an enjoyable time, exploring the shops and stalls. We talked with German gunsmiths and Tartar silk merchants, asking questions and poking our noses into everything. I was well acquainted with the rules of commerce from my trips with Heinrich, and took some pride in being able to display this knowledge to Vladimir. The exotic sights and odors were enough to make a young man long for adventure in all the many distant lands represented by the wide variety of goods. Vladya's lighthearted attitude did much to lighten the gloom which otherwise might have engulfed me, and for the moment I was able to push these darker thoughts into the deepest recesses of my mind.

Like myself, Vladimir had little in common with most of the fellows who joined in Ivan's revels. They were generally a shallow, ignorant lot, only three or four of whom knew how to read. In Vladya, I found a soul mate. Like his cousin, he was intellectually gifted, but he never indulged in the terrible displays of temper or fits of fury which had become frequent in Ivan's behavior. These unheralded changes of mood made it difficult to enjoy Ivan's company without being extremely careful to say nothing offensive. Vladya always seemed a veritable fountain of wit and exuberance, never asserting his rank as a barrier to our friendship.

As we came to know each other better, we discovered other areas of kindredness. . .aspects of our lives which presented similar problems. Vladya's mother, Euphrosyne, had used him all his life, and had imposed tasks upon him as premature to his age as those my mother had given me. At this particular juncture, both of us were in a mood to rebel against our respective dams, and to begin exercising some direction over our lives. That both women were working in various, nefarious ways to keep us apart, only added to the pleasure we continued to find in one another's company. Our physical likeness was only another factor, as I've noted before, and it was during these weeks that people first began mistaking us for brothers.

One evening we went to the Staritsky mansion, braving Euphrosyne's displeasure, but doing so as an act of open defiance. Vladya called it a proclamation of freedom. Like many other princely families, Vladya and his mother found the Sparrow Hills to be a convenient place to live. It permitted their being close to court, yet far enough away that they could escape the turmoil and frantic activity once their own gates had closed behind them. All the estates on this side of the river were large, with high walls and an almost country atmosphere.

Bordering Vladya's grounds was the enormous Glinski estate, where both George and Michael supposedly maintained residence. Michael spent more time in the large apartment provided for him within the royal residence, however, while George was often out of the city altogether. Their mother, the witch Anna Glinskaya, was the only permanent resident, living in regal splendor as matriarch of the family. Being Ivan's grandmother, she was honored as his only living forebear. No one was ever permitted to see her, although her years and her great rank would have exempted her from the usual female restrictions. Her seclusion was by her own choice, and this may have stimulated the rumors that she would often stand on her balcony, conversing with goblins and demons who lived in the woods behind the estate. Such stories naturally intrigued us.

On the night of my first visit to Vladya's home, we slipped over the wall and past the patrols of Glinski guards, hiding ourselves in some acacia bushes behind the mansion. From here we were able to watch the old woman as she paced the length of her fabled balcony, singing some strange songs in the language of her native Lithuania. In retrospect, I suppose she was probably mad, and merely acting according to God's dictates. But to us it seemed an evil mummery she practiced in the shadowy moonlight. Watching her, we became frightened, though neither of us wished to express his terror to the other. Finally, no longer able to withstand our unreasoned fear, we bolted from our hiding place and fled back the way we'd come.

Responding to a mutual panic, we simply ran, hurtling the wall and racing toward the sanctuary of Staritsky land. Our sudden motion must have startled the old lady, who began to shriek at our retreating figures. Assuming we were thieves who had crept in under cover of darkness, the guards set loose the dogs. Once over the wall, we fell to the ground, hugging each other and giggling hysterically as Anna's cries resounded through the night like the curses of a soul condemned. Then the baying of the hounds obliterated the sound of Glinskaya's voice and the Glinski guards began shouting to Vladya's, alerting them to the intruders' passage.

Later, when I told my mother about it, she snorted at me, laughing as usual at my stupidity. "Running like a scared rabbit," she howled, "because a poor old woman is singing to herself on a balcony. If you only realized it, the one real witch practicing the black arts in Moscow is that Staritsky crone you've become so found of!"

I sputtered a denial of her final accusation, because I knew she intended it as a further argument against my association with Vladya. While I disliked Euphrosyne – though not as much as Mother did – I was actually more afraid of her. Nor did I doubt the possibility of two witches. In my adolescent imagination I could picture the pair of them, each standing on her respective dais, hurling evil spells at one another through the gloomy darkness of the forests. But I was not to dwell overlong on any appraisal of witches. Ivan returned to the Kremlin with new ideas and plans.

I had turned sixteen, and the stubby golden hairs on my chin were finally forming into a proper beard. My voice had ceased to crack, and with the other evidences of manhood I had already experienced, I began inching into the influential role I dreamed about. Ivan started including me at meetings with his advisors, and several decisions he made, just after his return, were colored by my opinions. Ivan, of course, had also developed significantly during this period. With his full red beard and regal bearing, he was assuming the appearance of a tetrarch. He seldom took part in the wild rides of our friends, once the winter snows began to fall. Instead, he spent many hours composing ever grander plans for his realm. He still read voraciously, and he spent several afternoons each week playing chess. He even devised some variations to the classic openings and responses. He became so skilled I was hard pressed to beat him any more; Vladya never could.

One afternoon near the end of November, a company of us, including Vladimir and several other young men, rode out to hear Ivan address the people. He had been so secretive in preparing his text, none of us had any idea of its contents, the sense of mystery only tending to swell the crowd. Heralds had spread the word through the city, and as always when an event of importance was scheduled, a large throng of people crowded into the Square of Executions. We arrived a short while before Ivan made his appearance, dressed in a fine dark robe and riding his favorite black stallion. He rode slowly toward the Place of Skulls, sitting rigidly in his saddle and allowing his eyes to sweep the crowd with a practiced coldness.

When he reached the ring and dismounted, his guard formed into two columns, lining the steps he must climb to take the dais. I remained on my horse, where I had an excellent view of the people and all that might occur. In expectation of some major announcement, every member of the court was present – the group comprising close to half of all the boyars and princes in the realm. These gentlemen were now scattered in groups amidst the crowd, small islands of mounted nobility surrounded by the common tradesmen and peasants – the multitudes prevented from pressing too closely by the presence of armed retainers about each cluster of courtiers.

But this day Ivan spoke to the people, not to the princes. He apologized for the boyars' past behavior, and seemed to make a deliberate bid for the support of the populace against the established power of the aristocracy. "I lost my parents too early," he said. "The boyars took no thought of me, for they meant to govern themselves. They lined their bellies through injustice and they cruelly oppressed the people."

A roar of agreement burst from the crowd, while the nobles remained stony, few allowing any expression to show on their faces. Within my own group, I think each of us was too surprised to react. Ivan continued: "Nobody opposed them. But during my dreary childhood, I, too, was blind and deaf; I did not give ear to the lamentations of the poor, and no word of blame was on my lips."

He turned, then, imbued with the fire of his own accusations, and faced the largest group of princes. "You boyars!" he shouted. "You did as you liked, foul rebels and unjust judges that you were! What answers can you give me today? What tears have you not wrung from others; what blood have you not shed? I stand innocent of this wretchedness, but as for you. . .a terrible judgment of heaven awaits you!" He continued for a very long while, frequently evoking responses of surprise or approval from the crowd. The people began to edge a little closer to the various groups of mounted men, including our own.

When Ivan finished, a strange, uncertain silence hung in the air, the stinging echoes of his voice still seeming to reverberate against the stones. If he had given the word, I am certain that none of those who were mounted and well dressed would have left the square alive. But he said no more, simply turning toward the stairs, preparing to mount his stallion. An enormous cheer went up from the crowd. People rushed to the base of the platform and kissed his feet. Women held up their children, as if trying to expose them to some reflected glory. While this scene of peasant tumult continued, the groups of nobles turned silently away. Remaining in their original cliques, they slowly rode from the square. Only Vladya, Yuri, Andrew Kurbsky, and I remained to escort Ivan back to the Kremlin. On the way, he asked all of us to stay with him. I think we were too stunned to speak until we were in the courtyard near the faceted hall. I was closest to Ivan at this moment, and he turned to me. "Do you think your parents are home right now?" he asked.

I told him they were not, because I knew Mother had cajoled Heinrich into taking her on a hunt the previous morning. They were not due back until after dark.

"It might be well to go there," he said, directing this to everyone. "I'd like to remain away from the court for a few hours."

That was all he said until we were seated in Mother's comfortable *svyetlitsa*. I made sure all the servants were assigned tasks to keep them away from us, and I sent Frieda to supervise the women, lest any of them decide to spy. Once secure, knowing we could not be interrupted or overheard, Ivan looked at us and smiled with a little boy's guilty expression.

"Well, now that I've plunged my finger into the basket, I must pull out the biggest piece of fruit, mustn't I?"

Andrew slumped down into Mother's best armchair. "I don't know about the fruit in the basket," he remarked dryly, with his usual bluntness, "but there are going to be some unhappy boyars in the Kremlin this evening."

"Would you have a suggestion?" asked Ivan sardonically.

"Didn't you have a plan in mind when you made your speech?" I asked in surprise.

Ivan grinned again and pulled reflectively on his beard. "I went a little further than I'd intended," he said softly. Defiantly, then, in response to the looks of amazement on all our faces, he added, "But, it was an honest speech! All those people standing there, watching me as if I were God – expecting me to tell them how I felt! I had to do it, don't you understand? It was as if God, himself, put the words in my mouth."

Andrew pursed his lips and sat forward on the chair, elbows on his knees. "All of which does nothing to help the present situation," he said. "I also assumed you had a plan in mind."

Ivan smiled with a peculiarly expectant grin, watching Andrew, obviously toying with him.

"You're no fool, Ivashka," he said at length. "You've placed yourself in a position where you must be coronated, and soon."

Ivan nodded. "My thought, exactly," he admitted, ". . .but. . ." slyly smiling and looking at each of us in turn, ". . .not as Grand Duke."

There was a long silence. No one spoke, though each of us had his own thoughts as we waited for Ivan to finish his statement. "I shall be crowned as Caesar of the Third Rome," he said finally, ". . .as Czar!"

With no sign of surprise, and with no hesitation, Andrew agreed. "Which will make you undisputedly sovereign over all the boyars," he added. "Brilliant!" For an instant, I thought I detected a note of sarcasm, but perhaps I imagined it.

"Hail Caesar!" exclaimed Yuri, jumping to his feet and giving the Roman salute. He started to giggle, and his mirth infected me as well. Even Ivan seemed genuinely pleased.

Suddenly, Andrew stood up, his face white with emotion. "Keep still!" he barked. I think he was actually afraid. "You two infants would be better left out of this kind of thing!"

"At least we have enough faith in our Czar not to be scared pissless!" I snapped.

That surprised him, and he glowered at me.

"Enough!" said Ivan. "My followers must stand together."

Andrew backed down at this, and later claimed to have been joking. I did not think he really had been, but he never displayed any animosity toward me as a result of our exchange. On the contrary, he went out of his way to appease me the next few times the opportunity presented itself. We had reached a logical end to our discussion, although we had failed to formulate a suitable plan for placing Ivan's intention before the *Duma*. It had to be done properly, in a manner that would produce the least opposition, and we more or less agreed to consult the Metropolitan before making a decision. Nearly an hour later, Ivan still seemed reluctant to leave, so I ordered more drink and some cold meat to be brought. As she carried in the last of this, Frieda whispered to me that she had ordered a large enough dinner to take care of everyone. I told Ivan, and he readily agreed to stay. I realized he was delaying his departure in order to have a few words with Heinrich.

It was another couple of hours before my parents returned, and I was grateful when Mother had the propriety to retire without entering the roomful of men. I think her attire had something to do with it, for she had been riding a horse. Although she used the customary German lady's saddle, with a special covered hook permitting both legs to be kept on one side, she still had to wear skirts without the proper undergarments. Mother was never one to appear without her finest plumage.

Heinrich joined us immediately. Already aglow from the wind and from the mead he had been drinking all day, he was soon laughing and exchanging stories with us. He liked young people, and was at his best among them. But even half drunk, Heinrich was an astute observer. I could see him responding to the others' expressions as we spoke. With Ivan a little giddy and off his guard from a combination of wine and emotion, my stepfather eventually perceived a hint of what was happening. He drew Ivan aside, and the two of them sat on one of the benches along the wall, speaking together for a long time. When they returned to the group, Ivan had a smug, satisfied smile on his lips.

I was never sure how much of Ivan's clever maneuverings resulted from my stepfather's advice, nor how much he had actually planned prior to his speech. There can be little doubt that he would have faced serious resistance if he had simply announced his intentions to the assembled boyars, without a proper foundation to force their agreement. Taking the crown as Czar would irrevocably place every other prince and boyar into a position of clear subordination. They already were, in fact, but it had never been so blatantly rubbed in their faces.

Very few people were involved in formulating Ivan's intrigues. His Glinski cousins, for instance, were not informed – mostly, I think, because he was beginning to distrust them. Makari was consulted and eventually persuaded to enter as the most important participant. I knew that Vladimir worked many hours with the Metropolitan, assuring that every move was going to be made in precisely the proper sequence. Vladya even succeeded in keeping the secret from his mother until the last minute, which naturally infuriated her. When she did find out, she scoffed at the idea: "Czar, indeed," she sniggered. "Why every barbarian in Byzantium calls himself 'Kaiser-i-Rum', and every minor chieftain in the southern hills thinks of himself as Caesar. Just one more act of conceited stupidity!" I feared she might upset our plans, even at this late hour, but Vladya was so deeply involved she could not interfere without compromising him. There was also the possibility—in her mind, at least—that all these honors and titles would one day land on her son's shoulders. . .not an unpleasant prospect to assuage her greedy soul.

By the miracle of God's indulgence, no one with the power to oppose us learned the truth until Ivan's trap was fully baited and sprung. Our plans depended on the traditional influx of noble gentlemen who always came to Moscow for the holy days, the bulk of them arriving in early to mid–December. The time was just short enough for Ivan to make his move before any unfortunate consequences could result from his ill–considered speech—if, in fact, it was ill–considered.

Every omen and circumstance seemed to favor us; the fruit was ripe for the plucking. Over the past few months, discrete inquiries had been made in several foreign capitals, testing the possibility of finding a princess suitable to become Ivan's bride. The responses had not been favorable. The Western kings looked upon Russia as a land of barbarians, a condition for which the Shuiskys were largely responsible. With all the previous disorder a thing of the past, their western majesties' attitudes were insulting; however, in this instance, it worked to our advantage.

Makari called an assembly of nobles in the Cathedral of the Assumption, the second week in December. The real reason continued to be a carefully guarded secret, although rumors were rampant, including a few started by Vladimir. Some of the stories hinted at the truth, at least partially. This, too, was a part of the plan.

Once all the princes and boyars, the *voivodes* and *dyaks* stood in their proper places, the Metropolitan entered and went through a long liturgy, purposely repeating the lines with agonizing slowness. When the group was physically tired from standing, but with their curiosity thoroughly aroused, Makari led them into the great Hall of Facets, where Ivan awaited them. By now, the air of expectation was so heavy it seemed almost solid. Everyone knew a momentous decision was going to be announced, but of those who expected it to concern Ivan's marriage, most assumed he would simply tell which foreign princess he had chosen.

The men flocked into the room, joking and talking together, relieved to have the tedious church service behind them. Their dark mass completely filled the ornate, chilly hall, with a few of the *voivodes* and lesser gentlemen being forced to stand in the passageway. Ivan sat quietly upon his gold and ivory throne, waiting until everyone was present, allowing each ample time to find a place and become quiet before he spoke.

At length, still seated, he began his carefully rehearsed monologue. "Putting my trust in the Grace of God and His Immaculate Mother. . ." he said, turning to Makari, who stood beside him, ". . .in the Grace and Intercession of Sergey and of all the great Russian Miracle–workers: Peter, Alexi, Jonah. . .and with thy blessing, Oh Father, I have thought to marry."

He allowed the whispering of the nobles to fade before he continued. When he spoke again, the room was completely silent. Ivan stood up. "I first intended to seek marriage in a foreign court, in the house of some king or Czar; but I have foregone that intention because I was orphaned and left a small child after the death of my father and mother. If I were to take a wife in a foreign country and afterwards we did not get on well together, it would be difficult for us. Therefore, I wish to marry within my own realm – the one whom God will bless to be my wife. I shall do this with thy blessing, Oh Father." He turned again to Makari, this time with a smile on his face.

Ivan stepped around his throne and sat down beside the Metropolitan. They talked together for several minutes, while the boyars shifted about in the limited space, most of them whispering excitedly with their neighbors. Since Ivan had named no bride, it must mean he intended to choose from an assemblage of eligible virgins. In this event, any man present might become the father, brother, uncle, or be otherwise related to the new Grand Duchess. Within a few moments the popularity of Ivan's announcement culminated in a loud, spontaneous cheer of delight, eventually devolving into a thunderous roar of applause.

This was the signal Ivan had awaited. He rose again, and held up his hand for silence. "Before my marriage," he announced quietly, "I wish, again with thy blessing, Oh Father Metropolitan, to seek the ancestral rank—such as that of Our ancestors, the Czars and Grand Dukes, and Our kinsman Vladimir Vassilovich Monomakh. I also wish to be vested with that rank."

The nobles had been completely quiet before Ivan began to speak. Mostly out of surprise, they remained silent now. Then Vladimir, by prior arrangement, leaped up and shouted, "Yes! A Russian Czar! A Russian Czar, crowned and anointed to be the mightiest ruler of the mightiest land in the world, that we all may share in his glory!"

And that accomplished the desired result. The whole roomful of men took up the cry, first in small scattered groups, then in larger numbers until finally there came a cheering to nearly rock the building. It was settled! Ivan would be crowned as Czar, and any man in the room might be kin to the progeny of the royal house.

The cleverly developed mood had been properly exploited; the desired decision had been made.

For the next month, I spent nearly every waking hour with Ivan or with the Metropolitan, going over timeworn documents and questioning learned men. We sought to obtain a complete understanding of the ancient rituals. All the mysteries of the past must be joined, that nothing be omitted from the long coronation ceremony to allow any future doubts. As Ivan was to assume a title not formerly bestowed on a Muscovite Prince, it was necessary to alter the traditional ceremony for the coronation of a Grand Duke, and to incorporate certain elements from the more ancient Byzantine rites. There was some precedent for this, though not in Moscow. The ceremony used by Ivan's cousin Dmitri in Vladimir – about fifty years before – was almost identical to the form we decided upon.

I cannot emphasize too strongly just how daring a move it was for Ivan to assume this title. But the very audacity had the desired effect; no one spoke against it, because no one believed he could stop it from happening. Once he was anointed Czar, Ivan could make things go badly for any man who had tried to oppose him. Moreover, the Metropolitan had sanctioned the decision from the pulpit of the Great Cathedral. Who was to refute such authority?

For the celebrations preceding the coronation, Ivan suspended the rule which restricted peasants from remaining overnight in the city. With the harvest in, hundreds would journey to Moscow. They would offer up prayers for the successful reign of the Czar, and there would be liquor and food provided for them. Perhaps his idea was wise, even if I could not understand it, for Ivan was now the Vassal of God. The decisions he made could well have been directed by a power beyond my comprehension. At the very least, I reasoned, he had assured himself an audience of magnificent proportions – and unprecedented throng to celebrate the elevation of our first Russian Czar.

When the momentous day finally arrived, it burst upon us with furious impact. The coronation took place in January, immediately after Epiphany, as Makari thought it the earliest proper time. Our winter had been far from mild thus far, but on the night before the ceremonies a furious wind came down from the north, delivering a massive snowfall. In the hours before dawn, abruptly as it had started, the storm abated, but the temperature dropped to an unbelievable low.

I got up while the storm was still in its death throes, for it was part of the established ritual that Ivan speak with God, attended by his closest followers. He must beg for the Divine Guidance he would need for the rest of his life. I dressed hurriedly in my warmest clothes. The costume finery I would wear later in the day was still in the palace repository. The wind, at least, was gone by the time I left the house. Followed by two of Heinrich's men, I floundered through the heavy banks of snow. Servants had started clearing the courtyards, and my retainers called to them, holding lanterns above us on their long poles. Some workmen came with an equipment sledge; laughing at my mode of conveyance, they delivered me to the palace portal.

I waited outside Ivan's bedchamber until he came out, then accompanied him to his chapel where Yuri and the others joined us. Ivan was very restrained, hardly speaking to anyone. I sensed more than the expected nervousness in his attitude, but could only guess at the cause. The day before he had mentioned for the first time that he was unhappy about having to choose a Russian bride. Today's ceremony would be an irrevocable act, in accordance with his promise to the boyars. He would be forced to choose from the Russian maidens; a foreign bride, of a rank equal to his own, would be forever denied him. I think that circumstance was the only one which weighed heavily enough on his mind to explain his apparent depression.

After the prayer session, when everything was finally ready, he brightened only slightly. We were in Ivan's sitting room, all dressed in our fine robes. Downstairs, the first guests were beginning to arrive. Sleigh after sleigh tinkled across the icy crust of snow, depositing their noble passengers at the cathedral entrance. Ivan paced the floor, his heavy costume hardly stirred by the movement. He glittered with jewels, like stars on a summer night, but tiny pearls of sweat stood out upon his forehead and his jaw twitched as it did when he was frightened.

All of us in his entourage were weighted down with the voluminous robes, made of silver or gold cloth. Heavy festoons of gems hung from chains about our necks, with more stones sewn into our collars and the fabric of our garments. Ivan's anxiety infected us all, giving rise to a forced, superficial chatter, until we finally received word from a priest and started for the cathedral. We formed into a long, carefully ordered procession as we passed through the crowds and were joined by others who had parts to play in the rituals.

Ivan's confessor, the archpriest Feodor Barmin, went first, directly ahead of his Prince. He carried several sacred items to be used in the service. The rest of us followed Ivan, like the tail of the legendary peacock. People stood on every side, so awed by the majesty of the spectacle there was hardly a sound, only the soft howl of the wind through the towers and cupolas overhead. The sun beat strongly upon the glittering snow; as always, God acknowledged His awareness of a special moment in Ivan's life. Today He smiled on us from His heavenly throne, and rejoiced with the people of Moscow.

I walked in my designated position near the head of the line, much to the annoyance of several ranking courtiers. When the procession stopped I slipped into my place, toward the end of the second row of spectators. This put me near enough to step forward and perform my functions when the time came. The crowd completely filled the cathedral and overflowed into the courtyard, where they stood in frozen sunlight through the lengthy ceremony. The vault seemed jammed, even to the ceilings, because of the many religious frescoes staring down at us from the towering walls. Previously, whenever I had entered the building by myself, I had felt those accusing eyes of the saints. On this special day, they seemed to assume a more placid attitude, as if they rejoiced in having the true Czar anointed beneath their guardian beneficence.

The chorus had been enlarged by adding a number of young men and boys, making it sound more strident and powerful on the upper tones. They chanted exuberantly through the *In Plurimos Annos*, the hymn of greeting to a mighty ruler. Afterward came a long mass, at the end of which Ivan assumed his throne beside Makari, the two of them sitting together on a raised platform, twelve steps high, surrounded by flowing bolts of gold and silver cloth.

One by one, the Metropolitan conferred the various symbols of authority upon the Czar, lifting them from a long table and handing them to Ivan, or draping them about his slender body. Yuri assisted in placing the *barma* over his brother's shoulders, the tippet with seven medallions of gold, enamel and precious stones. I moved forward during this, and stood behind Yuri, holding the sacred chain. Once this was in place, Makari presented the crown and cross of Monomakh, each delivered with the appropriate prayer and blessing. The heavy crown, the "Cap of Monomakh," was made in three parts. At the bottom was a fur border, and above this an eight sided bell, comprised of triangular plates of gold filigree, linked together to make it flexible. The uppermost portion was the same shape, but smaller, topped with a cross and many precious stones. It was so heavy, a maxim had grown up among the people when they spoke of their ruler's having a weighty problem: *Oh, heavy thou art, oh Cap of Monomakh!*

And heavy, indeed, seemed my own cap of Monomakh before the afternoon was over! Glorious though it certainly was, I became forcefully aware how miserable traditional ceremonies can be. About half way through, I realized I should have urinated before I entered the church. By the time it was over I was in utter agony. In addition to this, my back ached from standing rigidly upright through the four hours of ritual, and my feet hurt from being crammed into boots that were much too small for me. I think my distress was shared by a good many others.

I was later ashamed to admit it, but other than the few moments when I had some minor service to perform, my thoughts strayed from the glittering scene before me. I was troubled by the peculiar circumstances of my own existence—now, more than ever before. Having no actual rank, I stood in attendance upon the Czar, shoulder–to–shoulder with the most noble blood in the empire. Outwardly, I was treated with respect and cordiality, for my friendship with Ivan required it be so. Neither was our blood relationship a secret, except that some now looked upon my face and smiled, whispering the name of Obolenski in their hearts.

Even Euphrosyne had changed her way of referring to me. She used to call me "Basil's bastard," until she began to realize the implications of this. She currently dubbed me "Eleanor's brat." Such names could not alter the nobility of my blood, regardless how I happened to possess it; yet I responded all day to the strangeness of my situation.

During the latter part of the ceremony I remained at the foot of the dais with Yuri and Vladimir. Beside us stood Andrew Kurbsky and Alexi Basmanov, Prince Pronsky, and the Glinski brothers. Surrounding us were other boyars and sons of boyars, princes, and most of the higher clergy. Behind them was a huge mass of faces, more boyars and nobles of the court, foreign ambassadors – each a man of noble birth. Even in the farthest reach of the cathedral there was no one who did not claim title to a brilliant lineage. The fact that my blood was as good as any could not assuage my feelings.

My mood changed when the ceremonies were finally over, and Ivan was Czar. It was possible for me to relieve the various aches and strains of my body, and I began to relax for the first time that day. The entire city had come to life, its populace bloated by the influx of visitors. Torches blossomed at every street corner, and enormous bonfires blazed in the market places and bazaars, even in the poorest districts. The gaggle of milling crowds had been increased by the large retinues of servants brought by the dignitaries and invited guests, and by the curious folk who streamed in from the surrounding areas.

The Kremlin gates were open and all the drawbridges were down, permitting the people to glimpse their Czar. A huge mass of humanity had been allowed to jam itself into the courtyards between the Savior's Gate and the bell tower. Guards had been posted in most of the open spaces to keep the great, unwashed herd from penetrating the residential areas, where in their drunken joy they might have been expected to steal anything in sight. The press of the crowd became so great it was finally impossible to keep them from coming as close as the palace steps.

It was only a few feet from the cathedral to the main palace portals. Ivan had already covered the distance, along with most of the guests, before the crowds broke through the cordon of guards. They shoved their way into the cathedral, now bereft of its noble occupants, and stole the decorations. The magnificent cloth of gold, covering the royal platform, was ripped to shreds by people who desired an amulet of the holy ceremony. In order to draw the mob outside again, several casketsfull of gold coins were tossed into the snow by the household guard.

A loud chant started after this, as the people did not realize the gift had been a ploy to get them out of the cathedral. They shouted and cheered, demanding that their Czar appear before them. Some of the foreign guests were startled by the uproar, not understanding the words. Ivan, not in the least disturbed, was flattered and greatly pleased. We were in the great Hall of Facets drinking to his welfare when the Czar made a sweeping bow to the assemblage and withdrew.

When Ivan stepped outside, a deafening roar thundered through the mass of closely packed bodies. The crowd surged forward as those in the rear, and those who were prevented from seeing their Czar because of the intervening buildings, shoved inward to obtain a better view. Several people were crushed to death, so great was the pressure and enthusiasm. Then Ivan spoke. He stood before his people, wearing the ermine robes and the Crown of Monomakh. He made so splendid a figure that this entire herd of common, ignorant people—louts who were usually insensitive to anything fine or beautiful—all were completely overwhelmed. They fell silent as soon as Ivan raised his arms, and starting from the front – gradually spreading to the rear, everyone dropped onto his knees. Torches flickered about the edges of the crowd, and from a few scattered places in its center. There was hardly any other light, only the reddish glow of these flames and the amber reflections from the palace windows. To me, it was a breath–taking tableau of devotion.

Ivan's comments were actually of little consequence, merely some words of humble thanks to God and to his people for the honor they did him. But he ended by promising to be a just and merciful autocrat. When the Czar finished, Makari stepped out to bless the crowd, allowing Ivan to withdraw. It was one of the Shuiskys – Peter, I believe – who announced the Czar's desire that all his people share in the joy and pleasure. Food and drink would be distributed in the Square of Executions, and in the major bazaars. His words brought another resounding cheer, after which the mob began to break up, retiring from the Kremlin enclosure, eager to glean their share of the promised bounty.

Within the palace, the only unhappy visage I noticed was George Glinski, who brooded that it should have been a Shuisky who made this announcement to the people.

Hardly had the crowds departed from Moscow after the coronation, than preparations were begun for the selection of Ivan's bride. Not only within the walls of the Kremlin, but throughout the entire city, people were busily employed, getting everything in readiness to receive the thousand virgins and their families. Ivan set up quarters for most of the girls in the building which had formerly been the women's palace. But for each maiden who came, it was anticipated there would be at least three others. Actually, in many cases the entourage ran closer to twenty. Everyone who had a spare room or who was willing to share a bedstead, was encouraged to offer it for use by the noble visitors and their retainers.

Our house was no exception. Heinrich invited the family of Zakharin to stay with us, as he had engaged in extensive trade with the venerable Gregory and considered him a very proper and respectable man. Of less than boyar rank, Gregory Zakharin still came from a well established, honorable family. His niece Anastasia was clearly covered by the definitions in Ivan's order, commanding all virgins of noble birth and marriageable age to assemble in Moscow for his inspection.

The Zakharins came early, due to some business Gregory had in the city. As final preparations had not been completed on the girls' dormitory, the entire group was to stay in our house that first night. I thought little about it, for I did not know Gregory, and I had no reason to anticipate involvement beyond the normal courtesies.

I spent the morning with Ivan, who was now in a state of high excitement. The coronation had done much to ease his qualms over selecting a Russian bride. With the huge flock of girls already on the way, he reverted to that same, rare mood of glee he had displayed after removing the Shuiskys. When morning prayers were over, he insisted on going to the baths. He was in such a hurry, I half ran to keep up with him, and Yuri kept falling behind. Ivan rubbed his hands together and fingered his magnificent beard, the golden–red hairs gleaming like silk from the constant brushing and attention it had received during the last few weeks. His eyes glistened brightly, as if with an eager fire.

Yuri caught up with us, and nudged me. "Hope he picks one that's worth all this trouble," he said.

Ivan spun around, executing the steps of a little peasant dance and poked playfully at his brother's face. "Out of a thousand heifers, I'm bound to find one! There might even be an extra left over for you," he added, dancing on ahead of us, bubbling with laughter.

Yuri's face turned white, except for the three lines where Ivan's fingers had pressed the flesh. "I don't think I want a wife, not just yet," he stammered, evoking another giggle from ahead of us.

"We'll see," Ivan called back. "We'll see!"

We passed the bottom of the stairs at the palace side entrance—the three of us with Adashev bringing up the rear. As we rounded the corner, Ivan skipped backward, making faces at us until he collided with Basmanov, who was engaged in an argument with three Italians who were working on the women's quarters. Ivan straightened and continued with a more dignified step. But he reached back, keeping his arms against his body so the bowing Italians couldn't see him, and quickly gave a sharp tug at Basmanov's beard. Yuri snatched at the tall boyar's hat, as I grabbed one of Alexi's arms. Yuri fastened on the other, and between us we managed to spin his huge bulk around in a complete circle. "We're going to have a Czarina!" we sang. "We're going to pick Ivashka's bride!" Basmanov roared at us in feigned anger.

We let go of him and ran after Ivan, Andrei struggling to catch up with us. Servants had cut several intersecting paths through the waist high snow, one of those from the rear of the palace to the bathhouse. We trotted the short distance, throwing snowballs at each other. As we reached the outside door of the bath, we could still hear Alexi bellowing obscene witticisms after us.

Inside, we flung our clothes to the attendants and ran naked into the steamy interior. Ivan stretched out on the highest shelf, Yuri and I sitting below him. Andrei busied himself by the door, carving the sharp nubs off several willow wands. As always, the hot, steamy room enervated us and we were soon half asleep. The only sound was an occasional crackling from the stove or a hiss of steam when one of the attendants dumped fresh snow into the caldron. The room was almost dark, dimly illuminated by a single lantern hanging from the ceiling.

Ivan's voice suddenly broke the silence. "She will be the most beautiful and virtuous woman in Russia," he said lazily, "and she will bear strong sons to wear the Cap of Monomakh."

Yuri, whose feet were close to mine, poked me with his toes and said nothing, probably afraid that reminding Ivan of his presence might encourage the promise of a second wedding. I looked up at Ivan, but could not see him clearly through the haze of steam. I wondered what expression showed on his features, and realized that without being able to see this, I could not be sure of pleasing him with my answer. For this reason I said nothing, lapsing instead into a consideration of this recent desire to please. It was true, I thought; I was becoming a toady, instead of feeling free to express myself openly as I used to. I lay back on the boards.

From the far side of the room, Andrei's voice quietly answered Ivan. "It is most important," he said, "that above all else she be intelligent and possess a grace of judgment."

I could feel rather than hear Ivan shift his position above me. He must have turned on his side to face Andrei. "Why do you say that?" he asked.

"How far do you wish to extend the borders of Muscovy?" was the servant's reply.

A thoughtful sigh and Ivan turned again, onto his back, I thought, with his hands beneath his head and his eyes focused on nothing. When he did answer his voice was firm, but calm, no tremble of emotion as when he had spoken of these things before. "Our realm must reach from the Urals to the Baltic coast – and more, perhaps beyond the Oder," he said, ". . .and from the frozen seas of the farthest north to the Empire of the Turks. I am the first Czar of the last Rome."

"And as Caesar left an empire for his heirs to expand upon," added Andrei, "so must you. But the sons you leave behind must not be indolent wastrels who will allow your empire to crumble, as did the sons of the Roman Caesars."

"And if you are away, at the head of your armies," I added, "it must be the Czarina who maintains your rule in Moscow."

Ivan swung his legs over the edge of his shelf, landing both feet on my stomach. A couple of playful pumps and he leaped over me onto the floor. "She must still be the most beautiful woman in the land," he said.

The attendants fell upon him with the willow wands, whipping his skin to bring all the poisons to the surface. The rest of us joined in, thrashing each other thoroughly and making it a game of war, in which each friend became a Tartar foe, to be beaten down with our supple swords. Later, as we rolled in the snow outside, Ivan grabbed me by the hair and shoved my face into a drift. "Your beard is getting long enough to merit a bride, too." he shouted. And to Yuri's discomfort, he went on: "Perhaps we shall have three weddings this winter!"

When I returned home, the sledges of the Zakharins were being unloaded at the front door. Several large chests had been carried in – clothes for the hopeful bride, gifts for the Czar should his choice fall upon the niece of Gregory. I had to wait for the doorway to be cleared before entering the hall. For a moment I was blinded, coming from the snow covered courtyard into the darkness of the atrium. As my eyes adjusted to the dim interior, I saw the outlines of several people, the smallest form standing closest to me. I was almost able to make out the features when Heinrich turned and noticed my arrival. He immediately presented me to Gregory.

"My son, Demetrius," he said, using the Germanic form as he usually did. "We are very proud of him."

"He looks to be a fine lad." Gregory's voice was surprisingly rich and mellow, much in contrast with his long, silver beard and deeply etched face.

I turned slightly, making a properly respectful bow to the older man. I could now see well enough to be strongly distracted by the other figure. This was, of course, Anastasia – a girl such as I had never seen before. Her hair was dark, almost raven, as were her eyes. She wore no flour upon her features, which were milky white, with just a suggestion of blush in the cheeks, an effect no skill with cosmetics could achieve. Her lips were full and generous, at this moment formed into the crescent of a friendly, innocent smile as she boldly returned my stare.

I am afraid our exchange of glances was not lost on either Heinrich or Gregory. The latter stepped forward, placing his arm protectively about his niece's shoulders. He seemed confused, for he was obviously a proper man. To introduce us in such a situation was not at all correct; Anastasia had not only removed her veil, she had even tossed back the hood which should have covered her head. Heinrich hesitated in indecision, and Mother, for some strange reason, was absent. The girl solved the awkward situation for herself. Taking a step toward me, she extended her hand gracefully, the beautifully tapered fingers pointing toward my heart.

"I am Anastasia," she said simply.

Her voice was husky, but cool like the fingers I now pressed to my lips in the western manner. "I am D–Dmitri," I stammered, "Heinrich's st–stepson."

"She already knows that!" Heinrich boomed, again in command of the situation. He laughed and stepped back to look up the stairway. "Eleanor!" he called. "Come take this young lady to her apartment before your son involves us in a breach of etiquette!"

My face must have burned crimson, and a little additional color appeared on Anastasia's cheeks, although she maintained her dignity. She smiled at me again, and unless the light deceived me, she winked! Mother hurried halfway down the stairs. "This way, my dear," she said. Anastasia turned to follow her, when to complete my discomfort, Mother had to add: "Dmitri, you had better go change clothes for dinner."

Anastasia had joined my mother on the staircase. I still stood in graceless embarrassment, for in order to obey Mother's last command I would have to follow them up. Heinrich saw my discomfort, however, and in a voice loud enough to reach my mother's ears he included me in the world of men. "Come have a hot drink with us first, son," he said. "I'm sure our guest would enjoy one after his weary ride across the ice."

We took seats about the end of the long table, its bare surface gleaming from hours of hard rubbing by the servant girls. Heinrich served us himself, taking the mugs of spiced wine from a tile shelf above the stove. He inserted a glowing poker into each, holding it there a moment before setting the drinks upon a silver tray and carrying them to the table.

Gregory sipped gingerly. "I've been looking forward to this for hours," he sighed. "I'm getting too old for these long trips during the winter."

Heinrich returned some complimentary remark about the old man's youthful appearance, but their conversation after that faded into the background of my thoughts. It was Anastasia who dominated my consciousness. I had never wanted anything so much in my life, and the sensation was almost painful. Strangely enough, it did not occur to me that she might evoke the same response in Ivan. I could only think of her exquisite features, her open friendliness; yet her grace in expressing this had been neither lewd nor vulgar. Her beauty was real and genuine. I also thought of Ivan's remark: time for me to marry. Why not this particular girl? There was a tightening in my belly, despite the warmth of the wine. I felt an almost convulsive constriction in my loins, but even this was different from the sensations I had felt for Sonya. It took a few more hours before I fully understood what had happened, but I was sorely stricken by the fever of love.

I visualized the procedure. I must wait until the Czar had selected his own bride from among the thousand girls assembled. When Ivan was in the height of excitement prior to his own nuptials, I could mention having found the bride I wanted. It would be a simple matter of the Czar's indicating his desire, and Gregory would place her hand in mine. I would possess her forever, her sweet innocent face, her virgin features. . . .

"Demetrius! Our guest is speaking to you!"

"I. . .I'm sorry," I said.

Heinrich's warning glance told me he knew, but the old man did not seem to connect my preoccupation with the recent encounter between his niece and myself.

"Your father tells me you are close to our young Czar," he said, a particularly sly expression forcing its way onto his face.

I nodded.

"They are like. . .brothers," Heinrich noted. For a moment he held my eyes with his stare, and there was a definite warning in his demeanor. Gregory brought his face close to mine. His eyes were blue and watery, faded as if by too much exposure to the sun. He spoke in a confidential tone. "I may sound like a foolish dreamer," he told me, "but it has recently been predicted by the holy Gennady of Kostroma, who was a guest in our home, that my niece is destined to be consort of the Czar."

A cold hand gripped my heart. If this most famous *yurodivy* had predicted it. . . . "She would be a most worthy Czarina," I replied.

My stepfather's look had brought me back to life, and I began to realize that the two men had purposely contrived my presence in the room. Nor had Gregory's remark about my being close to Ivan been just a passing comment. Both of them were watching me expectantly.

I folded my hands in front of me on the table and averted my gaze from their penetrating looks. I knew exactly what they wanted. This whole thing must have been planned for weeks, perhaps even longer, and I sensed my mother's devious wit behind it. The prediction by one of our holiest sages, I was to hint to Ivan. It was well known that such omens had great meaning for him. With this much to start, and with an agent such as I to whisper in Ivan's ear. I wanted to leave. I wanted to go up to my room and weep. Then I was angry! Why must I always be chosen to carry out the will of others? Why did the people who should be most concerned about my own desires and happiness. . .why should these be the very ones who constantly demanded I do exactly the thing I wanted least?

"It had occurred to us. . . ." Gregory began.

"I think Demetrius understands, don't you, son?" Heinrich spoke gently, and again his tone indicated he knew. He knew, and he understood. A diplomat all his life, he may have experienced these same emotions himself.

I looked up at him, unable to control the tears welling up in my eyes. "I understand," I replied resignedly. I stood up, anxious to leave. But I could not resist expressing a final bitterness. "Don't I always?" I muttered.

That night in bed I prayed with a sincerity I had seldom felt before. I beseeched Almighty God that I might fail in my mission to bring this unquestionably superior maiden to the Czar's attention. I had only caught a single glimpse of her since our first meeting, but I was at an age when the flames of love could blaze from the smallest scrap of tinder. Mother had called me to her chamber and explained exactly what I must do, what I must say to assure Ivan's recognizing Anastasia's charms. She concluded by cautioning me, lest I say too much and make my intentions obvious.

I sat staring at her for a few heartbeats, until I heard the door open behind me. I turned quickly enough to see my love withdraw. I am sure Heinrich had not related his suspicions to Mother, for she had made no comment. Now, my own face must have given me away. Mother seemed to coil, like a serpent about to strike. She watched me closely, her thoughts causing a series of strange expressions to pass across her features. Though obviously angry when she reached out her hand, I didn't pull away. Instead of a caress, she landed a stinging blow across my cheek. "You idiot!" she spat.

I made no move, no reaction to her outburst. My self–pity, my pride, my desire—at that moment were all as nothing. I had no feeling; even her blow had fallen on dead flesh, as if my face were frozen into insensibility. I knew my cause was hopeless, and nothing else mattered. I had found my love and lost her in almost the same instant. I felt my soul was dead.

But Mother was in no way distracted from her goal by any consideration for my feelings. "You stupid ass!" she continued, and I harkened back to by oldest, dimmest memories – the words she'd used to the tall dark–robed man that night so many years ago. Obolenski? When he tried to hide from his murderers? I couldn't remember. "You have the nerve to fall in love with the Czarina!" she rasped.

"She is not the Czarina yet," I muttered.

"And I suppose you intend seeing to it she never is!" My mother's eyes blazed with fury, almost with hatred. Could she really hold me in such contempt, I thought. But she got no further. I stood up, and she broke off her tirade, watching me fearfully. I realized she expected I might strike her, and the knowledge of her fear gave me strength.

"I shall do as you ask me," I said quietly. "I don`t know why, but I'll do it." I walked out without looking back.

I left her staring after me, and returned to my own room. Later, lying there in the dark I still did not know why. I knew, simply, that I would obey; and only by the will of God could I fail. All my fantasies of rapture would come to nothing, for how could Ivan possibly fail to note the qualities of Anastasia?" How could he possibly fail to choose her?

The next few days were a bitter trial for me. I experienced hot surges of hatred for everyone I had previously loved. The pretense of my mother revolted me, and I avoided her as much as possible. Heinrich tried to ease my feelings, but I fled from him, as well. Despite his enormous strength in everything else, I had seen his weakness before my mother's will. He was like a pawn in her game, and I despised him for it. And Ivan, bubbling over with the joy and anticipation of his coming choice, was absolute anathema. Every careless remark he uttered, every crude joke he made or laughed at when others made them – all this seemed a desecration of Anastasia's purity.

As can easily happen when one is separated from a desired object of beauty, that object begins to assume outlandish qualities of perfection. Naturally, I could not realize it at the time, but that was most certainly happening to me. Anastasia's face was seldom out of my thoughts. I would climb to the top of the Kremlin wall, where I would lie on my back, shielded from the snow by my heavy *shuba*. I would gaze at the sky, where her features could manifest themselves in cosmic proportions. I saw her face not only in the clouds above me, but when I was in church I could perceive her features in the icons of the Blessed Virgin. One day I tried to distract myself by reading, only to find her perfection along the illuminated borders of the manuscript. In short, I was experiencing the absolute epitome of adolescent love, surely the most soul consuming, painful form this emotion can take.

When the day came that I saw her again, I hardly recognized her. She was lovely, beautiful, graceful – yet somehow short of her image. My initial reaction was surprise, until I realized I had never seen her for any great length of time. And at this moment, my passion flamed anew. I was standing with Yuri beside the dais. Ivan was seated on his throne, above us. On the far side stood Vladimir, his mother Euphrosyne, the Metropolitan Makari, and Andrew Kurbsky. Other boyars and princes, as well as Archbishop Pimen of Novgorod and other high churchmen, were ranged along the walls, nearly filling the Hall of Facets. Everyone was splendidly attired; Ivan wore a full robe which sparkled with emeralds and rubies. Upon his head he bore a light crown of gold filigree, ringed at the base with sable. His robes were trimmed with ermine and his gold encased feet rested on a priceless rug of albino seal. I was wearing wine velvet, with a huge field of jewels about the collar. The design spilled down the front of my robe, to form a fiery river clear to my boots. These were of the finest soft leather, covered with a thick sheaf of beaten gold. Like all men of higher rank, I wore clothing from the royal treasury.

The clergy and lesser nobility wore their own costumes, many falling only slightly short of the magnificent display made by us. The gleaming white uniforms of the palace guard, standing in solid rows along the walls made a contrasting background to set off our splendor.

The court had assembled before Ivan entered, and immediately after he was seated the procession of girls began. Preliminary inspections had been completed the day before, eliminating all but one hundred. The others had been sent home with Ivan's thanks for coming, and each bore a small gift to assuage her disappointment. The remaining maidens were escorted to the foot of the imperial throne by their sponsors, usually the father or an uncle. These mentors formally presented their young wards to the Czar and made a short speech, extolling her virtues. Part of the test was how poised and graceful the girl could be in such embarrassing circumstances. Allowing just a few moments for each, the procession took a full two days. Anastasia appeared near the end of the second. By then, the field had been narrowed considerably.

Notwithstanding everyone's becoming a bit weary, Anastasia's appearance brought a murmur of comment from the assemblage. I could hear Basmanov's growl as he made some remark to Pronsky, who was seated two places distant. This was followed by knowing chuckles of satisfaction from their whole little group. Ivan leaned toward me as they approached, and shielding his lips with his heavily jeweled hand, asked, "Is this the girl you told me about?"

I nodded, and Ivan resumed his upright posture. I noticed Vladimir and his mother watching us curiously. There was a look of icy annoyance on Euphrosyne's face, but I took this as no more than an expression of ire, jealousy over my closeness to the Czar.

Then Anastasia was in front of us, dressed in white as a symbol of her purity. She wore no jewelry as the other maidens had, and her face was washed clean of any flour or artificial coloring. Her figure, displayed in a most refined manner by a cleverly designed gown, still presented a proper degree of voluptuous promise.

Gregory disengaged himself from his niece's arm and stepped forward. "If it may be permitted to speak without harm, Most Gracious Czar," he began, pausing until Ivan had gestured to indicate consent. "I, Gregory Zakharin, long a soldier in the service of Our Most Gracious Czar and of His Father Basilius before him, most humbly request Your Majesty's indulgence, that I may present my niece, Anastasia, daughter of the widowed Zakharina–Koshkina, a worthy descendent of the House of Romanov. With the Czar's permission, I would recommend to Your Majesty not only the obvious qualities of beauty and grace possessed by my niece, but would also mention that she, like Your Majesty himself, is an orphan, having lost her father at an early age. She was forced to grow into her present maturity without the guidance of this parent. Her soul, perhaps, may find its kindred likeness in Your Majesty's house."

With that, he stepped back beside Anastasia, bowing to the Czar. At Ivan's gesture, Anastasia allowed one side of the veil to fall from her face. Because she still wore her hood, as was required, her features were visible only to those of us who faced her, and a few of the princes seated most forward along the sides of the chamber. From this small privileged group there was an audible intake of breath, causing a great craning of necks and twisting of bodies from others too far in the rear to see.

I glanced up at Ivan, who had trouble concealing his pleasure as he uttered his formal appreciation of Gregory's loyalty in bringing this priceless treasure for his inspection. Anastasia refastened her veil before she backed away from the throne. Laying her hand gently on her uncle's arm, she turned to leave. But at the last moment her eyes made contact with mine, and this time I knew she winked! I looked at Ivan again, but fortunately he had missed this impropriety.

"You have excellent taste, Dmitri!" he murmured.

Once more, my gaze fell on Euphrosyne, whose malevolent expression was almost frightening. I tried to smile at her, but it did no good. Somehow, I had angered her and those wicked little pig's eyes looked venomously back at me from her ghastly, white–floured face.

A few more girls were presented after Anastasia, but she was the last to be included in the selected group of twenty, all that remained of the original thousand. It would still be days before the final selection was made, and they were days when I lived in constant dread of what I knew must be the final outcome. Regardless of my own desires, it was impossible not to say exactly the things about Anastasia that I knew would increase her chances of being chosen. When Ivan asked me which girl I thought he should pick, my reply was immediate. I had not yet developed the skills in subterfuge and diplomacy that later gained me some degree of renown.

Inevitably, the day came when Ivan dropped his handkerchief into Anastasia's lap, signifying he had made his choice. By then the field had been cut to five. When it was all over, I trudged home alone, through a new fall of snow. I tried to fathom the causes for my failure to do or to say something before it became too late. There had been one other girl who attracted Ivan's eye, and had I used my powers of persuasion, I might have swayed the choice. But in the end, it had gone where it properly should have gone. God had guided Ivan's judgment, and in this He had served His earthly shepherd well.

But what of me? I had prayed so hard and promised so much, if He would only grant me this single boon! I had hoped to find an ally in Euphrosyne, so great had become my desperation. Both she and my Mother had been on the inspection committee that assured the proper physical qualifications of the candidates. *Maultasch* knew I had promoted Anastasia, and I had a momentary hope she might find some blemish, that God might cause a bruise or scar to appear, even a wart! But no, she lacked such imperfection. God had forsaken me in my hour of greatest need. Very well then, I thought. He has failed me when I needed Him most; henceforth, I shall reject His works. And while this childish vow later became altered to a distrust of the clergy, I think I never fully enjoyed God's Grace from this day forward.

As the day of Ivan's wedding approached, I became more agitated and melancholy. Contributing to my distracted state of mind were other sources of frustration, major crises in the lives of people about me. I was doomed to see all this culminate into one terrible set of circumstances, the resulting horror being enough to completely crush the world of my own existence. It was surely God's just retribution for my rejection of Him, but I stupidly took it as further evidence that He cared nothing about me—if, in fact, He existed at all. I thus fell further into the quagmire of heresy and lack of Grace.

For several days I had noticed a peculiar, knowing attitude from everyone: my mother, Heinrich, Ivan – even Yuri, but no one would tell me the reason. One afternoon I passed Alfansy Buturlin, now recovered from the loss of his tongue. He was riding with some friends through the Arbat, the outer part of the city where most merchants had their warehouses and where they maintained the huge stables for pack animals. All around, the hovels of the city's poor were shoved together between the filthy alleyways. Since his moment of poor judgment, and the terrible retribution it had brought him, Alfansy had been much restrained. His openly boastful manner was largely gone, but I suspected his hatred of me had grown deeper. When I passed him and his friends this day, several of them shouted some very strange remarks at me – something about the "fair face of fortune smiling on me," and another remark to the effect of my being "about to receive the grace of nobility." I had no idea what they were talking about, and sick as I was in my own heart I soon forgot them. I took care of the business Heinrich had entrusted to me, tossed down a few vodkas in an Arbat tavern, and returned home just before dark.

When I entered the house I found my parents in the *svyetlitsa*, entertaining Alfansy's uncle, John Buturlin. All three looked up at me like guilty conspirators, and in that moment the horrible suspicion became manifest in my mind. They must be arranging my marriage!

I strode into the room, although certain I wasn't wanted, and without any word of greeting or respectful welcome for our guest, I demanded to know what they were doing.

"That is not your concern!" snapped my mother.

"If you're doing what I think you're doing, it's very much my concern," I shouted back at her. "And if you think I'm going to marry one of the Buturlins, you're very much mistaken!"

Alfansy's uncle looked quite taken back, and Mother assumed her shocked expression – the one meaning I had violated the most sacred protocol. I guessed it had to be Alfansy's sister Anna whom they were selecting for me, as she was the only marriageable daughter.

"It's a very good match for you, son," said Heinrich, confirming my suspicions.

"And something you need very badly to keep you from getting into trouble," added Mother. She looked piercingly into my face, as if reminding me of my many sins with women.

"Have you seen her?" I demanded.

"Of course not!" said Heinrich.

I glanced at Mother again. "It was naturally my duty to examine the girl," she said. "She is quite acceptable."

Old Buturlin stood quietly through all of this. He was exceptionally stupid, an ox of a man who acted as head of the family because Alfansy's father had recently died—and with him, most of the animosities toward Heinrich. At the time, my stepfather had some contracts with them and acted as their agent in two or three cities. With Alfansy unable to speak very well, all of these arrangements were made through Uncle John. The dolt now stood glaring at me, angry over my having insulted his blood, but too dense to make an adequate reply. He was undoubtedly anxious to marry Anna off, which also tended to restrain him.

Of course, I had not seen Anna Buturlin, either – not for several years. As a little girl she had been fat and pimply. From some past remarks of Alfansy and his friends, I assumed she had gotten fatter, achieving dimensions well in excess of any desirable plumpness. A year or so before, I recalled a joking conversation in which Alfansy had alluded to the enormous manhood it would require to penetrate his sister's layers of protective flesh. She had been among the maidens presented for Ivan's selection, of course, but had been rejected in the first elimination. I doubted if Ivan had even seen her. Far worse than the physical attributes of my negotiated bride, I could not imagine any people I would less desire as in–laws than the Buturlins. The whole family consisted of bloated, lazy wretches. In morals, they were almost as bad as the Shuiskys, except that they were neither as noble nor as rich.

"Well, you can make all the arrangements you want; I'm not going to marry her," I told them. I started to walk out, thinking to make my exit serve as an effective sign of finality.

"Just a moment, son," said Heinrich. He spoke quietly, but with a firm authority in his voice. I stopped and looked back at him. "What would you say if the Czar were to order this match?"

"He wouldn't," I said evenly. But he must have done just that, I realized, and my heart grew cold at the thought. Why else had he been acting so strangely, and why had Yuri seemed to bursting with news he wanted to tell and didn't dare? It had all been one, great, monstrous conspiracy! It was originally Mother's doing. Of this I was certain. She would never admit it, but she wanted me married before I got myself in trouble over Anastasia. She would have advanced my alleged promiscuity as the excuse to Heinrich, and the making of a "fine match" as the reason to everyone else.

I was so angry, the tears nearly came to my eyes. "If Ivan orders it, with his own lips," I said, "I'll have to obey him."

But Ivan did approve, and the next day I was informed – through Adashev – that everything was to be arranged as my parents had contracted. Andrei was sympathetic, although he had not seen Anna for himself. He therefore had no way of knowing just how cruel a blow fate was about to deal me. There were important political considerations to the match, he assured me in confidence, and I should be honored at the trust the Czar was placing upon me. As an in–law of the Buturlins, I would be in a position to see that their considerable wealth and land holdings, with all the attendant power this gave them, were used to Ivan's best interests.

After my conference with Andrei, I returned to the taverns in the Arbat and drank vodka with the peasants. I became so drunk I joined them in their songs, and for some few hours I forgot my troubles. But the next morning my misery started afresh. The marriage contract had been signed and the date was set for slightly over a month hence.

It was now common knowledge throughout the court that I was betrothed to Anna Buturlin. In keeping with custom, men were supposed to come forward and congratulate me, which they did...but not with the usual vulgar remarks and good–natured obscenities. Instead, my friends offered their best wishes in the tone one usually reserved for funerals. Alexi Basmanov hung his huge arm across my shoulders, and for one of the few times in our relationship he offered some fatherly advice, saying much the same things Andrei had said. Under normal circumstances, he would nearly have broken my back with exuberant congratulations.

Then there were those who were not my friends, and first among this group was my future brother–in–law. Smirking, triumphant as a soldier who had just made a slave of his enemy, he greeted me with a smile in the lower hallway of the palace. He was every bit as obnoxious as before, although he was forced to speak through his attendants.

This day, he was surrounded by the usual flock of bootlickers, men whose souls were as foul as his. I am sure they only bothered with him because of his wealth.

"Here's the lucky boy," said one of them. "Can you imagine anyone so fortunate as to win the hand of Alfansy's sister?"

"I hear she looks like you, Alfansy," called the tall skinny nincompoop who always trailed directly behind his master.

"If that's true, she must be lovely as an icon," said another. This was the one with the long, jackass ears.

"No one could be that lovely," cried a third, an effeminate fop named Mischa.

They all shrieked with laughter. "Lucky Dmitri!" they chanted. "Soon to mount the fairest mare in the empire!"

I shoved my way through them and walked briskly away, wishing I could silence their lunatic mirth with a few hefty strokes of my sword. I was furious with everyone, my parents included. I was even angry with Ivan, though I still retained enough fear of God to pray I be forgiven this sin. By the day of his own wedding I had been granted that much grace. I no longer blamed him. But I still cursed my mother, knowing it had all been her doing.

CHAPTER III

Ivan's marriage took place near the end of winter, during a brief period between the heavy storms that blanketed the capitol with layer after layer of snow. The ceremony was held in the small Cathedral of the Annunciation, with a service every bit as tedious as the coronation had been. Because it required fewer people to assist, I had no part to perform. Vladimir acted as sponsor for the groom. Distraught as I was, this seemed an act of heavenly pity. Had there been any way I could have avoided it, I would not have been present at all.

It was one of the most painful experiences of my life, watching my beloved Anastasia delivered with solemn vows to another man – albeit the Czar and my dearest friend. As I watched the service I had trouble keeping the emotion from showing on my face, but whatever did show was taken as evidence of my devotion to Ivan. No one ever criticized me for it. Only my mother and Heinrich knew how I really felt, and Mother told me later to control myself. Heinrich offered his sympathies without actually saying so. As for Andrei, no more was ever mentioned regarding my feelings toward Anastasia.

The wedding feast was loud and joyous, as it should have been. I drank far too much, until the sounds of merriment became a formless roar, emanating somewhere beyond the horizon of consciousness. When the Czar and Czarina finally left to ascend the nuptial couch, I was to have had the honor of holding Ivan's nightcap for him. However, my debilitated state precluded my moving quickly enough. At the last moment I was shouldered out of the way by Prince Shemiakin, who performed the task himself. Ivan was too preoccupied to notice. The curtains were drawn around the Czar's huge bed, and I slipped quietly away, finally wending my way home. The festivities lasted until the first day of Lent, when the bells of all the churches began to toll. Ivan and Anastasia then donned the cloaks of pilgrims and set out on foot for Sergey–Troitsky.

But before those bells sounded I was safely married off. The usual rituals were observed on the night before my marriage, and I went through them as rituals—nothing more. I moved in a trance and I continued to drink as if I could escape by entering into this unreal world. I refused to select any gifts to send to Anna the day before the wedding, but Mother took care of that. She also included the whip Old Buturlin was supposed to present to me after the ceremony.

The whole sequence of events is still a wretched, hazy, painful memory. My wedding day was foggy and chill, with a constant threat of rain. The weather precisely expressed my mood. I sat on the edge of my bed, wishing I could somehow flee to Poland, or that the Lord would visit some horrible plague upon me. Heinrich finally came in and helped me dress. He gave me a ruby ring as a wedding present, and I could hear the compassion in his tone. I am sure he had regretted his part in the arrangements ever since realizing how distasteful they were to me. Still, he could not understand the reasons for my being so upset. He had not yet seen my bride.

"Everything will be all right," he assured me. "Carry yourself proudly for your mother's sake, and if you need help later on we'll work it out." He winked and patted my shoulder. "Come," he said. "It's time to leave."

Like a lamb to slaughter, my parents led me into the chapel just outside the Kremlin walls. I was to be spared a service in one of the cathedrals, where I would have been forced to go through the thing in front of everyone. As it was, Ivan did not come; but Yuri was right in front of the group on my side of the church. I saw Ivor near the back when I entered, and Alexi Basmanov was about halfway up the aisle. As he had for Ivan, Vladya acted as my sponsor, Heinrich standing with him. I took my place beside them, facing the priest. I waited anxiously, hoping for the best, but my fearful dread was overwhelming.

When my bride was brought in, the catastrophe became complete. The chubby little girl I remembered had turned into the ugliest, most mountainous mass of flesh I had ever seen. She waddled down the aisle on her uncle's arm, resembling nothing so much as a fattened goose out of water. Her great breasts bulged against the front of her gown, protruding almost further than her belly. Her horrendous buttocks vibrated with every step. I looked at Vladya in absolute horror, and he shrugged, returning my glance with a grimace of pain. "It can't be helped," he muttered. "Of course, she might be one solid mass of passion," he added lightly.

Heinrich's eyes bulged when he saw her. He cast a quick, hard gaze at my mother, his angry frown enough to scorch her. I am sure she had convinced him that the bride's appearance would be less formidable than it was. Throughout the ceremony I could see Anna from the corner of my eye, leering at me greedily. At the end, when she was supposed to place her head on my foot, allowing me to cover it with the edge of my robe, she had to be assisted by two other women. Grunting like a hog in rut, she finally managed it. I dropped the hem over her as a sign that I accepted her vow of obedience, and in exchange assured her of my protection. When I stepped back she grinned up at me, displaying her blackened teeth and purple gums. Following archaic custom, her face was heavily floured, and she had used the Tartar formula to cause the whites of her eyes to become as black as her teeth. Her entire countenance was so ghastly I was nearly ill.

After the service came the usual wedding feast, during which we were supposed to slip away to the bridal chamber. This had been prepared in the newly refurbished wing of my parents' house. Several times, when I allowed her close enough to speak with me, Anna suggested we might retire.

"Not yet," I kept telling her. I ran my thumb along the whip her uncle had shoved into my hands, wishing I could use it on her. I continued to bolt down vodka until I was nearly as drunk as I had been the night our marriage contract was signed. Several people noticed this, as well as my reluctance to leave for the consummation – Alfansy among them. There was quite a bit of jeering and laughter, all very vulgar now, for everyone had been drinking heavily.

At last I could put it off no longer. I had reached a point where no matter how much I drank, I was getting no further effect. As much as I would have liked to pass out, it simply wasn't going to happen. We were hustled out of the banquet and up the stairs by a dozen or more helpful pairs of hands, suddenly finding ourselves alone in the bedroom, where I was immediately surrounded by the eager, fleshy arms of my wife.

"Shall we change for bed?" she asked coyly.

Like a man condemned, I nodded. We each went into our respective side chambers, where we changed into nightclothes. I was alone, for I had rejected any offers of help. Two or three women, including my mother, were probably in Anna's dressing room to assist her. I had not been interested enough to inquire.

Slowly, with unwilling, unsteady hands, I took off my clothes. Naked, I knelt before the little collection of crosses and icons, making a last desperate appeal to God that He might somehow give me the strength to fulfill the demands about to be made upon my flesh. I tossed the nightgown over my head, took a deep breath, and reentered the room. Anna was already in bed, her huge bulk raising a veritable mountain beneath the coverlet.

I extinguished the single lamp and gingerly slipped in beside her, cringing at the prospect of the inevitable physical contact. Almost at once, I was enveloped by her overpowering warmth. Her mouth sought mine, hungrily thrusting for my tongue, and her grasping hands kneaded my body. Reluctantly, I put an arm over her. Unable to work the other beneath her heavy form, I let it lie upwards on the pillow. I tried to make love to her, closing my eyes to further obscure the sight as there was still a ruddy glow coming from the stove. I finally kicked the covers off the bed, because the heat of her body was making me sweat. I fondled her with all the ardor I could muster, but the bloated skin sank inward at my slightest touch. At last I knew I was helpless, experiencing the same problem I had the day I tried to rape the merchant's daughter.

In desperation, Anna tried to help me, but there was no doubt she was a virgin. However much she might have been instructed by the older women, she had no conception whatever as to what she might have done. As it was, she only made it worse.

We had been in bed for over an hour, when the traditional knock came at the door. We could hear whispered laughter outside. "Everything all right?" called a voice. I think it was one of Alfansy's friends.

I didn't answer, for a positive response meant the marriage had been consummated. Yet to say otherwise would evoke further levity and depreciating remarks.

"In the Name of God, tell him we're fine," she whispered harshly, and when I still remained silent she poked me in the stomach. "Tell him!" she rasped. "You can't disgrace me in front of all my friends!"

I called out that all was well, and they answered with some more coarse humor, eventually returning downstairs to their drinking. Once it was quiet again in the hall, Anna resumed her futile efforts to coax a response from my body. When nothing happened she began to weep, blaming herself and saying all the cruel things about her appearance that I had been thinking all day. Had she continued in this vein, I would probably have felt sorry for her and eventually might have been able to do the expected. Unfortunately, in addition to her depressing physical attributes, she shared every other revolting trait of the Buturlins – the most notable being stupidity and a terrible disposition. Once the spell of weeping was past she began to revile me. She called me "not half a man," and a "poor excuse for a husband," a "fraud who paraded his masculinity before the admiring glances of the ladies, but who could not begin to satisfy a woman."

She finally made me angry, and I called her every name she had not thought to use on herself. I ended by threatening her with the whip if she did not keep still. Then she laughed at me, flicking my manhood with her finger. "Even a worm has more strength than this," she crowed.

"If you wish me to leave you on your wedding night, so you may explain to your friends how your charms entranced me," I said cruelly, "I will be happy to go."

She began to wail again, thinking of the morning. "What shall I do?" she bawled. "When your mother examines my shift, there will be no blood and she will think I wasn't a virgin."

"There can be little doubt of that," I muttered, but I slipped from the bed and returned to my dressing room. I took the ceremonial dagger I had worn at the wedding from its sheath, and reentered the bedroom. Sitting on the edge, I struck a light and turned the lamp up enough to see. As I picked up the dagger it glinted brightly in the flicker of the lantern.

"Dmitri!" she screamed. "You wouldn't. . . ." She drew herself into as tight a ball as her vast bulk would permit, tangling in the coverlet.

I looked at her in surprise, not realizing she might think I meant to harm her. "I'm not going to stab you," I said disgustedly. "Turn over on your belly."

She regarded me with questioning eyes.

"Just do as I tell you," I said. "I would also prefer our unhappy experience to remain a secret."

She obeyed me at last and flopped over on her stomach, her enormous rump making two jiggling mountains beneath her shift. I pulled up her skirt, trying not to see the huge white globes of fat. With the dagger, I punctured the little finger on my left hand, allowing the blood to penetrate the material of her shift. I made a fairly sizable puddle, not sure what it should look like, and pulled the cloth back into place. I put out the light and turned onto my side, as near the edge as I could get. "Now go to sleep," I said. "I'm too tired to discuss it any more tonight."

It took me a long while to doze off, as it did for her. But finally, just before I fell asleep, I heard her start to snore—a deep, resonant rumble. My sins were truly coming home to roost, I thought, for there was not a single fault missing in this woman I had been condemned to possess as wife.

I spent the first few days after the ceremony in my old room, feeling sorry for myself and dreaming of ways to circumvent harsh reality. The woman I loved was married to another man, and I was unable to face the woman I had been forced to take as my wife. I needed time to think, to be by myself while my mind recovered from its wounds. But I was not to be left in peace. There had been tremendous tension between my mother and Heinrich for a long time, stemming from a number of causes – personal as well as political.

Mother, quite naturally, was a staunch supporter of the Glinskis. Except for that one moment of weakness, when Feodor and the prospect of wealth had swayed her judgment, she had always favored their causes. She had been associated with the family since childhood, and now berated Heinrich to be more grateful for their help. My stepfather felt otherwise. They had tossed him a few bones, he said, but these in no way compensated for the losses he was suffering due to the general decline in trade – a condition brought about by the steadily escalating taxes imposed by the two brothers.

At first it had been only merchants who groaned beneath their burdens; now the complaints were universal. Traders avoided Moscow because of the gate tax, unless their goods were actually consigned for use within the city walls. Glinski avarice affected other communities as well, though to a lesser degree than was felt in the capital. Novgorod was the real beneficiary, receiving the bulk of goods for transshipment, which dumped gold into the coffers of the Shuiskys and Kubenskys. Buoyed by this sudden windfall, these families were making their power felt in other trade centers, particularly in the west, in Poland – to a lesser degree in the south, where the spices and silks of Cathay were exchanged for products of Russian fields and mines.

My parents had been at odds, and had argued about these problems prior to my marriage. Realizing the cruel trick Mother had played on me, Heinrich became increasingly vicious in his tirades against her. Their endless bickering threw the entire household into turmoil, with several of Heinrich's uncomplimentary remarks being overheard by my wife. One day, after a particularly violent exchange between my parents, Anna gathered her few possessions and fled to her uncle's home, outside the Kremlin, in the Kitaigorod. Mother tried persuading her to return, but Anna refused, saying she would not stay in a house where she was unwelcome. After her own failure, Mother came to me, insisting I personally fetch her back. I lay on my bed and laughed at her. "You bought that ripe sow for me," I told her. "*You* go bring her back. I'm glad she's gone!"

"You and your father are both impossible!" she ranted.

"Neither of you have to sleep with her," I retorted.

This multifaceted controversy between my parents raged for days, and several times Heinrich stormed out of the house. He would later return drunk, for Ivan's wedding festivities were still going on all over the city. Once outside, it was easier to drink than not. Like so many men who seldom indulged beyond their limits, Heinrich underwent a terrible change when he drank too much. Usually so gentle and understanding, spirits transformed him into a ferocious brute. He beat the servants who happened across his path, and once he even struck me – something he had never done before. When Mother slammed and locked her bedroom door against him, he smashed it off its hinges. Although I was afraid to look, I was sure he indulged his lust with no thought for her desires or resistance.

Mother left our house the next day, to take up residence with the Glinskis. I stayed behind with Heinrich, for if the truth be known, I felt more a son to him than I did to my mother. Had my choice been otherwise, my future life might have been very different. But on such seemingly unimportant decisions as this, hang the delicate determinates of a man's existence.

After Ivan and Anastasia completed their Lenten pilgrimage, they retired to the summer palace at Ostrovka to await the coming of spring, and to continue their honeymoon in private. Although this residence was less than a day's ride from the city, Ivan made it clear that he wished to be alone with his bride, and his wishes were naturally observed.

During late winter and early spring, grumblings continued on all economic levels. The Glinksi brothers were fast becoming more unpopular than the Shuiskys had ever been. At least the former regents had possessed a certain style and native charm, permitting them to mingle with all but the very lowest and to enchant many men of lesser station by their seeming humility. They had given large parties in their Kremlin *dacha*, inviting merchants and tradespeople and mingling with them as equals. The Glinskis, on the other hand, were foreigners – Lithuanians by birth, who still spoke Russian with an accent. While both brothers were good public speakers, neither bothered putting these talents to use. Few people ever saw them, except for occasional, brief glimpses when they rode by in a fine sleigh or carriage.

I was never able to prove it, but I have always suspected Euphrosyne of being responsible for some of the rumors starting to circulate at this time. The Shuiskys – always mortal enemies of Ivan's cousins – were probably involved, as well. If true, it constituted a strange alliance, but there was nothing new in that. People began talking about Ivan's grandmother, Anna Glinskaya, and how she openly practiced witchcraft on her estate. In April, as I recall – anyway, sometime shortly after Easter, a fire broke out in the Arbat. Immediately, rumor had it being set by a powerful sorceress, a mysterious woman dressed in black, who rode the wind with a black cat perched on her shoulder. Because snow was still piled heavily on the roofs, the fire did not spread very far. But it was said that the snow upon the ground showed no footprints, although the blaze was presumed to be arson.

Through May, Heinrich and I continued to live bachelor lives in our Kremlin *dacha*. My stepfather made several attempts at persuading Mother to return, but she stubbornly refused. The Glinskis finally issued orders to their guards, forbidding Heinrich's entry onto their grounds. My wife also remained away, although I am certain she would have returned had I asked her. Fortunately, Heinrich sympathized with me and did not pressure me to reclaim her. The property I had received as part of the dowry included a small country estate, south of the Dnepr, near the town of Dorogobuzh. When one of Alfansy's clerks came to see me one afternoon, trying to ascertain my intentions, I suggested Anna take up residence there. I intimated that I would join her at my earliest convenience. My next communication from her was a crudely written, tear stained note, in which Anna informed me she would not leave the city until I came for her. She begged my forgiveness and swore to be a good wife.

This must have been near the first of June. I tried to compose an answer, intending to delay a decision until I could see Ivan and persuade him to place Anna in a convent. As I had hopefully anticipated, an invitation arrived from Ostrovka a few days later, requesting a few of us to attend the Czar. Ivan's note made it clear that Heinrich was welcome, as well. Because neither of us shared the merry mood of our fellows, we departed early, traveling by ourselves with just our own retainers for company. I was doubly distressed, for my own domestic situation hung over me like a weight about to fall, while my parents' separation was beginning to look permanent. Heinrich, who had drunk heavily the night before, was nursing the usual combination of discomforts. Our trip was understandably quiet, with hardly a word spoken between us until we reached the imperial residence.

With our retainers, it was a different story. They chattered behind us, all along the way, repeating rumors now current in the city as a result of the latest outbreak of fires. There had been another the night before we left, and everyone seemed convinced they were caused by witchcraft. That they had occurred only since the beginning of Lent – none during the height of festivities, when great bonfires were lighted on nearly every corner – appeared as strong evidence of some malevolent cause. So far, snow–covered roofs had prevented any serious spread of the flames, but the last of this protective covering was gone. The people of Moscow were verging on panic. Fearing the powers of darkness, they would not venture outside at night to guard against the arsonist. Witchcraft or no, it seemed certain the fires were being deliberately set.

When we reached Ostrovka, the Czar came out personally to greet us. He wore a simple green tunic, reaching nearly to his knees, tied about the waist by a black leather band. His hose were of doeskin, loose fitting and designed for comfortable wear on horseback. He behaved as he was dressed, like a *szlachta*, or country squire. With only his closest friends in attendance, Ivan seemed completely at ease. I did notice, however, that the borders of his estate were heavily patrolled by white uniformed guardsmen.

I saw nothing of Anastasia, because she remained in the women's quarters. While this could not have been intentionally to spare my feelings, it served the same purpose. The possibility of seeing her, and thus rekindling the fires I had tried so hard to repress, had been my only fear in coming. Ivan was especially solicitous of me, as he attributed his good fortune in selecting Anastasia to my wisdom and loyal council. His joy was so overpowering, I eventually found myself succumbing to his influence. Observing his happiness made my own despair seem less. While my reverence for Anastasia never faded, I now began to accept the situation for what it was. I also resolved the other problem. When I had a chance to speak with Ivan alone, I succeeded in obtaining his permission to place Anna in a nunnery. Once I had described the full situation to him, including a vivid account of my wedding night, he laughed until he made me forget my anger and misery. I finally joined him in near hysterical mirth, both of us roaring until the tears ran down our cheeks. (We had been drinking a little vodka iuring the course of my tale, or course.) He suggested I might send her to the *Novodyevichi Monastery*, the New Maidens' Convent in the Kremlin. After she had been there a while, he would proclaim my freedom to remarry, after which Anna could remain or not, as she saw fit. Because the convent was new and modern, he said, there would be less objection from her family, and the location would make it possible for her to receive visitors.

I was not overjoyed at the prospect of having her this close to home, but I was so anxious to make the arrangements before Ivan changed his mind that I quickly agreed. There was never any mention of the matters Andrei had suggested as the reason for Ivan's having approved the match – that is, my marriage placing him in a better position to control the Buturlin assets – and under the circumstances I thought it best not to broach the subject. It did cause me to wonder about Adashev, however; I would never again consider him a really dependable friend.

The rest of Ivan's guests arrived before noon. There was the usual group; Yuri, Vladimir, Andrew Kurbsky, and Basmanov, who brought his young son, Fedka. Andrei Adashev and his father were the last to enter the gates, and the assemblage immediately drank to their health. Both father and son had been promoted to *okolnichi* – councilors "near to the throne."

Ivor, the former kennelmaster, attended the Czar as head of his personal guard retinue. I noticed several of our old friends from Ivor's group of boys, now dressed in the snow white uniforms, still serving both their masters.

We were to stay several days with Ivan, hunting deer and small game in the forests and lush meadowlands around his mansion. The thaws had removed the last vestige of snow, and while the soil was still damp in many places, it was generally dry enough to make riding a pleasure. The grasses were already a brilliant green, and most of the trees had burgeoned. Ivan had acquired several new kinds of musket, mostly from the gunsmiths of Luebeck. We were experimenting with them on the morning of the third or fourth day, all of us clustered about Heinrich's target in a field some distance from the house. Unexpectedly, Ivor limped hurriedly across the verdant meadow, approached the Czar without the usual ceremony, and whispered something into his ear. Ivan scowled, saying nothing as he started back toward the *dacha*. We were all on foot, and curious as to the cause of his guardsman's interruption, we followed the Czar. In the enclosed courtyard, we found a number of household guardsmen surrounding a group of eleven or twelve middle–aged men. From their dress I presumed they were merchants, probably from one of the western provinces. As we approached, we could see a great waving of arms and agitated conversation between the visitors and their captors.

I hung back with the others, not intruding upon the Czar as he conversed with the strangers. Suddenly, Ivan began to shout, his voice becoming high–pitched and rasping with anger. The group of merchants fell to their knees in the muddy courtyard, the leader slopping his forehead on the ground at Ivan's feet. For some reason, this did not seem sufficient to placate the Czar. His boot suddenly shot forward, toppling the man full–length on the ground. Ivor was standing beside me, and I cast him a questioning glance. The men's dress could have been Polish, so I wondered if they might be servants of Sigismund.

"Pskovians," whispered Ivor, hardly moving his mouth. "They came to complain about Turuntay–Pronsky."

I exchanged looks with Heinrich, who had also been watching with a quizzical expression. Now he nodded, knowingly. Prince Turuntay–Pronsky, the man we had recently had reason to suspect of being in league with Boris the Brigand—royal governor of Novgorod—was authorized by the Glinskis to collect taxes in Pskov. His reputation for thievery and excessive taxation had now become scandalous. Still, it did not excuse these men interrupting the final days of the Czar's hymeneal.

Whatever the Pskovians had said to him, they had driven Ivan into an uncontrollable rage. He shouted for his guards to strip the visitors naked, and he ordered another servant to bring a large vessel of warm vodka. In the time it took for these instructions to be carried out, his fury grew worse. When the liquor was handed to him, he went from man to man, leaning over the prostrate figures, pouring the warm liquor onto their beards. He called to Fedka Basmanov, and told the lad to follow him with a taper, which Ivan used to set the vodka aflame. The men were screaming in fear and pain, having to be held by the guardsmen as they were not secured by any stationary object. I think we were all a little surprised at the severity of the punishment, but when Ivan lost control of his temper he was capable of a good deal more. I could not really blame him, however, for the men had been completely out of place to come here.

The Czar was about halfway down the line of writhing figures, when a horseman galloped up from the Moscow road. His frantic shouts transcended the shrieks of agony and terror that came from the row of prisoners. "Fire!" he cried. "Fire! The whole city's ablaze!"

Ivan gaped, as I guess all of us did. Then, the Pskovians forgotten, the Czar shouted excitedly for his horse, and in less than a heartbeat he was leading us in a frenzied dash toward the house. He rushed up the stairs for a few words with his bride, and by the time he returned our horses were ready at the front gate. We were on the highway to Moscow within seconds, Ivan in the vanguard of the pack, Ivor and his men bringing up the rear. The road was still damp enough that the horses' hooves threw enormous clumps of mud in every direction, covering us with muck before we'd gone a league. One of the guardsmen went down soon after we started, but no one stopped to assist him. The second rider to fall was Heinrich. I pulled to one side and was going to stop, but looking back I could see he was not badly hurt. He was standing beside his mount and waved me on. His horse made no move to rise, so I yelled at one of Ivor's boys to go back and attend him. A moment later I was around a bend in the road, and soon after this I began to taste ashes in my mouth.

Ivan drew rein at the top of a small hill, some distance from the city walls. The rest of us gathered in a circle behind him. The entire horizon was cloaked in a heavy veil of smoke, and even at this distance we could feel heat from the hellish conflagration.

The fire had apparently started in a cluster of churches in the Arbat, but had now spread through the Bielgorod, the middle part of the city, and was licking at the walls of the Kitaigorod. A strong wind was spreading the blaze faster than I would have thought possible; but the last drop of snow had melted from the rooftops and there was nothing to hold it back. Several shafts of flame leaped so high we were unable to see beyond them for minutes at a time. The smoke rose black and heavy, boiling up like some huge genie; and through it all. . .through the heat, the terrible acrid smells, above the crackle of burning wood, came the horrified screams of the people. We could see small figures racing about the areas outside the city walls and in the cleared spaces that divided the three main sections of town. All along the river, mobs of hysterical people flung themselves into the current, both living and dead floating out the northern side of town.

So far, the fire had not leaped the main arm of the river. Nor, as best we could tell, had it reached the Kremlin. There were a few spot fires in the Kitaigorod, flames popping up here and there among the larger homes of the inner ring. We had arrived at dusk, and with the setting sun came a tremendous gust of wind, sending up a huge spiral of fire and sparks from the heaviest part of the inferno. This threw great chunks of flaming debris onto the roofs of the better houses, some of it flying over the Kremlin wall, onto *dachas* and government buildings inside. We could see a small fire, now, on the roof of the royal palace.

As Ivan turned his horse I caught only a glimpse of his face, for it was too dark to see clearly. I could make out his features only in the reflected, reddish glow from the city. He looked as if he had been beaten. "It is the wrath of God," he sighed. "It is my punishment for sin." He spurred his mount, calling to Ivor that he would spend the night at his father's old estate in the Sparrow Hills. This was the closest royal residence outside the Kremlin, and was located on the far side of the woods that bordered Vladya's and the Glinskis' estates. Most of the others followed him, but I held back. Vladya had also checked his mount, allowing it to prance in excitement while he decided what to do. Our eyes met, and I could see the anguish on his face. I am sure he felt as I did—that Ivan should have stayed, or at least ordered us to remain. On the other hand, he had not commanded us to leave.

"My mother. . . ." Vladya said at length.

I nodded. "Mine, too – and the Holy Father! He must still be there."

Together we started to gallop off in the opposite direction from the others, thinking to ford the river below the city walls on the north. Suddenly, above the roar of the flames and the continuous screams of the dying, we heard a tremendous crash. We stopped short, staring at the Kremlin where the sound seemed to originate. In just that few moments the fire had gained a foothold inside the fortress itself, and we could see the Bell Tower explode into a sheet of blazing red. The noise must have been the great bell falling from its lofty perch.

We both looked back at Ivan, who had also stopped and stood transfixed on top of another small rise, again watching the flames as they soared up from the citadel. Very slowly, his head sunk deep on his chest, he led the rest away. Vladya and I watched until they passed out of sight. We were sitting our mounts, knee to knee, and I nudged my friend to break his reverie. Together, we bounded down the slope toward the river, into the _Vorobiovo_ section. The flames were too intense to attempt a crossing. Instead, we separated outside the entrance to Vladya's grounds, and I continued through the open gates toward the Glinksi mansion. After pounding on the front door for several minutes, I was about to seek some other means of entry when an old man fumbled open the peep hole and stared out at me, his eyes wide with terror. The flames made an almost solid wall behind me, completely obscuring the sky across the river. I must have loomed dark and foreboding against this background.

"Where is my mother?" I shouted at him. Getting no answer, I slammed my fists against the oaken panel. "Open up!" I demanded.

I could hear him grappling with the latch on the other side as Vladya rode up behind me. "They've all left," he said. "Is your mother still here?"

I shrugged. "I don't know. Old fumble–fingers hasn't told me."

The door finally creaked open, and we both bounded inside. The old man leaned back against the door, and I heard the latch slide into place. Vladya grabbed him by the shoulders, shaking him. "Where is Lady Eleanor?" he shouted.

The old man stared at him vacantly.

"What do you want?" Her icy voice came from the darkness at the head of the staircase. Vladya and I both turned, startled. My mother stood in the shadows, looking down at us.

"We came to get you out of this inferno," I exclaimed, starting up.

"Just don't bother about me!" she said, still in that frigid tone. She evidenced no fear of the fire—no surprise, no joy that I had come for her. "You made your choice when you stayed with Heinrich. Go back to him. I hope you two are very happy together!"

I started up again. "Mother, you're leaving here if I have to carry you out!" I told her, trying to imitate Heinrich's firmness. From me, it didn't work.

"Get out of here!" she shouted, her eyes flashing like frozen points of blue ice. "Get out, and if you lay a hand on me I'll scratch that pretty face to shreds. You, too!" she thundered at Vladimir, who had come up the stairs behind me. "I don't need either of you, and I don't want you!"

"But the fire. . . ." I started lamely.

"The fire will never reach this house," she answered. She was rigidly calm again, sure that neither of us would try a heroic rescue.

"You can't be sure!" I cried.

"How do you know?" added Vladya, interrupting me.

She smiled mysteriously. "Perhaps I'm protected by Glinski witchcraft," she replied sarcastically.

"Where *are* the Glinskis?" demanded Vladya.

"In Rzhov," she said.

"And the Czar's grandmother?"

"The Czar's grandmother is a Glinski," replied Mother, as if to an annoying child. "She is where I told you the Glinskis went. Now, will you please leave!"

"But why are you still here?" I stammered.

"That is none of your business!" she shouted, her anger flaring out again. "Now get out!"

It was thus I parted from my mother, never to see her again except in death.

When we were back on the street, we could see the fire raging through both the inner city and the Kremlin. My own home, as well as the Buturlin mansion were surely destroyed, I thought, as they were situated in areas where the seas of flame were swirling, dancing masses. In considering the possibilities of Anna's fate, I did so with an uncertain mixture of feelings. Much as I detested her, I had never wished her dead. I felt I should do something...but what?

Across the river, we could see mobs of people crowding onto the banks, some with their clothing on fire. Women threw their children into the water, saving them from the flames only to have them sink out of sight before they could be found again. A very few men had been able to swim across. The only bridge sagged in ruins, I supposed because it had broken under the weight of those trying to flee across it. The river by the far shore was filled with bobbing heads, as thousands sought safety in its dark embrace. There were a few on both sides who knelt in prayer, making no further effort to escape.

"Maybe we should try to get across and help," I suggested.

Vladya shook his head. "We had better join the Czar," he said.

We remounted our restless horses and turned our backs on the holocaust. The smoke became still thicker as the high wind died down. Pungent billows of black settled lower over the entire city, until it was difficult to breathe. Heat, ashes, and smoke covered my face. I wrapped the cloak about my head and followed Vladya, our horses breaking into a gallop toward the royal residence on the other side of the woods.

Ivan was still in deep depression when we arrived. He had locked himself in his chambers, refusing to see anyone. Anastasia had arrived a few minutes ahead of us, accompanied by Heinrich, who had joined her entourage on the road. She had graciously invited him to ride in her carriage, as his horse had broken a leg and had to be put out of its pain. As soon as I was able to draw my stepfather aside I told him about Mother and her refusal to seek safety outside the threatened area. Surprisingly, he made no move to go after her. This later gave added credence to the story of her having taken a lover, who remained with her in the Glinski *dacha*.

That night, our sleeping arrangements were haphazard, as there were far too many refugees for the small palace to accommodate properly. I spent a restless night, sharing one large bedstead with Heinrich and Adashev. On one side, my stepfather tossed fitfully, mumbling in his dreams; on the other, Andrei snored delicately, making little whistling sounds with every breath. He never shifted position, lying flat on his back with his hands crossed on his chest as if he were dead.

In the morning, Ivan still refused to come out of his rooms until a messenger arrived, informing us that Makari had been seriously injured. In attempting to save the Icon of Our Lady from the Great Cathedral, the Metropolitan had been holding the sacred burden under his arm and had fallen when the monks tried to lower him on a rope into a wide passage that ran from inside the Kremlin to the river bank. This, incidentally, was not the same underwater passage I had used. I doubt if very many people knew of mine, and the elderly Metropolitan would never have been physically able to use it. Makari had been knocked unconscious by his fall, and as yet no one knew if he would live. Ivan bolted from his chambers when he heard the news and left immediately for the Novopassky Monastery, where the prelate had been taken.

Ivan departed so abruptly, hardly anyone knew he had gone. Only Yuri and a few retainers went with him. As soon as he left, I questioned the messenger and assured myself that the flames had still not crossed the river. There had been a few small fires, he told me, but they had been quickly extinguished. The worst seemed to be over, he said, and it was unlikely the flames would harm any of the large stone houses on the far side of the woods. I rode out a little later, onto a hilltop some distance from the city, where I could verify the fellow's account. The flames were indeed dying down, although the center of town was still a horrible mass of ferocious, blazing heat. I could also see spots of fire in the Kremlin. The blackened sides of the Bell Tower were still standing, although its wooden roof was missing. The palace also seemed fairly well intact, but there must have been considerable damage to the upper floors. I could not see the private houses, because they were not tall enough to show above the walls.

I was at the summer palace when Ivan returned later in the afternoon. Makari had not been mortally injured, he said, but had been badly shaken and must remain in bed to recover from his bruises. The Metropolitan's infirmities had serious implications, for Ivan badly needed his spiritual support. Without it, the Czar seemed unable to give coherent orders. His Glinski cousins were both absent, leaving us in chaos, for no one else had the authority to make necessary decisions. Almost as soon as he returned, Ivan went into his private chapel and knelt before the holy crosses and icons, begging God for help and forgiveness. He was feeling extremely repentant, blaming his cruelty to the Pskovian petitioners for the fire and refusing to consider that it had started well before the news reached him – certainly prior to his meeting with the western merchants. Nobody could convince him, although several of us tried. He would not listen to any of us.

Then, out of the cluster of monks who were forever underfoot, stepped Sylvester. This priest had come to Moscow with Makari, and was formerly a presbyter of Novgorod. He had been employed by the Metropolitan in the writing of his holy book. Ivan, his forehead bruised and covered with dust from beating it against the floor before the sacred images, had just come out of his chapel. He called for a flagon of wine, as Sylvester, in his black *schima* – the cassock worn by particularly holy, or "honest" monks – and with a heavy *klobuk*, or cowl, over his boney head, moved in front of his brother priests. He stood tall and threatening before the Czar. Pointing accusingly with his long, crooked finger, he berated Ivan unmercifully. "You, Oh Czar!" he rumbled. "The wrath of God is upon you!"

This accusation was so unexpected, everyone stopped to stare at him. Even at this early stage of his life, no one would have dared speak to Ivan like this, not any of us who were his closest friends. But the Czar was also taken by surprise, and he stood transfixed as the priest launched into a long, emotional tirade. He expanded upon Ivan's own belief that the fire had been visited upon Moscow as a result of its rulers' sins, cleverly indicating the nobility as well. He further implied that the fire, when it was finally put out, would have expiated the entire land. If Ivan took to heart this message from heaven, he could start afresh. As Our Savior had died on the cross for the love of man and the redemption of sinners, said the priest, so the fire would purge the evil from Muscovy.

I think Sylvester must have thoroughly terrified Ivan, by accusing him of the very things he had already confessed in his own prayers. When he suggested the hope of salvation – something the Czar had failed to think of himself – Ivan was more than happy to accept the priest's appearance at this particular moment as a sign from God. When Sylvester finished speaking, Ivan threw himself onto his knees before him. With the entire assemblage looking on, he begged for absolution.

"Your Heavenly Father has already indicated the path to your salvation," said Sylvester sternly. "You have but to follow it. I am only a poor priest, sent in this time of crisis to express His Will."

So it was that Sylvester joined our circle about the Czar—an unhappy moment for all of us. He was a cold, rigid man, incapable of worldly pleasure. He condemned any display of happiness as sin, and had a strange set of moral values. He even considered it immoral for a man to own slaves! He would later write a rather stupid, pompous book setting forth rules for proper household conduct between men and their wives, treatment of children, servants and the like. Although Ivan eventually recovered from his melancholy state, again engaging in pranks or other forms of pleasant relaxation with us, I always had the feeling that my motives were being picked apart by this hovering shadow of gloom. His accusing look could make the most innocent laugh seem blasphemous. In time we came to call him "Mad Sylvester," although Ivan disliked the name and it was never used in his presence.

The fire smoldered for another three days and two nights, finally burning itself out as God's Will changed the course of the wind, fanning the flames back across the previously blackened ruins. The destruction was total outside the Kremlin walls. Except for the suburbs – the "freedoms" – across the river, hardly a building remained in the city. Most of the government structures in the Kremlin were damaged, but none was destroyed. A large hole had been blown out of the north wall, when the armory exploded, and nearly all the houses around it, including ours, were burned to the ground. But odors! The stench of death was unbelievable! Thousands of people had burned to cinders, as well as horses, cows, pigs—all manner of livestock. This, mingled with the smell of singed moss – the material used to fill the chinks in log houses – and the rotting offal of animals—all of it added into a horrible, stinking putrification.

The Czar made a thorough tour of the devastated areas, accompanied by those of us who normally comprised his entourage...and Sylvester. The only conspicuous absentee was Michael Glinski, who remained in Rzhov with his mother. George had returned, and went with us. Predictably, in the group of boyars following behind us, was a Shuisky. The family had gradually drifted back into court circles, as Ivan's earlier strictures were relaxed. Except for Peter's brief moment of usurpation, when he announced the feeding of the crowds at the coronation, they had been restrained and respectful.

As we walked through the ruined city, and conversations within our own group lapsed from time to time, I could hear Prince Shopin–Shuisky speaking behind us. This was a sly, older man, who had remained in the background during the regency, gleaning what ripe fruit he could when his kinsmen had shaken the branches. While I could not hear all that was said, and was really not interested enough to try, I did catch a few strange phrases: "work of the devil," "sorcery as known only in the West," and the word "witchcraft" repeated several times.

Heinrich was with us on this tour of the city, but he hardly spoke to anyone. I knew he was sober, so his mood of depression was not the result of spirits. He still refused to go after Mother, although this situation was surely the cause of his brooding. I would have tried to help, but I was certain she would send word if she wanted to see me. Otherwise, I would only meet the same resistance as on the first night of the fire. I was worried about her – not that I felt she was in any danger – except people were saying unpleasant things, and her separation from Heinrich was creating a scandal. Preoccupied with these thoughts, I paid little attention to the small groups of dazed, bewildered people who approached us along the way, seeking the Czar's blessing. They believed that by touching his person they would somehow find an easier road into the future.

Heinrich spoke to me, finally, forcing my mind to focus more sharply on all that was going on around us. Together, we strayed from the others and talked with a number of people who were poking about in the ashes. Their faces were blackened with soot, and their clothes were stained by river water, some with large scorched patches. Most of these men sought some lost treasure or loved one in the ruins, their present mood being one of sorrow, capable later of turning to anger. Everyone believed the fire had been set deliberately, not by natural means. The word "witchcraft" was constantly whispered.

That evening, I discussed what I had heard with Andrei Adashev, who subsequently communicated my thoughts, along with his own, when he spoke with Ivan and Sylvester. I doubt that the claims of supernatural causes impressed Ivan very much, but he decided to conduct an inquiry. His choice of investigator surprised me, for he appointed Shopin–Shuisky. I think this resulted from a suggestion by Anastasia's Uncle Gregory, whose closest friend was John Chelydin. John was a vehement opponent of the Glinskis, but allied with the Shuiskys in business.

Shuisky sent his servants out immediately, questioning hundreds of people, particularly those who had lived in the Arbat. This was the area where all the fires seemed to have started, and where there was the greatest likelihood of finding someone who had seen the arsonist. How much these Shuisky men might have contributed to spreading the rumors, I cannot honestly say. I suspect it was a great deal. It was soon repeated all about the ruined city that the fire had been caused by a witch. She was said to have stolen the hearts from human corpses, soaked them in holy water – thereby consecrating them to Satan – and sprinkled this evil brew upon the churches and homes of the poor. This had ignited the horrible conflagration. And whispered more softly than the rest of the tale, the name of the witch was said to be Anna Glinskaya!

A day or two later Ivan made another of his inspection trips into the Kremlin, subsequently returning to the Sparrow Hills residence. I remained behind in the city to help some of my friends in the cathedrals. We were trying to remove the priceless works of art from the ruined churches before they could be damaged by the weather. I stayed at this task until dusk, when it became too dark to see what we were doing. Hungry, and in a hurry to join the others in the summer palace, I sloshed some water over my face and quickly mounted up. I exited via the Savior's Gate, which took me directly through the Square of Executions.

I was surprised to see a large crowd gathered about the *lobonoyo mesto*. Curious, I rode close enough to hear. The people were mostly peasants and beggars, men of the lowest orders. They held torches above their heads, and in the flickering light I recognized Prince Shopin–Shuisky upon the dais addressing them – or more precisely, exciting them.

"Who set fire to the city!" he shouted.

"The Glinskis!" roared the mob, which I am sure must have been liberally sprinkled with Shuisky henchmen.

"And what are we going to do about the murderers?" shouted a voice from the crowd.

"Kill them! Kill them!" came the frantic answers.

A small group of boyars and their servants came out of the Kremlin gate behind me, and I noted George Glinski's bulky figure among them. They could not have realized what was happening, although I tried to warn George of the mob's nasty mood. He would not turn tail and run, he said, not from any gang of vagabonds and fools. Contemptuously, he rode directly forward, into the milling knot of men. Because of his portly stature, he was recognized immediately. One huge peasant grabbed the bridle of his horse, and instinctively George struck him down with his riding crop. That set off the tinder box, for the mob reacted with uncontrolled violence. They swept forward, chanting, "Kill the Glinski! Kill the Glinski!"

George reined his mount backward, shocked by the unexpected anger and aggression. He turned toward the Kremlin, finally frightened enough to seek its safety. The *Spasskaya* mechanisms had been damaged during the fire, however, and although George made it inside, the gates remained open. The drawbridge was down, and the portcullis hung at an angle far above the planks. The mob continued its pursuit, moving so quickly they cut the rest of us off from the entrance. There was nothing to do but get out of the way, as George was chased up the steps and into the cathedral. His fat legs churned desperately, trying to propel his bulk inside the sanctuary. Two servants had managed to stay with him, and they assisted him the last few feet. I laughed, as did some of the others, for it was a humorous sight. We assumed George would be safe enough, now he was inside the church.

We did not laugh for long. Reaching the sacred area did not protect them, and the mob completed its work very quickly. Glinski and his servants were hacked to bits by the frenzied peasants! The first inkling of this was not communicated to us until we saw George's head being borne aloft by the mass of men who sallied forth from the church. One of the peasant leaders was holding it up by the beard, making the mouth hang open as if George were still screaming in agony from this upside–down position.

"We'd better get out of here," I said, waving at my own pair of men. The rest of the nobles followed in a frantic rush to reach the Czar and warn him. All of us, I think, anticipated a full scale rebellion, and Ivan's safety was foremost in our thoughts. For this reason, and this reason alone, it failed to cross my mind that the occupants of the Glinski *dacha* would be in danger. Like the others, I was close to panic. With the main bridges still unable to bear the weight of mounted men, we had to take a circuitous route, crossing the river to the south, then riding north again. All of this took the better part of an hour.

Heinrich was quick to respond the moment he heard the news. He left immediately, without a word to anyone, but his ashen face reminded me of Mother's danger. I followed him a few minutes later, after hurriedly answering Ivan's questions and receiving his permission to go.

The tableau at the Glinski *dacha* was one I shall never forget. Temporary repairs to the old bridge had allowed the mob to cross on foot. In the intervening time they had come and gone. We could hear their shouts from across the water, but on our side a deathly hush seemed to separate us from the world of the living. The iron gates hung in twisted masses from their hinges, and the front door had been smashed to splinters. Most of the furniture and wall hangings were gone; obscene marks had been drawn on the walls. The old man, who had so grudgingly admitted me a few days before, lay in a pool of blood just inside the doorway. I found Heinrich upstairs, in a room off the main landing. He knelt on the floor, cradling my mother's head in his arms. Her body had not yet stiffened in death, and her eyes were closed so I thought at first she was asleep. Her golden hair was disheveled and Heinrich was absently trying to stroke it smooth again. Her gown was torn, and there were several obvious marks on her body.

The only other occupant of the house, except for the servants who had been slain in their quarters, was a younger cousin of George and Michael. His body lay a few feet down the corridor, blood beginning to crust upon the numerous rents in his clothing. Heinrich carried my mother's body into a back bedroom, one of the few still containing usable furniture. Tenderly, he placed her upon the bed and pressed his lips to her forehead. Without a word he turned and started downstairs, kicking the body of the Glinski cousin as he passed.

I stood staring at my mother for a long time, until Heinrich's voice came to me from the darkness below. Slowly I turned and went down into the courtyard. I could once again hear the shouts and chants of the crowd across the river. They had reassembled in the Square of Executions, where they eventually expended their remaining energies and broke up into small, ravaging packs.

"We had better get back to the Czar," said Heinrich softly.

Heinrich would never discuss my mother after that day. She was buried in a simple ceremony, after the Orthodox faith both she and Heinrich had long since adopted. Actually, I do not think Heinrich was a very avid believer at this time, but at Mother's funeral he went through the proper forms and I knew he was sincerely saddened. Despite Euphrosyne's protest, Vladya stood by my side when Mother's casket was placed onto her bier and she was lowered into the ground. Andrei Adashev, Yuri, and Basmanov were there as well. No other members of the court attended, but I felt no malice. Mother had not been highly regarded by most, for she had always seemed a woman of improper forwardness. Many felt that this had been the cause of her untimely death.

Until now, there had been no report concerning my own wife, or her family. The most we had been able to learn was that both Anna and her brother had been in Moscow at the start of the fire. When Heinrich and I returned to the palace after Mother's funeral, we received word from one of the search parties that Alfansy's body had been found in the river. I never knew what became of Anna, and eventually she was declared officially dead. Had she obeyed me and gone to the country, she would have lived; so at least this sin does not lie upon my conscience.

The same day my mother was laid to her final rest, the wretched followers of Shuisky started agitating the people to further violence. Before we realized what they and their fellow conspirators were doing, the Shuiskys themselves had returned to Ivan's side. There they maintained a facade of innocence, pretending to offer the Czar their wholehearted support. The death of his Uncle George had thrown Ivan into such a fit of depression, he had hardly spoken to anyone. On this particular evening of which I speak, he had retired to his rooms, where he knelt at prayer with the black priest, Sylvester.

The rest of us had eaten dinner and were thinking of bed when a rampaging mob suddenly appeared outside the gates. They were shouting insults against the Glinskis, demanding the surrender of "the witch." As further, supposed proof of Shuisky innocence, the mob appeared to believe that Anna Glinskaya and Michael were with the Czar. As all of us, including the Shuiskys, were well aware, both of them were still in Rzhov. For the common peasantry to dare demand the life of the Czar's grandmother was an impossible affront. Thus the Shuiskys' crime was so gross and so vile it is understandable that people found it difficult to believe. Playing on this, they later suggested the improbable explanation of the idea's having sprung spontaneously from the dull, peasant minds of the mob leaders. Ivan chose to accept their statements, and he generously took no vengeance upon Shopin–Shuisky.

Now, with the howling mob about to break down the gates, the Czar stormed from his apartments, demanding to know what was happening. Playing his role of innocence to the hilt, Shuisky repeated the stated purpose of the rioters. In a raging fury, Ivan called Heinrich and Ivor, issuing specific instructions for silencing the criminals. I donned my own armor along with my stepfather and we assembled a mixed force of household guard, gentlemen volunteers, and retainers from our own and several other houses. Bursting out the front doors, we ordered the gates flung open. Seeing several ranks of armed men, the mob stopped where they were. It was easy enough to spot the organizers, as they began shouting for their flock to follow, and a few men actually started forward. Heinrich waded into them first, with the rest of us close behind him. We quickly seized every man who seemed to be a leader. With no ceremony and very few wasted words, we threw them to the ground, beheading them on the spot. The mob gaped in stark fear as we turned back to face them. They had obviously not been prepared to expect such severe or immediate retribution.

"Any of you who doesn't leave at once will share the fate of these brigands!" shouted Heinrich. "And if you ever dare return, you will not get this much warning."

"You have already brought the curse of Heaven upon your souls," came a voice from the balcony above us. I looked up and saw the dark form of Mad Sylvester in the shadows. Although I probably imagined it, his eyes seemed to glow like ruby coals.

Beaten, afraid for both their physical and spiritual survival, the mob broke up and drifted away into the night. I returned to the *dacha* with the others, and was met at the door by a chamberlain who politely asked me to attend upon the Czar at once. I started upstairs to Ivan's apartments, meeting a number of people coming down. Nearly the whole court had been at the upper windows, watching us disperse the peasants. Several men gripped my hand or patted my back as we passed on the stairs, congratulating me for my part in breaking up the mob. A few others, those who had previously been reluctant, expressed condolences over the loss of my mother. Something important was about to happen, I was sure. The way some of the men looked at me made it apparent. Ivan's mood had shifted abruptly. He received me at once and sent for some wine. He told me again how sorry he was that my mother had met such a fate, then spoke of the incident we had just concluded. "As you grow older, Dmitri," he added, "there will be many more things you can do for Us, even as you have done this evening."

"I would serve Your Majesty gladly in any way I can," I answered stiffly. Since the coronation, I had taken to using the proper forms in addressing the Czar.

Ivan laughed. "No one can hear us," he said casually. "You know I have made Adashev and his father *okolnichi*," he continued, and after a pause added, "What would you think of taking that rank as well?"

Although I was overwhelmed, I did not answer immediately. Keeping my emotion from showing, I replied simply: "You are the Czar."

After a moment Ivan began to laugh. Watching him, I could not hold it back and I joined him in his mirth. "If you can manage that much control over your expression," he said, "you'll be able to serve me sooner than I'd expected."

A servant entered with the wine, and Ivan gestured for him to serve us. "You understand," he continued, "I shall not vest you with boyar rank, although the position of *okolnich* might normally imply it."

I nodded. "I think such a rank would place me in the group I choose not to join."

We toasted that, and the Czar explained his reasons for placing men about him who were from lesser backgrounds than had been customary. Most of the *okolnichi* – those near the throne – would henceforth be men of less than boyar status. As the wine warmed his being, the Czar made some reference to the possibility of my one day assuming the title of Prince, since my father – my officially recorded father, Simon – was the only adopted son of old Prince Marensky. It would be stretching the rules of inheritance, he agreed, but who was to question the will of God's anointed Czar?

"I have also decided," he told me at length, "to appoint Adashev as my chancellor." He watched my expression before adding, "Would you have some thoughts on that, councilor?"

"You are the Czar," I repeated.

Ivan's mood changed, and he regarded me sharply. "That's not what I asked!" he snapped.

"I – I did not mean to be evasive," I answered. "I only meant that your power is absolute. You're the Autocrat. Andrei is probably the most faithful man you could find, and if it's your wish to appoint him, it becomes my duty—and my desire to support that decision." I withheld any mention of the nebulous doubts I had previously harbored. After all, Andrei had never failed Ivan. It had only been in his relationship with me – and that during the negotiations for my marriage – that his behavior had caused me to question his honor.

In another heartbeat Ivan's mood reverted to its former levity. He chuckled, sipping at his wine. "You are beginning to learn the graceful dance of words, as a courtier needs to do," he said. "As a matter of fact, you've answered me in almost the exact same phrases as the Metropolitan. By the way, I saw him this afternoon, and he seems to be feeling much better."

"I'm glad of that," I answered quickly. My first thought, of course, was to hope the Metropolitan's return to his duties might rid us of Sylvester. I suspect that Ivan understood, because he gave me a knowing look, grinning as he continued. "Makari also remarked, in discussing your appointment, that you are wise beyond your years."

"Sharing your moments of torment and fear may have aged me," I answered lightly.

Ivan roared with laughter, and I realized he was a little tipsy. He had obviously downed considerably more wine than the two or three beakers we consumed together. "You will make a first rate ambassador," he declared, refilling our goblets. He handed mine back to me – a singular honor, now that he was Czar. He hefted his drink, slopping some of the wine onto his sleeve. "To our glorious future!" he shouted.

I continued to sip the heavy red liquid as I listened to Ivan's further ramblings. Responding to his expansive mood, I ventured the question he had raised earlier in my mind. "What of Michael?" I asked. "I mean, isn't he still chancellor?"

"A messenger is on the way to Rzhov right now," said the Czar. "My cousin ceased to be an officer of Our government about two hours ago."

"I don't mean to appear critical of anything. . . ." I began.

Ivan looked up sharply, then withdrew the fire from his glance. "You may always speak without fear," he said soothingly. "That is why I have named you councilor. Do you think I'm wrong?"

"No, it isn't that. Only I wondered if you intend appointing Shuisky to—"

Now the fire did return to Ivan's eyes, but the anger was not directed toward me. "Never!" he declaimed violently. "Believe me, Dmitri, because I give you this oath today and I shall live by it for the rest of my life. No Shuisky, no Bielsky, no Glinski will ever – *ever* hold a post close to the Czar, not so long as I rule Russia. I may be forced to use them as military commanders, or to place them in charge of provincial administrations—only because their rank or experience demands it, or because it keeps them out of Moscow. But I'll never again allow any of them close enough to threaten my crown." As he spoke his eyes traveled to a large painting of the Blessed Virgin, hanging on the wall behind me. I had the impression of his directing his oath as much to Her as to me. Then his eyes returned to search my face, seeming to probe and seek within my soul.

"Dmitri, we have been children together. We've shared both hardship and danger, many pleasant experiences, as well. It is only by the Grace of God we are both still alive. By this, the Lord has made it clear He wishes me to live, and to rule. He has sent you, among others, to serve me. Do you feel this?

I nodded. "I have always felt that, Ivashka." I thought he started at my using the familiar form of address, for although I had called him this all our lives, I had not done so since his coronation. He said nothing, but I knew from that day hence not to call him "Ivashka" again – at least not for a very long time. It was but one of many small considerations I had to keep in mind, for Ivan would become ever more moody as the years went on. His sudden changes of temperament caused many other officials to fall abruptly from grace. Perhaps I had a greater advantage, having grown up with him and knowing his moods so well. As his personality changed with the years, it continued to be my duty to understand it and to anticipate its needs. On this night, when I achieved the coveted rank of councilor, I think I first became seriously aware of the responsibility carried by one who is friend to a king. Along with this came the realization that he really wasn't "Ivashka" any longer. The boyhood friend I had helped to keep from starving was now Ivan IV, Czar of Russia.

As we continued to drink, Ivan grew increasingly philosophic, then morose. He spoke at length of his sins, and how he must begin at once to fulfill his destiny lest God forget the promise of greatness made to his blood. I could not be sure how much of this was Sylvester's doing, but I assumed he was responsible for the sudden urgency.

"My eyes have been opened these last few days,' said the Czar, further confirming my suspicions. "I know I have sinned as no other man in Russia could have sinned, for I am Czar. I have allowed my people to be wronged by the very men I should have directed. But you will see, Dmitri, you will see changes you never dreamed possible. And you will see my greatness as a result of these changes."

He was so enraptured by his own thoughts I had no idea how to respond. Whatever I might have said would have sounded foolish and trite, following these statements from the greatest of Christian rulers. I allowed myself to sink farther in my chair, until Ivan paused and I knew I had to say something.

"I hope I may be of some small help," I added weakly.

"You will, Dmitri. Be sure of that! Would you care for some more wine?" he asked.

"Thank you, no," I said, taking the excuse to rise when Ivan again stepped to the decanter. "With your permission. . .it has been a very difficult day for me."

"By all means," said the Czar. "It was thoughtless of me to detain you on this day of grief. Please tell your father that my brother and I share his loss. I have already ordered eternal prayers for your mother's soul."

I felt a thickening in my throat. "Thank you," I mumbled.

Ivan grasped my shoulder as I stood by the door. "Without your mother's food during those black days of our childhood. . .I shall remember her in my own prayers," he assured me.

That night, in the privacy of my room – for I had finally been given my own quarters – I wept for my mother. I tried to pray for her soul, although prayers were becoming more difficult for me. Somehow, it was easier to imagine her love when she was no longer around to shatter the illusions I created in my mind. I think my feelings for her that night comprised a love she had never permitted me to feel when she was alive. Before I fell asleep, my thoughts turned to the Czar, and to the many glories I might achieve in his service.

CHAPTER IV

The dying embers of the great fire left many changes in their wake. With the leaders of the mob removed, the people of Moscow became sheep again, turning blackened faces toward their improvised hovels. Most walked each day to one of the various monasteries around the city, where they were fed and otherwise cared for by the monks. Fortunately, summer came early, in a rush of golden warmth. Most people found adequate shelter, although the nights remained chilly. Cold seems to bother a peasant very little, anyway, as they learn to live with it as suckling babes. Only our perfidious officials – whose mistreatment of the masses had created the climate for revolt – found reason to regret the advent of summer.

Shortly after I left the Czar on the evening of my mother's funeral day, his messenger returned from Rzhov. Michael Glinski had fled to Pskov, taking his mother and his treasure with him. Angered by this, Ivan sent men to arrest his cousin that very night. Glinski was seized a few days later on the road to the Lithuanian border. He was accompanied by Turuntay–Pronsky, who was also about to be stripped of his governorship. Between them they carried an enormous sum, which Ivan promptly confiscated. The two officials were imprisoned. It was several years before they were pardoned.

In the city, even before the last wisps of smoke ceased to drift from the ruins, Ivan issued orders to rebuild the government structures, the churches in the Kremlin, and much of the *Kitaigorod*. Andrei was appointed seneschal and oversaw most of the work. The Shuiskys, although in great disfavor again, were spared any direct punishment. I think this was due mostly to Sylvester's intervention. They were rarely seen at court. It was a new group of councilors around the Czar, now, and Kurbsky dubbed us "The Chosen Council." In addition to Andrew and myself, we had Andrei Adashev, Sylvester, Alexi Basmanov, and Vladimir. Michael Morozof completed our group, despite his former associations with the conspiring boyars. He gained Ivan's good will by his hard work and help following the fire. Like Basmanov, he had always refused to involve himself actively in any conspiracy against the Czar. I could appreciate Michael's potential value, for in addition to his skills as an army commander he was clever in dealing with foreigners. Far from being a handsome man, his appearance was still impressive. He was completely tonsured, short and stocky, with powerful arms that reached almost to his knees. I think he was only a few years older than Ivan, but I was never sure of his exact age. Over the years, he never seemed to change.

Anastasia's Uncle Gregory was raised to boyar rank during the early summer, but he had been overly friendly with the Shuiskys during the Glinski period, and I don't think Ivan ever fully trusted him. He was a silly old man, anyway, once one came to know him. He formulated all manner of grand plans for himself, never quite managing to bring them off. In commercial matters he was a consummate bungler, which accounted for his heavy dependence on Heinrich and my stepfather's people. Gregory's nephews, Anastasia's brothers, on the other hand, became quite close to the Czar. They were both weak, spineless creatures, afraid to express any opinion in opposition to Ivan's I never liked either of them very well, being especially contemptuous of Daniel, who had always been an effeminate fop, and was already causing some minor scandals by his sinful lusts. Nikita, at least, pretended to a modicum of manliness.

Makari, because of his station, was never a part of our secular group, and did not attend our meetings. Still, his advice was always heard with respect. Yuri, who frequently sat with us, was not able to contribute much; but, at this stage, neither did I. I needed some gray in my beard, Heinrich told me. My stepfather and I were living temporarily in the palace, while our house was being rebuilt. Ivan had given us a small, but comfortable suite of rooms in the wing where important foreign visitors were usually quartered.

Following my mother's death, Heinrich withdrew for a time, hardly seeing anyone except in the course of managing his business. Ivan had entrusted a large part of his commercial affairs to my stepfather, especially the transport of goods from the south. As a result of his own dealings being so involved with those of the Czar, Heinrich was becoming a very wealthy man. Ivan's current mood of compassion and piety made him less demanding upon his courtiers; Heinrich could be alone when he desired. It was months before he came completely to himself again.

Often deprived of my stepfather's company, and because I saw Ivan only when he called a meeting of his councilors – he was devoting most of his time to Anastasia – I was usually with Vladimir or Yuri. My friendship with Vladya had become even closer since his defiance of Euphrosyne to attend my mother's funeral, but we always had to meet someplace other than in his home. Euphrosyne no longer maintained any pretense of tolerance. She hated me, and would make my visits such miserable experiences it was far better to avoid her.

Vladya's life was further complicated that summer, all due to Euphrosyne's ambitions for him.   Several times she caused him terrible embarrassment by remarks she made to other people, and by her contemptuous attitude toward Yuri. This, in turn, made Ivan question Vladya's motives, since his cousin was next in line to the throne until the Czar should have a son. Confident of my own loyalty, I suspect that Ivan's subtle encouragement of my relationship with Vladya was due to his expecting me to relate any indications of impending treason. By early September, Euphrosyne had made herself so obnoxious that Ivan let it be known – without actually issuing a ban – that she was no longer welcome in the Kremlin. After this, she had no choice but to leave for Staritsa.

As to my passion for Anastasia, now the Czarina, I went through a period of gradually receding emotion. Presumptuous as it was, I had forgiven the Czar within my own heart. There was little I could ever say or do in opposition to him, nor could I harbor ill feeling toward him for very long. I seldom saw his bride, except for those few moments during the fire or at some public ceremony. Her absence, and the Czar's constant declarations of bliss, tended to dampen my desire. Without the threat of having to face my own wife, thus eliminating the constant temptation to compare, it became easier to forget. My new position, of course, gave me access to innumerable young maidens, which also helped lessen the sense of deprivation. I had confessed some of my feelings to Vladya, who did his best to provide additional diversions. My yearning, now, was to be Anastasia's servant, her knight errant, as Heinrich had described the heroes in his tales. Like Tristan was to Isabel, so I would be to her – without the tragic conclusion. The romantic foibles of youth! How wonderful it would be, if one could live his life in such purity and innocence!

As the city began to rise again, taking on a fresh appearance as new buildings grew upon the blackened sites of the old, so a change took place within the soul of the Czar. I attributed this to the dual influence of Sylvester and Anastasia. Ivan had always been given to long spells of depression, especially when he paused to review his sins. With a new bride to console him, these had become less frequent. The priest had assured him that his good works could expiate any past errors. As a result, Ivan became less easily agitated, not so prone to fits of anger, seldom morose or distant. Unfortunately, Sylvester's influence was not this beneficial in every instance.

Along with his benign effect upon the Czar's disposition, the black priest rekindled some old conflicts within the Church. Being a man of prosaic, fundamental beliefs, he tended to side with the hermits, or *yurodivy* – the "holy idiots" and "fools for Christ's sake." These men advocated the Church giving up its wealth, returning to the poverty of our original saints. Makari, who opposed Sylvester in very little else, was completely at odds with him over this. As Metropolitan, he represented the establishment of bishops and abbots who recognized the Church's need of material possessions to support its work. Had Makari been a younger man, this conflict would probably have become an open battle. But he never completely recovered from his fall during the fire. Even after he was up and about he seemed to tire easily, and much of his energy was gone. Although there were violent arguments among the other clergy, the Metropolitan said very little. Ivan, while taking no immediate action, never forgot the pleas of his new confessor. He was very much aware of the vast wealth in the hands of churchmen. I remember one evening, when Ivan had drunk far too much vodka – I had been drinking wine, so was better able to remember – he made a joke about Church resources being his reserve treasury.

Thus Sylvester was not successful – not within his own lifetime – in altering the fiscal balance of church and state. The only way he might have succeeded would have been to forsake his proper clerical garb for a beggar's rags. But his own ambition prevented this, as he would then have been forced to leave the comfort and security of the court, also his position of closeness to the Czar. I state this as the case, because it was the wild-eyed *yurodivy* whom Ivan feared more than anything else in the world. He was convinced of their strange ascetic powers, as were many other people. There was one, in particular, whom all of us feared. He was a cripple named Basil, who begged alms in the Square of Executions. During times of stress, he would harangue the crowds, even daring to approach the boyars and the Czar himself. Ivan was terrified of him, and would sometimes go out of his way to avoid having to pass him.

Basil was old, even in those days, and his body resembled a skeleton with loose hide covering the bones. In summer he wore only a breechclout, and not much more in winter. His hair was long and wild, tumbling down his back in a tangled mass of gray. His beard reached below his waist. He carried both a crutch and a cane, sometimes waving wildly with both as he accused the Shuiskys of perfidy and heresy, and later he said the same about the Glinskis. He would probably have been with the mobs after the fire, except for his inability to keep up with them. He said things no one else would have dared, because his holy state was so assured none could touch him for fear of God's wrath.

In my own lack of grace, I doubted the *yurodivy* and his holiness, as I had come to doubt my own God. Yet I still feared a fiery curse from one of these men, for I had somehow retained a belief in the devil. From a spiritual standpoint, I was going through a distraught period of my life. I survived it as well as I did, only because of my youth and its attendant frivolity. I harbored the fears and doubts within me, telling no one, for I dared not bare my secret. When I thought about it, I felt afraid and guilty – sometimes terribly alone.

Ivan, unaware of the turbulence in my heart, inadvertently set a new task for me which diverted my attention from religious matters. I must learn to speak Polish and Swedish, he told me. There would come a day when he would need an interpreter of the highest order. In addition to my native Russian, I already spoke fluent German and Lithuanian, being familiar with several dialects of each. Learning two new languages presented no great problem. I undertook my studies immediately, hiring a native of each land and spending several hours a day in conversation with one or the other. From time to time the Czar would join us, usually when I was with the Swede. This man was a follower of Luther, and Ivan enjoyed arguing scripture with him. It surprised me how quickly the Czar could pick up words and phrases in a foreign tongue, then hurl them back to support his religious convictions.

I continued these language lessons into the fall, restricting them mostly to the morning hours. In the late afternoons I would go a few practice rounds with Vladimir, because I also had to keep my sword arm in shape. Prior to this, my workouts had been mostly against men who trained in the German tradition, and who used weapons similar to those which Heinrich had given me. The Russian sword was larger and balanced differently, the armor heavier and more awkward.

As I would subsequently have to dress after the Russian fashion, for appearance sake if nothing else, these sessions were important. Although Vladya was my height, he was lighter by several pounds, this giving him some advantage in speed – a factor that had always been in my favor with previous partners. Although we generally used wooden swords, we still managed to buffet each other sufficiently to be constantly nursing a series of bruises in various states of healing.

Despite our vigorous exchanges in the practice yard, there was never an angry word between us. At night, the Czar's cousin and I often caroused the Arbat together. That neither of us contracted the pox was little short of miraculous. While we never took a woman who was not proffered as a virgin, some quite obviously were not.

A sense of peace had descended over the land in these final days before the onset of winter. Artisans and carpenters were busy rebuilding the Kremlin, and all over the city one heard the clatter of hammers and saws. Before the first snows, most people were settled into their new homes. Then the Czar announced another cause for celebration, tempering the winter's chill with joyful anticipation. He summoned another assembly of virgins, from which Yuri was to select a wife! Having observed the bliss in which his brother lived, the younger prince had now reconciled himself to taking a bride. Fortune certainly smiled upon him, for he found a paragon of the noblest sort – the Princess Ulyana, a woman of beauty, charm and grace, who almost rivaled Anastasia in her virtues.

The marriage ceremony was glorious and lively, an appropriate ending to our year of peace. For the banquet afterward, Ivan arranged a spectacular feast in the newly redecorated Hall of Facets. Anastasia made one of her rare appearances, looking as lovely as ever I remembered her. She seemed a little pale, but this added to her ethereal aura. Rumor had it she was with child.

The Czarina sat at the head of the table with Ivan, for marriage feasts were one of the few exceptions to the *terem* sanctions. I was especially honored when she sent me a succulent piece of meat from her own plate. Not many others were so thoughtfully remembered. We went through the usual toasts and laughter, although much of the customary vulgarity was omitted in deference to the Czarina's presence. So in this respect, the wedding dinner was not particularly boisterous. It was, as it happened, the proverbial "lull before a storm."

The women had just begun the traditional combing of the bride's hair, when a page whispered to Ivan that couriers had arrived from the Khan of Kazan. I remember Anastasia pouring the sacred wine into Ulyana's long black tresses while the boy leaned over the Czar's shoulder. The servant woman who handed her the golden comb seemed more interested in Ivan's discourse than with her duties. Everyone knew something had happened, and the room became quiet, except for Yuri's giggling. Several of us were about to start the ritual combing of his hair, so he had failed to note the Czar's momentary distraction.

I think Ivan's reactions might have been different had he not been so happy and expansive from the several hours of drinking and merry making. Instead of making the infidel swine wait to attend upon him in the morning, he laughed and ordered them shown in. I am certain he expected them to bear some gift for the newlyweds.

In came three richly accoutered Mussulmen, short swarthy men, with turbaned heads and grizzly black beards. They were singularly ugly, like most of their people, whose faces were said to be molded by the devil. They walked awkwardly, on legs bowed from earliest childhood by constant riding. They bent only slightly before the Czar, and stepped much closer than etiquette prescribed. The oldest one, obviously the leader, proffered a leather scroll which was taken by Adashev. The Tartar had mumbled some formal words of greeting, proper to an ambassador attending upon a Grand Duke, but not to a Caesar. The purposeful insult did not go unnoticed, and I saw Ivan tense as he listened. At first we ascribed this lapse to the ignorance of barbarians – until we heard the contents of the scroll. From the first word, it was obviously not a message to accompany any wedding gift.

At a gesture from Ivan, Adashev had broken the seal and glanced at the inscription, unable to read it. "It is in the infidel tongue," he said.

"Then the ambassador may read it and translate it for Us," said the Czar, still holding his annoyance in check. The leader bowed again, as best his misshapen body would permit. Grinning slyly, and speaking with a heavy accent, be began to singsong the words of his master. Gold must be sent, he commanded, and gifts worthy of a prince, else the Tartar Khan would lay waste the lands of the Muscovite Caesar. The insults that followed were almost unbelievable! Before the man finished speaking, Ivan's face was black with rage. He leaped up so violently he nearly overturned the table. As it was, dishes and goblets clattered in all directions. The Tartars were ordered seized and thrown into a cell. Within a week, three heads with gizzled black beards were on their way to the Kazanite ruler, thus launching Ivan's first holy crusade against the infidel Tartar.

Yuri's wedding had been in early November. Just one month later the Czar's army was ready to march. Ivan would lead the soldiers in person, ignoring Adashev's advice that he wait for spring. "We shall travel upon the frozen rivers," he said. "This insult cannot go unanswered for so many months. No Muscovite Czar will ever again pay tribute to the Mongol!" Ivan had been most decisive, and no amount of argument would dissuade him. Being too young to exercise any greater judgment than the Czar, I thoroughly agreed with his decision. In fact, I urged him to go. If he did not leave now, I said, he would have to wait until after the spring thaws, as the muddy roads would never permit transport of heavy supply wagons.

At this promise of military action, Heinrich finally came out of his seclusion and seemed to regain his former fire. I was eagerly preparing to accompany him, until fate dealt a tragic blow. I was in the practice yard, learning a new technique for handling a lance, when I fell off my horse – or rather was knocked off by my stepfather. In the tumble I broke an ankle, which resulted in my being left behind on this first of the Czar's campaigns of conquest.

Since none of the details are of much significance in my life, I am going to make only brief mention of the facts which are necessary to the understanding of my narrative. The Czar's army was successful in partially subduing the infidels, and he was able to reverse their arrogant demands, so that they once again paid tribute to Muscovy, instead of the reverse as had been demanded by the Khan's arrogant message. Of most significant moment in my life was the fact that the old Khan of Kazan, Saip Girei, had died shortly after sending his demand for tribute. His throne was promptly usurped by his kinsman Ulan Korshchak, a son of the Crimean Khan. But the old Khan had left an heir, his son, a little boy named Utemisch. He should rightfully have inherited the throne – and this created a situation very much like Ivan's own childhood, except that this little boy's cause did not prevail. As a result of our diplomatic efforts, however, he and his mother would eventually be granted safe passage into the Czar's protection, although they would technically be classified as "hostages." But this was still some time in the future. For the moment, the child remained in the citadel.

Andrei Adashev had been left to govern the Kazan district, setting up his headquarters in a new settlement called Svyazhsk, which soon grew into a city with a population to rival Kazan itself. It was situated at the estuary of the Svyaga River. Despite our Russian victory, there had also been a few unhappy incidents, including an accident when the ice on the Volga River broke, drowning a number of our men just beyond the island near Nizhny Novgorod where the Czar had set up his permanent camp. Then came an endless rain. Seeing much of this as the Lord's Will, Ivan began a long vigil of prayer immediately after returning to Moscow.

Still not properly defeated, the Tartars had been taught only a partial lesson. Even as they lined the battlements of Kazan, baring their backsides to our army, they had been frightened. Permitting a Russian town to be built less than half a day's ride from their citadel was certain proof of their weakness. Many tribes from the surrounding areas soon deserted the crescent banner of Islam, and swore fealty to the Czar. There were many Christian converts among these people, as most of them had been simple heathens, not even Mussulmen. In seeking the protection of the Christian Czar, they were also willing to accept his God. As everyone knew, a true Mussulman had already dedicated his soul to the devil. For them, redemption was especially hard, requiring extensive rites of purification before they could be properly baptized. Among those swearing loyalty to Ivan was Shig Ali, Khan of the Nogai Tartars.

For several months, Ivan insisted I remain with him. Both the Duma of Boyars and the Council of Bishops were to gather, at different times, to have the changes in secular and church law explained to them. The stripping away of boyar power had begun, and not without the expected grumbling. Among the loudest dissenters was Euphrosyne, who began making contact with other noble families, seeking to curb the reforms of the Czar. But Ivan was too fast for her. After a somewhat heated session with Vladya, he made it clear that Euphrosyne was to remain at Staritsa, with a large portion of her household guard comprised of the Czar's own men. While this arrangement was made to appear as an honor, a token of esteem by Ivan to his cousin, we all knew differently.

The new Khan of Kazan, of course, had only contrived his supposed surrender. In actuality, he was playing for time to gather sufficient strength to mount a proper defense. After our first great army had returned home, Ulan Korshchak arranged a series of clashes between our remaining forces and those of his subservient tribes. A clever conspirator, he carefully avoided any major affront or military challenge during the summer. Instead, he utilized this period of relative peace to arm himself, after which he planned to provoke the Czar into a final, great assault on the citadel.

During this respite between our two major campaigns, many captives were taken by either side. Most of the Russians seized by the infidels were not soldiers, but poor farmers and peasants who had braved the elements to cross the Volga and establish their meager homesteads in the virgin territories beyond. Our eastern settlements had greatly increased in recent years, much to the delight of the Tartar slave traders. These wretched parasites were overjoyed to find such a ready supply of fair Russian girls and boys to purvey in the great bazaars of the Turks. Eventually, the Tartar raids became so blatant they seriously annoyed the Czar and became a major factor in his decision to launch another attack. The threat of a Russian army descending upon them before they had time to complete their defenses caused serious political difficulties within the walls of Kazan. We made sure, of course, that rumors to this effect were circulated prior to our actions.

Political strife within the citadel continued to intensify, because many of their nobles had been unhappy with the decision to bring in a Crimean Tartar to rule them. Once Korshchak was installed, many more realized their error, for he was a cruel and ruthless man. He might still have succeeded in maintaining his rule, had he not cast lecherous eyes upon the beautiful young widow of the former Khan, the mother of the infant in whose name Korshchak ruled. The widow, Princess Suunbeka, wanted no part of this coarse, obese swine from the southern steppes. Through her subtle maneuverings, she was able to form a powerful coalition of dissenters, who planned to subdue Korshchak and his followers, bind them, and hand them over to us.

The Crimeans discovered their danger – not soon enough to reclaim control, but with sufficient time to escape. Korshchak and his party fled the city, planning to return south. But many of our soldiers had been posted into the area to fight the insurrectionist tribes. The group of exiles was quickly apprehended. They pretended to have been seeking a Russian war party, claiming they wanted to surrender. The subterfuge did them no good. They were quickly cast into chains and sent to Moscow, where the Czar placed them on public display in the Square of Executions. After being subjected to the customary indignities by the common people, they were beheaded.

Before doing away with the Tartars, the Czar had ordered them closely questioned in the chambers, after which we had a much clearer picture of the chaos existing in the home of our enemy. It was this knowledge, in addition to his mounting anger over the continued harassment of our garrisons and the slavers' raids on our settlements, that caused the Czar to lead another army against Kazan that winter.

For a while, it appeared I was going to miss this second campaign, as I had the first. On the eve of Ivan's departure, Heinrich was taken ill, suffering from a recurrence of the fever he had contracted on the previous sojourn. As I was to serve under my stepfather, I had to remain with his group until he was ready to travel. Although we feared for Heinrich's life during the first days after the Czar's departure, my stepfather recovered quickly enough that we were able to follow the others in less than a fortnight. I later wondered if the delay could have been God's Will, for it spared me what could have been the most embarrassing experience of my life. As it was, only Heinrich and his company bore witness to my humiliation.

Unencumbered by supply wagons, our small force made very good speed. The season of thaws had come early, so the roads were muddy and the ground was too wet for us to sleep comfortably in tents. As Heinrich was still recuperating from his fever, we planned to travel in stages that allowed our having a regular roof over our heads every night. One of the places we stayed was Nizhny Novgorod. We had all looked forward to stopping there, for it was a large city and offered many comforts not found in the smaller towns and villages. It was also capital of the territory belonging to the Obolenskis, ruled at this time by Ivan's vassal lord, Prince Peter Serebryanny–Obolenski. Prince Peter was a close kinsman of Basil's former master of the horse, Prince Ivan Obolenski, the same who had been the Grand Duchess Helena's ill–fated lover, the same whom some – Euphrosyne among them – would like to have believed my sire.

Our party reached Nizhny Novgorod just before dusk. We immediately made our way to the Obolenski *dacha*, where we requested shelter for the night. The Prince was most gracious, personally greeting us at the portal and escorting us inside. His house was large, but very old and even gloomier than the boyars' *dachas* in the capitol. The stone walls sweated from outside moisture, and the clammy air had a musty smell, reminiscent of a dungeon. Nevertheless, we were grateful for the warmth and for our host's apparent pleasure at our company.

Prince Peter did all he could to make us feel at home, and after a very fine meal he had some *skomorokhi* brought in for our entertainment. These were jugglers, who danced and sang, and performed feats of magic. There were a great many such entertainers on the road during those days, as there seemed a heavy demand for their skills. Large numbers of men, crowded together in their winter camps, were constantly in need of diversion—a good thing, too, I supposed, that these people were available. The situation in Svyazhsk had become so scandalous before the Czar returned to the field, that the Metropolitan had sent the priest Timothy, with a stern injunction against their immorality.

After the entertainment and a good many tankards of wine, we were about to retire when an old man, seated near the far end of the table – an elderly uncle of the Prince, I believe – suddenly spoke up. He had been watching me intently, between his periods of dozing, and once or twice his sharp stare had made me uncomfortable. Taking his behavior as no more than some peculiarity of the aged, I had avoided looking at him. Now, half rising from his chair, the old man pointed a gnarled finger in my direction. "Damned if he's not the spitting image of Ivan," he croaked.

At first I thought he meant the Czar, which was a strange comparison, for we looked nothing alike. Then, with a flush of embarrassment, I realized he meant the regent's lover, Prince Ivan Ovchina–Telepnef–Obolenski. I am sure my face must have burned crimson red; Heinrich told me later it did. Our host coughed uncomfortably, and rose to toast the Czar.

But the old man was not to be put off so easily. "Looks enough like your cousin to be his brother, Peter," he piped again.

I was greatly relieved when a young man seated near the oldster got up and escorted him to bed. But that night I pondered again the chronic annoyance of my life. Who was I? And finally I concluded, more firmly than I ever had before, that it mattered very little. To the Czar I was more than a brother; I was his friend. The opinion of others could not deprive me of that – birthright or no.

Three days before we arrived in Svyazhsk, the Czar had launched the single, heavy attack of the campaign. Catching the defenders off guard, our army killed at least a thousand Tartars, losing hardly a man itself. Immediately, the Kazanites sued for peace. When I reported to the Czar, he had just finished an interview with the infidel delegation, and he seemed amused at their credulity. We were in the strange position of having our enemy with its back against the wall, but lacking the requisite number of men to assure its total defeat. They were unaware of this, but would soon have discovered the truth if we had tried to press our military advantage.

On the advice of his councilors, Adashev in particular, Ivan had made more than the expected demands for tribute, also insisting the infant Khan and Suunbeka be delivered into our hands as hostages. No one believed the Tartars would agree, and Andrei's idea had been to use their refusal as an excuse to demand further military concessions. He wanted them to surrender sovereignty over certain lands east of the Volga River. Much to our surprise, the Tartars accepted Ivan's terms, both in regard to tribute and the surrender of Utemish and his mother.

I had heard many stories of Suunbeka's beauty, and with no immediate prospect for military action, I cajoled the Czar into giving me command of the party which was to escort the infant Khan to Moscow. Svyazhsk was only partially built at this time. The only military duties we had were routine patrols around the wall and environs of Kazan. The Czar was already making plans to depart, and all my friends except Adashev would be returning with him., or so I reasoned. In truth, the trip offered the prospect of command, which I could not otherwise obtain. I might justify my ambition by reference to the immortal Caesar: . . .*better first in a little Iberian village. . . .*

I was not, of course, departing Svyazhsk the day I arrived. It was August before the young widow and her son were sent to us. They left Kazan in an elegant gilded barge, launched from the far side of the city. As they moved toward the confluence of the Kazan River and the Volga, they traveled directly under the towering mud and timber walls, where thousands of infidels watched from the battlements. I was in a smaller boat, awaiting their arrival on the waters of the Volga.

The poor princess had been so terrified when told of her required sacrifice, she had cast herself upon her husband's grave and had sworn she envied him his peace. As her barge was rowed beneath the city walls, she huddled silently against the silken cushions, hardly noticing the crowds above her. She must have heard so many tales of the evil Russians, I am sure she expected me to have horns and a pointed tail when I came on board to offer the Czar's greetings and protection. But Suunbeka was both noble and brave. Clasping her child tightly to her bosom, she returned my complimentary salutations and exchanged the proper rituals. We transferred her Tartar guards to another boat, sending them back to Kazan and substituting *Streltsi*. Because the Czar had been anxious to depart for home, and would take the speedier overland route, he planned to receive his ward in Moscow. We therefore had no reason to land at Svyazhsk, which, as I have noted, was little more than a rough army camp at the time. My orders were to convey the princess by water, upstream, all the way to the capital. Thus, we traveled the wide expanse of the Volga to its junction with the Oka, and followed this to the Moskva River, stopping only at major cities along our way. By the time we reached Moscow, I was desperately in love for the second time in my life.

It is difficult to place the exact moment when I experienced the first pulse of desire, for everything happened quickly once the initial crack appeared in the wall of reserve between us. Suunbeka and her women were quartered on the upper deck, near the stern. In addition to the wooden superstructure, which was solidly built and provided protection against any inclement weather, there were several silken pavilions, all furnished in the elegant manner of the infidels. The princess remained within the largest of these enclosures during the first two or three days, seldom venturing outside the wall of gossamer draperies. I had restricted all of my men to the lower decks, with the exception of the *bulsha dwoaney* (Sergeant Major – literally "chief horseman"), the boat captain and, of course, myself.

I spent most of this initial period on the forward end of the upper deck, pretending not to look, but constantly fascinated by the shadowy movement inside the pavilions. The impasse might have continued to the end of our voyage, had little Utemish not been quite the problem he was for his mother. A very spoiled child, he took every opportunity to toddle onto the open deck. Usually, one of the women would see him and immediately fetch him back. If no one noticed his absence, he would deliberately flop onto the boards and start to howl, thus attracting the attention of several attendants who would promptly rush out to get him. One afternoon, however, he managed to slip away without being seen and started making his way toward me. This happened just at a time when the oarsmen were being shifted, and the barge lurched unexpectedly. Utemish toppled over the edge and into the water. I had already been moving toward him, so I had my hands on him while we were both still falling.

It was not a spectacular, nor an especially heroic rescue. The barge was barely moving, and the men hauled us aboard within seconds. I carried the child back to his mother, who awaited us on the upper deck. She had dashed out on the spur of fear, without thinking to cover her face or head with the usual veils and other wrappings. I had never seen quite so lovely a woman before. Nor, in truth, had I ever glimpsed a woman of noble birth in such an abbreviated costume – except for Anna, who could not have inflamed a man had she paraded herself stark naked in the bazaar. We stood facing one another for several heartbeats, the wet, wriggling child still in my arms. Suunbeka's dark brown eyes gazed deeply into mine, held as if some greater power enjoined us.

Perhaps I should not describe the subsequent events, and I would not if my words could still cause her injury. But Suunbeka is long since beyond the reach of human cruelty, and the hours I spent with her served to open my soul. I was exposed for the first time to the genuine blending of spiritual and physical love. Her body was an instrument, trained from its earliest moments to the pleasure of men. Its surface was a fragile smoothness, a warm and pliable velvet, scented with sandlewood. In the warm light of the lanterns, she glowed a deep hued rose, highlighted here and there by the moisture of my kisses. The darker tips of her breasts pointed proudly upward, above her firmly rounded flesh.

She had asked me to dine with her that same night, and afterward everything seemed to happen as if it were the most natural, unquestioned sequence. We lay together in the airy pavilion, her skin seeming to pucker at every pore. Warm summer breezes caressed our bodies, and her passion – so powerful and overwhelming at its height – seemed to hover in subtle restraint, tantalizing, like her perfume. Her every motion was a graceful act of beauty. She never hurried, nor did she make any outward sign to demand that I control my desire to reach the final, cascading moment of ecstatic attainment. Only by her own skillful actions did she cause me to pace my excitement in tempo with her own, and during the final moments I realized how little I had ever experienced before. She drew out the time, allowing me, almost forcing me to savor every delicious moment, every tiny element of sensual pleasure, until the final climax became like a goal long sought, its attainment achieved only after a lengthy, incomparably satisfying quest.

Every night I came to her, and during the day I prayed for the sun to speed along its course, hoping it might sink quickly into the rippling water before our bow. Suunbeka's women knew what passed between us, and I am certain my men suspected. But my own desire was so great, I hardly gave it a thought. Other than assuring they all remained on the lower deck at night, I took few precautions to guard against their knowing.

As the voyage drew near its end, I experienced a miserable dread, knowing we would be separated as soon as we entered the city. We had acquired enough common words by then to discuss our mutual desires, and with my love's permission I decided to ask the Czar for Suunbeka's hand as soon as the time seemed ripe. I knew I could not do this immediately, for the capital was full of Tartars and other barbarians who had sworn allegiance to Ivan. These newly attracted allies must not suspect, nor must the church – Sylvester particularly. I spoke to my *bulsha dwoaney* and threatened him with certain vengeance if any rumors should circulate about an improper relationship between the Princess and myself. He understood, and as best I knew, his men kept their counsel. The next day, our barge arrived at the river wharves of Moscow.

Ivor led a guard of honor at the pier, and John Mikhailof, Ivan's secretary, received the Princess. I conferred with him a few moments, long enough to learn most of the current news, and to receive an invitation to dine with the Czar that evening. Then Suunbeka appeared, heavily draped in veils and a velvet wrapper. One of her women carried the child. She stepped daintily into the waiting carriage, followed by her attendants. They were immediately whisked away to the palace *terem*, where – I thought with sinking heart – Suunbeka would soon be in Anastasia's company. I supervised the unloading of my men and their arms, following the route to the palace a few moments later. My anxiety was somewhat lessened when it occurred to me that the Czarina would only be able to converse with Suunbeka through an interpreter.

My heart was so preoccupied with thoughts of love, I hardly heard the greetings of my stepfather and my other friends. I wanted to shout the joyful tidings to them all, and yet I dared say nothing to anyone. The servants unpacked my bags, and I bathed leisurely before dinner, taking those solitary moments to plan how best I might approach the Czar. I could not allow him to suspect I had already tasted this forbidden fruit before obtaining his permission to pluck it.

The bath revived me, and I was looking forward to dinner. Realizing I was hungry brought me back to a proper awareness. I entered the hall, ready to drink and exchange stories with my friends, anticipating the rich foods and liquors, and anxious to see Ivan again. I sat with Vladya and Yuri, both of whom were questioning my trip, making veiled suggestions of how I must have enjoyed myself. I am certain neither suspected my having actually savored the pleasurable delights they were joking about. Several others joined in, chiding me, laughing at my feigned embarrassment. I laughed with them, and drank heavily of the wines.

When Ivan finally arrived, we all rose to bow and greet him. He came in with several Tartars, among whom was a great, fat lout of a man, whom I recognized as Shig Ali, the newly converted Khan of the Nogai tribes. He remained close to the Czar, who was obviously courting him, for Shig Ali was a powerful ally. His desertion of Islam had created a serious rift in the ranks of the infidels, and a large number of men had come over with him.

Before dinner was served, the Czar hammered the table to silence us and rose to make an announcement. It was his great honor, he said, to inform us of his decision to "reward his faithful vassal lord, Shig Ali, with the fairest plum of his native land." This very day there had arrived in the Kremlin the beautiful, widowed Queen of Kazan, a princess renowned for her beauty, no less than her virtue. As he spoke, my heart pounded in that terrible fearsome dread one experiences when he learns a loved one is about to die. I sat in an unreal world, as all about me became shades and shadows, fixtures in some distant chamber. I was alone, facing my friend, the Czar, who was in the process of cutting out my living heart. I wanted to scream at him to stop, or maybe to rush from the room and storm the *terem*, carrying my princess away before I heard the final words and became bound by them.

When he finished I stared vacantly ahead, as voices started up around me and curious faces turned in my direction. Someone was speaking to me, but I could not perceive the words. Almost violently, Vladya squeezed my arm, while Yuri stamped his heel against my foot. It was the Czar who had spoken, and his words slowly began to filter through the hazy confusion of forms and sounds. My head felt weightless, and I think I was about to swoon. Then I felt firm hands on both my arms, as Vladimir and Yuri each jumped up to hold me. Somehow I had gotten to my feet, though I do not remember doing it.

"Dmitri, are you all right?" asked Yuri.

"Come, sit down," Vladya urged. "He was all right a moment ago," he added, speaking to the Czar.

Slowly, absently, I slid into my chair, my hands grasping idly for the arms. Ivan, now seriously worried, stepped around the others and came to me.

"Dmitri, what's wrong with you?" he demanded.

"I must have . . . picked up a touch of fever," I said, recovering some presence of mind. "It seemed to start on the way back. I'll be all right in a moment," I added, turning my head to look up at him, trying to manage a smile. "Thank you – I'm – all right."

But again my world had been crushed. For a second time, the object of my heart's desire was taken from me and given to another man – and such a repulsive excuse for a man. There was no more ugly, no more ill–mannered swine in all of Muscovy than Shig Ali! Yet there was nothing I could do. The wedding took place two months later, without my ever seeing Suunbeka again. I might have arranged a clandestine meeting, and I almost gave in to my desire several times. But to what effect? I could never have her, unless I were willing to betray the Czar and carry her into some foreign land.

Instead, I tormented myself by imagining how that lovely, dainty princess must have felt, lying on her wedding couch, awaiting Shig Ali's sweaty embraces. Great as my own torment, I knew it could never compare to hers. Nor could I feel any anger toward Ivan, for he had no way of knowing, and once having expressed his wishes it would have been impossible to change his mind. I was fully aware of the political implications. He might have achieved the same ends without this marriage; but now the situation was hopeless. While I never discussed my feelings with the Czar, I did pour out my heart to Yuri.

Since his marriage to Ulyana, there had been a noticeable development in this younger prince. Always very slow and hesitating in his thoughts, he still tried his best to fulfill his role of councilor. At this time, he was staying at his country *dacha*, not far from the Czar's own summer palace at Ostrovka. I spent a few days with him after Suunbeka's wedding, for I needed to get away from the city. I reasoned that had there been a God, with a heart both pure and good, such a God could not have caused me this pain for a second time. I dared not mention to Yuri how I equated my loss as further proof of God's failure, though this was exactly how I felt.

Unlike wives in most homes, Ulyana was not closely restricted, and Yuri's intimate friends had a chance to meet her. This was partially because the prince never entertained great numbers of people. He was generally present when the Czar gave his banquets, and had his fill of large groups on these occasions. Most visitors to the *dacha* were men as myself, people who had grown up with Yuri, and toward whom he extended an affectionate, warm informality. When I arrived, I was shown to Yuri's personal chambers, where Ulyana sat in the background, sewing. At first, her presence – although I had experienced it before – inhibited my speech. But Yuri hastened to reassure me.

"You know what my life has always been, Dmitri," he said. "I lack the Czar's great wit, and I can't speak with the ease of a courtier. My dear Ulyana is my secret support. She can see into a man's heart as I have never been able to do."

"Then, in my heart, she's going to find a very sad and heavy burden," I replied.

"I think I already know of this burden," she said softly, not moving her eyes from the needle.

"You know – what?" I asked, perplexed.

She nodded, as Yuri watched us in seeming bewilderment. "What are you talking about?" He smiled, although our apparent understanding disturbed him.

"Dmitri wanted to wed Suunbeka," she said simply. "Their love has been the subject of women's gossip for months," she added by way of explanation. From her significant glance, I took it she was telling me that Anastasia knew, as well.

I regarded her closely, surprised, for I had no idea our secret was such common knowledge. If the women knew, surely many men did as well.

"The Czar –?" I asked.

She shrugged. "This I can't say," she replied reflectively. "The Czarina has surely heard the wagging tongues of others, and may have spoken about the Princess, herself. The girl was so heartbroken, it made all of us wonder, before we learned the truth. Of course, having to marry Shig Ali! Ugh!" She shuddered.

I must have blushed, because Ulyana quickly added, "But, as I said before, I do not know what words passed between the Czarina and Suunbeka."

I shrugged, spreading my palms and dropping down hard into a nearby chair. "Not only have I lost her, my plight has become the joke of every female in Moscow," I sighed.

Ulyana smiled mysteriously, as if to herself. "It is said that the blood of great lovers flows in your veins, Dmitri," she remarked softly. "I think it will not be too long before your heart finds a suitable substitute."

By this time my face must have been a bright scarlet, for even Yuri took notice. "You need a drink, my friend," he said. "You look about to burst."

There was a little ripple of laughter from Ulyana, now fast at work on her cloth. Yuri, probably not understanding why, responded with a giggle of his own. "No one can fall in love around the Kremlin without my wife knowing all about it," he said, handing me a goblet. "But seriously, why don't you get the Czar to find you a nice girl and get married to her. Anna's been declared officially dead, and, well, you can't appreciate the advantages of marriage until you actually live it." He looked at Ulyana, whose turn it was to blush.

Somewhat recovered, I began to return his banter. "Your own experience hasn't been as frightening as you'd thought, then?"

Yuri squirmed uncomfortably, especially as my words brought another tinkle of laughter from Ulyana.

"Was he really afraid of me?" she teased.

"I was never scared of marriage," Yuri blustered. "It was just – that the idea took a little time to work its way in – er, well – you know, I was very young."

Ulyana came up behind Yuri's chair, stroking his cheek with the back of her hand. "But you have been a marvelous husband. Although you *were* very young," she chided.

They were so wonderfully happy together, it made me wonder if I should approach the Czar and request another wife. But their relationship was far from typical. "Unfortunately, the fairest blooms have already been picked," I commented.

The tone of my words, and the compliment I meant to pay his wife, were lost on Yuri. "You know," he said, "I've never had to beat her?"

Despite the openness of my conversation with Yuri, I hesitated to discuss my feelings with anyone else. I finally did tell Vladya one evening, when we had been carousing the outer city and were both too drunk to care what we said. He answered with a vulgar remark about women being all the same in certain respects, and I almost poked him. But in the morning he had forgotten. Maybe because I had to hold so much within myself, or perhaps because I had actually possessed her, it took me longer to get over my passion for Suunbeka than it had for Anastasia. I was irritable and difficult with everyone. In cavalry drill I was overbearing with my subordinates, and I antagonized the other junior officers. I had a terrible row with Heinrich, which ended with our not speaking for several days. Eventually, even Ivan noticed my ill temper. Thinking it some residual effect of my illness, he arranged for me to visit with Vladimir, who had since returned to Staritsa. He did this without consulting me, and the first I knew about it I was, in effect, ordered to go.

I did not wish to offend Vladya by protesting, but I really had no desire to stay under the same roof with his mother. Of all the people in the world, I think she was the only one I really feared. But Ivan may have had more in mind than a simple trip to the country for my health. I still owned the farming estate I had received as part of Anna's dowry, and while I had never seen it, I knew it had a large comfortable house. I could easily have gone there instead. As it was, I left the Kremlin, wondering if I would live to see it again. That was near the end of September.

I need not have feared Euphrosyne, at least not this time. She tried to be cordial, and went out of her way to please Vladya. I was sure she had been lonely without him, and did not wish to drive him away. Even so, she was moody and frequently cold toward everyone, including her son. Still, with all this, she was not nearly as unpleasant as I had feared. She may also have suspected the Czar's motives in sending me. As it happened, I noticed nothing greatly amiss, although she had gradually managed to eliminate most of Ivan's men from the Staritsa household. I was certain her own men comprised nearly the entire current contingent of guards. Looking back, I have wondered if Ivan might have been going through one of his periodic spells, suspecting his cousin of evil thoughts. If so, Euphrosyne's handling of the guard situation could have contributed to his suspicions.

I stayed at Staritsa for a long time, much longer than I had intended. Vladya and I made several trips together, going north in the early winter to hunt bear and elk. We returned for the holy days, but later traveled the frozen rivers, leaving just after Epiphany. We fished the southern tributaries of the Dvina, and tried our hands at trapping ermine for their winter pelts. Euphrosyne threw a terrible tantrum when we left on the latter adventure, raving that she saw no reason for her son to brave the winter's cold for the sake of a few skins he could easily afford to buy. The huge collection we brought back, however, made her eyes bulge.We gave most of them to her, and she had an exquisite coat fashioned for herself – with enough pelts left over to make a fine *barma*, which Vladya wore for years afterward.

Soon after our return from the north, when the early spring colors were beginning to break through the frozen white of winter, a messenger in imperial livery drew rein in the courtyard outside Vladya's *dacha*. The warm, midday sun was just past its zenith, and the melancholy songs of peasants, working in the nearby woods, had started up again after their noontime rest. Vladya and I had been in the meadow, experimenting with a newly repaired matchlock rifle which my stepfather had sent. We were on our way back when we saw the white uniformed figure fly into the front courtyard at full gallop. We spurred our own horses to greater speed, and arrived before the fellow had fully dismounted.

"Sirs!" He bowed. "I have messages for Prince Vladimir Andreyevitch and for Lord Dmitri Marensky." He bowed again and turned to fumble in his saddlebags. The packet of papers he handed to me was sealed with Ivan's personal impression. I recognized the small chip over one of the heads on the Imperial Eagle, made when Ivan had angrily hurled the block at a servant. My note was brief, but it was written in Ivan's own hand.

"To Our Friend and Servant, Dmitri Simeonevitch," it read, "from Ivan, Autocrat of all Rus, Greetings. Know you that it is Our intention, before the new moon has waned, to lead a final expedition to gather in Our lands of the East, namely those held in vassalage by the infidel Tartar, Ediger, and his renegade brothers of the Nogai Tartars; most especially the City of Kazan, rightfully a part of Our Empire.

"It is Our further pleasure to request and demand your presence at Our side during the course of this adventure. You are commanded to come before Us at the soonest possible moment, that you may participate in the plans and preparations for this great undertaking. I."

Vladimir's letter was longer and more formal, written by another hand – probably Mikhailof, the Czar's secretary. It contained the standard request for a vassal lord to supply his quota of men–at–arms for the projected conflict. After reading our own messages, we exchanged papers and noted what the other had received. The contents were not unexpected, as Andrew Kurbsky had stopped by to tell us of the preparations almost a month before. He had been in Moscow since that time, supervising the efforts of the foreign craftsmen. Ivan had sent for a number of these men, to teach our people how to cast the huge bronze cannon he would need for his assault on the Tartar stronghold.

"It seems you are the Czar's favored, this time," said Vladya. His tone was purposely light, but I knew he was unhappy. Try as he would, this distance would always remain between himself and the Czar. He made no immediate comment, but I was sure many thoughts crossed his mind. Euphrosyne came outside, and Vladya absently handed her the two papers, which she read before saying anything to either of us. Her face reflected displeasure as she read her son's letter; anger when her gaze fell on mine. Without a word, she let the papers fall to the ground and went back inside.

I decided it best to leave at once and Vladimir rode out with me, escorting me beyond the edge of Staritsky land. He would be along in a few days, he said, as soon as he was able to get his peasants armed and arrange to have the harvest brought in that autumn. Extra fields had been cleared for the spring planting, and I knew Vladya was concerned lest the crops rot on the ground. The large levy he was required to produce would leave the estate short handed.

Ivan's messenger had left with us, staying a respectful distance behind. I waved him up, and took my leave of Vladya. Poorly as my visit had ended, the months I had spent with my friend had been an extremely pleasant interval, and I sincerely thanked him for it. We parted, each anxious for the great adventure now lying ahead of us. This would be the Czar's third attempt to subdue the infidels, and we knew it would be a battle worth describing to one's grandchildren.

CHAPTER V

I arrived in Moscow, dog tired after a full day's hard ride, to find the place a mass of bustling activity. Soldiers and boyars, princes and fortune seekers had flocked in from all over the empire, and beyond. The prospect of war, with its opportunities for bloodletting and plunder, has always attracted adventurers. Proclamations of the Czar's impending assault on Kazan had been carried far into the lands of Livonia and Lithuania well before Vladya and I had been summoned.

With the men had come the inevitable flocks of women: wives, mistresses and campfollowers. Several bands of nomads from the southern parts of Lithuania and Hungary, as well as every troop of wandering players, minstrels, and *skomorokhi* had converged on the city, further glutting the crowds. Because the courier and I arrived at dusk, we encountered the mobs at their worst and had to thread our horses through throngs of shouting, excited peasants, many of them seeing Moscow for the first time. Even the white uniform of my royal guardsman did little to speed our progress, as I suppose most of the visitors had no idea of the livery's significance. Cook fires glowed in many open squares and in nearly every bazaar. Sharp–nosed traders from the eastern steppes hawked their wares to the crowds, as they milled about in the narrow lanes between the clustered houses and shacks of the Arbat. Black– robed priests were everywhere. It seemed each abbey and monastery had sent its share of Godly men to care for the souls who were soon to ride forth on this boldest crusade against the infidel.

Tired as I was, the noise and delay were anything but pleasant. I wanted only to reach the Kremlin, and to sit on something softer than my jouncing saddle. My mouth fairly watered for some of the Czar's good wine. Adding further to the unpleasantness of our slow progress, the great numbers of people crowded into the narrow confines had increased the usual, sour, musty odors of the outer city to a staggering proportion. When we finally reached the Square of Executions and broke free of the press, I spurred my horse to a gallop, anxious to get inside the protective walls of the old fortress. I was almost thrown from my saddle by the unexpected appearance of guards, barring our way across the drawbridge.

I should have expected the gates to be watched more closely than usual, due to the large influx of curious country folks who might otherwise have flooded into the restricted confines. My greatest surprise was that none of the guards seemed to know me. Had I really been gone that long? Before I was put to the task of identifying myself, Ivan's messenger caught up with me. He spoke to the gatekeeper, who informed me that His Majesty requested my presence immediately upon my arrival.

Thinking it must be something urgent, I went directly to Ivan's apartments, without pausing to wash the road dust from my face and hands. But the Czar wanted nothing more than my report on conditions at Staritsa. Was Vladya to be trusted or not, he asked. What of his guards? Was he trying to form a personal army to threaten the throne? Was I aware of the messages being sent by Euphrosyne to other princes?

I did my best to reassure him, describing what I had seen, and laying all the blame I could at Euphrosyne's feet. I knew Vladya had no ambition to be Czar, and had never made any move to obtain the throne. Ivan should have realized this, I thought, although *Maultasch* made it seem otherwise. It was understandably difficult to believe that a woman could be this active in the affairs of men, and could stir up so much controversy without her son being involved. Ivan showed me some intercepted correspondence, both to and from Staritsa. None of it was in Vladya's hand, I noted. Euphrosyne must have sent or received these things while he and I were away on our hunting trips. I stated my feelings as strongly as I could, and apparently answered the necessary questions. When I left the Czar, he seemed convinced of his cousin's loyalty, and subsequently included Vladya in his personal entourage. Had he really feared some treachery, I was sure he would not have permitted this easy access to his person. For the moment, at least, Vladya had been returned to Ivan's good graces.

We were all kept busy for several more weeks, before the Czar's powerful army was finally ready to leave. On the morning of our scheduled departure a great crowd of warriors gathered in the meadows beyond the city walls. The lesser officers and junior commanders, each with a few dozen men, were crowded into the Square of Executions. The greater commanders – the princes, boyars, and other nobles – were assembled inside the Kremlin, waiting for the Czar in front of the Cathedral. Heinrich and I were with this group. The feverish excitement continued to mount, as men and boys roistered in anticipation of their impending adventure. Several landholders stood within the cluster of their own levies, joking and making wagers with other groups over the number of infidel heads they would take, or who would be the first over the walls of Kazan.

In addition to the *Streltsi*, in their special red–brown tunics, hundreds of arquebusiers, archers, and pikemen streamed into the meadows, where officers organized them into squadrons. Selected groups were led back into the city, further swelling the ranks of the Square. Most of these last minute maneuverings were at the instigation of the Kremlin clerks, who had been instructed to arrange a grand pageant for their departing warrior–Czar.

At last Ivan came out of the Cathedral and stood on the steps, as the Czarina appeared behind him. She was dressed all in white, except for the cloth of gold shawl about her head and shoulders. It had been rumored that she was *enceinte*, but there had been false rumors to this effect before, and as yet there had been no official announcement. In a public display of devotion, she encircled Ivan with her arms and kissed him, speaking formalized words of encouragement, asking God to send him home victorious and in good health.

We expected that Ivan would appoint Anastasia his regent, as he had before. Instead, he informed us that Yuri would act for him during his absence. He made no explanation for his decision, other than to take the heavy golden chain from about his neck and place it upon his wife's. I glanced at Vladya, for these were the keys to the prisons and the Czar's act evoked a thunderous cheer from the crowd. It was customary for most prisoners to be granted amnesty upon the birth of an heir to the throne. For Anastasia to be given the keys implied confirmation of the rumors.

The Czar spoke a few more words from the Cathedral steps, before commanding us to follow him into the Square of Executions. He was an inspiring sight as he galloped out the Kremlin gates, radiant in deep hued velvet robes, trimmed with the finest white furs. His silky red beard was fuller and longer than I had ever remembered seeing it. On his head he wore the steel helmet of a warrior, with a golden circle to denote his rank. Behind him rode the household guard, resplendent in newly designed white uniforms, mounted on milk–white horses. Ivan's huge black stallion reared magnificently before he cantered into the midst of his army. The men crowded forward, close about the Czar as he dismounted and climbed onto the *lobonoyo mesto*.

Almost unnoticed, the Metropolitan and his retinue of black–robed parish priests had followed the royal party. Makari rode a plodding gray gelding; but the *khorugvi*, the other monks were on foot, swinging pots of steaming incense or holding aloft their long poles topped with banners and holy images. Ivan waited until the priests were in place, encircling the dais below him. He raised his hands to silence the men, and following another roar of approbation the crowd finally became still. I noticed Anastasia had mounted the Kremlin wall above us, where she stood silently upon the ramparts to hear her husband's speech. She was on almost the exact spot where Euphrosyne had been to watch Feodor's execution.

Vladya and I remained mounted, crammed within the small group of officers which included Heinrich and Andrew Kurbsky. As we waited for the Czar to begin, the priests completed the final lines of the victory prayer they had chanted as they marched out. Now that Ivan had silenced the crowd, we could hear the words for the first time. The Czar permitted them to finish without any sign of impatience, as townspeople began to press upon us from all sides. We were assailed by the pungent scent of incense, mingled with the odors of the crowd – half human, half horse – like the centaurs of antiquity.

Finally, the Czar began to speak. "We depart this day," he shouted, "for the final conquest of Our enemies to the East, the infidel usurpers in Our City of Kazan." He paused for the prolonged cheer. "We leave in Our place, to oversee the welfare of Our people and Our realm, the hand of Our Most Beloved Brother, Yuri Basilevitch . . . and as his counselor and visor, as he had always been to Us, Our True Friend and Servant, Andrei Adashev."

Vladya snorted. "Why doesn't he just announce that Anastasia's about to whelp, instead of going through all this nonsense?" he mumbled.

I pretended not to hear, and hoped that none of the others had. Knowing Vladya as I did, I was certain he merely reflected his mother's evil influence, an effect which I hoped our time away from her on campaign would help to dull.

Yuri mounted the platform to stand beside his brother, and Andrei came up after him. I had not noticed either of them before. Yuri's eyes met mine almost immediately, and he grinned, very quickly, before turning to Ivan. The Czar handed him the scroll of authority and several other small items to symbolize his temporary office. Because Yuri disliked addressing the people, his speech was short and difficult to hear.

After the Prince, it came Makari's turn, but the religious observance was fairly short, and I was grateful that Ivan had not ordered a full mass in the Square. After a few more words to Yuri and Adashev, the Czar strode purposefully down the stairs and mounted his stallion, being immediately surrounded by the snowy uniforms of his guards. We followed them as they galloped out of the inner city, through the Bielgorod, turning onto the eastern highway as we left the Arbat gates.

Our huge army was soon strung out behind the Czar. The retinue was so enormous, the stragglers at the rear would sometimes camp in the same spot where the Czar had been the night before. We followed the trails to the Oka, and later paralleled the Volga. We passed through Kolomna, Riazan, Kasimov, Murmon – all the same cities where I had stopped with Suunbeka. The shimmering waters could not fail to awaken my recent recollections, and several times I seemed to detect a faint trace of sandlewood.

At least I was spared having to see Shig Ali's corpulent features when I dined with the Czar each night. He had gone ahead with a party of arquebusiers, under command of Prince Peter Bulgakov. They had been ordered to escort a party of bridge builders, in keeping with Ivan's overall scheme. Shig Ali's selection as a member of the advance party had been quite purposeful, as he was instructed to enter Kazan and try to arrange a treaty. His offer would be the infidels' last chance to avoid the devastation our army was sure to bring upon them.

Instead of following his instructions, Shig Ali thoroughly disgraced himself and greatly embarrassed the Czar. In his role of ambassador, he arranged a feast for many of the leading Kazanite nobles – the group including most of the leaders who might have been willing to treat with us. While they were seated at the table, he had them set upon and strangled, all this done in Ivan's name, thus destroying any possibility of negotiated peace. Had it not been for the number of men at Shig Ali's command, I think the Czar would have punished him severely. We learned of this perfidity four or five days after it happened, when the army was a little over halfway to Kazan. Ivan thought it expedient to keep Shig Ali away from his other officers until time dulled the memory of his deed. From a personal standpoint, no decision of the Czar ever pleased me more!

Because the weather was warm and mild, Ivan generally ordered his camp set up in the open, rather than staying in the small towns. Provincial *dachas* were never much to his liking, and Ivan differed from my stepfather in his attitude toward sleeping in a tent. As the Czar seldom had occasion to do so, it was a pleasant novelty for him. To soldiers who must endure the discomforts of foul weather inside a cold, flapping, leaky house of cloth, the prospect understandably tended to lose its appeal. I remember one night in particular, when we camped in the forest of Sakan, near the beginning of our journey. This was before the long days of marching began to tire the men who had to travel on foot. It was a beautiful evening, with a bright moon and stars shimmering in silvery brilliance upon the velvet blackness of heaven. My tent, which I shared with Heinrich, was close to the Czar's pavilion, and Vladimir's was directly across the open area which formed the main street of our camp. We were on a small knoll, overlooking the bulk of the army, spread for miles along the river bank. Hundreds of cook fires reflected in the rippling waters, while the heady aromas of bubbling stews and roasting meat drifted up to us, almost obliterating the musky, marshy smell of the river.

After dinner, we lolled about inside Ivan's pavilion, the sides of which had been rolled up to allow passage of the sweet, evening breeze. Below us, the men began to sing their wonderful peasant songs, their voices floating in lazy waves through the heavy moist air. Ivan lay half asleep on his couch, listening silently, mind and soul strangely at peace on this eve of his monumental campaign. The omens were good, and everyone expected this third attempt to be successful.

The army continued to swell as it moved eastward. The Princes of Kasimov and Temnikov joined us when we passed through their fiefs, each bringing a large retinue. Farmers and small landholders, seeing our column from their fields, dropped their plows and fell into the line of marching men. By July we reached Murmon, where we were joined by several infidel tribes, all wishing to add their strength to the army of the Christian Czar. Among these were Cheremisians and a few Don Cossacks from areas south of Kazan. By the middle of August we reached Svyazhsk, where our army was enlarged by the garrison detachments, to form the most powerful force ever to face the Mussulman usurpers within the mud and timber ramparts of the Tartar stronghold.

Svyazhsk had changed greatly since I had last seen it. The Czar's orders had been fully carried out, sometimes even exceeded. The town was no longer a rough army camp, comprising only crude cabins and pens for horses and other livestock. Now there were houses and churches, and large busy bazaars with stocks to rival the capital's *gostiny dvor*. Heinrich had established a thriving post here. As soon as we were free to leave the Czar, my stepfather and I settled our gear in the house where we were to lodge, and Heinrich took me to meet Abraham, his local representative.

This Abraham, a Jew from the western provinces, had been in Heinrich's service for many years. I remembered seeing him when I was a child, although Mother had detested him and had made quite a scene when Heinrich had insisted on bringing him to our home. At the time, Abraham had been on his way from Novgorod to Murmon, where he was to meet a caravan from the Crimea. I believe the incident had taken place during a period when Jews were held in special contempt because of their refusal to accept Christ as the Son of God and the Savior of mankind. Even at the time of which I speak, there were few of their race in the western areas of Russia, as the Czar was afraid they would contaminate his Christian peoples.

In Svyazhsk, old Abraham had established a very successful branch for my stepfather, including one of the busiest shops in the bazaar. Because of his need to maintain proper dignity as a soldier, Heinrich's ownership of the business was not generally known. This, I thought, was a notion properly relegated to the past. Even the noblest families, including the Czar himself, were actively engaged in trade. Ivan already maintained monopoly over certain commodities, and had made their sale the exclusive prerogative of the crown.

Pushing our way forward, we soon saw the familiar sign of the black, crowing cock on the banner above our shop. When we entered several of Abraham's assistants were busily trying to outshout their customers, haggling over the price of fodder and tent cloth, and the dozens of other items offered for sale. Strange, the thoughts that come to one at various times; but as I sat in the back of the stall, sipping tea with the nearsighted old Jew, the odor of sandlewood incense from the shop next door made me think of Suunbeka. In fact, for the rest of my life, I was never able to smell that particular scent without its having the same effect upon me. Later, when Heinrich and Abraham had fairly well completed their business, it suddenly occurred to me that Abraham had come to Moscow with his son – a lad about my age. I think I surprised him by my sudden question.

"You have a son, have you not?" I asked. "Jacob? Isn't that his name?"

The old man stopped speaking, and I noticed a look of consternation on Heinrich's face. Abraham peered sharply into my eyes, and for a moment he seemed almost angry. Finding no malice in my query, his face returned to its former unemotional mask, although the wrinkles seemed a little deeper and the flesh may have grayed a bit beneath its swarthy tan.

"My son is dead," he said quietly. But he spoke with a tone of finality that warned me not to ask him more.

As if my question had prompted a quick change of subject, Heinrich embarked on a fresh discourse on the war and the profits to be made from it. It seemed that Abraham had been dealing with some Novgorod merchants, the Stroganovs, who had advanced a grandiose plan to exploit the northeastern reaches, far beyond the Urals and into Siberia. In the beginning, Heinrich had looked upon their venture with some misgivings, but the profits would be so enormous if they were successful, he had finally authorized Abraham to cooperate with them, even to extend some credit. Now, the situation was much more promising. With Kazan in Russian hands, there would be no enemy powerful enough to prevent this eastward expansion.

After my apparently painful inquiry, I did not enter into the conversation. I wished they would finish so I could go home and get out of my armor, and I wondered if there was a decent bathhouse in Svyazhsk. Then Abraham began to describe the political situation within the walls of Kazan. For a few minutes I forgot my discomforts, listening to him enumerate our foe's strengths and weaknesses.

Ediger, the present Khan, ruled with the rigidity of a man who knew his cause was hopeless, Abraham told us. To keep his infidel followers from deserting, or taking some action to force a peaceful surrender, the Khan constantly made speeches, boasting of his invincibility. That Ivan was approaching with better than a hundred and fifty thousand men did not seem to alter Ediger's determination. At the time, Kazan could not have held more than thirty thousand defenders.

Throughout the city, his agents spread tales of great armies soon to arrive from the Crimea. The high walls of the citadel would withstand the disbelievers, he told his men, and he predicted the death of the Russian Czar in battle. Shig Ali had been proclaimed a traitor, with a huge reward offered for the man who could slay him and deliver his head to the Khan.

"A tempting offer," I muttered.

Heinrich frowned. "Don't even joke about it," he said seriously.

Following the plan he had outlined to me the night I was elevated to *okolnich*, Ivan suddenly announced a change in the army's organization. He suspended the old *mestnichestvo* seniority system, by which commanders had been chosen in the past. Dmitri Bielsky, who had led the previous assaults, had held his position for this reason. He had made several serious blunders during his military governorship, and had he not died of stomach cramps before the investigations were complete, we might have had a major scandal. Utilizing Bielsky's example to support his reasoning, the Czar encountered little opposition. Major commands would still go to men of boyar rank, but with two hundred families from which to choose, Ivan was able to select a cadre of extremely able men. All of this placed me in an odd situation with some of my own superiors, because I was frequently present when they were selected, or when the Czar and his other advisors discussed their relative strengths and weaknesses. I was careful to keep my own council, however, and I never embarrassed Ivan by allowing his decisions to be known prematurely. All in all, I think he appointed an exceptional staff of officers.

Andrew Kurbsky was to lead a large segment of the peasant levies, as was Peter Shuisky, a competent soldier despite his tendency to all the other weaknesses of his blood. Heinrich was in a position of secondary command, leading his own German–Livonian warriors, plus an assortment of other foreigners. A few local tribes joined the Czar at the last moment, and these were temporarily assigned to Heinrich, as well. Because of the language problems, my stepfather moved Abraham into his staff headquarters to act as interpreter.

Due to my age and lack of experience I did not assume any direct command, but served as adjutant to Heinrich. I anticipated a rapid advancement as I learned, however, for I was only a little younger than several of Ivan's choices, and Andrew Kurbsky was barely three years my senior. Heinrich encouraged me in my ambitions, expressing no doubt that I would earn my own command before the campaign was over.

How I enjoyed that summer, despite all that was to befall me! In the beginning, the only drawback was having to wear armor on the hot, dusty plains, proud as I was to so accoutered. One cannot imagine the discomforts until he experiences them for himself. It is impossible to mop your own sweat or scratch an itch. Responding to the calls of nature can present a major problem in metalcraft.

I had a busy few days before our initial assault, because Heinrich left most of his supply arrangements to me, with Abraham as advisor. Having his help should have lightened my burden, but the old man was reluctant to issue direct orders to any of the men. I was also responsible for maintaining discipline when my stepfather had to be in one of the interminable meetings with the Czar and the other commanders. None of these tasks were difficult, and I enjoyed the authority. Our greatest source of annoyance was the Church. Although I can now appreciate the value of having the Lord on one's side in time of war, I have always found it a nuisance to be constantly interrupted by priests. At this juncture, with my ill–conceived lack of faith and all the attendant guilt within me, I was sometimes short tempered with the men of God. I think Heinrich sympathized with me, although he said very little. Ivan was constantly calling upon Heaven for guidance, and with his priests conducting so many services, they were always swarming through the camp. The ones assigned to our unit would come every day to bless each weapon and piece of armor they could find. One nearsighted old fool even made the sign of the cross over Heinrich's chamberpot, mistaking it, no doubt, for a helmet.

At this point, I suppose, I should offer an explanation on a point which I have avoided until now. This has to do with the relationships which existed between men, both within and outside of the court. Although the Russian Orthodox Church does not accept the Old Testament teachings, as do the churches of the West – thus giving no credence to the laws as defined in Leviticus – it has always been deemed a mortal sin for a man to lie with another man, as if one were a woman. But such behavior was quite common in Russia, and especially among the armies it was to be found with alarming frequency. Honored almost as a tradition inherited from the ancient Greeks, many officers maintained handsome young men on their staffs, or as servants. In fact, some men were surprised to discover that Heinrich had not included me within his "household" for this reason. One of the most basic duties of the priests who accompanied the armies was to discourage this sort of situation – although many of them were as guilty as those they were supposed to lead. During this campaign, both my stepfather and I were completely innocent of such sin. But such situations later arose in both our lives, most especially in his.

When the final peasant levies and barbarian auxiliaries arrived, Svyazhsk could no longer accommodate the entire army. This forced the commanders to begin moving their units into areas closer to Kazan, where they set up strong emplacements on the sites where we anticipated the army would have to remain for the siege. Heinrich's force was moved out with the first of these detachments, and we were ordered to camp in a heavy forest, across the Kazan River from the city. Our assigned place was next to a *Streltsi* squadron, which gave me an opportunity to become acquainted with a number of these soldiers. Despite their humble origins, I soon came to respect their abilities and to greatly enjoy their company. Most of them were armed with a brand new type of arquebusk, capable of firing a very powerful shot. Their range was at least twice the distance of any Tartar bow. *Streltsi*, while nominally under direct command of the Czar, were actually led in the field by various boyars. Peter Bulgakov had been appointed General–in–charge. Ivor was now an officer of the corps, and seemed to be highly respected by the other men. Many of my boyhood playmates had continued to follow the former kennelmaster into the Czar's service, and several of them were in the nearby contingent.

Although Ivan was very proud of his men, I think his greatest passion was the cannon. We had the largest force of these ever assembled, over a hundred and fifty of the great machines. As the cannoneers were largely Germans or Danes, there were occasional language difficulties. When this happened, Heinrich was often the one to pass on instructions from the Czar's command post. Unless prevented by other duties, I always went with him. On several of these visits, I saw Ivan walking among the great, blunted snouts of his guns, patting them affectionately and speaking to them as if they were flesh and blood. Each had a name – Thunderer, Roaring Lion, or such – and the Czar knew every one. He also knew precisely how well each crew performed, eventually assigning clerks to keep a daily record as the battle progressed.

A day or so after the entire army was settled into permanent encampments, the officers were alerted to prepare for our first assault. We were all very excited, of course, and went through a series of furious preparations that evening – I, no less than the others. It was the junior officers' responsibility to assure each man had his proper equipment. Every bowman had to possess his quota of arrows, straight and of standard size. Bows had to be properly tied and restrung. Firearms were freshly cleaned. Every mount was closely inspected, especially if they were shod.

When I finally crawled into my blankets, I had difficulty getting to sleep, although I had consumed a goodly amount of vodka in Vladya's tent. It was close to dawn when I finally erased the many thoughts racing through my mind, and dropped off for a very brief rest.

Morning brought a fresh rush of activity. The warm August sun had completely dried the fields, allowing our artillery to be moved into position during the night. Kegs of powder and cast iron balls were being hauled up from the river as I came down to wash, prior to donning my armor. To keep the army supplied, great quantities of food and other materials were stored on barges, clustered along the river bank. The spirits of the men were high, and everyone expected a quick victory.

After an early mass and proper blessings by the priests, Ivan took his position on a small hill overlooking the walls of Kazan. Basmanov's son, Fedka, stood in front of the Czar, holding the staff with a huge banner at its head. On the flag, Anastasia had personally stitched the face of Our Beloved Lady. Focusing his eyes on this, the Czar called out the order to advance, asking God's final blessings upon his Christian army.

A great shout went up from the multitude of soldiers. With a deafening rattle of armor and shrieks of delight, we descended into the valley that separated us from the walls. Our artillery boomed behind us – all hundred and fifty pieces firing a steady stream of death and fear into the heart of Kazan. I remember wondering if any other army on earth could boast such power.

Our attack was not the disorganized charge of a Mongol horde. The men were divided into groups of ten, each team carrying the timbers for a siege tower to take them over the walls of the city. Every man had been given a metal token to be turned in at the end of the battle, thus assuring an accurate tally of our losses. Columns of priests streamed down the hill between the advancing soldiers, swinging their pots of incense and holding aloft the icons and *khorugvi*. At the very head of our host went the great, golden cross, while the heavy scent of incense almost obliterated the acrid pungency of gun powder.

From atop the city walls, hundreds of Tartars fired volleys of arrows from their stubby bows. But they wasted their shafts, for the missiles could not reach us. In a frenzy, the infidels lifted their robes – those who wore them – screaming obscenities as they turned, baring their backsides like a horde of drunken harlots. Some of them pissed over the side with their mutilated organs, shouting and shrieking, leaping up and down, calling upon the forces of evil to destroy us.

"It will take the full force of hell to defend that city," muttered Heinrich. He was mounted on a heavy, gray charger he had acquired the summer before – a very finely trained war horse. I rode the bay gelding Ivan had given me upon my return from Staritsa. He was a good horse, though not as steady as my stepfather's. The effort to keep his head down, to prevent his rearing up and prancing, was already making the sweat pour down my body. The sun had barely risen, and I knew it was going to be a very warm day.

As we advanced, the sun glimmered through the light mist rising from the ground, forcing it to dissipate. Wispy clouds floated upward, drifting over the battlements of the city. As the air cleared, we could see the slender minarets of the infidels, poking up beyond the walls. Black banners of Islam were hung from every tower and from the corners of the wall, flapping lazily in a sluggish breeze. From behind us came a chorus of trumpets, then a steady beat from the great brass battle drums. Looking back, I saw the Czar, stock still on his huge black stallion, dwarfing the figure of young Basmanov. The boy had now lowered his enormous banner, allowing the base of its staff to rest upon the ground. From their vantage point the scene must have been breathtaking in its glory, our mighty host descending onto the Arsky Plain.

Our army halted just outside range of the Tartar arrows, and again the priests led us in prayer. It was a short service, but when we looked up again it was as if the Lord had heard us. Not a single infidel was left upon the ramparts. The stillness was almost frightening. Even our own guns had ceased to fire while the holy words were spoken. A few seconds later, the silence was abruptly shattered. At a second signal from the Czar, the whole right hand, under Kurbsky's command, rushed toward the huge wooden gates. After a brief pounding from our heavy rams the portals gave and the entire city lay open before us.

Our army streamed through the gaping passage, the pieces of siege towers forgotten in the dust behind. Like Moscow, Kazan had its Kremlin, or inner fortress, and it was to here the defenders had withdrawn. The rest of the city and its treasures were ours for the taking. Most of the houses could only be locked from within, as was true of the public buildings. At first, even the bravest soldiers were fearful and suspicious at finding the place so deathly still and undefended. But the shouts of our men soon filled the void. Quickly regaining their courage, they began fanning out through the crooked streets and alleyways, destroying whatever they couldn't carry off. Our plans had not anticipated this lack of resistance, and the resultant disorganization almost caused our downfall. Before midday our men seemed to have completely forgotten their sacred mission, and sought only after the valuables they might obtain.

Bulgakov's *Streltsi* and our own group of Germans were the only troops to maintain discipline, though they also picked up a few items here and there. Our groups remained together, however, and the commanders maintained a semblance of order. The peasant levies were completely out of control, as were the barbarian auxiliaries. They quickly discovered a number of well–stocked wine cellars, and by mid afternoon most of our army was roaring drunk. As the heat of the day increased, many men collapsed on the street, too intoxicated to stand.

Heinrich led us into a square below the fortress, where we stood in advance of all the rest. From this position, we could see the ragged Tartars watching us from atop the soaring walls. Some taunted us, as they had before, but the noise did not seem as great. Somehow, there seemed too few men upon the parapets.

"This means trouble," said Heinrich grimly.

He dispatched a runner to contact the nearest *Streltsi* commander, and started to pull our men into a line which would defend against an attack from the fortress. We did not have time. With no warning, other than the sudden shriek of ungreased hinges, the gates above us thrust outward. Thousands of the most ugly creatures on two legs burst into the square. They bellowed their horrible paeans, rushing toward us in a flood of naked brown bodies. Few infidel soldiers wore more than a dirty turban and a ragged, filthy breechclout when they went into battle. They streamed out of the fortress, brandishing their curved swords and steel tipped lances. Small, bandy–legged men for the most part, so hairy they looked like malformed bears, their forward rush became a tumbling wave. Those in front had no choice but to charge, for the pressure of the men behind them. But I think they would have charged, anyway; a Tartar in battle loses all sense of being a man. He becomes a wild, senseless brute, responding only to his unreasoning lust for blood, the desire to kill. At first sight of these shrieking, blood lusting fiends, our Russian soldiers broke in terror. Those who were sensible enough to drop their booty were able to save themselves. The fools who continued to hug their new–found wealth to their bosoms were slain on the spot. Falling to the ground, they covered their fine silks and stolen brocades with the blood of their bellies, or from a neck which no longer supported a head. Heinrich's infidel detachments fled with the rest, but the discipline among our cadre of knights and squires persisted.

We quickly wedged ourselves into a narrow alley off one side of the square, presenting the infidels with a solid wall of steel. The line held, and Heinrich hurriedly ordered another group of men to block the far end of the street, thus preventing our being attacked from behind. For the moment we were safe enough, for we stood like the Spartans at the gates of Attica. We defended a small opening with a handful of warriors, while the horde of besieging barbarians could only attack in numbers equal to our own. Although a mob of the infidels continued to harry us, their main force pursued the peasant soldiers, whose flight led the enemy away from us. We could hear the pagan battle cries and the screams of butchered serfs growing softer as the slaughter moved into the distance.

"If Bulgakov can't turn them back, we'll never see another sunrise," Heinrich mumbled between labored breaths. He continued to shout orders to his men, who responded as competently as they had in drill. The great swords rose and fell, splitting skulls or severing limbs in a single stroke. The howling little men continued to throw themselves against our defenses, slowed only by the effort of climbing over their own dead. A few of our archers had managed to climb onto recesses and ledges of the buildings to either side, from which vantage points they poured a steady stream of arrows into the enemy faces. Heinrich looked up at the rooftops.

"Demetrius, you had better take a few men and get up there," he shouted. "If the infidels think to send bowmen onto the roofs, they can shoot down on us, like bears in a pit."

We still had two scaling ladders, and I used one to lead a small contingent up the steep wall, onto one of the roofs. Again, I cursed the heavy steel plates about my body, as they seriously hampered my movements. The armor was so heavy I could hardly haul myself up the rungs, which squeaked and groaned beneath my weight. Sweating, my lungs close to bursting, I made the top. I was second in line, behind the lightly armed lancer I had sent ahead to steady the ladder. He gave me a hand up, and as I came over the edge I saw it was not a moment too soon. A gizzled head appeared over the far side of the rooftop, directly across from me. Before he could move, I rushed him, swinging my sword in a fierce arc and bringing it down hard against the base of the man's neck. His head collapsed at the end of a half severed spine, splattering blood in every direction as his body slowly toppled backward, falling heavily against the infidels below him.

My own men were crowding up behind me, and within a few seconds we had control of the roof. I ordered our ladder drawn up and thrown across to the roof on the far side of the alley, forming a bridge so my small force could pass quickly from one to the other. Our defense devolved into a grim game of death. Each time an infidel head appeared at the edge of the roof, a heavy bolt of steel fell upon it. This was the first real battle for me, and I cannot seriously pretend to any sense of guilt or remorse, not at the time, not later. I struck at an enemy who had neither soul nor identity. I joked with my comrades as we kept account of the number of heads each man chopped. We wagered over who would claim the most, and I offered a skin of wine to the first man who could actually take a trophy. A few moments later a severed skull bounced across the roof, striking my boots. I kicked it away and watched it tumble over the edge, landing upon the frenzied mob below us.

Laughing aloud, I called acknowledgment to the man who'd won the prize, my voice becoming lost within the hysteria of battle. I was able to kill a man, now – an enemy, at least – without the slightest compunction. I could laugh and make jokes about my victims. It was merely one more step on the descending path my soul would take.

I did not know it at the time, but I was earning myself a reputation among the enemy. I wore a crimson plume on my helmet, as Heinrich did, and my own golden beard protruded from beneath the faceplate. With uncanny intelligence, the enemy knew who I was, probably from my having escorted their princess. They thought of me as Heinrich's son, and he was the warrior deemed most terrible of all the Russian host. The name they had for him meant something like "sword–of–the–flaming–blood." My title was the diminutive of that, a twisted series of unpronounceable sounds in their clacking, heathen tongue.

At length, there was a lull in our exercises. We had killed many of the enemy while only one of my men had sustained a serious wound, this being a fairly deep cut in his left arm. From the roof we were able to see some distance into the city, where our army had finally established a line. Our Russian leaders, Andrew Kurbsky more than any other, had rallied the *Streltsi*. They held at several important street intersections, allowing the boyars to reorganize their levies. Below us, Heinrich's group continued to hold its ground, although the number of infidels throwing themselves against the armored knights never slackened. A huge pile of bodies formed an almost defensive blockade at each end of our alley. Heinrich stood shoulder–to–shoulder with the others, sometimes climbing atop the mound of infidel dead to strike down more of the attackers.

On the far side of one building, we could see the Tartars begin to mill about. Their forward thrust had been broken farther on, I think by Kurbsky's forces. The infidels in the rear continued to shove forward, resulting in a tremendous crush. Eventually, none of them was able to move effectively, and in the end this saved us. In the frantic chaos, it became impossible for the Tartars to keep a ladder against our wall, thus preventing any attackers from climbing up after us.

I thought we were in fine shape, when suddenly some archers on the fortress wall began shooting at us. I first became aware of it when Carl, one of the young pikemen, crumpled onto the roof beside me. A bolt stuck out of his throat as he lay there, kicking for a few seconds before collapsing in death. For a moment I was shocked into immobility. Then I shoved my visor into place and shouted for the others to do the same. For the first time, I was grateful for my armor. A flurry of arrows descended upon on us, though not with any great force. We were too far away. The archers had to shoot upward, allowing for the distance, which caused their missiles to drop into our midst from above. By then, their energy was nearly spent, making them lethal only against unprotected flesh. The distance, of course, was too great for accuracy. One other man was wounded on the arm, just above the wrist, the result of a lucky shot. Later, the wind shifted and the arrows began to miss the roof more often than not, falling on the heads of the infidels below us.

From near the gates of the outer city, the deep boom of our drums began again, and we soon saw the defenders retreating in panic, the Czar's great army pressing them steadily backward. From our vantage point we could see the steady rise and fall of Russian swords, the sun glinting off polished steel. Flights of spears and arrows descended into the packed mass of naked brown bodies. The sharp reports of *Streltsi* arquebusks became more constant, finally growing to a steady, crackling rattle. We began hurling down everything we could move, tearing stones and timbers loose from the building, doing all we could to increase the confusion below. The attackers had withdrawn from the far end of Heinrich's alley, and all his men were concentrated at the forward opening.

Slowly, the armored knights began pushing out, into the congested square. The infidels shoved and struggled amongst themselves to regain the safety of the fortress walls. Heinrich told me later that his intentions had been to work around, behind the confusion of enemy soldiers, to block the fortress gate. Had he been able to do this, and to hold out long enough for the rest of our army to arrive, it might have ended the campaign. As it was, the press of struggling bodies was too great, and Heinrich's men were nearly exhausted. No one fought against them, now, as each of the terrified enemy tried to flee, only to find himself trapped by the mass of his own fellows. The wedge of knights never reached the gates. The Tartar commanders closed them long before the Russian army arrived, thus cutting off hundreds of their own men, who could easily have been saved.

The finish was sheer carnage. Fortunately, the rest of our army arrived before Heinrich and his men became too tired to lift their swords. They were close to that point, and counting the litter of infidel corpses left on the ground, it was understandable. Andrew Kurbsky led the troops into the square, riding proudly astride his heavy war horse. Behind him came Bulgakov, surrounded by his lieutenants and other mounted retainers. Swinging their swords in great arcs above their heads, the horsemen quickly dispatched the remaining infidels and shouted their victory to the stupefied defenders, who now watched dumbly from the walls. Only a few Tartar arrows were discharged during that final rush. The only effective weapons the Mussulmen employed were the caldrons of boiling water they poured on the few peasants who came too close to the fortress walls.

That evening, of course, Kurbsky was hailed as the victorious commander. Perhaps this was as it should have been. The victory was Russian, and it should have been a Russian who received the credit. I later made sure the Czar knew about Heinrich's heroic defense of his strategic position, and his honors came in good time.

CHAPTER VI

With our army standing victorious before the walls of the inner fortress, it seemed total triumph was immediately within our grasp. However, this was not to be; night would soon fall, and with it would come the problem of defending the conquered areas of Kazan. Within their stronghold there were still numerous defenders, capable of striking at us any time they chose. Heinrich was soon in close conference with Kurbsky, Bulgakov, and Gorbatov–Shuisky, who had been the fourth field commander that day. Their unanimous recommendation, forwarded by fast horse to the Czar and Prince Vorotinsky, our supreme commander, was to withdraw from the city.

I was dismayed, as were many others, when the orders were passed for an orderly exodus. Were we to remain as defenders, it was explained, we would never be able to sleep. We could have been set upon at any time by the infidel raiding parties, operating from the safety of the citadel. Before pulling back, we did as much damage as possible to the defenses, and took with us as many of the riches as came easily to hand. I looked up at the wall, the towering earth and wooden ramparts. The fortress stood on the crest of a steep hill, except for the one side where we had fought. Yet even here, there was not much level ground, hardly enough room to accommodate a force with the strength to threaten the gates. Just as the Kremlin in Moscow was considered impregnable, so was the fortress of Kazan. Only by siege and prolonged bombardment could we hope to dislodge the Tartar host.

Our horses were still skittish from the violent battle all around them. I had trouble holding my mount in check as we returned to camp. Our men, like all the rest, were loaded down with booty, and we led a few prisoners behind the horses. Other units had taken dozens of captives, mostly cowards who had hidden through the fiercest part of the battle, allowing themselves to be discovered only after the blind impulse to kill had subsided. Bound, with heads bowed, they were led on halters behind their new masters. I gazed backward once more, to the parapet where hundreds of tiny figures danced about, waving at us. But the obscene gestures and vulgar, shouted insults quickly ceased. Our engineers began blowing up the smaller walls of the outer city, leaving only the citadel intact as a bastion of defense.

I was astonished to discover how the first day of battle had sapped my energy. This sudden letdown after the excitement – the sense of total depletion – was a new experience for me. I returned to my tent seemingly drained of any vigor. Adding to the discomfort were a number of welts on my upper arms and thighs, where the armor bindings had cut into the flesh. Heinrich, though surely suffering from the same discomforts as I, was long since inured to them and did not evidence my degree of distress. Splashing some water on his face, he went off to make a full report to General Vorotinsky.

I stripped to the skin and stretched out on a piece of soft leather, atop a pile of cloth, while Heinrich's newly acquired manservant, Teshata, rubbed sweet oil into my aching muscles. Feeling much relieved, I slept for the hour or two that my stepfather was gone. He awakened me when he returned, saying that the Czar had asked us to come by later and bring Abraham. I was surprised at the request, but being refreshed by my nap, I was glad for the invitation. The Czar, with his peculiar curiosity and interest in the opinions of foreigners, had heard other officers mention Abraham, Heinrich explained. He suggested I get dressed and inform the old man.

Although visibly disturbed at the prospect of meeting the Czar – and having to enter a gentile lodging – Abraham had no choice but to obey. He was ready to leave when one of Ivan's servants arrived to light our way to the royal pavilion. Kurbsky was already there, as well as the General–in–charge, Prince Michael Vorotinsky. The Czar and his officers sat on camp chairs, probably in deference to their present soldierly occupations. The lowly stools had been supplied with cushions, and were heavily draped with skins and rich damask. Vorotinsky, a tall distinguished gentleman, with dappled black–gray hair and beard, was the perfect figure of a commanding officer. Gracious and polite, as only a proper leader can be, he smiled warmly at Abraham and myself, helping to relieve the old man's dread. Ivan allowed the General to act in his stead, as host, much as he acted in the Czar's name on the field of battle.

Fedka and another youngster were serving. I tossled the younger Basmanov's hair as I passed, and in the same motion bowed to the Czar. Ivan waved me to a seat beside him, while Heinrich presented his servant. Despite the old man's previous temerity, Vorotinsky's encouragement seemed to reassure him. Abraham's bearing before the Majesty of Russia was flawless, although I knew it distressed him to be there, in contravention of his strict religious prohibitions.

At Ivan's orders, Fedka brought a stack of cushions, placing them on a heavy carpet, in the center of the group. Abraham seated himself in the eastern fashion, drawing his legs up in front of him, waiting for the Czar and his generals to begin their inquiry. I caught myself dozing as they discussed the politics and personalities of our enemy, but came more fully awake when the conversation digressed to the infamies of the slave trade.

"This has been a most profitable business, most profitable," said Abraham. "Even now, there are at least fifty thousand Russians held in bondage behind those walls." He inclined his head in the general direction of Kazan, rubbing his palms together as he spoke.

Ivan nodded. Though the number was larger than I had heard mentioned before, the Czar was aware of the condition.

The center of the slave trade seems to be Kaffa –" Abraham continued, "– an infamous place, truly infamous! Most Russian captives pass through there on the way to one market or another. Many buyers travel to Kaffa from hundreds of miles away to have their pick of what amounts to a dealers' market. This is where the regular traders come to buy groups of fifty to a hundred, then transport them by caravan to other cities of the south. A dreadful trade in human souls! From Kaffa, slaves may be sent as far as Persia or India – or to the west, into Syria. I have heard tales of some being sent to Nubia, but I do not know this to be a fact."

"You have actually seen the market?" asked Kurbsky.

"Oh, yes – yes, indeed, My Lord," said Abraham, closing his eyes and nodding with his whole body. He seemed to conjure up a picture of the slave blocks in his mind. "The most prized captives are the young girls – and boys," he added quickly, "those who can be sold into harems. However, strong men are always in demand to work the mines, or to haul stone and timber for their masters' buildings. Even for an architect, it increases his prestige to have white bodies in the work force."

"And the women who are no longer suitable for the harem?" asked the Czar.

"They may be used as household servants, or if they have strong backs, as many peasant women do, they may find themselves working beside the men. It is only the elderly who are useless to the slavers, because they cannot withstand the long march to the market. The ordeal is terrible, of course. Slaves are chained at their wrists and ankles, joined together by halters about their necks. Old people who are deemed unfit to make the journey are turned over to the young men, who make – make sport of them."

"Perhaps His Majesty would like to know something of the other aspects of trade in the Crimea," Heinrich suggested. Abraham had paused for breath and to sip the wine Fedka had placed beside him.

I watched the intense interest displayed by the others, now, as Abraham continued his account, dwelling at some length on the commodities of the east and explaining how these treasures could be obtained. All four of the men had extensive investments in one aspect of trade or another. Their rapt attention encouraged Abraham to report in precise detail on methods of shipment, types of goods received from each port. He gave a long dissertation on price variations from area to area, and from one season of the year to another.

"Strange looking ships come from the east," he told us, "across the inland sea from Asterbad and Derbend. Goods may be shipped from these ports to Astrakhan, thence overland to Sarai or Tana, or they may be unloaded at Derbend, sent by caravan to Poti, and across the *Pontus Euxinus* to the Crimea."

Responding to further questions, he detailed the routes from Basra and Bokhara, and cities beyond the great rivers of India – places I had never heard of before. He not only knew the goods and their value, but was personally acquainted with several important merchants from Constantinople, Alexandria, and Venice. He knew the quantities each type of ship could carry, and how long a voyage should last.

When I thought the discussion was over, and was about to rise, Ivan suddenly returned to the subject of slavery. "I understand the slaves are branded," he remarked. His eyes seemed to gleam in anticipation of the answer.

Showing no wonder at the question, Abraham responded in the same pedantic tone he had used all evening. "This is true, Your Majesty," he said, "They are usually marked on both cheeks and on the forehead; sometimes the scars are gross, quite hideous."

"Doesn't this disfigure them for use in the harem?" Ivan persisted.

Had it been other than the Czar to whom he spoke, I think Abraham might have smiled at his naiveté. Or was it that? "Harem children are generally spared this treatment, Majesty," replied the Jew. "Frequently a metal collar is welded around their necks as a mark; their flesh is too valuable to be subjected to the iron."

Responding to further questions from the Czar, Abraham delved into an extensive explanation of the prices brought by light skinned Russian slaves, comparing their value with those of darker men from the southern deserts and Africa. Ivan alone seemed intensely interested in these descriptions. Common as slavery was in Moscow, I noted an expression of disdain on the faces of the others. The idea of brown hands mauling the fair flesh of Russian children was distasteful.

"It is even said," concluded the Jew, "that the rulers of Constantinople have forsaken the conquest of the Grecian Isles in order to expend their energies more profitably, by raiding into these areas along the Volga."

Ivan stood up. "It will become a part of Our Holy Crusade," he remarked grandly, "to free the Russian souls who now languish in slavery to the infidels." He pointed his *kisten* toward Kazan. "And later," he added, "We may drive the Tartar degenerates from their palaces in Astrakhan and Kaffa!"

For many weeks after this, the battle continued, stretching into a prolonged campaign and siege. Taking the inner fortress of Kazan presented all the difficulties one would face in trying to capture the Kremlin in Moscow. And Khan Ediger proved a formidable opponent – clever and deceitful in his desperation. Several times, he managed to slip a portion of his army out of the citadel and to coordinate attacks utilizing these forces in conjunction with frantic rushes by his frenzied Tartars from inside the walls. Once they even came close to Ivan's field camp, after which the Czar withdrew to his pavilion in the forest and remained there for the rest of the campaign.

Heinrich provided a great service, because several of his trading associates were inside Kazan, and they were able to send messages out to him, concealed in the shafts of arrows. These were always marked by having red tips on the feathers. Several times, he sent me out onto the plain to retrieve them, always making sure I was accompanied by a few of our own archers, who appeared to be collecting the spent bolts for reuse.

Vorotinsky proved an able commander, who earned the respect of the common soldiers, as well as his fellow officers. Moral among the men was still a problem, however, because the Musselmen set up a constant clamor from the walls, which made it difficult to get a full night's sleep, even during periods when the actual fighting was minimal. Our own great guns hammered the citadel all through the daylight hours. Andrew Kurbsky was in charge of these, and earned a great reputation for his skillful leadership.

For a while it appeared that our efforts to dislodge the Kazanites were going to drag on forever, for despite all our efforts the walls still stood and the Tartars continued their sniping attacks, seldom standing to fight. Then, through Heinrich's operatives, came word of a massive attack planned for the next day. As before, the Tartars would come at us both from within the citadel and from the woods on either side. But we were ready for them, with many men concealed in Kurbsky's trenches, just forward of his gun emplacements. The Czar had promised his officers a great banquet that evening, to celebrate the victory he knew we were bound to achieve.

The Tartars burst forth from Kazan and from the surrounding woodlands as expected, and we charged them from our places of concealment. When the little brown men were close to the guns, our men sprang from their hiding places, and the ensuing battle turned into a bloody rout. By evening our soldiers were busy stripping the enemy dead, or leading their captives back to their camps, as Heinrich and I returned to our tent to prepare for Ivan's celebration.

The banquet that evening was the grandest bacchanal I had ever attended—a Saturnalia, celebrated in the wilds of Tartary by the soldiers of victorious Caesar. True, I have since seen some entertainment more ribald, and some acts more extreme or violent. Yet this feast was to celebrate a magnificent victory over the infidel. It was given and attended in a spirit of sheer joy and pleasure. We were mostly very young men, and we had been subjected to the rigors of war. We had chafed under the tension of inactivity, and weeks of constant enemy harassment. Now, we suddenly found release in an artificial paradise. The Czar's pavilion and the huge tent set up beside it were fantasies of colored lanterns and silken drapes. Scented wood burned in several huge braziers, filling the forest with perfumed smoke. The Czar had selected the most attractive women in Svyazhsk to entertain us. The world of war and death and suffering was abruptly far away.

Food was plentiful and exotic. It came from every corner of the realm, and beyond. We had roasted lamb and veal, venison, and finely prepared dishes of beef and pork. There was fowl of every kind, including peacock and pheasant, dove and duck – and fish, sturgeon and trout from the southern Volga. There were sweetmeats and preserved delicacies captured from the Tartar stores in the southern district of the city. Also from this area below the fortress came honey and sweetened breads baked from the Khan's own stores of flour. There were several great pots of caviar, finer than I had ever tasted before. Wines of all kinds were served by the Czar's servants, supplemented and finally replaced – as the evening wore on – by the women of Svyazhsk.

The entertainment was the greatest surprise the Czar provided for us. In our own Russian *dachas* we might occasionally have jugglers or wrestlers. But since the capital had been freed from the Shuisky debauch, and especially since Sylvester had begun to lecture Ivan on his sinful ways, our dinner time entertainment had become understandably dull. For tonight, the admonitions of the priest had been disregarded. The performances of some of the troupes were intricate displays of heathen art. Mussulmen dancing girls, bred for the harem and trained all their lives in the sensual arts, knew exactly how to excite one's emotions. Though the infidel men were unquestionably the ugliest creatures to walk on legs – being bred in litters of two or three at a time, not opening their eyes until the third day – the women were like a different breed. Somehow, the Lord in His great wisdom had seen fit to compensate for the lack of symmetry in the male by endowing the women with exceptional charms—plump, dark–haired girls with rounded hips and enough flesh to make them sleek. Their heavy breasts were full, thrusting upward when bared in the early stages of their dances. One girl, a hill dweller, probably a Circassian from below the southern steppes, did a dance I shall never forget. Using tiny, silver finger cymbols, she echoed the rhythm of the drums, passing the sharp, flickering edges so close to her breasts it seemed she must nip the flesh. She spun and leaped, twisted her body into unbelievable contortions. She ended, finally, on Shig Ali's couch – probably mistaking the heavily jeweled swine for some fat, wealthy pasha.

We ate heavily and continued to drink until very late that night. With drunkenness came escape, fading memories of heat and dust, the sweet stench of the swamps—the smell of rotting corpses, and heathen sounds from within the fortress. Here we watched dancers who used their swords for pleasure. About the fire, men twirled their blades so fast one could hardly follow the movements. Girls leaped between them, always able to escape the keenly honed edges. Swirling skirts of gossamer silk over luscious, sensuous flesh, outlined their forms in the reflected red of glowing coals. The very air spoke a mummery of misty voluptuousness.

Heinrich had cautioned me to eat and drink sparingly. Over indulgence at night, he warned, made for a poor performance the next day. At first I tried to follow his advice, but I underestimated the power of these strange, new wines. Long before the evening ended, I was completely lost in drink. I could later remember only portions of all I saw and did after the fires burned low, and the dancers finally ceased to perform. I was on one of the rich carpets, my arms about one of the women, trying some impossible act of erotic mysticism on her breasts. My stepfather had slipped away, back to our tent and his own paramour, I supposed. With him went my final inhibitions.

My partner and I were far from alone, at times being pressed for room as other couples, or groups of couples, shoved close against us, their identities lost in the darkness. The braziers cast an intermittent flicker, leaving all the area beyond them dark and deep in shadow. A group of musicians continued to beat some exotic cadence on their pagan instruments, but I had lost all conscious perception. I knew only the warm, sensuous oblivion. Somehow, my passions overcame the deadening bliss of spirits. I was once again on the gently rolling barge, and Suunbeka was in my arms. I was experiencing the oriental arts of love, dozing perhaps in the darkness, reawakened by warm, enfolding arms. I was no longer with the same woman I had been with before, but it made no difference. Each body was the same to me; each woman was my love, while she lay in my embrace – then gone, and another fulfilled the memory. . .warmth, love, passion. . . .

Then clear in my memory, like a cold brilliant light—harsh rays through the warmth of misty fog. Suddenly, crackling with anger and hatred, a stern voice echoed against my brain. "The sins of Sodom and Gomorrah!" it shouted. "The Lord's wrath shall fall upon you! Sinners, sinners whose Holy Cause must fail before such evil!"

I became aware of Vladimir, a few feet away from me. The Prince raised his head out of the darkness. A ruddy glow outlined his features. A woman giggled, somewhere below him.

"What in the name of all the saints. . . ?" he grumbled.

"Sin! Sin!" came the voice again.

I lifted myself enough to see. Standing behind the chair which Ivan had occupied earlier in the evening, Sylvester held aloft a silver cross in one hand, a flickering lantern in the other. His eyes were wide and seemed aflame with zealous mania. I lay down again. "It's Mad Sylvester," I whispered, drawing back into the warmth of the woman beside me.

Vladya heaved himself to his knees, bracing his naked body against a table as he peered over the top, squinting in an effort to focus.

"Sodom and Gomorrah!" repeated the Czar's confessor.

"Sodom and Gomorrah be damned!" shouted Vladya. "That was a different kind of sin, as *you* well know –Monk!"

His emphasis on the proper words brought a choke of laughter from several men around us. Then the playful derision grew, until the priest could no longer make himself heard.

"Have a drink!" someone shouted.

"A little fuzzy might do you good!" yelled another.

In a rage, Sylvester withdrew. And with him it seemed, went the Grace of God. But we could not realize that until later.

Somehow, I found my way home. I awoke alone in the morning, but with a shred of silken veil in my bed. I could not remember. The demons of hell beat relentlessly upon anvils of steel within my skull – then some of Teshata's elixir—a vile, bitter brew of witches' herbs and disgusting ingredients I shuddered to think of swallowing. It helped me overcome the worst of my miseries, but the enthusiasm for battle was somewhat less than usual. I dressed, feeling better and assuming I appeared relatively normal until I saw my stepfather's expression. He said nothing, but his point had been eloquently made.

As if in response to Sylvester's anger, black storm clouds had gathered during the night. They now hung heavily on the southern horizon, making the entire day gloomy and foreboding. Regardless of the omens, we had to follow our advantage, allowing no time for the enemy to lick his wounds. The army assembled on the plain, under the leadership of Kurbsky on the left hand, Mikulinsky on the right. The huge copper drums, each suspended between four horses, set up their thunderous rumble. The tabors of the *bulsha dwoaney* beat out the order to advance.Priests in their black *skhimas*, lofting the crosses and holy standards, led us once more toward the fortress walls.

I rode easily, pacing my mount to the slow, steady rhythm. At length, the tempo of the great drums increased. Heinrich raised his scepter and we surged forward with the rest of the line. Men behind us carried pieces of scaling ladders; ahead loomed the towering walls with the frenzied, silhouetted figures on top. Ranks of Mussulman archers blackened the misty sky with arrows, the bolts landing a few rods ahead of us.

Our drum beat out the order to halt, immediately behind a row of posts which the Czar had ordered implanted before the walls, within easy hailing distance. Several score tightly bound Tartars were dragged forward, through the mass of Russian warriors, and tied upright to the stakes. With spears pressed hard against their backs, they were forced to call upon their comrades to surrender. "All is lost!" they wailed. "The might of the Czar is too great, but he is merciful. Those who surrender will be spared. To fight is to die."

The rain of Tartar arrows, which had ceased when they saw the prisoners among us, now answered their fellows' pleas. Taking careful aim, the Kazanite archers began to dispatch our prisoners. As one after another sagged in his bonds, the remaining captives besought their guards to release them. Instead, our men were ordered to withdraw out of range, while the last of the prisoners were dispatched by their own marksmen.

Through all this time, the black clouds had become denser, drifting closer to the walls of the citadel. When all the Tartar prisoners slumped dead against their posts, a peculiar motion began upon the walls, causing our own commanders to withhold further orders. Our priests moved forward and stood firmly before us, holding their holy symbols as a bar against the expected blasphemy. In a strange prelude to their act of necromancy, infidel priests and wisemen began shouldering their way into the jam of archers atop the wall. Waving their arms to form mysterious signs, shrieking out heathen curses, they evoked the forces of darkness to aid them. These weird rituals lasted for several minutes, while the storm clouds continued to grow, expanding across the sky as if in obedience to the infernal magicians. Suddenly, in the most shocking display of barbarian immorality, dozens of the defenders exposed themselves in unison and urinated over the side of the wall!

Our surprise at this strange behavior held us nearly speechless, and during these few moments the magic took effect. The heavens seemed to open, as if a knife had been plunged into the underside of a great sack. Satan had somehow responded to their shameless act. Momentarily gaining ascendancy into heaven, the evil one had joined them in their obscenities. The whole sky turned black. Torrents of rain fell so heavily that small rivulets were formed in seconds, and still the clouds continued to unleash the streams of water – warm, as if from the bladder of the Tartars' evil god.

The entire army raced for cover, for with the rain came a full storm of raging ferocity. The wind struck with a force that almost knocked us down. Then, before anyone could realize what had happened, the worst of the blow moved on, attacking our supply barges and tearing them loose from their moorings along the river. In a matter of moments we lost nearly all of our food supplies and the stacks of warm clothing the Czar had ordered for the cold winter months ahead. Minutes later the wind was gone, moving beyond the river to leave us immersed in the steady downpour.

We were in total chaos! There is something about rain to make the strongest men run for cover. Those who will face the wildest charge of the most terrifying servants of hell will flee before a pelting torrent of water. Heinrich's group pushed against the lee of a hill, seeking shelter from the overhang of a ruined cattle shed. The ground before us was already a sea of mud, but the sudden wind had raised a huge cloud of choking dust which the rain had not yet dissipated. We wound cloths about our faces, leaving only our eyes exposed as we waited for the storm to subside. Fortunately, the infidels lacked the wit to follow up their momentary advantage, else they might have destroyed the Czar's whole army – perhaps the Czar, himself. As it was, they remained within their fortress, unable to see us through the driving rain and dust.

I was convinced I had seen the handiwork of the evil one, and still in later years I wondered. Heinrich maintained otherwise, scoffing at the suggestion of the infidels' miraculous power. It was coincidence, an act of fate, he said—at most, an event foreseen by their astronomers. "What do you think that rain was?" he demanded sarcastically, "the devil pissing on us, along with the rest of the heathens? And the tornado. I suppose that was the result of Satan's breaking wind!"

But cynical as he was, I think he really wondered. To me it was the beginning of something more. To believe in the forces of hell is the first step toward accepting the power of God. Before the day was past, a second miracle was to further shake my resistance to the truth. The rain did not let up. It continued to fall with alternating intensity: hard beating squalls, between light misty showers. Heinrich organized our men and started leading them back to the camp. On the way we were met by a runner from Vorotinsky, who requested Heinrich's presence in the Czar's pavilion. Leaving me to return the troops to their quarters, my step-father galloped off.

I quickly settled the others and returned to our own tent. The structure had collapsed on one side, but was being reset by Teshata and another servant. I entered and stripped off my armor with the help of a retainer. Rain had penetrated everywhere, and I was soaked to the skin. I was about to change my wet undergarments, when Vladya poked his head through the half–secured flap, laughing at my appearance.

"The might of Russian arms," he chortled, squeezing through the opening. "You look more like a drowned slave!" Then seeing the scars from my armor straps, added, "Who's been beating you?"

"I suppose your lily skin is completely unmarked," I sneered.

"Well, I don't think it's in worse shape than yours. But you'd better get dressed again, or you're going to miss the excitement."

"What's that?" I asked.

The Prince flopped onto a corner of my bunk. "Ivan has all the chief merchants with him now. He's ordering replacements for the stuff we lost."

"That was fast," I remarked.

"God's anointed was never slow," he responded, "except, perhaps when it comes to exposing his ass to the enemy."

I glanced around to make sure the servants were out of hearing. "You shouldn't talk like that," I told him.

"Why not? It's the truth!"

"It smacks of sedition."

"From some perhaps. But I have no ambitions, and the Czar knows it. Who else could harm me?"

"You harm your soul!" I said, half seriously. "But what excitement am I going to miss?" I hunkered down beside the stove, trying to dry myself before getting dressed again. Teshata had taken my armor into the rear of the tent to wipe it before it rusted.

"The Czar has commanded our priests to make an end of this devil's holocaust," he told me.

"Whose idea was that?"

"Who else but the mad monk," he laughed. He stood up and looked about the tent. "Don't you people have anything to drink in this place?"

I called to Heinrich's concubine and had her bring us some of my stepfather's German liquor. Vladya grunted appreciatively as she turned to leave.

"Glad you approve of Heinrich's taste," I told him.

A few moments later we were in Ivan's pavilion. He had assembled every priest and holy man in the camp and from the surrounding hills. Of the latter he had a great many, for the wild hermits of the Volga had flocked to us, to bless our holy mission. Half–naked zealots, with hair uncropped and hanging nearly to their waists – beards so huge and unkempt a nest of sparrows could have lived in one undetected. They mingled, now, with their more conservative brethren, preparing to march together—brothers in Christian faith, to break the curse of the infidel. Of all the fiercely fanatic zealots, none looked more forbidding nor more demented than Sylvester. He stood to one side through all the commotion, holding a staff which was topped by the most holy of crosses from the Great Cathedral. Embedded in its center, amongst the gold and jewels, was a small piece of wood from the original cross of Our Savior. This most treasured and powerful Christian relic would be borne at the head of the procession.

Led by the highest bishops and abbots, the men of God crossed the river and filed down the hill to the plain. They spread out as they neared the walls, marching briskly in two lines, encircling the citadel. The army followed them, our weapons ready to guard the sacred procession. There were no drums or trumpets, only the chanting of the priests and the constant slosh of marching feet. Rain continued to fall in heavy, driving torrents. Finally, with their cassocks completely soaked and clinging in plastered wrinkles against their bodies, the heads of the two lines converged on the far side of the walls. Silently, a few feet behind them, stood the ranks of the Russian army.

There was no response from within the citadel. Above us, the Tartars stood mute atop the wall, as if they knew the forces of the Lord were at work. At a signal from the senior bishop, the chanting stopped, leaving only the sound of pelting rain. Then the priests began anew, chanting another psalm, another prayer. From beneath their robes they drew forth flasks of holy water. The naked hermits had also been provided with these miracle–working containers, and until now had kept them tied about their waists or necks. Slowly, and in time to the words, they began to sprinkle the blessed elixir upon the ground. From the walls, the infidels continued to watch in awe.

God's response was not long in coming. The remaining wind stopped completely, allowing the rain to fall in whispering, vertical shafts. Then these also began to lessen. The great black clouds dispersed. As the final drops of holy water fell upon the ground, a single ray of sunlight burst through the densely swirling overcast, illuminating the campsite behind us. The fortress remained shrouded in gloom. A few of our men began to shout at the infidels, boasting of God's favor and proclaiming the triumph of our true belief. An arrow flew at us from the wall, landing on the earth a short distance from one of the priests. The holy men withdrew, slowly and with dignity, as the air began to fill with flying missiles.

For myself, the battle of opposing forces – the good of God against the full powers of the evil one – left me bewildered. I should have seen that sudden ray of heavenly light as a certain sign, like Constantine before the eve of the battle. But I had existed too long in the mire of doubt and heresy. Within me, a faint, lingering flame of doubt still flickered.

CHAPTER VII

During the next few days we sent raiding parties into all the areas surrounding the city. Our guns were moved forward and continued to boom constantly, hurling fear and death into the fortress. Our cavalry swept in ever widening arcs to the south and west, where most of the crops were destroyed in the fields. Whatever had been harvested and was already in storage was brought in for the use of our own men. The raids also resulted in a heavy influx of prisoners, most of which were sent on to Moscow where they would be displayed for the amusement of the masses.

Although the Crimean Khan continued to make his threats, the Kazanites never saw any evidence of his sincerity. In the absence of promised reinforcements from the south, there remained only one large Tartar force outside the fortress. This was a barbarian group that made its headquarters within a walled area inside the huge swamp, two miles or so from the city. Most of the Tartar warriors who had recently wandered up from the steppes were massed there, unable to break through our lines to reach Kazan.

Vorotinsky ordered Prince Simon Mikulinsky, nominal commander of the right hand, to take a large force and purge the swamp. His instructions were to destroy the wall and its defenders. Mikulinsky, who was also the Prince of Tver, was ready to leave almost as soon as his orders were received, but Vorotinsky delayed them long enough to provide a supporting action by the rest of the army. His idea, I think, was to mask Mikulinsky's movements and allow his attack to be more of a surprise. Accordingly, the rest of us were ordered into positions about the walls, as if we were preparing to launch a major assault. This misdirected the Tartars and eliminated any possibility of assistance from the citadel.

Mikulinsky's force moved out amidst this purposeful confusion, and he accomplished his mission in less than two days. He then continued south to occupy the town of Arsky Gorod, some fifteen miles farther. By chance, his force encountered the advance guard of a small relief army which the Crimean Khan had finally dispatched. The battle was fierce and swift, with the Tartars losing nearly all their men. Expecting the rest of our army to be right behind Mikulinsky's force, the remainder of the Crimean Horde turned and fled, leaving such a wealth of booty it was almost too much for the smaller Russian contingent to transport. When they returned to camp, it was with laden camels and other pack animals, many of the men on foot so their horses could be used to carry the heavy bundles of supplies. These materials were more than enough to tide us over until our own replacement goods arrived. Again, God had favored our cause.

It became a great sport, now, to hunt down the Tartars whom we were able to lure out of the fortress. Small parties of Russians would approach to within a short distance of the walls, shouting insults at the defenders until some of them came out to chase their tormentors. The infidels would be led into the woods, where they would be fallen upon by a stronger force and either killed or captured. The Czar ordered that all men taken in these raids be bound to posts beneath the walls and forced to call out for the defenders to surrender. There were also men stationed beneath the corner turrets to whisper night and day: "Surrender, surrender, surrender!"

While these activities distracted the infidels, our engineers were tunneling beneath the walls, listening for the sound of water. The Kazanites had a good supply from two underground streams, and it was the Czar's plan to seal them off. Already, several charges had been exploded under the stronghold and had done considerable damage. Unfortunately, the fortress was so huge and the mud walls so thick, there was no hope of actually bringing them down.

Other engineers were at work in secret, constructing a great tower, tall and stout enough to mount several cannon, which would enable our gunners to fire down on the Tartars. But these activities did not involve any appreciable part of the army. After several weeks of vainly contemplating the wall, I – like many of the other younger officers – became bored and fretful. With the enemy raiders cleared from the forest and swamp, we had little or nothing to do. Ivan had settled into a routine, rising early as he always did, and praying for at least two hours before breakfast. Following this, he might have a conference with his commanders or conduct an inspection of the troops or gun emplacements. I spent several afternoons with him, playing chess or conversing with the other visitors. But I found a majority of the men who remained about the Czar to be unfit companions. Daniel Romanov, particularly, was a miserable bore. His constant, sniveling whine was obnoxious and irritating. Nor was his brother much better.

Finally, I approached the Czar with the request that he allow me to lead one of the bogus foraging parties. While this ploy had been used a number of times, it still seemed effective, generally drawing a few Tartars out of the citadel. Admittedly, it had become a little more dangerous. The notoriously stupid infidels were just wary enough by this time to hold back until their supposed quarry approached very near. Their greatest weakness seemed to be an inability to break off, once they'd taken up the chase. At this time, two of their parties had actually been successful in catching the smaller Russian units, thus giving them added confidence and a couple of "victories" to crow about from the parapet. Knowing all of this, I was convinced we could provoke them to additional foolishness.

The Czar was reluctant to let me go, but after I'd worked on him for a few days he grudgingly agreed. He insisted that I select at least half my force from Heinrich's men, however. The rest were to be *Streltsi*, with Ivor assigned to assist me. Heinrich told me I was crazy, but at the same time I knew he was proud of me. Both he and the Czar had secret words with Ivor prior to our departure, and from the big man's expression after leaving each conference, I am sure he was more afraid to come back without me than to face capture by the enemy.

Had I possessed the judgment to equal my youthful courage, I would have followed Ivor's lead rather than insisting he obey me, especially when his greater maturity found fault with my rashness. Actually, he would not have restricted me very much, as I think he had been as restless as I over the past few weeks. At least he seemed nearly as anxious for some immediate action.

Ivan had asked me to stop by the royal chapel before we left. I dismounted and trudged up the hill just as dawn was beginning to dissipate the heavy ground mist. The night's chill still lingered in the air, reminding us that winter was not far away. I remember thinking about this as I gazed up into the sky and saw the last stars fading before the aura of the sun. Despite my impatience to get started, I could not help responding to the peaceful contrast and the sense of tranquil stability engendered by this setting – this combination of secular and spiritual force, joined against a common enemy.

As I'd feared, the Czar insisted I join him at his prayers. Lacking proper internal grace, I did so impatiently, chafing to be underway now that I was inside and my semi–reverent mood had been shattered. Sylvester stood before us at the altar, making the proper signs and leading us through the liturgy. Glaring at me as if he were being forced to ask God's blessing on one of Satan's slaves, he mumbled prayers for my well–being along with those for the Czar. The priest's fiery gaze, even at this hour of the morning, was penetrating and accusative. Why Ivan put up with him, I never understood. The man's very appearance made one uncomfortable, while his searing glance could wither a person's spirit, making him feel guilty even if he hadn't done anything wrong.

When the Czar was finally satisfied with my exposure to God's Grace, he rose and walked with me to the vestibule outside the chapel. He picked up a beautifully carved scepter, handing it to me as my symbol of authority. It was as fine as those borne by any commander; even Kurbsky did not possess a more exquisite token of the Czar's favor.

"Carry this bravely," he said, "and return it to me safely."

I thanked him solemnly and broke away before emotion destroyed my composure. As I trotted down the slope, I looked back over my shoulder. Ivan stood in the entryway of his pavilion, framed to either side by the usual guards in white livery. Behind the Czar, hovering like the angel of death, stood the priest. His face was a mask of poorly concealed malevolence, bloodshot eyes protruding at either edge of his great bony nose. I mounted my horse with all the lightness my armor would allow and waved a casual salute to the Czar. He raised his hand in casual benediction, and turned back into the pavilion. It was almost as if he foresaw some catastrophe for me. The *Streltsi* soldier who held my reins mounted his own horse and followed me. The rest of our group was assembled below, at the base of the hill. Ivor grinned knowingly when I rode up, mumbling some witty vulgarity about my new "staff of power." In high spirits, we galloped across the bridge toward Kazan.

We had decided to approach the walls from the southern side, where the hill below the fortress was particularly steep. We made a wide circle to avoid being seen before reaching the area where we wished to be noticed. Heinrich had moved out ahead of us, leaving while I was with the Czar. He commanded a strong force of his own men, reinforced by more *Streltsi* and a few peasant boys. Like the rest of us, these fellows were all spoiling for action and several of them had told me to be sure I brought enough Tartars to go around. This group should have been setting up their ambush in the woods, some two miles below the citadel, about the same time we advanced to our selected position.

Despite the precautions, our movements were observed from the beginning. As soon as we passed within hailing distance of the walls, the infidels began shouting at us. I had been in the area just long enough to have a smattering grasp of their language – at least those parts used most frequently by their soldiers – and the names they called us that morning were the usual, vile expressions of their ignorance and stupidity.

The area I selected had been only sparsely settled before the siege. Now deserted by its few inhabitants, it had been completely razed by our troops during their raids on Khan Ediger's secret storage places. Once a garden spot, with handsome trees and fine houses, it was now little more than a rubbish heap, except for an arm of the old inner city wall between us and the fortress itself.

We began to poke around in the ruins as if we were looking for something. The defenders knew our engineers were tunneling, and I hoped to convince those who watched us that we were seeking another site for our digging. They shot a few arrows at us, but we were well out of range. Although the slope above us was nearly vertical, the span was half again the distance an archer could accurately handle.

We explored the ruins for a long time – close to two hours – and still no one made any move to attack us. Except for Ivor, all the men with me were young. Like myself, they were impatient for action. After a while, we began playing a game of tag, chasing one another in ever widening circles, riding farther and farther up the slope. Ivor didn't say much at first, but as we rode continuously closer to the walls he began shouting at us to keep back and to stay out of arrow range. With youthful carelessness, we laughed at him and called him an old woman.

After we had played our game for close to another hour, still failing to draw out the infidels, we grew even more rash and Ivor became increasingly agitated. Suddenly, after a particularly close dash beneath the walls, a shower of arrows pelted into our midst. There were five of us involved: three of Heinrich's men, one *Streltsi* soldier, and myself. The soldier, much more lightly armored than the rest of us, was struck in the chest and fell, rolling limply down the slope. A second shaft stuck in the rump of another fellow's horse, causing the animal to bolt out of control. This sobered us very quickly and we turned to flee down the sandy hillside, behind the wounded horse and rider. I could hear Ivor shouting frantically, and from the corner of my eye saw him start up after us.

Another rain of arrows streamed down from the wall. Because I had been farther up the hill than the rest, I was now at the rear of the group as it retreated. One arrow struck me on the back, shattering harmlessly on the steel plate. But a second bolt passed clear through the left rear leg of my mount. I do not know exactly what else happened during the next few seconds, as it was all a crazy mass of sound and light – rushing wind and spinning earth, as I was pitched over my horse's head. I landed in a tremendous crash of metal. I must have been senseless for two or three minutes, because the next I remembered was Ivor tugging at me, trying to get me up and moving. I saw my beautiful red geldling on his side, a few feet away, writhing in agony and fear. Arrows continued to fall behind us, but we were again too far away to be hit. There was a shout from high above us, and looking up I saw one of the small gates in the inner city wall – the kind the Tartars call "the eye of the needle" – swing open, and a stream of horsemen which had been hidden there rushed toward us.

The rest of our force, now clustered at the bottom of the slope, began struggling up to help us. Their progress was much slower than the Tartars, who had the advantage of descent in their favor. Before the others were half way to us, we were surrounded by the infidels. Their leader shouted an order, and the bulk of his force continued down, slamming into the rest of my men who were still too far away to offer Ivor and myself any assistance. The former kennelmaster had drawn his sword and was attempting to afford what defense he could. He had barely time for a single swing before the blade was knocked from his hand. Eight or nine of the attackers leaped upon him and carried Ivor to the ground beside me. In all, the Tartars took seven of us captive. Eight men were killed and the rest fled, eventually leading their pursuers into Heinrich's ambush. That much success, at least, was achieved by my sortie.

The infidels who had remained about us proceeded to secure our arms with ropes. One of them, displaying the mercy of a true horseman, dispatched my suffering mount. Then with rope halters about our necks, we were dragged back up the slope to the citadel. In these first moments of captivity, I could not fully believe it had happened. Like a champion who has just been staggered by a mortal blow, my mind sought to deny Fate's perversity. Perhaps I was still dazed by my fall, but everything seemed to be moving through a nightmare dream, just beyond the brink of reality.

We were dragged into a small square, near the gate from which our captors must have emerged. Once on level ground, we were forced to trot at the end of our leads in order to keep up with our mounted captors. Crowds gathered all along the route, shouting and spitting at us. On the way out of the square, one of my men fell. I think he had been tripped by someone in the crowd. The swine leading him never slackened his pace, although the captive screamed in anguish, his face turning black as he strangled at the end of his rope. Then his head hit a stone and the screams abruptly ceased. His skull had shattered into a spray of blood, which did more than anything else to shake me back to the present.

Six of us now remained as prisoners: three Germans, Ivor, one *Streltsi*, in addition to myself. As I emerged from my deep trance, I experienced the full, shameful weight of fear. My throat was parched and my mouth was as dry as if someone had shoved a piece of coarse cloth into it. Nor was this simply due to the rope halter. The dreadful terror I felt gripping my guts was beyond any fear a man can understand, unless he has been a prisoner, facing a completely unknown destiny. In my youthful ignorance, I made it even worse by attaching a heavier guilt to my own emotions than to the poor quality of my leadership. At length, the press of the crowd slowed our captors' pace. We were dragged through the milling, shouting mob, into a series of alleyways, and finally into another square. Here, we were made to halt before a very ornate facade, built in the Mussulman style with unshuttered windows and heavy iron scrollwork. Several of my fellow prisoners had sagged to their knees; but, while I was gasping for breath the same as they, I was determined to show no weakness. All along the way we had been jeered at, kicked, and spat upon by the half-naked savages. My one remaining asset, the single sustaining force within my soul, was the certain knowledge of my superiority over these filthy, uncivilized barbarians. I stood as straight as my waning strength would allow, taller than all of them. I forbid any expression of fear to show either on my face or by any bodily flinching before their torments.

Except for the moment it had taken the Tartar horseman to cut his dead prisoner loose, we had not paused long enough for the mob to seriously threaten us. Now, the ugly brown-skinned rabble swarmed all around, offering to tear us to shreds. They made every conceivable gesture, obscenely promising to cut, beat, or impale us. Our mounted captors were hard pressed to keep them back, while one of their number ran into the building to notify his superior of their catch. The remaining soldiers kicked my companions into a tighter group around me, properly taking my stance as a sign of leadership. After this, they wielded their staffs against the crowd, driving them back like so many dogs. Standing there amidst the chaos, I thought of Heinrich and the long hours of training, when he had forced me to run for miles in full armor. Had it not been for this, I might have been lying back near the gate, beside our dead companion. Reason and awareness were catching up with me then, and I wanted to weep in my fear and frustration. I began to curse myself for my stupidity, but it was far too late for that!

Eventually, a well dressed emir appeared on the stairs, accompanied by several others who were also wearing expensive Mussulman robes. But the emir's costume immediately marked him as being of higher rank than the others. His gleaming white gown was of silk brocade, probably brought from Cathay. Reflecting somewhat refined taste for an infidel barbarian, he wore no jewels other than the silver threads and pearls in his collar. He carried my scepter, and motioned with it for our captors to bring us inside. The infidel soldiers jerked roughly on our ropes and started dragging us up the stairs. Although they were leading us off to some dreadful unknown, it was a relief to be taken away from that howling mob. Within the structure, it was cool and much lighter than most Russian buildings. The Tartars, used to sleeping in drafty yurts on the steppes of their barbarian realm, always desired fresh air – even at the expense of warmth during the winter months. Consequently, their walls were mostly windows, and these were frequently open to the elements all year round.

I had first thought the building to be the Khan's palace, but soon realized it was not. There were uniformed men at every intersection of the halls, and in several rooms I could see Turkish *jannisaries* regarding us curiously as we were hurried past. We were dragged the full length of the structure, clear to the back wall, then up a long winding flight of stairs. At the top was a large bare room, its windows barred by intricate grills of black iron. Once we were inside, our captors gave our rope halters a final tug and shoved us down, onto our knees. Involuntarily, I found myself in the same supplicating position as the others. With my arms pinioned behind me, encased in the heavy armor, I could not get up, although I tried. The emir stood with a still larger group of Tartar officers and nobles, looking down at us contemptuously.

"And who have we here?" he asked sarcastically, speaking in lightly accented Russian. His voice was young, much younger than he appeared to be. But with his turban and heavy black beard it was difficult to see his features. The visible portions of his face were heavily tanned from the sun, making his already dusky complexion even darker. His hands seemed soft, almost effeminate, as they idly stroked the wooden shaft of my scepter. His delicate fingers tapered gracefully into long, pointed nails. "I think we have caught ourselves a minor prize," he gloated.

I continued to glower at him without speaking as I made another vain attempt to stand. One of the soldiers who was still behind me shoved his foot into my back, forcing me to lunge forward onto my face. Someone laughed, but I was so furious I couldn't tell who. Only after several moments' struggle was I able to raise myself enough to look at anything but the floor. By rolling onto my side and pushing downward where my hand could touch the tile, I was able to get into a sitting position. While awkward, this was the most disrespectful posture I could manage.

"From the yellow beard and the expensive armor, I would judge we have captured the beloved bastard brother of the Czar," he continued, "the stepson of Heinrich the Merchant."

I was surprised he knew so much about me and my face must have shown it, for he went on smugly, "Do not wonder at our knowledge. Muscovy has no secrets from its rightful overlords."

Ivor spat on the floor, and received a kick which would have broken the back of a weaker man. As it was, the blow knocked the wind from him and he lay struggling to catch his breath.

"Now you have us, what do you intend doing with us?" I asked, making my voice as surly as I could. My throat was still so dry it was difficult to speak, and I was sure my tone sounded pleading, which annoyed me all the more.

"I think we should devise some slow, painful death for you," he said smiling, "possibly something we can perform on the walls for the benefit of your brother."

"I would advise something quicker," I replied, trying to imitate his mannerisms, "else you may not finish before your city falls."

At my words, blood rushed to his face. If he had not already been black as a Nubian, he would have turned purple. "Kazan will never fall!" he barked, then lapsed into his heathen tongue as he instructed his lackeys. They seized me by the shoulders and dragged me upright.

Smiling, and in better control of himself, he spoke again in Russian. "I have ordered my men to give you a lesson in humility before I speak further with you." Turning on his heel, the emir departed, his robes floating gracefully about him like the gown of a Polish whore. Eyeing me sullenly, the other officers trod after their master. From behind, strong hands now began to rip at the laces and bucklings of my armor, pulling it off without regard to its fastenings. I didn't struggle; I knew it was useless. Besides, I was already considering the possibilities of escape, and knew I would be more agile without this hundred pounds of steel.

Ivor, who had regained some of his composure, sat cross–legged at my feet, staring after the departing figures. "Who was that, do you suppose?" he asked. I noticed his voice was also strained and taut.

"Maybe Ediger's son," I suggested.

"More likely his boy friend," sneered one of the Germans. His comment proved a mistake, for the infidel standing close behind him brought his fist down against the back of the boy's neck, using all the force of his body. Had he been a larger man, he might well have reduced our number to five.

"You offspring of pigs will learn many things in the short time left to you," said one of them in barely intelligible Russian. They had removed all of my armor, leaving just my hose and the soft leather shirt Heinrich had given me to relieve the pressure of the straps. More Mussulmen had come in behind us, and they now proceeded to relieve my companions of their gear. Only Ivor started to resist.

"Save your strength," I told him, using a farmers' dialect which I hoped the infidels wouldn't understand. "Our time will come."

Our captors had not removed the rope from my neck, nor the fetters from my wrists, for it had been unnecessary in their task of stripping away the armor.

Without warning, one little brown man seized the line. Unable to understand the jabber which had preceded his move, I did not realize he was going to drag me out of the room until I was actually through the portal. He forced me to trot behind him, my head bowed to a level just below his own. We went a long way, through seemingly endless passages, up stairs and down. I could not look back, but I knew my companions were not being brought along – at least not very close behind. We finally came to a heavy, ironbound door, set into the gray stone of a lower floor corridor. We seemed to be in a subbasement, as the atmosphere was clammy and droplets of moisture trickled down the walls. We were close to the southern embankment, I thought, for that was where underground streams flowed closest to the surface.

The Mussulman banged his fist against the door and it was opened from the inside. As I'd feared, it was an interrogation chamber, not unlike our own beneath the Kremlin palace. The single attendant wore a black robe and hood, similar to a monk's habit. Assisted by the little weasel who had dragged me there, he passed a chain through the circle of my arms. Without undoing my bonds, they looped the chain through an iron ring in the ceiling. Heaving together, they lifted me off the floor, causing my forearms to double up, against my shoulderblades, while chain and ropes cut harshly into my flesh. When my toes were nearly two feet off the ground, they secured the chain and left me dangling. As if wiping their hands after some disagreeable contact, they went through a ritual of cleaning their palms and faces. While I suspected their splashing about in the bowl of water was a deliberate attempt to make me more aware of my own thirst, neither man spoke to me or even looked in my direction. After this, they sat on a pair of stools, talking and laughing as they drank.

Finally, the weasel glanced up at me. "You will learn to speak respectfully to your master," he said harshly.

The other just grunted, like a hog. I do not believe he spoke Russian. By this time, the pain had become almost unbearable. I was no longer able to keep my arms flexed, so the full weight of my body was pulling against the shoulder muscles. Several more minutes passed, while I gritted my teeth and fought back the sounds of anguish which kept rising in my chest. The weasel was becoming impatient, obviously annoyed at my refusal to admit my misery. He motioned to the attendant, who brought a heavy square of iron from across the chamber. He attached this to a short length of chain, then lifted the weight while the weasel attached it to my ankles. When they released it, I could not suppress a groan, which seemed to please them.

My breath soon became labored; sweat was streaming down my face and upper body. The pain was so intense it blotted out every other sensation, and I remember thinking that if I was not taken down soon I would never use my arms again. I next recall lying naked on the stone floor of another room, a cell of some kind. My hands were free, but I was chained to the wall by an iron collar about my neck. I had the leeway to sit or lie, but I could not stand up. I knew I had been moved to a higher floor, because there was a window in the wall above me; but I had no way to judge my precise location. It was cold; night had fallen, and I could see the gray mist from the river drifting past the opening. My body was one great mass of pain, as I lay in shivering misery upon some musty, prickly straw.

Shortly after I had returned to my senses, I heard the bolt slide and the door to my prison creaked open. Someone was standing in the opening, holding a lantern; but when I tried to turn my head to look at him the pain was so great I gave up the effort. Before I could try again, the door was closed and I heard muffled footsteps leading away. I tried lifting my arms to rub my shoulders, but the strain was prohibitive. I rolled onto my back, trying to ease the ache that way, only to discover that the chain was too short without my being able to reposition the connection on the collar. Finally, I managed to struggle into a sitting position with my back against the stones. By bringing my knees up to my chin, I was able to ease the strain a little and to capture a suggestion of warmth.

A few minutes later I heard my jailer returning, a scuffling sound as he fitted a key into the lock, the creak of hinges as the door swung open. But instead of some tattered flunky, there stood the emir in his sparkling white robes! The contrast was startling. As if from a very great distance I heard his voice. "Are you comfortable, My Lord Dmitri?" Apparently fearful of contamination should he get too close, he stepped gingerly into the cell, remaining near the wall by the door. He grinned at me, triumphantly, waiting for me to beg his mercy. I merely stared at him, and even had I wished to speak, I did not think I could have.

"Not so talkative, now," he continued. "Well, no matter. I just thought you might like to know we have decided on your contribution to Our Most Glorious Khan's amusement." He paused again, waiting, obviously expecting some response from me. Receiving none, he spoke harshly: "You stubborn. . . ." But he checked himself and forced the smile to curl again on his lips. "You will be taken at first light," he said evenly, "and you will be impaled atop the wall, in full sight of your army."

I still made no response, although my blood no longer seemed warm and a feeling of utter hopelessness was beginning to penetrate my numbed senses.

"We have sent a message to your brother, the Czar, that he may be present should he wish to observe our ceremonies."

He remained another moment by the door, wallowing in his triumph. The jailer had been standing behind him, holding the lantern. The emir made a delicate, fluttering motion with his hand, commanding the servant to lift the light higher, allowing him to see me better. For all my internal response to his words, I suspected his act was to frighten me, and nothing would have pleased him more than to have me bolt forward, only to be brought down, strangling, by the chain about my neck. I kept perfectly still, hoping to deprive him of his full satisfaction.

His eyes wandered over my body. "Too bad you are not a few years younger," he sneered. "A slight operation, and you would have brought a good price in the Crimea."

Revolted by his remark, I moved slightly to better hide my nakedness and inadvertently I farted. It was a most eloquent answer! The emir stiffened at the sound. "Goat!" he rasped.

He spun about and was gone. The jailer stepped inside to pull the door shut, and for a moment he pressed flat against the wall. He gripped the wood, facing me as he pulled and I thought he formed a word or two with his lips. When he pivoted into the room and around the edge of the door, he passed within a foot or so of my face. From his free hand he dropped a tiny bit of material, which drifted slowly to the floor. Idly, my fingers strayed to the ground and curiosity overcame the pain of my movements. I lifted the material to my face, and despite the gloom I recognized it as a bit of red colored feather.

There was a heavy lump in my stomach, and I had still received nothing to ease the dryness of my throat and mouth. The cell had become colder, the night even darker. The tiny bit of feather was still in my hand, as my fingers absently rubbed and twisted its surface. It had been several hours – I do not know how long – since I had retrieved it, and I was almost afraid to hope for the salvation it implied. I tried to look at it, again, holding it close before my eyes; but it was too dark. I could barely see my own hands.

The pain in my shoulders and arms had now subsided to a dull, heavy ache. I experienced the previous, sharp agony only if I attempted to move. Caught between wild hope and utter despair, I tried not to dwell upon the emir's plans for me. Instead, I struggled to concentrate on my comrades and to generate some concern for them. But I was too frightened. Regardless how brave I might pretend to be, I was literally trembling at the prospect of dawn's arrival.

To be impaled was the most painful, and certainly the most humiliating death a man could endure. A stake is set in the ground, firmly implanted and gauged to stand at a height just short of the condemned man's waist. If the executioner is skilled, the victim will hardly bleed when he is lifted above the point and set down upon it, with the tip entering his fundament. His legs are then allowed to touch the ground, and as long as he can remain standing on his toes the point of the shaft will not penetrate the flesh of his guts. Frequently, the prisoner's hands are released, for the stake is greased and no amount of effort will permit the victim to lift free. The more he struggles, the greater the pleasure of the audience.

In the end, even the strongest man must weaken, gradually allowing himself to stand flat upon his feet. If the stake has been sharpened, the first flow of blood will begin seeping down; if dull, it requires longer for the distended organs to tear loose. Eventually, the whole performance picks up momentum, for pain increases fear and the victim will likely twirl himself around in an effort to be free of the stake. In so doing, he will cause it to cut more deeply into his remaining store of energy. Gradually, he will sink deeper onto the shaft, until it pierces a vital organ. In the most successful executions, the prisoner will sink to his knees before he dies, and this may take as long as three days. Impalement had long been a popular mode of punishment among the Mussulmen, although not yet the vogue in Muscovy.

Being inside the fortress, the constant racket from the Tartar barbarians on the walls was even louder than I had heard it before, and more annoying. Shortly after the emir's departure, the din became so great I had to concentrate to maintain my own thoughts. I was trying to raise myself enough to see out the window, when the door to my cell was opened. Distracted by the noise and the discomfort occasioned by my physical exertions, I did not hear it and jumped nearly the length of my chain when a warm, soft hand came to rest upon my back.

It was the same guard, and he whispered, "Take this," as he thrust a tiny bit of metal into my hand. "I do not have a key to your chain; you will have to cut it through yourself."

I tried to speak, but he silenced me. "No time, no time now. You may have less than an hour to free yourself!" He bolted nervously for the door. "Don't try to cut through the collar," he cautioned me. "Start at a worn spot, inside one of the links."

My mind was still dulled by pain and cold. Stupidly, I continued to sit, wasting several precious moments before I understood what he had said. The chain fastening me to the wall was old, and must have held innumerable loyal Christians before me. I felt along its surface and poked a finger inside several links before finding one which seemed more worn than the others. I groped about on the floor until my fingers closed on the bit of metal the guard had left. It was white iron, by the feel of it, with half a dozen saw teeth. Placing this against the bronze, I began the tedious process of trying to rub it through the unyielding metal.

I must have worked an hour without stopping. I had no feeling left in my fingers, but I seemed to have made progress. My eyes kept turning toward the window, where I could now detect a faint glow. Dawn was not far off. Frantically, I kept rubbing the scrap of steel against the link until the muscles of my left arm cramped into a knot. It was almost half an hour before I could force it to obey me again. I went back to work on the chain—rubbing, rubbing, rubbing, scratching metal on metal. The sky was definitely turning light; there could not be much time left. Finally, my improvised saw went through the link. Exhausted, I dropped my arms and began to breath regularly.

The cell door clicked and the guard appeared again. "Are you free?" he whispered.

He crept in, and I showed him where I had cut through. He fingered the link, twisted at it, but it would not separate. Although I had been able to slice through one side, the heavy bronze still retained its shape. The strength of twenty men would be needed to twist the link open.

The guard shook his head. "No time," he said. "You must cut through the other side of the link." He glanced furtively at the open door. "I'll try to get back." Quickly, he pressed a water bag against my mouth, giving me my first drink since being captured. "Drink what you can," he said. "I dare not leave it with you."

I swallowed nearly the whole bagful. Then, shoving a chunk of bread into my hand he fled.

Once the door closed behind him I wolfed down the bread, and desperately ran my fingers along the chain, trying to find the same link again. Forcing my fingernail into the slit, I set the teeth of my tiny saw against the opposite side and began rubbing. A ray of sunlight poked tenuously through the window. A moment later I started at the sudden cry of a Mussulman priest, calling from a minaret almost directly above me. The bit of steel slipped from my hands, falling into a crack between the stones of the floor. By the time I was able to retrieve it, using a bit of straw, the *muezzin* had finished calling the prayers. My time was nearly at hand, and I had hardly begun the second cut.

The door was flung open before I was a quarter way through. I had only time to hide my saw in a crack before two short, bow legged infidels came in. Without uttering a word, one of them grabbed my shoulder and forced me to my knees, facing the wall. The other seized my wrists and manacled them behind my back. They unlocked the collar and pulled me upright. One of them produced a grimy breechclout and held it open, jeering and motioning for me to step into it. Relieved at being spared the humiliation of walking to my death stark naked, I obeyed him. Once both legs were through the holes, he jammed it into position, nearly eliminating the parts he wished to cover. The other one shoved me into the corridor, where four more soldiers waited. They all wore the ornate gold uniform of the Khan's bodyguard, and carried lances in addition to their scimitars.

Surrounded by the infidels, I was marched through a musty stone hallway and out a small door, into a narrow uncovered passage between two very high walls. One of these proved to be the inside of the fortress, itself. We soon came to a wide, heavy-runged ladder. Two of the guards clambered up the first few steps; then one of them turned, motioning for me to follow. Someone shoved me from behind. I tried to climb up, but with my hands bound I could not keep my balance. The guards laughed and one of them slipped a noose around my neck, tossing the lead end to a man above. With this to steady me, I made my way upward, pulled by the rope and prodded from below by the point of a lance.

The ladder led to the top of the fortress wall, on the side facing the Kazan River. Soldiers quickly led me to the north edge, where the surface widened and a large number of infidel officials stood waiting. My fear began to mount, as again I felt the drawing and dryness in my mouth and throat. The tide of emotion seemed to enervate my brain, combined now with lack of sleep, thirst and hunger. Immediately after climbing the wall I experienced a few moments of dizziness, probably because of the rope's pressure around my throat. I know I had trouble focusing my eyes. Now I stumbled, falling hard against the timber surface.

The next I knew I was being held up by several pairs of hands, and being force-walked toward the waiting cluster of officers. I did not immediately see the emir, for he was on the far side of the group. Then the others parted to allow my escort to pass, and I was shoved face to face with my adversary. The rope was loosened about my neck and I regained enough of my senses to resist the final forward shove that would have thrown me onto my knees. My stance, however, was bent, due to fatigue and cramped muscles. When the emir drew himself up to his full height he was slightly taller than I, whereas I would normally have topped him by several inches. But today, he was able to look down on me. His haughty expression conveyed his contempt. Wrinkling his nose – indicating I smelled badly, which I undoubtedly did – he turned to look outward, toward the Arsky Plain. For the first time I became aware of the scene below us, and dazed as I was the sight made me gasp.

My view encompassed a complete panorama of the plain and all the areas beyond. Covering the sun bleached ground like ants, as far as the eye could see, were thousands of our soldiers. The trenches dug by Kurbsky's army stretched, two and three deep, as far as my view extended around the city. Russian artillery poked menacingly through the multitude of men, the evil looking snouts spaced not more than ten feet apart. A light haze still clung to the ground on my right, making the men on that side appear to stand as if in a dream, on drifting, misty clouds.

Directly before us, in the center of the Russian line, and only a few paces behind the first row of trenches, was a group of horsemen. I immediately recognized Ivan's great black. Next to him was Heinrich on his gray. Kurbsky, Bulgakov, and Vorotinsky were behind the Czar, while Vladya sat his mount on my stepfather's left. Behind the Czar's cousin I saw Basmanov, and beyond him stood a group of priests. I stared in awe and disbelief, nearly overcome at the display of concern.

I was paying no attention to the emir, so I did not hear him give any order. But I was suddenly seized again, and thrust to the very edge of the Parapet. At this, there was a noticeable stirring in the group below.

"See, mighty Czar, your kinsman stands naked and at my mercy," shouted the emir. "His fate will soon be yours!"

They were too far away for me to see the expressions on their faces, but the whole group of officers surged forward, past the foremost trenches. Bulgakov cupped his hands about his mouth and shouted back. "If you harm that boy, infidel, you forever renounce any hope of mercy from the Czar of Muscovy!"

More Mussulmen had mounted the walls, and I suddenly realized they were archers. The treacherous emir had used me to bait a trap for the Czar! "Get back!" I shrieked. "Get away from the walls!"

My guards yanked me backward, but I saw the whole leadership of our army still standing below us. I did not know if they understood me, but in the next moment it made no difference. The Tartar archers let fly a sky–darkening barrage of arrows, at which the group immediately closed about Ivan, protecting him with their bodies. I saw a shaft strike Kurbsky, but it must have shattered on his armor. The group withdrew, except for Heinrich and Andrew. They were both shouting, but whether their words were threats to the Tartars, or meant as encouragement to me, I didn't know. The noise and confusion was too great for me to hear them.

Then Andrew drew his sword, raised it high above his head and brought it down smartly. At that, all the cannon opened up at once. Before the infidels could move, the great iron balls were cutting through the tightly packed masses of archers. Huge chunks of clay and wood were splintering upward, as several shots bounced off the edge of the wall. Whatever display they intended to make, the cowardly Tartars had now forgotten it.

In a panic of fear and chaos, each man seemed interested only in saving himself, although – in fairness to the officers – I must admit those near me maintained a better control of themselves. Motioning for the guards to bring me along, the emir led the group away, all of them maintaining a display of dignity. I was led behind them, down a wide flight of stairs. Noting the damage being done above, I wondered if Kurbsky could have repositioned his guns during the night. Perhaps it was only because I was seeing it from inside, but his artillery had never seemed so effective in the past. Only a few shots had fallen short. That was all I had been able to see above, nor was I permitted to view much of the destruction below the walls. I was dragged into another building, through more halls and corridors, eventually emerging in a yard some distance beyond cannon range. I was startled to see several kinds of scaffolds in the otherwise bare enclosure, and I was sure my moment had arrived.

The emir turned on me in fury. "I had decided not to end your existence, after all, because it amused me to think of having the Czar's own blood for my slave."

I eyed him coldly, so drained of feeling I was beginning not to care what he did to me. "And now?" I asked.

His eyes turned from me to the guards behind. With no more instruction than that, blows began falling upon my back and sides, delivered by at least a dozen men. I tried to struggle away, but it did no good. I was eventually beaten unconscious, but just before I went out I heard one of the men say something in very

broken Russian: "Have respect for the Great Khan, unbelieving. . .(something). . . ."
Thus my final thought was to recognize my captor as the very incarnation of evil –
Ediger, the Khan of Kazan.

When I slowly returned to life I was in another cell, much larger than the
last. There was a thick layer of filthy straw on the floor and a shelf suspended from
the wall by chains. On this rested a large bucket of brackish water and a loaf of
black bread, on which a variety of vermin were feasting. These were the first items
I saw, but gradually I became aware of more. In the far wall was a huge, open
window, barred with heavy iron filigree.

I was completely unfettered, although I lay on the floor. I noticed I had
been placed on a cloth mat, separating me from the straw. As I started to rise, I
heard a loud commotion outside my window. Laboriously, I got to my feet and very
unsteadily reached for the shelf. I gulped a few swallows of water and tore off a
chunk of the bread, shaking the insects away as I staggered toward the window. In
addition to all my other woes, my feet were swollen and sore from going barefoot.
The spikes of straw made it seem I was walking on a bed of nails.

When I looked out the window, the sight was almost enough to overwhelm
me, and for a moment I thought I was going to swoon again. I was looking down
upon the courtyard where I had been beaten. It was now full of dancing, frenzied
infidels, who were celebrating the executions of two from my captured band. One
was the *Streltsi* soldier, a young man about my age whom I think they called
Nikola. The other was Franz, a squire to one of Heinrich's knights. Both were
naked and attached to separate scaffolds, Franz hanging by his feet, Nikola by his
wrists. Small beds of coals had been set beneath them, fed periodically with
additional scraps of tinder tossed by the reveling devils who became convulsed with
laughter each time one or the other victim winced or cried out in pain. The flames
were deliberately kept low, so as not to kill or render unconscious, yet hot enough
that the victim had constantly to struggle, keeping his body to one side or the other.
Once he allowed himself to hang motionless for more than a few seconds, his hair
or flesh began to sear. A part of me wanted to watch, but in the end I couldn't. The
bite of bread I'd taken tuned to bile in my mouth, and starved as I was I had to spit
it out. I sank to the floor, buried my head in my arms and wept. The whole thing
was my fault, I told myself. I had brought these poor wretches to this end, and
caused the deaths of those whose bodies still lay putrefying outside the walls. Ivor
and the others might also be dead, for all I knew, and this morning I had almost
seen the Czar, himself, fall victim to Tartar treachery.

Perhaps it was punishment for having laughed at the priests and mocked
the Czar's confessor. I had lately followed the ways of the evil one, and for too long
a time before this I had childishly forsaken my God altogether. I had sinned in
nearly every way before His eyes. I knelt there, in the blinding glare from the
window, and with the sounds of that horrible torment ringing in my ears. I prayed
to God for the salvation of my own soul, and for His mercy that my poor comrades
not be forced to suffer more for my sins.

I came away from the window in a trance, devoid of reasoned thought or
perception. Like some mindless being, I dropped to the straw, staring at the bleak
walls of my prison. Whatever additional abominations the infidels committed, I did
not see. Nor in my mental debility did I even hear them. My soul had been

withdrawn, much as they describe the condition of madmen. And at that time I may have been very close to madness. Certainly, it was hours before I could remember anything else. I am sure the Russian bombardment continued; at least I was told later that it had.

I must eventually have fallen asleep. My next memory was of being awakened, or perhaps being shaken from unconsciousness. Slowly, as if I were ascending from a deep dive through some warm, cloudy water, I began to perceive my surroundings. It was very dark outside, and the cell was dimly illuminated by the muted glow from a heavily covered lantern. The guard who had given me the saw blade the night before – or had it been the night before? – was frantically shaking my shoulders. He seemed frightened, but his fear was largely despair at being unable to waken me. When he saw the spirit returning to my body, he quickly fetched a dipper of water and forced me to drink. My mind began to function again, and abruptly I came fully awake. I bolted into a sitting position, then twisted in pain as every muscle protested the movement.

"Can you walk?" he asked in a harsh whisper.

"I think so," I replied. With his help I was able to get to my feet.

"Here," he said, shoving a pair of soft leather sandals into my hands. "Put these on." He steadied me as I stood on one foot, then the other, afraid to sit down again lest I be unable to rise.

He tossed a heavy brown cape of some harsh peasant material about my shoulders and pulled the cowl over my head. "Now lean on me," he whispered, "and hurry as much as you can."

Half dragging me, he led the way through a series of passages, alleys, and cellars of deserted buildings. I had no idea where I might be. I tried to question him several times, but he cautioned me to be still. "Later," he murmured. "I'll tell you everything later."

Our journey ended in another cellar, far below the normal depth for such rooms. Again, we were somewhere near the southern parapet. The earthen walls were so wet they glistened in the meager glow of a single taper, set in its own wax in the center of a crudely made table. Several men sat around the light, leaning together and talking in a muted drone. As we entered they spun about to face us, startled, regarding us with menacing expressions until they recognized my guide. After a few words in the infidel tongue, the guard motioned me to sit with them. "I'm sure you must be nearly starved," he said. "We will get you some food right away."

One of the men at the table, a short pudgy fellow with dark, pitted skin, shoved a wooden mug into my hands. He wore an expensive robe beneath his peasant's cloak, and I took him for a Tartar noble, or at least a wealthy merchant. The faces of the men around the table – there were five in all – regarded me intently as I sipped the liquor. None of them, apparently, could speak a language I would understand.

The guard, who had gone after food, returned a few moments later. He placed a loaf of bread, some grapes, and a large chunk of cheese on the table before me. Handing me the dagger from his girdle, he sat with us as I greedily attacked the food.

"These men," he said, "are some of the more substantial citizens of Kazan, dissidents who wish to dispose of Ediger. They've made it possible for me to be employed in the prisons, and they're willing to help you get out of the fortress."

"Can they really do this?" I asked, pausing just long enough between bites to frame the question.

"It is all arranged. Of course, I will have to go with you."

I looked at him, questioningly, still chewing on a large wad of bread. He was a man of medium height, slender but sinuous, with a swarthy complexion, not quite as dark as the others. His eyes were a lighter color, as well – more green than the usual Tartar brown. He was probably not much older than I. Behind his serious demeanor, I sensed a fleeting glimmer of amusement. "Have you really compromised yourself?" I asked.

He nodded. "They will know it was I who released you. They may know it already."

I washed down another mouthful of bread and cheese with a great gulp of liquor. "You're my stepfather's contact, then?'

"I am Jacob," he replied easily, ". . .son of Abraham."

I looked at him in surprise, as recognition began to dawn. "Yes, I remember – in Moscow, .maybe ten years ago. But – I mean, I thought. . .your father told me you were dead."

"I'm a Christian," he explained, "and I've married a gentile woman. I work for the *Freiherr*, just as my father works for him. But because I chose to embrace your faith, my father has had the prayers for the dead sung over my grave. For him, I am no longer alive."

The others were watching us, not understanding our words, but some of the meaning may have penetrated the void of language. The man nearest Jacob prodded him with his thumb and said something in Arabic.

"My friend is concerned that you understand who it is arranging your escape. He wishes your Czar to know of these. . .expressions of loyalty to him."

"Tell the gentleman that I am very grateful to them, and that once I am back with the Czar I will do everything I can to assure his mercy." The liquor, whatever it was, began having a tremendous impact. I felt extremely giddy, and the prospect of escaping the Tartar stronghold was almost enough to make me leap for joy. When I moved to face the men at the table, however, I was reminded of my strains and bruises—and the circumstances of my companions.

Jacob had translated my statement, and the others nodded solemnly. The man nearest me clasped his hands together against his chest, in the Mussulman sign of gratitude. I turned again to Jacob. "Where are the other men who came in with me?" I asked, ". . .other than the two who. . .the two they had in the courtyard this afternoon?"

"The large one is still in a cell next to the first one you were in," he replied. "The other has been given as slave to the *karach* who captured you. I do not know where he has been taken."

"If he has been given over to slavery, what will happen to him?" I asked. I could imagine many horrors for this last member of my group. It was Joachim, a lad of barely fifteen.

"He is very young," replied Jacob evenly. His eyes held on mine, but he offered no further explanation. I feared to contemplate his meaning. Bad enough if the boy was being subjected to the lusts of his barbarian master; it was an ordeal he could still survive. But I remembered the Khan's words to me – *a little younger. . . a slight operation. . . . .*

"We must free Ivor," I said simply. "He is also a favorite of the Czar." I hoped that my matter of fact tone would convince them. If the city fell in time, there was a good chance Joachim would be rescued. His beard had sprouted, and it was rare that boys were deprived of their manhood at such a stage of development. As a slave, he would probably suffer no more than humiliation in the interim.

"I do not know if it is possible to save your friend," Jacob answered. He turned to the others, and explained my question. There was a rush of words between the Tartars, a great flaying of hands as they argued. The well- dressed one gestured helplessly to Jacob, and spoke rapidly for several seconds. Jacob looked back at me. "They say it's impossible to rescue the large one. The Khan has plans for him, tomorrow."

"What plans?" I demanded.

Jacob looked despairingly at the others, cracking his knuckles as he tried to frame his words. "The Khan was stated his desire to observe the famous Russian sport of bear wrestling," he said at length. "There is a large, Siberian beast in his menagerie, and he announced the match. . . ."

"Then my friend must be freed tonight," I replied flatly.

"It is impossible," Jacob insisted. "It cannot be done."

The others were watching our conversation intently, absorbing what they could from our tone and gestures. Taking them all in with a single glance, I replied, "It *will* be done, because I won't leave without him. If these men expect the Czar's mercy, they must also free my servant."

My statement needed no translation, for the five Tartars were engaged in their animated conversation before Jacob had time to speak. Finally, their leader turned to us, and Jacob restated his lengthy discourse as simply: "They say they will do their best."

Perhaps I was being foolish, and even at the time I realized it, but I could not face my stepfather, or any of my other companions, knowing that I had left Ivor to such a cruel and certain death. Jacob had another long discussion with the Tartars, after which two of them got up to leave. Bowing respectfully, first to me, then to their leader, they withdrew.

"They are going to see what they can do about your friend," Jacob explained. "Now you must go with Yusuf Ali." He indicated the well dressed Mussulman. "If they have not already discovered your empty cell, they will very shortly."

"Where will you be?" I asked.

"I have one more task before we leave. I shall be safe enough."

"May I ask how you intend to get us out?"

"Your engineers are digging a tunnel beneath the city," he replied. "We will get you into it from this side, before they plant their explosives."

"Can you do this?" I asked, incredulous.

"I think we can," he said honestly. "They are seeking to destroy the water supply, and we have dug to within a few feet of their tunneling, going through the bottom of an old well."

Yusuf Ali made some remark to Jacob, gesturing to indicate his impatience. Jacob answered, nodding, and reached for his lantern. Its flame had been extinguished, and it stood on the floor by his feet. Taking a piece of dirty cloth, he wiped some soot from the chimney and approached me. "That yellow beard of yours," he said, starting to work on me with the cloth. "I have to make it darker."

When I left with the Tartar, my beard was black. My face and hands had been stained as well. Jacob's final warning was to keep the cowl over my face. "No Tartar has blue eyes," he reminded me.

Yusuf led me quickly through the fortress, speaking to me all the way as if we were two old friends, out upon some early business. The first, pinkish streaks of dawn were lacing the sky, and I knew we would have to get inside soon, before a *muezzin* began to call the prayers. I would be hard put to bluff my way through the ritual.

We reached Yusuf's door, and his knock was answered immediately by a huge African slave. Yusuf motioned for me to follow him through the lavishly furnished interior, toward a door behind some heavy draperies in the rear. I did not yet realize it, but I was being taken to the Harem. Yusuf clapped his hands, and seven lovely girls came running to him. All but one were dark, heavy–hipped beauties. The last was more slender, fair–skinned and blonde. They wore filmy harem garments, although several of the girls also had cloaks, because it was still chilly. They all recoiled in surprise at the sight of me, for their master was normally the only male permitted inside these doors. I knew that nothing less than mortal fear, the fervent desire to save his own skin, could have motivated such a breech of custom.

Yusuf waved his hand in annoyance, and spoke rapidly to the blonde. She giggled. Looking directly into my eyes, she said in halting Russian: "Our master says you are to come with us."

I looked at her, and back to Yusuf. "Go. Go!" he said, and gave me a gentle shove. "Maria. . .she tell. everything," he managed. He grinned nervously, then turned quickly and left. Over his shoulder he made some last remark to the girls, which started them laughing and squealing. I took this last to have been a warning not to make me too completely at home. Surrounded by the flock of chattering females, I was taken into the harem proper. Only the blonde Maria seemed impressed by the serious implications of my presence.

Once Yusuf was gone they led me to a soft, elegantly upholstered chaise, and Maria politely invited me to rest. Two of the girls hurried off to bring refreshments, while the others began plucking at my clothes. I wore little enough as it was, and in a panic of embarrassment I tried to draw my cape more tightly about me. This only evoked more shrieks of laughter, and a greater determination on the part of the girls to strip away my garments.

"It is proper," said Maria reassuringly. "Our master has instructed us to bathe you and to make you comfortable until this evening."

"But I can't display my nakedness to these women." I said.

"It is the custom of these people to treat an honored guest in this manner," she replied. "To refuse such hospitality is insulting to the host."

"*These people?*" I asked. "Then you are not one of them?"

"Do I appear to be one of them?"

"Only your clothes," I agreed, still struggling weakly against the others. They had now succeeded in removing my sandals, and had pulled the robe off my shoulders...would have removed it completely had I not continued to sit on it.

"I was taken from my parents seven years ago, and...oh!" she gasped, seeing the marks on my back and the clots of blood where the halter had rubbed the skin on my neck. The others were also speaking in hushed tones, running cool fingers across my skin to trace the scars and abrasions. Several of them spoke at once.

"My sisters say you must stand up," Maria told me.

"Are you sure?" I began feebly.

"Yes," she insisted, rising and pulling me gently. None of them were laughing any longer, and there seemed genuine sympathy in their expressions. "You have been very badly treated," said Maria. "My sisters and I will care for you."

I stood in just the breechclout, burning with embarrassment. Fully aware of my discomfort, Maria and two or three other girls led me gently to a huge, square pool of warm water, sunken below the level of the tile floor. When I reached the edge, I felt two pairs of hands begin to ease away my last item of clothing.

"It is all right," Maria assured me again, and in a moment I stood completely bare.

Two girls continued to steady me as I stepped into the bath, where warm water welcomed me with the subtle scents of roses and Oriental spices. The temperature was as great as I could have desired, and I sank luxuriously into its soothing embrace. Two of the dark–skinned girls pulled off their filmy coverings and glided over the edge, joining me in the water. Without protest, I watched them, too comfortable and relaxed to question. One on each side, all three of us hardly filling the pool, they began to rub my arms and shoulders with soothing, sweet–scented unguents. Maria sat behind me on the rim, and began dabbling water over my hair, rubbing another lotion into my scalp.

It was a form of sensual enjoyment I had never experienced before. As I started to lapse into a hazy, blissful state of semi–slumber, I happened to glance up at the side of the pool, startled to see a very fat, older woman standing there watching us. Feeling suddenly guilty, I tried to place my feet against something to steady me, and struggled to sit up. But Maria held my head gently in place. "That is Jasmine," she said, a trace of amusement in her tone. "She is the. . ..mistress of the. . .of us. . . ." She shrugged. "I have not spoken our language for a long time," she apologized. She said something in the infidel tongue to the older woman, at which Jasmine's entire, mountainous body quaked with mirth.

"You not fear me," she tittered. "I like big, light mens."

I lay back in the warm water, allowing the women to do what they wished with me, enjoying the explorations of their soft fingers, the rubbing of oils and ointments into my flesh. It came to my mind to ask why I was being hidden in the harem, but I felt too warm and calm – too safe, for the first time since my capture.

Finally, when they had cleansed every part of me, fat Jasmine sat on the lip of the pool, kicked off her sandals, and dangled her chubby toes in the water. The two girls who were in the pool with me began to giggle and play, splashing each other – and me, and anyone else who came close to the water's edge. After a while, Maria called softly for me to come out.

I could hardly pretend to modesty any longer, so after a minimum of urging I heaved myself out of the water and back onto the tiles. Amidst a chorus of tittering laughter, I walked into a huge towel, held out for me by the women. They led me to a low table, covered with a soft hide, and made me lie on my stomach while several of them began working on my wounded back and arms. They applied more fragrant lotions and oils, rubbing them into my skin with loving tenderness. Again, I nearly fell asleep.

They rolled me onto my back and continued their ministrations until I no longer felt the slightest suggestion of pain or fatigue. Much to my embarrassment, however, the stirring of other emotions was beyond my control. Even the girls' giggling could not inhibit me. Finally, Jasmine took over, with her plump, agile fingers. She soon worked me into that dreamy state between sleep and waking, lethargy, the peaceful sensation which one experiences only rarely. Eventually, their voices still tinkling with delicate laughter, the girls covered me with a silken sheet and I slept like one who was dead.

I am not sure how long I slept – two hours? Perhaps more. But near the end of my slumbers I had a strange, confusing dream, which I have never been able to understand – and which I feared ever to discuss. I found myself in the courtyard outside the prison cell, where Franz and Nikola had suffered their terrible tortures. I was naked as they were, but armed with a sword. I was trying desperately to hold back the rabble, while my free hand worked at the knots on the rope about the German's ankles. At one point in the struggle I managed to rake the tip of my sword through the coals beneath his head, and scatter them. He gasped his thanks, causing me to look down at him. Although his manhood remained intact, the rest of his body – his face and his voice – were Maria's!

The Tartar mob, somehow smaller now than before, was pressing in on my right, while the suspended body still swung on my left. In order to reach the rope about the ankles I had to press my nakedness against his body, and I somehow wished not to do this – wished not to make the physical contact. Both my arms were growing tired, and I knew it was only a matter of moments before the infidels overwhelmed me, when Maria's voice cried out to me, a whispered sound of terror: "Hurry," she urged, "hurry. They are going to search the house!"

"What? Who? Who's going to search. . .?"

She was pulling me after her, and in the few seconds it took me to waken fully, I realized I was running behind her, naked as the day I was born. As yet, the terror she was trying to communicate had not quite penetrated my brain.

"The Khan's soldiers," she gasped. "That is why Yusuf hid you here; they are not likely to search the harem. Such an intrusion would be most unseemly. But still, they might. The Khan must have been furious when he found you gone."

We were now in a small bedchamber, furnished in delicate silks and fine satin fabrics. "This is Jasmine's room," she whispered. "You should be safe here." She started to leave, and gestured helplessly.

"Maria, I. . .if they find me, I would at least like something to wear. And a sword, something. . . ."

She nodded. "All right. Just stay here; I'll be right back."

She fled from the room, and I could hear the harsh voices of several men in another part of the house. There was also the sound of heavy furniture being moved, and the audible clumping of feet. My first warning of real trouble was a resounding crash, as if some large glass object had been smashed. Unless Yusuf were in trouble, the soldiers would never have been so careless of his property. And if the search were more than mere routine, I could expect them at any moment. I began to search for a weapon and something to use to cover myself.

Then Maria returned, her arms loaded with clothing. Poking out of the cloth was the handle of a scimitar. Quickly, she helped me dress in the Tartar garments – obviously the gleanings of the Yusuf's wardrobe. The arms and legs were far too short, while the waist would have accommodated two of me. But I got into the things, ripping a seam or two about the shoulders, and stuffed my feet into the boots, which were soft and came closer to fitting than the rest. I was still stiff and sore, particularly across my shoulders. But fear lent strength, and I forced myself to move almost normally.

All the time, Maria was breathlessly telling me what she had seen. She was like a frightened child, and in her excitement she had trouble recalling the words she wished to use. "The soldiers – they have put the – .master in prison. But they do not know you are. . .I. . .I do not think they really look for you. They. . .they destroy. . .all."

I pulled her trembling form against my side and started for the door. "Is there a back way out?" I asked. Getting no answer, I shook her. "A back way – another door?" I demanded.

"Yes, yes," she stuttered. "We must go through the women's quarters to the kitchen. I will show you."

We hurried into the harem garden, starting around the lily pond with its fragile little marble columns supporting the roof, when the other girls came rushing toward us from the door leading to the main part of the house. Jasmine led the charge, her rolls of fat apparently no handicap. "They come; they come!" she shrieked, and collided so hard against me she would have knocked me down, had she not clung to my arm like her life depended upon it.

"Go on!" I shouted at Maria. "Lead the way."

She fled toward the rear exit, the other girls following her. Jasmine brought up the rear, still clinging tightly to my left arm. The girls must have been watching the intruders through a peephole in the harem door, but in their fright had neglected to lock it. This cost us the few moments delay it should have taken for the infidel soldiers to batter it down. As I slipped into the rear passageway, I saw several uniformed guards burst into the harem garden. They wore a red and blue livery, not of the Khan's household.

We bolted into the kitchen, and I slammed the heavy door shut behind us. The portal had a bar only on the other side, for it was intended to keep the kitchen help out of the harem. I seized a stool and smashed it against the wall, shoving an angled shaft of wood under the door in the hope it would delay our pursuers for a few extra moments. I rushed to the outside gate. Without stopping, we charged through into the street – the entire harem, increased now, by the cook and his two helpers. Less than an arrow's flight away, stood a squad of at least twenty soldiers.

For a moment, all of us – both my group and the soldiers – stood staring at each other. Then the leader of the guardsmen shouted and started running forward. I had taken about two steps backward, when there was a tremendous explosion. The whole earth shook, and the wall of the building across the street collapsed into a heap of rubble. Yusuf's house was half destroyed, with bits of brick and rubbish beginning to fall around us, through a choking cloud of dust and plaster. One of the girls was holding her face where she had been cut by some flying debris. Several others had been hit on the shoulders or arms. I realized what must have happened, for it could only be the result of our engineers' blasting. I did not know, however, whether it had been the blast to destroy the water supply, or another attempt to undermine the parapet.

Looking about quickly, I saw that we were near a section of the fortress facing Kurbsky's major artillery emplacements. Motioning my flock to follow me, I rushed down an alleyway in the general direction of the wall. We came out in a ruined marketplace, deserted except for a number of bodies. In the center of the square was a gaping hole, which must have been directly over the center of the explosion.

At first, I did not know what to do. To go back would surely land us in the arms of the troops, and there seemed no other exit from the square. The explosion had brought down most of the buildings on the other sides of the bazaar, and beyond them was the fortress wall. Going to the great crater, I looked in and thought I saw light! I jumped down the side, slipping on some loose rock, and slid to a stop at the bottom. Pulling what loose material I could from the hole, I saw a clear shaft leading downward. Beyond the vertical passage it seemed to angle off toward the wall. Somehow, the explosion had not completely blocked the passageway dug by our engineers. Or had it cut through to Jacob's tunnel? I didn't stop to question God's act of grace. The tunnel might collapse at any moment, but while it remained open it was a possible path to freedom.

Tugging at a large piece of rock, I realized I could not lift it by myself; but it did move. "Come on," I shouted. "Send the men down first."

In a moment the cook was beside me, his two boys sliding down behind him. Between us, we were able to shove the heavy block of granite to one side, leaving a passage large enough for a man to squeeze through. The others looked at me, waiting for my lead. The girls were already struggling down the slope, and as yet there was no sign of pursuit. I entered the hole head first, and wormed my way along the tunnel toward the light.

I made it all the way to the end, before encountering another stone that blocked the passage. It took all my strength to shove it out, which brought a trickle of earth down on top of me. But I was able to wriggle through.

I pulled myself out, and the cook emerged only seconds later, his two boys right after him. Maria came immediately behind the second boy. I had just hunkered down to help extricate the first of the dark–skinned harem girls, when someone shouted a challenge in Russian, and Maria dropped down beside me. I turned in time to meet the onrushing charge of a *Streltsi* patrol. "Wait! Wait!" I shouted. "We're Russians!"

The man nearest me slowed, for the combination of my words and blond hair convinced him. The cook, however, was struck down dead and one of his boys was injured before the *Streltsi* realized who I was. Then, with great glee, they helped pull the rest of my party from the tunnel – all except poor Jasmine. Her huge bulk proved too much, and she had been forced to remain behind. I wish I could say she was later found alive, but I never knew. I never saw her again.

Now the *Streltsi* surrounded us, laughing and pounding me on the back. They had approached us on foot, but the rest of their party soon brought up horses.

The leader offered me his own mount, and I was about to take it when a strange thought struck me. I had a golden opportunity, here, to create the kind of historical moment one hears immortalized in *byliny* and in stories told about campfires. I glanced at the top of the wall, making sure we were not about to be annihilated by archers. As yet, no one was there. Motioning for the girls to follow me, I started walking toward the Russian camp. We were well out of range before the first infidel arrow was shot at us from the parapet.

The reception I received was everything I had thought it might be. Vorotinsky personally kissed me on both cheeks, and congratulated my escape. Peter Bulgakov, his round face beaming, escorted me, and laughed until the tears rolled down his face. By the time I had finished telling my story, Vladya was rocking off his cushion, holding his sides with laughter. Heinrich nearly wept for joy. The only solemn face was Sylvester's. The black priest stood at the rear of the group, trying to condemn our levity with his bleak stare. After a short time, I noted a subtle play of muscles about his lips, before he turned his back and left.

The Czar gave another of his grand banquets that night, and my girls contributed to the entertainment. Maria so pleased the Czar, he took her into his household for the rest of the campaign. This was a singular honor, for to the best of my knowledge she was the first woman he had known who was not a virgin.

As if my return had not already been triumph enough, Jacob was able to slip out of the city later in the evening. Heinrich was notified of his capture by the *Streltsi,* who took him for an infidel and would have treated him as such, had Ivor not come crawling out behind him. My stepfather ordered them brought directly to the Czar's pavilion, where Ivan gave Jacob a magnificent golden cloak to cover his tattered rags, and had him tell his story to the whole assemblage. Everyone was well on his way to a glorious drunken state by then, and Jacob's tale evoked many loud roars of laughter, especially when he told of my second encounter with Ediger. By morning, every soldier in the Russian army was joking about the time Dmitri broke wind in the face of the Great Khan, and returned to camp with half his harem. Many men have earned fame in more dignified ways; but none, I think, has earned it with more genuine comradeship than I. By my earthy answer to Khan Ediger, and the exaggerated story of my escape, I soon found my ability to command unquestioned. Men no longer feared to follow me because of my youth. When the army was organized for the final assault, I was given a regular command under Heinrich, who now carried a general's scepter.

CHAPTER VIII

The explosion which facilitated my escape from the citadel had, indeed, been the blast intended to destroy the water supply. Fortunately for me, it had not been completely successful, else the tunnels would have been flooded. But our engineers had been fairly close in their calculations, and water was becoming scarce within the walls. More detailed information than this was hard to come by, for with Jacob's flight Heinrich no longer had a first–rate spy inside the walls. Ivan and Kurbsky both had several operatives, but they were not as resourceful in transmitting their information.

For the first few days after my escape, the girls presented a problem. I had no proper way to care for them, and they seemed to feel they were mine by right of capture. Gradually, I was able to give them away to other officers, where I knew they would be looked after and not mistreated. I kept two, both of whom adored Heinrich, and saw to his every wish whenever he was in camp. His former mistress had returned to Svyazhsk during my imprisonment, because my stepfather – in a moment of self–recrimination and remorse – had vowed to forego all pleasures of the flesh until I was safe. He had blamed himself for the catastrophe.

As the season gradually turned to winter, with the promise of freezing weather manifest in the nightly frosts, the Czar stepped up his campaign. I think he was as much concerned about the impending birth of his heir as anything else, for the sages had promised a son.

I served for a time under Kurbsky, and was in command of the men who formed the furthermost portion of his line, on the extreme right hand. His brother Roman commanded the unit next to mine. Andrew, himself, was very involved with the engineers, supervising completion of a great tower, on which he told us we would mount a dozen cannon, with fifty or sixty bowmen and arquebusiers. During this time, Tartar sorties from the fortress became frequent and frantic. They knew their days were numbered, and sought desperately to frighten our soldiers. Within the citadel, water continued in short supply. The food stores were so low, their fighting men did not have enough to eat. On our side, the Czar's orders had been fulfilled and provisions were arriving in plenty. The prices charged by unscrupulous local merchants had fallen sharply. One could buy a whole cow for ten squirrel skins, whereas the price a few weeks before had been as high as forty.

Our men were now seasoned warriors, and our units were better organized. Kurbsky's artillery had mutilated the battlements and gates, until it was difficult for the Mussulmen to sally forth against us. To keep us out, they had barricaded the openings, which deprived them of easy passage.

The final undermining of the walls was underway, through a tunnel running from the side by the swamps. Forty–eight barrels of powder were placed beneath the battlements. On the afternoon of the day preceding the explosion, we were told to hold ourselves in readiness. That night the great tower was moved into place, and ten cannon were installed. Although the infidels suspected our purpose, they were appalled when dawn found our huge structure, firmly implanted and powerfully manned, standing face to face with their highest turret. The fire power from this machine was fearsome! It ripped into the fortress with an impact greater than any force we had yet brought to bear. Our bowmen and arquebusiers maintained such a deadly rain, no infidel dared to mount the walls.

Early that morning the Czar went to his prayers as usual, but those of us who commanded were not summoned to attend him. Vladya was there, and he told me later that just as the priest was reading the liturgy, saying: "There shall be one fold –" the great explosion went off under the walls. Ivan did not stir from his place, but remained with his head bowed, praying fervently for our victory.

As the infidels' defenses crumbled to rubble, Andrew leaped to the head of his men, charging his horse down the slope, into the gully, and up the hill to the remains of the fortress wall. New debris covered the old ruins of the outer city, and part way up the incline we reached the broken pieces of dried mud and timber. These lay scattered about in heaps, and here we crashed into the first of the Mussulman defenders. Their line crumbled so quickly, it hardly slowed our progress. Kurbsky's agility in armor was amazing! He leaped his horse through the breach and mounted the remainder of the parapet on foot, shouting for his men to follow. Roman and I were right behind him, our men in good order at our heels. It was Roman who actually reached the highest point of the wall first, and from there we rushed into combat with the main body of the infidel army.

Like fear crazed animals in a trap, they fought desperately, and at times succeeded in driving us back. But we never retreated through the opening in the wall, and eventually the press of our men was great enough to give us the needed advantage. The lighter weapons of the infidels gave them some purchase in speed, but in striking us they had to find a weak place and hit us with a sure stroke. With the huge swords we carried, it was possible to split a fully armed Mussulman in two. Soon, rivers of blood flowed through the streets of the fortress. No mercy was shown on either side, as we gradually made our way toward the great iron gates on the northern end of the enclosure, allowing the army to pour in from two sides.

The steep walls of the Khan's residence were even more fiercely defended than those of the fortress, itself. The infidels dumped huge, flaming pots of oil on the men trying to climb the siege ladders. They heaved heavy timbers upon us, and flurries of stones nearly blotted out the sky. A great number of the enemy had been trapped to one side of Ediger's stronghold, not far from Yusuf Ali's house. Through this area the fighting was so fierce, one forgot anything save the desperate need to kill. We began to be pushed back once, for many of our peasant soldiers had started looting. There were great riches on every side in this neighborhood of wealthy homes. Some of our men actually made several trips into the fortress and back to camp loaded with booty. Kurbsky sent a message to Vorotinsky, requesting reinforcements.

It was past midday, and the sun was already casting long shadows from the west, when we learned that the Czar was going to take the field. He was back on his hillock, where he could watch the battle. About a third of the army was with him, all the rest of the troops having been committed. The only available reinforcements were from this group. After consulting his commanders, the Czar did a very brave thing. He decided to approach the battle, where his very presence would help inspire the men to fight.

At this announcement, the high officers and commanders who had remained with the Czar doffed their finery and garbed themselves for battle. Leading the troops who had stood guard over Ivan, they flung themselves into the fray. Even the cooks and stewards and other servants followed them, all except the Romanov brothers. This pair was never seen until the final victory.

The sight of so many clean uniforms startled the Tartars, who now fled in confusion. Once the outside force had been pushed away from the walls of the Khan's castle, we soon had ladders against its sides and our men began to enter the sanctum sanctorum. All the great emirs and advisors to the Khan had gathered here, and our men pursued them through the marble halls, into the lush gardens and pleasure rooms. At last, pressed into the central court, they begged to send a delegation to Kurbsky.

The infidels proposed to surrender their Khan alive, but requested that we allow them to take the field, themselves, and live or die as warriors. Kurbsky was not very pleased with their offer, as I knew the Czar had instructed him to shed as little noble blood as possible. Andrew finally agreed, however, and Ediger became our prisoner. He passed quite close to me as he was led away, to bow before the Czar. He did not recognize me in my helmet and armor, or at least pretended not to. I wished greatly to throw a harness about his neck and lead him forth, but that was not my prerogative.

Once he was gone, we had but a moment to wait. Tartar bowmen began shooting arrows at us, and our archers quickly returned their fire. The fierce battle continued, as we made quick work of the remaining defenders. Before the fall of darkness, the Czar's pennant flew from the highest pole in his newly conquered city, while the crescent banners of Islam had fluttered onto the stones, to be trampled underfoot by the victorious Muscovite army.

We were a happy, tired group as we returned to camp that night. It was hard to realize that Kazan was really ours. Many of us had stood about in the streets, uncertain whether to leave or not, as around us the looting had turned into a wild scramble. Men fought with each other for possession of valuables and for the innumerable women found cringing in harems all over the inner fortress. My unit had become hopelessly separated, and after a few vain attempts to gather the men, I joined some other officers and returned to the Czar's pavilion. In camp, at least, we were able to maintain some control.

Kurbsky had been wounded near the end of the fighting. Two horses were shot from under him during the course of the afternoon, and the second time his mount fell, Andrew was unconscious for several minutes. In the tumble, he had sustained a deep gash in his arm. At first, his men had thought him dead, but he revived in time to receive the Khan's surrender and the deputation of nobles. He had been brought back to camp, and now lay propped up in a large ornate bed, his arm in a sling, head swathed in bandages. Because his part in the victory had been so substantial, the Czar ordered him carried in, bed and all, to celebrate with the rest of us. Andrew amazed everyone, I think, by leading the revelry from his couch, toasting the Czar and Vorotinsky, Bulgakov, and many others. He was later carried back to his tent, where he slept four or five hours, bounding out of bed the next morning with his arm sling the only evidence of his injuries.

I was kept busy this next day, setting up a special camp for the thousands of Russians we had freed from bondage. Some of these, though now adults, had been taken prisoner when small children and did not speak their own language. Of the others, there were some who had endured captivity and slavery for many years. Most had been physically abused; nearly all bore the scars of Tartar brands on their faces and lash marks on their bodies. Among those set free was Joachim, the last of my raiding party to be accounted for. I had him released from the camp at once, and assigned him light duties until he had recovered from his ordeal. I did not question him about the details of his captivity, for the scars he bore were not of the flesh. The iron collar about his neck, in lieu of a brand, spoke the story. To judge from his subsequent bragging, he had not suffered greatly.

There now followed a few days of turmoil and temporary assignments for many of us, while Ivan decided on the division of lands and more permanent arrangements for governing his new domain. It was also time for offering thanks to God, and for relaxing the tensions we had been under during the siege. Once I had made full confession to a priest – not Sylvester – I felt a great weight taken from my heart, and was able to join the Czar in some of his revels. With the great curiosity Ivan had always possessed, it was necessary for him to see everything in the captured lands, and to interview a good many of the foreigners who were constantly coming into camp. He also displayed an interest in the growing mound of booty. Among these materials were a number of animals, horses for the most part, but also camels, asses, and oxen. There was one large, ugly camel, in particular, that had become a source of annoyance to the Czar. It would not obey his commands, although it behaved beautifully for its driver. The matter finally became a bitter contest, and a number of other officers had been joking about it, even wagering on whose stubbornness would win out – the Czar's or the camel's.

I went with Ivan on one of his early morning rounds, on what proved to be the first day of the heavy rains. The morning had dawned chill and overcast, the sky completely black, as one sees it only in the eastern lands. Scattered droplets of water fell in several brief, uncertain showers; then stopped, as if God were undecided whether to unleash the deluge or not. I accompanied Ivan and a few others to the storage areas, where much of the wealth of Kazan was being loaded onto barges for transportation to the capital. In the nearby animal pens, I noted Ivan's antagonist. The beast seemed to be watching us, haughtily. I thought the Czar was going to ignore it this time, but some of the other officers encouraged Fedka to point the animal out, assuring that Ivan saw him. After speaking to the men in charge of the loading details, Ivan rode toward the pens, where the stench alone should have discouraged him. Much to the amusement of everyone, he dismounted and ordered the keeper to bring the camel out to him. At this point, even the Czar was joking about their contest.

Slowly, with deliberate steps, the horrid beast was led up to the Czar. Ivan snatched the prod from its driver and shouted an infidel command at the camel. The foul smelling demon stared at him, stupidly. The Czar repeated his command several times, and still the beast refused to obey. Then one of the pages tittered – I'm sure it was Fedka – and Ivan started to lose his temper. His red beard seemed to bristle. His eyes took on a wildness I had not seen for a long time, not since that day before the great fire. He shouted once more at the camel, slamming the prod into its neck. The animal jerked its head back and spit a huge wad of vile, greenish liquid onto the front of Ivan's robe. The Czar's scream of rage stifled any sounds of levity from his staff. Losing complete control of himself, he drew his sword, blindly hacking and stabbing at the stupid brute. I was sure he killed it with his second or third stroke, but he continued to harass the carcass until he was fairly covered with blood. Several keepers came running, only to stand stupefied, watching the Czar without daring to interfere.

Eventually, Ivan became short of breath and I was able to approach him. Gently, I took the sword from his hand and led him back to his horse. The Czar was close to tears now that his rage had subsided. In fact, I think he was afraid. He mumbled something about not understanding why he had done it. He followed without protest and mounted his stallion while I held the stirrup for him. As we started back to camp, the rains began to fall. Before the Czar could reach his pavilion the heavy deluge had almost washed the blood from his robes.

It continued to pour for day after dreary day, hardly letting up even for an hour. But we still had work to do. I was assigned to command one of the fourteen units that hunted the remaining hostile Tartars. Each morning I would rise to dress myself in the freezing darkness, putting on clothes still wet from the day before, and set forth after the elusive enemy. In the marshy lands the mud became so deep there were places where a horse could not get through with a rider on its back. We would be forced to dismount and lead them, sinking to our hips in mud. Still the rain continued. Half the army was sick with fever, while the other half pretended to be. It became all but impossible to assemble a proper company every day.

Inevitably, I became sick, myself. My nose was so stuffed I could hardly breathe. My eyes smarted, and my ears began to ache – ringing with a terrible humming sound, until I nearly went berserk from the constant pain and noise. I had trouble sleeping because of it, and the resulting fatigue made it worse. When I finally did sleep, my dreams were horrible and frightening.

During this time, Heinrich was ordered on an expedition south, chasing some renegade bands of Nogai Tartars, who still threatened to attack once the great army had withdrawn, a moment that was not far off. As winter set in, the Czar made plans for his return to Moscow. He announced the appointment of Gorbatof–Shuisky to be governor of Kazan, which was no great surprise to anyone. His rigidity and relentless concern for conformity in every detail made him a good choice to supervise these subject peoples – or so we reasoned. These same traits of character made him so obnoxious that I was glad to hear of Ivan's decision, and suspect it may have been partially the reason for it. I knew the Czar disliked him, and I remembered his oath to use such men where their rank and abilities could be put to use, but to keep them far enough away not to threaten the throne.

Trading concessions were granted to many Moscow and Nizhny Novgorod merchants, with a very fine charter being given to Heinrich and myself. Provisions were made to bring in Russian settlers, while some of the bravest soldiers were given land grants or estates within the city. Many Tartar women followed the example of Ediger, who had decided to become Christian. These were mostly the young girls and widows who had found favor in the eyes of one or another Russian soldier. Before leaving with his troops, Heinrich had asked me to arrange for the return of our possessions to Moscow. This included the two Tartar girls. I sent everything off with Roman Kurbsky, who was one of the first to leave. I continued on duty all this while, but the cold now went into my chest and became a true fever. Because I was constantly on the move, no one noticed my infirmities until Ivan sent for me to go over some of Heinrich's business. This was three or four days after my stepfather had left for the south. The Czar took one look and ordered me taken off active duty.

After this, I would probably have been all right if I could have gotten dry. But the miserable weather continued for several more days. Rain poured upon us with such vicious strength, even the stoutest tents began to leak, and there was not a dry spot to be found in all the camp. Most ominous of all, the river began to rise. The swiftly flowing water crept ever higher, threatening to inundate the surrounding land. Mud became so deep on all the roads it was impossible to move the supply wagons. Although Ivan had moved his headquarters into the Khan's palace, those of us who commanded field units felt compelled to remain with our men.

With all of this, my fever continued to worsen. The humors had taken complete possession of my chest, and I could hear a deep, rasping rattle with every breath I drew. My face was florid; my entire body felt as if it were on fire, and I ached so badly it was an effort to move. I no longer remember exactly why I went, but I made my way to the Czar's apartments one morning, two or three days after he had relieved me of duty. I can recall making my way gingerly through a sea of mud, groping along a wall from the stable where I left my horse, half blinded by a sudden torrent of rain. By the time I entered the palace, I could hardly see through the dreary gray light and the pounding downpour. One of the guards stepped out and grabbed my arm as I stumbled on the last step.

"His Imperial Majesty is still in chapel," the fellow told me, as we entered the antechamber. A meager fire smoldered in an enamel stove, giving off hardly a suggestion of warmth. The guard assisted me to a couch, as I burst into a spasm of coughing. The man bowed himself out. "I shall inform the Czar of your presence as soon as he returns," he said.

I pulled the couch closer to the stove and lay down on the end nearest the heat. Even the cushions seemed soggy, for Tartar buildings do not hold out the elements much better than a tent. Shivering with cold, I must have fallen asleep. I can remember the next few weeks only through a haze of alternating consciousness and deep, fantastic imaginings. Ivan came back and found me; this much I know for certain. I vaguely recall his standing in the background as an old man in a long robe, covered with curious symbols of stars and moon shaped objects bent over me, pouring some foul elixir down my throat. Then somewhere, at some later time, Vladimir was sitting next to the bed where I was lying. He said something to the effect that I was going to live, that his mother would take care of me.

The prospect of Euphrosyne's tending me was so frightening, I must have tried to sit up before fainting. Then I was in a jouncing vehicle of some sort, still on my back, but held in place with straps as the contrivance bounced in seemingly every direction at once. An old woman was watching me, leaning close to my face. When she saw my eyes open, she said something in a language I did not understand and tried to poke some sour gruel between my lips. I immediately vomited, and swooned again. There were several more vague memories – people looking at me, poking objects into my mouth and ears. I seemed to remember a black–robed priest making the sign of the cross above my head, but Vladya told me later this had never happened.

There were dreams, too, terrible dreams of screaming Tartars riding over me on horses of fire . . . black imps of hell leaping from each other's backs, great clouds of sulfurous smoke belching from the yawning chasm out of which the malevolent army had sprung. Ivan was there, cutting into the flesh of some monstrous flaming demon, with a huge two handed sword that dripped fiery red with blood. Huge drops of gore fell upon me, burning my flesh as I tried to call out to him. But I had no voice. An enormous black stallion reared above me, ebony hoofs slicing through the air. A faceless rider swung his heavy, curved blade in a wide arc, suddenly severing Ivan's head from his body. With a deafening, shrieking scream, the Czar's skull crashed against my face, engulfed me, as I struggled to get up and away from the horrors of hell.

I somehow found my voice and cried out in terror, fighting the bonds that held me in place. The wild rush of wind and the pounding horses' hoofs became the throbbing of my own temples. From nowhere, Vladya appeared to push me back upon the bed.

"It's all right, Dmitri," he said soothingly. "We're almost home."

He was still speaking when the blackness came over me again, but this time without the terror of my feverish wanderings. I awoke to the coarse sounds of sparrows outside the window of a bright, sunlit room. A young servant girl got up from beside the bed and ran into the hallway, calling to someone that I was awake. Then, as if my nightmare were about to resume, the very room seemed to sway and Euphrosyne stood in the doorway. Her smile was probably intended to be friendly, but it sent cold shivers racing down my spine. In my first irrational wave of thought, I was sure she intended to poison me.

But Euphrosyne shared the same strange quality many women have – perhaps it is more correctly termed instinct. Be that as it may, she now sought to mother me, or so she made it appear. If her pretense of concern was the result of her own conniving, I had no way to know it. Still, standing in the doorway, looking at me over the foot of the bed, she seemed taller, darker, and more forboding than in my most unflattering recollections.

Forcing herself to continue smiling, she assumed her most gracious manner and came around the side of my bed. She sat gently on the edge and placed an icy palm against my forehead. "The fever has finally broken," she said, as softly as her raspy voice would permit. "I was afraid the trip might have been too much for you."

I looked about, but could not orient myself. "Are we in Moscow?" I asked weakly.

"Oh, no," she laughed. "You are at Staritsa. Vladya brought you home to recover."

I am really in her power, then, I thought. I seemed to feel the hatred emanating from her, and I had to fight back my instinctive urge to recoil from her touch. She patted my arm as she stood up. "It's so nice to have both my boys back home again," she said.

"Could I see Vladya?" I asked hopefully.

"Not right now, my dear," she said sweetly. "He is in Moscow until tomorrow night."

"Oh?"

"Yes," she finished. The smile faded from her face, and the unfamiliar lightness dissolved from her voice. Almost choking on the words, she said, "The Czar has had a son."

"When . . . . really? When?" I asked excitedly.

"Four weeks ago," she said. "A messenger met him with the news at Nizhny Novgorod, when he was on the way back to Moscow."

"I wish I could be there," I sighed, leaning back against the pillows.

"You will soon, my dear," she said, returning to her former sweetness. "But you must rest now. I will send the girl up with some broth."

"But there's so much I have to know!" I started, and broke off in a sharp fit of coughing. "How long have I been ill?"

"According to Vladya, you took sick just after the fall of Kazan. That was near the end of January; tomorrow is the first of March." She started to leave the room, and I panicked, because questions now began flooding my mind.

"Wait!" I called, coughing again, pawing the air to keep her attention. "You have to tell me –"

"We shall have a long visit later," she said soothingly, then changed her tone to the familiar commanding crackle. "Now you are going to rest!" This time, she did leave.

The young girl returned with a bowl of soup, and spooned it down my throat. I tried to question her, but she must have been so terrified of her mistress she would only shake her head. The effort of drinking the broth was enough to exhaust me, and I fell asleep almost as soon as the bowl was empty. I awoke again after dark. It must have been very late, for I could not hear a sound in the house. My room was fairly warm, heated from the corner stove. I could see coals through the grill in the door, and they had been banked several hours before. I went back to sleep, aware of nothing else until daylight.

The next morning Vladya's mother settled into a chair beside my bed. "Now, Dmitri," she began, "what is it you would like to know?"

"My father," I asked. "Has he returned yet?"

"I understand he is back in Kazan," she replied. "I sent a messenger to him yesterday, informing him of your recovery."

"And the Czarina?" I asked. "Is she well?"

There was only the slight movement about Euphrosyne's eyes to betray her awareness of my former feelings. "The birth was difficult, but the Czarina is doing nicely." Her tone, I thought, was icy. She had never liked Anastasia, and now that the Czar's bride had presented the State with an heir, she undoubtedly liked her even less.

The girl came in with my breakfast, but Euphrosyne made no move to leave. "There must be something else you would like to ask me," she said. By her attitude I knew there was another bit of news she wished to impart, but I could not think what to ask. The girl started to feed me, but I waved her away.

"You may leave us," Euphrosyne commanded.

I began to nibble at the bread, and took a few sips of tea. Euphrosyne sat silent, waiting for me to speak. At length, I gazed directly into her eyes and replaced my cup on the tray without breaking the contact. I spread my hands in a gesture of helplessness. "You wish to tell me something else?" I asked.

She merely watched me, playing with me, knowing I could not get up and leave. I felt a rising swell of anger, but controlled my words. "What is it, Madam? What has happened?"

Her smile was not quite triumphant, but it certainly came close. "Your friend, the Czar," she said, "has fallen ill. He seems to suffer the same malady as you."

"How serious is it?" I demanded. Forgetting my own condition, I sat up too suddenly. The whole room seemed to spin and grow darker. When my head cleared I continued to sit upright, regarding Euphrosyne with as stern a look as I could manage. "The Czar!" I nearly shouted. "How sick is he?"

"He has taken to his bed," she replied, "and although he is still himself, his fever grows worse every day." Her smug expression, more than her words, convinced me that Ivan's illness was serious.

"You will excuse me, Madam," I said. "I must go to him." I swung my feet over the edge of the bed and started to get up.

She stood over me. "You are in no condition to go anyplace," she boomed. Her large form blocked my way.

"Do you intend to hold me against my will?" I demanded.

"I shall do only what is best for you," she replied coolly.

"Then order a carriage and have some clothes sent to me," I commanded. I had somehow gotten to my feet, and by holding firmly to the bedpost was able to maintain a wobbly, upright stance. I was so intent on our conversation I did not think about standing before so great a lady in my nightshirt.

"You are being very foolish, Dmitri!" she warned.

"Woman, as much as I appreciate your hospitality, I am going to do my duty, and that means going to my Czar when he needs me," I insisted, matching the firmness of her tone. "You will either help me, or I shall do it on my own."

She stood watching me for another moment, before allowing her face to relax. "So be it," she said. She turned abruptly and left. A short time later, one of Vladya's manservants came in with an armload of clothes. As he helped me to dress in his master's apparel, I realized how much weight I had lost. Vladya's tunic was loose on me. Leaning on the servant's shoulder, I crossed to the window and saw that Euphrosyne had fulfilled my demand. A *troika* stood by the front portal. In my befuddlement of recent awakening, I had forgotten it was still winter.

"Are you to accompany me?" I asked the servant.

"Yes, my lord."

"Then bring some warm blankets and a flask of spirits. I want to get started."

Within half an hour I was warmly bundled into the sleigh, with the servant cracking his whip at the three horses. Two retainers rode ahead of us. The bells jingled merrily as we flew across the white, frozen fields, following the barely discernible course of the road. Although I had won, I thought, Euphrosyne was being an unusually good loser. Or perhaps it was her pride; she wanted to assure my returning from her estates in proper style. The hour was still early, and we should have been able to reach Moscow before dark. The excitement of the moment had kept me awake and alert, but I was still very weak, and the motion of the *troika* began to lull me asleep. Several times I dozed off, only to be awakened by a sudden lurch or bump, as the runners passed over some obstacle buried in the snow. The last fall had been heavy, but it had been several days before. On the more traveled sections of road, the sleigh occasionally grated across patches of bare earth. Sometime during the late afternoon, when I had been asleep for an hour or so, I was jolted awake by the sled's coming to an abrupt halt. I looked about, not sure where I was, although I had traveled this road many times before. The sun was nearly set, and long blue shadows stretched out from the skeleton forms of trees on either side of the highway.

"Why have we stopped?" I demanded.

The driver turned to look at me, a cruel grin on his face; but he didn't answer. The mounted retainers had now come up on either side of the *troika*.

"What do you men think you're doing?" I bluffed. In that moment I realized perfectly well what they were doing. Fool that I was, I should have known better than to cross Euphrosyne. One of the retainers had dismounted and started to climb onto the sleigh, when there was a loud hail from back on the road. "Thank God!" I whispered. Then my doubts returned. It was Vladya! The Prince rode up, trailed by a party of seven or eight soldiers. "I thought I recognized my own livery," he said. "What are you doing on the – Dmitri!" he shouted.

"I was on the way to the Czar," I said.

"And I had been sent by God's Anointed to fetch you," he laughed. "How are you feeling?"

"If you are rescuing me," I said, "I feel fine."

"What do you mean?" He looked genuinely puzzled.

"I am going to the Czar against your mother's wishes." I said no more, nor did Vladya make any further comment to me. He understood, and his face blushed scarlet. He shouted an order to his soldiers, who immediately seized the three servants. One of them put up a struggle and was knocked to the ground. Taking his crop, Vladya started after one of the villains, while a couple of his men took care of the others. After being stripped of Staritsky livery, the three were thrown to the ground and given a sound whipping. Half naked, they were chased across the snow by Vladya's mounted men, slashing at them as they raced out of sight, into the frozen forests. The last I could see of them, their tormentors were still striking at them with whips and staffs.

The Prince rode back to me, out of breath. "I'd better not set eyes on them again," he said. "I'll also settle with Mother, later. Er, you will, of course, keep this between us?"

"We have many secrets, my friend," I said simply.

He clapped me on the shoulder and ordered one of his men to drive the *troika*. He rode beside me the rest of the way and filled me in on the happenings since I had dropped from the world of the living. By his casual attitude and offhand answers to my questions, he implied that Ivan's condition was no cause for alarm. Because of this, the worst of my anxiety dissipated, and with it, the internal tensions which maintained my energies.

"The Czarevitch bears your name," he told me. "Officially he is named after Dmitri Donskoi, but I think the Czar had you in mind." He chattered on and on, giving me all the news he could think of, as well as all the gossip, until it finally began to fall on deaf ears. I knew enough to piece together what must be happening, but as yet did not wish to try discussing it, even with Vladya. Whether Ivan was seriously – mortally ill – or not, his incapacitation had obviously given rise to a series of palace conspiracies. If only Heinrich had been there, I thought; or if I were not so weak from this damned fever! I was useless as a woman!

It was dark when we approached the outskirts of Moscow, but we could see the lights from far away, reflected off the gleaming mantle of snow. A new moon hung low in the sky, and lights from the Kremlin glinted off the many cupolas. It made them appear as fat stubby fingers, the extremities of a crowd, reaching heavenward in futile appeal toward the uncaring face of the moon.

"Vladya," I said, interrupting his description of the Russian occupation in Kazan, "I must *ride* into the Kremlin."

"Dmitri, you can't!" he protested. "You'll never be able to sit on a horse after more than a month in bed!"

"It is not what I *can* do," I told him. "It's what I *must*! Stop this sled!"

When he still hesitated, I repeated my demand. With a shrug of resignation, the Prince called to his men, and our group came to a halt.

"Pick out a peaceful animal for me, then have your men help me up," I directed.

Several of the soldiers drifted back into earshot, and at a nod from their commander three of them dismounted. I struggled into the sleeves of my *shuba*, and the men lifted me out.

Moscow had been completely rebuilt since the fire, now seeming to have spread beyond its former limits. After so long an absence, the sight of the Kremlin, towering proudly above all the rest, brought a feeling of warmth and pride to my belly. I vowed inwardly to succeed in riding through the gates on my own. I had a bad moment when my mount slipped on a patch of ice, and again when some boys ran across our path, forcing us to stop short. But in the end, stubborn determination carried me through. We passed into the Kremlin grounds without serious mishap. At the foot of the palace stairs, Vladya dismounted and motioned for his men to help me. I leaned on them to climb the distance, because my legs refused to work. Once on level floor, however, I was able to walk, leaning on just one of them.

Vladimir regarded me critically, a twinkle in his eye. "Now what, mighty warrior?" he laughed.

"If I weren't an invalid, I'd poke you," I said. "Aren't you supposed to get me to the Czar?"

My arrival was quickly announced to a number of people, as the Czar's summons had been no secret. Vladya was immediately the center of a group, mostly palace officials and *dyaks*. I wondered if they were seeking favor with the man who might be their next Czar. Another cluster of men descended on me, Basmanov being the first.

"I feared we'd never see you again!" he bellowed, lumbering toward me like some huge, charging beast. His hand was upraised, I am sure with the intention of administering one of his crushing blows to my back. I shied away. "Don't you dare!" I said, smiling. "It's all I can do to stay on my feet."

Others came now: Andrei Adashev and Gregory Zakharin, who had been on their way upstairs. Ivor appeared from behind me, leading a company of palace guardsmen. Beyond his company was a group of priests who knew me from my days as an altar boy. Not all of these people had come specifically to greet me, but each of them stopped to exchange a few words. Mostly, they inquired after my health and said they were glad I was still alive. Underneath the customary smalltalk, I sensed an unmistakable tension. It was a condition affecting everyone, especially Adashev. The Czar's minister seemed almost furtive as he spoke, leaving me with the impression that he would like a word with me later, in private. As for Gregory, the Czarina's uncle was almost too glad to see me; it was obvious he regarded me as an ally. Whatever the rift, it was undoubtedly the result of Ivan's illness. The court was drifting into factions. As soon as I was able, I drew Ivor aside. "If you can get a message off to Heinrich," I whispered, "tell him to get here as fast as he can."

Ivor nodded. "I'll take care of it tonight," he said.

I looked around for Vladya, but he was still in the center of an agitated group of courtiers, everyone talking at once, each trying to be more charming than the next. Among others, I saw the fat rear of Shig Ali. Nikita Romanov stood silently at the edge of the clustered figures.

"Well, Father Bear," I called to Basmanov, "how about helping me up to see His Majesty?"

The boyar ordered two of his retainers to bring a straight backed chair. Once I was seated, they lifted me, and amidst some muted laughter, carried me through the brightly lighted corridors. This was my first view of the completed renovations following the fire, and I observed them with interest. The work had been only half finished when we left for Kazan. I was pleased to note how the old somberness had been lessened by more pleasing colors on the walls and ceilings. Even the carpets reflected a happier tone. The new appointments were rich, and being new they had lost the ragged appearance of age. Still lacking the light, airy look of a Tartar building, the palace was far less oppressive than before.

Only the attitude of those around me dampened the cheerfulness. The underlying sense of concern became more apparent as we approached the royal suite. The mood of the men keeping vigil outside Ivan's bedchamber was anything but happy. Adashev had gone ahead to make sure the Czar was awake and would receive me. As I was carried into the outer rooms I was struck by the solemnity of the hovering figures. The atmosphere confirmed the worst of my fears. These men expected the Czar to die!

The diversity of postures and emotions was astounding. Various groups had gathered unto themselves, not mixing with those of different rank or political affiliation. Some of the higher serving gentry – men of *dyak* and even *voivode* rank – had gathered in the hall outside the Czar's apartments. Some of them were actually weeping. The clusters of priests, these groups being divided according to the form of their habits, stood with heads together, murmuring prayers for salvation. Others knelt in pairs – or threes or fours – in front of little niches in the corridors where crosses or icons had been set up.

Inside the apartment were the higher ranks, or men of lesser station who were particularly close to the Czar. Here, the attitudes were much less consistent. Men stood in small groups, whispering together, some in obvious grief. Others seemed fearful, and some were surely engaged in avaricious plotting. The latter groups cast suspicious glances at the others, and many jealous looks were turned in my direction. With the Czar apparently near death, the hostilities harbored against me by many of the courtiers – something none had dared express since the day Buturlin lost his tongue – were beginning to show in their expressions. As yet, they were displayed only to the extent of a few unfriendly looks.

Andrei stood at the doorway to Ivan's bedchamber. He nodded to me, and I was carried through before I could give the disaffection more careful appraisal.

The men started to place my chair at the foot of the Czar's bed, but Ivan gestured weakly for them to bring me closer. Twice they tried to set me down, but each time the Czar insisted I be brought nearer until my chair was finally set directly beside his pillow. Satisfied, he motioned Basmanov's retainers away.

Andrei remained just inside the door. Sylvester hovered darkly on the other side of the bed, while Anastasia was seated in the shadows at the far end of the room. Otherwise we were alone. The Czarina had greeted me with the wan semblance of a smile, the priest by only a hunching of his shoulders and by taking a more protective stance over his sovereign. To my eyes, the black priest still resembled the angel of death. At the moment he seemed to anticipate the time when he might reach out a bony hand to clasp the heart of his dying benefactor.

And Ivan did look close to death! His complexion was sallow. His shaven head, where it showed beneath the disordered nightcap, was sweaty and covered with reddish stubble. His cheeks were deeply sunken, and his eyes stared at me from rheumy black puddles, surrounded by puffy, stricken flesh. It took him a few moments to speak. His labored breathing, raspy and rattling from the effort of moving closer to me, brought on a spasm of coughing. My first reaction was fear.

"Dmitri—" he managed at last. "I knew. When I need you, I always know—" He fought again for air, like a runner who had exceeded his limits. He watched me, desperately trying to establish some controllable rhythm in his respiration. As for myself, I was gripping hard at the arms of my chair. The combined effects of being carried along at the bouncy pace of the two men, plus my own inner reactions to all I had seen, including the stricken Czar, had caused another dizzy spell.

Ivan heaved a sigh and pressed his head against the pillows. He reached out a fumbling hand to touch my knuckles where they fastened hard to the wooden chair arm. "God has seen fit to afflict us both," he gasped. "I pray your strength returns that you may defend Our right."

"For such a holy cause," I replied awkwardly, "surely God will hear." I noted Sylvester's movement as we spoke, but I ignored him. My foremost concern was the Czar. "By God's help," I continued, "I am nearly recovered and need only to rebuild my strength."

The Czar rolled his head on the pillow, again casting his ghastly gaze in my direction. "I am going to die, Dmitri," he said.

His words froze me, and a coldness seemed to close about me. I heard Anastasia sob, with a sharp intake of breath. For the first time I noticed she held the infant Czarevitch in her arms, clasping him to her bosom. The child made a little gurgling sound at his mother's tightened grip. The priest, towering above everyone else, made the sign of the cross over Ivan's head.

Andrei was now standing behind me. I could hear his own labored breathing, almost as heavy as the Czar's.

"I cannot believe our sins so great," I said firmly. "Surely, God in His mercy and wisdom, would not take you from us before you were able to fulfill His mission on earth. Why else would He have spared you through all the years of childhood torment and danger?"

Ivan closed his eyes, allowing his head to drop backward. "Perhaps," he whispered, "perhaps."

Then, to my very great annoyance, that wretched priest began mumbling an unseemly series of lamentations. "The Will of God," he whispered, and "The Lord's Will shall be done," – a whole gamut of such phrases. He showed no inclination to stop, and I felt his conduct completely uncalled for. He made me so angry I wanted to pitch him out. I looked across at Anastasia, but her gaze was on the child. She seemed oblivious to us. It was frustrating for me to be so helpless. I couldn't even get out of my chair, although I now tried to do so. The Czar lay deathly still, gathering his strength to speak again.

Looking up at Sylvester, Ivan surprised me by managing an authoritative command for the priest to leave. "I would speak to Dmitri alone," he said.

Whether the remark was meant to include Andrei or not was unclear, but the minister hesitated only a moment before following the priest. Anastasia also started to rise, but Ivan turned his head slightly in her direction. "No, let her remain," he mumbled. Once the others had withdrawn, Ivan struggled closer to the edge of his bed and began speaking to me in harsh whispers, displaying more strength than I'd expected. "They are all sure I'm going to die," he began, "and even among my closest advisors there is dissent. Many refuse to recognize my son as heir. Even that priest with his holy vows seeks only after worldly gain."

"Who opposes you?" I asked.

"All – almost all," he whispered sadly, his voice trailing off. Then he continued more stridently, his anger giving him the necessary stamina. "But these two," he snarled, "these two men who stand like harbingers of doom beside my bed, wearing the fine robes I've given them, they, of all the people in my realm, men I've raised from obscurity to the highest office. They have refused to take the oath."

"Who has taken it?" I asked, not sure exactly what oath he meant. At the moment it did not matter; I could find out later.

He gestured helplessly. "Oh, the Zakharins, the Romanovichi – naturally, the Romanovichi, some of my officers, and Basmanov. Alexi is always faithful."

"What of Vladimir?" I asked.

Ivan smiled wanly. "My cousin? The potential heir?"

"But Vladya has no desire to be Czar," I protested.

"Dmitri, Dmitri, you are so naive sometimes. Can you imagine that any man would reject the Crown of Monomakh?"

"It's his mother," I insisted. "She wishes him on the throne." I went on to tell the Czar of my near brush with death at Euphrosyne's hands. Even as I spoke I realized it was violating the assurance I had given Vladya, but by telling the Czar at this time I was using the information for my friend's own benefit. I emphasized how Euphrosyne's plan had nearly ended my existence and removed me as his servant, but her own son had saved me.

"He would *surely* not have done that," I concluded, "were he really ambitious for the throne."

The Czar remained thoughtful, absorbing the knowledge I had given him. "Dmitri," he began hesitatingly, "I, I have given some thought to . . . to a move I am now convinced I must make. I have decided to raise you to boyar rank."

Without thinking, I responded immediately. "No!" I almost shouted. "No, you can't do that!"

"You, too, would refuse the orders of your Czar?" he asked in surprise.

"You and I," I told him. "You and I have always shared our hatred for the boyars. Oh, certainly, we have friends among them. But they are an evil class. See what they're doing to you now. Please! Don't force me to be one of them, to become like they are. Besides, I'm not fitted by birth or deed, or by any station. I would never be accepted."

"I am still the Czar," he growled. "If I decree it, then you must be accepted."

"It is still wrong," I insisted. "It must not be."

"With you in the *Duma*," he went on, "and with you to speak for me in the council chambers, my own voice would never be stilled, even if I should die. Can't you understand? You would continue to serve me."

"I will always serve you," I assured him, "whether you live or die. I will do everything the Lord permits to carry out your wishes; but please don't ask this of me. Besides, you're not going to die. If you bestow this rank on me today, you will grow to hate me tomorrow. I would become a part of the group we have both sworn to destroy."

Ivan lay there, sighing and laboriously struggling for breath. "I have already recognized you as heir to the title of old Prince Marensky," he gasped. "Boyar or not, you are a Prince." As wearing as our discourse had been on me, its effect upon the Czar was more profound. Ivan, in the earlier stages of his illness, had still to face the crisis I had already survived.

"I have told you my wishes," he added at length. "You must now do as you think best. I don't have the strength to fight both my enemies and my friends. But always remember, *you speak for me,* and now with the authority of a Prince."

I thought he had fallen asleep, he lay so still and his breathing had become such a regular, labored rumble. But once again he opened his eyes and called weakly for Anastasia. The Czarina slipped immediately to her feet. Still cradling the infant Czarevitch, she moved silently up beside me.

The fever was taking hold of Ivan, and his face began to glow with it. His hands shook. The effort of speaking was almost too much for his failing vigor. "My little heifer," he gasped, his hand wandering across the coverlet in search of hers. "You must always trust Dmitri. Listen to him, and be sure your uncle and brothers do the same. He is wise for his years, and his, his –" The Czar's feeble thoughts trailed off into the misty hell of delirium. I paused a moment, allowing my mind to accept the fact that I now ranked as high – or nearly as high – as any other member of the court. Strange sensation, satisfying under other circumstances, but now, especially if the Czar should die . . . .

Anastasia stood motionless, idly allowing her left hand to rest on my shoulder. I looked up at her, but neither of us spoke. Words would have destroyed the fragile threads of our communication, for it was as if our minds had met and merged. We each could sense the other's love. Not in any physical way. I have no wish to imply this. But there had always been a kind of love between us. Now, when neither of us knew how long the Czar might live, we were drawn together in support of his wishes.

I reached up and took her hand from my arm, awkwardly pressing it to my lips. "You had better call the others," I whispered.

She started to pull away, but paused as if a thought had suddenly entered her mind. Her voice was unexpectedly strident. "The doctors," she said. "Twice now, they've bled him and each time he grows weaker. Can you stop them?"

"I'll try," I said. "Go ahead now; open the door. If Ivor is there, tell him the Czar wishes to speak with him a moment before the others come in."

Anastasia obeyed, and Ivor entered immediately. I could see several figures in the outer room, craning their necks to peer over Ivor's hulking frame. The Czarina closed the door behind him, and the old soldier approached the bed to make his proper obeisance.

"Never mind that," I said. "His Majesty's asleep. There are several things you've got to do, and as you love the Czar, you must not fail."

Ivor regarded me quizzically. I had assumed he would follow me without question, but strong as his friendship might be for me, his primary loyalty was to the Czar. Others had already approached him, I learned later, trying to give him a variety of conflicting orders.

It was Anastasia who convinced him of my right to demand his obedience. "The last word spoken by the Czar was that I, and every other person who wishes to serve him, must take Dmitri's – Prince Marensky's – commands as his own," she said. "Please, Ivor . . . ." Tears glistened in her eyes. "Please, do not forsake Us now."

"May God forgive my doubts," he said, almost weeping himself. "What do you want of me?"

"First," I said, "have you sent for Heinrich?"

"That was done an hour ago."

"And Prince Yuri? Where is he?" I asked.

"He went to his own apartments just before you arrived," said the Czarina. "He had been here without sleep for so long, he couldn't stay awake."

"Then it must be your task," I told Ivor, "to assure the safety of those who remain loyal to the Czar. Have you enough men you can count on?"

"I think so," he said, but his tone belied the words.

"Use only men you are completely sure of," I instructed him. "You must see to the safety of Prince Yuri, Gregory Zakharin, Basmanov, and the Metropolitan – and any others who take the oath. Basmanov must have some men you can use. But most important of all, we must protect the Czarina and her child."

Anastasia had eased herself gently onto a corner at the foot of Ivan's bed. "But after the Czarevitch," she said, "you must first of all guard Dmitri."

"I will see to it," he assured us.

There was a gentle tap at the door.

"We have to let the others in," said Anastasia.

"One more thing," I added quickly. "Ivor, you must be sure I can communicate with you at any time. I have no retainers, because they're all with my stepfather. Find me a few men, not household guards. I want a couple of fellows who can pass as servants, who won't attract attention moving about the palace."

Anastasia was at the door, preparing to open it. "The doctors," she hissed. "Don't forget about them!"

"Yes, the Czar must not be bled again," I mused. "Ivor, go to the Metropolitan. Tell him the Czar may need his blessing, but when he comes direct him to me as quickly as you can."

I had not experienced such an ominous dread since the days of the Shuiskys. Two guardsmen helped me out of Ivan's bedchamber. This time I walked, leaning on them, for I was over the effects of my foolish horseback ride. Anastasia remained with the Czar, and Sylvester stayed with her. The rest seemed content to sit in the outer chamber, so long as the door was left open between them and the Czar.

Both Vladimir and Andrei Adashev were there, neither speaking to anyone, each staring off into space as if lost in his own thoughts. I did not have the energy to keep going much longer, so I asked them both to step into an alcove with me. "Andrei," I began without further preamble, "why do you refuse to swear fealty to the Czarevitch?"

Caught off guard by my directness, he stammered, "The, the Czar may die," he said.

"In which case?"

"In which case we would find ourselves in the same situation we were in twenty years ago," he declared flatly. "For the good of Russia, I cannot take the oath."

"And you, Vladya?" I continued, turning to the Czar's cousin.

The Prince hung his head. "You know how I feel," he said, not looking up. "For myself, I have no wish to rule. But if Ivan dies, it will be the Zakharins and the Romanovs who hold the whip over all of Russia."

"We could have a far worse regent than Gregory Zakharin," I replied.

"But who would follow him?" demanded Andrei. "Can't you see, Dmitri? If the Czar should die, we would have nothing but continuous civil strife, with an infant and a woman to rule."

"And as for the welfare of the child," added Vladimir, "who is to guarantee he would be as fortunate as Ivan?"

Ivor looked in, interrupting us. He beckoned for me to come. "Excuse me," I said coldly. "I must tend to some business for my Czar."

My exit, though opportune and effective, was anything but graceful. Ivor helped me into the hall and across to an empty bedroom, where he had persuaded Makari to wait. The Metropolitan had been accompanied by several black-robed priests, who now milled about in the corridor. They looked at me curiously, as I limped past on Ivor's shoulder, breathing like an old man climbing a high flight of stairs.

"Please grant me the boon of your patience, Fathers," I begged them. "I must have a brief word with the Metropolitan. The Czar has entrusted me with a message."

Their response could have been a murmur of assent or a grumble of disapproval. They stepped aside as Ivor opened the door. I had not seen Makari for several months, and he had aged many fold in that time. He sat quietly on an unpadded chair, staring vacantly toward the window where frost clung tenaciously outside the mica panes. I had to speak to him before he seemed aware of my presence.

"Holy Father," I said gently.

He turned his rheumy gaze in my direction. I was sure he could not see me, for white shades of blindness were growing across both his eyes. He tilted his chin upward, allowing his pupils to stare out under the milky curtains.

"Is it really you, Dmitri? I had heard you were too ill to come." His voice crackled and broke; his palsied hands gripped tightly about his stick.

"Yes, it's me. But I've asked to see you for the sake of our Mother Russia, and our Anointed Czar," I said.

"Come, my son, and let me bless you," he replied, completely ignoring my words.

Not knowing what else to do, I worked my way over to him, leaning on various pieces of furniture for support. I knelt before him and allowed the aged priest to say a benediction over me. I tried to speak to him again, but it was no use. I had heard how the Metropolitan vacillated these days. He had moments of great lucidity, when God seemed to speak through him in ringing tones. Then there were periods like this. Tonight, when I needed his mind, it was simply not there.

At length, I thanked the Metropolitan for his divine blessing and asked permission to withdraw. He graciously consented, and I called Ivor to help me. I could not get up from my knees. "Get me to bed," I whispered to him. "I can't do any more today."

Ivor started down the hall with me. "I've arranged for you to stay in one of the chambers off Prince Yuri's suite," he said. "It will ease the job of guarding you."

He escorted me into the apartments of the Czar's brother, where one of Yuri's servants would see to getting me into bed. Everything would keep until morning, I thought – unless, of course, the Czar should expire during the night. I had to keep those doctors away! If I could accomplish that much –.

"Ivor!" I called, just in time to catch him at the door. "One more thing. I'm sorry to lean so heavily on you, but, if you can find Basmanov ask him to come see me for a moment."

Alexi was there in less than fifteen minutes. I explained my anxiety about the bleeding, telling him I feared for the Czar's recovery if it continued.

"I am not a man of great knowledge," he said humbly, "but if you think it best the Czar not be bled again, he shall not be! Good night, Dmitri."

My sleep was heavy and undisturbed. Ivor posted two men outside the door, and six more inside to surprise any forceful intruders. None came. I awoke at daybreak, much refreshed and feeling a good deal stronger. Yuri called to me as I was dressing. I went immediately to his bedroom, surprising Ulyana, who was just coming in from the other door.

"It is good to see you, Dmitri," she said, not at all embarrassed to be seen in her robe. Her hair had been combed out and lay like raven's wings across her shoulders. She sat down on the bed, beside Yuri, who had not yet risen. The Prince wriggled himself into a sitting position, leaning against the headboard. He seemed little changed, still radiating a childish innocence. With the nightcap hiding his tonsured skull, he looked like a stripling. His beard had finally developed some fullness, but it would have been more in place on an adolescent than on a man in his twenty–second year.

We chatted for a few minutes, and Yuri commented in his boyish voice: "I wish I could understand what is going on. Ivan isn't going to die." He made the statement with such assurance I could almost believe him.

"Why do you say that?" I asked. "Have you a sign from Heaven?"

"No, no – nothing like that. I just know! I would know, wouldn't I, if my own brother were going to die?"

"I am sure you would," I replied, uncertain what else to answer.

"You'll see," he told me. "In a day or so he will be up, as strong as ever."

"I hope your faith is justified," I said sincerely, and then to change the subject, I remarked: "I only wish my stepfather were here."

"He should arrive today," said the Prince, a note of surprise in his voice, as if I should have known.

"But I only sent for him yesterday," I said.

"Yuri sent a message on the first day of Ivan's illness," said Ulyana softly. "We thought you'd be too sick to come, and we wanted someone we could trust."

"Yes," added Yuri. "In good weather, a messenger using post horses can make the trip in eight days. The man we sent – left – he left –" The Prince tried counting on his fingers, and looked helplessly at his wife.

"This is the sixteenth day," she explained. "With luck, Heinrich will arrive by sundown."

A servant brought in a breakfast tray, and I ate with them, all three of us sitting on Yuri's bed. I smiled to myself, thinking of the shocked expression this would bring to certain faces. Ulyana noticed and questioned me. We all giggled like children at the idea of Euphrosyne's being able to see us.

When we finished I felt much better, and excused myself. I had many things to do. Two of the men who had been on guard inside the apartments followed me, for Ivor had seen to my wishes. They were both burly fellows, wearing Yuri's livery, and they stuck close to me all day.

I went directly to the Czar's chambers, walking into a near riot in the hallway. Alexi had taken me at my word, and had stationed himself outside Ivan's door. When the doctors arrived that morning, he had sent them sprawling, despite the protests of several officials. In addition to the confusion following this episode, Vorotinsky had come up, accompanied by Roman Kurbsky. They intended to take their oaths of fealty to the Czarevitch and had encountered Vladya in the anteroom. The General had made some insulting remarks to the Czar's cousin, with the result that they nearly came to blows. Basmanov and Andrei were still holding them apart when I came in.

My appearance helped quiet them, for Basmanov's admonitions had only added to both men's anger. I calmed them, and eventually persuaded Vladya to leave. He had been there all night, and regardless of the strange situation the Lord had imposed upon him, I knew he would have guarded the Czar with his life, had it been necessary. Still, he had not taken the oath; nor would he. If the Czar should die. . . ? It would mean civil war, I supposed, and we would likely be on opposite sides.

Vorotinsky and Roman Kurbsky went into Ivan's chamber, where they kissed the golden cross at the foot of his bed. In addition to them, myself, and those mentioned by Ivan the previous evening, we could only count on John Sheremetief, Michael Morozof, Mstislavsky, and Dmitri Paletsky. Against us would be most of the boyars, including John Pronsky, the Shcenatofs, the Obolinskis, the Shuiskys and all the other Novgorod families. Kurlyatev and the treasurer, Fumikov, were yet to be heard from. Both claimed to be ill. The situation was tenuous, but as long as Ivan lived there was no man brave enough to move against him.

I stayed outside the Czar's door most of the day, being called in once to speak with him. He seemed the same as before, though perhaps a little more feverish. Anastasia remained in her chair against the far wall, but the child had been taken into the alcove behind her, where he was attended by other women. The Czarina smiled weakly at me when I entered and when I left. No other communication passed between us.

The only time I left the chamber was when I saw Vladya slip into the empty apartment across the hall. He had been outside the palace, and must have come directly here without going to his own rooms. He was fully armed, and went into the chamber to divest himself of weapons before coming into Ivan's suite. I followed him in and waited until his retainers had left with his gear. Then I launched into my lecture. We argued back and forth for quite a while, Vladya becoming more agitated as we talked. He kept looking over his shoulder as if expecting someone to appear.

"Dmitri, please try to understand," he said, almost begging.

"I can only understand that our Anointed Czar has made his will, and named his successor. He now orders all his loyal vassals to take a holy vow to fulfill its conditions. You are refusing to obey."

"Don't be an idiot!" he shouted. "I have no desire to unseat Ivan, and I don't want to be Czar, myself. There are too many things I enjoy doing that I couldn't do as Czar. You know this better than anyone else. And if I assumed the office, my mother would never leave me in peace. I'm not thinking about myself, but of this same beloved Russia you keep throwing up to me. Do you think I want to see it run by the Romanovs? Look how those sniveling swine have acted during the Czar's illness. And before. They've always fawned on him like dogs. Remember how they were at Kazan, always *behind* the Czar? Even during the worst battles, when we needed every man, there they were, dressed in their golden armor, shoving sweetmeats down their throats and carrying the chamberpot for Ivan!"

"It is still the Czar's will," I said quietly, "and we are both sworn to obey."

"Are you telling me I should take the oath to humor him, and break it later if circumstances indicate it?"

"Let me express it this way," I said. "I am not convinced that the Czar is going to die. If he lives, you may lose your head over this. Ivan is magnanimous, but your failure now could be called treason!" I paused, staring at him. "I'm your friend, Vladya, else I wouldn't say this," I added.

"And were you not my friend, I wouldn't listen," he returned. "However, your first point is well taken, and I know the risk I'm running. But what if the Czar *should* die?"

"All right!" I said. "If the Czar were to die, Anastasia would become regent until the Czarevitch is of age –"

"And her senile uncle, her cowardly brothers become rulers, in fact," he finished for me.

"As I have said before," I replied, "Gregory, who is neither senile nor cowardly, would probably hold the reins. He would not be the worst ruler we ever had."

"Except that he—" Vladya began, his voice still loud and harsh. He had forgotten to look behind him for several minutes, having become too involved in our argument. As he stared at me, his mouth curled slyly, and wagging his finger at me he chuckled. "Except that I begin to see," he said in a knowing tone, "Once the Czar is dead, the Regent's lover, perhaps? The young man with the Obolenski face, the Staritsky heart – and now the Marensky title? Are you trying to outmaneuver me, Dmitri?"

This made me angry enough that I almost struck him, but I controlled myself. "You should know better than that!" I snapped. The idea was insulting, and yet I cannot deny the thought had crossed my mind, which only made my friend's perception all the more aggravating. Still, Anastasia was a saint to me. To make love to her would be akin to violating something sacred. I didn't even know if I'd be capable of it. "Regardless what thoughts may have occurred to me," I continued, "which I deny, the Czarina would find them outrageous and immoral."

Vladya smirked. "Any woman, under the proper circumstances . . . ."

"Stop it!" I shouted. "All you're trying to do is excuse your treachery, and there isn't any excuse for it!"

Over the Prince's shoulder, I saw Ivor enter the room. He stood quietly, waiting for us to finish. At last my words stung Vladya, for his anger drained away and a look of wounded feelings came across his face. "Can you really call me a traitor?" he asked, his voice tight with emotion.

"I don't know," I said sadly. "I only know that my Czar lies in that room, breathing what may be his last, and it's within your power to make it easier for him. What happens after that . . . ." I shrugged. my voice trailing off.

"Then you *are* suggesting I take an oath I later intend to violate?"

"If that is the only condition under which you will take it, yes," I replied. "Regardless of the reason, you must do it!"

I think he was weakening, although he still argued. I wanted Ivor to leave before Vladya saw him, and looking past the Prince's shoulder when I thought he wouldn't notice, I grimaced at the old soldier to go. But Vladya saw me and, turning, he also saw Ivor. That ended our conversation.

"I must think," said Vladya, fixing his steely eyes on me. "Perhaps I'm wrong, but I must make my own decision without your emotional appeals."

"May I speak to you later?" I asked.

"This evening, perhaps," he muttered. "Yes, I will come to a decision by tonight." He shouldered his way past Ivor, hardly acknowledging his salute.

As we returned to the Czar's apartments, I kept wondering how close Vladya had come to the truth. Was I really ambitious? I had protested accepting boyar rank, but had still become a Prince. Would I seek to become Anastasia's lover? I resumed my vigil outside Ivan's door, silently praying to God for guidance. I asked Him to forgive me, if I really harbored such evil within my soul.

As the chill north wind brought darkness hurrying through the Kremlin, two powerful forces converged upon the court. For me, the arrival of the first was unexpected. Euphrosyne came by sleigh and stormed into the palace as if she were already its mistress. She went immediately to the apartments given over to her son, where she soon had dozens of traitors groveling at her feet, lackeys who stumbled over each other to lick her shoes. My spirits fell, for I knew Vladya was lost to any words from me.

An hour later, Heinrich pounded into the courtyard, followed by a score of men–at–arms. I was never so glad to see anyone in my life! He had met Euphrosyne's messenger on the way, but had somehow missed the man Ivor sent.

Thus he knew I was alive, but was surprised to find me in the palace. He was dumfounded that I met him standing up, shaky though I was. We retired at once to Yuri's rooms. In the Prince's presence, I related everything I knew of the Czar's condition, and of the conspiracy, now centered around Euphrosyne.

"That bitch should have been executed with her husband," Heinrich growled in German. "What do you think Vladimir really wants to do?"

"If his mother had not arrived," I said, "between us we might have persuaded him to take the oath."

"That is undoubtedly why she came," said Heinrich grimly.

"It's too bad Kurbsky and Bulgakov are still in Kazan," I remarked. "Perhaps they could tip the balance in our favor."

"I wouldn't be too sure. Kurbsky's an opportunist. His whole family is that way. If you'll remember, they never stood up for Ivan against the Shuiskys, not until the very last moment."

"Nor were they ever against him," I added. "Roman has taken the oath as his brother's proxy."

"That's good news, but if it really appears the Czar will die, who can tell?" he sighed. "As for Bulgakov, the man is a fine soldier, but he knows nothing of politics. Without the army he wouldn't be much help. The Czar sent everyone home except for the force he needs at Kazan and the few *Streltsi* who are still under Vorotinsky's command."

"Then we have the army!" I said quickly.

"What there is of it," replied Heinrich depreciatingly. "The force isn't large enough to be much value – and won't be, until the Czar completes his plans for recruiting a permanent force. That's a good year away. Right now, one rich boyar could field twice the men."

"Then, what shall we do?" I asked.

"We shall pray," said my stepfather sarcastically, "and we shall also guard the Czar. Most important, we must convince him not to die."

"That doesn't sound very practical." I commented. I wasn't sure whether Heinrich was serious or not.

"It's more practical than you think," he snapped. "I've seen men die when they shouldn't, simply because they were convinced they were going to die. I've also seen men with their guts torn out, men who should already be dead, return to life because they never intended doing anything else. Besides, you and Basmanov have done the best thing anyone could do for him, by throwing those stupid doctors out. I never saw a man recover yet who had half his life's blood drained out of him."

Ivor came in later, while Heinrich was eating, and told my stepfather that something was happening. Too many people were congregating in Vladimir's apartments. Leaving a sizable guard on Yuri's door, and cautioning both the Prince and Ulyana to remain inside, the three of us hurried across the palace to Ivan's chambers. Basmanov had come back with his son, Fedka, who was now serving as senior page to the Czar. Andrei Adashev was outside, conversing with John Mikhailof, Ivan's fussy little secretary. Sylvester was in the bedchamber. Other than a few servants and the usual priests, no one else was there. The only armed men were the household guard, down the hall, and the retainers following Heinrich and me. I carried only a dagger, as did my stepfather, although the ruling made several years ago, allowing him to bear arms in the Czar's presence, had never been rescinded.

"Send someone for Vorotinsky," said Heinrich to Ivor. "We may need all the help we can get. Tell him to bring some men."

Nor was the guess far wrong. A short time later, Euphrosyne appeared in the doorway. Behind her, nearly filling the hall, were several score of men. They were a strange mixture of nobles, soldiers, servants, clerks, and what appeared to be a few hired bullies. Vladimir was not with them. Ignoring me, *Maultasch* strode into the antechamber, demanding Adashev announce her to the Czar. Andrei, although he would not swear to support the Czarevitch, was horrified by her brazen behavior. He ordered her to leave.

"We have no way of knowing the Czar is still alive," she said, breaking into a cunning smile that showed her crooked, yellow teeth. "For all we know he may have died yesterday, and his alleged orders may really be yours. No one has been permitted to see him since last night."

"I have seen him, and he is very certainly alive," I said.

She snorted. "When I need the word of a base–born cur, I shall give him permission to address me," she replied haughtily. "Prince, indeed!"

Basmanov and Ivor moved quietly in front of Ivan's door to block her entrance. Heinrich now placed himself directly in her path. Andrei withdrew to the window.

"No one is going to disturb the Czar this evening, Madam." said Heinrich, speaking in firm, controlled tones.

She remained toe–to–toe with him, glowering.

"I have never struck a woman before," Heinrich continued, "but no one, Madam, is going to pass me until this carpet is red with my blood."

"Foreigner!" she shrieked. "Adventurer! Mercenary! How dare you threaten the widow of the Czar's own uncle?"

"If you are indeed the Czar's kinswoman, you had better act like it," Heinrich barked.

The two of them stared into each other's faces like a pair of angry beasts. There was a stirring in the hallway, where we could hear the ominous mutterings from her small army of lackeys. I think we might have been exchanging blows in another few heartbeats if Andrei had not called out.

"Look below," he said. Everyone in the room turned toward the window. Andrei pushed the casement outward and there, below us, reaching as far as the Kremlin wall, were thousands of people. They knelt in the snow, or stood holding torches, looking up at the Czar's windows. Even as far as the hallway, their murmured prayers formed a rolling swell of sound. It looked as if the entire population of the capital had been allowed inside to pray for their Czar's recovery. The previous day's crowd had been barred at the Kremlin gates. Tonight's display, I thought, was Ivor's doing.

I was the first to speak. "Can you equal the number of the Czar's loyal servants?" I asked. "Do you dare make a move to stir that mob?"

"Herds of cattle!" she replied scornfully, but she had taken a few steps backward.

"Have you ever seen a man trampled by a herd of rampaging cattle?" asked Heinrich.

"It would be better if you left, Madam," added Andrei quietly. "The Czar still lives."

"All of you had better pray to God that he continues to live," she said harshly, turning to leave.

"As fervently," I muttered, "as a murderess prays to the devil."

She stormed out, blasting a path through her followers. Leaderless, they slowly turned and trailed in back of her, dropping into single file to get past Vorotinsky's men, who filled the hall behind them.

Once she was gone I sat down beside Andrei Adashev, who was still on the bench by the window. He was watching the multitude below.

"You surprise me," I said.

"How so?"

"You opposed Staritskaya," I replied.

He moved his slender shoulders to face me, his expression sad and stricken. "Dmitri, you do not understand my soul, do you? I would not oppose the Czar, or permit anyone to harm him. But I cannot see the sense of throwing the land into civil war to assure a succession which can never be assured."

"Then, while Ivan lives, you will side with us?" I asked.

"It is not a question of siding," he explained, as if speaking to a child. "I am a loyal servant of the Czar. If he lives I hope to continue as such. If he dies, I must do what I think is best to fulfill his dreams and plans, not just his desires as a father."

"Then as a loyal servant of the Czar," said Heinrich, a suggestion of malice in his tone, "what would you suggest we do to keep him safe from that woman?"

Andrei sat silently, biting his upper lip. He shrugged in despair.

"I have a thought," I said, "but I hesitate to suggest it."

"Any suggestion would be welcome," said Heinrich.

"That crowd," I replied thoughtfully. "If they believed the Czar's illness was the result of sorcery. . . ."

"And that *Maultasch* was the witch!" Heinrich picked up my train of thought.

"That is a dangerous weapon," Andrei commented.

"If they burn her, so much the better," I said bitterly. "Ivor, can your men start the rumor?"

"I will gladly start the rumor myself," he told us, grinning. "I would even be happy to light the fire under her."

We all looked at Heinrich. He was silent, now, perhaps remembering the results of the last cry of witchery in the city. Then he shrugged. "We must try it," he said.

Ivor started for the door, and I decided to go with him. We gathered a half dozen of his men along the way, explaining to them what they must do. Leaving Vorotinsky to guard the Czar, we wound our way through the palace corridors. I had only a moment of misgiving. What I was about to do could result in the assassination of my best friend's mother. For his sake, I hoped it would not come to that, but she had placed herself in a position where we had to stop her.

Within an hour, we had the crowd chanting outside the palace: "Drive out the witch and save the Czar; drive out the witch. . . ."

Our rumormongering was so successful, the problem was to prevent violence. Some of the townspeople became unreasonably agitated as our story spread from mouth to mouth, although it had taken all of us shouting together to get the chant started. There were now individual shouts, men threatening to storm the palace and seize Euphrosyne.

"As long as we keep them chanting," said Ivor, "no one will be able to harangue them into acting."

The night grew very chill, with the threat of snow before morning. Finally, a few people began to leave. The chant continued, but gradually, as more people left, it began to fade. In the end, the freezing cold dissolved the mob and assured that nothing would happen immediately.

I returned to the Czar's apartments before the crowd broke up. Except for the noise outside, the chant clearly audible through the closed windows, everything was quiet. After speaking with Heinrich, Vorotinsky left with his *Streltsi*, but he set up a guard post downstairs. I doubt if Euphrosyne slept until the people finally left, and by then it was very close to dawn. At daybreak she was in her sleigh, on the way back to Staritsa.

Once she was gone, I went to Vladya's apartments and had a long talk with him. Later in the morning he took the oath. Once he had done so, most of the others followed, including Andrei Adashev. But Sylvester never did, for he said it would only be an oath he might have to break later, and he could not violate a promise to God.

By the following morning, it all made little difference. When I entered the royal bedchamber, I found the Czar propped up on his pillows. His fever had gone. While weak, he was obviously going to live.

CHAPTER IX

Ivan's recovery progressed more slowly than mine, and it was several weeks before he completely overcame the aftereffects. At least it was that long before he admitted feeling well enough to receive people he did not wish to receive, or before he participated in any public functions. The routine of government was carried on by Adashev, and by the numerous clerks within the Kremlin bureaus. Only a day after Vladya had taken the oath, he was confronted by Ivan sitting up in bed. He immediately fell on his knees, touching his forehead to the coverlet. The Czar, in a moment of magnanimous majesty, placed a trembling hand over his cousin's curly hair. Vladya was forgiven. The Czar added a blessing, along with a prayer that his kinsman might be a better servant in the future.

Vladimir left for Staritsa that afternoon, where he remained for several days. Through the gossip of servants, I heard about the terrible scene he had with his mother. He upbraided her, not only for appearing to threaten the Czar, but for her attempted murder of me. From other sources, I had already heard of Vladya's trying to dissuade Euphrosyne from leading her motley group into Ivan's apartments. But *Maultasch* had never been amenable to verbal argument. As a result of their subsequent disagreement, she made her son's life so miserable he was forced to leave his own estates and return to the capital.

On one important subject, my informants failed me. I did not discover the most interesting bit of gossip until Vladya told me himself, and by then the public announcement was only hours away. Vladya had decided to take a wife. A few days after his return to Moscow, he was granted the Czar's permission to sign a marriage contract with Nikita Odoievsky – the man who now replaced Bulgakov as Michael Vorotinsky's second–in–command. Evdokia Odoievskaya, Nikita's sister, was said to be extremely beautiful, and her family enjoyed a reputable position. Again through backstairs gossip, I heard that Euphrosyne's reaction to this news was so violent, no servant dared approach her for days. She pitched every piece of her son's clothing into the snow, tore out half her own hair in rage, and almost burned down the stables by throwing a lighted lantern at a groom. Her fury stemmed not so much from disapproval of the match as from not being informed, much less consulted, beforehand.

As the Czar slowly regained his strength, he was constantly attended by the Czarina's brothers, and by Gregory Zakharin. All these royal in–laws had many axes to grind. As a result of their tenacious displays of loyalty to Ivan while he was ill – although it was obvious they had no other choice – they had been subjected to insults and ridicule. They now sought revenge, and began pointing out traitors to the Czar. If these were men of lesser rank, Ivan simply had them arrested, relying solely on the evidence of his in–laws' accusations. From my own conversations with the Czar, I knew he had no wish to create more dissension by any immediate venting of anger against the higher nobility, particularly the boyars. Both Anastasia and Sylvester harped at him constantly, insisting that he should forgive these men their errors. Ivan heeded their pleas, although the arrests of lesser persons drove a shaft of fear into the hearts of several guilty men, those who knew within themselves how far their sedition had gone. It would be some time before any of them slept easily at night.

In my own haste to reach the Czar's side in his time of need, and because I had been needed in the palace during the crisis of his illness, I had not even seen our new *dacha* in Kitaigorod. Now, with the Czar's recovery, Heinrich and I were able to move in. While I knew Ivan would have preferred us in residence a few more days, our presence was superfluous. Ivor had everything well in hand. As the new commander of the household guard, his power was akin to a Praetorian Perfect.

When I finally saw our house, I could hardly believe the magnificence. Heinrich and I had become two of the richest men in Muscovy, for the concessions given us in Kazan and Svyazhsk were affiliated with those of the Czar. The contracts prevented the grasping Shuiskys who governed the two cities – Peter in Svyazhsk and Gorbatov–Shuisky in Kazan – from laying a finger on our operations. Nor could they levy taxes upon us. By the Czar's order, my name had been entered on all the charters, and I was appointed Heinrich's heir. My poor mother would have been ecstatic, could she have shared our present good fortune. Our household arrangements, on the other hand, might have presented a problem. Roman Kurbsky had faithfully transported our goods and property. When we arrived at the house, my two harem girls had prepared an extraordinary welcome.

In the matter of names, it was customary within many infidel harems for the women to take for themselves the names of flowers or other lovely manifestations of nature. Both of our girls had done this, with the result that each was called by a series of syllables no Muscovite could ever pronounce. We therefore gave them Russian equivalents. The chubby little girl we called Lotus Flower, while her more slender "sister" became Lily.

A week or two before, Jacob had come north with a huge caravan to supply our stores in Moscow, Novgorod, and Pskov. Because there were too many pack animals for our Arbat facilities, he had quartered the overflow in the stables behind our new house, prior to sending them off to the west. The girls had cajoled him into diverting enough of the trade goods to bankrupt a poorer merchant, but the effects they produced turned our home into a veritable oriental paradise – thick Persian carpets, Chinese urns, and dark carved teak furniture. They had used yards and yards of raw silk and heavy, precious brocade to drape the rooms. Except for the Czar, Heinrich had become the major importer of silks and art works from Cathay. These came mostly through Bakhara and Samarkand, where Abraham had established connections with other Hebrew merchants. During the hostilities at Kazan, these commodities had backlogged in the southern cities. With caravans able to move again, the materials came in a great flood, and our home became the most envied in Moscow.

The influx of goods from the south was already beginning to create another situation, a situation which was soon to result in a second war. Muscovy had no port on the Baltic Sea. An unwritten agreement between the Poles, Swedes, and Danes made it nearly impossible for us to ship into the Western countries, where our goods could bring the best prices. What little did get through was subject to ruinous taxes, making their resale prohibitive to any but the wealthiest. Our fine fabrics sometimes lay in warehouses until they were covered with mold and fungus.

Spices would frequently spoil or lose flavor through age. With other nations bringing in the same materials by ship, routed through the sea lanes between Byzantium and Italy – even by some new route they had discovered south of Ethiopia – we faced a growing competition. Unless we acquired a port in the west, we would never be able to supply the market. Our only alternative at the moment was to ship through the chain of Hanseatic cities, starting at Novgorod.

Jacob, who had lingered in Moscow to confer with us after sending most of the caravan westward, reported on his own observations in Kazan and beyond. Though Heinrich had just come from the area, himself, we both recognized Jacob's greater ability to mingle with the native populations, and to see things we could not. He spoke of new stirrings among the Tartars, and the many tribes remaining unconquered. The Crimean Khan had belatedly realized how the loss of Kazan was going to disrupt his control over portions of his own realm. He had started sending spies and provocateurs into Russian held provinces to stir up trouble. He was also actively trying to woo the Cossacks back into his own fold.

The avaricious Shuiskys had already created unnecessary tensions by their corrupt tax methods, while the flood of Christian priests had done poorly in converting the Mussulmen to a belief in the true God. "It is difficult to convince the people they should adore the Prince of Peace," said Jacob, "when the catechism is read beneath the dangling feet of a corpse."

But we did not dwell on problems so far from Moscow. Such was not the Russian way. After Jacob's departure, we entered into a round of festivities, celebrating our victory over the infidels, the miraculous recovery of the Czar, the birth of his heir – and, more personally, my own elevation in rank. One of the first guests in our house was that fat swine, Shig Ali. At first I refused to be there when Heinrich told me he had been invited. But my stepfather insisted I remain, claiming it was essential to our continued prosperity. Thus I was forced to sit next to this disgusting man, watching him gorge his bloated face, devouring every morsel of food that came within his reach. His obese, greasy body reeked of sweat. But through the pungent, sour odors, I kept imagining I could detect the delicate suggestion of sandlewood. With my best friend about to marry, I suppose I was particularly sensitive regarding my own status. I envied the tranquillity of each man who had been fortunate enough to wed the proper woman: Ivan, Yuri – even Shig Ali, and now Vladya. I wanted this badly for myself, yet I knew several other men whose wives were almost as unsatisfactory as Anna. In truth, I was afraid to take the chance of being bound forever to a woman I might grow to despise. I kept thinking of this as I sat beside the man who had stolen the one woman I might have taken as my own. At length I had to leave the room, for the little food I had been able to consume did not wish to remain with me.

Heinrich glowered angrily when I excused myself, and I knew there would be trouble later. But I didn't care; nor could I later bring myself to return. This marked the first in a series of arguments with my stepfather, for he was furious with me, and we had some heated words later that same evening. I don't know whether he had intended to invite the man, anyway, or whether his announcement was to serve as my ultimate punishment, but Heinrich terminated our verbal altercation by informing me that Ediger, the former Khan of Kazan, would be our guest the next evening.

"How can you invite that man into our house?" I demanded. "This is the *Oberschwein* who was going to shove a stake up my ass and plant me on top of the city walls, to bleed my guts out—"

"It doesn't matter what he *almost* did," Heinrich bellowed back. "Right now he's in a position to make us the wealthiest merchants in Christendom."

We continued arguing until our shouting brought the servants, and then our violence scared them away. It ended when I tried to strike Heinrich. Still too weak from my illness to be very effective, my blow was easily deflected by his arm. He then delivered a punch to my chest which sent me tumbling over several pieces of furniture.

The next day we were more or less back to normal, although an unusual tension remained between us. I had started managing some of our accounts, and thus kept myself occupied during most of the day. Heinrich always left me alone when I worked on these records, mostly, I think – though he would never admit it – because his eyesight was not quite what it had been. Trying to read the figures was a strain on him, and he was sometimes unable to decipher my writing without holding the sheet suspiciously close to his face. I found the books in very bad condition, as they had not been properly maintained since prior to the army's departure for Kazan. This offered me the excuse to stay in the accounts room all morning and into the afternoon. But as the hour of Ediger's impending arrival drew closer, I started to fidget, finally becoming so restless I had to stop.

I went for a walk in the *gostiny dvor*, ostensibly to look over our shop, only to find it impossible to keep my mind on trade goods. Every time I thought of the need to be gracious to a man who had so humiliated me, my stomach drew into a knot. I walked through the marketplace and into the Square of Executions, where workmen were surveying the site for a new cathedral Ivan had ordered to commemorate the conquest of Kazan. It was to be consecrated to the Blessed Mother of God, and would be the most extensive construction undertaken since the days of his grandfather.

I dallied until close to sunset, passing the *lobonoyo mesto*, which had been especially busy the last few weeks, executing those whom the Romanovs accused. I walked to the river, watching the golden pockets of sunlight change and glitter amongst the black ripples of the water's surface. The end of another winter was near, I realized. Tiny patches of green poked out here and there, while in many places the snow had melted into the ground.

I turned back, starting to cross the square again. Workmen were packing up their tools, making ready to leave for home. The usual evening tangle had started, for the city was becoming a modern Tower of Babel. Mercenaries from Poland, Germany, Denmark, Sweden, Hungary came in droves to fill the openings in our army. There were groups of Tartars and Cossacks, as well as Moravians, Cheremisians, Circassians, and barbarians from innumerable other tribes. It must have been very like the First Rome, in the days of the great Caesars, when soldiers of fortune from all over Europe had swarmed into the Capital of the World. Also, like the first Rome, we were organizing these foreigners into a huge standing army. Their voices in the streets blended into an inharmonious rumble. As Rome had done before us, we were in the process of changing from a small provincial state into a powerful nation.

Nor was our growth exemplified merely by the buildings or the army. In addition to recruiting foreign troops, the Czar was exercising clever diplomacy in dealing with his brother rulers. Ediger was an outstanding example. Since he had decided to become a Christian, and the time of his baptism had been set just a few days hence, the Czar had already heaped many honors and riches upon him. I knew my attitude was wrong, that Heinrich had good reason for what he was doing. Ediger had been Khan, ruler over thousands of infidels, many of whom still roamed the steppes south of his former domain. These people inhabited the banks of the Volga, the Dnieper, the Don – all the great southern rivers. From these areas, or at least through them, would pass the richest transports in the history of trade. Whoever controlled these peoples, or could bargain with them for safe passage, could foresee a brilliant, profitable future. Ediger could be valuable, and Heinrich meant to obtain full measure from him.

I had resolved, finally, to return to the house and perform my duties. I had just turned toward home when I heard a commotion in the bazaar, and most of the crowd began edging in that direction. Swept along like some flotsam in the river, I soon saw a messenger who was shouting something to the people. I could make out the word "catastrophe," but the noise of the mob prevented my hearing the rest. The fellow wore a blue livery which I didn't recognize, and had no doubt taken it upon himself to deliver his news to the populace. "Plague!" someone shouted. "Pskov is destroyed by the plague!"

The reaction of the crowd was immediate – fearful panic and a milling confusion. Gradually, the mob melted away, each man going into his own home and bolting his door. I watched the messenger gallop through the Kremlin gates. Assuming the Czar would receive the news in a few minutes, I hurried home to find my stepfather involved in an argument with one of the Shuisky representatives. It was the same fellow who had come before, trying to negotiate a joint caravan with us. The man was sly and surly, which only increased Heinrich's aversion to him.

"Tell your masters I shall consider their proposal," said Heinrich, at last, getting up to indicate the man should leave.

"But I must return with an answer," he whined.

"You have your answer!" snapped Heinrich. He started from the room, motioning me to follow. The man finally slumped away.

"There is plague in Pskov," I whispered.

I might as well have shoved a knife into Heinrich's belly. He gritted his teeth, emitting every Russian, German, and Polish oath he knew, slamming his fist again and again against the table.

"How did you find out?" he demanded, once the first wave of frustrated anger had passed.

"A messenger just rode in with the news," I said. "He shouted it in the bazaar."

"Whose messenger?"

"I don't know. I didn't recognize the livery."

"Then you don't know for sure. How do you know he spoke the truth?"

"Well, everyone believed him, and he rode into the Kremlin afterward. Why should someone spread a lie like that?" I asked defensively.

"You have much to learn, Demetrius." Heinrich went to his writing table and took out a scrap of parchment, scratching out a note to Andrei Adashev. He called a servant to deliver it, then dropped into a chair, bellowing for some vodka. He sat pensively, hand on his chin.

"Are we in trouble?" I asked.

"We have enough merchandise in Pskov and Novgorod – or on the road between them by now – to ruin us if we lose it," he sighed.

"Will we necessarily lose it?"

"Do you know how they stop the plague? he growled. "They burn the city. There's no other way. They burn the city and everything in it!"

"And if the plague is in Pskov now, it will be in Novgorod next, won't it?"

"It could hardly fail to spread at least that far. And, God have mercy on us, it could hit Moscow after that."

"With the number of men flocking in from the west, it could already be amongst us," I suggested.

"Not likely," he replied thoughtfully. "It moves slowly, like a great storm, and it decimates one town after another. It would have to hit Novgorod and Klin before it came here." Then Heinrich bounded toward the back of the house, shouting for some horsemen. He dispatched two of them after Jacob's caravan, ordering its return. We were sitting together in the nearly darkened room when Ediger arrived.

With an effort, Heinrich heaved himself to his feet and walked heavily toward the hall to welcome our guest. As always, the Tartar was attended by a dozen servants and retainers. I had never spoken to Ediger since escaping from Kazan. He had made himself very hard to find during the turmoil in the palace, for the Czar's death could well have meant his own. Vladimir, or course, hated him as much as I did.

But this evening, the dark–skinned Ediger was a strange surprise for me. After speaking with Heinrich in the entrance hall, he accompanied my stepfather back into the room. During the interim, servants had lighted tapers and replenished a fire in the hearth. The room was pleasantly warm, and possibly because of this and the familiar decor, Ediger seemed very much at home. I rose when he entered, and as soon as he saw me he smiled, approaching with an apparently sincere display of pleasure.

"Prince Dmitri," he said warmly, extending his right hand. "I have wished to speak to you for such a long time!" Unabashed by my lack of enthusiasm, he went on: "The fortunes of war place us in such unfortunate circumstances! Please believe me when I say how greatly I regret that unhappy experience in Kazan."

"You regret it no more than I would, had your plans been carried out," I responded coldly.

"No, no, no," he said, gesturing with both hands. He moved them gracefully, like two spread fans. "At that time we were at war and you were not Dmitri, the son of Heinrich, who in turn was the friend of Ediger." He glanced at my stepfather for support. Heinrich nodded, and our former adversary continued: "The attitude of the Khan of Kazan to an unknown enemy soldier must be far different from that between two men who are soon to be joined, not only in allegiance to the One True Czar, but also in the brotherhood of Christian faith."

"What our guest would say," added Heinrich meaningfully, "is that between the three of us there are many areas of mutual interest. For the good of all, it would behoove us to solidify the bonds of friendship."

I continued to look coldly at both of them, but I didn't answer.

"I am learning many things," added Ediger, "and one of them is understanding the Christian soul."

"Remember, son," said Heinrich, "Prince Ediger has undergone many changes in his recent life. Where he was once supreme ruler, he is now a subject of the Czar. He would like to make amends for his past."

I began to feel very boorish, with both of them working on me. They were really asking for nothing more than a gesture of acceptance. It would have been most unseemly to continue my resistance, so I went to Ediger and placed my hands on his shoulders, intending to give him the traditional welcome. This produced a comical moment, for to a Mussulman the left hand is unclean and should never touch another. Ediger flinched involuntarily. However, he was the first to laugh. "I am no longer an infidel misbeliever," he said, gripping my forearms with both his hands. "You see, I exercise the bond of friendship without my former superstitions."

"Good!" shouted Heinrich. "You will also join us in a goblet of wine, then."

"Ha! I confess that wine was always a secret vice," said Ediger, "even when my former religion forbade it." He accepted the goblet and made a proper toast to our new home. "To symbolize my true repentance, Prince Dmitri," he said, "and to compensate for your loss, I have brought you a gift. Come," he motioned to me, "you must step to the door."

His people were still loitering in the entryway, as Heinrich had not yet told our servants what to do with the retinue. They stood aside as we passed, the nearest opening the door for us. Outside, a groom held the bridle of the most spectacular white stallion I had ever seen. The horse had been combed and rubbed until his coat gleamed like the live white flames of steel. On his back was a silver saddle with patterns of gold beaten into its surface.

If this gift were truly for me. . . ? I looked questioningly at Ediger, hardly able to believe he would present me with anything so fine. "If you would honor me by accepting . . . ." he said. "His name is Gabriel."

As if in a dream, I went up to the animal, fondling his nose and face to reassure him. I was dressed in light clothing, but I mounted and rode him on a wild flight to the Kremlin gates and back. I had never known such a mount! He was from the finest Arabian stock, obviously bred on the steppes, for his breathing was heavy, deep – typical of horses from that area. He was perfectly trained, yet there was spirit beneath his glorious exterior. On the way back I felt more than a twinge of embarrassment. It was such a magnificent gift – really a gift fit for the Czar, himself – I wondered if it would be right to accept it.

When I reentered our front court, everyone had gone inside except for the groom. He stepped forward immediately to take the stallion's head, holding him as I dismounted.

"He pleases you?" asked the little man, bowing in Tartar fashion.

"Very much," I said.

"Then you will keep us?"

"Us?" I replied, puzzled.

"It was my master's – my *former* master's desire that we both enter your service together," he replied respectfully.

"Was it you who trained the animal?" I asked.

"Yes, Master, it was."

"Then I suppose I will have to keep you, if I am going to keep the horse. What are you called?"

"The Russians call me Serge," he replied grinning, "for my real name is beyond their ability to pronounce."

"Then Serge it shall be," I told him, laughing in a sudden surge of glee. "Do you know where the stables are?"

"Yes, Master. And I shall see to Gabriel's needs."

Gabriel, I thought, the messenger of God. An appropriate name! "You may go then, Serge, and when you have finished tell the cook to give you a good meal. I'll speak to you again in the morning."

He bowed himself away, walking backward and leading the horse, all in the Mussulman fashion. "Serge," I called as he reached the corner. He stopped, waiting expectantly. "Are you a Christian?" I asked.

His round little body shook with mirth, and a broad grin broke across his features. He bowed, bobbing up and down several times. "Oh yes," he laughed. "I am a good Christian. I have been a Christian for almost two months."

The rest of the evening with Ediger was pleasant enough, although I struggled against the sense of having been bought. But our guest had such a remarkable ability to deal with people, he quickly forced all negative thought from my mind. After a few goblets of wine, he became witty and entertaining, losing his saturnine demeanor. He enthralled us with tales of his visits to the Sultan of Turkey and his many experiences in the court of the Crimean Khan. My growing acceptance of him was significantly advanced when I realized that he shared my opinion of Shig Ali. Only force of circumstances required Ediger to maintain an appearance of friendliness toward him. (Let me make a note here for clarification. Henceforth in my narrative, I shall have other occasions to refer to "The Sultan," of which there is only one – Suleyman Kanuni, an Osmanli Turk - the Tartars' ruler of Turkey, who resides in Byzantium and is the sworn archenemy of the Czar.)

After dinner, we had quite an extensive discussion regarding the hostility of certain Mongol-allied tribes, the Cheremisians and Bashkirs particularly. Ediger explained why the Mordvins, Chivaches, and Votiaks had refused to pay their tribute, although the amount was the same they had formerly paid the Khan of Kazan.

"The answer to this has several roots," Ediger told us, "for the tribute is paid in furs. This same situation faced my own tax collectors, and I found it necessary to employ only men of means, and of exceptional loyalty to me. This, I do not believe has been done by your governors. Instead, they have hired evil, greedy men, which would matter little if the levy were assessed in coin. Each man would know exactly what he must pay. In furs, the tax is uncertain, for the value of a pelt can vary according to its size, the quality of the hair, the color. It will depend, too, on the time of year the fur was taken, winter coats being more desirable, as you know. If the tax collectors are dishonest, they create the very problems your governors are now experiencing."

"This only goes to prove you should never trust a Shuisky," I said sourly.

"One more facet to the problem," continued Ediger, "is the present scarcity of animals. I have heard reports that thousands of Russian peasants are moving down the Volga, claiming land for farms. My informants were amazed at the size of this migration, especially during the cold of winter. But these people have trapped and otherwise taken many of the animals for food, as well as for their skins."

"Do you expect a major uprising of any kind?" asked Heinrich.

"I am afraid there may be trouble," Ediger replied thoughtfully, "for the remnants of my – Kazanite army have built a fort some fifty miles to the south. This may merely be a wintering place, but I fear the worst, especially after the news I received today."

"You mean about the plague?" I asked, wondering how that could affect Kazan.

"Plague!" said Ediger, shocked. "No, where is there plague?"

"In Pskov," said Heinrich softly, "but as yet the story is unconfirmed."

"Let us hope it is a false report!" he replied. His expression was suddenly grim. "But no, the news I meant was the massacre of your fur collectors in Kazan. I assumed you knew about it."

It was Heinrich's turn to gasp. "When was this?" he asked.

"About a week ago," Ediger told us. "I am surprised your own sources had not already informed you. I was asked to question the Czar's messenger this afternoon."

"Well, what happened?" I asked.

"From the best we have been able to learn, a number of people staged an uprising over the fur tax. It grew, as mob actions will, until it involved a whole section of the city."

"How many men did we lose?" asked Heinrich.

"Something over three hundred Russians, and a number of Cossacks. I do not know exactly."

"Shuiskys!" I muttered.

"I fear your governors know little about managing subject peoples." added Ediger.

"If they treat the Tartars as they treated the citizens of Moscow, and every other area they've ever ruled," I said bitterly, "they won't make any friends for the Czar."

"To rule one must be firm." Ediger remarked.

"There have been too many hangings," said Heinrich with a sigh. "My last caravan brought news of seventy–some men hanged at one time – bandits and insurrectionists. I can't believe a good governor would have to do this. It only serves to excite the lower elements."

"Fear is a valuable tool, and used wisely it can preserve order – foolishly, it can create chaos," said Ediger. He had been drinking very heavily as we talked but still seemed completely sober. Our two harem girls were serving, and we continued to sit a little longer, as the conversation gradually drifted onto other subjects.

At length, Ediger stood up, stretching his slender body. "The hour grows late," he said. "I must thank you for your hospitality, and leave before I impose upon it." He was remarkably steady on his feet, as Heinrich ordered a servant to alert his retainers. After the usual exchange of amenities, all done in proper Russian form – with another profuse expression of gratitude from me – Ediger left. I could still not understand exactly how it happened, but he departed as my friend.

Within two days the Czar ordered the Novgorod highway sealed off, assigning a strong force of *Streltsi* to enforce his edict. The soldiers posted notice that anyone avoiding the roadblock to enter areas around Moscow would be burned alive, with all his possessions. Our messenger had found Jacob's caravan before it reached Novgorod, and they started back, only to encounter the *Streltsi* guard post. After considerable argument and protestation, Jacob finally convinced the commander that he had not been in tainted country. His return to the capital was a great relief to Heinrich. Although we had no local market for most of the goods, at least they would not be consumed by the plague fires.

The governor of Novgorod also issued an edict. In an attempt to save his own city, he forbade all travel to and from Pskov. Still the plague struck, and we soon heard that people were dying by the thousands. In Pskov, the dead were legion, without enough survivors to bury them. In Moscow, life went on as usual behind the *Streltsi* blockade. The people were restless and fearful, but there was nothing they could do. The Lord would decide their fate.

Vladimir opened his mansion across the river, and took up permanent residence away from his mother. There had been some residual coolness between my friend and me for several weeks, but it gradually subsided. The Prince was very impressed with Gabriel, and offered me a huge sum if I would sell him, which, of course, I would not do. I think it rankled Vladya to have people stare at my mount, remarking on its magnificence, when none of his horses could create half the comment. I persuaded Heinrich to contact Abraham in Svyazhsk, who sent a very fine gray for Vladya. It arrived near the end of March, just in time for the round of baptisms.

Together, Vladya and I attended three christenings within a week's time. First, the infant Czarevitch was baptized at the Sergey–Troitsky Monastery, with nearly the whole court riding out in an enormous column of sleighs. Everyone wore gaily colored finery, drinking heavily to overcome the cold. We were a merry crowd long before reaching the monastery – leaping off our sleighs to jump onto the one behind or beside us. All the way, the bells chattered on the horses' harnesses, while one group would sing in competition with another. Black and white frames of birch reached naked fingers up through the drifts of winter snow, whizzing past in ever more blinding rushes as the vodka clouded my brain and made it difficult to focus my eyes.

Mercifully, the ceremony was simple and brief; but held in the impressive atmosphere of this sacred shrine, it still tended to sober me. The bones and other relics of Saint Sergey were housed here, and the knowledge always made the chapel seem especially awe inspiring. Adding to the somber aura was the same ascetic monk who had slept in his coffin outside the door for as long as any of us could remember. Whatever dreadful sin he had committed to require such expiation, it made my own seem less.

The words were spoken by the venerable Archbishop Nikander of Rostov, a fat gnarled old priest, who spoke very slowly and seemed to creak under his own weight when he moved. Following the ritual, Ivan decide to remain an extra day to pray at the shrine and to visit with Joseph, the former Metropolitan. Most of us left, traveling through a heavy fall of snow which did little to dampen the revels of our return trip.

The day after Ivan came back, the Metropolitan baptized Suunbeka's son, Utemish, who was henceforth called Alexander. The ceremony took place in the Czar's private chapel, with Ivan and Anastasia standing up for the child, whom the Czar decreed would be raised as his own. All of the court that could squeeze into the tiny area was present, again in all their finest raiment. Makari, having one of his good days, delivered a brief, almost inspired speech, welcoming the child into the grace of Holy Church and into the brotherhood of Christianity. Suunbeka, her lovely face veiled, but wearing heavy Russian clothes, stood beside her corpulent husband, Shig Ali. Although I watched her closely, she never looked in my direction. The one woman I had loved in every sense, I thought, watching her. How long before I met another?

The third ceremony – Ediger's christening – makes my blood freeze to this day, whenever I think about it. A large hole was cut through the ice of the Moskva River, for only small children were spared the proper immersion during winter months. Adults, especially converting infidels, had to endure it. Most people chose to wait for warmer weather, but for political reasons Ediger could not delay. Early in the morning, Vladimir and I rode out with a boisterous, noisy group of friends. Everyone was teasing Vladya about his coming marriage, expressing the vulgar ideas they could not mention in front of the Czar. The day was bitter cold, coming as it did during the last heavy freeze. It was the kind of day when people say "It's too cold to snow."

An icy wind screamed in from the north, making one's breath form large, gray clouds before his face – but briefly, for the sharp wind quickly whipped them away. My group remained mounted, watching from an embankment along the water's edge. From our position we could see everything, but still be first to leave when it was over. Even this far from the frozen surface, dressed in heavy felts and sables, we found the deep chill uncomfortable. Everyone came wrapped in his warmest furs and heaviest coats, except for Ediger. He stood barefoot before God, shivering on the ice, covered only by a linen shroud. Makari was to be his Godfather, although this naturally implied no responsibility for sin, as Ediger was not a child.

The service began with a bishop – I think he was the rector of the new cathedral at Kolomna – bellowing his words into the gale. Hardly anyone could hear him. At the proper time, Ediger shouted: "I hate and renounce Mohammed. I love God, Christ and the Holy Trinity! Today I die as a Mussulman, and rise again as a Christian!"

Then in he went, through the nearly freezing water beneath. "In the name of the Father," called the bishop, shoving Ediger's head under the water; "the Son," and down again; "and the Holy Ghost." He pushed Ediger under for the third time. The new Christian came out, assisted by two sturdy altar boys. His shift clung to his trembling frame, and his dark hair covered his face, plastered against his skull. He looked nearly drowned. As he later told me, he had not only died as a Mussulman; during the third dunking he had doubted his Christian existence would be very long–lived. As it was, he came down with a terrible cold which lasted for several weeks. It never developed into the disabling fevers experienced by Ivan and myself, however, and our new Christian remained in bed only a few days.

Ediger was now called Simon Bekbulatovich, or simply Prince Simon. Ivan gave him a beautiful house inside the Kremlin, and made him wealthy enough to live in comfort for the rest of his days. The Czar also blessed his betrothal to Maria, the daughter of Prince John Mstislavsky, a kinsman of the royal family. Maria was, therefore, of extremely good birth and a woman of high Christian morals. Vladya, who had an aversion to all dark–skinned people, made some harsh comments about their coming union; but I was eventually able to persuade him into a reasonable acceptance of Ediger, now Simon. At the banquet following the Christening, we all became gloriously drunk, and in the end Prince Vladimir toasted Prince Simon. The Czar blessed us all, for Makari had fallen asleep.

Ivan was convinced he had one more duty to perform, and in a way I blame myself for the catastrophe that resulted from his decision. I could probably have dissuaded him, had I started soon enough, and not gotten involved in a wild round of drinking bouts with Vladimir and our other friends. But with Vladya and Simon both about to marry, we seemed on a never–ending crusade to drain every wine barrel in Moscow. Our only real achievement was to suppress the underlying concern we all felt over the ominous potential danger from Pskov. With enough spirits, they say, there is escape from any fear or terror.

During Ivan's illness he had prayed to his patron Saint Cyril for intercession, swearing that if he were spared he would make a pilgrimage to the monastery at Kirilof. Such a journey meant traveling through the snow–covered northern wilds, to the shore of the Frozen Sea. Now, with his health restored and the three baptisms behind him, the Czar announced his intention to go. Weather not withstanding, he planned to take his family. Several of us remonstrated with him after the public announcement was made, one of these being Kurbsky, who had just returned from Kazan. Adashev talked for the better part of an hour, and even Anastasia pleaded with him to leave the Czarevitch in Moscow. But Ivan had promised the saint, and no one could weaken his resolve. Disregarding all advice to the contrary, the Czar set the date of departure. As he did not plan to be absent very long, no regent was appointed to take his place though the duty nominally devolved on Yuri. Once Ivan's intentions were announced, I noted an underlying carnival spirit throughout the court, for ever since his illness the Czar had become much more serious, tending to frown on any behavior he considered ungodly among his courtiers. Most people blamed this on Anastasia, but I think it was more Sylvester's doing. Fortunately, the monk was too self–satisfied to see his own faults, and his bullying was becoming obnoxious even to the Czar.

Ivan sent for me the day before he was due to leave. When the messenger arrived I had just returned from the public bathhouse, where Vladya and I had steamed out from our night's carouse. Since the fire, there had been several very nice places built on the sites of the old baths in the inner city. The one we used was especially modern and well designed. Whereas the older building had been a gathering place for elderly men and their wives, the new one attracted many younger people, largely lower court officials and others from the wealthier merchant classes. During the day a good many women would bring their daughters. While everything was done quite properly, it did give one an opportunity to see some nice young ladies who were otherwise secluded in the women's quarters.

Vladya and I had parted when we left the bathhouse, and he had also gone home. We were planning to meet later that evening at a new gaming house in the

Arbat. When I received the Czar's message, I sent word to Vladya that I might be delayed and went at once to the Kremlin. Mikhailof took me to Ivan, who was sitting on the floor with Fedka Basmanov. They had a chess set between them, with pieces the size of beer tankards. The Czar was teaching the lad some advanced moves in their game. The other page brought me a cushion, and I joined them, the three of us sitting like Turks around the board. With the Czar advising him, Fedka was winning. The child had a ready mind, and seemed to absorb Ivan's teachings very quickly. He was extremely pleased with himself for beating the Czar.

"No, no," Ivan told him. "If you do that you are going to lose a castle."

The lad seemed to consider a moment, and grinning delightedly made the move anyway. Ivan took his castle, removing his hand from the board before he saw the trap Fedka had laid for him. "Too late," growled the Czar unhappily. "You have beaten me, son."

"Do you wish to play another, sire?"

Ivan got up, holding his hip. Two servants rushed forward to assist him. "Not just now, Fedka," he said. Then to me, he remarked, "I have not been getting enough exercise, my friend. I am like an old man." He shook himself free of the servants. "But I'm not that old, yet. Get away!"

"Your Majesty looks the bloom of health," I answered grinning.

"Are you going to become another spittal–licking courtier?" he groaned. "I look the shadow of death, and you know it." He did look weary, and his eyes were very bloodshot. However, this was not unusual; Ivan still read a great deal, frequently at night. He always had trouble sleeping.

I had been joking when I made my first remark, and I would have made another, except that the servants were still in the room. Court etiquette had become so rigid, Mikhailof had even distributed a list of rules and rituals, much of it based on Byzantine standards. Unfortunately, Ivan had approved this, which committed himself and all of us to its observance. Finally, the Czar motioned his servants and pages out. "Put the pieces away, Fedka. And all of you leave us."

That was a compliment to me, I thought. The Czar was seldom unattended these days, and there were only a handful of us who were permitted into his presence without at least one guard in the room.

"That little Basmanov is a fine lad," Ivan remarked after the others were gone. "I hope my own son may grow like him."

"He is a good child," I agreed. "You should assign him to the Czarevitch's household."

Ivan nodded assent. He eased himself into his great chair, pulling his robe open and scratching at the hairs on his chest. "Oh, that feels good," he sighed. "Terrible, the things one can't do in front of these damned attendants! You look all fresh and pinky; been to the bathhouse, eh?"

"You aren't supposed to know that," I replied.

"I know everything," he said seriously. "My informers tell me too much. Incidentally, I am going to speak to Vladimir. He should begin to remember his rank. You, too, for that matter. Do you realize how you are regarded by the people around me?"

"I would not like to think how bad that might be," I said lightly.

"I think you might be pleased," he returned, still speaking seriously. "Oh, there is jealousy, of course; that's to be expected. You are wealthy – newly elevated – and you stand high in my favor. But you are highly regarded by most of them, and visiting public bathhouses is not the most respectable form of behavior."

"I learn many things from the lower classes," I replied. "In the future, who knows what value this could be."

"As always, you pretend to answer in wisdom. Still, I would like you to be more conscious of your position." He leaned forward and lowered his voice to a more confidential tone. "I'm going to entrust you with a further bit of knowledge. As you know, the realm is beset with difficulties: problems in Kazan, a pending uprising in the south. We have plague in the west, and our trade is nearly at a standstill. I fear that God has withdrawn His favor, and that is why I must make this pilgrimage."

It was at this point that I should have tried to persuade Ivan not to make the trip. We were alone and relaxed, and it is just possible he would have listened to me, at least postponed the journey until warmer weather. Instead, I made some stupid response, expressing agreement – "further proof of worthiness" – some such nonsense.

"Hum!" he grunted. "You make noises like Adashev! None of you want me to go, and I know it. But you're all missing the real significance. I went to this shrine once before. No, don't look at me as if I were having feverish imaginings. I was carried there in my mother's womb, when she made the trip to pray before my birth. Now that I have been reborn, so to speak – restored to life – I must repeat the act of grace." He suddenly gestured wildly, as if to ward off a swarm of bees. "Compared to mine, your own soul is pure, Dmitri. You cannot understand the effort I must put forth to cleanse myself of sin, because you can't see into my soul. You don't know all the evil hidden there to threaten me. I hope you may never learn to know it."

"I am sure it cannot be so much —"

"It doesn't matter!" he interrupted sharply, cutting me off. "One day you may understand. But back to my reason for asking you here. While I do my best to fulfill the requirements of God and His Holy Church, I must leave certain mundane responsibilities to you and a few others."

"I'm always available," I replied eagerly.

Without acknowledging my enthusiasm, he went on: "As you may be aware, Andrei and others are urging me to pursue the war in the south, even to seizing Astrakhan from the Crimean Horde. I have sent Boris Saltikov to Kazan, with enough men to punish the insurrectionists; but this is not enough to satisfy them. They want war and further conquest."

"I know," I said thoughtfully. "I can't decide whether they're right or not."

"Then you can appreciate that I'm also torn between the alternatives. As yet, the Lord has not made His Will known to me. We must either push toward the south, continue our Holy War against the infidels, or We must reassert Our rights in the west."

"Don't you regard the plague as a sign?" I asked.

"Adashev says I should, and Sylvester harangues me every day. He swears the Lord has spoken by bringing the plague, leaving the way open for us to move farther into Tartar territory below Kazan, while being assured our enemies can't attack us across the afflicted areas. At the same time, the plague prevents us from moving west."

"It is quite a convincing argument," I replied.

"Yes, it is," he sighed. "And yet, Dmitri, the Lord moves in strange ways. His Word is not always easily read. I want to hear a few more holy men before I decide. Nor is there any need to hurry. Spring thaws will mire the roads, and we won't be able to move, anyway.

"Do you expect a sign at Kirilof, then?" I asked.

"Perhaps, but I also intend to confer with people at Sergey–Troitsky. I'll go there first, and when I return from Kirilof I will have made up my mind," he said firmly.

"And in the interim, what do you wish me to do?"

"Regardless of the way the Lord instructs me, I am sure it means war again this year. You've seen the flood of men entering the city every day. There may be fewer, now, until the bans are lifted; but they'll still come – especially from the south: Tartars, Cossacks, as well as other barbarians. All of them must be organized and instructed. I've assigned Ediger . . . er, Prince Simon to do this." He watched me closely for my reaction.

I shrugged. "It was a reasonable choice," I responded.

"It was the best I could have made. This is why I've heaped so many honors on him. I find him a charming companion, by the way. Still, I can't bring myself to trust him without some control. Less than a year ago, he was my bitterest foe."

"Then, I'm to work with him?"

"You will be his second–in–command," said Ivan. "Michael Vorotinsky will remain in charge of the whole army; I anticipate no change there. But Michael dislikes Simon, as do the Kurbskys. Otherwise, Roman might be a suitable second, although he lacks your ability to observe and interpret. Andrew couldn't be degraded to serve under a man he defeated, and I can't put him in charge of Simon, or I'll defeat my entire purpose. All in all, you're the best choice, and I know I can depend on you to assure nothing untoward occurs."

From the first, the prospect displeased me. Drilling troops can be a terrible drudgery. Still, the Czar could not be denied, and I accepted my post without question. As soon as I had seen the royal entourage off the following morning, I reported to Simon's house.

The Prince's residence was only a few steps from the site of the old Vorontsof *dacha*, which had been destroyed in the fire. The new structures in the section were quite elegant and very modern. The Czar had ordered huge quantities of timber, sparing no effort or expense in the construction. Many of the homes had glass windows throughout the upper floors, where these faced toward the center of the Kremlin. Some, like Simon's, had stone foundations. Others were faced in brick or fitted stone.

My arrangements with Simon did not take long. He knew, naturally, that I had been assigned to work with him, and very likely had been maneuvered into requesting me. The servant who admitted me went through the full ritual for greeting a man of great rank, then led me through the house to the practice yard, where his master was attempting to familiarize himself with our heavier, Christian weapons. I noted he was not very skilled with them.

"Come, have a bout with me!" he called merrily.

"You give me too great an advantage," I replied. "Use your own weapons. They're more suited to your build."

I think he may have misunderstood me, for a heavy frown crossed his dark brow.

"I mean no offense," I added quickly, "but you're rather smaller and weigh less than I do. You're a master at using the weapons you've always used. Why try to change?"

"I have changed all things," he said sharply, trying to catch his breath. He walked over to me, tossing the shield to his sparring partner and placing his sword on the table. "Do you think it seemly I should use the weapons of an infidel?"

"You'll be leading infidels," I said. "At least, they'll be men who were born infidels. We certainly don't want to retrain all of them in the use of Russian weapons! It would only complicate what we have to do, and would make them poorer soldiers in the end."

"Maybe you're right," he said, snapping his finger to bring a servant. The man handed him a towel. Thoughtfully, he wiped the sweat and dust from his glistening face. "If I lead the foreign levies, maybe I won't look out of place bearing the same weapons."

"Do we have any problems, yet?" I asked.

"Nothing serious," he told me, "except the Cossacks. They will follow only their own officers, which is all right, except their officers dislike taking orders from anyone else."

"Kurbsky handled that at Kazan," I said. "He called the leaders together and talked to them – gave them plenty to drink while he was at it. Then he challenged them to a game on horseback. You know, if you can beat them on a horse they'll never question your leadership, again."

"And did he beat them?" asked Simon incredulously.

"Well, he did get them terribly drunk," I said, "and as you know, Andrew is no mean horseman."

"I shall leave it to you, then, my friend," he said. "With Gabriel, you should have no trouble at all. Now, as to organizing the men. . . ."

We talked at some length, deciding on officer assignments and division of the various groups and tribes into units. Old hostilities between individual chiefs and between one clan and another had to be considered, but Simon seemed well versed in all of this. When we finished, Simon asked me to inform Kurbsky of our tentative decisions, mostly, I think, to give our commander a chance to voice any objections before the lists were made public.

I had to wait until evening to see Andrew, as he had ridden part way with the Czar. There had been another fresh fall of snow – hopefully the last of the winter – and Andrew did not get back until after dark. I left word at his house that I wished to speak with him, and a servant came with an invitation to join the general for a late supper.

Andrew was very upset when I arrived. His usually ruddy features were blanched, and his slender cheeks were drawn with anxiety. Following the Czar's example, he had recently shaved his head, which gave him an oriental appearance. His beard, light brown and sparse to begin with, had been trimmed short to form a point, like a Pollack's. He paced the room while we spoke, pausing in his motion only long enough to bolt down an occasional swallow of vodka – an unusual indulgence for Andrew.

"Only harm can come of this trip," he told me. "All of us have tried to persuade the Czar not to go, but he won't listen to anybody."

"His decision surprised me, too," I said, "but he feels he has good reason – seeking divine guidance, like he always does. Andrei was worried, too, of course. Did you speak with him?"

"Yes," Andrew sighed, "but I fear Adashev has seen his day," he added regretfully. "You know, Dmitri, I never liked the fellow when we were children, but of late I've come to respect his judgment. He's a very mortal man, with all the human weaknesses, except he's uncommonly good – a miserable administrator, but still honest and intelligent. You couldn't find a better advisor. If he'd only taken that stupid oath when the Czar first fell ill!"

"He was afraid he might have to break it later," I said.

"What difference does that make!" he almost shouted. "Any of us might have had to break it. I certainly wouldn't have served Daniel Romanov! Would you?"

I answered slowly, not really wanting to say anything. "No," I agreed at length. "I suppose not."

"But since Andrei refused to obey him, the Czar has taken every opportunity to ignore his advice. If he'd favored the trip, the Czar would probably have remained in Moscow until spring."

"You really foresee danger, then?" I asked.

"Of course I foresee danger!" he snapped, starting to count off the difficulties on his fingers. "The road is covered with snow. Then they're going to travel the rivers. This time of year the currents are treacherous where there isn't ice, and where there is ice you can't be sure it's solid. They could easily capsize, or get swamped by a sudden storm, and that would be the end of them all."

I finished my business with Andrew and left soon after dinner, really beginning to worry for the first time, also beginning to blame myself for not doing more to oppose the trip. The first news of their journey arrived several days later, after the party had left Sergey–Troitsky and started its northward trek. As best we could fit the story together, Sylvester – who had been left behind for the first time since Ivan appointed him confessor – had sent another warning of disaster. Adashev, who was with the royal party, delivered Sylvester's message to Ivan. The Czar had flown into a rage, venting his anger on Adashev and ordering him home. Other than this, everything seemed to be in order.

As Andrew had projected, the Czar's trip had to proceed in stages, utilizing different modes of transportation. The river was still frozen in the south, although the ice was no longer thick enough to bear the weight of a sleigh. Therefore, the Czar's party traveled overland to Uglitch, where the river widened to provide an open channel. They were to use this, traveling north by barge to Shcherbakov, and thence along the Upper Volga, through a hundred miles of wild, desolate country before reaching Kirilof on the Frozen Sea.

They never completed the journey. Two days out of Shcherbakov, the Czarevitch Dmitri died.

The Czar's grief was a terrible, dreadful thing. Rushing back to Moscow, Ivan personally bore the tiny coffin into the Uspensky Cathedral. He laid it before the alter and remained praying beneath the crosses and icons through the night – until well past dawn the following morning. No one could console him. He could not understand why God's wrath should have fallen on him when he was in the process of fulfilling a holy vow. He asked what sins he'd committed that were great enough to demand such expiation.

Naturally, the whole city mourned with him. People had perceived Ivan's child as the heir who would one day rule them with the same stern wisdom as his father. The Czar's suffering was so intense none of us did more than kneel beside him to pray. Even Mad Sylvester had the good sense to keep quiet. Had he spoken his usual words of condemnation, explaining the child's death as the result of any evil on the part of the Czar, Ivan would probably have run him through with his *kisten*.

Finally, between Andrew Kurbsky and myself, we were able to get Ivan away from the body to allow its preparation for burial. It was a dreadful ordeal for everyone, with not a single dry eye in the whole cathedral as Makari celebrated the mass for the dead. The little Czarevitch was buried in the Cathedral of the Archangel Michael, right at the foot of his grandfather's crypt. It was more than a week before Ivan recovered enough to resume any of his duties. And he did so then only because it was necessary. We had received more bad news from Kazan. I believe that it was this period in Ivan's life when something permanent happened within his soul. Whether this was due to his being abruptly forced to break off his solitary mourning or not, I have no way to know. I am sure that he changed – somehow, deeply and irrevocably. It was as if God's cruelty had left a bitter brand upon his soul.

The army sent to punish the insurrectionists in Kazan had been badly beaten. The commander, Saltikoff, had been captured by the barbarians. The Czar ordered Kurbsky to take a sizable army east again, although Ivan himself would remain in the Kremlin. Simon's force was a part of this command. Daniel Adashev, Andrei's brother, was assigned to us, and I talked Simon into giving him charge of the Cossacks, thus relieving me of having to compete with them on horseback. As Simon's total force was almost half Cossack, he divided it by giving me charge of everything else.

Daniel, being very slight and having grown up in the south country, rode like a plainsman and did very well with his charges. Heinrich did not go with us, as he was too involved in business, much of it the Czar's. With a large part of our market still cut off by the plague, my stepfather faced as great a challenge as any man commanding an army in the field. Whereas the epidemic showed some signs of letting up, the western areas remained in quarantine.

The battles we fought were even more bloody than before, and we killed thousands of infidels. Simon proved himself an excellent field commander, as well as a loyal Christian servant of the Czar. He thoroughly earned everyone's respect. In the course of the war we destroyed the Tartar fort below Kazan, situated on a plain called the *Mesh*. We killed Aleka, the Cheremisian leader, in battle. Later, we captured the commander of the Tartars, Prince Yanchura, whom we promptly hanged. Near the end of July we had extinguished all armed opposition. My part of the army returned to Svyazhsk, for Simon did not wish to enter Kazan.

Ivan was so pleased he sent medals of gold to all of us. With the messenger came a short letter to me, in Adashev's handwriting. It said simply:

"Dmitri – please return to me in all haste. I have an interesting adventure for you, and require your particular skills. Ivan." The signature appeared to be the Czar's.

I left the following morning, loading Gabriel onto a barge. In the long run, it was the fastest way. While I might make better time on land during the day, I would have had to stop at night, as well as several times during the day to rest my mount. The boat could travel continuously. The only delay occurred when we passed another barge headed south, and I recognized the black cock painted on the side. I hailed them and found it was Abraham, on his way to Kazan with a load of supplies Heinrich had sold to the army. I ordered both boats beached, and once out of the others' hearing, I told the old man about the Czar's message. I asked him if he had any idea what it was about. He scratched his white hair for a moment, thinking.

"I have heard a story," he said, "of a great ship. It was supposed to have arrived at Kholmagora, on the mouth of the Dvina. A messenger came in from Saint Nicholas Monastery about the time the Czar sent the medals to you. It might be that."

A ship! I thought. I had never seen a great ship, and trying to picture it excited my imagination. "Of what country was this vessel?" I asked.

"A land far to the west," said Abraham, "called England."

"England!" I exclaimed. "That is the legendary land of chivalry!"

Abraham drew back with a grimace. "Of what?" he asked.

"Oh, of the tales Heinrich used to tell me as a child," I said. "England was the land of great ships and knights. Haven't you ever heard of the crusades, and *Coeur de Lion,* the great knight of the cross?"

"I have heard these things," replied the old man, "but they are only legends."

"I was never sure, myself," I told him, "but if the strangers are truly Englishmen it will certainly be worth finding out."

I broke off our conversation as quickly as courtesy would permit. Once on the water, again, I ordered the oarsmen encouraged to their greatest effort. I was on a military barge, not a merchant vessel, so the rowers were all slaves. The master, by using his whip less sparingly than usual, was able to cut half a day from our travel time. As soon as I was within a day's ride of the capital I left the barge, riding Gabriel nearly to exhaustion in my eagerness. I was afraid if I took too long, the Czar might send someone else. I don't know why I assumed the ship to be my mission, but as it turned out I was right.

I rode directly into the Kremlin, reining up sharply in front of the palace. A retainer ran to take Gabriel's head, while another helped me down from the saddle. I looked at my mount, and even in my rush I could see he was badly in need of attention. I ordered him sent home with one of the servants, then ran inside. The whole place was so strangely quiet, I had the horrible thought that the Czar might have left on a pilgrimage or some other business. I went up to one of the guards standing like pieces of statuary on either side of the main portal. "Where is the Czar?" I asked.

"The Czar and his entire court are at table, sir," he replied.

"Go and inform the Czar that Prince Marensky is here," I told him.

The fellow did not move. "I cannot leave my post, sir," he replied stiffly.

"Have I been gone so long?" I asked. "When did this begin?"

"A few weeks ago, sir." He squirmed in discomfort at my questioning. "There are servants and pages in the antechamber," he added, barely moving his arm to indicate the direction.

I walked across and opened the door. At least two dozen servants sat primly along a row of straight–backed chairs. If they had been speaking at all it had been very softly, for I heard nothing as I approached the portal. They looked at me curiously, for I was covered with dust and grime from my ride, and flecked with lather from Gabriel's sweating hide. One of them recognized me, however, and got up. He was in Basmanov's livery.

"May I be of some service, sir?" he asked.

"Inform the Czar of my presence," I commanded him. I was afraid he might also refuse to obey, so I spoke almost harshly to him.

He bowed and withdrew, going through the door on the far side of the chamber, and into the great dining hall. As he opened the door I could hear the voices of the guests and the clicking of knives against platters. The odor of roasted meat drifted through the room, reminding me that I had not eaten since dawn. The servant returned moments later. "The Czar commands your immediate presence," he said.

I started to go through the way he had gone, but he plucked at my sleeve in embarrassment. "No, sir, not that way," he said, almost in fear. "That is the servants' entrance."

"I know that," I growled, impatiently. "I grew up in this palace."

"Please, sir, this way," said the man. He led me to another small room, where a bowl of scented water and a towel had been laid out. He helped me sponge my face and hands, then took a brush to remove the worst of the road dust. Some major changes had certainly been initiated in court etiquette! "Tell me," I said, "what's going on? Why is everything so formal?"

"It is not for me to say, sir," he replied. I had frightened him by my previous tone, "But," he added finally, "the Czar is presently entertaining the Polish ambassador."

"Oh, well, maybe I'd better change before I go in," I suggested.

"You mustn't take the time, sir!" exclaimed the servant. "The Czar has commanded your presence."

"Then present me," I told him, resignedly.

My name was called as I entered the door, and every head in the room turned to stare at me. Very conscious of my dirty clothes and horsy odor, I looked at no one but the Czar as I walked the full length of the room and stopped in front of him, making the three bows as required by the rules established prior to my departure. I hoped the number had not been raised or the postures redefined. Apparently I did everything right, for the Czar smiled at me through the entire process. He sat in the center of the head table, dressed in more than his usual splendor. He wore a ceremonial crown, much grander than the Cap of Monomakh, and he glistened with rubies and other precious stones. On either side of him sat men I did not recognize, but from their dress I assumed they were the Poles.

"This is one of Our most honored servants," said Ivan, " a commander from Our great army in the east."

I bowed perfunctorily to each of the gentlemen.

"You will note," continued the Czar, "that despite Our only having dispatched the summons a few days ago, Our commander has obeyed at once – has come directly into Our presence without even stopping to refresh himself."

"True devotion," mumbled one of the Pollacks.

"A fine display of loyalty," said the other.

"Come, Dmitri," cried the Czar, a definite twinkle in his eye, "sit down with Us." He motioned for one of his richly garbed servants to make a place for me, beside the Pollack on his left. Kurbsky was sitting there, and I did not think he was very pleased. As he told me later, I smelled like a sour stable. The Polish gentleman, who was a *pan* – their equivalent of a *voivode* – named Tishkovitch, grudgingly moved his elbow from the board, allowing his chair to be pushed a few inches closer to the Czar. He sniffed significantly as I sat down, then turned his head away and spoke not a word to me for the rest of the meal. The whole situation was unfortunate, I thought, although I knew that Ivan had deliberately contrived it to annoy the Poles. I received several extremely unpleasant glances from Mikhailof, the Czar's secretary. It had been he, in his pedantic manner, who had instituted the new rules of decorum.

After a few minutes, Kurbsky seemed to get over his annoyance, and among other things he whispered to me that Anastasia was again with child – an explanation for the Czar's lighthearted mood. Andrew and I spoke together until the meal was over, and Ivan retired to his rooms. Anxious as I was over the prospect of meeting these strange foreigners and seeing their ship, I said nothing about them. Probably because the Czar had made no mention of his reason for calling me back, I had a feeling he would not wish to discuss it in front of the Pollacks. As it happened, my assumption proved correct. Before I could leave the palace, I received a request to attend the Czar in his rooms.

He explained the arrival of the ship to me, and laughed as he showed me the reports he had received from the people of the Dvina Delta. They had taken the Englishmen to be angels of the Lord, as they had never seen such a ship, described as "towering to the clouds." As it turned out, these simple peasants had never seen any kind of cannon, either, for they called the ship's guns: "armaments as only God, Himself, could command." In actuality, these pieces were much smaller than many of our own field guns.

"I sent for you, Dmitri," said the Czar, "because you are a master of languages – but more so because I can trust you. If you feel these men are honest traders, which they claim to be, bring them to me. If they appear to be spies or the forerunners of some great armada, they must be destroyed."

"When may I leave?" I asked.

"The prospect excites you?"

"Very much," I said. "I have never seen such a ship, and I have heard many tales of England."

"Then I'm glad I awaited your return," he returned. "Fumikov has been instructed to advance you what you need, as I want these men brought in some pomp, if you decide to bring them in at all. Take whomever you wish with you."

"I'll be ready tomorrow," I told him.

"Not too fast," he cautioned. "It's now midsummer, but you have a long way to go. Be sure to take winter equipment, and do not be in such a hurry you forget something you may need. These men have traveled a great distance and have been at sea for months. They will wait for you."

"Have you sent word that someone is coming for them?" I asked.

The Czar nodded. "The Abbot of Saint Nicholas has been instructed to look after their comfort until you arrive. Go home, now, and get some rest. Be sure you see me again before you depart."

I got up to leave. "What of these Pollacks?" I asked.

Ivan's face went white with anger. "That creaking old goat on his rickety Polish throne still refuses to recognize me as Czar!" he spat. "He will one day lick my boots!"

I laughed. "I hope the army doesn't march before I return," I said.

"You'll be with us when we go," he assured me. "The day will come, and you will see it."

CHAPTER X

It was now necessary to plan a route of travel, allowing my party to reach Kholmagora quickly and to cover as much return ground as possible before the snows. I decided to go on horseback, sending sleighs and other winter equipment by water. That way, I could have them available at some appointed place along our route south.

I assumed that our return would necessarily be slower than the ride north, for we would be hauling carts with whatever trade goods the English merchants were bringing. It would be best, therefore, to connect with one of the main rivers – probably the Sukhona. I had never been above Kostroma, myself, and I did not know anything about the condition of the roads, nor was I familiar with the villages north of that point. Even the indigenous peoples were unfamiliar to me, except that I knew of several hostile, barbarian tribes, plus the usual quota of brigands.

Heinrich was no help, either. The northern trade was almost entirely in the hands of the Stroganovs. Except for the few contracts whereby we traded for their furs, neither Heinrich nor I had much to do with them.

"What you need," said my stepfather, "is some kind of a guide. Otherwise you're never going to reach the White Sea before winter."

"Maybe I could pick one up along the way," I suggested.

"Possibly," he said, "but that would be strictly a last resort. You're as apt to pick a robber as a guide. Why don't you let me send a man to Tver, and see if one of the Stroganovs can lend you someone?"

"Do you want a Stroganov involved?" I asked. "What if there's a valuable trade to be built with these people?"

"It's immaterial," he said. "The Stroganovs already have the north country, and it won't be taken from them. But you have something better. You have the Czar."

Heinrich spoke slowly, emphasizing each word by tapping his finger against the table. "Never forget this, Demetrius; you are one of the few men the Czar completely trusts. You can count the rest on the digits of one hand. If you keep faith with him, the day may come when you are the *only* man he trusts."

He paused, watching me, I suppose because my face reflected some doubt. "Look," he said, "the Czar is still a very young man. You're two years younger. Most of the men who are close to him are fifteen or twenty years his senior, except for Adashev and Andrew Kurbsky. And after that mess with the oath – who knows? And as for Sylvester – I'd wager the Czar ships him off to a monastery before very long. Then, who else is there? Vladimir? He will never have Ivan's complete trust, certainly not while Euphrosyne's alive. You stand in a unique position."

"I've thought about all these things," I confessed, "but – well, it's the uncertainty of my birth," I blurted out. "The Czar has made me a Prince, but there are many people who still look down on me, sneer at my title."

"This is nonsense. Every noble family in Russia, or anyplace else, for that matter, started off with a commoner obtaining a title," he replied vehemently. "It takes several generations before you're at the top of the roster of nobles. But even now you are one of the most powerful men in court. And in battle, in palace intrigues, you've proven yourself the equal of any. Your loyalty is unquestioned. Do you realize the honor the Czar's conferring on you by sending you on this particular mission? He is as anxious as you to find out about these strange men from the West; but he delayed appointing his ambassador until you could get back here. It won't be long," he added sagely, "before you stand closer than any other man to the greatest ruler on the face of the earth."

"You really believe that strongly in – in our destiny?" I asked, surprised at his depth of expression. Like all Germans, Heinrich was usually reticent to express his innermost feelings.

"Of course, I believe it! Why do you think I've forsaken my ties with the League? Why have I embraced the Orthodox faith and given up my papist allegiances? I've demonstrated many times I would gladly spill my blood for him. In return for this I have been substantially rewarded, and I see no reason why this bounty shouldn't continue – and it's right that it should. I'm honest in my loyalties and in my faith, the same as it is with you, no?"

"Yes," I replied softly. I knew I would risk my life for the Czar without a second thought. Heinrich's remarks had also reaffirmed a proper pride in my heritage, reminding me that my soul was Russian.

I requested Ivor as a member of my party. Ivan agreed, and along with the former kennelmaster I obtained a small company of his men – some twenty in all. Then I looked over the supplies Fumikov had assembled, and found them pitifully incomplete. The wily treasurer protested like a squealing pig when I told him what I would need.

"One would think the Czar a pauper, the way you pinch the purse strings," I remonstrated with him. "Do you want to disgrace him by your stinginess, or shall I have him come down here to see just how parsimonious he's being made to appear?"

Fumikov wrung his hands. "Trade has not been good . . ." he began.

"You fat rodent," I said laughing. "Who do you think keeps the records on the Czar's trade ventures? You've been ordered to outfit this party in proper style. I'm giving you a list of my needs, and I want them ready for shipment tomorrow. That includes the barges on which to send them."

When he still protested I grabbed the fat at the base of his cheek, twisting it slightly between my fingers. "Tomorrow, Chubby," I added, "or the Czar may have to find a new paper–scratcher to guard his treasure house." I left him mumbling his curses, but I had known him too long for any real anger to pass between us. I could remember as a child, when Fumikov was still a clerk; I used to run up behind him and grab at the roll of flesh about his waist, pinching it and running away before he could catch me. It had become a regular game between us, until the day he heard me coming and caught me. He'd shoved me down and sat on my stomach, jouncing up and down until I could hardly breathe. Since then we had always joked with each other, although the dignity of his new position demanded we speak properly in public.

My supplies were assembled the next day, and we left the following morning, my saddlebags stuffed with several maps Mikhailof had found for me. The chief of Ivan's Bureau of the Lands had asked me to make any corrections I felt appropriate. With that reassurance as to the accuracy of my charts, I led my troop out of Moscow, following the northern highway where it paralleled the river.

I prefer not to think of all that befell me on this horrible journey. It took us so long to travel north that the English had finally grown tired of waiting, and started south. We came upon them in the wilderness, finding ourselves suddenly face to face with this strange group of foreigners. They were being guided by some natives who appeared to be Finns or Lats, although they spoke a dialect of our own language. After some mutual suspicions, I used hand signs and drawings in the snow to convince the visitors that we had been sent by the Czar to escort them. We also discovered some commonality between their native speech and German.

The English had dog sleds, something I had seen only as children's toys in the royal kennels. They traveled more easily than we did over the powdery snow, which now began to fall in seemingly endless storms. In most places the wind kept the river ice fairly clear, and the increasing cold had made the water freeze clear to the bottom, allowing us a smoother, faster roadbed.

With our supplies and those brought by the English, we were able to travel in reasonable comfort to Velikiy Ustug, where by God's grace our own equipment had arrived. During the trip south I tried to establish some communication with our strange visitors. This being my first experience with Englishmen, I did not know of their peculiar attitudes regarding peoples of other races. They looked down on everyone who was foreign to them. If one did not speak English, or possibly French, he was considered heathen and beneath them.

The commander of the group, who was also the captain of the vessel – the *Eduard Bonaventura* – was called Chancellor. Unfortunately, he was so paralyzed by the cold I could hardly get him to speak, and hence learned little more than the basic commercial reasons for this trip. Once inside shelter at Velikiy Ustug, however, our guests expressed the first humor I saw in them. The village name seemed to strike them as funny, and they made several references to it in their own language, laughing and sparing playfully with one another. I think this was partially because they were able to remove their heavy clothing for the first time since leaving the White Sea. I knew that Parkinson, who seemed to be Chancellor's second–in–command, had been even more miserable than his superior. He had been completely silenced by the cold.

In this little port city was a very fine merchant's lodge. It was extremely well built, with whole logs stacked to form the walls, and heavily sealed with moss and mud to keep out the cold. It had a wooden floor, on which the caretaker had spread a thick layer of rushes. Because the lodge sold spirits it had to belong to the Czar; but it was maintained by the Stroganovs and a few smaller groups of merchants who traveled the river routes.

After their experiences in the desolate lands of the north, I did not know what the English expected; but I think when we first arrived in the settlement they took it to be the capital. They thought the Imperial Administrator was the Czar! To them, it seemed the end of a very long journey. I had learned just a few words of their language, which is extremely difficult, being in some ways similar to low

German. I was finally able to explain that Moscow lay far to the south, almost three times the distance they had already come. That seriously dampened their spirits.

Chancellor especially liked Serge, probably because the little Tartar was always happy and clowning. For this reason, he was able to make himself understood better than any of us, although he had learned even fewer words than I. The northmen who had come with the English party were too stupid even to speak Russian very well. Their leader was an extremely old man who had brought his son, two grandsons, and a variety of cousins as helpers. I sent them all home, for we no longer needed them or their equipment.

I did envy them the opportunity of seeing the great ship, something I was not able to do after all the hard travel. Because I was sure the Czar would want an accurate description of the vessel, I sent two of my guardsmen back with the old man. I instructed them to make drawings and to note measurements of everything they could. One of the fellows I sent was a Novgorodski, a highly skilled lad by the name of Vladimir, who later became widely respected for his icon painting.

The Sukhona River was completely frozen when we left Velikiy Ustug, as it was then late November. Our fifteen sleighs were retrieved from the sheds where the boatmen had stored them, and rigged for the trip south. The goods being transported by the English required only a portion of the space I had expected they would, which allowed plenty of room for our guests to ride in ease, and permitted us to carry enough equipment for excellent camps each night. With these added comforts, I found my visitors more relaxed and anxious to converse whenever they could. Before we reached Moscow, I learned to speak enough of their language to make myself understood. Although I later mastered English fluently, I always considered it terribly harsh. I also found it difficult to express myself completely, as it lacks the fine delineations of the Slavic.

Once I could more or less converse with Chancellor, I learned that he had originally started with three ships, trying to find a northern passage to Cathay. The other two vessels had been wrecked somewhere along the Finnish coast, lost forever in the icy blackness of the sea.

We arrived in Moscow a few days before Christmas. This seemed greatly to please the English, for they regard the anniversary of Our Savior's birth to be the major holy day of the year. They celebrate it with festivities and gifts, much as we do Easter. Word of our progress had been sent ahead by post rider, and the Czar ordered a fine house put in order for the Englishmen. Adashev had been instructed to make all arrangements for their comfort, and my orders were to report to Ivan immediately that I had seen our visitors settled. I left Serge with them to translate their desires to the other servants, and went directly to the palace, having to endure several delays before reaching the Czar. The rigid court ritual had been further formalized during my absence, and I wondered when Mikhailof was finally going to reach his limit.

I finally progressed to the inner corridors, where I passed a group of Polish emissaries waiting outside Ivan's door. They had apparently returned to their homeland while I was gone, and had been sent back. This time their group had been enlarged to include representatives of the merchant interests. Pollacks were much different from us in their attitude toward trade, considering such enterprises beneath the dignity of gentlemen. They preferred to relegate the conduct of business to Germans and Jews. For that reason the Polish nobility was always poor, except those who were able to rob the traders, either by taxes or outright brigandage. Having learned of the Englishmen's arrival, they had increased their diplomatic pressure to obtain concessions from the Czar.

I found Ivan in a jubilant mood, but very haggard in appearance. As Adashev informed me, he had been spending long hours at prayer, thanking God for the remission of his sins and granting him another son. The boy, named after his father, had been born two months before. Apparently, the Czar had been allowed little time for unhampered rejoicing. He had decided to finish gathering in the Tartar lands south of Kazan, at the same time giving serious consideration to the Polish requests for a peace treaty. Still angry with King Sigismund, the Czar had also needed time to consolidate our eastern and southern forces. Only after accomplishing this, could he think of involving himself in the west.

I soon found the court factions to be strangely aligned, and this was reflected in the grouping of men about the Czar on the evening of my return. The Church was pressing for a further acquisition of infidel lands, calling it a holy crusade. The major traders wanted the Baltic ports, the warm water windows to the West. When I entered Ivan's presence, I was thrown immediately into the middle of this controversy. Mikhailof had already intercepted me in the hallway. Drawing me out of the Pollacks' hearing, he had tried to fill me in on developments since my departure. He was anxious that I support the merchants' cause, but his reasoning was so confused and complicated I could not absorb it all at once. He did clarify the positions of the major interests, however, which I greatly appreciated. Gorbatof–Shuisky was with the Czar, as was Prince Mikulinsky of Tver, Daniel Adashev, and a representative of the Obolenskis whose name I have forgotten. They had all been drinking.

"Now the circle is complete," Ivan bellowed, by way of greeting. "The Marensky–vonStaden interests are represented, along with all the rest." He never gave me time to bow or kiss his hand before signaling a servant to shove a goblet of wine into my fist. I immediately toasted the new heir, and was unhesitatingly supported by the rest. Apparently the lesson had been learned. Young Ivan's birthright would never be questioned.

"A taste from the vineyards of France," laughed Ivan jovially, when I commented on the fine quality of the wine. "It comes to Us through the courtesy of the Polish Ambassador."

This seemed to strike everyone as very humorous, and the room rocked with their laughter. I drained the goblet and handed it back to the servant, who promptly refilled it.

"Our mirth seems lost on Dmitri," said Shuisky, still chuckling. He had gotten quite fat since taking up residence in Kazan, and his belly vibrated beneath the rich satin of his robes. It was an outlandish, infidel costume to be worn by a Russian officer, I thought.

"Dmitri has the wit to appreciate our humor," Ivan corrected him, "though the cold north may have dulled his passions."

"Not our old harem thief," quipped Mikulinsky. The Prince was seated on a long padded bench, and he beckoned for me to join him. "How did you make out with the English?" he asked.

"A very long tale, my friends," I said, settling wearily against the velvet cushions. "I will need more than a few of these to carry me through the telling." I held up the goblet again. A servant took it from behind, returning it almost at once. The wine was deceptively mellow, and my head was already spinning.

"First off," I said, "I got lost."

That brought another chorus of laughter, and everything I said from then on they found so funny they were rocking back and forth before I finished. Ivan wiped his eyes when I described Chancellor's respectful attitude toward the administrator in Velikiy Ustug, mistaking him for the Czar and the little merchant post for the capital of all Russia.

"We must give these fellows the grandest reception ever extended," roared Ivan. "We shall show them magnificence to outdo the Sultan, himself."

"You'd better get rid of those Pollacks, first," I said, "or Old Goat–face will be insulted enough to start a war before we're ready for him."

"Our curse on Sigismund August," shouted the Czar. He tried to stand and make a bow in imitation of Polish foppery, and almost fell on his face. Daniel was closest and caught him, helping the Czar back into his chair, at which point he grew more serious. "That old bag of bones is still calling me 'Duke' and signing himself 'King.' I sent him an answer to his last letter, addressed to the Grand Duke of Lithuania. Nothing else, just Grand Duke."

"I'll wager he bleated for an hour over that," said Shuisky sarcastically. He was not quite as drunk as Ivan, and anyway he considered himself above all of us.

Ivan chose to ignore his pompous superiority. "Enough of the Pollacks!" he shouted. "Dmitri, what of these Englishmen? Have they anything to offer us?"

"From the little I have been able to understand of their barbarous tongue," I told him, "they are a great merchant power, with more ships than Sweden and Denmark combined. Their Queen is bound by marriage to the King of Spain, another great trading nation on the far side of Europe. Between them they rule half the continent. The Spanish King, as I understand it, is the grandson – or great–grandson – of the Emperor Maximillan. He is named Phillip; she is named Mary."

"Then we shall make good use of our opportunity. Perhaps it's the answer to our Polish problems," the Czar added thoughtfully.

"It can only mean trouble," Shuisky asserted bluntly.

Mikulinsky stirred beside me. I know he disliked the Shuiskys and considered them upstarts. "With whom are the English allied?" he asked.

"I don't know," I answered honestly. "Apparently they have no ties with any northern power, but their language is very difficult and I haven't mastered it yet. I will try to get this type of information later."

"You will, you will," Ivan chanted, then cocked his head as a servant bent over to whisper something in his ear. The Czar called for silence. "I am informed," he said gleefully, "that the Polish delegation is still awaiting Us. In fact, the Ambassador wishes to remind Us that they have been waiting for over two hours!"

We all roared with laughter and someone made a remark about their leader having arrived, mounted on a white pig. With surprisingly little difficulty I was able to excuse myself, thus avoiding a prolonged contact with the Pollacks on this occasion.

"We will have you involved with them later," Ivan remarked. "Right now, your problem is the English. We will let them cool their heels for a few days, lest they find Us too anxious to receive them."

I was not able to avoid the Polish delegation completely, for they were still in the antechamber when I left. Since I had come directly to the palace, I had not changed clothes, although I was better dressed than the last time I confronted a Pollack. As I brushed past Pan Tishkovitch, who refused to extend the courtesy of stepping back from my path, I was amused to hear another significant "sniff." As I went through the door he mumbled to one of his companions, questioning whether I ever attended upon my Czar in other than soiled traveling garb.

Once in my own home, I was taken in charge by the girls. Heinrich was in Novgorod, where he had gone with Simon. This was his first trip since the plague, and apparently the results were satisfactory. A letter was waiting for me, noting that our losses had not been as great as we had feared. It also listed a number of details I should take care of as soon as I returned.

In my stepfather's absence, I had the full attention of both Lily and Lotus Flower, who bustled about, attending to my comfort. I was soon immersed in our huge Roman tub. This had been constructed at Heinrich's order by one of the Italian architects, a man whom Ivan had summoned to help with the reconstruction of the Kremlin and inner city. Even in the middle of winter, the water in this small pond was kept warm by a clever arrangement of pipes which ran through a stove and vent arrangement. As I eased myself into the steaming embrace, I was grateful for my stepfather's undying love of comfort. No travel is so lacking in rigor as not to require some solace once a man reaches his destination.

The girls had all sorts of gossip to impart. While scrubbing me with their scented unguents, they told me about Vladya's wedding, among other things. It seemed that the relationship between the Czar and his cousin had continued to improve during my absence. Vladya had consummated his marriage within the royal palace, and Ivan had been very generous in arranging the ceremony. Jacob arrived in the middle of this discussion, and perched on a nearby stool. He was able to supply some information the girls lacked, as he had been among the crowd observing the ceremonies inside the Kremlin; Heinrich had taken him. For the occasion, Ivan had lifted the ban on Euphrosyne, allowing her to return to court. During the betrothal, she must have reconciled herself to the match. At least she made a great show of affection toward her future daughter–in–law, even bringing some of the Staritsky jewels and traditional wedding paraphernalia with her. She personally assisted the bride into the trappings she had worn when she wed the Czar's uncle. But she could not sustain her gracious behavior; after the ceremony, she proceeded to enrage Ivan by some affront to Anastasia and was again banished to Staritsa.

Shortly after Vladya's wedding, Anastasia had presented Ivan with the second Czarevitch – "Vanya," as he was called within the family. Because he was born exactly nine months after the death of little Dmitri, there was some whispered nonsense about the spirit of the first child having entered into the second. I never believed it, of course, for the two boys were nothing alike. From the very first, Vanya was much stronger than his brother had been.

Jacob also told me about the signing of a formal document between the Czar and Vladya, which I supposed Heinrich had described to him. Following the birth of the second Czarevitch, Vladimir recognized him as the legitimate heir to the throne, and agreed to support him in the event of the Czar's death while the child was still a minor. In turn, Ivan named Vladya as regent, and heir after all his own sons. Implicit in the agreement was Vladimir's oath to protect the Czarevitch, with his own life if necessary. It specifically mentioned Euphrosyne as one source of danger against whom the Prince would protect his little cousin. Listening to Jacob's recitation, I laughed at the thought of Euphrosyne's face when she was told of these conditions.

I had finished my bath and, still naked, was being kneaded with oil when a servant came to tell me that Andrew Kurbsky was downstairs. It was not Andrew's custom to come unannounced, and as it would have taken me several minutes to dress, I told the servant to ask him up. I was sure he must have had something important to discuss with me. Jacob slipped out the back way.

When Andrew entered the chamber, he must have been totally unprepared for the scene that met his eyes. It was the first time he had seen any part of my home beyond the first floor dining halls, and he stared for several moments before speaking.

"I must say, Dmitri," he began, "your household arrangements are . . . ." He hesitated.

"Barbaric," I finished for him, laughing.

"To say the least!"

"If you'd like a rub –?" I offered. The girls had not stopped massaging me.

"No . . . no, but go right ahead." He was obviously amused. While he tended to be overly proper and rigid in his own code of behavior, he seldom criticized his friends – unless they far exceeded the bounds of propriety. I knew he had chided the Czar into censuring both Vladya and myself for our frivolities in public places, but private conduct was another matter.

"If you can overlook the, er – environment," I said casually, "we can speak as you wish. The girls do not understand enough to compromise us."

Andrew cleared his throat. "No, I imagine their compromising qualities are in another direction," he remarked.

I had a comfortable chair brought in for him, and sent for a pitcher of good wine. Once the surprise had worn off he seemed almost to enjoy the harem atmosphere, and readily went into the reason for his call. "Sorry to come like this," he said, "but I wanted to speak to you without our Polish friends being aware of it. Since they've been coming to Moscow *en masse*, a man can't trust his own servants not to carry tales to them."

"Are they that active?" I asked.

"They have spies in places you'd never suspect," he told me. "They're so afraid of us, it's almost tempting to persuade the Czar to attack them right now. They must be completely unprepared."

"I see benefits either way – south or west," I replied.

"Benefits or profits?"

I was now lying on my back and looked at him upside down. "Do you find my motives so avaricious?" I asked lightly.

"Not really. As you say, you would profit in either case. I think you are honest enough not to let commercial motives influence you immoderately."

"Probably not," I replied, still watching him over the top of my head. The girls were pounding my stomach and thighs.

"That is –" He twisted his neck to look directly at me, but could not. "That is the –" he started again, then gave up. "Dmitri," he said, "will you please get rid of these females, and come down off that table? You're looking up at me like a dead fish and I'm trying to talk seriously."

"Good enough," I agreed. Sitting on the edge of the table, I waved the girls away. "We can go into another room, if this bothers you," I offered.

"No, it's quite comfortable here, one of the few warm rooms in the city," he said. "Besides, I'm sure we are completely private." His last remark was more a question than a statement. I nodded reassurance.

"Then let me explain," he went on. I filled his cup again, and settled back to listen. "We are going to take Astrakhan this summer," he said flatly, "and the Czar has offered the command to me." He seemed to await my reaction.

"Excellent! Couldn't be better!"

That seemed to satisfy him. "Good. This brings me to the problem of staff," he said. "Would you like to be my second?"

I was very flattered and wanted to jump at the offer, but I restrained myself. "Have you discussed this with the Czar?" I asked.

"Not fully," he admitted. "I think he might be considering Adashev's brother, or – God forbid! – that stupid Romanov. If I propose your name before Ivan expresses his wishes. . . ."

"You do me great honor," I said sincerely, "but you know the Czar has given me over to the Englishmen."

"We won't be departing for several months," he replied. "Surely, your involvement with these foreigners will be finished by spring!"

His tone answered my question. He was most anxious for me to accept. "I should expect to be free of them by then," I said.

"Then shall I count on you?" He was striving to make his voice as casual as mine, but he was pressing me with an uncharacteristic anxiety. Something was troubling him, and I suspected it was not so much a need for me as to avoid getting someone he didn't want. Kurbsky could be devious, and I doubted that either of the alternatives he had suggested was his most likely second–in–command.

"Are you being honest with me, Andrew?" I asked directly.

"As honest as I can be right now," he replied, looking me straight in the face. "Are you with me?"

"Pending the Czar's approval," I said, "it would please me very much."

"Then it pleases me, too," he said. "You will. . . be discreet?"

"Am I known to gossip?"

He shook his head. "That is one reason I came to you."

I spent the next few days with the Englishmen. They were easier to escort than most visitors, for no one but myself could speak with them. I had left Serge in their house where he served as interpreter while keeping me informed of their conversations. The weather had turned warmer and the English no longer wrapped themselves in the heavy Russian coats I had given them. Instead, they went abroad in the peculiar costumes of their own land. These were something similar to Polish outfits: tailored jackets, or doublets, much shorter than our peasant jerkins, and of a material they called "broadcloth." I was given to understand that their better classes did not always wear this type of woolen material, but it was their major item of export. Wearing it in public, they claimed, would demonstrate its practicability and enhance its future as a commercial item. The rest of their dress consisted of hose, coming to above the knee, where a tight fitting pair of pants filled the distance between. They wore elegant plumes stuck into their strangely shaped hats, and sometimes their costumes were further embellished by tassels at the tops of their stockings. The ruffled collars about their necks were a good deal smaller than the enormous fans of the Pollacks, but were of the same general shape.

The Czar had made it clear, although he had not issued an order, that the Englishmen were not to be feted by anyone other than myself until after he had received them. Otherwise, he placed no restrictions on their movements, except to instruct me to stay with them whenever they went into the city.

Because their house was inside the Kremlin walls, I usually conducted them through the Savior's Gate. It was inevitable that we should encounter the Polish Ambassador on one of these trips, especially as he was fully aware of their presence and must have been curious. While I assumed the meeting was intentional, therefore, there was no discourse, only the questioning stares of the Pollacks. To Chancellor, Tishkovitch and his party looked like a group of foppishly dressed Russians, so I did not advise him differently. For once, I was better attired than the Poles, and could not resist the opportunity to "sniff" as we passed. They had been out for a morning ride and were a bit horsy.

The English were impressed by the size of Moscow, but being a very phlegmatic people, they tried not to show it. They did not direct their remarks to me, and they always controlled their tone. As I could now understand what they were saying to each other, however, I was aware of their surprise at the extent of the city's outer walls. They commented at length on other matters, too; things I had never particularly thought about. One of these was the drunkenness of the average citizen.

Even early in the day, we would commonly see a number of drunks, especially in areas outside Kitaigorod where the lower classes had their hovels. This was nothing unusual, and any person of quality tended to ignore it. I had assumed from their dignified, almost pompous attitudes, that the English would be even less concerned. For some reason they were not.

"Shocking!" I heard Chancellor comment. "Why the (something I did not understand) are drunk from dawn 'til dusk!"

"Demetrius, why do your people drink so much?" asked Parkinson.

"The lot of the peasant is hard," I replied. "They have their God and their vodka. With this they are happy. Is it not so in England?"

"Rather not," said the captain. "The Queen's law makes public intemperance an offense."

I laughed. "In Russia," I said, "the crown owns the taverns. To counsel a man to desist from drink is the offense; it robs the Czar of his revenue."

"Does your Church not preach against drunkenness?" asked Parkinson.

"That is another matter," I explained. "To be drunk in church, of course, is a sin. Beyond this, some priests speak against immoderation, but when a man drinks, he forgets, and he continues drinking to further forget his forgetfulness."

"What do these people do for food?" asked another of the party.

"Grains, bread, fish, sometimes fowl," I said. "There is occasionally game, and other fruits of the fields. Cabbages and roots. There is meat, of course, for those who can buy it. In difficult times they make a fairly tasty broth from the bark of trees."

"They are not unhappy?"

"We are on this earth to be unhappy," I replied. "If we can achieve our goodness here, despite adversity, our reward will come from God. Is that not the teaching of your Church?"

My answer was perfectly reasonable, but they did not understand. Each land had its own peculiar customs, I supposed, and the farther one traveled from his own home, the more bizarre the attitudes of the natives appeared.

I remember we passed an old man one day who walked naked in the streets. He had drunk away even his clothes, and was begging alms about the city. The English were so disturbed by him I gave the fellow a coin and told him to spend it on clothing. I suspect he quickly drank it away once we were out of sight.

Touring the city, of course, could not satisfy these visitors indefinitely. Chancellor began questioning me, asking why the Czar did not receive them. I explained that he was a monarch with such boundless territories as always to be busy with his governors and ambassadors. It was sometimes months before even the highest could obtain an audience. I assured them, however, that through the esteem in which the Czar held me, I would do my best to arrange a meeting at the earliest possible moment. This attitude of anxiety was the sign Ivan awaited. When I communicated it to him that evening, he promptly set a date for the reception. It would be a week hence, he announced; the Pollacks would be gone by then.

I waited two days before informing the Englishmen, allowing them to believe there were complications. Chancellor, in desperation, gave me one of the letters he bore from his sovereign, asking me to deliver it to the Czar. I did just that, immediately. Together, Ivan and I were able to read it, for it had been prepared in several languages, including Swedish and Greek.

Ivan was most impressed by the power and extent of the possessions represented by our visitors. The letter was signed jointly by: Phillip and Mary, King and Queen of England, France, Naples, Jerusalem and Ireland, Princes of Spain and Sicily, Archdukes of Austria, Dukes of Milan and Brabant. Some of these were places we had never heard of, and we assumed the English Empire must be vast, indeed. Ivan did question how they could be King and Queen of France, however, for the House of Valois sat that throne in the person of Henry II and his Medici wife – this much we did know of the West! When I questioned Chancellor the next day, he instructed me regarding the peninsular possessions and the blood lines of the various royal houses. By his reasoning, the Kings of England could rightfully claim France as their own.

I informed Chancellor this same afternoon that the Czar had appointed the day for his audience. Although the man was surely excited, he would not let me see it. He maintained a perfectly calm exterior, telling me to inform the Czar of his pleasure in accepting the invitation. After I left, as Serge later informed me, the English were in great glee, hugging themselves and expressing their pleasure in quick sentences my servant was unable to understand. The English questioned him asking why the Czar had delayed so long, and Serge led them to believe it was because the great Christian Czar was concerned to know whether they were proper, God fearing men. I thought this an exceptionally intelligent response, as I had not prompted him to say it. The next day, I carefully instructed the Englishmen on the proper rituals they should follow in the upcoming ceremony.

On the day of the Czar's reception, before the English were due to arrive, the entire court assembled and Fumikov distributed costly costumes from the royal treasury. Since the Czar's wedding – the last time I had occasion to wear anything from this store – there had been many additions. The robes were so brilliant it was difficult to look at them in sunlight. Those to be worn by the boyars, especially members of the council, were made of pure gold, beaten thin and stitched onto cloth backings. Mounted against these surfaces were many precious stones, all of which glittered to catch every light and reflect it in a hundred directions at once. Because I was to escort the English to the palace, the Czar ordered that my robes be retained on the premises. I was to leave the visitors in an antechamber for the few minutes it would take me to change.

I did this, and when I returned, dressed in the Czar's golden robes, I saw the Englishmen's eyes widen. But none of them made any remark to betray their awe. Chancellor's only comment referred to the fine workmanship. I told him we always wore our best for formal audiences with the Czar. The door was thrown open, and the visitors' names were called, including their titles as ambassadors from the Great Queen. The reaction of the English as they entered the reception hall was most disappointing. I am sure they had never beheld such grandeur, but their cold natures permitted them to accept what they saw with little or no show of emotion. As I had told him he should, Chancellor led his group to the foot of the dais, and doffed his hat before the Czar, bowing three times.

Ivan was wearing the Crown of Monomakh, and because of its weight I knew he intended this to be a short audience. Yuri sat next to Ivan, with Mikhailof standing on the Czar's other side. The boyars, in their multi–colored magnificence, were arranged along either wall. Chancellor went through the prescribed rituals without flaw, finally dropping to one knee and kissing the Czar's hand. I translated his words of greetings and reverence, which Mikhailof repeated in a loud voice for the Czar and all the company to hear. The full reception took less than two hours, during which time the Czar asked many questions of his visitors. Before he terminated the interview he began to sag under the weight of his crown. I withdrew with the Englishmen to rest before dinner.

The meal, itself, was even grander than the earlier reception, and I was finally gratified to see our visitors' eyes traveling furtively from one rich item to the next. Ivan had changed robes – as the rest of us had – and now wore the Crown of Kazan. Many of the boyars had added more jewelry, heavy gold bracelets and immense finger rings. Ivan had ordered the servants to be clad in cloth of gold, and the table was set with heavily carved golden vessels. Our wine goblets were of the same, set with precious stones – huge flagons by English standards, richly ornamented with enamel insets to represent heroic deeds from Byzantine history and legend. The Czar had made sure his wealth was displayed in every possible corner of the room. It was impressive, even to those of us who knew the contents of the royal treasure vaults. I heard a good many jokes about it later, for few could understand the Czar's determination to impress these half–impoverished foreigners. Some even called him "The English Czar."

I was seated with Vladimir, the first chance I had to speak with him since his wedding. He was one who made several remarks about Ivan's having stripped the treasury. He seemed genuinely annoyed when Ivan made it clear he intended going through the full Byzantine ritual, having everything tasted before he ate it. For once, I agreed with Vladya in opposition to the Czar. I had been busy all day, and was very hungry – as I'm sure the English were – and all this ceremony took so long we were nearly drooling before we were finally served.

But I think the banquet properly impressed the English; at least they spoke together in more respectful tones when referring to Russia and to the Czar. In the weeks that followed, they were entertained by a number of princes and boyars. Chancellor was taken to Novgorod and Yaroslavl to observe the bazaars and trading methods. I saw them frequently, continuing to acquire what I could of their language. Serge remained as their interpreter until they departed.

The papers Ivan sent home with Chancellor founded a mutually profitable trade, and although it was some time before I saw the captain again, I occasionally visited the men who remained in Moscow. The Kremlin Bureau of Secret Affairs – the "third bureau" – had been instructed to assure the safety of the English post, for there were many factions, including the Pollacks, who would have liked to see them destroyed.

Gradually, my own visits fell off, as I became more deeply involved in other affairs. Heinrich had left many details for me to handle. I spent hours with Jacob, arranging for materials we had stored in local warehouses to be packed onto wagons and moved toward the west. Part of this merchandise was the Czar's, in accordance with agreements we had made with him, and this gave us priority over the other merchants who were also anxious to transship their goods through the former plague area.

Heinrich returned with Simon just before our last shipment went out, and was very pleased to learn that I had managed to get our goods moving while the Shuisky interests still awaited official clearance. He said he had passed three of our caravans on the road and he was sure we would have the first merchandise into the Hanseatic ports. The only sour note was sounded by Simon, who was troubled by the unrest generated over the Czar's demand for tribute from Dorpat.

Heinrich tried to reassure him, as he felt the prospect of war with the Livonians to be remote. Sigismund had no intention of involving Poland–Lithuania in a battle over rights of the German states. The question he had raised about Ivan's right to be called "Czar" was the basis of all the tension between Moscow and Krakow. The Pollack was simply jealous, as his own background was not nearly as impressive.

King Sigismund August was nine or ten years older than Ivan, and had been appointed to reign by his father, the Great Sigismund. He was already showing signs of madness, although he was never quite deranged enough to be deposed. His mother, Bona Sforza, had been an Italian princess, related to a family which was second only to the Borgias in political perfidy. She had reared her son in luxury and effeminacy, hoping one day to rule through him. She no doubt took the Medici woman in France as her model. Sigismund proved a great disappointment, for he displayed the weakness of many Western monarchs by allowing his nobles to assume extraordinary freedoms. When he finally saw the danger of this, he made a feeble attempt to curtail his vassals' power. It was already too late. The Polish nobles tried to overthrow him, and while the attempt was unsuccessful, Sigismund's security had been badly shaken. His mother fled back to Italy, taking a sizable slice of the royal treasury with her. At the time of which I speak she was still living in luxury – I believe in Florence. She was poisoned by her lover some four or five years later.

Once rid of his mother, Sigismund was able to concentrate enough support to bring his most important nobles into line. He then contrived to assume the Dukedom of Lithuania, as well as the crown of Poland. Although supposedly a Christian of the Roman persuasion, he allowed such freedom to the Protestant reformers that many of his greatest landholders and senators – even bishops and other clergy – exchanged their Roman vows for the heresy of Luther. While Ivan, himself, tended to be rather tolerant of other Christian beliefs, he was never foolish enough to allow such potentially dangerous divisions to develop. After all, Protestants and Roman Catholics were constantly at each other's throats all over Europe.

I never saw Sigismund in person, but he was described as small in stature, with a narrow little face that ended in a scraggly, pointed beard. His general appearance, it was said, reminded many of a nanny goat. His voice tended to break when he had to raise it to address a group of people. He was the last of the House of Jagellon, founder of a mighty race of warriors. They were fallen very low, indeed, when this miserable example was all that stood between their former greatness and complete extinction. With so weak a king on the throne, I doubted we would have much trouble in obtaining our desires in the west. Simon feared we would provoke a war by our demand for tribute, but if this happened I welcomed it. The Germans of Livonia should be worthy foes.

Heinrich told us he had information that some of his former associates in the Hanseatic League were on the way to Moscow. Although Tishkovitch had made it clear how Poland disapproved of our demands for tribute from Livonia, the Czar had not backed down. The Grand Master was apparently going to negotiate the payment, and there was no great buildup of Polish arms in support of her supposed ally. Then the Czar made a decision which further assured me of his intent to move westward. I was called to the palace and confirmed in my post, second–in–command of the expedition against Astrakhan. But I was to serve under General George Shemiakin. Kurbsky had been posted to examine and report on the terrain beyond Pskov. He was to give the Czar his recommendations for future disposition of forces around Dorpat and Riga. Adashev, who had lately fallen into lesser favor, was assigned as Ambassador to Livonia. From all this, I was sure that I would one day serve in a campaign against the Livonians – and eventually against the Pollacks. But for the moment, I was to face another enemy: my old foe, the Crimean Khan.

CHAPTER XI

In the spring, after the baptism of the Czarevitch, I departed south with the army. In addition to my military duties, I was loaded with instructions from both the Czar and Heinrich, regarding our commercial operations. I suspect this was largely Ivan's reason for sending me – Kurbsky's opinions to the contrary. Once Astrakhan was ours, there would be tremendous booty to be disposed of, and numerous trade negotiations to be made. Subject to the immediate approval of my commander, I was charged with making these arrangements, the final forms to be confirmed by the Czar. Before departing south, I sought what advice I could from Simon, and even endured a long, detailed dissertation from Shig Ali.

My interview with Suunbeka's corpulent husband, incidentally, had concluded on a most unpleasant note. I neither knew nor cared whether the man was aware of my intense contempt – which surely meant he knew, as I'd taken few pains to hide my feelings. Suddenly, just as I was preparing to leave, he flopped onto his knees and wrapped his arms about my legs. With tears flooding his eyes, he begged me to do all in my power to see no harm befell the Khan of Astrakhan. Because I knew the request came from Suunbeka, the Khan being her father, I assured Shig Ali I would do what I could. His sincerity and obvious devotion to his wife almost made me repent my detestation. Life in the Kremlin had wrought great changes in him, and I knew I was overly harsh in my attitude – even in my descriptions of his flabbiness. He had taken to regular participation in exercises with the soldiers, and much of his fat was beginning to harden into muscle. To give him his due, he was a competent, even a clever military commander, as he was soon to demonstrate in the west. I was aware of several remarks by Simon, indicating that he, too, felt a grudging respect.

On the long trip south, I had ample time to think and to attempt a revaluation of my rigid and unrelenting opinions. There had been many on–going changes in my life: my own maturation and that of my friends, a growing awareness of elemental good in several men I wished to hate, as well as the weaknesses I saw in those I respected. Beneath it all, I realized, was my own failure to find a woman I could truly love. I had forced myself to relegate Anastasia to the status of an inaccessible saint, yet my unfettered mind continued to evoke unthinkable images when I dreamed of her at night. Suunbeka remained as the only woman I had fully possessed in love, but she was equally beyond my reach. My other affairs, before and since, had been meaningless. I could observe my closest friends living in marital bliss, but I was too cowardly to take the chance myself. As a man does in deciding to take another's life, he makes an irrevocable decision when selecting the woman he wishes to marry.

The army we led south was a strikingly elite guard, comprised largely of Cossacks, *Streltsi,* and *dvoryanstro.* We went nearly the entire distance by water, for the thaws had freed the rivers, while leaving the roads deep in mud. Once we reached the Volga, and were being rowed in our great galleys, the campaign seemed more a pleasure trip than the prelude to battle. With George Shemiakin – the Prince of Pronsk – in command, my role as second assumed a greater than normal importance. George was lazy, and left many of his command detals to me. However, he had earned an enviable reputation during the siege of kazan, when he and his friend Feodor Lv'ov had ridden down more than one mob of screaming infidels. As a result, the men respected him and the Tartars were afrad of him

The campaign, however, was not particularly glorious. The enemy had fled in terror, leaving the bleached, sandstone walls of Astrakhan undefended. Thus our conquest of the city and much of the vast territory it controlled was simply a matter of moving in and setting up an administrative center with a large enough garrison to assure its survival. After weeks of ranging across the steppes, George and I led the bulk of the army back to Astrakhan. We had, of course, continued to send reports of our progress to Moscow, using post–riders.

Abraham had come down river on my step–father's instructions, arriving a day or two after we returned from gathering in the steppes. He brought pack animals by boat, and bore a package of letters from Heinrich, who had thought up several commercial tasks for me. He also bore a commission from the Czar, officially naming me his representative in the disposition of spoils. In this, my authority was to exceed Shemiakin's.

When I returned to camp and showed the Czar's charter to George, I expected he would be annoyed. Instead, he seemed delighted. He had been involved in constant arguments with the lesser commanders over possession of the booty. To settle these disputes, I had Abraham take up residence in the camp, and assigned a half dozen clerks to assist him. If an argument ensued, I made a decision behind closed doors, then refused to discuss the points of dispute with the contestants. I also let it be known that Abraham was under the personal protection of the Czar and for this reason he was never molested, despite his unpopular office. My use of this shrewd Jew was a fortunate choice, for he insisted on arranging the trade in caviar, that rare delicacy made from the roe of sturgeon. The Lower Volga later became famous for it, and while we enjoyed it as part of the spoils at Kazan, none of us had fully appreciated its commercial value. In the Czar's treaty, we inserted a clause whereby the city would pay a tribute of ten times one hundred sturgeon, and forty times one thousand altines. This was subject to increase as demand for the commodities grew. Once all the details were formulated, George and I decided upon a Tartar named Derbish to rule the conquered territory in the Czar's name.

News of our victory had reached Moscow on August twenty–fifth, the Czar's birthday. He took this as an omen of great good, and ordered a tumultuous celebration. I was told that even the Czarina and old Makari were at the banquet that evening. The following day the Czar dispatched orders calling us home, including the commission, appointing me to the rank of general. Ivan had been so pleased with our quick and bloodless victory, he began all his official statements: "In this, the twenty first year of Our reign over Russia, the third over Kazan, and the first over Astrakhan. . . ."

Leaving a sizable garrison in the city, we started north shortly before the onset of colder weather. The Russian domain now stretched from the Frozen Sea to the great inland ocean. We were indisputably the most powerful empire in

Christendom! I laughed to think what excuse old Sigismund would have to give, if he wished to continue denying Ivan the title of Czar.

On our way back, we stopped at both Kazan and Svyazhsk, where the government was now in firm control. However, it was easy to see that Shuiskys ruled both places. People in the streets stared dumbly at our soldiers, and when any of us appeared wearing armor and insignia of higher rank, the peasants turned their backs, afraid to look upon us. They acted as if the Czar's officers were deified avengers.

But there was little we could do about these conditions, other than to report them to the Czar when we were back in the capital. So George and I embarked via river barge as soon as we could, on what certainly became the most pleasurable part of our entire trip north. Among the spoils of our conquest, of course, were a number of slaves, including some extraordinarily handsome women. George had selected several for our amusement – a sufficient number, in fact, that there were always companions for the other officers who occasionally joned us for dinenr. I had noticed one very wild, spirited hill girl among the throng of female captives and I made sure to have her included among those who were to serve us on the way back to Moscow. George also made sure that the Bishop – whom Ivan had sent to assure our spiritual welfare – and all his priests were several boats ahead of us in line of vessels going home.

Our barge was much larger than most people would think a river boat to be. I can best express the size by noting that the ones used to transport horses could easily accommodate ninety animals, with all the fodder necessary for a trip of at least one hundred miles. Our boat was appointed like a fine *dacha*, with velvet draperies, and well–furnished sleeping quarters. The banquet room was as large as that of a modest home.

My hill girl, whom we called by the Russian name of Tamya, was not at all sure she wished to surrender to me that first night. Like all hill people, she considered city dwellers to be less than men. In the dining hall, she spat contemptuously when I dragged her down beside me. Twice, I had to jump up and chase her, for she bolted away whenever she had a chance. After the second time I beat her soundly, much to the amusement of the other officers. This seemed the one language she understood. Although she bit me when I tried to kiss her, there was little further resistance until I took her to my room. By then we had both drunk a good deal.

Again we had a scuffle before I took my way with her, ripping the clothing from her back and assaulting her cruelly until her own passion burst into flame. Then she clung to me in a desperate embrace, her nails scratching deeply into my back, while her supple body bent into unbelievable contortions to accommodate mine. She was able to assume positions I had never known were possible, and once aroused her lust was unquenchable. I was never able to complete our love making on the couch, for she always forced us to roll off, onto the deep Persian carpets. Each fall from the bed seemed to excite her more, and she never relaxed her grip. She continued to bite me in her wanton lust, but I returned her nips until we were both covered with love bruises about our necks and shoulders. After that first night she was mine. She became so jealous and possessive no other woman dared come near. I had many sins to confess by the end of the trip, for I did all the forbidden acts with this woman, more blatantly than I had with any other. I was thankful I did not have to explain myself to Sylvester.

When I left the boat in Moscow, Tamya did not want to let me go, fearing I would send her away. This was exactly what I intended to do, for I was afraid to take her home. The other girls would be no match for her, and I knew Heinrich would never permit me to get rid of them. I was ready to end the affair, anyway, as she was exhausting me. She demanded fulfillment whenever I came into the room, and embarrassed me before the other men by her immodesty. She was rightfully mine by then, for I had purchased her from the spoils. When we docked, I ordered my servants to keep her confined to the boat until further orders.

I had an immediate interview with the Czar, during the course of which I mentioned Tamya to him. I did not actually offer her, because it did not seem right to present the Czar with a wench I had used so many times, myself. But my description amused Ivan, and so excited him he asked me for her. His own retainers were dispatched to take her from the boat. I do not know exactly what happened to Tamya after that. She was carried away, screaming and struggling, cursing me with every infidel profanity. She never appeared again, to my knowledge, nor did Ivan ever make mention of her. There were stories told, even then, of things the Czar was supposed to be doing in his chambers below the palace. I am sure they were exaggerated; certainly they were premature. At this time, however, Anastasia was again with child and the Czar was in need of diversion. I hoped that whatever pleasure he derived from Tamya might partially expiate my own sins. Perhaps it did, for no heavenly punishment was immediately visited upon me.

To my surprise, the Czar reciprocated my gift. That evening, he sent a stately blonde Swedish girl to my house. She had been taken when our armies drove the forces of King Gustavus out of Wiborg. He sent a note along with her, something to the effect of allowing me to play the white while he took the black. After Tamya, I found the pale Swede unexciting and dull. She was afraid of me, and unwilling to do more than tolerate my advances. However, Serge was nearly wild with desire for her. Because he had been deprived of adventure in Astrakhan, due to his duties with the English, I rewarded his labors by giving the girl to him. They made a strange couple, for she was easily half a head taller. But they seemed to get on well, and were eventually married in a proper Christian ceremony.

Ivan's second son, little Fedya, was born just after the army's triumphal return. To celebrate the royal birth, as well as our victory, the Czar declared a massive public display. This was followed by a number of banquets, given by other officials living in and around the Kremlin. The Czar distributed such a flood of medals to the commanders and heroes of the campaign, we were hard pressed to justify all the awards. For political reasons it was important to decorate a goodly number of soldiers, especially among the Cossacks, where such honors were highly esteemed. As a result of Adashev's activities, Muscovy now had the rudiments of a proper coinage system, and some of these novel pieces were also distributed to the most deserving of the Czar's troops. It was apparent that the Czar had some further plans for his armies in the coming months.

I spent most of the winter with my friends: visiting Yuri and Ulyana, playing chess with the Czar, and frolicking on the floor with the Czarevitch. I stayed with Vladya and Evdokia at Staritsa for several weeks, returning to the

Kremlin just before Christmas. A child was born to Simon a day or two before Epiphany, and this gave us cause for still further celebration. It was during one of these informal gatherings – I think in Simon's house – that the Czar casually informed me I would soon be posted to assist Kurbsky in Pskov. I looked at him questioningly, but he put me off. Anxious for an explanation, I went to the palace before sunrise the next day, hoping to catch Ivan going into his chapel. But this was Epiphany, and the Czar refused to discuss anything, insisting we allow temporal matters to wait until after the holy days. Instead, he invited me to accompany him to the sacred ceremonies at the river.

This was the last time old Makari performed the rites; he died a few months later. For this reason, probably, I particularly remember the occasion. Ivan and I arrived at the river in the first gray light of dawn, just in time to see the young acolytes carry their tapers out onto the ice, following the boy who bore the sacred lantern. Then came the priests, carrying the cross and the icons of Our Lady and of Saint Nicholas, the wonder worker. Behind them were more than the usual hundred monks, all chanting in unison. Although it was very cold, and the layers of snow were exceptionally deep, the wind had fallen off, making it almost pleasant for this time of year. In the misty gloom of morning, people lined both banks of the river, watching the procession as it assembled around the huge hole cut in the ice the previous afternoon. All the hundred torches were held aloft, forming a perfect circle as the flames leapt skyward to welcome the rising sun.

Once the priests were in their places, the main procession began. The Metropolitan went first, wearing his gleaming golden robes, beneath a huge coat of silver fox. The poor old man had become so feeble he had to be assisted by a pair of priests. They helped him from his sleigh and supported him as he crossed the frozen river. When Makari had taken his position before the others, I walked out with the Czar, leading the procession of boyars. Streaming out behind us was the entire court, everyone wearing his best sable or ermine *shuba*. Tall boyar hats bobbed up and down as all the great nobles marched behind their Czar. I had a chuckle with Ivan on the way, because we were both wearing new military boots with leather soles, instead of the softer skins we were used to. We were keeping score to see who would have to catch the other the most times. As our feet slipped to the side, he had to turn, looking sternly at those behind to quell the ripple of laughter.

A wooden platform had been built for Makari, which he stood upon as we came up. Custom demanded that the Czar and all his court stand on the ice. This had been the reason for our wearing the boots, as our feet had nearly frozen the year before. The ceremony of sanctification began with the priests singing lengthy prayers to bless the water. At the conclusion of their ritual, Makari dipped a bumperful from the river and dashed it over the Czar. He then refilled the container, pouring frigid water over me and a number of others who stood close by. Following some additional prayers, each of the priests and monks approached the hole, dipping out a large cup of the sanctified river water as they withdrew. The rest of the court, those who had not been close enough to the Metropolitan to receive the blessing at his hands, now came forward. They dipped their own containers into the water, everyone dashing some of the blessed liquid onto his face.

Those whose sins were especially heavy cast off their furs and leaped in, clad only in their shifts.

When the court and other people of quality had withdrawn, the peasants and shopkeepers came down to dip out the holy water. Many of them, men and women alike, bathed naked in the freezing river. No heavy sinner could afford to miss this opportunity of gaining God's forgiveness. On the way back to the palace, the Czar relented his former reticence, mumbling something about the holy days being concluded. He told me to be ready for departure the next morning, and to come to him before dawn for my final instructions. That evening, I discussed my pending assignment with Heinrich, but he had no better idea than I of the Czar's intentions. There had been fairly extensive campaigns during the summer, going deeper into German–Livonian territory than Ivan had thought possible. We had also driven the Swedes from our northern lands. Kurbsky's army was currently bolstered by units from my Astrakhan command, and a number of Cossack companies had already been sent west.

It appeared that we were about to annex the desperately needed Baltic ports. Furious as Sigismund must have been, there was nothing he could do. He was far too weak to stop us, and if he tried he would risk extensive portions of his own domain. While I had been with our army in the south, Shig Ali had led a large force of Tartars and Circassians into Livonia, taking a number of small towns along the border, including that portion of Narva which lay east of the Narova River. This comprised a fair–sized city by itself, and after it had been captured it was renamed Ivangorod. Its absorption into the Czar's empire was uncomplicated, as it was already populated mostly by Russians.

The greater portion of those areas taken by Shig Ali had been parts of a disputed territory, land claimed both by the Czar and the Grand Master. What lay beyond was Russian only by the severest stretch of history. All of us admitted that. But it was an area we badly needed, and we should easily have been able to take it. The Livonians were afraid of our barbarian soldiers, especially the Tartars, who were more ruthless than any other. But even this terrible threat failed to awaken the decadent knights. They were so sunk in effeminacy and debauchery they would hardly bestir themselves to defend a neighboring city.

I felt that much of this Livonian degeneracy stemmed from their having been converted from the Church of Rome, into the errors of Luther. When Shig Ali invaded Livonia, the great knights were assembled in Revel to celebrate the marriage of a rich merchant. They did not even interrupt their toasts when word was brought of the Russian advance, and because of their apathy Altenhorn, Neihaus, and Marienburg were all reduced to ashes.

At Dorpat, the Livonians finally offered some resistance. This was quickly overcome by our army, but the commander's orders were not to take the city. He was to proceed down the coast to Wesenberg, rather than tie up the entire force in a long siege. Meeting very weak resistance, he advanced almost to Riga, burning everything that could not be carried away. But while the Livonians would seldom fight, neither would they surrender. When cold weather forced the Czar to order his armies to withdraw into more defensible positions, many of the areas we had taken fell back into German hands. Kurbsky had been in overall command, supervising both the campaign in Livonia and the one farther north, against the Swedes. Thus it was Shig Ali who gained the greatest glory and reputation.

I could imagine how Andrew must have chafed at the progress of the battles. Overseeing two campaigns, in widely separated areas, he had been forced to remain in Pskov, where he was accessible to both field commanders. His position was rather like Vorotinsky's, who commanded all the armies, but who never saw a battlefield because his position forced him to remain in the Kremlin. Under Andrew, other, lesser commanders, like John Sheremetief – the same who had commanded the peasant levies during our punitive sortie into Kazan the year before – were able to wade into the heat of battle and cover themselves with glory. All Andrew could do was pace his command post, receiving and dispatching messages. Whatever the Czar had in mind for me, I hoped it would entail some action.

"But you're a general, now," laughed the Czar. "What do you mean, 'fight'? I need your mind, not your brawn. Besides, you're not a boy anymore. You should be happy to stay away from the butchery and the dust – all the blood and mess of battle."

"A soldier lives for battle," I replied stiffly. I was taken aback by his remarks, and embarrassed that he berated me in front of several other people – Mikhailof among them.

"Look," he said, taking me to the wall where he had a large map of the West. "While you were gathering in the southern source of wealth, my other generals were pushing toward the Western windows. These ports will give us access to the great marketplaces of the world! It was the greatest piece of diplomacy Adashev ever accomplished when he backed the Grand Master against the wall with his threats. He made the old man so angry he refused tribute from Dorpat. That gave me the excuse I needed to invade. Now I've given him the choice of swearing fealty to me or continuing a war he knows he's going to lose."

"Even if Poland jumps in?" I asked.

"Poland!" he scoffed. "Do you think that scraggly old goat would dare challenge me? Why the very mention of Tartar troops sends him scurrying to hide under his mistress's bed. No, Poland won't attack us – not unless we make it impossible for them to avoid it." He watched me significantly. Obtaining only a blank stare, he began again, poking his finger into my chest. "That is going to be one of your responsibilities, Dmitri. Andrew keeps telling me we must march into Poland and subdue her while she's still too weak to offer much resistance."

I shrugged. "And you don't wish to do this?" I was puzzled.

Ivan sighed, flopping into a chair. "You are becoming too much the general," he said unhappily. "Sigismund is not the only European monarch who is afraid of Us. Do you know I lost thirty craftsmen in Luebeck last year? Yes, yes I did! I'd made all the arrangements to bring them here – gunsmiths, metal workers, even a printer. They were all ready to come, until the Emperor – the Austrian Emperor, mind you – requested they be refused passage into Livonia."

"Do you think the Emperor would go to war for Sigismund?"

"Who knows?" he shrugged. "Sigismund is not a well man. What if he dies? With that stupid Pollack system of electing a king, it could be the Emperor – or one of his sons – who sits on the Polish throne a year or two from now. Then what?"

It was my turn to shrug. "I'll just stay a soldier." I said.

Ivan laughed again. "No, this time you must be a merchant," he told me. "You will carry a packet of sealed orders for Kurbsky, but no one must know you carry them."

"Why not use a regular courier?"

"I could," he said, "but we have lost a few messengers lately, and if I send the orders by heavy guard, the enemy will know I'm up to something. But you, traveling with a load of valuable merchandise, you can maintain a heavy guard without arousing notice. You can visit Andrew. Nothing would be more natural than that, and there are ample business reasons for your being in Pskov. I am ordering an advance into Livonia again, but it will come before the spring thaw. That should catch them by surprise, especially if they don't know I've sent the orders."

"Am I to have a part in the campaign?" I asked.

"I have left that up to Andrew. If he feels you could be of help, by all means remain. Otherwise, return to me. I can always use you."

With that, I set out on my journey, taking Serge as groom, and a small detachment of mounted retainers in my own livery. We had a caravan two days out toward Novgorod, and would be able to join it long before coming to any major settlement. Afterward, there would be nothing to indicate I was other than a prosperous merchant on a routine commercial venture. Because it was the very middle of winter, the roads were all but impassable, and we traveled the rivers as much as we could. After joining the caravan we made fairly good time, as the weather held all the way to Novgorod.

Along the way, I was surprised to discover many vacant cabins, even whole villages deserted by their inhabitants. At first, I thought the residents must have been victims of the plague, but a fellow who had made several trips with Heinrich told me that these were cabins and villages of families who had been moved into new lands along the Volga. I had known of Ivan's having ordered large migrations, but the extent had never struck me so poignantly. So many people!

At Novgorod I was received in the home of Archbishop Pimen, who, in his usual nosy way, tried to discover if I had any mission to perform other than the obvious commercial one. His silky white beard seemed to flutter beneath petulant lips as he spoke in a pious, confidential manner. One could almost believe him honest, but I knew better. Although Pimen might sound like Sylvester, he did not have the dogmatic sincerity of the Czar's confessor. As much as I detested Sylvester, I had to admit he believed in what he said. With Pimen, I always felt he pretended to be an honest priest, while actually involving himself in very worldly matters.

I assured the Archbishop that I had come solely on a commercial mission, and hinted that I handled the Czar's interests as well as my own. My story seemed to satisfy him, but when I returned to my lodgings I discovered someone had gone through my baggage. Nothing was stolen. The Czar's papers were perfectly safe, for they had been sewn into the lining of my shift. I made no outcry, and went right to bed. I was tired from the day's travel, and from Pimen's long lecture on the evils of sin. He had started immediately after dinner, and continued until it was finally late enough for me to excuse myself. His principal theme had been the great offense we would commit against the Lord if we continued to bear arms against our fellow Christians in Livonia.

"We should pursue the holy wars in the South," Pimen had thundered, "where we may achieve that which the Western crusaders were unable to do." I think he seriously expected we could rescue the Holy Sepulcher from the Turks.

I departed again the next morning, thankful to be away from the Archbishop, although I had to admit he set a very fine table. It had been so fine, in fact, I was up twice during the night with stomach cramps. The harsh jouncing of Gabriel's pace across the snow created horrible pains within my belly all morning. By afternoon I was sure I was poisoned. We took refuge in a monastery that night, just in time to escape a heavy snow storm. Both snow and flux lasted two full days, after which we continued to Pskov.

Word of my trip must have preceded me. When we arrived within the city gates, we were met by a delegation of junior officers from Kurbsky's command, who seemed to know I was bearing some kind of message. One fellow even asked which town we were to attack first. I was greatly relieved to get the Czar's letters into Kurbsky's hands. Andrew looked extremely well. His chestnut beard was fuller, his face ruddy and glowing. His blue eyes sparkled as they traced the lines of the Czar's messages, but he made no comment until he had read them all. Then he leaned back with a look of pleasure on his face. "Action again!" he said. "We are to reoccupy the entire coast from Narva to Riga. At my discretion we are to take the cities, starting when I think I can do it, but having them all by summer."

"And the Pollacks?" I asked.

He gestured with his hands, helplessly. "We are ordered not to provoke an incident. But it will come! They are already sending a few supplies to the Germans. Later, it will be more. And it will be war!"

"Maybe you can take the whole coast, cities and all, fast enough to avoid . . . ."

"Exactly what I intend!" he snapped. "I have just been waiting for Ivan's permission. No troops move better than ours through snow, and if I'm going to accomplish what the Czar wants me to do, we must start now."

Although the prospect of action was enthusiastically received, Kurbsky maintained such good discipline among his officers there was little drunkenness to celebrate the coming campaign. Order among the troops was also good, but I ascribed this to Andrew's knowing two days in advance of my coming. He had gotten everything in readiness for the orders he expected to receive. As soon as I was able to get him alone, I requested a place on his staff, and was assigned to command the force being sent to take Narva.

For several days I floated on a cloud of exhilaration, especially pleased by Andrew's apparent expression of faith in me. Narva was the northernmost of the towns we needed to take, and hence, my assignment was to an important post. What I did not know at the time was that Ivan had sent a note among the papers I carried, telling Andrew to give me a good command. I have never known whether I would have gotten it on my own.

I led my forces north to the Russian stronghold of Ivangorod, directly across the river from Livonian Narva. My intention was to make a show of strength, and to demand surrender of the town. I had no qualms as to our ability to take the city by force, but I hoped the Germans would be sensible and allow it to fall without further bloodshed. Unfortunately, the political mess within the League did not work in my favor. The Grand Master, von Plettenberg, was an old man. He was too senile to have sense enough to step down, allowing a more able commander to replace him. In his fumbling dotage, he again allowed the Russian forces under Kurbsky to take some twenty small towns and many hectares of land. The Germans had offered only token resistance to Andrew's advance, and by the time I reached Ivangorod the Grand Master was already asking for a six–month truce. He claimed he needed that much time to arrange a surrender as demanded by the Czar.

This was the news which greeted me when I entered Ivangorod. I quickly ordered my artillery placed on the walls, where I hoped I could bombard Narva before the truce was negotiated. The placing of the field pieces took a full two days, and during that time I sent an envoy to the city, demanding its surrender. They refused, as I knew they would. I ordered my men to stand ready, intending to attack at first light of dawn. But I was too slow; the Czar's order arrived while I was still at morning prayers.

Faced with a half–year's ban on any military action, I soon discovered how really dull and wretched the command of an outlying post can be. There was nothing to do, and the Lenten abstinences made it worse. I had heard of another English ship having landed at Kholmagora, and for a while I harbored the hope that Ivan would send for me. He did not.

I began to take long walks by myself, going for miles along the sandy shores of the Baltic, inhaling the peculiar odors of the sea. I was fascinated by the strange power of the surf and the boundless expanse of dark, choppy water. My one diversion during that season of Lent was a girl I met on one of my strolls. She was a fisherman's daughter, a wench of such low origins I did not dare bring her to my quarters. I confess it was a sordid affair, frequently conducted on the floor in the back of her father's shack all stinking of saltwater and fish. I would return home covered with oil from the tarpaulins on which we lay, so ashamed of myself I would vow never to return to her again. But my lust was too great, and I gave in. Since I was born in greater sin than most, I wondered if I was condemned to live accordingly.

Finally so bored and miserable within my soul, I could hardly bear to think about it, I arranged to leave my post and spend the Eastertide with Andrew. The truce was still in effect, and there should have been no difficulty. It was, therefore, my second who took Narva, after the Germans opened fire on Easter day! I hurried back, but the fighting was long since over.

Out of all this, however, there came a strange story. It seems that one of the houses in Narva, occupied by Orthodox Russians, had been burned by the Germans. The house had been completely destroyed, but an icon was found to have survived, unscathed, from the family chapel. I had the relic carefully wrapped and sent to the Czar, who was so pleased he ignored the report in which I disclaimed the honor of having taken the city. It had still been my command, he insisted, and he bestowed several costly gifts upon me, including some very extensive estates south of Marienburg. Many years before, these had belonged to Simon, my mother's first husband, the man who was recorded as my father in the Kremlin archives.

I was now assigned a staff post with Kurbsky, and commanded his right hand in several skirmishes, before another truce was imposed upon us. I was about to settle into a new routine of boredom and inactivity, this time without even the fisherman's daughter, for Andrew would never have approved such frivolous behavior, when a courier arrived from the Kremlin delivering an unhappy message. Before the General had time to open the scroll, the messenger had spread its news about the camp. The Czarina was very ill, and the doctors feared for her life. Moscow was already in mourning.

The response of our Russian troops was immediate and uniform. No one in all the realm was more beloved than Anastasia. Men stopped where they stood, bowing their heads to pray for her recovery. The Cossacks, too, remained quiet and respectful, although their concern was not as great as ours. Andrew called me to his quarters as soon as he had read the letter.

"I can't leave," he said, "but I think you should go as quickly as you can."

"Did the Czar send for me?" I asked.

"The letter is from Mikhailof," said Andrew. "He writes that the Czar is too depressed for anything but grief. I am sure he would want you, so go as my representative. Offer my proper respects, whatever happens."

The ride to Moscow took a fortnight, over slippery, muddy highways. I had forsaken Gabriel's great strength and utilized the Czar's post horses. My last mount was nearly done in when I reached the outskirts of the city and clattered into *Kitaigorod.* I knew Anastasia was still alive, as the church bells were silent and a huge crowd stood in the Square of Executions. There were still more people inside the Kremlin court, making it necessary to bully my way through the tightly packed mass, trying not to trample those who knelt in prayer. I finally left my mount a short distance from the Savior's Gate, and walked the remaining few steps to the palace.

Guards opened the doors for me without question, and I hurried through the darkened passages to the Czarina's apartments. There was a heavy murmur as I approached her door – dozens of people praying in the hall and outer chambers. The crowd of nobles about Anastasia's bedchamber was so thick, it was hard to tell who stood beyond the nearest figures. I was finally able to catch a glimpse of Heinrich in the middle of the room. Beside him was Michael Vorotinsky, his hands clasped in front, two huge tears running down his cheeks. Gently, I pushed my way through to them and whispered an inquiry as to how she was.

Heinrich shook his head. "It is very near the end," he told me. "The last rites have already been given."

"Is she awake?" I asked.

"I don't think there's any pain," said Michael, misunderstanding my question. If Anastasia were conscious, I hoped for a final word with her.

"See if you can get to the door, son," said Heinrich. "I think the Czar left word to admit you."

With some difficulty I was able to get close enough to the portal for the guards to see me. I gestured silently with my hands, asking if I might enter. One of them nodded and asked those nearest the door to step back for me. Mikhailof was one of these, and he patted my shoulder as I passed. Many others were clustered there, as well: Vladimir and Evdokia, Euphrosyne, Fumikov, Fedka. Euphrosyne was the last to step aside, and I remember wondering why she was there. The last I had known, the Czar's ban still restricted her to Staritsa.

Anastasia's room was nearly dark, with heavy curtains pulled across the windows. The only light came from two candles in tall holders on either side of the bed. Her eyes were closed and she seemed hardly to breathe, her face waxen as if life had already departed. Ivan knelt beside the bed, his face buried in the covers, kneading her hand with both of his. The Czar looked up at me briefly, hardly seeming to recognize me. I had never seen him look so ghastly, not even when he lay close to death himself. His beard seemed dull and tinged with gray. He shoved his forehead down again, and his deep, racking sobs were the only sound, except for the droning of the Metropolitan and three priests who stood several feet away. Gregory Zakharin and the Romanovs stood silently at her feet, their lips moving as they silently repeated the prayers of the priests.

In order to reach Anastasia I would have to step between Ivan's legs, then lean over him. Even in this moment of anguish, I hesitated to commit such an act of familiarity without his permission. With his head against the sheets, he seemed to have forgotten I was there. Uncertainly, I stood behind him for a few moments. Then he spoke quietly, without looking up.

"Come ahead, Dmitri," he whispered. "She wanted to see you before – the end."

As I leaned over her, Anastasia opened her eyes, gazing up with that expression that always made me want to fall on my knees before her and beg her blessing as if from a saint. That this angelic woman could die so young was a terrible display of fate's perversity! The Czar released his hold on her hand, and as a second thought placed it in mine. He patted the two together, and moved enough to allow me next to the bed. For a moment I thought he was going to sit on the edge, but if such an impulse crossed his mind he quickly suppressed it. It would be akin to sitting on God's Holy Alter.

Weakly, the Czarina pulled me toward her, and when my head was close to her face she whispered something about my staying close to the Czar and not allowing him to fall into the black pit of despair. "Stay by his side," she said, "this is why I wanted you to come."

She coughed gently, and from somewhere in the dark recesses at the far end of the room a doctor appeared. He took her hand away from me. I stepped back, allowing the man to examine her fingers and her face. The Czar stirred beside me, causing me to glance into his saddened, haggard face. His eyes were red from weeping, sunken deeply into their darkened sockets. His whole body trembled, and he gave off a sour, sweaty odor.

I wanted to ask what had happened, but this was not the time. Then Ivan began to tell me. "It was so sudden," he mumbled. "One moment she was playing with the children, laughing in that quiet way of hers, and telling them fairy stories. The next, she had fallen to the ground. She has been like this ever since." He swallowed hard, and made no attempt to wipe away the tears.

The word "poison" came immediately to my mind, but again it was not the time to say it. "Did you hear what she told me?" I asked.

Ivan nodded, brushing my elbow with the back of his hand. "You know my soul, Dmitri." This was all he said.

The doctor stood up slowly, his head on his chest. He dared not look at the Czar. "She is gone," he said.

Ivan bolted around the doctor, who seemed in a daze, just standing where he no longer belonged. He threw himself across the wasted body, weeping loudly, almost strangling on his sobs. The priests stepped forward and began the ritual following death. They glanced up at me, for Ivan was in their way and they were afraid to touch him. I allowed him a few more minutes, then took his shoulder and firmly pulled him back. "She is no longer with us," I told him. "You must be the bravest of all."

"My little heifer; my little heifer," he repeated over and over again.

I opened the door for him, and the crowd fell back as we passed. From his face everyone knew. I could hear the women and a few of the men weeping before we reached the hall. As I helped Ivan into his own chambers bells began to toll all over the city. No professional mourners were needed; all Moscow expressed its anguish that night. Runners went out to every city in the land, so the clarion bells of death sounded from Kholmagora to Astrakhan, from Kazan to Narva.

I stayed with Ivan for a long time, thinking as I did how I was following Anastasia's last wish. No one disturbed us; Fedka Basmanov stood just outside the door, where he was soon joined by Heinrich and a few others. They turned away everyone who tried to get in. I left for a few moments to confer with Mikhailof in making the funeral arrangements, and told him not to bother the Czar with the details. The ceremony itself was so formalized there would be little to ask him, anyway. After this, I returned and did not leave again until the next morning, when Ivan finally fell into a fitful slumber.

Heinrich had gone home, where I found him napping in the front room. He awoke and called to me, ordering a servant to bring some warm wine. Anastasia had suffered several attacks, he explained. They were caused by a strange malady no one could understand or cure. The English doctor, Standish, who had arrived with the group from Kholmagora while I was in Livonia, had been unable to diagnose it. Several weeks before, the Czar had taken Anastasia with him on a pilgrimage to Mozhaisk, thinking she was well enough to make the trip. In fact, the main reason for going was to offer prayers of gratitude for her renewed health and vigor. On the way back to Moscow, while the royal family was spending a few days at one of Ivan's country *dachas,* Anastasia fell ill again. Due to lack of foresight on the part of the royal retainers, there was no doctor and no medicine available. The trip had been easy, and made in comfortable stages, so there should have been no cause for anyone to become ill.

Still, the Czar was furious. His anger was only further increased when Sylvester suggested the attack had been the result of God's displeasure over Ivan's campaigns against the Christian powers of the West. In a fit of rage, the Czar ordered Sylvester out of his sight and forbade him to enter the palace. Once back in Moscow, Anastasia seemed to rally a bit, as she had done before. But while she lay ill, a fire broke out in the Arbat and became so threatening everyone feared the city would burn again. Smoke filled the palace corridors, and became so heavy in Anastasia's rooms she screamed in her delirium. Not knowing what else to do, the Czar ordered her removed to the summer palace in the Sparrow Hills, while most of the court remained to direct the fire fighters. Once the flames were put out, Anastasia was brought back. By then she was obviously going to die, and it had been at this point Mikhailof sent messages to Kurbsky and all the provincial governors.

I do not know how long I had been asleep, probably an hour or so. I had been dreaming – a heavy, dreadfilled fantasy, in a world full of dark, misty clouds, trying to escape some unknown horror. I was unable to move my arms, and the horse, which seemed somehow to be a part of me, was sliding backward over a slippery surface. A servant woke me, shaking me desperately and whispering, "Sir! Please wake up, sir! It's important!" When I was sitting up, the man told me Prince Vladimir was downstairs.

I was not conscious enough to question the hour. My man held out a robe, and I hurriedly shoved my arms into the sleeves while my feet fumbled on the floor, trying to slip into a pair of sandals. Then Vladya came into my room, instead of waiting downstairs for me to join him. In the reddish light of a single, flickering taper, I could see my friend's face was ashen. His eyes were wild with fright, and his whole body seemed to be responding to some unmentionable terror. I drew him to a seat by the stove, which still gave off a narrow aura of warmth. I sent my man to fetch us some of Heinrich's brandy. Not until the fellow had served us and withdrawn did Vladimir begin his explanation.

"You are the only one I can come to," he started. I thought he wanted to weep, but was too frightened.

"Vladya . . . anything I can do –" I stammered uncertainly.

He stared for a moment, as if still struggling with a conflict of impulse – to tell, or to withhold his story. Then he blurted out the dreadful tale. "It's Mother," he managed in a constricted voice. "I know she poisoned the Czarina – I mean, she had it done. I only just found out."

My utter shock held me motionless, until it began to melt into a blaze of anger. I'm certain it had to show on my face.

"But I didn't know," he protested. His voice was squeaky, almost a whine. "I had no idea until she boasted of it to me this evening. Somehow she placed a maid in Anastasia's household, and she's been poisoning the Czarina for months. What am I going to do, Dmitri? Ivan would never believe me. If he finds out, I'll be as guilty as she is. And she's my own mother!" he almost shouted. "I can't tell the Czar. What am I going to do?"

"But . . . but, why?" I asked at length. Why even Euphrosyne – cruel and evil as I knew her to be – why even she would wish to take Anastasia's life. I couldn't understand it.

"I suppose it's my fault," he said remorsefully. "Mother is half mad. I've known it for a long time. But I never thought she'd do a thing like this! She had some idea that Anastasia was Ivan's strength. She called her 'Samson's hair.'"

The brandy helped to awaken me, and the cold horror was beginning to drain away. "Who else knows?" I asked.

Vladya shrugged. "The maid," he said simply. "I guess that's all, except for you and me . . . and Mother."

"If you are truly innocent. . . ." I began, fixing him squarely with my gaze. He looked back unflinchingly. The only reaction was a slight twitch of his jaw, an expression of wounded feelings.

"If even you doubt me—" he said helplessly.

I moved closer and gripped his forearm, ashamed of my own lack of faith. "I don't doubt you," I said sincerely.

He looked down at the floor. "Thank you," he muttered.

We said nothing more for a while, each of us deep in his own thoughts. I was trying to reason with myself. I knew I should tell the Czar, and yet I knew just as surely that I couldn't. Euphrosyne had destroyed her own soul, and her hatred had made her life a misery. It was inexcusable she also be allowed to destroy her son. But her vile depravity could carry the destruction further that that. Vladya had now involved me in his confession.

"The maid," I said finally, "where is she now? Has she been questioned by the guard or the third bureau?"

Vladya shook his head. "No one has mentioned poison, and the bureau isn't involved as far as I know. The girl must still be in the *terem*."

"Her silence must be assured," I said flatly, "– and your mother must be confined to Staritsa."

Vladya looked at me, trembling. He seemed numb, too distraught to do anything. "If she were to leave before the funera l. . . it would . . . could . . . look strange," he replied.

I agreed. "The most important thing is the girl," I said thoughtfully. "Your mother has been involved in so many plots she should know how to keep silent, at least long enough for you to get her away after the funeral."

"Are you suggesting I murder the girl?" he asked in horror.

"You are more important than she is," I replied grimly. "If you can get her out of the palace and into some safe place without killing her, fine. But she's a murderess, anyway. She deserves to die."

"And my mother?" he asked. Now his eyes fixed mine, his gaze like a bird of prey.

"You must decide that," I told him. "I would not suggest you harm your own mother, but you must keep her away from Moscow. If she is truly mad, you can never know what she might say to someone. But the greatest sin you could commit would be to deprive the Czar of your help and loyalty at a time when he badly needs you. For Ivan's sake, let alone yours, I would prefer he never knows."

"Then you'll help me?" he asked.

"Yes," I said simply. "If it comes to that, I'll help you."

CHAPTER XII

The memory of Anastasia's funeral stayed foremost in my mind for many, many months. I would find myself speaking to someone, only half knowing what I said, while tears ran down my face. Because of this, many thought I was crazed; but since it was a malady I shared with the Czar, no one said anything publicly. I had no further conversations with Vladya on any subject even remotely related to the murder. I tried to tell myself I had dreamed the whole episode, but that didn't help. I am not sure how it had been arranged, or if there had been any arrangement to it; but one of Anastasia's handmaidens hanged herself in the early morning hours, following her mistress's burial. Everyone assumed she killed herself in a fit of despair and sorrow. Nor did there seem to be any suspicion of the truth. Vladya left for Staritsa the day after the services, taking Euphrosyne with him. To my knowledge, she was never permitted inside the Kremlin again.

Neither Ivan nor I had the heart for political or military activities for several months. But life continued around us, despite our heavy loss. The English had come in a large group, this time with a charter from their new Queen Elizabeth, the sister of the previous ruler. In the group was a man named Anthony Jenkinson, who was destined to become the Czar's favorite. His mission on this trip was to travel as far south as he could, to establish some new trade routes beyond Bokhara. Although I was later closely associated with Jenkinson, I met him only briefly during this period. . .while he was anxiously awaiting the Czar's permission to begin his journey.

The war with Livonia dragged on, interrupted by one truce after another. The Czar, feeling the need of Kurbsky's presence in Moscow, replaced him in his command by Peter Shuisky, recently recalled from the governorship of Svyazhsk. The Grand Master had also been replaced – finally. A younger knight, von Ketler, had assumed the robes of his office. He mounted a slightly more effective resistance than his predecessor, and he sent ambassadors to nearly every nation in Europe, seeking allies against us. We were afraid that Emperor Charles of Austria, who had been a friend of Ketler's, was going to come to his aid. But for some strange reason, the Emperor suddenly renounced the world and retired into some peculiar madness, refusing to engage in any contest of arms. The Swedes were afraid to fight us again, and the Danish king delayed a long time without giving the Grand Master an answer. The Knights of the Golden Fleece were too jealous of the Teutonic Knights to accept Ketler's leadership. This left only Sigismund as a potential ally. Too weak and cowardly to do more than bleat in protest, the King wrote to his brother monarchs warning them of the Russian threat. He compared us to the Mongol Horde and claimed we sought to conquer all of Europe!

He even wrote to England, bemoaning our intention to "destroy the Christian nations of the West." But for all his verbiage, Sigismund offered no real resistance. Shuisky's armies soon took Dorpat and all the land to the east. Before the first snow, our forces were again at the gates of Riga.

Only now was I beginning to recover from the Czarina's death. . .as was Ivan. Lest it seem strange I should have been so affected, I can only suggest that as long as Anastasia lived, no other woman could ever fully possess my soul. She had been my first love, and she had always been something inaccessible to me. I could not explain my passion more explicitly than this. My love for her was a pure, unique condition. I think Ivan understood how I felt, for he made several remarks to acknowledge his appreciation of my devotion to his wife. Nor was there ever a suggestion he felt it improper. The depth of my own soul, and the vastly deeper complex of the Czar's were different from most other men. We shared a level of understanding that was incomprehensible to any other.

During the period of mourning for Anastasia, Makari passed away. He went quietly in his sleep, leaving this world with very little comment or ceremony. Ivan chose Alfansy, Abbot of the Chudov Monastery, to be the new Metropolitan, and he was duly elected by the Council of Bishops. I do not think the choice would have fallen on this poor, weak man, if the Czar had not still been deep in his despair. While much respected for his piety, this old man was certainly not an influential leader, not even within the brotherhood of the Church.

By Christmas, the court was functioning normally again, although a great change had come over the Czar. His look was more stern, his temper short. He never appeared without his *kisten* – the tall, steel pointed staff. Those who aroused his displeasure were quickly punished. It was as if the evil fires of his spirit, those which had caused him to cut out my brother–in–law's tongue, or to pour flaming liquor into the beards of the Pskovian emissaries, had suddenly sprung to life.

I tried to honor Anastasia's last request by staying close to his side, but I could not always dispel the misery which tortured his soul. I knew his wounds required a more potent salve than words – from me or from anyone else. While I regretted the form it had to take, I—and many others—assumed the situation to be a temporary one. I refer, of course, to the chambers. If the healing balm could only be produced by Ivan's destruction of lesser beings, we thought, then so it must be. The Will of God must be fulfilled. His Anointed Czar must make what use he needed of his subjects.

Adding to Ivan's woes, we began to have serious troubles with Poland soon after the first of the year. Tartars had again entered our southern territories. When Sigismund learned of this he immediately offered his protection to Livonia, assuming that our armies would be committed to a defense of the south. This, in turn, encouraged the Danes to announce their intention to intercede if our war in the German states continued. Pressed on both sides, Ivan agreed to continue the truce. Then the wily Pollack pressed too far. He suggested the Czar return Smolensk to Poland, after which he would join us in a Holy War against the infidels. Ivan went into a towering, frightening rage.

"Smolensk!" he shrieked. "That has been Russian territory since before either of us was born! He will rue the day he insulted the Czar of Russia with such a proposal. I shall not only keep every city I now possess, I shall add more from the Kingdom of Poland!"

Not satisfied at having annoyed the Czar with one foolish suggestion, Sigismund officially proclaimed himself Protector of Livonia, ordering us to withdraw our forces at once. This further enraged the Czar, and only increased harassment in the south prevented his taking action during the summer months. Unfortunately, Tartar legions were being mustered and supplied from both the Crimea and by the Sultan, himself.

I led our army against the Tartars that summer, and was assisted in my command by Prince Vishnevetsky, a Lithuanian who had transferred his allegiance to the Czar. . .disgusted, he said, with the feeble promises of a king who seldom put his bragging words into action. At the beginning of our journey I was in a mood to enjoy Vishnevetsky's company. He was young and very witty, full of ribald, vulgar stories about Sigismund and his court. But the man had a manner about him...an underlying slyness that belied his facetious exterior. As time passed I began to grow weary of him, and his superior attitude toward everyone and anything. When we were together he never stopped talking and eventually his accent became an irritation. I knew within myself that all was not well with the Czar, and the few stories which filtered south confirmed this. There were many times when I wished to be alone, when I would have liked to sort out the pieces of news and relate them to my own thoughts. To Vishnevetsky, all life was amusing. While he was careful never to poke fun at the Czar in my presence, I am certain he did this in other circumstances.

While we were chasing the Mussulman hordes across the steppes, Ketler began to take the offensive in Livonia, thus violating his own truce. Expecting Sigismund to fulfill his promises, the Grand Master laid siege to Dorpat and a few other fortresses. Kurbsky was returned to command, and struck back immediately. With Daniel Adashev as his second, Andrew pushed the foolish knights from one castle stronghold to the next. The Grand Master sent plea after plea to the King, begging for assistance that never came.

Kurbsky's victories in the west coincided with ours in the south. I was recalled to Moscow for the celebration, leaving my army under Vishnevetsky's command. There was little more for them to do, other than remain in the region and keep the Tartars from returning. It was the situation I found in the capital that distressed me more than anything else, and this was more a matter of attitude and general atmosphere, I suppose, than any tangible change. Regardless, I was unprepared for what I found. The Czar's summons had not indicated his serious motives for ordering us assembled...the first item of business being his insistence on a new oath of allegiance from all his major nobles and commanders.

Change is always a source of concern; I knew this, but I was uncomfortable with all the subtle, minor differences I noted within the palace—new men in clerical posts, where I had known the incumbents for years—rigid enforcement of all the petty rules about the palace, and new restrictions on one's movements within its confines. Thus a goodly number of familiar faces were missing, the most significant absentee being Sylvester – no cause for tears, of course, in my estimation. Like many others, I was relieved to learn of the Czar's having finally gotten rid of the mad priest. Ivan had been angry with him for his diatribes during Anastasia's illness, and for implying that her death was the result of our wars in the west. He had now been exiled to the farthest, coldest monastery in all the realm – Solovetsky, standing in frigid solitude on an island in the Frozen Sea.

The Czar's wrath had also fallen on Andrei Adashev, who was now in prison in Dorpat, the city where he had last served as governor. Andrei had been found guilty by a boyar court, convicted of several serious crimes. Ivan told me of this himself, and from his expression I was certain he expected some kind of argument. I was surprised at the news, but I did not question his wisdom. I had been disturbed with Andrei, myself, ever since his refusal to take the oath during Ivan's illness. I had liked Adashev personally, but I had never fully trusted him after that episode. Neither, apparently, had the Czar. I might have been tempted, even then, to say something in his defense, but Ivan's words and facial expressions made it clear that I had best keep still.

"The dog!" said the Czar adamantly. "The man I raised from a dung heap! He's failed me when I needed him most. He's opposed me in the council, and he allowed my little heifer to die because he failed to perform his duty by sending doctors and medicines with us. He knew she was ill, but he never liked her. I'm sure he wished her dead!"

I shuddered inwardly to think of Vladya's fate should the Czar ever unearth the true cause of Anastasia's death.

Just before the scheduled assemblage, where all the nobles were to take their new oaths, word arrived of Andrei's death. At this, I must admit a sincere feeling of sadness – and regret. He had been my friend, and the Czar's friend, although he had claimed to place his perception of Russia's welfare above everything else. Some whispered of his having been poisoned, but I think it unlikely. Disappointed as the Czar may have been with his minister, I could not believe he intended for Andrei to die. I had seen that castle at Dorpat, and I knew how easy it would be for a man of Andrei's frail constitution to perish there. Like most German prisons it was very dirty and full of rats. The walls were so poorly constructed they failed to stop the wind, and a prisoner on one of the lower levels was constantly exposed to heavy seepage from the swamps. The cold, foul water was sometimes more than a foot deep on the floors of the dungeon cells.

There was some grumbling among the masses, for to the common people Andrei had been a saint. It had been he who received their petitions, and who had acted in the Czar's name to correct anything he felt unjust. Unlike those of us who knew him, the peasants were unaware of his weaknesses. For instance, there was a rumor at the time of his death that he kept ten lepers in his house, and that he personally washed them every day as an act of humility. This was most certainly untrue, for Andrei was deathly afraid of lepers. Likewise, the alms he distributed, which had caused him to be so beloved of the beggars, had been bounty from the Czar's treasury; distributed by Ivan's order. But such is the way of history and legend. Sorry as I was for the way it had ended, I knew the Czar was right. His decision had been inevitable and fully supported by his boyars.

Among those who came to take the oath was Daniel Adashev, Andrei's brother. I did not know what Ivan intended doing with Daniel – probably nothing, although he would likely never have commanded an army again. But Daniel was young, and not as wise as his brother had been. He made several remarks, mostly when he was drunk, about the unfairness and ingratitude of the Czar. Without trial or further comment – as was his right – Ivan ordered Daniel arrested along with his twelve year old son. A few days later, both were beheaded in the Square of

Executions – an example to others who might question the Czar's divine right and judgment.

Despite the unquestioned propriety of his actions, the necessity of ordering men to their deaths – especially those who had been close to him – all of this weighed heavily on Ivan's mind. He tried to find escape from torment in drink, and in the arms of women brought by several courtiers. Nothing seemed to help. I spoke to him at great length following Daniel's execution, but the Czar was inconsolable. His actions also frightened a number of people, especially Vladya, who suffered from the weight of his mother's guilt. The Czar's cousin found an excuse to leave Moscow as soon as he had completed his oath. He was foolish, I felt, because his only open offense had been at the first oath–taking – something for which the Czar had long since forgiven him. Running away could only cause more suspicion to fall on him, as happened later. At this time there was no discussion of disloyalty, for all of us knew Evdokia was about to bear another child.

The one action Ivan took at this time that I might have questioned was his execution of a certain witch, referred to by many as "Maria Maddalena." Several advisors, Nikita Romanov and Alexi Basmanov among them, had long considered this woman to be an evil influence on Adashev, for she had lived in the servants' quarters behind his *dacha*. In her madness she had loaded her body with chains, mortifying her flesh and making a great display of her supposed holiness. She would sit in the bazaars, clothed in her wretched rags, telling everyone about her fasting and other sacrifices. She was not a virgin, as she was commonly known to be a widow with five sons. She had probably taken up this mockery of asceticism in order to beg more successfully. Whatever evil power she might have exerted over Andrei could only be surmised. I felt certain she was no more than a harmless lunatic.

After listening to his advisors, especially the Romanovs, Ivan decided to have Maria Maddalena burned at the stake. Then, to assure the end of her malevolent lineage, her five sons were executed as well, all of them buried in unhallowed ground. I voiced no open objection, as I did not care one way or the other, but I remained convinced that her only crime was in pretending to be something she was not. And in this there were few of us who should not have shared her punishment.

With the period of official mourning for Anastasia long past, the Czar should have been over the worst of his suffering. Obviously, he was not, as evidenced by the increased executions and his sudden need to drink more heavily than he ever had before, not with a light–hearted enjoyment, but with a morose attitude and heavy depression. He also developed a tremendous craving for food, and began to put on fat until his condition engendered serious concern among those of us who were closest to him. There were many whispered discussions as to what would be best for him, the result of these being our consensus that the best remedy would be for the Czar to marry again. If he could find another wife to fill the void left by Anastasia, perhaps his soul would be at rest.

Because Ivan was more likely to heed my advice, the others elected me spokesman. I was to approach the Czar and persuade him to call another assemblage of maidens. I was not very pleased with the assignment, because I was certain the Czar would refuse. It would be too reminiscent of the ritual he had gone through to find Anastasia. I was also afraid that in his present state of mind, he might expect God to have duplicated her among the assembled girls – assuming that he did take our advice. If the gaggle of females failed to produce another such bride – and how could there be another? – it could well produce a further passionate fit of despair.

But they pushed me into it, and I approached Ivan one morning when he came out of chapel. His eyes were so deep in their blackened sockets it was painful to look at him. Despite his fullness of face, there was a distressing sag to his jaw, and small wrinkles crisscrossed his entire countenance. His skin was dry and sallow; the red beard looked faded and somehow thinner than it should have been. He seemed pleased to see me, and I was invited to break bread with him. Knowing me so well, he may have guessed my mission; I could not be sure. But as we sat together, the Czar broached the subject of marriage on his own, the object of his desire being one I would never have considered.

"I don't know how you have been able to live all these years without a wife, Dmitri," he began. "I know you were not so fortunate as I in the original selection of a bride, but I should think by now you would have chosen another."

"I have thought this myself," I told him, "but each man is different. Some have a greater need for matrimonial ties than others." I watched him carefully, not knowing if I dared push further. For the moment he seemed at peace, munching heartily on a huge slice of black bread. I took a chance and continued. "Some of our closest friends have expressed their concern that perhaps your own needs. . . ."

He laughed, his mouth full of crumbs which he sprayed across the table. "You always think to anticipate me," he boomed lustily. "I *have* thought to wed again," he continued, "and without telling any of you I have sent inquiries to Our brother in Poland." He looked at me expectantly.

I returned his gaze blankly. "Sigismund?" I fumbled. "How could he. . .his sisters?" I asked incredulously.

"Why not one of his sisters? Such a match would do much to reduce the tensions between our nations, and I am told they do not share their brother's unfortunate disposition."

"Aren't they a little. . .er. . .elderly?" I asked.

"I am told that one is less than five–and–twenty," he said. "I sent Pissemsky to look them over and tell me which is the plumpest. If he considers either sister a suitable match, he has my permission to offer a contract of marriage."

This unexpected development completely silenced me, as I am sure Ivan intended it should. I sat there as he continued to laugh at me, and to poke playfully with cutting words, very pleased to have caught me so off guard. It was also a moment of great relief, although I kept this to myself. Whether or not the Czar obtained his desired alliance with the House of Jagellon, the prospect had restored his humor. There was little more I could wish. When I left I asked if I might inform the others, and the Czar merrily granted permission. "Tell them all," he shouted gleefully. "Tell them the Czar will soon end his celibate existence!"

But Ivan's joy was not to be. Sigismund did not reply directly. Instead, he sent one of his most clever ambassadors, a certain Marshal Simkovic. This was a sly, greasy, subtly insulting man, who arrived with a sheaf of proposals. Each of these outlined a different set of conditions under which the King of Poland would permit one of his beloved sisters to marry the Czar of Russia. Pissemsky had selected the older sister, Catherine, as being the most suitable, although he later admitted to me how relieved he was that the Czar never actually set eyes on her. She was considerably older than Sigismund claimed, and was far from attractive. She had bad teeth and an unpleasant odor, but she had been the best of a poor choice. She would also have brought the larger dowry. Fortunately, the Polish demands were so unreasonable as to be insulting. The cheapest price Sigismund would accept required Ivan to relinquish Novgorod and all the Russian lands to the west.

Simkovic remained in Moscow for a full ten days, finally being ordered by the Czar to leave. By this time, he had worked Ivan into a frothing rage. I would gladly have strangled the Pollack with my own hands, for his visit produced exactly the opposite of our desired effect upon the Czar. For days afterward, none of us dared try to speak or reason with him.

It was Simon who finally supplied the answer. Among the Circassian princes who now served the Czar, Simon had befriended a chieftain named Temgryuk, who claimed to have the most beautiful sister in the world. I gave a banquet for Ivan in my home as soon as I could after Simkovic's departure, and I saw to it that the Circassian was seated near the Czar. During the course of the evening, we guided the conversation into proper areas, and Temgryuk began bragging about the beautiful women in his family. The Czar heard him when he started to rave about the charms of his sister.

Soon after this, things moved a little faster than I had expected. Ivan stood up, raised his goblet, and took an oath that if the Circassian's sister was really as beautiful as Temgryuk claimed, he would marry her. So great a beauty, he told us, should be Czarina of all Russia. Everyone laughed, and many lewd comments were shouted at Temgryuk. None of us believed his sister could possibly be as lovely as he claimed – certainly not on the basis of family resemblance.

But the Lord works in strange ways, and time soon proved us wrong. A week or so later, the Circassian presented his sister to the Czar. She entered the audience chamber with her face completely veiled and dressed in the Mussulman custom, for she was still unbaptized. The Czar rose from his throne and descended to her, lifting the draperies with his own hands. I was one of the few who could see her face, as I was seated just a few feet from Ivan's dais. She was extremely lovely – fair skinned with blue eyes, as were many of her race.

Now, by rights, Ivan should have taken her as a concubine. She was not the daughter of an important chieftain, and her rank did not demand the Czar possess her in marriage. But Ivan had given his word. While he had been more than a little drunk when he made the promise, he refused to go back on it. In a very short time the Circassian princess was baptized with the name Maria, after which she was wed to the Czar.

When the ceremony took place, Maria did not speak much Russian, but she acquired the language in an amazingly short time, even learning to read and write. Once she could speak for others to understand, she astounded everyone with her incredible vulgarity. Despite her baptism, her soul was never Christian. She certainly brought none of Anastasia's virtues to the palace. Her one contribution to the tranquillity of the realm seemed to be in the royal bedchamber, where the Czar finally found solace from his unhappiness.

As the political implications of Ivan's second marriage became apparent, I realized he had not acted purely out of lust or in a moment of drunken indiscretion.

Soon after the wedding, Temgryuk was sent home on some fanciful mission for the Czar. Returning to his own country as Ivan's brother–in–law, he naturally spread the story of the mighty Czar of Russia having married his sister. The barbarian Circassians were so flattered by this, they soon began flocking to our banner. Their lands lay between the Cossacks of the Terek, to the south of Astrakhan, and the domains of the Crimean Khan. Thus their alliance was extremely beneficial to us.

Once the Czar was married, I entered into my own period of emptiness and depression. More than ever before, I seriously contemplated taking a wife – and probably would have, had there been a sufficiently exciting possibility. Finally, for lack of something better to do, I made the trip to Novgorod in time for its annual fair. Fortunately for the English, I arrived just after they did. It was my second encounter with Jenkinson, and this time I found him in jail.

A peculiar set of circumstances had led to his incarceration. As Novgorod had been one of the Hanseatic cities before being annexed by Muscovy, it had been allied with the other major cities along the Baltic coast. Even after the annexation, the Czar and the Grand Dukes before him had interfered as little as possible with the local government. This was due to the amount of trade which continued to flourish in Novgorod, resulting in much of our national prosperity. There was a strange kind of electoral system for selecting certain city officials, much like the manner of selecting the Polish King. Although the Czar disliked it, he had not changed anything, mostly due to Adashev's advice. Andrei had always defended the burghers' right to maintain their old customs as long as they did not interfere with the authority of the Czar.

This autonomy had permitted other ancient traditions to prevail in Novgorod, whereby certain foreign merchants were entitled to specific privileges. The rules of seniority were strictly adhered to, with the length of time each group maintained trade ties with the city determining its position of preference within the merchants' community. Of these groups, the Flemish stood the highest, for they had always maintained a lively trade with both Novgorod and Pskov. Ignoring this, the Czar had granted some of the same privileges to the English, thus causing many hard feelings. When Anthony Jenkinson and his party rode into Novgorod, the Flemish merchants made protest against them to the city officials. On the Englishmen's previous trip the Czar had ordered all local governors and other administrators to extend them every courtesy, but there had been no new orders issued since Chancellor's departure. Without instructions to the contrary, the city elders promptly threw the Jenkinson party into prison.

I knew that this failure to reissue the orders had been an oversight on the part of the Czar's clerks, and I quickly set it right. Jenkinson took it all very well, as he had not been in the cell for very long. He seemed less on his guard with me than he had been in Moscow, and eventually we were able to laugh about the incident. We spent quite a bit of time together, in and about Novgorod, finally returning to Moscow in each other's company. Anthony complained that after more than a year's stay in Russia, he was still trying to obtain the Czar's permission to travel through Tartar lands into Persia. I was surprised the English had been so neglected, but soon discovered the fine hands of several Shuisky agents at work in the various bureaus. As soon as possible, I arranged a personal conference for Jenkinson with the Czar.

Ivan was especially interested in learning everything he could about the new Queen of England, questioning Anthony at length regarding her age, appearance, and temperament. He had never forgotten the impressive signatures on those first papers brought by Chancellor, when Queen Mary had been united with the Prince of Spain. Although Ivan was newly married, I knew he was considering the possibility of an alliance. It would be no great problem to put the Circassian aside, as I knew he was already tiring of her coarse humor and complete lack of decorum.

After several visits with the Czar, Jenkinson received permission to depart as soon as spring thaws opened the waterways. As Heinrich was acquainted with the Persian Ambassador, I arranged for Anthony to meet him, which resulted in satisfactory arrangements for his reception once he arrived at his destination.

In the spring, I was also assigned a mission into the steppes. After the several campaigns I had led against the Tartars, I suddenly found myself our most experienced commander when it came to knowing the infidel ways and the areas west of Astrakhan. Ivan received news near the end of winter that the Lord had visited a great pestilence upon the Nogai Horde. In the course of this, they had lost many thousands of their horses. As these barbarians lived largely on the milk of their animals, from which they made a horrible, sour concoction of mold, the loss of the horses resulted in famine. Desperately, the Nogai survivors had gone to the Crimean Khan, Perekop, seeking food. But there was hunger here, too. A severe drought had dried the water holes, resulting in the Crimean Horde's also losing much of their livestock. Taking all this as an omen from God, the Czar authorized an army of some eight thousand men to move against both Hordes, hoping to destroy them once and for all.

As I was to leave at the same time as Jenkinson, I invited him to share my barge. During the intervening weeks, prior to our departure, I assisted Anthony in organizing his party, and Heinrich entertained the English quite lavishly in our home. This gave Jenkinson an opportunity to see how we lived, and to observe our customs as he had been ordered by his Queen. Because I had also been instructed by the Czar to learn what I could of the English, such a close relationship served both purposes.

By the end of April, the ice had melted enough for us to launch our larger galleys. I loaded my troops, and taking Anthony with me in the lead boat, we set our for Kazan. From there we went to Astrakhan, where I parted from the English. They continued south to their wondrous adventures in the infidel lands beyond Bokhara and Samarkand. They were exceedingly brave men, and I wished them well. As their shrinking figures disappeared into the vastness of the steppes, I wondered if I would ever see them again.

But I had little time to think about it. I had requested Basmanov as one of my staff, and it proved an excellent choice. Alexi was no longer young, and as I have previously noted, he was never very quick of mind. But he was always steady in an emergency, and made a fine balance within my group of officers. Most of the others were completely inexperienced youths, sent with me to learn the tactics of fighting the infidel. The Czar had expected it to be a light campaign, which to a large extent it was.

The Tartars were so weak from lack of food and mounts they could not effectively oppose us. Still, when they were cornered, or when they were able to fall upon a small detachment of my army, they fought with the same fierceness and desperation I had seen during the battles for Kazan. I knew of a great many Christian prisoners within the Crimean Horde of Perekop, and it was my intention to free as many as possible. I had also learned of meadows and foothills below the Khanate of the Lesser Nogai, where we could find several vast herds of horses. I wanted to capture these, as the heavy losses of animals in Livonia had considerably raised the price of horseflesh. Both Heinrich and Ivan had urged me to send back as many mounts as possible.

In the first instance, I was not very successful. I sent my army after Tartars as quickly as I could get them unloaded from the boats. As we usually spent several days organizing our troops, I hoped my haste would take the Horde by surprise. I had not foreseen the Tartar determination to prevent their slaves being freed. When my army finally trapped the infidels against the river, they fought us to the death, slaughtering their prisoners before we overran the camp.

As punishment for this, and as an example to the other Mussulman leaders, I publicly executed every ranking Tartar who fell into our hands. At the same time, I offered clemency to those who agreed to surrender. It did no good. I spent most of the summer, well into autumn, chasing scattered bands of infidels through the southern steppes and into the mountains. I was successful in capturing many thousands of horses although most of them were hill ponies, good only as mounts for common soldiers. I began sending them north in groups of five hundred. In all, there were less than two hundred mounts fit for a gentleman to ride, and I shipped these back by water.

By October I had completed as much destruction as I could, and my men were weary from the long hours of hard riding. I sent word to the Czar that my mission was completed, and began to load the army for its return. We were in the midst of this when Jenkinson returned to Astrakhan. He had reached Persia without difficulty, as the ambassador's letters had been honored by the other infidels. His trade had been good, and he brought many things back with him, including an Islamic beauty named Sultana Aura, whose presence during the return trip upset me considerably. I would gladly have bedded her the first night.

With classic English stoicism, Anthony neither touched the girl himself, nor permitted anyone else to do so. In fact, the English were so straightlaced about this sort of thing, I felt guilty at having my own harem girl on board. I asked Anthony why he had brought the wench if he had no intention of using her, and he explained he wished to return to his Queen with this example of infidel beauty. He thought Elizabeth would enjoy having such a picturesque creature about her court. I could not understand the man's reasoning, but he did exactly as he said he would.

We reached Moscow after the first snows, and when the ice was already forming on the rivers. If we had delayed our departure another week, it would have been necessary to unload the galleys and march the last few miles overland. Ivan had been very pleased to receive the horses and other booty we had taken. All of us were sure it would be some time before the Tartars troubled us again. Between the heavy destruction I had caused, and the stand now taken by the Circassians, there was little chance of their being able to raid us in the spring. All in all, it had been a very successful summer.

In the Kremlin, however, the situation was not very happy. Ivan was thoroughly disgusted with his choice of a bride. Despite her skills in the bedchamber, she had begun to annoy him greatly. She refused to remain in the *terem,* although she had been reared in a harem, where the restrictions were much more rigid. Here, she was impressed with her supposed dignity as Czarina.

With the Czar's flagging interest in her, she began seeking elsewhere for solace. I do not know how many men succumbed to her charms, but it was scandalous. Although the Czar pretended not to know, it was impossible for him not to. I suppose he felt it beneath his dignity to make a display of being an outraged husband, nor did I think he really cared. While she committed her petty sins, the Czar was having a number of serious conferences with Jenkinson, preparatory to making a fervent bid for the hand of Queen Elizabeth. The more freedom he allowed the Circassian, the easier it would be to catch her in such guilt there could be no criticism when he cast her aside.

Another matter was pressing on Ivan's mind as well. Ever since he had lost Anastasia, he had been concerned over the need to establish a place of sanctuary, should he ever become the victim of treachery. When he first mentioned this to me, I misunderstood, and fear squeezed tightly about my heart. I was certain he had discovered Euphrosyne's crime and was about to avenge himself on Vladya. But this was not the case at all. Ivan was one of the richest rulers in the world, and if he ever ceased to rule he did not intend to wallow in poverty, or have to rely on the charity of another king. In his first letters to Queen Mary, which had been delivered to her successor, Ivan had proposed an agreement between himself and the Queen of England. If either of them should ever be in need, the other should extend the sanctuary of his realm. Elizabeth's answer had been most gracious, although she had hinted at the necessity of the Czar's providing for his own expenses should he ever avail himself of the agreement. Why Ivan should have felt it necessary to have such a place of refuge, I could not really understand. But somehow, it had become an obsession with him, and he intended to have it.

While aware of Ivan's peculiar anxiety, I thought little about it until he called me to the palace one day near the end of winter. He was sending me to England, he announced, after which he proceeded very calmly to explain how I would go and what I was expected to do. As there had been no previous hint of his intention, I stood facing him in a shock of disbelief, listening without knowing how to answer.

After he had spoken for a long time, I managed to find my tongue. "Are you really going to send me all the way to England?" I gasped.

"You will sail with Jenkinson when he departs this spring," said the Czar. "I am sending Pissemsky as my ambassador, and you will be with him. You will have no official standing, other than as a respected member of my court. That should leave you free to carry out my instructions."

He then continued his description of what I must do. He presented me with a finely carved trunk to be used on the trip. It was large enough to hold almost everything I would need to take. Making sure we were alone, the Czar tripped a concealed spring near the top of one leg, sliding out a long tray hidden in the bottom.

"In here, you will carry a collection of gems," he said. "Because they are small they will not be difficult to transport. Nor will their weight give away their hiding place. When you get to England, you are to sell them and deposit the gold with a reliable banker for my use, should I ever find it necessary to go there."

I still gaped in utter perplexity. How could he place such a responsibility in my hands, I thought. I had no idea how to find a buyer for such a collection, and I knew nothing of the bankers' trade. But I was very excited by the prospect. After listening to him for the better part of the afternoon, I had caught the intensity of his own fervor and told him I would gladly accept his assignment.

"And no one must know!" he cautioned me. "I would rather lose the jewels than have it nosed about that I was concerned with such a negotiation."

"May I discuss it with no one, then?" I asked unhappily.

"Only those with whom you must deal," he said. "I know I can trust you to do what is right. Be sure you tell each person with whom you act no more than he must know to perform whatever it is you wish him to do. Sigismund and Our enemies would make great sport of this if they discovered what we were about."

When I left the palace, I was still dazed. I went home and downed several beakers of vodka before I began to recover my senses. I chased the girls away, for their chatter bothered me when I was trying to think. By chance, Abraham came to the house, bearing messages from Heinrich in Novgorod. I invited the old man to stay and sup with me, which he seemed delighted to do. In the course of the evening, I questioned him to get his advise in handling the assignment Ivan had given me. Or course, I did not tell him I was on any business but my own.

The old man listened to me, his wise face showing no sign that he perceived more than I thought I was telling. It would matter little, anyway, because I knew he could be trusted even if I told him everything. When I finished, he sat silent, mulling over all I had said.

"There are many of my people in the lands of the West," he said at length, "though I know little of this nation you are to visit. Frequently, the Jewish quarter will be a center of banking and other transactions with gold and valuables. You should go to them, and you must use the words I shall teach you. Unless you are very unfortunate, or unless you fail to make a proper judgment of the men with whom you deal, you will be able to accomplish your business without being robbed or otherwise taken advantage of."

He then spent several hours instructing me in the phrases I must know of the Hebrew language. When we had finished, I felt much more confident of my ability to fulfill the Czar's desires.

While there continued to be minor conflicts in Livonia, some involving the niggardly, inconsequential forces sent by the King of Poland, the Czar did not assign me to any military duty. Instead, he had me at the palace almost every day, where I was involved in the councils with his principal ministers. Kurbsky was also called into these, as I think the void left by Adashev was beginning to trouble Ivan. No one had previously realized the enormous quantity of work Andrei had done, or had arranged for various clerks to do. No other individual possessed his knowledge. There was a deluge of petitions, requests for permits, and questions of administrative matters by the local governors. On top of these were the usual visits by delegates of foreign powers, which caused a great deal of work. They also placed Ivan in direct contact with people who had previously been kept away from him. And from all this a strange fact became apparent. Ivan was greatly feared.

For several years, the common people had called him *Ivan Grozny* – the terrible, or the dread. But in this they had referred to the terror he struck in the hearts of his foes: the Tartars, the Poles, and the barbarians who threatened our borders – enemies from whom the Czar had exacted his dues. No one had ever implied that Ivan was to be feared by his own subjects, any more than a properly stern father should be feared by his children. That they would be punished if they transgressed was something to be understood and expected. Unreasoning fear was something else again.

Adashev had never been afraid of Ivan, for like Yuri and Andrew. . .or myself, for that matter, they had grown up together. Each had shared the heart of the other. Now, we discovered, many officials dared not assume any authority which had not been specifically granted by the Czar. Even the officious bureaucrats would handle only routine matters. Any complication was immediately referred to their superiors, who in turn passed it along until the great mass of it came directly before Ivan. Mikhailof brought this to my attention first, and because it amused me I mentioned it to the Czar. I suspected he would be displeased, for he had always enjoyed being called "Ivan the Good." I was wrong.

Officially, he took great pains to reassure those who managed his many bureaus, and told them to look upon him as a loving father. Still the fear persisted, and in hidden, secret ways, the Czar encouraged it – and enjoyed it. He was the true autocrat of Russia, a man whose glance could wither, whose displeasure could destroy. He took time to explain this to me, and I understood the wisdom of his attitude. The strength of our nation lay with its Czar, on whose authority all order and progress depended.

My other duties during these months prior to departure concerned my projected traveling companions. The Czar assigned me to the English, my task to assure their receiving whatever they needed from the clerks. Feodor Pissemsky, who was to be our ambassador, also spent time with them. His particular concern was to learn all he could of their language.

A few weeks before we were to leave, there was a great furor over a Pollack insult. As its gross character would surely result in war, I was on the verge of asking to remain. Having missed their opportunity for an alliance, the Poles now attempted to humiliate the Czar by an incredibly crude jest. As a belated wedding gift, their king sent Ivan a white mare. . .a sway–backed, decrepit animal, not fit to pull a plow. This gift had no sooner arrived than we received word of further Polish forces being sent into Livonia. However, these troops did not join with the armies of the Grand Master. Instead, they simply occupied certain territories along the Lithuanian border. The King's greed was thus proclaimed. He was attempting to seize what he could under the pretense of defending Livonia.

Ivan was greatly angered, his final irritation being the news that Catherine, the wife denied him by Sigismund, had been betrothed to John of Finland, heir to the throne of Sweden. Ivan could brook no further insults from Sigismund, whom he now hated with unabated passion. Because the troops sent to Livonia had actually been Lithuanian, Ivan declared war against the Grand Duchy of Lithuania. He did not declare war on Poland, itself. He thus placed Sigismund in a most awkward position. Separately holding both titles – King of Poland and Grand Duke of Lithuania – Sigismund was not free to use the forces of one nation in a war involving only the other. And the Polish barons had no desire to fight us. When the Czar made it clear he did not wish to engage Poland, he nearly placed Sigismund in checkmate.

While the Polish–Lithuanian nobles milled about the King–Duke–Buffoon in argument and confusion, Ivan fielded an enormous army – more than two hundred thousand men. As a declaration of his intent, the Czar sent a brief note to Sigismund, informing him of a hole, dug in the Kremlin court. "It is large enough to accommodate Your Grace's Head," Ivan wrote.

I watched with burning envy from the Kremlin wall as the Czar moved out with his huge host. The commands had gone largely to Tartars, and in fact the composition of troops was more eastern than any army assembled in the past. John Mstislavsky and Peter Shuisky were in command of the largest contingents of Russian troops. Kurbsky acted as supreme commander, under the direct supervision of the Czar and Vorotinsky. But included among the senior generals were Shig Ali and the Czar's brother–in–law, Michael Temgryuk. Under them were such names as Bekbulat, Kaibula, and Ibak.

Looking forward with great expectancy to my English voyage, my hands still trembled for the heft of a sword. Heinrich was attached to the Czar's staff, and watching him ride off was the hardest of all. He was mounted on Gabriel, for I had insisted he should use him. This made it easy to follow his progress in the mass of darker colors. I stood there watching until the last rider had vanished across the snow, and the army had faded into the forests along the western highway.

Ivan had ordered us to depart for England as soon as the winter broke, regardless of whether he had returned. For this reason I did not see the Czar again before I left. Each day I waited anxiously for news, hoping the conflict would be resolved before I started north. Sigismund had put an army of thirty or forty thousand men into the field, commanded by his cousin Radziwell. Neither the army nor the commander were any match for us. Word soon reached the capital that the stronghold of Polotsk had fallen. If the Czar could take this, he could conquer the entire land.

Reports began to arrive, telling how the entire Lithuanian army had fled, commanders leading the terrified troops in their flight. Our spies in the Crimea sent word of envoys arriving from Sigismund, urging the Khan to attack us from the south while the great army was occupied in Lithuania. I laughed at Sigismund's desperate pleas. After the destruction I had wrought only a few months before, the Tartars would be hard pressed to place ten thousand men in the field. Adding some of my comments in the margin, I sent the messages along to Ivan.

Now a huge stream of booty poured into the capital. Sleigh after sleigh arrived, laden with gold and the treasures from Lithuanian noble homes. Slaves, too, were brought in large numbers. The Czar wrote me, gleefully boasting about the addition of "Grand Duke of Polotsk" to his growing list of titles. As the war progressed, a number of clerics were requested from the front, for the numerous Roman Churches all needed reconstruction and new priests to conduct Orthodox services.

To the very eve of my departure, we continued to receive news and stories of our glorious victories. It was on this last night that Temgryuk returned, bringing many details of the battles. He bore a huge, jeweled cross, taken from the cathedral at Polotsk, as a gift for the Metropolitan. He was very friendly with me, of course, because he know I had been instrumental in bringing his sister to the Czar's attention. In confidence, he assured me I need not be overly concerned at not being involved in the fighting, as the Czar was wearying of the war and was favorably considering Sigismund's overtures for peace. Thoroughly enjoying the triumph, Ivan had demanded the person of the King's sister, Catherine, as hostage, although she was now married to the Duke of Finland.

So I spent my last night in Moscow, drinking with Temgryuk and his sister. The Czarina made bold to wander through the entire palace while the Czar was not present to chastise her. She sat with us in the banquet hall, where we were mostly attended by Tartars and other barbarians. She was several months pregnant, her belly protruding as if she carried a young calf, but she still possessed the passion of a wild beast, and that evening, she directed her attentions at me.

Had I been sober enough to consider the possible consequences, I would not have refused her as coldly as I did. The fury of a woman's heart can sometimes be deadly. But she was in such gross disfavor with the Czar, her word should have made little difference. She ended the evening in her apartments with two or three young officers who had returned with her brother. She was disgusting! I sincerely hoped she would be in a convent before I returned.

The next morning I began the northward trek with Pissemsky and our English companions. I looked back fondly at Moscow as it glittered in the bright morning sunlight; a great, powerful giant, just awakening from its slumbers. I always missed the city when I had to be away for long periods, and it now assumed an especially endearing attraction as I realized how terribly far I was going from home.

Interlude

The Blue Stone

CHAPTER ONE

The sight of land at last! Like the promise of salvation, a faint mist hovered upon the horizon, and within its nebulous mass I could see the solid line of earth. Beneath my feet, the slimy deck still pitched in all directions. Choppy waves slapped against the hull, while a stinking lixivium churned and slopped within the bilge.

I had long since surrendered any romantic sense of adventure; my eager anticipation had faded after the first few days aboard the great ship. Although my English companions had assured me that our trip had been unusually quick and uneventful, their words only served to emphasize how thoroughly wretched a sailor's life must be. Strangely enough, I was never really sick – never sick enough to vomit up the horrible, queasy lack of ease within my guts. Instead, I spent the entire voyage with a lump pressing inside my stomach, wishing I could have one, good, solid spell of being honestly and completely ill.

The ship was smaller than I had originally expected, and without its towering masts it would not have been much larger than the river boats with which I was familiar. My greatest discomfort, I think, was in never being completely dry. After a time, one became used to the stench from the holds, and the complete lack of privacy. Even the boredom – days on end with nothing to do – was something a man could grow accustomed to. But whenever I dressed in the morning, it was like putting on clothes from a battle the day before, still damp with sweat and sour from the fear of death. And, of course, there had been genuine fear aboard the ship, for there was no way to avoid the stormy seas in making this northern passage. It took so long to traverse these vast distances that no matter when one started his voyage it was impossible to avoid the winter weather.

We approached the shores of England during the fifth year of the reign of the Great Queen. Standing at the rail while our ship was guided up the Thames to London, Pissemsky and I were both seized by the unfounded dread one experiences when he is about to become a foreigner in a strange land. Watching the buildings glide past us along the shore, this feeling could only be emphasized by the peculiar architecture – the cold, gray facades of the city. At this distance one could observe only the majesty of mighty structures and overall a forbidding orderliness. That London's sounds, like its odors, would not vary greatly from any other large city, we could not yet observe. The few shouts and answers which crackled across the waters seemed harsh and alien to our ears.

Pissemsky gripped the railing with both hands, hunched his slender shoulders as he stared at the moving shoreline. "I am glad you have come with me," he muttered. He seemed unable to rip his gaze from the fantastic collection of huge buildings now coming into our view.

It was near the end of April, for we had made an exceptionally quick passage – a bare eight months. Yet the weather was warm. We were standing on deck without our heavy coats, and while I sensed a tremor through my companion's body, I knew it was not a response to the chill.

"That people from so warm a land should be so frigid in their discourses. It disquiets me," he remarked.

"I think you may find greater frivolity at the Queen's court," I said.

From conversations I had heard among the crew, I was convinced that the reserved demeanor of Jenkinson and his friend, Fletcher, must not characterize all Englishmen. Still, except for the low born servants and crewmen, they were out–wardly a sober lot, at least when they knew we could observe them. Once, however, when Fletcher referred to their Virgin Queen, I had imagined I detected a slight twinkle about his eyes. It was from a series of such subtle clues that I garnered a ray of hope.

Pissemsky finally turned his back on the city and leaned against the rail. "Have you decided not to separate yourself from the rest of us?" he asked suddenly.

"I don't understand," I answered innocently.

"I would be a poor ambassador," he replied, "if I could not perceive that the Czar has entrusted some mission to you. I am not asking you to violate a confidence; but whatever you need to tell me, you may be sure it will go no farther."

I frowned, and he added quickly, "Our basic assignments are the same, Dmitri – to carry out the Czar's desires. I only mean to offer my assistance, if there is some way this can be accomplished without compromising your instructions."

"I think it best I simply remain with the rest of you until I know my way around," I said. "What I have to do need not be done immediately, and I doubt it will ever require my leaving the group – at least not for any extended period." Watching his face, I realized my decision had not pleased him. Feodor was the accredited ambassador of the Czar, but my position in our own court far exceeded his. As long as I stayed with him, many people would defer to me. In the end, it could undermine his authority.

He twisted his mouth thoughtfully. "I shall not trespass upon your judgment. You will do as you think best, in any event. Just remember, you have no need to fear an indiscretion on my part, if you find that I can help you."

I thanked him, and we returned our attention to the city. The rest of our little group was on the lower deck, also watching the strange land slip past. We were only five, in all, as there had been no accommodation on the ship for servants. In addition to Pissemsky and myself, we had two clerks and a priest, Father Thomas. The clerks were of lesser backgrounds, one from the Bureau of Secret Affairs, the other from Mikhailof's secretariat staff. I did not care for either of them, and we had had little contact during the voyage. I found Father Thomas pleasant, though perhaps a little dull. He had been sick during much of the trip so I had not seen a great deal of him. As a former chaplain with my army in the south, he was inured to the discomforts of travel. He had suffered in silence and without complaint. When well enough to perform his duties, he had seemed a good and Godly man.

Our ship was nearing the wharf now, and the shouts from men in the small boats were being answered by others standing along the shore. Despite the fabled amount of commerce in and out of these London docks, our arrival had attracted a crowd. Workmen and clerks and a number of immodestly dressed women stood facing us on the wood planks, laughing and calling out to the sailors who eased the ship into its berth. These sounds of levity were mingled with the cadence of hammers and saws and other, unidentified evidences of industry from all along the shore. I must admit to a feeling of awe as I glanced up and down the river, surveying the forest of masts and rigging that seemed to extend for many miles.

I soon became aware of a sour stench, which grew stronger as we approached the dock, a rather brackish essence, well matched to the inky surfaces of the water. In my own thoughts, I kept comparing the strength of the Czar's landlocked armies with the potential power of this seagoing nation. In such considerations lay the greatest proof of Ivan's wisdom in seeking to provide his merchants with year–round ports and to seek an alliance with the Great Queen.

We were soon able to hear a murmur of voices from the waiting crowd, and to identify the words of individual speech. Mostly people from the laboring classes, they enunciated their English syllables with a peculiar accent, very different from the aristocratic adventurers who had visited Moscow. Still, their manner of speaking was not completely new to me, for many members of the crew spoke the same way.

Pissemsky had wandered off, down the few steps to the larger deck, where men were already preparing to unload the cargo. Watching him, I began mulling over his offer of assistance. I knew it was genuine, although a bit pompous. I also knew my baggage had been rifled during the voyage. I had said nothing about it, and it could have been a crewman – or even one of our clerks. Yet a crewman would likely have stolen something. It must have been one of our group, I reasoned – probably that clerk from the Third Bureau. Whether he was responsible to Pissemsky or not, I had no way to know. But the false bottom on my trunk had gone unnoticed; of this I was certain, so no one could suspect the huge fortune I carried.

I think I did very well during the unloading, for I managed to hide my anxiety as the trunk was hoisted from the deck on the backs of two strong men and borne to a waiting carriage. Had it been dropped, it could have spewed gems all over the dock, causing an unprecedented furor.

Pissemsky went down the gangplank with Jenkinson; Fletcher followed them, then stood looking back, apparently waiting for me. While his action was merely a gesture of courtesy, it called unwanted attention upon me. My status was supposed to be unofficial and unobtrusive. Instead, I was being treated from this first moment as if I were a second ambassador.

Fletcher, protective now that we were in his own land, took hold of my elbow as I started to cover the last few feet of planking. There was no rail, so perhaps his action was justified. However, I discouraged him. "I'm all right," I said, pulling a little ahead, just enough that I did slip on the damp wood. I thus made a very ungraceful entrance into England, stepping onto her shores by one hand and a foot.

"Lesson number one," Fletcher chortled. "Never refuse a helping hand."

"I apologize," I replied, "and I shall profit by your instruction." This was said lightly, but within my mind the thoughts were more serious. The offer of a helping hand which concerned me was not Fletcher's; it was the earlier suggestion from my colleague.

I really need not have worried, as things turned out. Pissemsky was soon so involved in rituals and conferences at the royal palace he hardly had time to tell me about his own doings, much less question me about mine. Our English traveling companions spent the next few days helping us to get settled. A house had been provided – we thought, by the government. But we were surprised to discover that the parsimonious Queen of England did not intend to pay our rent! In Pissemsky's absence, I negotiated with the landlord, a middle–aged merchant gentleman who made his living largely in rental properties. I had almost turned him over to one of the clerks, whose English was good enough to handle the transactions, then decided to do it myself. I was later glad I had, as the man was a fund of information. Some of the things I learned caused me to form a much different picture of England. The most outstanding impression I retained of our landlord was his very casual way of discussing the Queen. He willingly related very intimate details and gossip about her personal habits: her supposed love affair with her Master of the Horse, and the suspicion that his first wife had recently been murdered to leave him free for whatever might be desired of him in the future. Shocking comments, especially to a foreigner! In fact, the man was so open with his treasonous suggestions I wondered if he might have been a plant.

The day after we arrived, Jenkinson made a tour of the city with me, borrowing a carriage and horses from the royal stables. This caused my first view of London to be from a strangely warped viewpoint. People on the street were at least as interested in me as I was in them. We were accompanied on our ride by Father Thomas, more than ever the retiring, scholarly cleric, for he had yet to acquire any knowledge of the language. He was not one to intrude where he was unwanted, anyway, so there were times I almost forgot he was with us. Had Ivan sent someone like Sylvester, it would have greatly upset our entire group – and might well have compromised my mission.

In trying to see the city, we found our robes always attracted attention, making it difficult to step out of the carriage without a flock of people gathering about to stare at us. Much to Father Thomas's chagrin, the garb of an Orthodox priest provoked even more comment than my attire. For this reason, I am certain he heaved a sigh of relief when I decided to remain in the house until I could get some English clothes.

Our clerks cared nothing for people's stares, and having little to do in the first days, they probably saw more of the city than I. They went out every day on foot, returning home full of drink and impressions by nightfall. I did not question them, though they may have learned some things that could be useful to me. I was more concerned that they not dwell on my reasons for being in London.

I was secretly glad when Jenkinson left, for it allowed me the freedom I needed. He had remained out of friendship – or duty, or possibly both. But he had a family some hundred miles away, and he had not seen them in over three years. Trying to be a good host, he took up so much of my time I could not get any inquiries started. Then, when he finally left, I found Pissemsky was having difficulties.

It was not long before the ambassador's generous offer of assistance to me became, instead, a desperate cry for help. He had been granted one audience with the Queen, had been through two sessions with her ministers, and things were definitely not going well. Now Fletcher and Jenkinson had left London to visit their families, we were without our only friends. This left us like orphan children in a strange household.

And as for humor – whereas I had hoped to find a break in the stoic demeanor of our English associates, we now suffered from an over abundance of British levity. First, Pissemsky was dubbed with an unfortunate nickname. This type of humor was common among them; but to an Imperial ambassador it was distressing, to say the least. Although I had tried to persuade Feodor to use an interpreter, he proudly insisted on trying to carry out his own discourses in this unfamiliar tongue. It made him appear a complete buffoon. Because a Russian accent was new to these gentlemen of the court, they found the ambassador's outlandish grammar and unique mispronunciations extremely funny. As can often happen when a man speaks a foreign language badly, Pissemsky, who was a most intelligent, sober man in Russian, sounded like a dolt in English.

At first, I think he was embarrassed to come to me. He, too, remembered our conversation that last day aboard ship. Finally, it became nearly impossible for him to continue his work, and he had no place else to turn. Almost at the point of shedding tears and renting his garments, he explained to me everything that had happened. What should he do, he asked.

I knew he had mixed feelings in requesting anything from me. He feared my possible usurpation of his position and dignity, but he was attaining neither by his own efforts. Finally, he asked that I accompany him to his next conference, scheduled for the morrow. It was then I began to have my own doubts. The less attention I attracted the better, I felt, at least until I had finished by chore. Now, after being in London only a few days, I had discovered another disturbing fact. The Queen was poor! It was hard to believe, but I had been informed by several reliable people, including our landlord. The royal treasury was nearly empty. Nor was this just a temporary state of affairs; it was apparently a situation old enough to be traditional to the English crown. If the agents of a bankrupt monarch were to discover such a fortune as mine existing in her realm, and this in the hands of a foreigner who was not even an accredited ambassador! The very prospect terrified me, and I wished I could discuss it with Pissemsky. But that was out of the question.

As I listened to him, though, and sifted his words through my own thoughts, I began to realize his request was, in itself, the very justification I needed for helping him. If I went with our ambassador to the palace, and entered into discussions with the English ministers, I would thereby assume a certain diplomatic status. Then, if I should be discovered in the act of transporting the treasure, it would place the Queen in a difficult position to do anything about it. I became so engrossed in my own thoughts I did not realize Pissemsky had stopped talking.

"In the name of Our Most Holy Father, Dmitri," he shouted, "are you paying any attention at all to what I am trying to tell you?"

"Yes, calm down, my friend," I said soothingly. "General Demetrius has decided to help defend your posterior."

"You have?" he asked in surprise.

"Well, isn't that what you wanted?"

"Yes. Yes, of course, but I didn't think – You mean, when you say 'help,' you are coming with me tomorrow?"

"Not only that," I said, very pleased with myself, "I am going to strike a heavy blow for your mission." I struck him square in the chest with my finger. "And for *my* mission as well," I finished. "What do you think of that?"

"I only hope they don't laugh at your speech, too," he sighed.

"If they do," I said, "I shall simply start speaking in German, and they will have to get someone to translate it. Then I'll switch to Polish, or maybe Swedish. By the time I get through with them they'll be relieved to hear even butchered English from me," I laughed.

Gradually, Pissemsky's sour, tortured grimace melted into a grin. I stood up and patted his shoulder. "Let's betake ourselves into London for a taste of their local wine, friend Feodor," I said. "I've discovered a very fine tavern not far from our front door."

He looked at me uncertainly; in his heart he was probably saying "No." Feodor was a little older than I, slender and already gray. A clerk at heart, he had little adventure in his soul. "Come on," I urged. "There is no better way to learn a language than in a native tavern."

He came.

Our appointment at the palace was for the following afternoon. In preparation for this, I took the first of several blundering, innocent appearing steps, that nearly put an early end to my English adventure. I had heard of a very fine barber, a man much in vogue with many gentlemen of the court. By sending a small bribe, I was able to secure his services for the morning, as I was anxious to appear my best. I tried to tell him this, but unfortunately he was a Frenchman, and his knowledge of English was extremely limited. That, combined with my own accent, led to an unfortunate misunderstanding. I allowed him to start to work, not realizing that my instructions had been seriously misinterpreted. When he had finished cutting my hair, he washed it, and began packing my face and neck with hot towels. Still being a bit tired from my previous night's activities, I fell asleep as he worked on me. When I awoke, my beard was gone!

The barber had tapped me gently on the shoulder when he finished, and proudly held up a mirror that I could survey his handiwork. I could only stare for several seconds. First, there was frozen disbelief; then I shouted in horror.

"Oh Merciful God, forgive me!" I think that was what I screamed. My shock was akin to a man recovering from battle wounds, coming back to his senses to discover an arm is missing. I shrieked in such dreadful helplessness that Pissemsky came running, certain the barber had turned assassin, and I had just caught him trying to slit my throat. Instead, the poor man stood white and trembling against the wall, not knowing exactly what he had done wrong. Naturally, everything I said had been in Russian.

Pissemsky also stared for a few moments before he could react. The he started to laugh. "Like a sheared sheep!" he hooted. "Ha, ha, ha. . .face as smooth as a maiden's breast!"

"What am I going to do?" I bawled at him. "I can't go to the palace like this!" I grabbed the mirror back from the barber. I looked at my face again, hoping, I suppose, to see a few hairs beginning to sprout.

But my remark had sobered Pissemsky. "What do you mean, 'you can't go?' You must go!"

"I'd as soon enter the house of God without my hose," I replied.

"Don't be ridiculous, Dmitri," he cajoled. "This is England, not Russia. Many men go about with shaven faces. Half the men at court wear no beards, especially the younger men – men your age."

"What do you mean, `younger men?'" I shouted desperately. "I am over thirty years old! I can't go out in public without a beard, any more than I could walk the streets stark naked. Besides, it's a mortal sin!"

As we had continued to holler at each other in Russian we so badly frightened the barber that he slipped away unnoticed, leaving most of his equipment behind. He never did come back for it; but he spread the tale about the palace. In retrospect, he had been able to figure out what had happened. This made me the object of some humorous remarks; but mostly, I became an item of curiosity. Everyone, it seemed, wanted to see a Russian without his beard. More than this, it greatly enhanced my ability to attract the English ladies. They were much less modest than our women, and were permitted to associate freely with men, displaying their bodies in quite revealing dresses. In all humility, I must admit that the loss of my beard made a striking improvement in my appearance – at least by western standards.

In the end, I finally weakened and went with Pissemsky. This proved the second step on my road to near disaster; nor was my beardless appearance as terrible an experience as I had expected. The English do not share our beliefs or reasons for wearing a beard. It is not commanded by their Church, nor do they maintain that decency, alone, should dictate it. In Russia, a man without a beard is not properly masculine. He appears foppish and effeminate. It is said the sight of a beardless man will give rise to improper thoughts in other men, for the shaved appearance is too like a woman. In England, however, many ladies – including the Queen – seemed to enjoy the company of such unmanly men. On my first trip to the palace, I was made almost painfully aware of this.

Pissemsky and I had been in our meeting for only a short while, seated about a long, rectangular table with several of the Queen's ministers. Suddenly, with no warning or announcement, Her Majesty stormed into the room in her riding costume! She had just been informed of some misdeed by one of her servants, and her fury would not wait on propriety.

I had already been standing when she entered, for I was speaking to the group, trying to explain our need for English arms in the war against Sigismund of Poland. At first, Elizabeth hardly noticed anyone except the unfortunate minister she had come after. She broke into my discourse with a flood of angry words. Everyone had jumped to his feet when she entered, and they stood uncomfortably while she spoke. Her own words seemed to increase her anger, and she finally began to harangue the whole group. Her eyes traveled from one to another, until they reached me. Here, she stopped.

"Who is this?" she asked, pointing her finger in my direction.

I bowed to Her Grace; and Lord Cecil, who was never daunted by any adversity replied calmly: "Madam, may I present General Prince Demetrius Marensky, emissary of His Majesty, the Czar."

"You may indeed," she said, but her tone was still cold. She acknowledged my bow, and after a few more angry cuts at her ministers she left. I think she had not realized there would be foreigners with them, and it embarrassed her that we should have witnessed the royal outburst. After her departure we tried to continue the meeting, but the mood was shattered and we accomplished very little. Lord Cecil suggested we adjourn until the following day.

To fully appreciate what happened next, one must understand a little about this woman who was the Queen of England. She was about thirty years of age at this time, and while her greatest pride was supposed to have been her virgin condition, it was rumored – even by people who should not have said such things – that her purity was more fantasy than actual fact. The Queen was then, and for two or three years previous, supposed to have been having an affair with one of her lords. This was an effeminate fellow named Robert – or "Robin" – Dudley, later the Earl of Leicester. On that day when I first encountered the Queen, Dudley was also present, for he was one of Her Majesty's most trusted advisors. Although I think Lord Cecil frequently overruled Dudley's suggestions, he being the ranking member of the inner council, a queen's lover has certain obvious advantages in getting his ideas heard. Dudley was surely accustomed to doing this.

As a queen, Elizabeth struck me from the start as magnificent. She was stately, both in physical bearing and in her very regal attitude toward everyone around her. In this respect she was a handsome creature. As a woman, she left considerable to be desired. Her face was certainly not pretty, and her complexion was very bad – much too rough and ruddy for proper feminine charm. Her figure was ample, but not in a truly buxom sense. I suspect that beneath her flaring skirts was a pair of rather skinny legs. It was also rumored she was bald, but of this I have no personal knowledge. She was tall, domineering, and possessed of an iron will – all excellent qualities for a queen. But they are unfortunate disasters for a woman.

Some two days after this first meeting a liveried messenger appeared at our house and delivered a letter to me. He had refused to give it into any hands but mine. He did not wear the colors of the royal household, and whose they were I did not immediately recognize. I learned later that he was in the service of a family whose eldest daughter was one of the Queen's ladies–in–waiting. The letter contained an invitation for me to attend upon this lady that evening. It further requested that I return my answer via the bearer.

I went to Pissemsky and asked him if he knew who the lady was. Feodor thought a moment, then told me he believed her to be the small, auburn–haired girl who was always in such close attendance upon Her Majesty. Considering myself fortunate to have received such an invitation, I sent an affirmative answer back with the servant. That was step three on the road to near destruction, for when the fellow returned that evening to guide me, it was not the lady–in–waiting, but the Queen herself to whom I was taken.

Her majesty was dressed in a beautiful gown of pink and lavender, split at the waist to reveal a swath of lighter fabric, all stitched with gems and intricate embroidery. I felt her costume might better have been worn by a woman of tenderer years, but it was, nonetheless, well suited to her form. Before reaching the door I had become suspicious; there would have been no reason for such stealth in a simple liaison with a lady of the court. With this much forewarning of the possibility, I think I was quite poised during the exchange of greetings.

There was a light supper on the sideboard, and a small round table set for two. It was in no way an ostentatious display; the knives were only silver handled, and the plates of base metal, obviously of domestic manufacture. My eyes took in as much as they could, and the Queen followed my every move. It also occurred to me that she might have someone watching us.

"We are completely alone," she said as if reading my thoughts. "Pray seat yourself."

If I could have, I would have feigned an ignorance of the language. But I sat down as she directed, and trying not to evidence my nervousness, I asked her of what service I might be.

"Service?" she asked. "Surely, even a beardless Russian should surmise the implications." There was a glint of levity in her tone, but I must confess to being more distraught than my outward appearance would indicate. I could not appreciate whatever humor there may have been in her remark. In my own conceit, I was certain I had been summoned as a stallion to a mare, and if Elizabeth should ever wed the Czar – I shuddered at the thought.

"Being closely associated with another head of state, Madam, I can appreciate the delicacy of some special matters," I responded stiffly. At the moment, my feelings must have been quite similar to those experienced by the young virgins whom Adashev had brought to Ivan's bedchamber.

"You are very glib for one not brought up to speak our language," she said, sitting next to me on the couch. She was teasing me, although I did not realize it. However, to do her justice, she remained a good arm's length away.

"I enjoy learning languages," I told her. "It permits one many more opportunities to acquire knowledge."

"You are a scholar, then?"

"Only of languages, I fear."

"And what languages do you speak?" she asked, smiling.

"Several dialects of my own Russian, German, Polish, and a little Swedish," I replied. "I can also make myself understood in some of the infidel tongues."

She watched me for a few more moments. She seemed like a cat toying with an insect, and I began to realize it was something else she wanted.

"Why do you think I brought you here?" she asked suddenly.

Taking a great chance, I answered, "I would like to believe it was for myself, but I think my first assumption must have been correct; you have a matter of business to discuss with me."

"Not exactly business," she sighed, and again she paused. It appeared she was now uncertain. She stood, motioning for me to remain seated. She brushed past me, her fingers barely touching my shoulders, and I must admit a tremor passed through my body. "You know, of course," she continued at last, "that your Czar has done me the honor to . . . make inquiries, regarding the possibility of . . . a marriage."

"I know the Czar would receive no news more gladly than Your Grace's consent to such a match," I replied hopefully.

She cleared her throat; it was a significant gesture, and a slight blush deepened her already ruddy complexion. "Tell me," she went on hesitatingly, "is it true that you are . . . kin to your Czar?"

It was now my turn to blush, and I was still trying to decide how to word my response when she suddenly dropped down beside me again, and smiled as if divulging a confidence. "I know the stories surrounding your birth," she said pleasantly, "and far from being the detriment you probably feel it to be, let me remind you that it can be a . . . a kindred thing."

She was trying to tell me we were both bastards, I thought, and the idea made me chuckle. I almost expressed my feelings, but restrained so presumptuous a remark. Still, the suggestion had been made and we both started laughing merrily, the tension melting away with our levity.

"Your . . . brother, the Czar," she began at length. "Is there a family resemblance? I know my ambassadors say not, yet brothers must somehow share a few features."

"It is rumored," I said, "that my illegitimacy extends even further than Your Grace would know."

Her laughter stopped abruptly; she stared, then hugged herself in a convulsive peal of mirth. "I think we will be able to speak quite frankly, you and I," she said.

"Nothing would please me . . . or my Czar, more than that," I told her. I was now a little disconcerted by her directness.

Abruptly, she controlled her laughter and looked at me more seriously. "I have not the slightest intention of contracting marriage with your Czar," she said, almost sharply. "At least, not just yet."

"I beg Your Grace's pardon," I began, "but from Your. . . ."

"That need not concern you, Demetrius," she went on. "Understand, I am not so poor a statesman as to tell you this, if I were not perfectly confident you will never repeat it to your Czar. No, no," she said, lifting her finger to silence me. "Do not protest my words, for I know more of your Czar Ivan than you may realize. Were you to take such news to him, even you could well face his wrath. And if that were not sufficient deterrent, then I many count upon your loyalty not to wound his pride. In either way, my confidence is safe with you." She continued watching me.

"Your Grace is probably correct," I replied feebly.

"Good; we may proceed." She described at some length her desires regarding the commercial treaties, showing an amazing business head for a woman. I saw the merits of her ideas, and expressed agreement. Then she broached another subject.

"It puzzles my advisors that you have come to England," she said, "for they are aware of this unique relationship you bear to your master." She paused, obviously expecting an answer.

"I wished to see your country," I replied evasively.

"That hardly seems adequate reason for a first-rate general to be absent from the realm in time of war," she countered softly.

I shrugged. "We seem always to be at war," I replied. "Besides, I am more a merchant than a general."

"Are you seeking, then, to establish trade contacts on your own?"

"That would be most improper," I said, begging the question as my feelings of discomfort crept back. "I am not trying to be evasive, Madam, but both the Czar and my stepfather have great hopes for a successful trade with your nation. For this reason, it is important to understand all we can about England."

"And your Czar shares this interest?"

"I can assure Your Grace there is no person in all Russia who is more interested in learning about England and the West."

"Are you aware of any other . . . er, personal requests made by your Czar to me?" she asked suddenly.

I knew she had to refer to Ivan's request for sanctuary, should he ever require it. Discussing this would come too close to my own reason for being there. "I have been instructed not to discuss it," I answered in the same blunt tone as she had used. Then smiling, I added: "You see, Madam, I am being most honest. When I may not speak, I say this openly. I make no attempt at subterfuge."

"You are so disarming, I could almost believe you," she said. "Except that my envoys to Russia seem to feel you handled them very cleverly, and allowed them to believe what was convenient for you – or your Czar – to have them believe."

"I have always tried to do my duty," I said.

The Queen rose, which meant I must also. "I truly wish, Demetrius, that you were English." She led me to the sideboard without attempting a further explanation of her comment, and insisted that I partake of some food. We each ate a bit of meat and drank a glass of white Spanish wine. "If you are uncomfortable and wish to leave," she said, "I shall not insist on your remaining."

"I would leave only if Your Grace desires," I replied.

"Then know that Her Grace would enjoy your company a while longer," she told me. "Do you find Our realm as you expected?"

I told her it was far different from my expectations, and we discussed my impressions, some of which seemed greatly to amuse her. I stayed another hour or so, and when it came time to leave I realized I had thoroughly enjoyed her company. But we had spoken of so many different things, I was still not really sure why she had sent for me. Whatever she had wished to discover, she apparently had; or at least she had satisfied herself as far as I would permit.

Elizabeth was a remarkable woman, and she seemed as interested in learning what she could of Russia as Ivan had been in discovering the essence of her land when he questioned the English visitors. I realized that to some extent I was in the same position as they had been, and yet there was something else. One would have had to know the Great Queen much better than I to estimate her motives for many things she did. Whether she had actually intended an affair and changed her mind, possibly fearing my refusal, I did not know. But I doubted it. Perhaps there had been some scrap of information I could give. The only certain thought I had when I left her presence was that she could not have perceived the real reason for my being in England. I hoped her spies were not going to be overly active in watching me.

It had been dark when I arrived, and it was pitch black outside as I left. The messenger who had brought me waited at the foot of the stairs, and escorted me to a carriage. We rode through the twisting streets of London, stopping a few blocks away from the house. We walked the rest of the way. Several times I thought I heard footfalls and rustling sounds as we covered the final distance, but we were not molested and I finally ascribed the impression to imagination, or perhaps some intemperate Englishman staggering home under cover of darkness.

Pissemsky had already retired, so I went directly to bed. I could not sleep, as the thoughts of the day – and most particularly the evening – kept running through my head. It must have been God's will, for this restlessness saved my life. Through the dark stillness of the house I heard a slight tinkle of breaking glass. It came from somewhere downstairs, about an hour after I had put out my light. I lay very still, listening. After a few moments there was a definite creak, as of a floor board.

Immediately, I was up and moved on bare feet to the rack where my sword was hanging. I had also purchased a brace of pistols since my arrival, and I pulled one of them from its case. I quietly put my bedroom door slightly ajar and peered through the crack into the gloom of the hallway. A dim night light burned at the far end, and I could just make out the head of the stairs. Soon there was a dim form moving toward me. I waited, and saw a second; but there did not appear to be any more. When the first man was at my door, I flattened myself against the wall and shouted, "Hold!"

Without waiting, the man fired a pistol directly into my room. Had I not been back against the wall, his shot would surely have killed me. Then it was my turn. I fired into the blur of darkness, for I was blinded by the flash from his shot. After this second blast, I could really see nothing. I heard a body crash to the floor, followed by the panicked footfalls of the other man as he fled down the stairs. I started after him, but I was unable to see and blundered into the banister. It was no use. The second intruder was out the window and gone before the servants came running from their quarters below. Pissemsky stumbled out of his room, directly across from mine, and the rest of our party clumped into the hall from every direction.

When we finally had a light, we examined the man I had shot. I had sheared off most of his face, so there was no chance to recognize him. His clothes gave no clue either: they were simply old and very soiled. He had one thing, however, to mark him as an assassin rather than a common thief. In a leather pouch tied about his neck were twenty, newly minted, Spanish gold pieces.

CHAPTER II

There was little we could have done at that hour, so we ordered the body removed to the basement. One of the maids wanted to clean up the hall, but I told her to cover the stains with a sheet to save them for the authorities – this to preserve the evidence of my having slain the man in self-defense, outside the door to my bedroom. After assigning the two clerks to stand watch, Pissemsky and I went back to bed. I doubt either of us slept well; I know I did not, and in the morning the Ambassador's eyes were red and swollen.

Who had done this thing? That was the first question when Feodor and I sat down to breakfast. I had not been able to explain the details of my meeting the night before, as I did not wish any but Pissemsky to know it had been the Queen I had met. Nor did I think I should tell even him very much of what transpired. Her Majesty of England had presumed correctly; I felt compelled to keep my silence.

Because the rest of our group, including the priest, were of lower rank, they did not eat at the same table with the Ambassador and me. We had our meal in the small dining alcove, while the others ate at a table on the far side of the adjacent room. They were distant enough not to hear us. I briefly explained what I could of my adventure, prior to the attack by the unknown assassins.

"Could it have been the Queen, herself, who sent them?" asked Feodor at length.

"I cannot imagine why she should, and I can think of several reasons why she should not," I replied.

The Ambassador agreed, after thinking about it for a few seconds. "Who, then?" he asked.

I shrugged, no better able than my companion to make a reasonable guess. "It has become common knowledge," I ventured, "at least among the higher court officials, that Ivan seeks the Queen's hand. As we know, there are many others."

"Sweden, Spain, Orange. . . ." he supplied.

"And France, just to start the list," I said. "And the coins were Spanish."

"I thought Spanish coins were in common usage here."

"They are," I agreed. "The fact they were paid does not necessarily point to Spain. Quite the opposite, I should think."

"But if it were Spain, or some other contender for the Queen's hand, would they not have tried to kill the Czar's Ambassador? Why were they after you?"

"I don't know," I admitted.

"Perhaps you were to be first," he suggested. "After all, there were two assassins."

"If I were to hire a killer for myself," I said boastfully, though not unjustifiably, "I think I would send more than one man."

"But who would be interested in killing you?"

"I had just come from a private nighttime session with the Queen," I replied. "Are you aware she has a lover?"

"But you said nothing of an . . . er . . . intimate nature—" He tried to flash a knowing grin, but it came out forced and sour. I ignored it.

"Would someone unable to see into the room be aware of this?" I asked. "What if Lord Dudley were convinced I posed a threat to his own relationship?"

"He seems such a fop. Would he be capable?"

"Before the Queen assumed the throne, and the realm was ruled by her sister, Lord Dudley was married to a woman named Amy. It is said she fell down a flight of stone stairs and was killed."

"Such things happen," said Pissemsky sagely.

"This happened near the beginning of Lord Dudley's liaison with the Queen. Do you not find it suspicious? Most members of the court seem to."

"And the Queen?" he asked.

"I imagine the Queen prefers to ignore the possibilities."

"Then let us say it was Lord Dudley who sent the men. What now?"

"First," I replied, "the Queen must be advised. We have not enough men to mount a proper guard, and in so strange a land there is no way to procure retainers we could count on not to murder us themselves."

"Are you certain the Queen would protect us?"

"Her Majesty is most anxious for a profitable trade with the Czar; she could hardly accomplish this by allowing his emissaries to be murdered," I said.

"I shall request an audience at once," said Feodor, starting to get up.

"You'll never get it," I said calmly.

"Why?"

"If we are right, Dudley will see to it you don't."

"Then you?" he asked. He was crestfallen that I might have an entry whereas he did not.

"I don't think it will be necessary," I told him. "The Queen must have eyes and ears of her own. And you have the best way to contact them."

That seemed to please him. "Lord Cecil?"

"I would guess that Old Cecil and 'Dear Sweet Robin' are not on the best of terms," I said. "I would ask him, if I were you, what should be done about that body in our cellar."

Pissemsky agreed to seek an urgent interview with Lord Cecil that morning. He went to his room to change, as I did. But my plans were quite different. I decided to garb myself as much like an Englishman as possible. I wanted to go out into the streets before the activities of the previous night brought me such notoriety that I would attract more than casual attention. As I still had to find a banker, I assumed a good time to start the search would be under cover of the confusion over this attempt to murder me. By being away during the course of the investigation, I also thought to appear haughty and indifferent. A boastful attitude, perhaps, but one which might throw my enemies off guard.

I had ordered an outfit of English clothes, which had been delivered the day before. I had not yet tried them on, but did so now. I found the fit was fine though the colors bothered me a little. I had chosen a deep blue doublet, with a lighter shade for the hose – this on the advice of the tailor, who had assured me that "blue was my color, as it complimented my blondness." I had also let him talk me into some heavy silver stitching and ribbons at the knees, all of which appeared a bit gaudy as I stood before my mirror. But I had no choice; bright as my English plumage might be, it was far less conspicuous than a Russian robe.

I waited in my room until I heard Pissemsky leave. Then, feeling more than a little awkward in my unaccustomed attire, I went downstairs. I had originally intended going alone, but thought better of it when I reached the door. Not only was it quite literally the threshold of an alien world; I felt so unnatural in my flashing blue velvet and ribbons that I simply needed the moral support of a companion. I would have preferred a Russian to accompany me, but they all looked like Russians – or rather, like Jews, for that was the normal error made by the common people in England. Our beards and clothes seemed more like those of Hebrews than any other race they had ever seen. My problem was to select one from the English servants whom I felt I could trust.

I thought a moment and remembered our footman, a fellow named Alfred, who seemed the most reasonable choice. He was about my own age, and appeared a stout enough fellow. He also seemed quite open, incapable of any great deceit. I called him and said I wanted him to come along to carry my purse. This was the prevailing custom in England, I had noticed. A gentleman seldom handled money, simply making his selection of goods and instructing his servant to settle the reckoning.

"Be right with you, sir," he beamed, and ran into the back of the house to get his jacket. He had been repairing the broken window pane when I called him, working in his shirtsleeves.

I waited a few moments at the door, and Alfred did not return. "Come on," I shouted. "I have many things to do."

A little boy peeped out from the pantry door – a child of perhaps seven years. "Da says he'll be right there, beggin' your Lordship's pardon, but he's ripped his jacket and Cook's takin' a stitch that he don't disgrace you."

I plopped onto a bench in the entryway, puffing my cheeks and exhaling my impatience. When I looked back toward the rear of the house, the child was still there, staring at me.

"Well, now what do you want?" I asked. I had spoken sharply, and immediately regretted it when a trace of anxiety appeared on the little boy's features. But he displayed a steadfast courage for one so young, and instead of running away he answered me.

"Oh, I don't want nothing, sir," he said, "but I have never seen a Roosky before."

"Am I so different?" I asked, more amused than annoyed with him.

"Oh no, sir," he answered. He took a faltering step into the room, allowing the door to close behind him. "Fact is the kitchen girls think you're quite like human English people."

I laughed aloud. "Come here, boy," I called.

He walked uncertainly across the carpet. "I am not supposed to enter the front parlor," he whispered.

"That's all right! Come here. What's your name?" I asked.

"I am Toby, sir," he told me. He stood directly in front of me, meeting my gaze with a mixture of awe and curiosity. Two or three times he glanced back nervously at the pantry door, finally trying to force a smile onto his features.

"Do I frighten you?" I asked.

"No, sir. It is just that Cook is very strict."

"Don't worry about Cook," I told him. "So, you are Alfred's boy?"

"Yessir."

"And is your mother employed here as well?"

He looked at his feet. "My mother is dead, sir," he said softly.

"I am very sorry, Toby," I replied, and for some reason I really was.

"Toby!" came a sharp voice from the pantry. It startled us both.

A large, scowling woman stood in the open doorway, hands against her ample hips. "Beggin' your pardon, sir," she smiled toothily, "but the boy has been told not to leave his place."

"But the boy is coming with us," I said. "Tell his father to hurry along."

She looked at us in surprise. "Yes, sir," she said, and went back into the kitchen, shaking her head.

I did not know why I had said it, but the boy beamed at the prospect. Well, no harm, I thought. He was wearing a well–made suit of clothing, and would not appear out of place. His father came running out of the pantry, pulling a jacket on and apologizing for the delay.

We were a block or two from the house, when Toby pulled at his father's sleeve and pointed back. "Look!" he said. "The watch is stopping at our door."

We all looked back, and saw a company of the Queen's guard at the portal.

"Good," I said. "They will take care of things."

"Don't you want to go back, sir?" asked Alfred.

"It isn't necessary," I told him.

The servant shrugged. "Good enough, sir," he said.

We walked into the city, which was not far distant. I kept an eye open for someone following us, but there did not appear to be anyone. I had not been into London proper very often, never on my own; so was completely at a loss where to go. What I wanted, of course, was the section of Jewish merchants. Although I hesitated to ask Alfred directly, there seemed no other way.

"Where do the Jews keep their shops?" I asked at length.

"Jews?" he responded in surprise. "Why, there are no Jews in England since old King Edward threw them out – hundreds of years ago."

I stopped walking. It was as if lightening had struck me. "There are no Jews at all?" I asked at last.

He scratched his head in thought. "There are a few've come back, scattered here and there," he said, "and some as works for the foreign money lenders, mostly Italians and Venetians," he added, pronouncing the words so strangely I had to ask him to repeat.

I told him to direct us into the district where the money lenders might be found. I explained that I wished to purchase a small trinket for a lady. Good values could frequently be found where items were sold out of pawn. To make con-versation, I asked him if he found prices to be fair from these Italians.

"That would not be for me to say, sir," he answered humbly. "I have little cause to seek after golden trinkets."

"Ah, affairs of the heart can be expensive, Alfred," I said, thinking how I wished I might have been speaking the truth. I had been without the company of women since my last night in Kholmagora – almost nine months.

Alfred winked. "Aye, sir; expensive they are, or so I hear." He grinned in a companionable way. "I heard –."

"You heard I went out last evening?" I finished for him.

He forced the smile from his lips. "Aye, sir," he said.

"That's all right, Alfred," I reassured him. "Let this be our secret."

He brightened again, nodding agreement. "Then, shall we seek out a Jew among the Italians?"

"Let's try," I replied. "They are a people I am used to dealing with."

The money lending, or banking section, was some distance away. I instructed Alfred to hire a carriage. "Have the driver take a roundabout route," I said, and in answer to Alfred's questioning look I added: "lest our friends from last night –"

He understood and instructed the cabby. There was still no sign of pursuit, and eventually we wound our way into the areas where many foreigners had their shops and other places of business. It was a strange hodgepodge of buildings and stalls, some rather humble, others with imposing gates across heavy, solid wooden doors. There were many well–dressed people on the streets, I noticed, for these merchants apparently gave good value for their money. Instructing the cab to wait, we began to saunter through the stalls.

No actual goldsmithing was done here, Alfred explained to me, for the London guilds would not permit it. However, a great many imported items were to be had, as well as pieces of local craftsmanship which had been taken in pawn. There was one particularly prosperous looking establishment that caught my eye, and I decided to try it. Inside, we were greeted by a young man in a full beard, black like a Tartar's. He was dressed in a drab, gray coat, and Alfred whispered "Jew" as we entered.

The clerk clasped his hands and bowed after the fashion of the east. When I had browsed about the shop for a few moments, allowing Alfred and Toby to lag a little behind me, I spoke the words Abraham had taught me.

The Jew's eyes bulged out. He emitted a long flood of phrases in the same language, which I could not begin to understand. Then he turned, and almost ran into the back room. Alfred was watching me curiously, as was Toby.

"I just used some of my desert traders' language on him," I laughed. "I guess he hadn't heard it from a gentleman."

That seemed to satisfy the situation, and the Jew returned before Alfred could say anything more. He spoke again in the Hebrew tongue, and motioned for me to come with him.

"I'll be back in a few minutes," I said, leaving my companions in the shop.

An old man, with the gray beard of wisdom rose to welcome me when I entered the room behind the shop. I took him to be the younger man's father. Respectfully, he bid me peace and asked if I would sit with him. I replied in the proper form, and eased myself into a chair. Beyond these formal words of the ritual greeting, however, I could not understand him.

"I do not mean to deceive you, Good Father," I said in English, "but I am an honest trader like yourself, come from the far lands of Russia."

"How came you by our rites?" asked the old man.

"I have in my employ several of your people," I told him, "and because I have found them the most trustworthy of servants, I decided to seek out their kindred here."

"And the words you spoke to my son?"

"They were taught to me by an old and trusted friend," I replied, "who told me they would convey to you, his brother, the affection he has for me."

The old man sat back, regarding me thoughtfully before he spoke again. "You did not know, before you left your native Russia, that Jews are forbidden on English soil?" he asked.

I shook my head. "It is unfortunate," I said, "but not so different from my own land."

"True. Everywhere we are looked upon as accused. My son and I are here, only because we serve our master."

"And who might that be?" I asked.

The old man glanced up in surprise. "The greatest banker in all the world," he replied, almost smiling. "Ridolfi of Florence."

"Then I have come to the right place," I told him.

"Your visit has to do with the transfer of moneys?"

"It has," I told him.

"A large sum?" he asked cautiously.

"A very large sum."

"I must arrange to acquaint you with my master," he said, "but as you came with the blessing of one from my own brotherhood, I would first offer a suggestion."

His words seemed ominous. "You imply your master is not to be fully trusted?" I asked.

"No, my master is the most honest of men." he assured me. "Whatever arrangement you make will be done in proper form, and it will involve a written contract. But – be sure you understand each and every clause, and that the paper says exactly what you wish it to say. In years to come, a man can forget his momentary thoughts or spoken words of promise. The contract must state your agreement without doubtful phrases, or omission of alternatives."

"I thank you, friend," I said. I waited expectantly for him to direct me.

Instead, he fingered his beard and regarded me thoughtfully. "Your business," he began slowly, "– you say it involves a large sum?"

"An extremely large sum," I returned.

"In that case, it might be better if I undertook some preliminary arrangements. I will make an appointment for you to see the master, rather than take you to him now. It will place you on a more . . . dignified basis."

"Good," I told him. "Shall we say tomorrow morning?"

"Fine, fine," he nodded. "It will be arranged."

I rose to leave, then remembered my companions waiting outside. I turned back to the Jew. "Incidentally, I am supposed to have come here to purchase a small gift for a lady," I told him.

The old man got up and went to a chest in the rear of the room. He brought out a tray of finely worked gold brooches. "Perhaps one of these?"

I selected one. "Yes, this will do," I said. "The price?"

He named a ridiculously low figure.

"I cannot take advantage of your master," I said lightly. "State a fair price to my man, and let him pay you."

Before leaving the back room I wrote my name for the old man and learned he was called Ephram. Back in the shop, he collected a small sum from Alfred, who carefully examined the coins he received for change.

"Did you get a good price, sir?" he asked me, giving Ephram a threatening look.

"Yes, a very good price," I assured him. "Thank you, Ephram. I shall come again."

On the street once more, I looked down at Toby, who was trailing happily along behind us. "What should I see next?" I asked him. I was determined to stay away from the house as long as possible, hopefully allowing the furor to subside. I was also becoming reasonably comfortable in my English clothes, no longer experiencing the urge to cross my hands in front of me to better accouter my body.

The lad smiled brightly at my question. "There are many beautiful swans by the river park," he said, "and wondrous shops along the bridge."

"Shops of the toymakers," added Alfred. "I doubt if they would be —"

"Nonsense!" I said. "We have time to see it all. Come along, Toby."

True to the lad's words, there were indeed some marvelous sights along the river, and a whole string of shops on the great bridge which spanned the water. I had Alfred buy us some sweets, made from a wondrously delicious essence, culled from the sap of a cane plant. It was much different from the sugars we imported from China and India.

In all, it was a very pleasant day. We returned home only a little before dark, having made a number of purchases. I left Alfred to settle with the driver and went directly into the house by myself.

A maid had opened the door for me, and although she said nothing I could see by her expression that something was terribly wrong. Then I saw Pissemsky, sitting rigidly in the parlor. With him were several uniformed gentlemen. The Ambassador was on his feet at once.

"In God's name, where have you been, Dmitri?" he exclaimed in Russian. "The Queen must be in a fine state by this time."

"The Queen? What about the Queen?"

"She sent for you over two hours ago. These men came to fetch you."

"Then I must go at once," I said in English. "Gentlemen, shall we—"

As they stood I saw two sets of irons in the hands of one man.

"Surely, those are not intended for me," I protested, struggling to keep a lightness in my tone.

"Only if they should prove necessary, sir," replied the captain.

"I assure you, they will not," I told him, managing to match his dignified cadence. I paused at the door, looking back at Pissemsky. "Are you coming?" I asked.

"They did not say. . . . Should I?" he stammered.

"You are the Czar's Ambassador," I said firmly. "When one of His subjects is on the verge of incarceration, I should think you would be concerned enough to come along."

He came, to the obvious annoyance of the soldiers. The carriage they had brought, and which they had prudently left hidden around the side of the house, was too small for all of us. Two of the men had to walk behind. Alfred and Toby stood dumbly in front of the house, watching us being taken away.

"No problem," I called to them. "We shall be back in a short while." Inwardly, I was not so confident, although I could not imagine why the Queen should have sent soldiers.

At the palace there was no delay, and I was escorted immediately into Her Majesty's presence. Pissemsky was left in the antechamber, much to his annoyance.

This time, Elizabeth was not alone. With her were both Dudley and Lord Cecil. For the second time, I was treated to a display of the royal temper. "We are pleased," she began sarcastically, "that Our Russian guest has finally seen fit to answer Our summons!"

"I have only just received it, Madam," I replied, making the proper obeisance. "I made all haste to obey."

"Don't ply thy oily tongue with me!" she stormed. "How dare you insult my confidence, to embarrass me before my court? Am I some poor harem girl, for you to compromise and then brag about to your . . . your troops?"

"I am very honestly at a loss to understand how I have offended –"

"It appears that English and Russian standards of temperance and decency are quite diverse," she snapped. "It also appears that my entire court is gossiping about your being alone – with me – last night! If you did not allow it to be known, who did?" She had been pacing as she spoke, and finished directly in front of me, shouting the last words in my face.

I looked directly into her eyes, and quietly said: "Lord Dudley, Madam."

She started, for she obviously had not expected an answer. Turning uncertainly toward her paramour, she asked: "Robin?"

Robin lounged comfortably against a chest, his slender body arched sideways, his rose clad legs crossed at the ankles. It was not a very manly pose. His sweetly pretty lips formed a half smile, but he made no attempt to answer.

"Is Her Majesty aware that I was nearly murdered after returning home last night?" I continued, softly.

She looked back at me sharply. "How? Some sneak thief?"

"With twenty pieces–of–eight about his neck?" I asked, my tone still much softer than hers. "No, I think not, Madam. What is the price of an assassin's blade in London?"

"What has all this to do with your violating my confidence?" she demanded.

"Whoever sent the assassin, Madam, knew where I had been. I heard men following me on my return from the palace. I have spoken of our encounter only to Prince Pissemsky, and to no one else. Even to him, I made it clear we had discussed only Your Grace's affection for the Czar. From my lips, Madam, there have been no scandalous insinuations."

"Cecil?" she said, uncertain now.

Lord Cecil, gray and balding, but ever the dignified statesman, moved casually into a position of attention. His voice was cool, very soothing, and well modulated. "I have spoken to the Russian Ambassador," he said, "and he corroborates Prince Marensky's statement. I think we may have been hasty."

Dudley wiped daintily at his brow with a silken kerchief. "It still appears strange to me, Your Grace, that a man can murder one of Your subjects, and then be so unconcerned about it as to go on a shopping spree, leaving before the watch have even come to investigate."

"In my country, My Lord," I answered him, "the life of a paid assassin is of too little value for a gentleman to squander his time in mourning. I left the disposal of his remains to my servants." As I spoke, I remembered how easily I had evoked laughter from the Queen the night before. Taking a chance that it might work again, I shifted my weight to one foot. This caused the opposite hip to rise, and by resting the back of my wrist against it, I assumed a pose in imitation of Robin.

Our argument persisted for a few minutes more, but each time he changed his posture I continued to mimic him. It finally broke his aplomb, because the Queen began to titter.

"Oh dear, Cecil," she giggled, "I think we have terribly wronged the Prince."

She kept laughing, at which Dudley began to sweat more profusely, and his face turned a deep shade of red. The Queen's laughter was reflected in Cecil's eyes, although he was too controlled to join her. Finally, she gestured for me to stop, and Dudley stood as if to leave. His face was burning red with shame and anger.

"With Your Grace's permission," he said, bowing.

"Oh no, Robin," she replied, catching her breath. "You are not going to leave Us yet. What of this assassin? Did you send him?"

Dudley looked at her uncomfortably. I did not know if he would have been forced to lie or not, but I spared him the necessity. There was no reason to make him any more of a violent enemy than I already had. "I think, Madam," I said softly, "that – if I may be so presumptuous – in Your Majesty's place, I would not wish that question answered."

"You do presume," she said tartly. "But let Us hear your reasoning."

"If I may, Lord Dudley is assuredly the most loyal of Your Grace's subjects, and Her most ardent admirer. May we agree to this?"

"Fairly stated," she said.

"Then, if Lord Dudley were to send an assassin to remove another man, must we not assume he did this for reasons other than those which he perceived would harm his Queen?"

"You are saying that My Lord Dudley was jealous?" she gasped in surprise. Then she started to giggle again. "Cecil, I have never heard the like. I told him last night that I wished he were English. He has proved the wisdom of my admission. Really, Robin, this man is a fitting companion for you; he has wit enough to match the best of your friends."

"I shall remember Your Grace's impression," he replied coldly.

"There is really no cause for animosity between us, My Lord," I added. "Nothing has been offered me that is yours, and I covet only Her Majesty's gracious indulgence for the duration of my visit."

"Tell me," asked the Queen, "are all Russians as bold as you? If so, I would fear an eastern invasion."

"I have been brought up in palaces," I said evenly, "and perhaps I am overly aware of the humanity of kings."

"Well spoken," said Cecil. "If Your Grace will permit us. . . ?"

"Yes, by all means go before you reduce me to a giggling school girl. Not you, Robin!" she said more sternly. "We still have a matter to discuss!"

Lord Cecil and I bowed ourselves out of the royal presence, and left Lord Dudley to Her Majesty's graces. But he must have handled the situation satisfactorily, for only a few weeks later he was created Earl of Leicester. However, I had occasion to encounter him again, prior to his elevation.

After my meeting with the Queen and her two favorite advisors, I returned home to find a note from Ephram, apologetically postponing my appointment. Ridolfi had been unexpectedly called out of London, he explained, but he did not give any more detail than that. Anxious though I was to complete the Czar's business, it was pleasant to have this respite.

During the next few days, Pissemsky spoke several times with Lord Cecil, and reported to me that all seemed well at the palace. Dudley made no further contact with us. It was rumored at court, at least according to Pissemsky, that the Queen had firmly chastised her pet, but had forgiven him, being secretly pleased at his display of concern and jealousy. His later elevation to boyar rank would seem to confirm this.

After several days I sent a message to Ephram, reminding him that I would like to get our transaction started. I was trying to plan my next move. Before I could properly discuss the treasure with Ridolfi, I thought, I should take a part of it to him for his appraisal. To do this, I had two choices of method. I could enlist the aid of several men to act as guards, thus attracting unwanted attention. As an alternative, I could go alone, at the risk of being set upon and robbed. No one would know what I carried, I supposed, but robbery was common even in London, especially if one ventured into the poorer sections. Even in a carriage, I would have to travel through a very bad part of town in order to reach the bankers' quarters. In the end I compromised, having Alfred accompany me again. I was fairly well convinced by now that he was what he appeared to be, that he was not a spy for the Queen, her ministers, or any foreign power.

And this was another matter of constant concern to me. If none of the people within the house were spies – and none of them seemed to be – who was watching us? I could never detect anyone I suspected of maintaining surveillance on the house or trailing me when I went out. I could not understand how this was possible. Visitors in Russia were always followed; it was an expected and time-honored practice. I could not believe we were unguarded! To test this, I made several trips into town, just visiting places of amusement and making a few purchases. Still no spy. Then Ephram answered my note, setting a date for me to meet with him, although Ridolfi was still away.

On the appointed day I called Alfred without warning him beforehand, and said simply that I wanted his company. It was a little past noon when I went to my room to change clothes. I had not, as yet, become sufficiently accustomed to English costume to wear it about the house. Just before leaving I extracted one case of jewels – there were four in all – and stuffed it under my waistband, against the flesh of my belly. I was wearing a less ostentatious outfit than I had the time before. It was also of a thicker velvet, which did a better job of hiding my contraband. I strapped on an English sword, utilizing the waistpiece as the final bit of camouflage. There was really no other reason to carry such a weapon, I thought. I was extremely uncomfortable with it, because it was a very light foil, called a rapier. It required a special skill to use, but other than a pistol it was the only weapon which a gentleman might carry. My regular sword would most certainly attract attention; to the English it looked like something from their legendary past. When Alfred met me in the lower hall, I noted he had stuck a dagger into his belt.

We went directly to Ephram's shop, which was actually the back end of a large building that filled the entire area between two streets. Ridolfi owned it all, frequenting only the forward portion, where he had both his home and offices. The master's section faced on a more fashionable street. Still guarding against my companion's being a spy, I made a casual remark about having seen another item in the shop I wanted, and hoped it had not yet been sold.

We arrived without incident, and were greeted by the old man himself. Again, I went into the back with him, risking whatever suspicion this might arouse in Alfred's mind. In truth, it would have required a more complex man than Alfred to wonder what I was about; he seemed perfectly satisfied to wait for me, never questioning my actions by word or sign. Still, I made it a point to purchase a small item on this and each subsequent trip, again having him make the actual payment.

Ephram was extremely impressed with the materials I had to show him. When I told him it was less than a fourth part of the whole he gloated, assuring me his still absent master could handle it. "He will be delighted with the collection," Ephram assured me. "Jewels are so much more easily transported than gold, as I am sure you are aware." He glanced up at me, for the first time displaying a hint of his degree of understanding. "This might almost be the treasure of a king," he added significantly.

"I trust you will exercise proper discretion," I said, making no other attempt to explain or deny his implications.

"Never fear, my friend; discretion is our business. Do you – do you wish to leave them in my keeping?" he suggested slowly. "I realize you do not know my master or myself, and the value is great. Yet the risk of transporting . . . ."

"I have every intention of leaving them with you," I replied. "If I am to trust you with the whole before I leave England, it would make little sense not to trust you with a part of it now."

Ephram had hardly looked at me as we spoke, his eyes drawn to the gleaming pile of gems. This first segment was mostly emeralds and rubies, the most precious of fiery reds and the cool, mysterious pools of green. There was one very large diamond, however, a stone I had tried to discourage Ivan from sending. Its value was very great, and now its size bothered Ephram. Usually, I did not care for diamonds, preferring the more vital hues of the other stones. But this particular gem was exceptional. It was blue, and so deep a color I had first taken it to be a sapphire. It was also the only item over which we had a serious disagreement in placing our tentative values.

"The risk of transporting such a stone, let alone finding a buyer for it," Ephram said, "must restrict its worth."

Ephram looked at the elegant blue surface with sad, appreciative eyes. He sighed. "Of all the gems you have brought, this is the one I wish I might possess, if only for a short time." He shrugged and glanced up sharply; his tone changed back to its proper quality. "But you are right. It is better for you to keep it."

He provided me with a soft leather pouch, so I could suspend the diamond around my neck, thus taking no chance of losing it from my clothing. Certain I could trust him, I left the rest of the gems in his possession. Ephram assured me a second time that I could depend upon him to safeguard them. I suggested the time for my next visit, and Ephram gestured with open palms, expressing his doubt that Ridolfi would have returned so quickly. As I had decided to transport the entire collection, one fourth at a time, and to entrust them to the old man's keeping, I insisted that I would take my chances. It was far better, I thought, to get the transfer accomplished as quickly as possible.

When Alfred and I returned to our house, I immediately placed the great diamond back into its hiding place. I made my second delivery two days later, again reaching the shop with no difficulty. Ridolfi had not returned, but in the interim I had discovered a partial reason for his absence. The Florentine, so the rumors went, was involved in his own political intrigues. He was related by blood to Catherine d'Medici, Dowager of France. Ridolfi was trying to arrange a marriage between Catherine's son and the Queen of England!

To confirm the information I had already received, I made passing reference to Ridolfi's Medici blood as I stood with Ephram in the back room, examining the second collection of jewels.

"Oh yes," the old man assured me. "That is why I cautioned you. When you deal with the Medicis, you must be sure your contract is clearly written."

"If I cannot trust him. . . ."

"It is not that," Ephram assured me quickly. "Ridolfi must abide by the terms of the contracts he makes, for his business depends on such matters as yours. His reputation is more precious to him than even the enormous value of your treasure. You may rely on this, and you may rely on my master's being completely true to the contract he makes with you."

Still apprehensive because of Ridolfi's being in a position of competition – his candidate versus mine, so to speak, for the hand of the Queen, I made my next appointment for two evenings hence. Ephram said he expected Ridolfi's return by then. He also made another remark which did not immediately penetrate, but which I later understood when I had time to think about it. He had referred to the complexity of politics and the lessening of regal power over vast areas of earth. He was telling me, I later decided, that Ivan was not a serious rival. Had his realm been geographically closer to England, I might have had something to fear from another contender. On the basis of the Queen's own words to me, I knew he was right. The truth rankled me, but I could not help feeling grateful for Ephram's honesty. He had taken the risk of offending me in order to communicate this additional bit of reassurance.

Neither during our return that day, nor in the course of the next trip to Ephram's shop, did Alfred give me any reason to suspect his questioning my activities. He appeared content to obey. Yet I was extremely discomforted that neither he nor anyone else seemed the least concerned over what I was doing. The lack of attention caused ponderous worry for me. The Queen's ministers, at the very least, had to suspect that I was in England to conduct some kind of business, either personal or for the Czar. Surely they – or someone – would be curious enough about my activities to make some sort of inquiry or conduct an investigation. I needed more than ever to discuss my apprehensions with someone, but I had no person to whom I could turn.

When we left the shop after the third trip, with Ridolfi still absent, I was in an even higher state of anxiety. In fact, I was so preoccupied with my own thoughts that I hardly realized how long I had been inside. I was somewhat surprised to step outside and discover it was already dark. There were no carriages about for me to hire, as I had not thought to ask our man to stay. During daylight hours, the street had always been busy and bustling with people, and there had always been several drivers looking for fares.

We left the section of shops on foot, and began to wind our way back into the central part of town. It was at this juncture that my concern over the lack of obstacles abruptly ended. We were set upon by a gang of ruffians!

They came at us from either end of a narrow alleyway, striking first from the back. Alfred, always wary when we passed through any less prosperous area, had heard them coming. He turned to meet the first man with a hard knee to the groin and a quick thrust with his dagger. I pulled out my flimsy excuse for a sword, by which time two more of the robbers had come at us from in front. There were still two behind us, struggling with Alfred. For a few moments we were in desperate straits, for my companion's dagger was a poor defense against two men armed with similar weapons. Nor was I in the least skilled with a rapier. Only the narrow confines of the alley allowed us to fend them off long enough for help to arrive – this from an unexpected source.

Ephram, without mentioning it to me, had been concerned about my traveling to and from the shop with only a single attendant. Fortunately for us, he had stationed his son on the street to watch. The younger man had been following us – and doing a good job of it, for I had never noticed him despite my wariness. As soon as he saw what had happened he fled down another street and summoned the watch. The Queen's soldiers arrived in time to keep us from being overwhelmed. All was well after that, except that I knew the incident was certain to be reported, creating a record of my having been in the bankers' district. I wondered how much longer I had before I could expect some official interference. One telling point had been made, however, and the quieting effect of this outweighed the rest. Had Ephram wished to cheat me, he would not have kept watch over us. Had I perished that night in the alley, he could simply have kept three parts of the Czar's treasure with no one the wiser.

Neither Alfred nor I had been badly hurt, although my companion did sustain a fairly deep gash in his thigh. The soldiers carried him to a physician, who drained the wound and ordered him to remain in bed for several days. This left me without an attendant for the next trip.

My sojourns into the city had not gone unnoticed by everyone in our party, as it turned out. The clerks, being silly and frivolous, had not thought much about it. They were simply envious of my freedom and ability to purchase whatever I wished. Pissemsky was too busy to pay much attention, although by now he must have begun to wonder. Knowing I had work to perform for the Czar, and having been instructed by Ivan not to interfere with me, he said nothing. It was the priest, who had found me his only companion since the voyage, who surprised me by knocking on my door the evening after the attack.

"May I come in, Highness?" he asked.

"Certainly," I told him. I had been lying, fully clothed across the bed, one arm over my eyes to blot out the light while I considered my next move.

Father Thomas stepped gingerly into the room, looking as if he expected someone to be with me. I do not know how old our chaplain was, probably not much past forty; but his quiet piety gave the appearance of a sage. There was a fair amount of gray in his black beard; his head, of course, was completely shaved, for he was a monk of the same Novgorod order as Sylvester. His face and body were typical of most clerics who had forsaken their youthful fanaticism: sleek and given to an almost effeminate plumpness.

"I have not seen much of you these past few days," he said softly.

"I have been very busy, Father. I hope the time has not weighed too heavily on your hands."

"It has given me an opportunity for . . . meditation," he said tentatively. I thought he wanted to add something else, but seemed to hold back pending a lead from me.

"Did you just wish to visit, Father?" I asked, "Or have I been remiss in my religious duties?"

"Your piety is unquestioned," he replied in the same, modulated tone. "I would have no cause to censure, I am sure. But I know you are disturbed, and as your friend I thought to help lighten the burden."

"I am afraid my problems are of a more secular nature," I told him. Then before he could ask, I thought to supply an explanation for my visits into the city. "I have been so involved in the business of learning, I have had little time to sin."

"Dmitri, you must not think me unobservant because I choose not to intrude into the worldly pursuits of my flock. I know your feelings about the clergy, and I understand how this may influence your attitudes toward one such as myself." He paused, knowing his phrasing was awkward, but at the same time he radiated sincerity. "Although I am your confessor," he continued cautiously, "I would also be your friend. As a fellow countryman, I also have my responsibilities to the Czar. He is, when all else is forgotten, our earthly bridge to heaven and God's anointed shepherd. I know you serve him in whatever it is you do."

I smiled reassuringly at him, thinking to myself that I was again receiving an offer of unwanted assistance. Or was it unwanted? "Do I understand you to say, Father, that you would consider any help rendered me in the name of the Czar to be a part of your holy commission?"

"That would be another way to phrase it, yes. May I sit down?" He had remained standing at the foot of my bed, and I had swung my legs over the edge, where I sat looking up at him.

"Certainly, Father," I apologized. "I did not mean to appear undesirous of your company."

He picked up a wooden chair and moved it closer to the bed, sitting with his knees together and his hands folded in his lap. He waited silently for me to continue.

"If I were to avail myself of your offer," I began, "how might we consider it sealed? As under the rules of the confessional?"

"Do you feel it must be so bound?" He seemed surprised that I considered my business this serious.

"My own oath to the Czar is nearly that binding," I told him. "But at the moment I badly need someone to help me. Would you be willing to accept my statement under the seal of the confessional, hearing as much as I need tell you and accepting the rest without explanation? I would swear a holy oath that my unexplained activities constitute no sin, and are done in the Czar's service."

"If your activities require such secrecy, I think this would be incumbent upon me."

"Then hear my confession, Father," I said.

The priest left to get his holy trappings, and I used the intervening moments to phrase the confession I would give him. I decided to tell him of my having a great fortune to deposit in England for the Czar, but I would not go so far as to explain the full reasons for his wanting it left here. While a man's confession is supposed to be repeated to no one, there were instances where I am sure the information could find its way upward in the hierarchy of priests – especially where such information would serve the Church. Father Thomas returned; I knelt before him, and made my confession.

When we had finished and I was once again seated on the bed, I told him of my appointment two days hence. "If we were to leave the house early," I said, "we could stop at one of the holy shrines in the city. A visiting man of God might be expected to do this. If we then go into a place of business, it would not seem necessarily strange."

"Do you think you have been followed on your trips into the city?"

"Strangely enough, it appears I have not," I said. "But after today, I think it very possible I will be."

"It would give me great pleasure to see Saint Paul's Church," said Father Thomas.

On the morning of the appointed day, we left in the small, open carriage which Pissemsky had acquired for us. "You should have had the brains to do this for yourself," he had scolded. "Depending on the chance hiring of a carriage, indeed." Toby, I noticed, had come along dressed as footman, in livery to match the driver`s. Having children play these roles was a popular custom with the English, and he had probably worked in a similar capacity with his father. I did not know the fellow who drove us, but assumed he had been sent by the Queen's ministry, as had our other English servants.

We went first to the great church, threading our way through the early morning crowds: clerks on their way to work, farmers and housewives hurrying to the marketplace to buy or sell vegetables and fruit.

At Saint Paul's, there were a few worshipers at prayer when we entered, and our appearance caused some immediate consternation. A Protestant priest was performing some rituals at the alter, which stood in front of the congregation, unscreened from the body of the church. He was assisted by two acolytes, one of whom had been the first to notice us. He whispered something to the priest, who hurriedly completed whatever he was doing and rushed back to intercept us. We stood just inside the door, uncertain as to the proper way of displaying our respect within the shrine.

The priest, wearing a white smock over his black cassock, approached us with a surly sneer. "Jews are not welcomed here," he whispered. "I am surprised you would dare to violate the house of Our Lord Jesus Christ!"

Thomas looked at me in confusion, not understanding the priest's ungracious greeting.

"We are not Jews," I told him, "but visitors from the land of Russia. My companion is a priest of the Orthodox faith, and a servant of Our Lord and Savior, even as yourself."

"A papist, then?" questioned the priest, still standing as if to bar the entrance of the evil one. His eyes had now fastened upon the heavy silver cross hanging from Thomas's waist.

"We are not of the Roman Church, either," I said sternly, "and such a poor welcome to guests of your Queen is not only insulting to Her Majesty, but to the God you are sworn to serve."

"You are truly guests of the Queen?" he asked, beginning to soften a little. The two altar boys had come up to stand behind him, listening intently.

"I have had two interviews with Her Majesty within the last ten days," I said, "and she has extended to me the hospitality of her realm. Acting on Her Majesty's invitation, I have brought my –" I hesitated to say "confessor," for this would smack of papistry – "friend and spiritual advisor to view this famous shrine. Its renown has spread even into our own, distant land," I lied.

The priest still seemed reluctant, but taking the safest course he turned us over to one of the boys, telling him to show us the building. The lad was very nervous at first, but as I kept speaking to him he realized he was not in imminent danger of being struck from above. He guided us as the priest had instructed.

After touring the ground floors, we climbed the high tower, from which we enjoyed a spectacular vista of the entire city. I did not think London was quite as large as Moscow, but the amount of commerce was very great. The ships in the river compensated for whatever the city lacked in size, and the very orderly construction of stone houses, as well as the paved streets, contrasted sharply with our own capital. Across the busy waterway we could see the Savior's Church, and the towers of Westchester House near the end of the bridge of shops. The Tower of London dominated the scene to our left on the near shore of the Thames.

I think Thomas was impressed with the size of the church, for it was very large, though not really any bigger than the Great Cathedral in the Kremlin. Inside, the ornaments and holy vessels were very poor by comparison, and there were no icons. The Protestant religion, in its ignorance, forbade them as graven images condemned by the Lord. Devout as these people claimed to be, I was amused to note the many rows of benches lining the nave. To sit before the holy throne of God was a luxury denied even the Czar in our own churches. In England, a beggar might repose in ease through the divine service.

When we left, the priest stood by the door, apparently having reconsidered his previous discourtesy. "I hope Your Lordships have found proper inspiration here," he said pompously. "Our doors are never closed to fellow Christians."

I thanked him, and we returned to the carriage. Toby held the door for us, and I settled back comfortably on the leather cushions. There was a threat of rain, now that the morning fog had lifted. Afraid we might find ourselves in a downpour, I decided not to waste much time in my scheduled ploy of taking a drive through the city. Still, I though it best not to go directly to the Florentine's. I had not noticed anyone following us, but the driver was new to the household. I had to assume he might be a spy.

"Where are the houses of the great merchants?" I asked. "I would like to see some of their places of business."

"Not far, sir," replied the driver. "I'll point them out to you."

Thomas, unused to intrigue, sat stiffly beside me. I leaned back and told him, in Russian, to do the same. His hand stole cautiously to his middle, where I had helped him strap the final container of gems. "It is a wondrous city," I commented in English. Without changing my tone, I added in Russian: "Stop fidgeting. No one is going to suspect a priest of carrying the Czar's treasury."

We soon came to the merchants' section, and the driver began picking out the houses of the major traders. "It is true," I asked, "that there are foreign firms represented here . . . Dutch, and Italian, and the like?"

"I am not much the man for business," he replied, "but I know there are foreign bankers."

"Oh, I have heard of the . . . the . . . what is that Italian banking house? I believe they are related to the Dowager of France."

"They are on the next street," he said. "That large, gray building is the House of Ridolfi."

"Do you suppose they would change foreign money?" I asked, hoping his ignorance would shield me. "I would like to obtain some easier coin to spend than this Russian money I have."

He seemed to think they could help me, and his expression – what I could see of it – betrayed no hint that he might know about Russia's lack of coinage. I am sure there would have been little exchange value for squirrel skins in an Italian banking house.

"Good," I said. "Stop and we shall go in. Father, would you like to come with me? Perhaps you would enjoy seeing some modern money–changers at work."

I had continued to speak in English for the driver's benefit. I did not expect Father Thomas to understand the words, although I was certain he would know what I meant. He surprised me by responding: "I would be glad to, my son."

Entering the Florentine house from its elegant side, I found it not exactly as I expected. For some reason I had assumed it would be elaborate and showy, with well dressed people conversing in Latin tongues. Instead, the reception hall was small and dusty. The clerk on duty was definitely English.

I asked for Ephram, and the clerk sent a boy to fetch him from the far side of the building. The Jew, surprised to see me so early, escorted us immediately into an empty office. It, too, was small and cramped, with stacks of dusty books piled on shelves about the walls.

"I understand you had some difficulties after leaving us, last time," said Ephram. "My son told me."

"Thanks to you – and him – we survived it." I replied.

"You have brought the rest of the treasure?"

I patted Thomas's belly. "Safe in my confessor's – heart," I said.

With some difficulty I was able to extricate the gems from under Father Thomas's gown – not, I'm afraid, without sacrificing a degree of his dignity. Ephram had just taken the fourth packet into his hand when the clerk tapped on our door. The master would see us, he said. This was my first indication that Ridolfi had returned.

Ephram led us through the front office, and out a door on the other side. We went down a passage into a very large hall, where the entire character of the building seemed to change. It became as I had expected it to be. There was a heavy wrought iron grill across another arched entryway, blocking our exit from the solarium. Sunlight streamed into the room from a huge, frosted window in the ceiling. Our heels clicked on the marble floor as we approached the barrier, passing a heavy piece of statuary in the center of the hall: a rather wanton depiction of debauchery, a naked male with enormous genitals and the tendrils of grape vines dragging at his legs like the clutching fingers of the evil one.

A servant opened the gate and closed it behind us, as we passed down a heavily carpeted passage into another large room. This one was darkly paneled and appointed with an extraordinary style of furniture, the like of which I had never seen before. The pieces were massive, yet delicately carved – chairs, tables, chests. All stood on slender, highly ornamented legs that seemed hardly stout enough to hold the weight. Seated at a huge, gold leafed desk which could easily have served as an alter, was a strikingly handsome man in his early fifties. He was dressed in an expensive doublet of sleek, black velvet, with elegant accents of silver. The rest of his costume was the same dark hue, complimenting his silvery gray, black–streaked hair.

But it was the second person in the room who attracted my immediate attention, making it necessary for Ephram to repeat his introduction. Roberto Ridolfi, substantial banker and highly respected man of business, smiled condescendingly when I finally went through the proper forms of greeting. It was only with an effort that I took my eyes off the young woman who stood beside the desk.

Signore Ridolfi did not miss the lingering interplay, for it had been something less than subtle. Indeed, the lady had responded in an apparently favorable manner, boldly returning my glances. Ridolfi, amused, introduced me to his daughter, Antonina. She then greeted me formally, executing that most graceful, Italian form of curtsy. As she moved, she caused a delicate aura of perfume to engulf me.

Her father spoke a few words to Antonina in Italian. She responded with a little tinkle of mirth, and withdrew. But she gave me a most knowing and provocative smile as she passed. This, too, was observed by her father. To my later chagrin, it was also noted by Father Thomas, who was to make some uncharacteristically harsh comments on her lack of modesty and decorum.

Whatever Ephram had told Signore Ridolfi, it left little for me to explain. He had seen the jewels – all but the last packet – and he seemed satisfied with the values his servant and I had agreed upon. Since I had allowed Ephram to assume I was dealing for my father, the subject of the Russian Czar had never been mentioned. However, I was dealing now with one of the shrewdest men in the world, involved in the most discreet businesses. The tremendous fortune I had brought must have hinted at the source. It was well known that Ivan was the wealthiest monarch on earth, his only possible rival being the Sultan, the usurper of Byzantium.

Thomas, after being presented, and hearing Signore Ridolfi exchange a few polite phrases with me, moved unobtrusively toward the open windows at the far side of the room. These gave entrance to a tastefully beautiful garden court. The sun had now broken through the earlier cover of clouds, and it lighted the profusion of plants and flowers, producing exactly the effect the architect must have planned. The priest turned back to us, and managed enough English to request permission to examine the enclosure. Naturally, Ridolfi was more than happy to extend the invitation.

At a slight gesture from his master, Ephram also left us. I was now alone with the Florentine, and for a moment I felt afraid, unsure of my ground. But Ridolfi was a man of such grace and charm, he soon forced these apprehensions from my mind.

"Now, My Lord," he began, speaking English with only the barest trace of an accent, "perhaps we can establish the exact arrangements you wish to make."

"I shall be most relieved to have it all completed," I told him, "and to have no further concern for the safety of my funds."

"I understand your . . . friend wishes to establish a reserve here in England, against a time of possible – er, crisis in his own land?" he began. I noticed he had not said "father." It was obvious he had surmised the truth.

"That is correct," I responded.

"And this person, if he should wish to avail himself of these funds . . . he would act on his own, or do you wish it established that he must act through you?" He was making pointed reference to conditions I should consider before the contract was drawn.

There was no point in further subterfuge, and taking Ephram's advice, I stated my wishes with no equivocation. "Let me be perfectly frank, sir," I replied. "Although I am also a man of business, and have been involved in both political and financial intrigues all my life, I feel I must forego all subtleties in this negotiation. You must understand exactly what it is I want done, and this leaves me no choice but to rely on your discretion – and, of course, your honesty."

"You need have no misgivings –" he began.

"If I had misgivings, I would not have come to you," I responded, cutting him off. "Still, I am a man from a different country, dealing in a type of business with which I have no experience. I must depend upon you to fill the cracks in my armor, so to speak."

"I understand your situation," he responded slowly. My sharpness of speech had taken him off guard, as I had intended it should. After all, I was not coming to him as a beggar. It was necessary that he understand our dealings would have to be done as I wished them done.

"The sum we are discussing is very large," he continued. "I do not wish to intrude into areas of confidence, but we are discussing what might well be termed a 'king's ransom.'"

"As you have undoubtedly guessed," I replied bluntly, "I am acting on behalf of the Czar."

He nodded. "I had thought it possible." He did not appear the least surprised.

"Then you are aware of the political repercussions if our transaction should be other than the most confidential."

"As I understand it, you wish this fund established for the use of the Czar, who may act either for himself, or through you?" Again there was that significant look. It continued to puzzle me.

My expression must have conveyed my lack of comprehension. "Let me put it more plainly, my friend," Ridolfi said, hunching forward with his elbows on the desk. "These funds will be placed with us for an indefinite time, and will be held in security for the Czar's use if he should ever require them in England. Or in any other country where our firm has offices, for that matter. But what if the Czar should never require them? Perhaps political developments will be such that he never needs to leave his state. Let us hope this is the case. What then? How shall we dispose of the funds? Once the Czar is dead, let us say," He gestured with open palms, "of the natural processes of old age, who then inherits his interest? To whom is he going to confide ownership of such a sum? There is a son, I understand —"

"There are two sons," I replied absently. I pondered the alternatives before saying more. "Suppose we were to leave it," I added at length, "that the Czar, his sons – and their sons for so long as the line shall survive – may direct you in the disbursement of the funds?"

"That would be a practical arrangement," he said, "but I might suggest that you not forget yourself. You act as an agent now; why not allow your name to remain in the contract? Your Czar may wish you to act for him later."

"I would prefer to leave that to him," I said.

Ridolfi shook his finger at me and clucked his tongue. "Do not forego the advantages inherent in such an arrangement," he cautioned me. "You have acted as the Czar's instrument in setting up the fund. You are one of the few men to know about it. You are the likely agent to act on it later. It will be easier for you if your name appears there now. I may be in my tomb by then, and the only instructions my successors will have to go on will be the contract we sign today."

His advice was obviously good, and I agreed. I began to have a greater confidence in him, too, for he did not *need* to point these things out to me. I felt sure I had selected the proper repository for Ivan's treasure. However, my decision that day was to prove of more consequence than I could possibly have imagined, and its repercussions were to haunt me to the end of my days.

We spoke, then, of a great many subjects, developing a mutual acceptance of each other, and respect for the differing skills we possessed. After a while, Ridolfi picked up a silver bell from his desk and at its tone a slender young man appeared through a side door. Ridolfi spoke to him in rapid Italian, as the young man took notes on a pad of paper.

"Our contract will be drawn within the hour," said the Florentine. "May I extend to you the hospitality of my home while we wait?"

"Nothing would please me more," I said happily.

"I should . . . ummm, think not," he remarked under his breath. Aloud, he said, "My daughter appears quite taken with you."

I openly smiled in pleasure at that. "Do you –. I mean, you would not object to my paying my respects? I hope this is the custom in your land, as it appears to be in England."

"It is, Lord – Demetrius? Am I pronouncing that correctly?" He spoke my name as if it were Greek, which gave its German version an odd, but strangely romantic sound.

"Quite correct, sir," I replied.

"I never object to young gentlemen of means calling upon my daughter," he replied, leaving the end of his sentence on such a tone that I caught the definite impression it was a question.

"My father and I are quite successful merchants," I answered, as if to a direct inquiry. "I am also a Prince and an officer of General rank in the Czar's army," I added standing to face him.

"Your presence would do my house great honor," he said graciously. "You see, I, too, can be a man of forthright directness." He laughed as if to discount our entire exchange, yet I knew he had been completely serious.

Now that my social status had been established, he shepherded me into the garden. Thomas had seated himself on a stone bench, obviously enjoying the beauty of the flowers. He seemed lost in some deep meditation.

"Would the reverend gentleman join us in a glass of wine?" asked our host. He looked from one to the other of us, not knowing whether Thomas would understand him or not.

The priest rose slowly, not fully comprehending Ridolfi's invitation. He looked questioningly at me.

"We have been invited to join our host in a glass of wine," I explained in Russian. I then added in English: "There is no sin in drink, Signore, only in drunkenness."

"So it is among our own men of God," he replied, leading us through the doorway across the garden, "although I fear some of our Italian friars do not always set the best example of moderation."

We entered the other room, furnished even more magnificently than Ridolfi's office. I had never seen such items! There were finely carved woods, with gold inlaid into the surfaces; skillfully painted figures adorned the panels; and behind glass doors was a huge collection of crystal goblets and dainty stemware, mingled with exquisite figurines of animals and people – all done in a variety of porcelain and china. Yet none of the glory of the appointments could overshadow Antonina. She received us when we entered, carrying a silver tray with a decanter and several small stemmed goblets.

"I have anticipated your request, Papa," she said in a soft, mellow voice. Her appearance, her manner of speaking and moving – all were so completely right and complimentary to her loveliness, I was already in love. I realized later that she resembled Anastasia, for she had an angelic face, framed by gleaming black hair, highlighted here and there with deep, auburn red. Her figure was a bit more slender, and there was no excess fleshiness. Yet her hips were plump and round as they should have been, and her firm breasts were not as small as her tightly laced bodice would suggest. Her form was gloriously outlined by a pink satin gown, trimmed with rich, wine–red velvet. She wore no jewelry, except for a small golden cross on a slender chain about her neck. She was young, though certainly no child. I correctly guessed her age at just under twenty years. A little older than Anastasia had been when I first saw her, but the resemblance was uncanny – so alike in appearance, but so different as I later grew to know her and to perceive her personality.

She handed me a glass of wine, gave one to her father, who was closer to her than Thomas. She hesitated, looking at Ridolfi before giving one to the priest. She took the fourth glass for herself, at which I noted Thomas glared in disapproval.

"This is not Russia," I reminded him in our own language.

"It certainly is not!" he replied sternly.

"What did the Father say?" asked Antonina slyly, knowing with her womanly senses what had passed between us.

"Father Thomas wishes to drink to your health," I said, and to the priest I added, again in Russian: "Now behave yourself!"

We remained in the banker's house for better than two hours. In the tensions of negotiations, followed by the delightful company of Antonina, I had lost all track of time. When the contracts had been prepared and signed, I had no further excuse to delay departure. The banker saw us personally to the door, his final parting words to reassure me that I would always be welcome in his home.

Once back in the carriage, I felt a great sense of relief, knowing so much of my task was completed. I was also very involved in thinking about the banker's daughter and I started when the driver turned in his seat, speaking most presumptuously. "Quite a long visit, sir! Did you get your money changed?"

"You may take us to the Thames Bridge," I told him sharply, "and mind your driving!"

He gave me a surly, knowing look and whipped up the horses. I was confused enough by the twisting streets that I did not immediately realize the driver was taking us in the opposite direction from the bridge. I was thinking of other things, more or less lost in my own reverie, when it suddenly occurred to me we had been traveling for too long a time. I looked at the unfamiliar landscape and shouted at the driver. "I said the Thames bridge, you clod!"

The driver did not answer, and Toby, seated beside him, began tugging at his arm. "His Lordship's speaking to you," he shouted shrilly. "He wants to know where we're going."

The driver shook him loose, knocking the lad half off the seat. I reached up and grabbed the boy's arm, pulling him through the air and into the coach, just as the driver whipped the horses into full gallop. Toby landed hard against the priest. "Are you all right?" I asked him.

A stout lad, he replied, "Yes, sir," but he had a cut on his forehead and held his elbow where he had struck it against the carriage door.

I was already angry, and the sight of the boy's injuries made me go into a flash of red, blinding rage. Without considering the consequences, I threw myself against the driver's back, hooking an arm about his neck, and hauled him downward against the forward seat. He landed upside down, his feet flailing wildly in the air, his neck and shoulders pressed against the leather. The carriage began careening crazily, for the horses were now unguided by the reins, which flapped about in empty air. But I was not even aware of it; I started pounding on the villainous brute with both fists, digging my knee into his neck. I landed several blows against his belly as he sagged limply onto the floor. I had been shouting all the while, using my newly acquired English oaths: "What do you think we are, you son of a bitch, a flock of defenseless women?"

While I had been engaged with the driver, Toby, with amazing presence of mind, had managed to climb back onto the bench and was pulling with all his strength at the brake. It did little good, although I suppose it had slowed us a bit. The reins had fallen completely out of reach after I grabbed the driver, and they were now trailing on the ground, between the backs of the panicked horses. Trees and buildings flashed by, as we were carried out of the city and headed into the countryside, fairly flying along one of the Queen's highways.

My first coherent memory was of Toby screaming, desperately trying to attract my attention. "I can't stop them, sir!" I caught only a glimpse of Thomas as I went over the front seat to join the boy. The priest, with one foot planted on the driver's neck to hold him to the floor, was praying fervently.

Our horses were now running completely unchecked, the carriage swaying wildly from side to side. We were moving much too fast for any thought of leaping out, and Toby shouted something about hills and sharp bends ahead. There was no other choice; I threw myself onto the back of one horse, nearly rendering myself a eunuch. By gripping his mane with one hand, I was able to reach down and grasp the reins with the other. I tossed the loose ends back to Toby, keeping hold of the center part myself. Between the two of us, we were able to bring the horses to a careening halt. The carriage swung around in a scittering arc, until it bumped to rest against a tree.

I slid down onto wobbly legs, coughing and trying to brush the dirt from my clothes. A great swirl of dust was settling around us.

"A most heroic display!" came a familiar voice from somewhere beyond the cloud of dust. "I did not think you were going to pull it off!"

I came around the carriage, to face the elegant figure of Lord Dudley – not quite yet the Earl of Leicester. I glared at him, standing in the roadway as he towered above me, mounted on a fine chestnut gelding. He was wearing a bright array of very foppish clothing, and headed a group of some half dozen young men. Most of the others competed with him in the brightness and poor taste of their outfits.

"So, the Russian knows something about horses," he sneered. "I understand many barbarians are born on them."

That remark brought a tittering giggle from his companions.

"Were you responsible for this?" I demanded angrily.

"Oh, hardly anything so crude," he replied, as if my words did him injury. "Were I to do away with you it would be accomplished with far more . . . grace, more finesse."

I turned my back on him and returned to the carriage. Toby had gotten inside with Father Thomas, who was now nursing a bump on his head. Otherwise, they both appeared to be all right. The driver was lying on the floor, groaning.

Thomas had been watching me and the activities on the road, probably understanding little of the verbiage, though the mutual hostility between Robin and myself needed little by way of translation. Suddenly, the priest shouted: "Look out, Dmitri!" I spun just in time to miss a slash from Dudley's crop.

"No foreign bastard turns his back on –" He never finished. I grabbed his arm and yanked him down from the horse. The animal continued on without him, colliding with our team.

I let go of Dudley, who came up from the ground in a fury. I checked him with an outstretched arm, keeping a sharp lookout for interference from his friends. They all crowded around, but none made a move to assist him.

"I think you would like to challenge me, would you not?" I demanded.

"Nothing would give me more pleasure, sir," he gasped. His girlish face was crimson, and his breath came in short, uneven snorts.

"Well, I shall not throw down the gauntlet," I said flatly. "Not only am I a guest in your land, but I am also unfamiliar with your rapiers. Any time you wish to challenge me, of course, I stand at your service. But I warn you, sir, when the choice of weapons is mine I shall choose broadswords!"

I let go of him then, and he took a step backward to get his balance. "I want no further trouble with you," I went on. "I thought I made this clear the last time we spoke. I seek in no way to harm you; now, will you let it go at that?"

"He's got you, you know, Robin," called one of his friends.

"Yes, let him have his way," shouted another, a merry tone of laughter in his voice.

Dudley stood without making a reply for several minutes, while his companions continued their banter. Except in a contest of skill with the rapier, Dudley would have had little chance against me. Less than three fourths my bulk, he was soft from his easy life. I also suspected that the discomforture of rising before dawn, which was the British custom in scheduling a duel, was more distressing to him than the possibility of his being killed. "Broadswords," he muttered. "Messy! Sheer barbarism!" Then, like the sun breaking through a cloudy sky, a smile spread across his face. With that peculiar code of honor, so typical of the English, he stepped toward me with his hand extended! "Fair enough," he said. Not knowing what else to do, I exchanged the grip of friendship with him.

A fact of which I was unaware at the time, and which Robin confided to me much later, was an injunction placed upon him by the Queen. Following the attempt on my life and the subsequent scene at the palace, Elizabeth had instructed her favorite to make no move against me. Thus, his pretended willingness to duel with me was nothing more than bluster. With the touch of our hands on that dusty road, all malice seemed to slip away. Robin draped an arm about my shoulder as if we had been lifelong friends, and drew me away from the others. "You have shown yourself a man," he said, " which all of us are, despite what you may think. But I feel I should warn you of something – and I do this because it would be the Queen's pleasure. The attack on you the other night was not ordered by me, although I have since discovered that it was done by a friend who thought to render me a service. What happened today was in no way my doing."

"Who, then?" I asked.

"Who, indeed?" he said. "I would guess the Spaniards."

"Why?"

"They have friends at court, powerful men left over from the reign of Mary Tudor. There is little you have done which they – and myself for that matter – do not know about. We are aware of your trips to the Florentine, and we know you are dealing in large sums. I cannot say this does not interest us; gold always does. Still, the Queen is cognizant of your Czar's motives and will not interfere. For this reason, our only concern is to prevent your disturbing the balances within the court. There are others who would profit from your total failure."

"Could I really disturb the balance?" I asked.

"With enough gold, you could." he said honestly.

"That is the farthest thing from my mind," I assured him.

"Then we shall leave it at that," he said, starting to walk back toward the road. "And one more thing, Demetrius. Regardless of my past suspect behavior, if you should ever need my help. . . ."

"Thank you," I said.

He paused, thoughtful again. "Ah, this incident . . . I think for all concerned it might be best if it were never mentioned."

I agreed.

"Now, let us see if your carriage is all right," he continued. "We don't want to leave you stranded."

I climbed into the driver's seat and prodded the horses. They seemed firmly hitched, and the carriage moved as usual except that the rear axle seemed a little bent.

"You will get back all right," said Dudley, mounted again. He pointed at the driver, still moaning in the floor. "Better throw that rubbish out before he causes you more trouble."

"I think I'll bring him back with me," I said. "Maybe he can tell us something."

"Perhaps you're right," Dudley replied. He gripped his chin as his gaze focused on the captive. He circled us on his prancing mount – a truly beautiful animal. "Tell you what. Follow us to the watch headquarters. Maybe we *can* get something from him." He added this last as a casual afterthought.

Dudley and his friends rode ahead of us, chattering and joking among themselves. Robin dropped back twice to say something to me, then rejoined the others. His attitude was strange, but it was English; it seemed against their way for a man to hold a grudge. Our encounter had been quite by chance, incidentally; the group had been racing their mounts on a training track nearby. They had seen the carriage speed past and had followed out of curiosity.

We entered London and followed a course through the less traveled back alleys. Dudley certainly knew the city, even areas where I would not expect he had ever been. Our journey ended at the Tower of London, for many generations the residence of English Kings. As a fortress it fit the need; as a king's palace it was horrid. The tiny, single entrance served everyone – prisoners on the way to dungeon cells, as well as noble gentlemen and ladies who came on state business. Elizabeth, showing a greater delicacy of taste, never stayed there, though I think it was still her official home.

Just prior to arriving at the Tower, we had passed through a busier section of town. Our captive had come to his senses and tried to leap out, but Father Thomas had clouted him soundly on the head with the chunk of tree limb I had tossed onto the seat for that purpose. Thus the fellow was still only half conscious when we halted before the narrow doorway. Robin and I dragged him out and turned him over to a pair of husky guardsmen. He would be taken to one of the interrogation chambers, the captain told us – a place equipped with the necessary persuasive instruments.

The rest of Robin's group awaited us, milling about on their mounts. They were still laughing about the priest's manner of "converting the prisoner." Father Thomas had chosen to remain in the carriage. Robin called to his friends, and all of us trooped into the Tower.

It took the English jailer less than half an hour to produce a flood of information from the driver. The fellow was bound down on his back upon a cross–shaped table, his wrists secured with leather thongs. The interrogators used a screw device, crushing his fingers one after the other – a most effective means. I might note that during my stay in England I had several occasions to witness their methods for punishing criminals, although this was my only experience with an interrogation. In general, their procedures were no less severe than ours – although quite different.

After being assigned by the ministry clerks to take Alfred's place, the driver had been approached by two different gentlemen, he told us. Each of these had offered a good price for my murder. The man had taken gold from each. One was Spanish, he said, confirming Robin's guess. The other was an Englishman, and the driver did not know whom he represented. One of Dudley's friends supplied the probable answer. He had seen a man he knew to be an agent of the Swedes, coming from the stable yard that morning. Comparing descriptions, it would appear to have been the same person.

"Many princes seek the hand of our Queen," Robin remarked. "Since the rumor has become widespread that your Czar is also a suitor, the 'establishment of swains' is bound to be disturbed about it."

"I should think they would have gone after Pissemsky, our Ambassador," I said innocently.

Robin cleared his throat, embarrassed. "I do not wish to be offensive, but your blood relationship –"

"Even that is known?" I laughed, but I think I blushed a bit, as well.

"There are few secrets in a royal court, especially a hag–ridden court," said one of the others.

Everyone laughed at that – even Dudley, which surprised me. But they all seemed to feel I had little to worry about. My visits to the Florentine had also disturbed the situation, Robin reasoned, especially as Ridolfi was openly involved in trying to supply a suitor, himself.

"It is the Swedes who puzzle me," he admitted. "Gustof is not a leading candidate – never has been, and the Swedish ambassador knows it. What his people hoped to gain, I can't imagine."

"I can answer that," I told him. "Russia has been at war with Sweden, on and off, for the last two years. Since one of our purposes in being here is to procure weapons –"

"I am perishing from thirst, Robin," shouted one of his fellows. "Can't you discuss this over a tankard of ale?"

There was general agreement to this, and we immediately retired to a nearby tavern – a terrible, dingy establishment on the waterfront, frequented mostly by laborers and seamen. Yet my companions did not seem strangers, for the crone who ran the place greeted them like old friends. We had brought Father Thomas along, and the men spent nearly two hours trying to get him drunk, paying for the drinks with the Spanish and Swedish gold we had taken from my would–be assassin. Like most of our countrymen, the priest had been brought up on spirits. In the end, it was he and I who remained coherent. Two of our companions were already unconscious, while the other four and Robin remained barely aware of their circumstances.

This evening of drinking and good fellowship marked the beginning of my friendship with several of these men – and others whom I was to meet through them. I also began calling on Nina Ridolfi soon after this, following Robin's guidance in matters of dress and manners. I think it pleased him to have such an opportunity to act as instructor. He assured that we received numerous invitations to parties and social gatherings all over the city. He also arranged opportunities for me to speak with several great men of learning. And however it was accomplished, I was not bothered with foreign paid murderers again.

For all the pleasure I took from these various activities, I felt I was fulfilling the Czar's desires. He had told me to learn all I could of the English ways, and of their philosophies. That I should also find it the most enjoyable period of my life was, in my opinion, no sin. Even my relationship with Nina was more than proper – strangely enough, more my doing than hers.

I had been in England for nearly six months when I wrote the Czar, requesting his permission to marry Nina. I sent the letter off with Sir Jerome Bowes, who was returning to Russia in Fletcher's stead. Anthony Jenkinson, who was a little older than the others – I suppose in his early forties – had decided the journey was more than he wanted to take. I knew the Czar would be disappointed; Anthony had always been his favorite. For this reason, I would also have preferred him to act as my spokesman.

CHAPTER III

My third notable encounter with the Queen occurred several months after Robin had been created Earl of Leicester. By this time I had seen a good deal of him and his friends, and through his tutelage I had entered fully into the social life of London, including many court functions. On these occasions I would frequently see the Queen, but had little opportunity to speak more than a greeting. My beard, of course, had grown out by this time, but I was having it trimmed in the English fashion. I was also wearing Western dress all the time, now, and would have felt foolish and out of place in my heavy Russian robes.

My business with Nina's father being long since completed, my calls at his home were for the obvious purpose of courting his daughter. I think Ridolfi was having some second thoughts, now that the relationship between Nina and me had progressed to the point where I was only waiting permission from the Car to marry her. It was not that he objected to me as a prospective son–in–law; he was troubled by the thought of his only child being taken away to the distant cold of Russia. For this reason, in my letter to the Czar I had requested him to allow me an additional year in England. Regardless of this, Nina and I were definitely bound. Her father, decisive as he was in business and in his political dabblings, was like unresisting honey in her hands. His expressions of disapproval, therefore, were minimal. I saw Nina nearly every day.

I have avoided any attempt to explain my own emotions during this time, because I cannot honestly interpret them. The overpowering love I felt for Nina seemed to rob me of my manhood, to make me weak; it gave rise to an almost immoral willingness to accept her woman's soul as the equal of any other. I found myself hearing her and heeding the advice she gave as if these ideas had sprung from the mouth of a holy sage. The most disturbing of all was a realization I kept hidden, even from my confessor – the knowledge that no other person in all the world could mean as much to me as she. I knew deep within myself that Nina held the power to command my spirit and to extract a loyalty which rightly belonged only to God or my Czar.

As for Robin, I cannot overstate the pleasure I took in our friendship. I had never before enjoyed such a cultured and well–informed companion. He seemed to delight in showing me the wonders of his homeland, in addition to being as unrestrained a reveler as Vladya had ever been. Robin and Nina had also formed a bond, with the result that a good many invitations were extended to us jointly: picnics, sightseeing trips, and balls, especially balls! I learned all the popular dance steps, mostly in the privacy of Ridolfi`s parlor, where the banker's own musicians would play for us. Nina was a wonderful dancer, and she taught me so well that we were frequently called upon to lead the quadrilles.

In the late spring, almost exactly a year after my arrival in England, we were extended an invitation to spend a few days at Robin's new home in Leicester. The purpose of this fete was to belatedly celebrate his elevation to the Earldom. The

Queen was expected to attend, making it an especially exciting prospect. Our only obstacle was Ridolfi, who suddenly became stubborn about granting his permission for Nina to go. Feeling as he did about losing his precious child, he had lately become very protective of her and seemed reluctant to permit us the degree of freedom we had been enjoying. This time, he voiced his objections in no uncertain terms. Our being together for several days, without a proper chaperone, was impossible, he said. Unlike the Spanish ladies, who were always attended by an elderly aunt or other kinswoman – I believe they are called *Duenas* – Italians of Ridolfi's class did not normally bother with such things. Nonetheless, the chastity of a daughter was no less a consideration. With his Medici kinswoman still the dowager Queen of France, Ridolfi considered his daughter's position to be in danger of serious compromise if she should go unattended. The prospective presence of the Queen did not lessen his resolve. Without someone specifically assigned to safeguard her virtue, he flatly refused. Finally, I appealed to Robin, and arranged that Nina's father also receive an invitation. This, of course, delighted him, and may have been what he wanted right along.

Now I had Ridolfi pacified, there came some trouble in my own household. Pissemsky and Thomas banded together, and the two of them cornered me one afternoon, taking me to task for my frivolity. I think the real sore point, at least from Feodor's standpoint, was my being invited to so many more social functions than he. In this instance, the ambassadors of several other countries had been asked to Leicester, and Pissemsky had been neglected. Attacking from a different angle, Thomas accused me of neglecting my religious devotions. He also brought up the question of my beard, the fact that I was having it severely trimmed and shaped.

"But I cannot grow back a great Russian bush," I explained. "In England it would be out of place, and I would look ill groomed."

"You are associating with these ungodly men," the priest berated me. "You are assuming the mannerisms of their effeminacy and indulging in their debauche‐ries. You are further imperiling your soul by your relationship with that papist Italian woman."

"I am going to marry that Italian woman," I said flatly. Prior to this, I had not told either of them, because I was afraid Pissemsky might write the Czar, expressing an adverse opinion.

My statement shocked both of them mute. Taking advantage of their silence, I went on: "The condition of my soul," I assured them, "is quite as secure as it was the day I set foot on these shores. I have performed the tasks assigned me by the Czar, and I have done all I can to assist the Czar's Ambassador to complete his own duties. I have befriended the Queen's favorite, and through him have done more to forward the cause of our anointed Czar than you could ever have accomplished if I had remained home at prayer. As for this 'Italian woman,' she is as pure and virtuous as any lady I have ever met. As a priest, Thomas, you should rejoice that I shall soon bring another soul into the bosom of the true, Orthodox Church."

There was little more they could say, and it was with their grudging approval that I left with Nina and her father two days later. We traveled in Ridolfi's very elegantly appointed coach, manned by his regular driver and footman, but with Toby and his father added as my contribution to the staff. We had six outriders, two of Ridolfi's men and four retainers from Leicester's guard. With all of this, our trip to and from Leicester should have been swift, comfortable, and completely safe. Unfortunately, I was guilty of a bit of foolishness which was to cause considerable trouble. At the time I decided upon my course of action, I did not stop to realize how great a sin I might be committing. What followed was no more than a just visitation of God's well–deserved wrath.

Because this would be the most elegant and formal occasion either of us had ever attended, I decided that Nina should wear the great, blue diamond I had left over from Ivan's collection. It was to be a surprise for her, worked out by her father and myself. I brought the gem to Ridolfi the day he received his invitation, and he had seen to having it mounted as a pendant. (It was far too heavy for anything else.) When we started out for Leicester, I had it in a velvet box with some of my personal possessions, on the floor of the carriage. With such a gem about her neck, Nina would be the greatest sensation at the ball; she would undoubtedly attract the attention and envy of every woman there, including the Queen. The prospect made me so eager for the event, I could not keep the secret once we were underway.

"I have a surprise for you, my dear," I said, fumbling on the floor for my case. "Your father and I have prepared something to make you the grandest lady in the castle."

"Oh?" she said teasingly. "I thought you considered me that, anyway."

"Of course," I replied, "but this adornment to the already glorious plumage will only enforce my judgment, and will prove to the others how great my devotion really is."

"Then it is to make yourself the grandest gentleman you have done it," she laughed. But I could see she was eagerly awaiting my surprise.

I found the box and placed it on my lap. "This is a great treasure, belonging to my Czar," I said, lest there be any misunderstanding about its ownership. "But he has entrusted its safekeeping to me. Now, for a few hours, I pass the task on to you." With that, I opened the box. The sparkling pool of icy blue, set in a circle of finely wrought gold, brought an involuntary gasp from Nina.

She slowly reached out her hand and gently lifted the precious medallion from its case. "I have never seen anything so . . . so overwhelmingly beautiful!"

"About your neck, my dear it will be set off to its greatest glory," I said.

She held it to herself and reached for her own case to get a mirror. She viewed her reflection, still awed at the magnificence of the jewel. Then she looked at me, a worried expression on her face. "Is it not true that all great diamonds have tales of evil curses attached to them?"

"I have heard this," I said, "but it is only the greed of men that causes such things. This stone has lain in the coffers of the Princes of Muscovy for a great many years. Before that, I know only that it came from Bukhara, taken as booty from a Mongol chieftain."

"And did this Mongol die?" she asked.

"Probably," I said casually. "I am not sure. By now he would be dead in any event, so why does it matter?"

She leaned across Ridolfi and kissed me on the cheek. Showing no favoritism, she then did the same to her father. "I shall trust you two fine gentlemen to protect me from whatever curse the stone may carry," she said. "It is much too pretty to be evil." She watched in almost childish disappointment when, at her father's insistence, I placed the necklace back into its hiding place.

The road to Leicester took us north through Middlesex, then westerly into Buckingham. Because we had left London so early, it was still light when we arrived at this halfway point, where Ridolfi had arranged for us to stay with friends of his. Nina and I wandered through the old village and browsed in a few shops, pausing to view the river from the city walls. Our sole attendant was Toby, who followed behind us. Nina had formed a great attachment for the lad, and preferred him to any other retainer. As I liked the boy, myself, and found him honest and well mannered, I was happy to indulge her.

Nina and I found Buckinghamtown especially interesting, for we had recently seen a play by one of the better established masters. It had concerned the life of King Henry VI, an English monarch of the previous century. Much of the story had taken place here and in nearby Saint Albens, but with the theater's poor trappings it had been difficult to visualize the area. Now that we could see it, we found the real place quite enchanting, a setting well suited to romantic imaginations.

It was dark when we returned to our host's manor, and we found that Nina's father had seen to it that the romance of the region did not bring about any lack of propriety. His bedchamber was between those assigned to Nina and me.

In the morning we again left early, traveling toward Northampton, which city we reached at noon. We had our midday meal at a little tavern on the edge of town, and afterward set out on the last leg of our trip, hoping to arrive in Leicester before dark. We made excellent speed, of course, for the Queen's highways were well tended and the ground was completely dry.

We were not many miles out of Northampton when we encountered another coach traveling in our same direction. From the livery of the driver and the outriders I recognized it as belonging to Warwick. We journeyed along in a procession of two, increasing the column as we met still more coaches along the way. We were seven in all when we arrived, amid much laughter and joking, the occupants leaning out and calling back and forth to one another. I think Ridolfi was happy for the company, for he was deathly afraid of highwaymen. The seven coaches had provided us with a small army of retainers.

The gathering at Leicester was quite the merriest I had ever attended. The castle was very large, surrounded by vast stretches of lawn and closely shaped hedges. Its furnishings were a mixture of the old, heavy pieces, not unlike our own in Russia; and the more delicate, fancy finery I had grown accustomed to in London.

Again, Ridolfi arranged to have his room located between Nina's and mine. Why he had suddenly become so concerned was more a matter of amusement than annoyance to us, for we had never engaged in any compromising activities. For me, the idea of committing such a sin with this woman was enough to keep me well within the bounds of propriety. I will admit, though, that with her father attempting to assure our continued restraint, the forbidden fruit was beginning to appear sweeter to us both.

The grand ball was to be on the evening after our arrival; Her Majesty was also due on the morrow. Leicester, himself, had been delayed and was now coming with the Queen, thus leaving his guests free to entertain themselves that first night.

Robin had not been neglectful in any way, I might add, for his master of revels had gone to great lengths in decorating and provisioning the castle with food and drink. The guests, themselves, seemed a peculiar mix. But the guest list had been made up solely of people who were popular with the Queen or our host. Many of us were foreigners who found it difficult to converse in any mutual language; and on this first evening not all the party had arrived.

The Italians were well represented, and a number of them turned out to be friends of Ridolfi. The most outstanding figure in this group was Guido Cavalcanti, a wily little Florentine in the service of Catherine d'Medici. He was an agent whom the Dowager Queen frequently entrusted with her foreign intrigues. At the present, these concerned an attempt to arrange the marriage of Elizabeth to the Duc d'Anjou, the same cause which had delayed my original introduction to Ridolfi. The two men were immediately engaged in a lively conversation. Henri, the Duc d'Anjou, was the younger brother of the present French King. While his advocates were never successful in arranging the marriage to Elizabeth, I was still destined to have some association with him, because he later became King of Poland. The stories I heard that night from Guido did not interest me as they would have, had I known what the future held for this young man. Still, Henri's life was lurid enough to provide a number of interesting anecdotes. It appeared he was the most intemperate of men, completely given over to strange, voluptuous pursuits. Even his mother's ambassador found it difficult to formulate a complimentary description of him. Among his fellow Italians, Cavalcanti was quite candid, making his remarks in their native tongue, which – despite my efforts to learn the language – involved many terms I could not understand. Nina translated these in a whispered voice, until some of it made her blush. After that, she refused to continue.

Our group was standing near the windows of a large salon, overlooking the gardens behind the building. Servants were busy below us, lighting colored lanterns which they placed at intervals throughout the park. The moon had not yet risen, and the movement of men from station to station was visible only inside the circles of light from their torches.

"I would like some fresh air," whispered Nina.

I agreed. "So would I." Without bothering to excuse ourselves, we slipped away from the group of chattering Italians, none of whom seemed to notice our departure.

Although such things were apparently as common in Italy as in England, and nothing new to Nina, I never ceased to marvel at the beautifully kept lawns and hedges. In the Leicester park there was an exceptional arrangement of these, with a most intricate maze formed by the placement and shaping of the shrubs. It was supposed to be a game to find your way into the very center, where there was a statue and some benches. Nina and I became lost several times, trying to achieve the innermost point. By using the maze as the designers must have intended, we frequently pressed our lips together at the dark end of some false passage. In the inky blackness we did not have to fear being seen, even from the heights of the castle. Thus, from my standpoint, the game became more a search for the patches of darkness than for our original goal of the center. Nina finally led me in the proper direction, amidst sounds of laughter and giggling from other couples lost in the twisting confusion of hedgerows. We were calling to some unseen companions, laughing at our own wit, when we almost collided with the back of a white, iron bench. Above us was the goddess of love on her pedestal. Obviously, we had found the center.

"Victory deserves a little reward," I said, pulling Nina against me.

Her willing lips met mine, and as always I could feel her long lashes against my cheek when she closed her eyes. Only a moment later, I felt them open again, and a little squeal sounded deep in her throat. Our mouths parted and I saw she was looking at a shadow, a dark form seated on a bench across the clearing from us.

"I thought I heard someone," she whispered. "Is that a man sitting there? I can't see well enough –"

"Have no fear, My Lady," came a suave, slightly accented voice from the darkness. "I mean nobody any harm, but like yourselves I have wandered in here and know not how to get out."

"Who are you, sir?" I asked sharply.

A pudgy little man stepped out of the shadows, bowing deeply before us. He was of middle age, with a smooth face and shiny, bald head, edged by a light fringe of white hair. A pair of strangely shaped lenses, called spectacles, were perched on the end of his long, pointed nose. He was dressed in somber black, as if in mourning, except for a brightly striped waistcoat beneath his doublet. My hand had strayed to the hilt of my rapier – which I had now learned to use – but I let it drop when I saw the shape of our little specter.

"Permit me to introduce myself, sir, and madam," he began grandly. "I am Doctor Elysius Bomel, late of His Majesty's court in Westphalia, doctor of medicine from the College of Cambridge in this fair land, and student in the arts of astronomy, astrology, philosophy and alchemy. And I have the great honor of addressing . . . ?"

"The Lady Antonina d'Ridolfi," I replied, as Nina made a playful, exaggerated curtsy. "And I am General Prince Dmitri Simeonevitch Marensky, from the Imperial Court of His Majesty the Czar." I also bowed, and in my clowning I nearly fell on my head.

"Ah, such titles and honors, my children, all gathered here in this tiny space, from whence I fear we may never escape!" The doctor waved his arms about the enclosure. "But as a general, my dear sir, I have no doubt your sense of direction will prove our salvation. Think you, it may be possible to lead us from this place?"

"It could probably be done, Doctor," I replied. "But for such a service, what reward might I expect? I am nursing a right formidable thirst, sir!" I _was_ thirsty, and I knew he had something to drink, for he fairly reeked of wine.

"Then permit me, sir," he replied at once. From the bench where he had been seated he produced a flask of Malmsey. "The very grape in which the Duke of Clarence met his end, yea these many years ago," he said, handing me the bottle. "I beg you, sir, to forgive my informality, but I did not think to bring a glass, never expecting such a flower of the Mediterranean." He swept another very unbalanced bow to Nina, and this time he did topple onto the ground. "I am ever so slightly tipsy," he apologized.

I offered the flask to Nina, but she shook her head. I tipped it to my lips and took a deep drought. It was the first of this particular wine I had ever tasted, and I found it most agreeable. "I know now, Doctor," I remarked, "Why the good duke elected such an end. This is delicious."

"Perhaps it will also excuse my unfortunate condition," he replied. Now that he was attempting to stand without leaning on the bench, I realized how very unsteady he was.

Our conversation had been overheard by another couple, just over the hedgerow from us. "Beware the good doctor, Demetrius," called a feminine voice. "He can drink more wine than any three men!"

Doctor Bomel laughed with us, and together we made our way back through the maze. I was very taken with the man, as was Nina, for he possessed wit and great skill with words. While we were outside, musicians had set up in the large salon, where they were now playing some of the more popular dance music. Many people were already making use of this, although several couples still wandered in and out of the doors to the various terraces and gardens. I had expected the doctor would leave us, once we were back in the castle; but he showed no inclination to do so. Instead, he attached himself to us, and to the Italian group, when we rejoined it. We introduced him all 'round, and he surprised us by speaking to Ridolfi and his friends in their own dialect. He was apparently as skilled in this tongue as English. Both Nina and I continued to be impressed.

That night in Robin's castle marked a peculiar high spot in my English adventure. It was almost the pinnacle of pleasure, almost the end of this tranquil period in my life. Nina and I danced together, not much concerned with Doctor Bomel or anyone else. Some of the later pieces required a bodily touching which all but set me aflame, for I had never desired anyone as I craved Nina during these final hours. It was very late when we finally retired, having outlasted Ridolfi, the doctor, and nearly everyone else. Only by the greatest self–restraint did I keep from committing the grossest of mortal sins, for so it would have seemed to me had I taken advantage of the opportunity. My love for Nina – and my near veneration of her purity – transcended any physical lusts, though just barely.

The next day we were all up bright and early. Leaving our rooms, we were quickly caught up in the dual excitement. There was a fox hunt scheduled for the morning, and in the afternoon the Queen was expected to arrive. I tapped on Nina's door, but she and her father had gone down ahead of me. I found them breaking fast in the main hall, sitting at a long table with Doctor Bomel and some others. I was surprised to be introduced to Anne Richards, the doctor's wife. She had not been among the guests the night before, and Elysius explained that she had been indisposed. Actually, I think she disapproved of her husband's heavy drinking, and had retired to their room so as not to see it. Considerably younger than the doctor, Anne was quite plain, with a sallow complexion and drab, brownish hair. However, she made up for her physical shortcomings by an almost motherly sweetness, which had already worked its charm on Nina. The two women were soon whispering together, exchanging gossip and confidences. They appeared to have formed an immediate attachment for one another.

The hunt was a spectacular success, especially enjoyable because of Robin's fine stables. The riders, dressed mostly in greens and browns, galloped like a horde of Cossacks across the meadows and fields. Even the ladies, hampered as they were by the awkwardly shaped sidesaddles, rode as if part of their respective mounts. I stayed near the rear of the group with Nina, who was not as confident as she might have been of her horsemanship. Still, speeding across the open countryside, raven hair streaming loose from beneath her feathered cap, face flushed from the excitement, she was lovely as I had ever perceived her to be.

The Queen arrived shortly after we had returned to the castle, and with her came most of the court. The noisy, boisterous flock swept into the hall of Leicester in a glittering burst of sound and color. Robin greeted those guests who had preceded him, and personally conducted Elizabeth to her rooms. The other latecomers were quickly attended by servants, who guided them to their quarters and the raucous flurry subsided almost as soon as it began. I had been standing to one side, alone because Nina and her father had gone upstairs to refresh themselves and the Bomels had remained in their quarters during the hunt. Although I had now grown used to the mannerisms of the gentlemen who surrounded the Queen, I was still distressed to hear their high–pitched voices, mingled with the chatter of the females. As the last of the incoming group dispersed, an overpowering aura of perfume lingered behind. They had not traveled far, having remained the night in Northampton. Yet everyone seemed to require some rest before the grand ball. For the next few hours the castle was silent, except for the muted discourses of the servants.

With the fall of darkness, the rejuvenated court streamed down for the evening's festivities. In all, it was the merriest assembly I had ever seen: ladies in their full, gaudy gowns, gentlemen in the finest silks and velvets. The Queen danced with a joyous, almost girlish abandon, completely at odds with her usual, restrained demeanor. Later in the evening, she retired to her place of honor, on a low dais against the long wall. Once in place she remained there, receiving the homage of Robin's other guests. At the end of one quadrille, Nina and I ended almost directly in front of her, and Elizabeth beckoned for us to approach. "I hope Our Brother, the Czar, will quickly grant his permission for your union," she said.

I thanked Her Grace and immediately presented Nina, who had not previously been so honored. I could see the Queen's eyes fasten on the great diamond, though she said nothing about it. During this pause we had become the center of attention, and following it I noticed nearly every woman in the hall made a point of coming forward to wish us well – using this excuse to make a closer inspection of the huge stone. The effect was exactly as I had hoped, and Nina was in absolute ecstasy.

In one respect, my own pleasure seemed too great to be real. I kept contrasting this lighthearted mingling of the sexes with the restrictive customs followed by my own people, wondering how Nina was going to accept the drab role of a Russian noblewoman. Perhaps I had drunk too much, but as the night wore on an ominous weight began to form in my gut. I am not certain if I recognized the source just then, but it could have been due to the troubled thoughts emerging through the joyous revelry, the knowledge of how transitory these pleasure had to be. As much as I tried to deny it, I thoroughly enjoyed the freedom of Elizabeth's court and I secretly dreaded the moment when I would have to leave. Such an admission – even to myself – was wrong, sinful; and against the background of levity I felt the dark, looming specter of guilt.

I must have projected some of this distraction, for Robin noticed it. Taking me by one hand, Nina with the other, he led us back to the Queen's dais. With Her Majesty's permission, the Earl of Leicester announced our plans – publicly, for the first time. He proposed a toast to our lifelong happiness, and the Great Queen raised her glass with all the rest.

The revels continued for another two days, with very few of the guests departing early. Unfortunately, Ridolfi's business required his being among the first to leave. At his insistence we set out early in the morning – this because of his heightened fear of highwaymen. Now that everyone had seen the diamond, Ridolfi wanted to take no chances by traveling after dark.

Doctor Bomel and his wife had come to the castle with some other people and had no conveyance of their own – or so they told Nina, who invited them to accompany us back to London. With five of us in the carriage it was a little crowded, but both women were small and they sat close together, gossiping and discussing the other females. Bomel passed the first day alternating between a wheezing doze and several long expositions of his many adventures within the intellectual circles of England, Germany and France. Our time slipped by very quickly.

There had been several other carriages with us when we left, but ours was the only one going all the way to London. When we reached Buckingham we were alone, with just our six outriders and the regular carriage attendants. We spent another night with Ridolfi's friends, setting out early the following morning. All went well until we came close to a small hamlet called Henley, where the road turned to follow the Thames into London.

Our driver had maintained a steady pace all day, making as good speed as he could without a change of post horses. Suddenly, one of the outriders shouted a warning, and the driver yanked on the reins. Before we could stop, the carriage clumped heavily onto its left side. We were all pitched against the door, and it was only by the greatest of good fortune that no one was seriously injured. Nina bumped her head; Bomel sustained a bruise on his hip – nothing more. I struggled to get the door open on the upper side, pulled myself through and jumped to the ground. The carriage was listing badly, with a broken front wheel.

Two or three of the men dismounted and tried to heave the chassis off the ground, using a long pole for leverage. The rest of our party climbed out to watch as the men continued to struggle with the damaged wheel. Ridolfi called to his driver.

"What happened?" he asked in a dazed voice.

"There must have been a deep pot hole in the road, sir," answered the servant.

"We couldn't see anything," added Toby. He had perched on the sloping carriage boot, but jumped down now and ran back along the highway. Alfred was among those trying to remove the wheel. We were in a deserted area, with lightly forested meadow land on either side of the road. I could see a farmer's cottage in the distance, but that was the nearest structure. The sun was low on the horizon, casting long shadows from the nearby oaks across the roadway.

Soon all our retainers had dismounted and gathered around the men who were trying to lift the heavy carriage. All but two were helping in one way or another, and this pair was standing closet to the rest. Ridolfi, Bomel and I were watching them from a few feet away, while the women had found a grassy spot across the road. They had seated themselves, pulling their cloaks more tightly about their shoulders against the advancing chill from the river.

Then Toby called from down the road. "Sir, oh sir! The hole! Come see it!"

Bomel and I started back toward Toby, who had picked up something that appeared to be a large sheet of parchment. It looked as if someone had deliberately dug a pit, fastened the piece of material across the top and covered it with a light layer of road dust, thus making it invisible to the driver. It took only that single glance before I started running back toward the carriage, calling for the men to prepare against an attack by bandits. I never reached them. One moment I was racing along the dusty highway; the next I knew I was in my bedroom at the house in London.

I came back to life with a violent lurch, still trying to do something. I could not remember what. I knew only that there should be a great urgency in my motion. A firm hand pushed me back, and I looked up into Doctor Bomel's chubby face. Pissemsky stood on the other side of the bed, and Nina was beside him. I tried to question what had happened and where I was, but the effort to speak brought a sharp pain to the left side of my face. I realized I was swathed in bandages.

"You were creased by a shot," explained Pissemsky.

"You are lucky to be alive," added the doctor. "A hair's breadth farther and it would have penetrated your skull."

I groaned. "Was anyone hurt? The diamond!" I did bolt up at that, ignoring the pain in my head and the pressure of the doctor's hands. "What happened?" I demanded.

"We were attacked by brigands," said Nina. "Some of them were hidden along the road, and the rest were mounted. They came from behind us, and as soon as these men got close the ones in the ditches leaped out. Two of our men were killed, and they took everything – including the pendant."

"The Czar's diamond," I groaned.

"What do you mean, the Czar's diamond?" demanded Pissemsky. "I thought it was your diamond!"

I looked helplessly at the three people clustered about my bed, while through the haze and throbbing pain I tried to think. Nina knew only that she had worn a pendant, made from a diamond belonging to the Czar. Pissemsky knew I had the stone; I had been afraid not to tell him, lest he hear from others that Nina had worn it. But he thought it was my own property. Bomel knew only that Nina wore a piece of jewelry I had given her. There was no single statement I could make to satisfy all three, as I had thoroughly tangled myself into a web of half truths. "God be merciful!" I moaned.

"Never mind appealing to the Almighty!" said Pissemsky sharply. "What is this about the Czar's diamond?"

"Don't try to bully me," I snapped back at him. "This is my problem and has nothing to do with you!"

"I think the others had better leave us," said the Ambassador. He spoke in a more controlled voice, but his slender frame had begun to tremble, whether from fear or anger – or whatever other emotion – I could not yet tell. "Dmitri and I have a few things to discuss," he added when the others hesitated to go, deferring to me with their glances.

"I don't think we have anything to discuss," I insisted. I was still unreasonably angry, more at myself for my stupidity than over anything Feodor had said.

Pissemsky herded the others toward the door, gently propelling them with his outstretched arms. "Please," he urged.

"He must lie back," said Bomel, looking over his shoulder.

"He will lie down," Pissemsky assured him. He came up to the bed as soon as the door was closed and shoved me back, none too gently. "Now, please stay still and listen to me," he said firmly. His tone was just stern enough that I ceased trying to resist.

"I do not know what this business about the diamond is," he began, "but there are some other matters of urgency I must discuss with you. Are you well enough to understand me?"

"What's happened?" I asked.

"There has been a ship from home," he answered haltingly. "All is not . . . well."

"The war?" I asked.

"It is not the war," he responded slowly. "I have some other news which will. . .disturb you." he looked at me compassionately, hesitant to explain further. "I hope you are well enough. . . ."

"Curse you, Pissemsky!" I shouted. "I am perfectly well enough for whatever it is you have to tell me. Not knowing is much worse, now you've gone this far!"

"We have both been ordered home," he began. "Andrei Savin has been sent to replace me."

"Is that the disturbing news?" I asked.

"There is more," he said, almost in a whisper, and a great sadness crept into his voice. "It concerns your friend, Prince Vladimir. He is dead."

"Vladya?" I exclaimed. The same cold wave of horror clutched at my guts as I had experienced in the Khan's prison cell. "How? In battle?" I watched Feodor's face and I knew. ". . . executed?"

Pissemsky nodded. "I have not received anything in writing, but Savin tells me he was executed by personal order of the Czar."

"Tell me!" I insisted.

"There was a plot, as I understand it, involving the Prince and his mother."

"The witch!" I moaned. "I knew it! I knew someday she would destroy him."

"The Prince, his wife, both sons – there was a second born soon after our departure – and Euphrosyne. All of them, taken to the summer palace and forced to drink poison."

I groaned. I beat a rhythm with my fists against the coverlet, and rocked my head from side to side in grief. I wanted to weep, but no tears would come in my paralysis of shock, disbelief and sorrow. My friend, my lifelong, closest friend was gone! More than any other, Vladya had been not just a friend, but a close companion. The thought of his death was pain as I had never known it; not even the loss of my mother could compare, nor any of the others I had known and who

were dead in battle or by execution. But Vladya, the happiest, most carefree of any –
a man who did not lust for power, and who would gladly have lived out his life on
his country estates, surrounded by his family and his friends.

I felt a surge of hatred for Euphrosyne. She had brought her son to this!
All her life, all the things she had ever done had only contributed to this moment.
Then my rage against her subsided, as my mind's horizons seemed to expand and a
cold fear swelled through my body – a fear that sent a sharp pain twisting into my
bowels. My throat was parched from it, and my tongue seemed thick and heavy.
What if Ivan had learned of Vladya's visit to my house that night? What if he
thought I had some part in poisoning the Czarina? Even if he suspected I knew and
hadn't told him, Ivan would look on this as sin. And it *was* sin. My punishment
must come, if not from the Czar, from God.

I became aware of Pissemsky again. He sat quietly, waiting for me to
absorb his news. It suddenly occurred to me that I was presuming too much, that it
might not have been Anastasia's murder, but something else Euphrosyne had done.
"What charge . . . I mean, what did the plot involve?" I asked.

"The Czar seems to have been convinced Staritskaya had poisoned the
Czarina," he said.

Again cold fear, but I managed to look at him in puzzlement. "The
Czarina? She poisoned Anastasia?"

"No, the Czar is said to have mumbled something about Euphrosyne
having taken his 'little heifer' as well; but His Majesty executed the Staritskys for
the murder of Maria, the Circassian."

"Then she is dead, too?" I mused. The warmth of relief began to trickle
into my hands and feet. It seemed I could suddenly breathe again. Yet even the
suspicion that Euphrosyne had also poisoned Anastasia . . . it could still involve me.

"The Czar never loved Maria as he did Anastasia," I remarked. "If he
mentioned the death of the first Czarina as murder, too, then there must have been
some new evidence. We always suspected Euphrosyne might have – given the
chance —"

"There was no further evidence," said the Ambassador evenly. "The Czar
is not – um – exactly as we remember him." In response to a sharp look from me,
he hastily added: "His Majesty appears to have, er, aged, according to Savin.
Perhaps the strain of conflict . . . ."

"How long before we must depart?" I asked, keeping some sharpness in my
voice to hide the despair, and the fear.

"There is a ship leaving in three or four weeks," he said. "I have made
arrangements for us to be on it."

"And there was no message for me?" I asked.

Pissemsky handed me a thin packet of hide, which I tore open with eager,
trembling fingers. Inside was just one sheet of parchment, with the double–headed
eagle on the seal. Written in the Czar's own hand was the single sentence: *Dmitri
– You are to return at once. Ivan.*

I handed it to Pissemsky, who glanced at the paper and then at me. In
response to my questioning look, he said only, "That is not much different from
mine." He rose to leave. "Shall I tell Antonina?"

"Ask her to come back," I said.

Nina must have remained in the hall, right outside my door. She returned immediately, her face sad and drawn.

"You have heard?" I said.

She nodded. "In less than a month. There was not time for the Czar to answer your request?"

"No. My message is barely nearing Russia now, unless bad weather delayed the ship."

"What are we to do?" she asked.

"Did the Ambassador tell you about – anything?"

"Only that there was serious trouble in your homeland." She watched me anxiously, her eyes huge with tears.

"If it were not for this other," I mumbled, "I would take the risk. The Czar would forgive me, I'm sure. But now –"

"I am willing to risk it," she said softly.

"I may be in extreme . . . disfavor," I replied.

"If I do not leave with you," she said, "I know I will never see you again." She leaned over me, pressing her body against mine, cradling my head in her arms. "I do not think I could survive it," she whispered. "You must take me, Demetrius."

A rush of lust overcame my reasoning. Blood pounded so hard against my temples that I could hear nothing else. The dull, heavy pain of my wound threatened to engulf me, but I was the victim of such powerful cravings my body refused to surrender. Instead, I drew Nina tightly against me, crushing her fragile being until my arms began to tremble and a dark veil fell across my eyes. I felt myself slipping from consciousness and fought against it – may actually have been senseless for several moments. "You may be placing your life in my hands," I remember telling her. "It may be –"

Her mouth came down on mine, working frantically until her lips forced mine to part and her tongue curled up, touching the insides of my teeth. Her outgoing breath filled my lungs, and the passions boiled in my loins until I was helpless to dispute her. I turned onto my side and held her to me, barely able to restrain the tide of desire. "If I could only be sure I am not leading you to your death," I whispered.

"It doesn't matter," she answered firmly. "Without you, I am already dead."

"What of your father?"

"He understands that I *must* go with you. He isn't happy, but he understands."

I could not say anything for several moments. The swelling mixture of emotions was more than my mind could handle. I had just learned that my best friend was dead, and in the next breath I was arranging to marry. I was caught in such a conglomeration of sadness and joy I really did not know what to do – only that I wanted Nina. Through my tangled thoughts ran a flashing memory of the other women I had wanted as wife – how each time she had been taken from me. Now it was about to happen again, unless I were willing to risk her very existence for the sake of my own lusts.

Yet I told myself that it was not completely true. I could determine the circumstances myself, at least for the moment. What happened later would be in the hands of God. My love for Nina was greater than any past remembrances, and this time no other man stood able to take her from me. The decision was mine. There was no one to stop us.

"I want you," I whispered, and we kissed each other many times. Her tears were falling against my cheek, touching my lips with a trace of salty sweetness, mingled with the honeyed scent of her breath.

Again I must have slept. I had been unconscious for nearly an entire day, and it had been late morning when I had first come to my senses. The next I remember, the room was filled with deepening shadows, hardly a trace of light remaining. I was roused by a gentle tapping at the door. Nina kissed me and slipped off the bed, quickly patting her hair into shape and dabbing at her eyes. "Come in," she called.

The door opened and Toby stood there, holding a long taper in both his hands. The flame jumped from the trembling of his fingers; his face, glowing in the aura of yellow light, was a mask of tear–streaked grief.

"Your father?" asked Nina.

The boy slipped his candle into a holder on the table and ran to her, throwing himself against her bosom and sobbing into her enfolding body. She looked at me over the top of the boy's head. "Alfred was sorely wounded," she whispered. "Now three men are dead."

"This is a day for grief," I muttered.

"And joy?" she added questioningly.

"And joy," I agreed. "They sometimes come together."

Toby pulled his head back and looked up at Nina. "I will always be your servant," he sobbed.

She patted his back and cast a helpless glance in my direction. "Of course you will," she whispered. The boy buried his face against her once again. "Do you suppose . . . ?" Her own eyes were bulging with emotion, pleading with me.

"To Russia?" I asked. "We may be taking the boy to his death! Toby," I said more firmly, "have you any family?"

"There is my father's sister," he admitted unhappily. "But I would so much rather serve you, sir."

"Do you know we are leaving England?" I asked.

He nodded. "I know. You are going back to Russeland, where it is always cold and where the houses are made of precious silver and gold. Please, sir, let me go with you!" He pulled gently away from Nina, hesitantly approached the side of my bed. "Please, sir?"

"I don't know, Toby. What of your aunt? Have you spoken to her?"

"No, sir. She has not come yet. But Cook sent a message that she should."

"We must talk to her first, then," I told him.

The boy left a little later, and Doctor Bomel came in. He made some remark about the dark and quickly lighted some more candles. He looked questioningly at Nina, who shook her head.

"Well, how is our patient," he said, jovially poking at my bandages. "Do you feel ready for another bout with your favorite Malmsey?"

"What are you two plotting?" I asked, ignoring the cover of his levity.

"Why, what do you mean?" he asked innocently.

"I saw that bit of interchange when you came in. What have you been plotting?" I asked again.

"Ah, you are a man of great perception," said the doctor. "But I feel I may intrude upon some sacred communications if I discuss the matter without knowing if – ah, congratulations are in order." He looked again at Nina.

"Demetrius and I will be married as soon as he recovers from his wound," she said. "We have decided to risk the Czar's displeasure."

"And you have discussed the other matter? No, it is obvious you have not," he answered himself.

"All right! That's enough!" I exclaimed. "What other matter? What more are you after?"

"Doctor Bomel had discussed with me the possibility of his also going to Russia," said Nina, raising a finger to stifle my protest. "Before you say 'no' let me explain. In addition to being a very fine doctor, and an accomplished mathematician and astrologist, there is the question of my going into a strange land without friends or attendants, without even knowing the language. If Elysius and Anne were to come with us, I should not feel so lonely when you were gone for months in battle."

"So, instead of just a wife I am to bring home a private physician, a female companion for my spouse, and a young servant boy. And all I may accomplish in the end is to cost my Czar the price of four extra executions."

"Executions? My word!" said Bomel. "Are you taking us all to our deaths, Demetrius?"

"I am not sure I am taking *all* of you anyplace," I said. "It is beginning to sound like the story of the chicken and the falling sky."

"I think Demetrius is exaggerating the dangers," said Nina.

"I *hope* I am exaggerating the dangers," I corrected her. "Would you place your head on the block beside mine, Doctor?"

"My friend, I cannot believe. . . . I mean, your position in the court of the Majesty of Russia – surely, you are not truly in danger?" he flustered.

"The Czar's cousin, my closest friend, has just been executed for treason," I answered coldly. "I am ordered home and no explanation is given. How does that sound to you?"

Bomel smiled as if much relieved. "It is only that you are missed," he assured me. "Your Czar has need of your great talents and judgment. I am sure it can be no more than that, however ominous it may sound."

"Then you would like to take the risk?"

"Most assuredly, sir," he responded, rubbing his palms together.

I lay back silently. I had worked him to the point where I wanted him. I had anticipated the request, for I knew more about the doctor than he thought I did. Several people at the castle had warned me against him, seeing that he had singled me out during the course of the revels. Even the source of his invitation seemed nebulous, and had Robin not been so involved in entertaining his guests, he might well have investigated the circumstances and asked the intruder to leave. On the other hand, Bomel did possess the very qualities and skills which would most please Ivan. I had even considered the possibility of inviting him to return with me, should he not broach the subject on his own. At the moment, though, I had use of these skills myself.

"If you are so desirous of going to Russia, doctor, I would suggest a slight service you might perform to help assure our welcome there."

"Anything, my Prince," he replied gracefully. "Anything at all."

"My suggestion would be, doctor," I said, allowing my tone to deepen as I spoke, "that we make every effort to recover the Czar's property before we leave. I have sufficient funds of my own to make a fairly good offer to whomever is holding it; but I would not know how to initiate such a transaction. I do not exaggerate when I tell you that without the stone we may, none of us, survive the Czar's displeasure. I think you have a far better idea than I how such things are arranged."

"Indeed, sir, I hardly know what you expect of me," he sputtered, much taken back by my tone as well as my words.

"I have heard, doctor," I continued, "that your associates have not been entirely among the most eminent and noble. In fact, is this not partially the reason for your wishing to leave England?"

"Why, whatever can you be implying?" he asked indignantly.

"Yes, Demetrius, what do you mean?" added Nina.

"I mean that Doctor Bomel has a knowledge of more than just medicine and the stars. He has instructed mathematics at Cambridge, but he has had a bit of experience here and there with people in slightly different professions, have you not, doctor?" I made this last remark most pointedly.

He continued to regard me with a distressed expression.

"Let me assure you, Elysius," I consoled him, "your past is not in any way a detriment to my taking you with me, as I am sure both the Czar and I can find use for your talents, assuming, of course, my Czar permits either of us to survive long enough to make use of them. Nevertheless, I must make this a condition to my taking you out of a land where your freedom is already a subject of some question. I understand there is a little matter still before the magistrates."

"Very well, Demetrius," he responded quickly. "I see we understand each other, and that your degree of perceptiveness may exceed even my generous evaluations. You may be assured I shall do my best to recover your stone."

"Not *my* stone, Doctor, the Czar's stone. And, incidentally, your passport to Russia. I think you might leave us now, and get started. You have barely three weeks to complete your task."

The doctor left, his face reflecting the confusion of his soul. Nina came back to sit on the bed. "How did you know all those things about him?" she asked. "Is he really such an evil man?"

"I do not think he is especially evil," I said, "He has been placed in the unfortunate position of having to live by his wits. He is rather a brilliant and talented man, and I think he can be of value to me – and to my Czar. If you had not spoken of taking him with us, I would have done so myself."

"Demetrius, you are a very devious man!"

"How so?" I asked innocently.

"How so, indeed! Why, you made us practically beg you to take him, when you wanted him all the time. But, how did you know all of these things about his past?"

As I explained I could see the trace of a satisfied smile crease her lips. "You display a certain . . . Oriental guile," she said at length, "in many ways not unlike the Medicis. Have you also investigated me?" she added, half joking.

"I made a fortunate guess in going to your father," I said seriously, "and it proved how God's Grace smiled upon my work. But you, your face was too lovely to question. I always accept beauty as I find it. In this, God has also shown me His Favor."

I pulled her head down and kissed her. "But do not be deceived," I added. "It is important that I have the diamond before I return to Russia."

"I do not understand why it's so urgent. You told me you made a better bargain than either you or your Czar had thought possible, and you have a greater credit of gold established than you had planned. The Czar need never know."

"There is something you must understand about me from the very beginning," I explained sternly. "I am a loyal servant of the Czar. I will never lie to him, nor do anything which I consider harmful to him. His wish, however slight, is of more value than my life. He is the Anointed Caesar, the Right Hand of God in this world."

My words silenced her completely. Then her Medici mind started her on another tack to solve my problem. "But you are not a poor man," she suggested. "Could you not just pay the Czar for his diamond? Surely this would satisfy him."

"That is still not the answer," I said, trying to find the words to express my feelings. "The stone was not mine to use. Had I done so and had no harm come of it, it would have mattered little to anyone. I could have told the tale to the Czar and he would have laughed, considering it no more than a prank. Now that the diamond has been lost as a result of my foolishness, I must recover it. I must do this for the Czar; he would expect it of me."

"And Pissemsky might carry the tale?" she asked.

"It is possible."

"And then, if you should produce the stone, it would make him out the fool?"

"Your Italian teaching?"

"I have seen such things happen among people of many races," she answered defensively.

"Then understand," I said. "It is Pissemsky's duty to inform the Czar. Whatever he knows, and whatever he suspects; this he must tell. I hold no malice toward Feodor, and I do not seek to embarrass him. I simply must have the diamond back before I leave for Russia. Otherwise, it is my own soul which will be in torment. Can you understand?"

"I think perhaps I do," she said. "But your Russian soul is not an easy thing to comprehend."

"Now, let us see if I can get up," I said. "Where is your father?"

"He is home," she replied quickly. "Demetrius, are you sure you should get up so soon?"

"I have no choice," I told her, putting my feet gingerly on the floor. My head did not ache badly any more, and although I was a little unsteady I was able to walk without assistance.

"If you will excuse me, my dear," I said, pulling self-consciously at my night shirt. "You might call one of the servants to help me."

She nodded. "I will meet you downstairs," she said.

Nina sent a servant woman back with a pitcher of warm water. I washed and unwound the bandages from about my head, finding that the doctor had applied far more linen than necessary. The furrow left by the bullet started just behind my left temple and extended forward the length of my head. It would probably have been the source of the heaviest bleeding, and was responsible for frightening everyone so badly. I tore off the cleanest part of the doctor's wrappings and reapplied as small a covering as possible, just over the wound itself. The rest of my injuries were minimal. I had scraped the skin on my face and neck, as well as bruising the side of my body when I had fallen on the road. I washed these areas as best I could and hurriedly dressed myself in a clean outfit of dark–hued, English clothes.

I forced the thoughts of Vladya from my mind, considering other, more immediate problems. It had occurred to me that the theft of the diamond could have been instigated by some other foreign power. After all, both Sweden and Spain had attempted to eliminate me once before. But that possibility seemed remote. Since Robin had applied pressure on the other embassies, there had not been a hint of trouble from them. No, it was more likely the work of native highwaymen, and I harbored more than a flickering suspicion that Doctor Bomel could have been involved. He surely knew people whom he could have contacted, and he could have arranged it all through one or two messengers. I did not really think he had, yet his past was quite unsavory – if one believed all the accounts and stories.

When I went down I found that Nina had ordered the cook to make a light supper for me. As I sat eating it, Savin came in. He was much changed from the time I had last seen him as *voivode*, commanding the unit at Riga. Then he had been quite dashing, though already of stocky build. His hair had been chestnut, and his beard had been full and silky. Now, he was corpulent. His face was beefy red about a gray–streaked beard. He seemed very happy to see me, however, and greeted me as a long–lost companion. Roaring like a bull in rut, he launched into an immediate, lengthy discourse. Naturally, he did not miss the opportunity to poke fun at my English dress and stylishly trimmed beard. He hinted that my injuries would not have been nearly as extensive if I had not committed the sin of going about practically beardless, thus leaving my flesh exposed to the just punishments of God. As he spoke, I tried to translate for Nina.

The subject of Prince Vladimir was one of the first he touched upon, but I told him I already knew about it and would prefer he spoke of other things. He respected my feelings, adding only that he felt I had nothing to fear as a result of my friendship with the Prince. The Czar's only comments regarding me had implied my continued favor, he insisted.

"How did the Czarina Maria's death come to be blamed on poison?" I asked, in spite of myself.

"At first it was said she died of gluttony," he replied. "But it occurred so suddenly the Czar soon convinced himself that it had to be poison. You can imagine the rest for yourself. In my own opinion, if she really was poisoned, it could well have been . . . well, let us say it could have been done to please the Czar. At least, there was no remorse on His Majesty's part and he has already taken another."

"He is married again?"

"Not exactly, although the court is extending the lady all the privileges of rank."

"What else happened?" I asked tenuously.

"Your father has done well," he said, "and still enjoys the Czar's closest confidence, along with Andrew Kurbsky. I think these two may be closest of all right now, possibly excepting the Basmanovs. Oh yes, the Metropolitan Afansey died, you know."

"I expected he would; he was ill when I left."

"It was the Lord's mercy," said Savin. "The Czar has selected the Abbot of Solovetsky to replace him."

"Phillip?" I asked in surprise. "I would have thought Pimen of Novgorod."

"I would have, too," he said, chuckling, "and so did Pimen. In fact, he was so sure of his appointment he had already let it be know whom he wanted as his successor in Novgorod. But he was starting to sound too much like Sylvester, if you ask me, and you know how the Czar feels about that!"

"In which I fully concur. How is Prince Yuri?" I asked.

"He has not been well," said Savin, concerned. "You know, all his life he has had that strange affliction, making him speak so slowly everyone thinks him stupid. Whatever it is, it has grown worse of late, and he is seldom seen about the palace."

"Has the court stayed mostly in Moscow?"

"No, not really. The Czar has made several pilgrimages to the western monasteries. He has even appeared to watch a few battles when the war picks up from time to time. It's been lagging badly, you know. Whenever there's some distraction within the realm, the Czar pulls back the western forces. That old goat in Poland hasn't the guts to take the offensive, though he's always issuing statements about marching on Moscow."

"And he never will," I said depreciatingly. "But one of these days Sigismund is going to face his maker, and things may change."

"It all depends on who takes the throne," said Savin.

"With that silly system of electing a king, it could be anyone. Who is thought most likely? Is it still Batory?" I referred, of course, to the Hungarian.

"That is still my guess, but Pollacks being as they are, they could pick almost anyone, even Ivan."

"That would be too much to hope!" I laughed. "Can you see Tishkovitch on his belly, kissing the Czar's foot?" I looked at Nina as I translated the last, but she did not understand enough of our politics to appreciate the humor. I could see she was growing impatient with our discourse.

"Andrei," I said, "did Pissemsky tell you that I am planning to marry Nina?"

"No!" he bellowed. "Not really! I am delighted you have finally decided to become an honest man, and to give up your old, harem-stealing ways!" He leered at Nina, in what was intended as a friendly smile. She shrank back at his sudden gesture, unable to understand the words accompanying it. I explained his remarks, and she responded with her usual dignity, thanking the Ambassador for his compliments.

"Tell your future wife that I, Andrei Savin, claim the honor of standing with you in place of your father, Dmitri. We shall have a proper ceremony, even if we are in a heathen land. We'll do it right here in the embassy!" He stopped then, having thought of the difficulty I had thus far hesitated to bring up. "She is going to join the true faith, is she not?"

"Although Nina has been a very religious woman, and closely reared in the Church of Rome, she has indicated her willingness," I said, hoping I would not have to back down later. As I spoke, however, a partial solution occurred to me and I added: "In order to please her father, we have decided on two ceremonies, one Orthodox, performed by Father Thomas – the other Papist, by one of the chaplains from the Italian colony."

Nina did not understand my explanation, which gave me time to discuss it with her alone. When I did mention the problem later that evening, she agreed to the wisdom of my quick decision. She even suggested the first ceremony be the Roman, and that it be done quietly, in secret. That would satisfy her father. Then, since the English seemed to harbor no ill will against our Russian Church, the second marriage could be performed in the embassy and attended by whatever English friends we might wish to invite. Even Robin might come to this, although he probably would not have attended a Roman ceremony.

"I think it might be wise not to say anything of the first wedding to Father Thomas, either," I suggested, "and just let him assume you are going to convert to the True Church without any problems."

"Is this what you wish me to do?" she asked simply.

"It has to be," I told her. "The wife must take the husband's faith."

"I have given this some thought," she admitted, "and I knew it would come to this. I will embrace your faith once we have reached Russia. Until then, I hope you will permit my father to assume I remain true to the Church of Rome."

And so it was settled. I know our subterfuge must have been offensive to God, for it is never excusable to deny Him, even for love. But such was the foolishness of my more youthful years. Certainly, this sin was but a paltry offense, compared with those I was yet to commit.

CHAPTER IV

Our marriage plans were announced the next day. Neither Pissemsky nor Thomas was pleased about it, but they did not try to dissuade us. Robin led a large retinue into our front enclosure late one afternoon, and I was kidnapped for the most monstrous drinking bout I had endured since leaving Russia. I did myself proud, being among the last to remain upright and proposing the last toast, when I was nearly the only one left to drink it. Doctor Bomel, who as usual had managed to get himself included, was unconscious on the floor at my feet, and had to be carried out to the surrey which Pissemsky had sent after us. Andrei Savin gave me a terrible dressing down for not having him along, but he had been at the palace with Feodor when my friends arrived. There was nothing I could have done about it.

The following morning, Doctor Bomel went out long before I was up, so I had no opportunity to discuss his progress in the quest for the diamond. I hoped his absence indicated some continued efforts. I vaguely remembered some mention of the search during our heavy drinking the night before, but what was said, let alone who said it, completely escaped me. Naturally, everyone knew about the theft, and several fellows had questioned me on the particulars. It was Robin, himself, I think, who had commented on the stone's being so large it would be impossible to sell in England. It would have to be cut, he said, and he did not believe anyone capable of doing it, unless he were a foreigner, unknown to the local guilds. That Leicester should be thus informed led me to believe I had still another ally, doing his best to locate the Czar's gem.

Nina came to our house early, using the excuse of an interview with Thomas. The priest sat with us, although he never ate before noon and merely watched as we dallied over our meal. As always, he had difficulty conversing with Nina. She had a heavier accent in English than I had, while Father Thomas's knowledge of the language was still sparse. His pronunciation was so atrocious it was impossible to understand him. Despite my monumental hangover, I spent most of the morning translating for them. In the end, we arrived at a workable agreement for the ceremony.

Nina and I had planned some shopping in London, gathering together the items we wished to take back to Russia. Shortly before we were to depart, Toby knocked on the open door, telling me his aunt and her husband had arrived. Casting an anxious glance at Nina, he asked if I would speak to them. I told him to bring them in.

The aunt was a very pleasant woman in her early thirties, her husband a few years older. They both appeared sober, hardworking farm people, with coarse calluses on their hands and with faces heavily wrinkled from too much time in the open sun and wind. They were dressed for the occasion in heavy English broadcloth, obviously having put on their best. Both appeared ill at ease in the finely appointed parlor, although Nina and I tried to make them comfortable. I think we eventually succeeded.

"Would you object to my wife and me taking Toby into our service?" I asked at length. "The boy seems to have his heart set on it."

"We would be happy to provide a home for him, ourselves," replied the aunt, "but we are poor people, as your Lordship can see. We have three sons of our own, and one more –" She broke off self–consciously and glanced at her husband. "Well, perhaps one more would make little difference."

"But we hardly know the boy," added the man, "and if it is his wish, we would not object, except that Russeland is so far away."

"Would the boy receive his proper training, as an honorable, God fearing man?" asked his aunt. "It is this we fear the most, that he may become heathen and disowned by the Lord."

"You are of the Protestant faith?" I asked.

They both nodded. "We are of the Queen's Church," she replied.

"Of course, we are of the Orthodox faith in Russia," I told them, "but I find our beliefs are closely akin to yours. Whereas the Protestants have broken away from the Church of Rome, because the Papists fail to adhere to the old principals of God, it is our Church which maintains these early concepts. Like you, we refuse to rejoin the Romans until they, too, return to the old ways."

My words had the proper effect on the simple country folk; but I saw from the corner of my eye that I had not pleased Nina. No matter, I thought, for I have spoken the truth. The Protestant church in England was very like ours. They had taken up the old creeds and adhered to the purity of the original beliefs. All I had learned of these religious theories was going to make for interesting discourses when I had the opportunity to relay them to Ivan. The English Protestants bore little resemblance to the heretics of the German states, who preached the word of God, while following the ways of the evil one.

As I had continued to talk with Toby's aunt and uncle, I began to formulate another thought. It appeared they were perfectly willing for the boy to accompany us, now they had been assured on the score of his religious training. They were asking for nothing, themselves, but I felt I might be able to do something for them – and for myself as well. I ended our interview by requesting the husband – Henry Fowler was his name – to return and speak to me again within the next few days. Otherwise, the matter was settled when they departed. Toby was definitely coming with us.

All this assembling of an entourage was having its effects on Pissemsky. An evening or two later, after I had returned from Ridolfi's, the Ambassador and I had some half–serious words about it.

"What are you doing, putting together a traveling carnival to take back to Russia?" he hollered. "How many people do you think a boat can hold?" He made some further references to Noah's ark and wanted to know if I contemplated returning with some samples of native flora, as well.

"That ship will take a good many more people than I plan to ask," I told him. "You just see to the arrangements. And remember, if I manage to retain my head after we return, I shall likely be in a position to have the Czar ship you off to Siberia with the Stroganovs, if you don't behave yourself!"

"My lord and master!" he roared. "Here, let me display my humility!" At this, he flopped onto his belly and grabbed my foot, placing it upon the back of his neck. We were engaged in this ridiculous posturing when a servant opened the door, escorting Robin, who had come in unannounced.

"By the soul of Saint George and all the other sinners!" he exclaimed. "Now I have seen everything! A true Oriental blessing!"

The Ambassador quickly retracted into a sitting position, scurrying for his hat, which he clapped atop his shaven head.

"I never believed those tales about you fellows running around without any hair on your crowns," Robin continued, bowing to Feodor who had managed to set his hat on backward. As he lifted it again I could see he had turned a deep red, on top of his head as well as his face.

"We were in jest, My Lord," he muttered, grunting himself to his feet.

Robin extended a hand to help him up, taking a couple of swipes to help brush off the dust. "We will miss you, Sir Ambassador," he said. "It is seldom that our foreign delegations present such an interesting array of – talents. Well, my friend," he said, turning to me, "you look like you've been staying out of trouble."

"I am too busy to allow time for sin," I replied. "I can't afford those extra moments each day to atone for the previous night's pleasure."

The Earl of Leicester swung one leg over a straight–backed wooden chair, draping his elegant form backwards into the seat. He propped his chin against the upper rung and grinned as if bursting with some secret knowledge. As always, his clothes were just a shade ahead of fashion. This evening he wore plum colored doublet and hose, all of the finest velvet, with a wide, sparkling collar, fanned out almost like a Pollack's.

"I have engaged in a rare exercise on your behalf," he said. "I passed up a brilliant party in order that I might spend a few hours in quiet thought. I actually retired to my own, monklike cell and meditated."

"A rare experience, I'm sure!"

"Of late, I fear it is," he said seriously. "But I find the skill not completely atrophied." He turned to Pissemsky. "Are you fully informed, sir, of the difficulty in which our friend, here, finds himself?"

"Although I am excluded from many of Demetrius's confidences," said Feodor with a touch of bitterness, "I know he lost the diamond, and stands in danger of the Czar's displeasure." The Ambassador seemed proud of himself for this display of fluency, but his tone still expressed some of the injury he felt. It offended him not to be at least as privy to my confidences as the Earl.

"I am afraid I have not told anyone the full details of my activities in England," I said, "because it was not my place to reveal them. While I have given slightly different accounts to different people, I have not really lied. I have merely restricted my words to that part of the truth which I needed to tell."

"This is more or less the conclusion I had reached," said Robin, "and in adding together the stories of several people, I achieved what appeared to be a large portion of the truth. Had you placed your faith in your friends, as you should have, Demetrius, you should have saved me this trouble," he scolded. "But let me recite to you my theory. To begin with, you brought into England a certain number of gems. I do not know how many, but a goodly fortune by all reckoning. These were pawned with the Florentine, Ridolfi, for gold. Certain foreign negotiations make it appear the vast bulk of your gems have already left the country. But no matter. The credit you acquired is now deposited with the House of Ridolfi. I would hesitate to explain these facts in any company but this. . . . Well, let that go for a moment."

He looked from one to the other of us, back and forth, enjoying the consternation on Pissemsky's face and the expectant suspense on mine. "From other remarks," he continued, "including those made concerning the diamond – the last of the original treasure remaining to you – I must conclude the entire fund belongs to your Czar, rather than to you."

Pissemsky had listened without comment, nodding now and again. At this juncture he looked at me with an approving smile. "Without knowing the details of his transactions, it is more or less what I suspected Demetrius must have been doing."

"And it was well done," said Robin. "Although the facts may now become known, at least to a few, the act is completed. Had the knowledge been acquired sooner, someone might have felt compelled to interfere. After all," he said, looking me directly in the face, "you may have deprived the royal treasurer of considerable funds by providing the Florentine with an easy method of removing great amounts of wealth in small units, units capable of being concealed on one's person, let us say.

"But again, what is done is done. We now come to the most crucial point. The three of us are the only ones, beside Her Majesty and Lord Cecil, who know of a certain request made by your Czar, regarding a somewhat delicate, reciprocal agreement. I may presume too much, but if your Czar were to avail himself of the terms of this agreement, these funds would be. . . most advantageous to him."

I said nothing, watching Leicester with as blank an expression as I could. There was a tickle of laughter just below the surface of my bland countenance, for Robin was an extremely clever fellow.

Pissemsky remarked, "If our friend, here, has indeed accomplished such a feat, he is to be complimented."

"This may be true," agreed Robin casually, "but it leaves one question unanswered in the Queen's mind. Is the Czar about to avail himself of our treaty? The amount involved here must be very great."

"The Czar is very wealthy," I said simply.

"He is so wealthy he can leave this fortune, idle, in a foreign land, just as a possible refuge?" The Earl seemed amazed.

"As I have said, our Czar is very wealthy. This might be a matter to be taken into account by Her Majesty, in considering . . . some other matters," I added.

"Then may we presume it was not all intended to remain a secret? At least not a secret from the higher levels?" asked Robin. "Was the Czar's wealth meant to be displayed to us in this way, being cast, so to speak, upon a distant shore to remain there both as . . . a fund for a remote contingency, but also as a monument to his golden treasure house?"

"We have an interesting possibility, do we not?" I said, beginning to enjoy the possession of an iota of information denied my English friend. I was also beginning to see how my great bungle could be turned into a triumph. If the English could be left with the belief that my clumsy handling of the diamond had been a deliberate and vainglorious display of Ivan's wealth, and if in fact it did proclaim such wealth, it might eventually persuade the Queen to give more serious consideration to the Czar's offer of marriage. I knew this to be much dearer to Ivan's heart than any amount of gold I might deposit for him.

"Then following from this," Robin was saying, "we come to the matter of the diamond. Was its loss necessarily such a tragedy? I cannot imagine it was contrived as it cost three men their lives and nearly landed Demetrius in his grave as well. But do you really want it back?" He watched Pissemsky and me intently, but neither of us answered him.

"Ah, the inscrutable Russe," he said. "Either way, gentlemen, you stand to profit. And your Czar stands to profit."

Slowly, without any apparent importance to his action, he reached under his doublet and drew forth the golden chain. He gradually pulled it out, and at the end, sparkling in all its magnificent brilliance, was the diamond.

"I have here your property. May I ask what disposition you wish me to make of it?"

"How did you –?" began Pissemsky.

"As I told Demetrius a few nights ago, the stone is too large to sell in England. The Queen simply let it be known how great her displeasure would be should any loyal Englishman attempt to remove it from the realm. The first time the thief attempted to sell it, it was in our hands."

"Who was the thief?" I asked.

Robin gestured delicately with his hands. "A common form of native vermin," he chuckled. "Nothing of any meaning to you, and possibly more significant, a man not acquainted with your Doctor Bomel."

"Bomel is innocent, then?" I asked, relieved and pleased.

"I think so," said the Earl. "In any event, he does not know the stone has been recovered, and he is making a frantic canvas of all know dealers in stolen goods." He grinned crookedly, still holding the chain from which the pendant swung back and forth, glowing in its deep blue fire.

I knew very well what he was after, now, for I had seen Elizabeth's eyes when they had fastened upon the stone. As it was presently in Robin's possession, I wondered how much chance I would have to get it back, were I willing to try. "Such a gem," I said graciously, "belongs only on the person of a Queen."

"Then may we presume the Czar intended it as a final token of his esteem for the Majesty of England?" asked the Earl.

"I am sure His Majesty of Russia could have intended nothing else," I replied.

Robin handed the pendant to Pissemsky. "You will have a farewell audience with the Queen," he said. "Lest there be talk of our having been responsible for its theft. . . ."

The Ambassador took the jewel in his hands, fondling the cool surface with loving awe. "It will be my pleasure to make the presentation," he said, "unless Her Majesty might feel slighted, since it has been worn publicly by another."

"A gem this size need never be looked upon as a hand–me–down," he said, laughing. "But I shall arrange a small, intimate audience." The Earl stood up, stretching. "The hour grows late," he remarked. "If either of you gentlemen would care to join me, there is still entertainment to be had."

"I think a good night's rest would be better for us both," said Pissemsky.

Robin looked disappointed, but I knew the Ambassador wanted to question me further. I complied with the unspoken suggestion, also declining the Earl's invitation.

"Perhaps tomorrow, then," he said lightly.

When he had left, I had a long discussion with Pissemsky; but I refused to explain any further details of my transactions. Since so much had already come to light in Robin's discourse, I allowed Feodor to presume I had intentionally permitted it to become known, with the knowledge restricted to a very select group. Later, to compound my sin, I convinced myself it would be best if I also allowed the Czar to think the same. It would do no harm, I reasoned, and in the end it would likely be for the best. How easily an evil man deludes himself! When I decided to practice a small deception on one man, it grew larger toward the next, and monumental when perpetrated upon the anointed Czar. It was surely another irrevocable step toward eternal damnation.

There still remained a few things I wished to do before leaving England. My wedding was one week off, and I wanted all this other business completed beforehand. First, there was the matter of Toby and his family. The second concern was my own funds. I still had a considerable amount with me, although it was paltry beside the fortune of the Czar. I was able to resolve both problems with one stroke, for my plans worked out exactly as I had hoped.

Nina and I had gone on our final shopping spree, during which I warned her it would be the last chance to buy everything she wanted to take back with us. I purchased the gifts I needed for Ivan and my other friends and servants. I had all of it crated and taken to the ship.

The only moment of sadness came when I had to sort through the items I had already acquired. I came upon the fine brace of pistols I had purchased, early in my stay, for Prince Vladimir. I could hardly bear to look at them, and was going to send them back to the shop where I had bought them. I happened to look up at Toby, who was helping me. He was much too young for such a gift, but he was staring at them with such fondness I impulsively shoved the case into his hands. "Keep these in the box until your beard begins to grow," I said.

He hugged the case to himself, speechless – at first, not even able to thank me. "I will, sir," he said finally. "I shall promise not to take them out until I am old enough to use them."

"Good lad," I said.

When all of these expenditures were completed, and I knew how much cash would be left – including, of course, Nina's rather considerable dowry – I had a serious discussion with Robin. While his new estates were very extensive, and he was high in the Queen's favor – in an excellent position to make himself a wealthy man – he, like all his class, was constantly short of funds. Tactfully, I suggested that if it should ever come to pass that the Czar would actually flee Russia, I would naturally wish to accompany him. Once the Earl had accepted this, I went on to describe the beauty I had observed on his new estates, how I had grown to love the great groves of oaks and the rolling meadows of Leicester. "If I could not live in my own land," I told him, "my first choice would be the hills of your central England."

In the end, I arranged to purchase a fine tract of farmland, with a small village and a mill. He was more than pleased with the transaction. It gave him ample funds for his current endeavors and as he put it: "The prospect of merrie company for his declining years." When Toby's aunt and uncle came the next day in response to my summons, the contracts were already prepared. I installed them as managers of my new properties, under Ridolfi's supervision. Needless to say, their expressions of joy and gratitude were both sincere and touching.

With this business completed, I was left with very little cash. But I anticipated no great expenses before I reached home, and Savin's reports eased my anxieties on what I would find there. My only remaining concern was the marriage, now three days hence. As proof of my true love and devotion, I experienced the symptoms of cowardice. My knees trembled at the very thought!

I had almost forgotten about Doctor Bomel and the impossible task I had set him. As Pissemsky's audience with the Queen was scheduled a day or two after my wedding, there had not been even a rumor about the gem's recovery. I had told no one, not even Nina. It was, therefore, on the day before my wedding, that Bomel all but threw himself at my feet, begging me to relieve him of his assignment.

"I know you have charged me with this task because you suspect I might have been involved in the actual theft," he pleaded, "but please believe me, good sir, such a crime against a friend is beyond even my evil means."

"I never suspected you of such miserable deceit," I replied, denying the fact, now my former suspicions had proved ill founded.

"Then allow me to tell you what I have discovered," he continued, "and perhaps you can understand my dilemma. The theft was committed by two groups of highwaymen, who banded together for this one assault. This gave them the force of numbers. They had nearly exhausted themselves, and despaired of catching us at an auspicious moment, when that moment – in fact – occurred. They had followed us both days, waiting for our carriage to be in a location where there was no one about and where we were far from all approaching vehicles. They wanted none to disturb them in the course of their felonious act. A group of them raced ahead, going across fields and meadows, to get onto the road before us. There they dug the pit and hid themselves in the nearest cover.

"If they had not gotten us at Henley, they would have failed altogether, for beyond this village the highway is too heavily populated. This much information I have learned, at great expense and risk of my very life. I have turned my findings over to the proper officials, and the leaders, at least, are already in custody."

"And will be duly executed?" I asked.

"They should be drawn and quartered, sir," he said. "I only wish I could remain long enough to see it."

"That could be arranged," I said coldly.

"Oh, no – no, please sir! After what I have done for you, and what I have achieved to the detriment of the worst thieves in London, it would be impossible for me to survive long without your most gracious protection.

"But to continue," he resumed hastily, "once I found the identities of the thieves – and no easy task, either, I assure you – I then attempted to trace the diamond, itself. I found it was taken, under cover of night, into a section of London not frequently traversed by honest, Christian people. . . ."

"And it was turned over to a known dealer in stolen goods," I continued, "who subsequently disappeared, along with the stone. No one knows where he is, although rumors are circulating that he now resides in a cell, somewhere in the Tower."

Bomel gaped at me in amazement. "How do you know these things?" he squeaked.

"It is you who are supposed to supply the information," I said, still keeping any suggestion of levity out of my tone. "Pray continue."

"The diamond appears to have been stolen from the thieves," he said, bewildered, "but by whom, I cannot discover."

"And you dare to bring this pitiful information to me?" I shouted. "Do you really expect this to serve as your safe conduct to Russia? Why, I should turn you over to the public prosecutor right now, and tell him to throw you into prison for complicity in the crime!"

He was on the verge of a seizure, so I relented. I had intended allowing him to pursue his search until we were ready to depart, but his pitiful pleas wore me down. I told him I already knew the whereabouts of the stone, though I did not reveal that to him. Relieved, he drank himself into a stupor and thus missed the party Robin gave that evening to celebrate my last night as a bachelor.

Andrei Savin, however, assured his own invitation this time, and even supplied a whole cask of vodka. He dared anyone to match him drink for drink, creating such a distraction I was able to imbibe only moderate amounts of wine, thus keeping my head clear for the morrow. Finally, roaring drunk, Savin shouted. "The gifts for the bride! Gifts must be sent to the bride!"

"What's this?" asked Robin.

"It is our custom," I told him. "In Russia, a bride must receive a parcel of trinkets on the night before her wedding."

"And a whip!" bellowed Savin. "She must have the whip, so her father can present it to the groom."

"If you send a whip to Nina, you will scare her away from the wedding," Robin howled, laughing merrily, "and her father will probably use it on you!"

"It must be done," Savin insisted, staggering up from the table. "Wait!"

He went out to the stables, returning a few moments later with a carriage whip. "Have you no wedding presents for your bride?" he shouted at me.

"I have," I told him. "They have already been sent."

"Without a whip?" he shouted again. "Dmitri, your life in England has softened you!" He went to the door, still hollering, and gave the coil of leather to Toby. "Take this to your new mistress," he said.

The boy started to take it, but looked around the bulk of Savin's body to see if I consented.

"It's all right," I assured him.

"And take this parcel along with it," added Savin, pulling a felt case from under his tunic. Toby departed with both items, and Andrei returned to the table. He proceeded to demonstrate his capacity, outdrinking everyone, including the waiters and the barmaid. I pretended to reach my limits long before I really would have, for nothing would have amused them more than my being unable to face the ceremony the next day.

Early the following morning, I made my way to Ridolfi's house. In the chapel, just off the garden where Thomas had sat during my first meeting with her father, Nina and I were married according to the Roman ritual.

The entire household, including the banker, was in tears. The priest was not happy about performing the ceremony, as he apparently doubted I would ever become a member of his Church. He made several questioning remarks before I left, but my answers were vague. Mostly, I pretended not to understand him. Besides, I though it was important to be back at the embassy before I was missed by too many people. The subject of the whip, incidentally, was not mentioned at this time, except that Nina showed me the necklace Andrei had sent with it. His gift was very Russian, a long, heavy gold chain with a sapphire broach – beautiful, but something she would wear only later, in Moscow, where such things were the style.

On returning to the embassy, I found the house fairly bursting with people. It seemed half of London had come to see the Russian ritual, for it was something new to them. Pissemsky was beside himself, not knowing how to eliminate the unwanted, and uninvited guests. Savin supplied a partial answer by physically ejecting the most obnoxious. After that, I made a short speech to those remaining, requesting that the sacred character of the ceremony – and the privacy of my bride and myself – be respected. There were many roars of laughter, and a number of vulgar comments; but I was able to get rid of a few more. By then, it was possible to move about inside the house, and Pissemsky personally asked the remainder of the overflow to leave. I went upstairs to change, posting our two clerks to guard the stairway.

Pissemsky had outdone himself in making preparations, for he wanted our wedding to be perfect. Few of the traditional trappings were lacking, although Nina was spared the embarrassment of the customary processions from her house to mine, in which she would have been preceded by symbols of her chastity, docility, and fertility. Pissemsky simply sent our carriage to convey her and Ridolfi, having explained to them that it was the proper form. The only symbolic item was a small sack of hops, placed on the seat beside the bride, to assure her bearing sons.

Nina wore a magnificent gown of white silk and satin, with yards of gossamer veils. The entire Italian community turned out to wish her well, and this flock, added to the still congested quarters, brought us back to the situation I had found when I returned earlier. Somehow, we got them all in, and the ceremony began. I wore the full–length robe of a Russian Prince, and Father Thomas appeared in the elegant, brocaded regalia he had not worn since leaving Russia. I think this helped still some of the truculence on the part of the Roman Catholics, for I know they considered our service to be less than valid.

Nina and I exchanged the rings, and she repeated her vows in Russian, as Thomas had instructed her. At the end of the service Nina knelt, as our ritual prescribed, and touched her forehead to my boot to signify her submission. I then covered her head with the edge of my robe to symbolize my assuming the duty of protection, and the responsibility of cherishing her.

The banquet following the wedding was to have been held in the house, but with the great number of people it was necessary to take over a nearby tavern. Before and during the ceremony, our servants had been busy carting supplies out the back door, and into the large hall down the street. The distance was not great, and afterward we all trooped over on foot. As I led Nina to the door, I was surprised to have that damned whip shoved into my hand by Ridolfi.

"I hope this is just a symbol," he whispered, laughing nervously.

I assured him it was. But because we were just leaving the house I could not get rid of it. There was no place to put it, nor anyone to whom I could hand it. Consequently, I carried it all the way to the tavern, much to the amusement of everyone. I finally managed to toss it to Toby, who put it away.

At the tavern, decorations had been hastily strung along the walls and musicians had been assembled. After the first few rounds of wine had been served, Savin surprised me again by calling for the "special songs." At this, all the Russian people present – there were now fourteen, including the priest – gathered into a group beside the musicians. They began to play the traditional, sad songs, while my countrymen sang the words to Nina. It was a scene of great beauty – or at least we were drunk enough to think it was. The songs told of girlhood's end, and the beginning of a woman's life. When the sadness of the melodies – or perhaps the poor quality of singing – had brought tears to all the female eyes, Savin considered his enterprise complete. We returned to the wine.

Nina and I slipped away without being noticed, something we had feared we might not be able to do. Robin had offered us a wing of his own house, but knowing his peculiar sense of humor, I expected he might play some trick on us. I had declined his kindness in favor of a small cottage belonging to some of Ridolfi's friends. It was located near the mouth of the Thames, where we could see the channel and the many ships which plied its waters. No one but Nina's father and the owners of the house knew we were going there, so we escaped the customary harassment and lewd remarks. We still had a week before the ship was due to sail, and we stayed in our private world until the eve of departure. To describe the bliss of those last six days in England would be beyond the words of any language. They were the last truly pleasant days we were to know for a long, long time.

BOOK THREE

Ivan Grozny

CHAPTER I

From the outset, our voyage home was a terrible ordeal. The ship was even smaller than the one on which I had come to England. In order to reach the Russian northland during a month when the port was open, and when overland travel was possible, we had left London during a season of rough water and storms. The ship rolled from the moment it left the Thames, moving in every possible direction – from side to side, up and down, and finally rocked from bow to stern like an enormous cradle. As we sailed north it became bitterly cold, and everything aboard was damp every hour of the day. For Nina, I think the most distressing aspect was the complete lack of bathing facilities. Neither was there any privacy, except within the narrow confines of our tiny cabin. Yet even this was no sanctuary, for the air became heavy and fetid if we stayed with the door closed for any length of time.

In a way, Feodor had been right about space; the passenger capacity of the vessel was extremely limited. In addition to Nina and myself, our group included: Pissemsky, the Bomels, Toby, two officers of the newly chartered London and Muscovite Company – Randolph and Horsey – plus some dozen clerks and lesser officials. For the first week nearly everybody, including Horsey, was too ill to get out of bed. The odors in the passenger corridor were beyond description. With each violent motion of the ship, our prayers alternated between pleas for survival and beseeching the Lord to grant a less painful death. Randolph was the only true sailor among us, though he almost succumbed several times when forced to observe our miseries.

After these initial tortures, we gradually acclimated ourselves to the sea and fell into a dreadfully weary routine, the major object of which was to pass the time as quickly as possible. The voyage took a full nine months, again less than it might have been. Surely, it was an experience to try the bravest soul! The dark waters of the northern seas were never still. They formed themselves into mountainous pits, and sometimes the ship would plummet into these, being so deeply inside a valley of water one could see nothing but a patch of dark gray sky above, and black threatening waves all around. To travel without sight of land was always frightening, for I did not trust the compass when the ship's motion was so extreme. When we did sail within view of the shore, we were in imminent danger from rocks and ice floes. Further north we encountered enormous mountains of floating crystals, some of which loomed above us and occasionally traveled as rapidly as we did.

During the long, trying voyage, we all became well acquainted. I had known Randolph previously, as this was his second trip to Russia. He was quiet and reserved, but a stout fellow and a good companion. Horsey was agreeable, but another sort altogether. He came from a wealthy family, although I do not think he possessed much himself, being a second or third son. On first acquaintance, I took him to be overly pedantic, almost rigid in his insistence on all proprieties. Beneath this facade of a proper English gentleman he possessed a ribald sense of humor and a vast store of bawdy stories. I spent many hours in conversation with him and found him well informed on all the modern arts and sciences.

Among our own group, I considered it most important to instruct Nina, Toby and the Bomels in Russian language and customs. Before we reached Kholmagora they had all progressed enough to make themselves understood, with the doctor and Toby almost fluent. Three months before we reached port, Nina informed me – in Russian – that she was with child.

We landed at Kholmagora – a perfect landfall, despite my reservations – in the late part of June. No other ship had come in as yet, although the *Sparrow* had left port one month ahead of us. I later learned that this ill–fated vessel had carried Chancellor, our original English visitor, to a watery grave. Naturally, our arrival created much excitement among the native Lapps and Samoyeds, and all the inhabitants for many miles around came to meet the ship. For us, it was the greatest boon of our lives to be able to walk down the gangplank and set foot on solid ground. Although my Russian soil was cold and the last of the winter's ice had not yet melted, stepping on it was like entering the gates of heaven. In the two days we spent at the traders' lodge, we were finally able to dry ourselves and our clothes.

The English had established a fairly substantial post here, maintained by one of their own men and several Russian employees. I was surprised at the number of warehouses they had built since my departure. They also had a good bathhouse, and while the idea of community bathing was strange to Nina, we all went in at once. None of us could wait another hour. We stank like peasants and would not have been able to endure one another's presence, except each was as offensive as the next.

Pissemsky and I led them through the full routine, although we allowed the women the privacy of a dark corner and an improvised drapery suspended from the beams of the ceiling. We were all laughing and reveling in the luxury of dry land and clean bodies, thrashing one another with supple wands, dashing water over ourselves and our companions. Only when Feodor and I ran outside did we lose our apprentice bathers. We had been sweating for over an hour when we bolted across the hard packed earth and into the icy water of the river. To a man, our companions refused to follow. Doctor Bomel, who had previously boasted that he would do everything we did, came as far as the bank, stuck his foot into the water and returned to the bathhouse defeated. Even Toby balked, until Feodor grabbed him and both of us pitched his struggling, squirming body into the river.

News of our arrival had immediately been carried to the Monastery of Saint Nicholas, where an escort sent by the Czar was awaiting us. They had brought both sleighs and wagons, not knowing when we would arrive, and had been there for almost two months. In charge of the group was a young captain named Skuratof, who had apparently been associated with Basmanov during the Kazan campaign. I did not remember him, for he must have been of inferior rank, though related somehow to the Bielskys. He was almost too respectful when he greeted me, but I took this as a favorable sign. It did not necessarily mean I was in good graces with the Czar, but for an escort to be sent at all – sent by Ivan instead of Heinrich – helped to ease my fears. Before we departed Kholmagora, a messenger was sent ahead to inform the Czar of our arrival. To better prepare him for the news of my marriage and the companions I had brought back with me, I sent a long, detailed letter with the rider.

Because it would take the English several days to unload their cargo, and because their travel south would be even slower than ours, I decided we should go ahead without them. The Czar's instructions to Skuratof had been to bring us immediately. In fact, the captain chafed at the extra day's delay, necessary to get our own trunks and crates unloaded from the vessel and packed into the wagons. It would be a long trip, at best, as we had to use plodding draft horses to pull the heavy cargo vehicles.

As a matter of propriety, Pissemsky decided to remain with the English, else they would have had no other escort. Skuratof left half his men to accompany this second group. This far north, the roads were not badly rutted, although they were damp. In addition to their being little traveled, thus sparing our having to jounce over hardened tracks left by previous users, there was always frozen ground not far below the surface. With the powerful horses, used to hauling the Czar's cannon, and with carts as heavy as these, we did not have much trouble with surface holes or excessive sliding in the mud. Our wheels pressed deeply into the muck, to rest firmly on the perpetual frost underneath. Our difficulties would come later, when we had traveled far enough south to encounter softer marshes.

Having been there before, I knew we faced a protracted, rigorous trip; but the prospect of returning home made it less depressing for me. For my companions, anticipation of the unknown served much the same purpose. To Nina and the Bomels, it was also frightening. I think the doctor, looking at the unfriendly wilderness on all sides, had some misgivings that he had ever come. For Toby, of course, it was a great adventure. It was his enthusiasm that helped to make the entire trip more bearable for the others. Skuratof's troops, who were *Streltsi,* were well–mounted horsemen. Once we had been underway for a few days, I borrowed mounts for the boy and myself. Together we explored the countryside while our caravan plodded slowly along the roadway.

There were several men among the soldiers who had served in campaigns where I had commanded. This helped my relationship with them, but it also created some problems with Skuratof, who was fast proving to be a surly mentor despite his inferior rank. He was resentful of me, for my presence tended to usurp his authority. The men seemed more willing to take orders from me than from him. I did my best to avoid words with him, as I felt the others would be less uncomfortable without an open controversy between us. Although the wagons were large and well appointed, Nina was already starting to show signs of strain and fatigue from the constant motion.

Still, it was inevitable that Skuratof and I should have a showdown. Both my wife and Doctor Bomel were afraid of him, which he soon realized and attempted to use to his advantage. As a younger man, Skuratof must have had an open, innocent expression; but his face was now becoming etched with lines of cruelty and avarice. He was still called Malyuta, however, which meant "baby." But his disposition was more like a savage Tartar, possibly having altered through the years while his once angelic features became hardened and wrinkled by exposure to the sun – and by reflecting the evil of his own soul. At the time of this first meeting – regardless of the causes – Malyuta Skuratof now was certainly not an attractive man, physically or otherwise. He had a full head of black, grimy–looking hair. He wore this in braids down either side of his face, where it blended into his heavy mustache and beard. His skin was dark from the sun, and he followed the barbaric custom of rubbing fat into his scalp and facial hair whenever he ate meat. A man of neither taste nor decency, he was a true harbinger of things to come – perhaps a portrait of what my own soul was to become.

For the first few days of the trip I kept my silence, allowing the captain to carry out his duties without interference. He must have taken this as a sign of weakness, for he soon began to bully us and to exercise the same hard authority over my party as he imposed upon his men. It displeased him to see me engage in a casual, friendly conversation with any of his subordinates. The further south we traveled, the less courtesy he showed us and the more overbearing he became.

Our unspoken antagonism came to confrontation about two weeks after we had left Kholmagora. We were following the Dvina, as we would for some time, and I had ridden ahead with Toby to scout out a suitable campsite. Both Nina and Anne had been uncomfortable the last few stops, because we generally camped very close to the river bank, where it was damp and chilly. We were just coming into a swampy area, which meant our camp would be invaded by the thousands of insects which rose from the bogs at dusk. I was determined to spare the women as many of these discomforts as possible. I did not seek trouble with Skuratof. To the contrary, I made every effort to avoid it. For instance, I knew he had been making lewd remarks about my wife to his men, for the women had made no effort to conceal their faces and generally forgot to wear a proper covering on their heads. I had ignored these insults, pretending to be unaware of them. I had chided Nina gently, but when she seemed irritable over "those silly rules," I ceased to pester her about it.

Toby and I discovered a perfect campsite, not far from the river. The ground rose high enough to provide good drainage, yet was still close enough to the bank not to make water hauling a serious chore. The slope from the road was gradual enough to offer easy access for the wagons. Once satisfied with our find, we rode back to the troop and I told Skuratof where I wished to stop.

He refused, saying we still had another hour of daylight and he wanted to keep going. I reminded him of Nina's condition, insisting she not be over taxed by needlessly long rides each day. Skuratof was adamant; we should press further.

"I have no intention of arguing with you, Captain," I told him. "This is where we are going to camp for the night."

We had been speaking long enough and loudly enough that our words were being overheard by the soldiers. Several of the men had pressed closer to listen, and the whole caravan had halted until we came to a decision.

"My orders are to get you to the Czar with all possible haste," he shouted back.

I sat looking at him for several moments before I replied. His horse shifted its weight, and taking that as an excuse he flicked his eyes away from contact with mine. Now, as anyone experienced in matters concerning the human mind will confirm, a man who can be outstared by you is a man who will eventually obey you – although you may occasionally have to whip him into line. Speaking very evenly, but loud enough for the soldiers to hear me, I asked: "Do you know to whom you speak? Do you really wish to challenge me . . . to incur my anger?" I stopped to let it penetrate, then shouted: "How dare you speak to me like this! You will obey me, or I'll order these men to flay the skin off your back! Do you understand me?"

A quick glance at the men assured me they would follow, for Malyuta was not a popular leader. He glared back, but did not answer. Still with a surly expression on his face, he started to turn his back on me. I didn't let him get away with it. I spurred my mount forward, causing it to collide with Skuratof's, almost knocking him down. Edging up beside him, I grabbed the fur collar of his jacket. Holding his face close to mine – not the most pleasant experience – I continued: "I asked you a question, Captain! Do you always ignore a General's question?"

"I obey my Czar," he replied, but in a weaker tone.

"And you will obey the Czar's generals as the extensions of the Czar's will! And when you speak to the Czar's generals, you *will* do so with proper respect."

I saw his hand creep toward his waist. Taking a chance on falling, should our mounts suddenly pull apart, I leaned over and grabbed his wrist with my other hand. "This scene is not a good thing for your men to see," I said quietly. "If I must throw you into the mud before them, you will never command their respect again. Now, are you going to obey me or not?"

"I shall report your actions to the Czar," he replied stubbornly, "but until then I shall obey."

"*I shall obey, 'Sir!'*" I growled. This, the others couldn't hear.

Again he hesitated and I increased the grip on his wrist.

"Sir," he said at last.

I let him go and he began shouting orders for the men to make camp on the hillock. We were never to become friends, but I had no more trouble with the captain during the rest of the trip. I was not to discover until much later how truly miserable a person he really was. Typical of most men who tend to be disrespectful and overbearing toward their betters when they think they can get away with it, Skuratof now began to fawn upon us, being almost comically solicitous of Nina for the entire two months it took us to reach Vologda, in late August.

While the rest of us were impatient for the journey to end, Toby seemed to enjoy every minute. He rode with the soldiers most of the time, chattering with them in Russian. He even learned one of the dialects spoken by the men who came from Pskovian territories. I eventually had to caution him not to use certain words he picked up, for soldiers' speech is notoriously vulgar. He had also learned to handle a bow very well, and frequently supplied us with hares for the dinner pot. Once, he managed to bring down a deer. The men called him "Little Dmitri," as his hair was as fair as mine and we shared a certain similarity in facial features. It was the soldiers' humor to imply he was my son; but as this was done in the spirit of good comrades and friends, I did not chastise them for it.

When we were a couple of days from Vologda, Skuratof sent a man ahead to order suitable quarters prepared for us, and to alert the boat captains who would ferry us the rest of the way. I was grateful for this, as the trip was eroding our tempers and sharpening our tongues. It had rained for several days, making it necessary to hitch extra horses to the wagons, sometimes moving them in shifts to utilize double or triple teams in hauling us through the deepest ooze. Nina had started to swell quite perceptibly, but refused to stay inside the wagon where both propriety and her own well–being dictated she should have been.

Doctor Bomel attempted to depreciate my concern, telling me she was a very healthy girl and would be a good mother. I had no cause for worry, he said, repeating all the usual things a doctor will tell a prospective father. Still, it bothered me to see her body swaying back and forth on the wagon seat. When I remonstrated with her, she refused to go inside and lie down. It was too close and stuffy, she insisted. It made her upset to her stomach and gave her a headache.

I indulged Nina in these whims while we were on the road, but at the same time I tried to prepare her for the life she would be expected to lead in Moscow. I had already explained the manner in which a good Russian wife was supposed to behave, although foreign women were generally permitted a little greater degree of freedom. She seemed to understand how necessary it would be to observe the basic proprieties. In deference to my wishes, she had started keeping a shawl over her head and wearing at least three petticoats. This latter concession was made under protest, however, as Nina claimed the extra clothing made her look fat. That a certain degree of plumpness was desirable on a woman was another aspect of our culture she found difficult to accept. I knew there would be much for her to learn and many new ideas to be absorbed. For the moment I refused to upset her with too many demands. I was more concerned with her comfort.

The next day, a lone rider came galloping toward us from the direction of the city. As I was driving the wagon in which Nina and the Bomels were riding, I saw the horseman when he approached the group of soldiers ahead of us and stopped to speak with them. His horse pranced proudly about as he paced the troop, full of spirit even after the long gallop. Well mounted as he was, I knew it had to be a gentleman. One of the men pointed back toward our vehicle, and the fellow started in our direction, acknowledging Skuratof with a casual wave of his hand. The captain had ridden out from behind the line of wagons, making his way up the column in one of his periodic checks on the men. Other than this simple gesture, the new arrival ignored Malyuta – another indication of his rank. A few moments later I caught a glimpse of his face, and was surprised to recognize Daniel Romanov, Anastasia's disgustingly effeminate, younger brother.

As if we had always been the best of friends, Daniel pounded up to the wagon and declaimed his pleasure at seeing me back in Russia. Glancing at Nina, he grinned crookedly and congratulated me on the beauty of my bride – this before I had a chance to introduce him. My letter from Kholmagora had obviously been received by the Czar.

Daniel was overly gracious when I presented Doctor Bomel, and made an embarrassing display of his regard for me. This excessively solicitous attitude puzzled me almost as much as his act of coming. He was lazy and indolent, and we had never been close. In fact, I had always rather disliked him. Regardless of these reservations, I was impressed and appreciative. Toby had ridden back to discover who our visitor was, so I asked him to take the reins and invited Daniel to join us inside the wagon. The interior was quite spacious, appointed with several couches attached to the floor with staves to prevent their sliding. I offered Daniel some wine, which he drank greedily, and after a few more preliminary remarks he more or less came to the point of his trip.

He had journeyed here at the order of the Czar, he told us, but his selection as emissary had been at his own request. The court had only recently returned from the summer palace at Alexandrov, where Ivan now stayed for increasingly prolonged periods. The tale Daniel had to tell was disturbing to the others, and while it seemed exaggerated to me when I heard it, I was soon to find a good portion of it based on fact, badly distorted as it was by Daniel's interpretations. This younger Romanov, I should note, was still a relatively handsome man, in a somewhat uninspired way. He reminded me of a statue Ridolfi had in his garden, a copy I was told, after a great sculptor from his native Florence. The carving depicted the heathen god, Bacchus, curator of the vineyards and patron of drunkards. The face was youthful, but dissipation and lack of proper exercise tended to enervate the entire form. It lacked the muscular strength proper to a man of less than middle years. The contours of the stone face had brought Daniel to mind when I originally gazed upon it, and his presence reinforced the impression.

"Many things have changed since you left," Daniel said at length, "and the Czar has changed most of all. That man Skuratof who commands your horse is typical of the people who now surround him."

"You surely cannot compare Malyuta Skuratof to Kurbsky and my stepfather," I replied defensively.

"They are the exceptions," he said quickly. "But they, too, have changed, as you will see. I live in fear, Dmitri! As the uncle of the Czarevitch I should, by rights, hold a position of respect and honor among the nobility. Instead, I am frequently ignored and forced to pay homage to men of the lowest rank, men whom the Czar has elevated during some moment of intemperance."

His insinuations – as well as his mannerisms – annoyed me, and my expression must have shown it. Not only did I feel he spoke unwisely in referring to the Czar, his words had an immediately adverse effect on my companions, serving only to magnify the apprehensions I had previously observed. Nina glanced at Anne, and Bomel fidgeted nervously. I had taken a seat next to my wife on one of the couches, and now felt impelled to slip my arm around her shoulders. She responded with a stifled little sound in her throat and pressed herself against me. I could feel her trembling, however, which only added to my irritation at Daniel's lack of judgment.

"You should exercise some care in what you say," I warned him softly, trying not to alarm the others by appearing to threaten him. "You know I am completely loyal to the Czar, and I've already explained his virtues to my friends."

"The virtue of the Czar is unquestioned," Daniel whined, "but there are moments when the fires of hell seem to burn in his eyes, and the torments of his soul are frightening."

I bit my lips to keep from shouting at him, but there was obviously no way to silence Daniel without frightening Nina. More than this, he had piqued my curiosity. I was already wondering why he had come at all, and the only way to find out was going to be by listening to him. I wished I had had the foresight to take him aside and speak with him outside the others' hearing. Too late for that – too late . . . . And then, I really didn't wish to halt his discourse. He was revealing himself, though his motives remained obscure, and I found my own suspicion of the man fading into the background of my thoughts as I listened in fascination to his slanted account.

"Andrei Savin must have told you about the murder of your friend, Vladimir," he began. "Yes, it was murder," he insisted quickly. "The Prince had gone to live on his estates. The turmoil of the court was more than he could stomach. He never came to Moscow unless the Czar demanded it, and he had no communication with anyone within the royal household, other than the handful of friends who still dared visit him. His mother had already been sent into exile by the Czar – to Beelozersk, of all places – but the Prince made no effort to oppose the Czar. Then suddenly, one day when Ivan was drunk, he sent soldiers to arrest Vladimir and Evdokia, and both their sons – one less than two years old, and had them brought to Moscow. Ivan accused Vladimir of plotting against him and of poisoning Maria. The exact charge was *nepravda* – falseness. After a terrible harangue – I was there; I heard it – he made them all drink poison, even the smallest child. He sent orders to Beelozersk that Euphrosyne be drowned in the lake, and then sent more soldiers to Staritsa. He ordered them to hang all the servants, and he had them burn out the peasants who lived closest to the *dacha*."

He paused for breath, sweat beading on his brow, and I found myself asking, "The little girls, Vladya's daughters . . . what of them?"

Daniel snorted. "In his great benevolence, the Czar has taken them into his household. But they are paupers, completely dependent upon him. He has confiscated all the Staritsky property, even the servants' plate and his cousin's clothing, which he has ordered sold in the public bazaars for the benefit of the royal treasury."

There was a terrible conflict arising within my thoughts: anger at this contemptible man, my own desire not to believe him, my unbidden acceptance of his tale as basically true. I suppose these feelings were reflective of the confused attitude I had always had toward Daniel. I simply did not like him, although I had tried many times to find some positive aspect, some spark of manhood to command my respect. He was, after all, the brother of the most noble woman I had ever known, whom I still revered and would always hold in fondest remembrance. In certain lights, I could catch a trace of Anastasia in Daniel's features, and it may have been this – more than anything else – that forced me to tolerate him, and to feign a friendship which I really never felt.

His rekindling of my grief over Vladya's death had brought me almost to the point of weeping, something I refused to do in Daniel's presence. Afraid that my voice might betray me, I waited a few seconds before saying anything, covering the interval by pouring more wine into the bumpers of all my companions. I realized, too, that I was morbidly fascinated by these details of Vladya's fall. I would question Daniel later, in private. For the moment, I thought it best to change the subject. "I suppose you have observed other sins?" I asked, not really expecting much of an answer. My conversations with Andrei Savin had left me with the impression of little change, but Andrei having not lived at court, may not have known everything in such detail as Daniel.

He took my remark as encouragement, and I am certain the wine was causing him to feel very much at home with us, dulling his senses to a point where he missed any underlying derision or sarcasm in my tone. "How about the *medvedi* – the bears?" he asked loudly.

Nina looked at me curiously, not understanding him. I translated for her.

"Bears?" she exclaimed. "You mean real, live, wild bears?"

"Yes, bears!" Daniel repeated. "Ferocious beasts from the wildest parts of Siberia. The Czar has a standing order with the Stroganovs to keep a supply of them coming to him. It has become a favorite sport to have contests between man and beasts after dinner. Sometimes, even in the dining hall! And sometimes the men he orders to fight the animals are people who have just broken bread with him.

"And the staff, that terrible *kisten!* He carries it with him at all times. He strikes out in anger whenever he wishes, hitting anyone within his reach, sometimes with the side, as with a club, other times with the steel of the point. You don't know what fear we live with, Dmitri! You can't even imagine it!"

As before, I had the urge to strike out at him. I didn't want to believe any of this, and kept trying to deny it in my mind. I was certain he must be taking some skeletal facts and loading them with the flesh of his imaginings. Daniel filled his own cup from the wine cask and flopped back onto the couch. I might still have kept quiet had his expression not reflected such satisfaction, and had I not been able to feel the terror range in tremors through Nina's body. "Why do you tell me this?" I demanded. "Does it give you some twisted pleasure to lay such treason at my feet?"

"I speak not only to warn you, as befits an old friend," he whined, "but because you, of all men, possess the skill to soothe the Czar. You can speak to him almost as my sister was able to do." He glanced up at me, his dark, effeminate lashes wet with tears, and I realized he had used some cosmetic to blacken them. Again, through the distortion of Daniel's features by drink and emotion, I caught a fleeting image of Anastasia. This alone stayed my hand as he continued. "If you are aware what horrors have come to pass in your absence, you will be better prepared to meet them," he added softly.

It suddenly occurred to me that there might be more behind Daniel's visit than I first suspected. "You didn't come completely on your own, did you?" I asked. "There are. . . others who feel as you do?"

"There are many who fear the Czar," he answered evasively. "But we all remain loyal to him," he added quickly. "We seek nothing more than our continued existence, that we may go on serving him."

"You seem to imply more."

"I speak only in factual truth," he insisted, interrupting me. "Let me tell you a little more, and perhaps you will understand." He sighed and moved forward on the couch, the drunkenness seeming to fade with the intensity of his plea. "In the cold of winter," he began, his voice falling into the cadence of a professional storyteller – possibly indicating a careful preparation, ". . .with the snow heavy on the ground, the Czar suddenly ordered all his treasures and the wonder–working icons loaded into sleighs. Taking his sons and a few trusted servants, he ordered them to drive off into the countryside. It was early morning when he left, and the faithful were just coming out of the churches. Calling out to him, we asked where he was going. The Czar ordered the column to halt, and from his *troika* he spoke to us, accusing us of disloyalty, claiming that he was surrounded by treachery. He said he was leaving Moscow forever, giving up his crown, although he took it with him. He did not wish to be Czar, he said, if he was not allowed to rule without constantly having to unravel the plots and ploys of his nobles and his bishops. He did not know where he would go, he told us, but would follow wherever the Will of God should lead him.

"With that, he ordered his drivers on and they raced away, leaving us standing in the snow. No one knew what to do. Without the Czar there is no State, no nation, no leaders. He passed through the city, of course, so all the people saw him go. When they came to us and asked what they should do, we told them we didn't know. We went to the bishops and the Metropolitan Alfanasy, and we asked their advice, for if the truth be known it had been their opposition that most grievously offended the Czar. Alfanasy said we must follow after him and beg him to return.

"Not a single shop was open in the city that day, and all of us – nobles and peasants, churchmen from the highest bishop to the lowest monk – all of us followed the tracks left by Ivan's sleighs. John Bielsky, son of Johannes, Mstislavsky . . . my brother and myself, all of us did as the Metropolitan said we should. A few of us started out on horseback, but Alfanasy chastised us. We must go on foot, he said, in all humility, if we wished to persuade the Czar to return. Then the old man personally set the pace at the head of the long column.

"We walked for days through the snow, following his trail. The wind was cold and we had little to eat, for few had thought to bring supplies. But we never faltered. We loved the Czar and we wanted him to return.

"At last we came to the village of Alexandrov, and there we saw the sleighs of the royal household. All of us knelt in the snow, begging the grace of the Czar, beseeching him to forgive us. The Metropolitan cried out the loudest of all, encouraging the others until Ivan came outside. He stood before us with his face composed into lines of innocence and concern. He listened to us without comment, standing like an unmoving statue. Finally, he agreed to return – only if all restrictions were removed from his office and if the Church promised upon the most sacred oath not to interfere with his leadership. Everyone agreed, including the Metropolitan, who knelt directly in front of the Czar, weeping and nodding to every demand.

"The Czar returned to Moscow, bringing back all his treasure and his family. But he did not remain for long. He soon returned to Alexandrov and ordered a palace built upon the site where the Church and people had promised their obedience. The construction is almost completed, and already the things that happen there are too frightening—"

"What of the conflict between the Czar and the new Metropolitan?" I demanded sharply. I refrained from making any comment on his tale, though I now felt an ominous pressure within my own gut. I was trying to divert him onto another subject.

"The long walk to Alexandrov and the cold weather were too much for Alfanasy," said Daniel. "Soon after returning to Moscow, he took sick and died. Everyone expected Pimen to be named Metropolitan, but Ivan selected Phillip instead. At first, the priest refused; but the Czar demanded and Phillip had no choice. As you know, this is a very holy man. He has already done things and said things that disturb the Czar."

"Has he gone back on the assurances given by Alfanasy?" I asked.

"Not really," said Daniel thoughtfully. "He has only spoken in private about the excesses of the court. He has questioned the ungodliness of the Czar's activities at Alexandrov, and has referred to the Czar's attendants as ruffians. He is most particularly critical of the monastic travesty. . . ."

"Monastic what?" I interrupted.

"It hasn't been officially proclaimed," explained the Romanov, "but Ivan has made it known that he intends to surround himself with exactly one thousand loyal followers, all of whom will take monastic vows and will live with the Czar as monks about their abbot. The name of this group, I'm told, will be 'The Ones Who Serve' – *Opritchina.* Your stepfather is already a member."

"Then I am sure it must be an honorable group of men," I answered. "You, I take it, have not been invited to join."

Daniel hung his head as if defeated, finally responding to the contempt which I allowed to show in my expression. "There is nothing else for me to say," he mumbled.

"I should hope not!" I told him. "You've sat here, slandering the Czar and prostituting your honor before my wife and friends. You've heaped dishonor on me, and unforgivable sin upon your own soul! You should pray for God's mercy."

"I have only spoken the truth," he answered in a flat, emotionless voice. "But I should have known. You have never liked me, although I know the love you bore for my sister. . . ."

Nina looked at me curiously, but I commented in English: "'Twas like the love of a warrior knight who serves his sovereign's lady."

"Your friend," she said dryly, "makes it sound more like Tristram and Isabel."

Daniel looked from one to the other of us. "Your wife does not speak Russian?" he asked stupidly.

"Well enough to have understood your unhallowed words!" I said, "And to have wondered, since she's a foreigner, knowing only what I've been able to tell her of the Czar, whether she's in a land of madmen, or whether she's listened to one who differs from the rest." I spoke so disparagingly that, had he been half a man, he would have hit me. Instead, he continued to sit with his head drooping forward in despair. At length he began to weep, and I finally asked him to leave. We were still a full day's travel from Vologda, and I should have asked Daniel to stay with us. Instead, I followed him outside the wagon, which had now been positioned for the night, and glowered at him until he mounted and rode away.

When I climbed into the wagon, I was besieged with questions: Were they really safe, or should we turn now and leave? Might my own life be in danger, after all? What of the unborn child? How could it survive in Russia if I were in prison – or no longer alive to offer it protection?

I soothed their fears as best I could, cursing Daniel under my breath, but blaming myself as well. Angry as I was with him, I knew it had been my fault for allowing him to speak in front of Nina and the others. I felt disloyal – unclean for having spent the last few hours with him. Later, I stayed at prayer much longer than I usually did, and I begged the Lord God to look deep within me, to examine my soul before attaching Daniel's guilt to me. Even so, I continued to feel corrupted, as if Daniel had somehow befouled my spirit by forcing me to hear his blasphemy.

In Vologda, we transferred ourselves and our baggage into the waiting boats, and embarked on the last leg of our trip. Daniel did not show himself again, and followed us later, arriving in Moscow with Pissemsky and the English. I tried not to think about him, but his words kept returning to my mind. Some of the things he'd said disturbed me even in sleep.

On the whole, our passage along the rivers was pleasant. The weather turned warm, and the boats were extremely well appointed. Ivan had sent the very finest conveyances at his command. Unfortunately, Daniel had been the Czar's only representative. Now, in the Romanov's absence there was no one to supply us with intimate information about the court, to confirm or deny the accounts we had already heard. The boatmen and other retainers either did not know, or would have been loath to discuss such things with a man of my position, even if I had thought it fitting to approach them. Doctor Bomel, having fewer scruples, engaged several of the hands in conversation; but he did not tell me what he had learned. I was not overly concerned about him, and I spent most of the time writing out my recollections of England.

When we arrived in Moscow, we were treated to a very gala reception. It would have been beneath the dignity of the Czar to meet us in person, but he sent Kurbsky in his place. And behind Andrew were Simon and Sheremetief, in addition to many other members of the court. They all wore their brilliant brocaded robes, with heavy fur capes and the tall hats of their rank. I think Nina found them a little frightening, although I was repeatedly hugged by all these old companions and each was most respectful when I presented my new bride.

Andrew escorted us to the door of my house, telling me that the Czar had ordered a banquet for that evening to celebrate my arrival. Ivan had also expressed interest in meeting the famous magician whom I had brought all the way from England. We had ridden in a tall, gilded coach, passing along the outer side of the Kitaigorod wall, and entering the gate to the inner city a short distance from my property. Nina and the Bomels were so taken with the sights of their new home, they hardly noted the words passing between Andrew and me. Toby was riding with the driver atop the coach,.

Among other things, I learned from Kurbsky that Heinrich had been sent to Lithuania a few weeks before, and so would not be at the house to greet us. I think Andrew was genuinely glad to see me, although he was always reserved in any expression of feelings. It was difficult to tell what he really thought. I sensed some inner reservations, for instance, over my having married a foreigner – this, despite his display of courtesy. When he left us at the door he told me I should go to the palace as soon as I was settled. Mikhailof would have some information to impart.

Except for Heinrich's absence, the household was exactly as it had always been. The first to greet me on the threshold were the harem girls, on whose score I must confess I had completely forgotten to warn Nina. When they ran forward, throwing their arms about my neck covering my face with kisses, I think my wife would gladly have stabbed them both – and me as well. As soon as I was able to untangle myself, I presented them to their new mistress, explaining to Nina that these were the Tartar girls I had rescued from Kazan. In lame excuse for their behavior, I further suggested that they had never ceased to display their gratitude to me. Happily, Nina's annoyance with them lasted only a short while. Both girls had aged, as Tartar women will, and Lotus Flower had gotten almost as fat as Jasmine had been. They were hardly a threat, nor in any way competition for her. With their harem training they fell immediately into the role of handmaidens.

As Doctor Bomel and Anne were to remain with us, at least until the Czar ordered otherwise, Nina was not without ample company. Still, she was unhappy that I must leave her so soon after our arrival. She was uncomfortable in these strange surroundings, and while her condition would have precluded her accompanying me to the palace in any event, she was disturbed by this first encounter with the restriction against women at a banquet table.

I no longer recall just how it happened, but my impending departure led us into our first real argument – the exchange ending only when I left the room. Still fuming, I walked back to the stables. There I was greeted enthusiastically by Serge, who immediately led Gabriel out for my inspection. The snowy stallion had been groomed to perfection, his coat brushed until it gleamed like creamy milk. He was getting on in years, nearly fifteen according to Serge, but he still held his head as proudly as ever. From the way he snorted and nuzzled my hand, I was sure he remembered me. I could not resist mounting him and taking a short ride around the city, much as I had done that first day after Simon had given him to me. He was a shade slower now, and I could feel him strain slightly when he galloped. But he was still the most magnificent mount in all the empire.

Many people turned to look at me, and a number of them waved or called out – mostly common people whom I did not know, but who appeared to know me. The greatest change I noticed was the great church in the Square of Executions. It had been nearly finished during my absence, and it was a breath–taking structure. The spiraling towers ended in enormous cupolas, the entire building white and sparkling in the sunlight. What a glorious monument! It seemed almost impossible one could doubt the godliness of a man who was capable of inspiring such a design.

I stopped before the building and admired its facade, comparing it in my mind with the dinginess of Saint Paul's Church in London. My reverie was interrupted by a beggar man, who hobbled up to me, pleading for alms. I had no money on my person, but feeling the sanctity of the moment, I pulled a ring from my finger and pressed it into his hand, hardly looking at him when I did so.

"Bless you, my son," he said, "and the holy Basil will bless you as well."

I still was not paying much attention to him, and the remark about Basil took a moment to reach my consciousness. "Holy one!" I called to him, realizing it had not been just a beggar, but one of the Fools for Christ who had spoken to me. "What do you mean, 'Basil will bless me?'"

He seemed puzzled I should ask. "You stand before his church," he answered.

I still failed to understand, as Ivan had spoken of consecrating his cathedral to the Mother of God. My answer came that evening, when the Czar himself explained to me that the people already considered Basil a saint, although he still lived to beg alms in the Square. "The church is consecrated to the Holy Virgin," he explained, "but people call it Basil's Church, and I suppose it will one day be his shrine. He is certain to be canonized when he dies." I made no com–ment, just shook my head in amazement.

"Have you ever beheld such magnificence?" the Czar asked me proudly. "I told the architects I would put out their eyes if they ever dared duplicate it elsewhere."

"I am sure they never could," I told him. "It is the inspiration as much as the builders' art that makes it what it is."

But when I returned from the Square of Executions I did not know this. I mulled over the holy man's words and their implication. How ironic it would be, I thought, should Ivan's great church, built to commemorate his first mighty conquest, be named for the only zealot he really feared – and disliked. How mysterious the ways of the Lord!

In my house everything was quiet. The Bomels were in the wing I had turned over to them. Toby was in Nina's bedroom helping her unpack. I went up quietly and watched them from the hall. My wife's anger had turned to a less violent mood of irritation. The greatest annoyance was her belly, preventing her from doing for herself, as she could not bend to retrieve an item if she dropped it. I saw how gingerly she moved as she pulled her dresses and other cloth items from the trunks. Adding to her aggravation, she found a number of them damaged beyond repair by mildew or water stains. At last she dropped heavily onto the bed, sighing deeply. She still had not noticed me.

Toby, who had been pulling things from a trunk on the other side of the room, suddenly held up the whip Ridolfi had given me at the end of our wedding ceremony.

"What shall I do with this, Mistress Nina?" he asked.

"Put it in the stable," I told him, entering the room.

Nina looked up at me, the last embers of fury still in her eyes. "No," she said haughtily. "I believe Russian custom dictates the marriage whip be hung on the bedroom wall, over the bridal couch. Isn't that right, Dmitri?"

"Few of the better families carry the custom that far, anymore," I replied evenly.

"But we are a most conservative family," she retorted. "I insist the sign of your authority be given a place of honor." She took the coil of leather from Toby and held it against the wall above the bed, placing it here and there, as if studying the aesthetic effect in various positions. "I think we shall have it hung right here," she said. "Toby, will you see to it, please?"

He left to fetch hammer and nails.

"Where are the girls?" I asked her.

"I sent them away," she said. "They kept chattering about everything that came out of the trunks until they gave me a headache."

"It seems many things are giving you headaches," I replied meaningfully.

She turned to me, then, and pressed her swollen body against me. Her face was on my shoulder, but she didn't weep. She trembled slightly, and I knew she was frightened – already a little lonely.

"You will become accustomed to our ways in time," I told her, "and you will see there are many pleasant occupations for a woman."

"I hope so," she whispered. "I guess it's being with child more than anything else. I'll be all right, once the effects of the trip wear off. You go ahead, now; I want to lie down awhile."

I went into the bathing room and cleansed myself thoroughly, dressing in my best and most expensive clothing. Lotus Flower trimmed my beard, which had completely grown back during the voyage. It was still as blond as ever, but coarser and more crinkled. She also clipped my hair, cutting it down almost to the scalp. She giggled to Lily, who was busy brushing my robe and applying sweet essence to the necessary points.

"What are you laughing at?" I asked her.

"Your hair," she told me, giggling again. "At the very top of your head, you will soon not need my services."

I resisted vanity's impulse, and did not examine my scalp in a mirror, pretending not to care. "You had better cultivate what's there," I told her lightly. "When I have no hair left for you to cut, you may find yourself on the auction block."

Their reaction – simply a continued gabble and laughter – was very different, I thought, from that of many other houses. Had the master made such a threat, even in jest, his slaves would have been frightened enough to question the seriousness of his intent. I had always been much too kind to my servants, as a number of friends had told me in the past. I resolved to be stricter in the future. It really was not good practice for a household to become as undisciplined as mine.

CHAPTER II

I went to the palace, expecting to find it much as I had left it, despite the several surprises I'd sustained on previous returns after much shorter absences. But I had succeeded in pushing Romanov's whining account from my thoughts, and once inside I found the superficial trappings unchanged. The white uniformed household guard still maintained their positions at stiff attention; the heavy, colorful furnishings were the same as I remembered. Upon my arrival I was taken in hand by Mikhailof, although the Czar's secretary did not greet me personally at the portal. Instead, I was escorted to his office by a servant who had been waiting for me in the atrium.

As I followed the man through the series of passageways, I became aware of the first noticeable innovation: the odor of burning incense, which had rarely been used in the palace prior to my departure. It gave the whole place an air of Tartary. There were fewer people about and through the halls. Except for the guards, the palace seemed nearly deserted. Mikhailof explained this to me, speaking cautiously and fidgeting with his hands all the while. "The Czar has reason to suspect a conspiracy," said the little man.

"From whom?" I asked.

The secretary looked at the ceiling and sighed. "From whom, indeed?"

"Do you imply criticism of the Czar's judgment?" I asked.

"Not at all," he replied too quickly. He continued to watch me warily, now, as he spoke. "It seems we are surrounded by conspirators, of whom I am unaware," he added. I could not tell whether his tone was sincere or sarcastic.

"Is there some reason why you, above anyone else, should be aware of conspirators?"

"I am not only the Czar's secretary, Dmitri," he replied, "but I also have been assigned to supervise the Bureau of Secret Affairs." His beady little eyes shot here and there about the room, like a mouse in search of grain.

"I didn't know the third bureau ranked so highly," I remarked.

"In this, the Czar would seem to disagree with you," he returned, almost triumphantly.

"And the chief snoop has an opportunity to mark down one black check against poor Dmitri," I said lightly. I had always found this type of gentle bantering to be the best way of handling Mikhailof, at least in private. With others present he was always fussy and proper. A small, busy little man, he had previously responded in a way which made me feel he was my friend. Now I sensed something more. In the past his officious manner had indicated a degree of certainty, of confidence in his own authority. At the moment I had the uncomfortable impression that he was afraid of me.

"Ah, Dmitri," he said at length, seeming to relax his guard. He sat down heavily, as if the act relieved tremendous pressure. "It's been so long since I've spoken to someone in jest! It's a refreshing change to have you back."

"I have heard many strange tales," I suggested cautiously.

"From that idiot Romanov?" he asked, nodding. "Yes, well you might. The Czar is also tiring of his constant whining. I tried to intervene when he asked to be sent to greet you . . . knew you'd never liked him, but the Czar had already consented before I could speak. Mostly, I think, he did it to get rid of Daniel for a few weeks."

"I suppose you've gotten Pissemsky's report by now?"

"Yes, and as usual you've added some spice to the adventure. How do you always manage to get yourself into so much trouble?"

"My greatest concern, now, is whether I'm in trouble with the Czar," I admitted flatly. I watched him closely, seeking any reaction which might confirm my apprehensions.

Instead, Mikhailof laughed, spreading his palms and shaking his head. "With Ivan? You? In trouble? I should hope not! The Czar has been waiting for your return like an impatient bride. He asks me at least twice a day if there's been a message from you. I admit, if anyone else had presumed to give away his diamond, even to the Queen of England, the man's head might be on the block. But you, my friend, have nothing to fear."

"You know about the diamond?" I asked in surprise.

"Yes. From your letter to the czar from Kholmagora. So, I know – you and Pissemsky, the Czar of course. No one else."

"Why was I summoned back so urgently?"

"Because you're needed," he said seriously. "Not that your abilities as a commander or a diplomat are so irreplaceable – and don't think I depreciate them. You're more competent than most. But the Czar now stands alone. Nearly every man he had thought to trust has turned on him, or at least he believes they have. Even now, Polish agents are in contact with Kurbsky. We know this, though Kurbsky isn't aware that we know."

"Do you really believe Andrew would betray the Czar?" I asked in amazement.

"We don't know. Probably not, and with the Czar as suspicious as he is of everyone, I can understand why Andrew hasn't mentioned the contacts made by Tishkovitch and others. Yet, in these trying times, who knows?" He shrugged.

"And what of Heinrich?" I asked.

"Oh, your stepfather has proven his loyalty many times," he answered casually, "but you must remember, Dmitri, Heinrich is a much older man than the Czar. Nor is he Russian, however faithful he may be. He enjoys the Czar's confidence only to a degree. As much as a foreigner ever could. But you! You're the companion of his youth, very probably of his own blood. With Yuri as good as in his grave —"

"Yuri is really going to die?"

"There is little doubt," he said sadly. "The physicians have done everything they can, but nothing seems to help. It's a wasting sickness, without much pain. But the Prince is now so weak he can't get out of bed."

"How is Ivan taking it?"

"It disturbs him more than most people realize. It's increased his trouble sleeping – you know the problem he's always had. And his only solace is – is that unfortunate remedy." His eyes avoided mine, and he looked down at his hands.

"You mean the chambers," I said casually. "Yes, I know. It was beginning to be so before he married Anastasia, and it started again after her death. But, what if a few useless criminals meet their ends to provide the Czar with strength to carry on God's work?"

"True, true," he agreed piously. "But lately, it's more than just a few."

"There are many useless men," I remarked, "but only one Czar."

"You understand him better than anyone else. Perhaps he'll be able to relax without these . . . distractions, or at least with fewer of them," said the secretary. "He cannot go on as he is. The strain is too great."

When I saw the Czar that evening, I discovered some of the meanings behind Mikhailof's innuendoes. Ivan, as I remembered him, had always been majestic: tall even when he stooped, his red beard cascading down his chest like a river of flame. His sharp nose and piercing eyes had given him the appearance of a proper autocrat, striking fear into the hearts of those who harbored evil thoughts against him. Now, the beard was scraggly. What little remained of it was almost dingy, yellow gray. His eyes, still penetrating and intense, were so red they seemed to glow from some unearthly, internal fire. His forehead was bruised, as I had seen it before, from being struck against the floor during his devotions. He was no longer lean; he now ate and drank much more than he used to. His face was blotchy; the regal nose was red. What puzzled me most was the condition of his beard, however, for as yet I had never seen him in such a rage that he tore at it, plucking out chunks of hair in his fury.

His face brightened when he saw me. I was already seated when he entered, and I stood respectfully, as did everyone else. There had been a group of men around me, asking all manner of questions about England and the Great Queen. The Czar let out a roar that echoed through the hall, and startled me so I almost dropped the goblet I was holding. The sound, in addition to Ivan's severely altered appearance, was unnerving. He raced forward to enfold me in a bear hug, nearly crushing a rib or two, then insisted I take the seat beside him. This pushed two others down the table: Kurbsky, who scowled; and Simon, who didn't seem to care.

Ivan had already been drinking, but this in no way inhibited his consumption of vodka at the table. Before any food was served he had led us into a high state of drunkenness. Unfortunately, in drinking with the Czar, I could not depend upon my usual ploys to avoid intoxication – pouring a goodly portion of the liquor into another container, or onto the floor – or merely by never drinking the goblet more than half empty. This night I felt no need to be on my guard, anyway, and I became as uproariously drunk as the rest – more so perhaps, as I was no longer used to these vast amounts of vodka – surely, the strongest drink in the world.

Doctor Bomel had come to the palace after I did, for I had left early to confer with Mikhailof. Elysius was escorted by Serge as far as the royal portals, and received there by household servants whom I had alerted to his coming. He had been entertained with a brief tour of the palace, and was led into the banquet hall a short while after the Czar had seated himself. Ivan was so involved in questioning me, I did not interrupt him when the Doctor was quietly seated at the other end of the main table. Beside him was Michael Saltikoff, on the side toward the Czar; and on his other hand, at the very end of the table, was Malyuta Skuratof. I had not expected the captain to be in such company, certainly not at the head table. Yet, he seemed very much at home, soon laughing and exchanging stories with Elysius.

It was a little while before I had an opening to introduce the doctor. "Your Most Gracious Majesty," I shouted, swaying very badly as I stood, clinging to the table for support, "if I may be permitted to speak without harm. . . ." This brought a huge roar of laughter, for it was well known I could always speak before the Czar. The crowd did not quiet quickly enough to suit Ivan, however, and he bellowed at them, at which the room became like a tomb.

"For the entertainment and enlightenment of Your Most Gracious Majesty." I repeated, "it is my great pleasure to announce the arrival in Your Majesty's court of that noble and eminent Doctor, Elysius Bomel, late of the Court of Her Majesty of England, and previously astrologer and mathematician supreme to His Grace, the whatever–he–is of Westphalia."

Doctor Bomel stood up, also unsteadily I noticed. He bowed low over the table, and in doing so succeeded in trailing his lacy ruffles through a platter of meat. His speech of greeting to the Czar was not only proper, but eloquent, despite his speaking in Russian. I was proud of having taught him so well, and the Czar seemed impressed.

"Prince Marensky, you have done Us a great service, I think," he said, winking. "Your Czar is greatly pleased with you." At that, he signaled to a servant. The fellow stepped behind him, and Ivan indicated he should take the remainder of a very succulent joint from his own plate. The servant took it to a side table, where he carved it in two, delivering one piece to me, the other to Doctor Bomel.

"Would it be proper for me to propose a toast to Your Majesty's health, and to a further increase in Your Majesty's realm?" asked Doctor Bomel, raising his goblet.

"It would be most *improper*, good Doctor!" Ivan roared with laughter, "But as you are a foreigner, and a good fellow, by all reports, We shall permit it!"

The bantering went on for quite a while, with many toasts being drunk, and with everyone laughing and seeming to have a good time. Yet, beneath the levity there was something else – a tension, perhaps. I could not immediately place it, but the laughter was not the same as it used to be, nor was the comradeship as real. The new ingredient was fear, although it was a few more days before I could name it. But on this evening, Doctor Bomel was a huge success. He carried on a lengthy, animated conversation with several of the Skuratof cronies. They were all joking with him, and seemed genuinely to like him, as did the Czar. Then, as the evening wore on, Ivan had his fill of the doctor's adventures in England, and returned his attention to me.

"What is this they tell me of your marrying without my permission?" he bellowed unexpectedly. This came after I had just parried a few questions about Elizabeth, and whether I thought she would be a fit bride for him. His roar had been so sudden, and sounded so serious, everyone fell silent to listen.

"I had to make a decision," I said calmly, though I could feel my heart pounding against my ribs. "In Your Majesty's absence, I asked the advice of Your Majesty's sister, the Great Queen herself. She told me it would be foolish to leave such a perfect flower unplucked, and in effect gave me her blessing, as if she stood in Your Own Stead."

"A very clever answer," howled the Czar, laughing again. "And I understand you have shown good taste. Except that she might be a little plumper, from the reports I've received."

More laughter, and a toast to my new bride. Then the Czar leaned heavily upon the table. "But there is one more matter," he growled. "Dmitri, what of my diamond?"

I stared at him a moment in silence. I could not answer this before the entire court, and I think Ivan's drunken state was the only reason he had asked it. To explain about the stone would have required my telling everyone why I had it in the first place. I cleared my throat. "The stone you gave me," I began, and as I spoke I could tell by his expression that the Czar had realized his error, "as a token to be presented to the lady of my choice, was too fine a gift for any but a Queen. I gave it to Elizabeth in Your Majesty's name, for I could find no more suitable way to use it."

The others cheered and hooted, and the Czar laughed, partially in relief that I had covered his slip of the tongue. Pressing my advantage, I playfully added: "Now, of course, I have given away the great stone, so I have been unable to present my bride with a proper token of my Czar's affection."

Ivan looked at me with a blank stare, as I continued to smile innocently at him. He grunted and finally broke into merry laughter, for the Czar could still enjoy a joke at his own expense. The others echoed this, though they were never to understand the reason.

"You have outdone me, Dmitri," he whispered, pulling a large ruby brooch from his robe. Then, in a loud voice he continued, "Here, present this to your lady with the compliments of the Czar, and with his wishes for a long and happy marriage!" Under his breath he added, "You fox!"

By this maneuver I had now accomplished two things. The brooch, valuable as it was, made no difference. But by getting Ivan to give it to me, I had reestablished my nearness to him and confirmed Mikhailof's opinions. More important, I had allowed newcomers – like Skuratof – to see just how close I was to the Czar.

The finale of the evening came when the men about Elysius set up a sudden chorus of very boisterous laughter, attracting the attention of everyone in the room. The Czar was immediately curious.

"This man has never seen a bear!" shouted Michael Saltikoff.

"Should we not remedy that?" asked one of the others.

"A match, a match!" came a loud voice from the other side of the room – Alexi Basmanov, I think. Then many others joined in. "A wrestling match!" they cried. "Bring on the bear!"

Through it all, I could hear Elysius. "It is really not necessary, good sirs," he pleaded. "It could wait until the morrow." This only brought more laughter.

Ivan signaled a servant, who approached him on the far side from me. I could hear the Czar questioning who was available to fight the bear. The names of several prisoners were mentioned, but they must all have been men of no consequence; the names I heard meant nothing to me. At last one was decided upon, and the Czar ordered him brought over from the prison.

While we waited for the contestants, more liquor was poured and I shouted at the doctor to tell us another of his stories. After a little persuasion from his nearest companions, he tried to stand up. Unable to, he remained in his chair and regaled the company with a most obscene, hilarious tale about a priest and the wife of a sea captain. As he was speaking my gaze happened to fall upon Kurbsky, and I noted he was the only person in the room who did not enjoy the situation. He struggled to maintain a cheerful expression, but I saw the mask slip – just once, when all the others laughed at a particularly vulgar part of Bomel's story. Andrew looked stonily at the doctor for a single, fleeting second. Then he returned his features to their schooled control. Evidence of another dissident voice was the Metropolitan's table, separate from the others and laid with the finest service on a sparkling white cloth. It stood empty, unoccupied by Phillip or his priests. I felt a slight twinge of nostalgia, as if Makari's ghost had materialized. I knew this new patriarch only by repute, and from seeing him once at a congress of churchmen.

My own attention was diverted, then, for the keepers had brought in a huge, shaggy brown bear. I had seen many such animals before, but I gasped at this one's size. "Where did you find such a monster?" I asked the Czar.

"The latest arrival from Siberia," he chuckled, "by the goodness of Prince Stroganov. Magnificent, is he not?"

I watched the animal as the keepers tried to hold him still. The noise and odors of food had excited him, until it took all four of the regular keepers, plus several additional servants to hold the ropes restraining the beast at the far end of the room. A heavy muzzle covered his mouth, and I could see his claws had been cut. Even so, he remained a mountain of brute strength, and I wondered how much contest it would be to pit a human against him.

Soon the door opened again, and a large wild–looking man was brought in, naked except for a breechclout and nearly as hairy as the bear. The fellow's arms were fastened to a block of wood behind his back, and he blinked in the bright light of the dining chamber. His full brown beard was uncombed and filthy from the dungeon; his bald head glistened with sweat, as did his muscular, warrior's body.

"This is a servant of our illustrious Radziwell, General of the Polish army," shouted Ivan. "What say you, we pit this Pollack hero against a Russian bear?"

The room resounded with shouts of assent and catcalls directed at the prisoner. He might have been just a Pollack, and an extremely ugly one at that; yet I felt a certain compassion for him, and admiration as well. He was brave enough to shout above the roar of the Czar's court: "And if I win, what will be my reward? Freedom? Gold? Surely, the Great and Generous Czar will not ask me to fight for nothing!" He stood straight, now, glaring at the head table.

Ivan's mood was generous and he chuckled at the fellow's audacity. "You may name your reward in advance," he replied. "Tell Us what you'd like, fellow, and if you defeat the beast it shall be yours – within reason, of course," he added with a laugh.

"Freedom," the prisoner said simply. "Freedom and a safe conduct to my own lines." He looked so serious one would have thought he expected not to die.

"Done!" exclaimed the Czar. Then he shouted to the servants to free the Pole. Once his hands were released, the man was given a heavy cudgel, after which the bear was turned loose. I noted, too, how quickly and precisely the white uniformed guardsmen filed into the room, positioning themselves so their heavy lances would assure neither bear nor man would suddenly charge the Czar.

The guards also had a secondary function, this to assure the bear faced the right direction – though in this instance, they need not have been concerned. Without waiting for the animal to attack, the Pollack ran at him. He delivered a crashing blow against the brute's body with his club, then retreated. The bear grunted in pain and surprise; emitting a horrible roar, he turned on the man, charging toward him on all fours. When he was close enough, he raised up, flaying the air with his front feet, towering above his antagonist. The man swung his club once more, pounding another hard blow, but this time striking only the right paw. The beast lunged, smashing his other foot against the Pollack, knocking him down. When the man fell, the club clattered away from him, sliding across the floor.

The uneven struggle went on for several more minutes, as the man used his greater agility to worry the animal and try to tire him. Several deep gashes appeared on his body, where the bear had raked him with the stubs of his claws. Then finally, the bear was on him, trying to bite, but prevented by the leather muzzle. He wrapped his great forelegs around the Pollack's chest, and after a couple of trys he managed to roll onto his back, pulling the man over, on top of him. The Pollack lay with his back against the bear's chest, his legs and arms waving uselessly in the air. Slowly, with tremendous strength, the bear squeezed tighter, ever tighter. Clear at my end of the room, I could hear the Pollack's bones begin to crack. One after the other, the huge bear crushed his ribs. At first the man struggled, but made no sound other than a groan or straining gasp. After a few moments he began to moan horribly, expressing his pain and agony as loudly as he could. But his lungs were crushed along with his bones. Before his courage was spent to a point where he would have shouted his terror, his body was unable to produce the sound. At length, the bear let go. The man's body fell heavily onto the floor as the animal rolled back onto his feet, looking for his next antagonist. One of the keepers held out a bucket of honey on the end of a long stick. After a few more sniffs at the broken body, the bear followed this lure into an antechamber, while other retainers grabbed the ropes trailing from his collar. The door closed, and it was over.

There was a loud cheer for the victor, as a couple of servants dragged out the body of the dead Pollack. I looked down the table at Doctor Bomel, who seemed a little green after his first experience with bear wrestling. "You'll get used to it, Elysius," I called, and added in English. "Bear up, old man!" I was terribly drunk.

The doctor smiled sickly and waved back. Someone shoved a full goblet into his hands, and he drained it without taking a breath. After that, he seemed himself again. The banquet ended soon afterward, as the Czar excused himself and left with Fedka Basmanov.

When Elysius and I returned home that night Nina was still awake, trying to read. Anne had fallen asleep in a nearby chair, but she opened her eyes as we entered. Doctor Bomel was very excited about his first visit to the Czar's palace, and most particularly enthusiastic in describing the gold and precious gems which were so commonly used on the Imperial table.

I presented the Czar's gift to Nina, who fondled it sleepily. Like all Russian jewelry, it was heavy and lacked the delicate workmanship she was used to. Solid gold, it featured one quite large ruby surrounded by six smaller ones, with diamonds outlining the medallion's outer edge. It was a piece the Czar had often worn prior to my departure to England, and I knew it was one of his favorite pieces, and extremely valuable. "We can have the stones reset," I told her.

"Did they have wrestling bears?" asked Nina, obviously not expecting an affirmative answer.

"Bears!" shouted the doctor, eager to describe it now that he was safely removed from its presence. "Such a bear as you have never seen! A huge, shaggy brown monster, with enormous hairy ears and feet as big as a man's head!"

When the doctor paused for breath, Anne quickly interjected the question uppermost in her mind. "You were well received, then, Demetrius?"

"More so than I dared hope," I said. "I am to see the Czar tomorrow, and discuss the things he wishes me to do."

Despite my assurance that all was well, Nina still seemed disturbed, as if her mind were troubled by many anxieties. Later that evening, as we lay beside each other in my great bed, she enumerated her fears and other concerns. The household arrangements were her first complaint. While the girls accepted her as the senior wife, something would have to be done about "that harem," she insisted. They seemed to expect they would spell her in the conjugal bed, as well as remaining available for my stepfather. I assured her that language problems had created a misunderstanding, and promised to explain the principals of Christian marriage to them in the morning.

Then, she added, the Russian rules of seclusion for women were outrageous. She was not going to live that way. I told her we could work something out. Then there was that "horrid little Chinaman" – I discovered she meant Serge – whom she had caught peering at her through one of the grilled windows in the rear of the house. I promised to speak to him.

I must also get rid of the insects from the stables. They were all over the house, horseflies particularly, so large they looked like birds. All of this I promised to remedy, though I explained I could not simply discharge the servants who were displeasing to her; they were slaves who belonged to me, and if I threw them out they would have no place to go. Besides, they had been in my household for a long time, and were very loyal. This, I emphasized, could be an extremely valuable asset some day. At last she agreed, but made me promise to speak to them. After that, I thought she was finished. I kissed her forehead, and started to doze off. I was very tired, and very, very drunk.

But all the other anxieties had been preliminary; her real fear was of the Czar – this stemming from the stories she had already heard of him. "There was a priest called Sylvester," she said suddenly, her voice startling me in the stillness. "Isn't he the one you mentioned as the Czar's confessor?"

"Yes, he's no longer at court," I mumbled, already half asleep.

"Did you know the Czar recently executed his brother, and his brother's children?"

"No, I had not heard about it," I sighed, forcing myself awake again. "But what does it matter? He was a man of little consequence, and was related to one who had been highly placed. Sylvester was removed from his position of closeness to the Czar, and could someday become an enemy. It is only proper for the Czar to dispose of his brother."

"But why the wife and the poor, innocent children?" she asked, almost with tears in her voice.

In the darkness of our bedroom, I drew her closer to me. "What if the children were to grow up?" I asked her. "Would they not say, 'look at this man who has killed my father'? Children who lose their parents will usually feel anger at the man responsible, even if the executions were justified. It is possible that one of these children, through the misconceptions of youth, or the stories told him as a child, might forsake his holy teachings which bind every man in loyalty to the Czar."

Nina was silent, but I heard her catch her breath once or twice as if about to say something more. After a few minutes I lay back and quickly fell asleep. I knew she did not understand; our ways were still strange to her.

The next morning I left early for the palace after giving my entire household staff a dressing down and leaving no doubt in anyone's mind that I meant what I said. At the palace I was taken immediately to the Czar, who had returned from chapel some time before and was just finishing breakfast in his own apartments. We had a great many subjects to discuss, among them the further details of my adventures in England and the impressions I had formed of the Great Queen. Ivan was very displeased that she had been evasive in answering his proposal of marriage.

"I think it much more a matter of political consideration than anything else," I told him. "The Queen uses her sex and her half–promises of marriage to retain the friendship of several nations."

"Whom do you think she is going to marry?" asked the Czar.

"No one," I told him frankly. "There is something strange about her, and while I spent much time with the man who is reputed to be her lover, he never said a word to imply any relationship other than friendship."

"I should hope not!" said Ivan stiffly. He seemed surprised I would expect differently.

"A man in such a position would be reticent to boast of his sexual adventures with so great a Queen," I assured him, "but any man who is having an affair with a woman is bound to let some remark drop, sometime. If you are in his company long enough, and if you are listening for such things, you would detect it. Or if he did not, one of his friends would say something. Really, in my own mind, I do not think there has ever been intimacy between them."

"Then she is truly a virgin?"

"I would say so," I told him. I wanted to say more, but I knew it would be impossible to make anyone understand what I sensed about Elizabeth. A person would have to meet her for himself. Nor was I sure enough of what I felt to try explaining it. I knew the Czar was going to vent his displeasure on the Queen's emissaries, but for the moment that would have to be their concern. In addition to their failure to return with the answer Ivan wanted regarding his proposal of marriage, the English group that was now on its way to Moscow did not include Anthony Jenkinson. This alone was enough to offend the Czar. Anthony was a singular person, as I had discovered for myself, and Ivan was annoyed by his failure to return.

But we went on to other matters. With the Queen's answer a fairly definite "no," Ivan indicated his intention to marry again. While we were discussing this, Fedka tapped on the door and came in to stand quietly in the background until the Czar turned to him.

Many rumors were already beginning to circulate about this young man, and his relationship to the Czar. Seeing him this day and the night before, I could understand how such ideas had started. He was no longer a boy, being well into manhood, though he still had no beard. I do not know whether he shaved it or not. And his tousled blond hair was much too long for a man. His face and hands were smooth, like a woman's. His skin was a golden brown from the sun, and his general appearance was like the Italian statue of Apollo that stood in Ridolfi's garden. I knew he regularly slept in the Czar's rooms, but he had been named *postelnik* – gentleman of the bedchamber. I had to assume he slept there to be close at hand if Ivan needed something during the night. Still, his manner of speaking to the Czar, and his overall attitude, I thought, were too familiar. But again, he had been like a son to Ivan, and had spent most of his life in the Czar's household. He came now to inform us that the Czarevitch wished to speak to his father.

"By all means," said Ivan. Looking at me, he added enthusiastically, "You did not see Our Vanya last night, as he was on a little adventure of his. . . ." He was interrupted by the youngster's entrance, and I gave an involuntary gasp. It had been well over three years since I last saw the Czarevitch; the change was astonishing. It was as if I gazed back over the last two decades. Vanya was the very essence of the youth who had bested the bullies and assumed the throne of his fathers. The Czarevitch was surely the son of Ivan IV, a fact no man could refute. Vanya made the brief semblance of a bow and came to sit beside his father. I had half risen when he came in, but both father and son gestured me down.

"I am told there is a resemblance," Ivan laughed, watching my expression.

"More than that!" I said. I looked at them carefully as they sat together, purposely assuming the same pose to enhance the similarities in their features. I could see a suggestion here and there of Anastasia; Vanya's ears and jawline were hers, but the eyes and nose were his father's. The hair was a shade darker than Ivan's had been, and his frame was a little slighter. "You could never deny him," I said at length.

Ivan placed an arm about his son's shoulders and squeezed affectionately. "I should never wish to do that," he said smiling, the pride of a father in his son. Vanya must have been about ten, maybe twelve, at the time.

"I hear there is a little one on the way in your own house," said the Czarevitch, courteously. "Is your bride really as beautiful as We have heard?"

"More so," I replied, thanking him for his inquiry. I was not sure just how I should react to this boy. As close as I was to the father, the son was another person, becoming a man. Someday, he would be Czar. He seemed to accept me as Ivan did, as a friend to whom, in private, the rigid rules of Byzantine court behavior did not apply. As I had always been willing to play with Vanya when he was little, I felt it likely that he looked on me much as I had on Vorontsof. I hoped not to prove such a disappointment.

"I would not have interrupted you," said the Czarevitch, including me in his remarks, a further indication of favor, "but Mikhailof had a message from the

Pollacks, and he was afraid to bother you with it. I thought it was funny." He grinned, almost cruelly, handing the small scroll to his father.

Ivan pulled the string and unrolled the parchment, squinting a bit as he read. "Ah!" he roared. "Good enough for him!" He read to the end and dropped the scroll on the table. "Do you remember Vishnevetsky?" he asked me.

I started, for the man had been a subaltern and companion in battle, second in command when I defeated Perekop. "Of course I know him," I replied. "He served under me that whole summer in the steppes."

"That's right, he did serve with you. I'd forgotten – chased the Nogais all the way to hell, didn't you?" The Czarevitch watched us, grinning as his father spoke. By his expression, it was clear he understood everything we said, and that he was already aware of the campaigns we mentioned – a very penetrating mind in that youthful body.

"Yes, he also served a short while in Livonia," I remarked, "before the Lithuanians came into it."

"Did you know he deserted Us – went back to Sigismund?" asked Ivan.

"I had heard something about it," I replied casually. In fact, I knew all about it. Vishnevetsky had been a Lithuanian baron, but had refused to accept Sigismund as Duke. He had exercised his ancient privilege as a free noble, transferring his allegiance to the Czar. While I was in England there had been some difficulties – apparently with newcomers in the court, and Vishnevetsky had returned to Lithuania. He made his peace with Sigismund August, but when the King ordered him to command a force against the Russians, he claimed we were his former comrades–in–arms and refused to fight us.

"His desertion has been well rewarded," smiled the Czar. "Sigismund ordered him to lead an army against Us, but the coward refused, claiming it would be against his honor to fight former friends. The last I heard of him, he had been sent to the Sultan – I thought as an emissary." He continued to laugh, a hoarse, unpleasant chuckle. "But even the Sultan seems to have no use for traitors. He strung Vishnevetsky up in the marketplace and had a bit sliced off each day, until there wasn't very much left."

It saddened me to hear this, but I knew God would not wish me to further burden the Czar by refusing to reflect the proper attitude. "A poor way to contaminate a marketplace," I commented coldly.

"But a good example to others who would betray Us to the King of Poland," said Ivan. He paused, then, which gave me a chance to lead us into something else.

"Do you plan to renew the conflict in the near future?" I asked.

"What do you mean, 'renew it?'" asked the Czarevitch, almost sharply. "It hasn't ever stopped."

"I mean, we are not making any major assaults at present," I replied cautiously. "I had assumed this to be the reason for my recall."

"We may soon have use for your skills as a general," replied the Czar, "but right now We have another duty in mind for you." He grinned knowingly at his son, and looked back at me. "You have heard of the group We are forming to protect Us from traitors and Polish spies?"

"The *Opritchina*," I replied simply.

"You are always well informed," he said, a little surprised I knew about it. "It will be more secret than this," he continued. "Some members will be acknowledged, of course, but many others will not. I knew you would wish to be on hand when I consecrate the abbey."

"As much as I feared being relegated to holy orders in my youth, it now appears I'm to receive the call, after all," I quipped.

"But only as a holy limb of God's earthly emissary," noted the Czarevitch seriously. This time, he sounded as if he were repeating a liturgy, repeating words by rote that had little meaning for him.

I acknowledged his comment and turned again to Ivan. Their lack of humor sobered me – frightened me, too. An ominous dread pulled at my gut. "What of the others?" I asked. "I mean, those nobles and boyars who are not to be of the *Opritchina?* Have you devised some special duties for them?" I had heard a partial answer to this the night before, but I wanted it directly from the Czar.

Ivan assumed a satisfied expression, as if glad I should have asked. "For many years," he said, "there has been a silent struggle between myself and the boyars, to determine who will truly rule the realm – and more than that, to determine whose ability is supreme. It is my intention to force a contest, of sorts. The lands of Russia will be effectively divided. There will be the lands of the *Opritchina,* which will hence be mine as the *Opritchniki* themselves are mine. Added to the lands I already possess, and discounting that portion of the realm which belongs to the Church, I will thus own half of Russia. I shall be sure this includes all the border areas and all the major cities. The remainder will be left for the boyars and other nobles. We shall call them the *Zemschina,* the Society of the Land, for most that remains will be farm country and small towns. Within the *Opritchina,* lest you misunderstand my intent, Dmitri, there will be a few who are now boyars. I intend to select young men, some noble, some common, but all fellows who are loyal to me. The oath will place their service to the Czar above their families, above their very lives. With such a brotherhood to help me rule, we shall see whose ability to govern is really blessed by God." He looked at me smugly, a fire such as I had never seen before seeming to leap within the orbs of his eyes. "An effective scheme, eh?"

I was aghast at the magnitude of his plan, but I controlled my expression and answered as evenly as I could. "It sounds like a good test," I remarked thoughtfully, "but what assurance is there of a continued loyalty among the *Zemschina?* With all those you fully trust in the brotherhood, are you not organizing your own opposition?"

"I am going to pardon your old commander, Michael Vorotinsky. He displeased me some time ago, as you may remember, and I packed his saucy carcass off to Beelozersk. I would have executed him, but I knew I should want him one day. By now, I hope he has learned his lesson and will behave properly as leader of this other group. As an ex–prisoner, he should fit the role very well."

"You surely don't doubt his loyalty?" I asked, making no effort to hide my surprise. I had not known Vorotinsky was in exile, nor could I imagine Michael being anything but loyal. It was on the tip of my tongue to remind Ivan that this man had been one of the few to take the oath when the Czar was thought close to death; but I checked myself. It seemed almost as if I had come back to madness.

Those I considered most devoted to the Czar were the very men he feared, while the toadies in highest favor were largely churls like Skuratof.

"I might question Vorotinsky's loyalty to *me*," Ivan explained, "but to Russia there can be no doubt. He cannot harm Us, I think, and if his opposition should become offensive, there will always be a good headsman in my employ."

Again I tried to change from an unpleasant subject. The Czar's doubts about my old commander disturbed me deeply, and a hard lump seemed to be growing in my bowels. "It is always the boyars, isn't it?" I sighed. "I can remember how we used to plan their destruction when we were boys – about your age," I added to the Czarevitch. "I can also remember an evening a few years ago when I told your father he would grow to hate me if I allowed him to bestow such rank on me."

Ivan pursed his lips, smiling, pleased at my statement. "You are the only man ever to refuse a gift from me," he said. "I even had to force the rank of Prince upon you. Perhaps that is why I know I can trust you. But at the moment," he added, going on to still another problem, "it is not the boyars who concern me. You know of my trouble with that damnable priest?"

"Which priest?" I asked.

"You see?" roared the Czar, suddenly bubbling with laughter. He gestured violently to his son. "I told you he hated all priests. When I mention one who is damned, he knows of so many fitting the description he cannot guess which I mean."

"But he loves God?" added the boy uncertainly.

"I am sure there is none who loves Him more," said Ivan, "but a priest is not God, though they would have you think they are. On this you must never be deceived." He turned back to me. "To answer your question, my friend, I refer to that wretch whom I caused to be appointed Metropolitan. He is a sorry disappointment!"

"Daniel Romanov mentioned some – conflict, or something," I replied cautiously.

"Conflict! That is how I'd expect such a ninny to describe it! The fool Phillip has seen fit to renew the harassment I thought I had ended – you heard of my trip to Alexandrov, when I made them all think I left them? – Yes, I thought you would. Well, I'd intended to teach them a lesson, like a husband who walks out on a nagging wife, leaves her to starve for a while. That is exactly what I did to them – nobles, merchants . . . priests – most of all the priests. But they came after me, on their knees! And they begged me to return. All of them, the Church more than any, promised on the most sacred oaths not to interfere with my rule, or with my methods of discipline."

"That was a different Metropolitan," I commented.

"What difference does that make? The word of one is binding on the next, is it not? Won't foreign kings and emperors expect my son to keep faith, by fulfilling the terms of treaties I've made? Isn't that right, Dmitri?" he demanded heatedly.

I agreed. "The word of God's priests should be no less honored than a promise by His secular rulers," I conceded. "Perhaps Phillip needs only time to become more – settled in his position," I suggested hopefully.

"He will become settled soon, or I'll settle him permanently, in a sepulcher!" Ivan barked.

His words startled me – or at least his vehemence. I could not imagine he would seriously offer violence against the Metropolitan; yet, it was not like Ivan to make idle threats. The thought of Phillip had angered him, and fury contorted his features as he continued to speak of the Metropolitan's treachery. Then he stopped, and his rage was gone as quickly as it had come. A calm, almost serene expression fell over him.

"Have you spoken to him? I mean, privately?" I asked.

Ivan sighed, shaking his head. "He is the most stubborn man I have ever had to deal with. Besides, I do not wish to speak to him. He insults me by finding excuses to be late, or by not coming at all when I send for him. And I certainly am not going to him!"

The Czarevitch spoke up. "You are skilled in persuading people, Dmitri. Why don't you have a visit with him?"

"Yes," Ivan agreed loudly. "Go see him! You won't accomplish anything, but you'll learn what a stubborn ass he really is."

While Ivan's anger did not show itself again that afternoon, I knew I would henceforth be dealing with a much different man from the one I had known before. He had been wounded and scarred within his soul – scarred as badly as any soldier who might be wounded on the field of battle. Most of those who had brought pleasure to his life, or helped ease his burdens, were gone, either dead by God's will, or removed because they proved or were thought disloyal: Anastasia, Vorontsof, Adashev, Sylvester, Makari and his predecessors . . . Vladya, and now Yuri was close to death.

Just before I took my leave, I inquired about the health of the Czar's brother. Ivan's face fell at the mention of Yuri's name, and he seemed close to weeping. "It is so sad," he said wearily. "Each day he grows weaker, and none can offer hope."

"I wonder if Doctor Bomel might be able to help," I suggested. "He is reputed to possess certain skills, unknown to many physicians, even in England."

"Tell him to come," said Ivan quickly. "He can certainly do no harm; but I hold no great hope. God has clearly marked my brother's soul, and even now must wait his coming."

Because it was late when I arrived home that evening, I informed the doctor he should attend upon the Czar's brother first thing in the morning.

"You will come with me?" he asked.

"By all means," I said. "I only hope you can help; it would certainly ease one of the Czar's cruelest burdens."

That night I entertained a few friends at dinner, among them Prince Simon and Alexi Basmanov. Simon seemed smaller than I remembered him, I suppose because of the heavy Russian clothing. Otherwise, he was unchanged. His skin and beard were as dark as ever, with no sign of gray or age. Alexi, twice Simon's size to begin with, had become so enormously fat I feared he would not fit into my dining chairs. Aside from his obesity, he looked fine – a glowing picture of health. If anything, he appeared younger than when I'd seen him last, and I made a point to tell him so.

He snorted disparagingly, though I knew my remarks had pleased him. "It's the good, pure life I'm living," he boomed. "Do you know the Czarevitch had me out hunting wolves? No, don't laugh! I've slept more nights in the woods than at home, the last month or two. My wife accuses me of finding another love!"

His comment reminded Simon of a parcel his wife had sent to Nina, and he called for one of his servants to bring it in. Because my wife was so close to her time, she had remained in our apartments without my having to discuss it with her. Even in her own country it was improper for pregnant women to make a public display. Anne Bomel stayed with her while Elysius, naturally, was with us. "These are just a few items Maria thought would be useful," he said.

I had not given much thought to Simon's place in this new set of organizations being formed by the Czar. Early in the evening he opened the subject, and I let him speak without interruption. The secret had been more poorly kept than Ivan seemed to think, for Simon certainly knew what was going on. "I shall not be a member of either group," he said, "because I am still a foreigner, of sorts. As I understand it, the area within the Kremlin is sacrosanct, so those who live there are under the personal protection of the Czar. I do not expect either group will bother me."

"Do you really expect you would be 'bothered' if you lived elsewhere?" asked Alexi.

"I am still a 'wily Tartar,' according to some," he said, "and I know how hostile many are toward my race, especially the lower orders. And the Czar has selected a number of his followers from these. Without the sanctuary of the Kremlin I should live in constant fear."

"I tell you now," I said firmly, "and before I drink enough that my promise may be mistaken for drunken ravings; you will always find protection in this house. You must never forget it."

"My doors are always open to you, as well," said Basmanov. "You are an old enemy turned friend, of which there is none better."

Elysius, who had been out of the room when my guests arrived, had joined us in the middle of this conversation. "Why is there such fear?" he asked, directing his question particularly at Simon.

"I am a foreigner," he repeated, "and by blood a Tartar. For this reason some men hate me. Those who sat close to you at dinner last night, on the other side of the Czar from me – these men would destroy someone like me for the sheer joy of committing the act."

"Will they have such power?" Doctor Bomel asked.

Simon looked thoughtfully at each of us. "I place my life in your hands to describe these feelings," he said, holding out his hands, empty palms turned upward. "There are evil men surrounding the Czar. Malyuta Skuratof, though distantly related to the Bielskys, is an ambitious man of the lowest order and vices. Yet Ivan seems under his spell, constantly increasing his rank, heaping honors and riches upon him. Then there is Alfansy Viazemsky and Michael Saltikoff, both men of noble birth, but with the souls of peasants. Their only talents seem to be their skills as torturers. In different circumstances, all three would be paid assassins."

He stared at Alexi and me, abruptly stopping his flow of words as if he feared he had gone too far. "But you must know this," he sighed, more to

Basmanov than to me, "even if you do not wish to admit it. Not only I, but you – all of you – will have cause to fear these men more than I do before all of this is over. I was once a powerful ruler, but I was forced to surrender, and I've given myself into the protection of the Czar. If I must die, so be it. Perhaps it was the Will of God that I should have perished after the fall of Kazan. In that case, my continued existence has been but an extension of His Grace."

"I think you fear without cause," I said, and Alexi agreed with me.

"I hope you're right," said Simon. He sipped thoughtfully at his wine. "I would not bring up such an unpleasant subject, but there are many who have perished already, simply because someone has been able to convince the Czar he should suspect them."

"The Czar's judgment is unquestioned!" I insisted.

"I do not cast aspersions on his wisdom," Simon continued, "but the Czar does not communicate with anyone except through those around him. It is so with any great ruler. The men who stand by his side wield tremendous power, because they can bring certain facts to their lord's attention and neglect to inform him of others."

"Mikhailof is above any suspicion of such disloyalty," I said defensively.

"Yes, Mikhailof is an honest man," Simon agreed, "but for that very reason I fear he may not last much longer. Fumikov is already gone, you know, and the treasury is in the hands of another."

"He grew old and tired," Basmanov growled. "All of this concern is for nothing, Simon. You aren't in any danger, and neither is anyone else who stands loyal to the Czar. That's all he asks from any of us."

Simon clasped his hands in the oriental manner. "I hope with all my heart that you are right," he said.

Perhaps I was naive. Certainly, there were many who later called me such, and worse. But who could have foreseen the dreadful specter of death that hovered behind the Czar's grand scheme? I doubt if Ivan, himself, with all his God–given wisdom, suspected what lay ahead. I quickly put aside the fears of my friends, and I slept well following the evening's conversation. At the time, it seemed no more important than many other political discussions I had shared with various companions over the years.

The next morning, I accompanied Doctor Bomel when he attended Yuri. The Prince was expecting us, lying propped up against his pillows; but only his eyes seemed alive. His complexion was yellow, and even the hairs of his scrubby beard looked wilted. Ulyana, wane and anxious, stood beside the bed. I grasped her hands, looking reassuringly into her brimming eyes.

"I have brought one of the finest doctors from England," I whispered. I started to reach for Yuri's shoulder, but Doctor Bomel waved me away. "You must not touch him," he told me in English.

Yuri tried to smile, a brave but unsuccessful attempt. With an effort, he moved his arm, curling the fingers. Ignoring the doctor's warning, I took the wasted flesh and pressed it in both my hands, encouraging him as best I could. "Doctor Bomel will know how to help you," I told him. I stood aside, then, speaking quietly with Ulyana as Doctor Bomel felt Yuri's arms and chest, finally pressed his ear against the Prince's heart.

"I am certain it's no use," she whispered despairingly. "Many magicians and doctors have examined him, and none can do more than draw his blood."

At length the doctor stood up, sadly shaking his head. "It is too late for any cure I might have offered," he told us. "It is a disease we call jaundice – quite common in the warmer climes, where it is frequently treated by having the patient consume vast amounts of sweet roots and bitter vitch. He should then be bled daily, to remove the excess humors. Had this been done when he first fell ill, he would now have been recovered."

I looked at Yuri, but he had fallen asleep before Elysius started to speak. After a few more words to Ulyana we left. There was nothing else to do. Watching my friend and his wife saddened me more than I could bear. On our way out of the Kremlin, Doctor Bomel tried to explain his diagnosis. I was very impressed with his knowledge, for as he pointed out to me, he was one of the few doctors in the world to have completely catalogued the parts of a human body.

"I have seen all the organs," he told me pedantically, "and I find that the form and placement of these varies only slightly from one man to the next. A noble person seems to have a larger heart and liver than others, but of course I have not been able to measure the entrails of such a person very often. Usually, only bodies of the poor are available for examination. We may never discover all there is to know about the functions of these parts; and I believe there are some things we are not meant to know. However, I am convinced the liver is the second most important organ of all. Only the heart, which produces the blood and other fluids, is more vital. Once the blood is formed, the heart pumps it to all parts of the body, where it is absorbed into the tissues. The liver is attached to the heart by a series of small tubes. It is my belief that the evil humors of the body are generally absorbed by the liver, forming yellow bile. This eventually finds its way into the bladder, where it is eliminated. In a disease such as Prince Yuri's the humors build up, forming so much bile that the organ can no longer remove it. Eventually, this poison will consume the flesh. There are some who do not agree with my theories," he admitted, "but my observations support the conclusions."

I was disappointed that with all his knowledge Doctor Bomel could offer no hope. I returned to visit the Prince several times during the next few days, but he seldom awoke enough to recognize me. By the end of summer, God had claimed his soul.

Well before Yuri died, however, the Czar had completed his reorganization of the realm, this accomplishment being capped by the return of Michael Vorotinsky to Moscow. Gaunt and shrunken from his months of exile, the old soldier quickly regenerated his energies. Within a few weeks he started to form his Society of the Land – the *Zemschina*. I was so occupied with the Czar's commercial dealings, on top of my own that finding an evening when both Vorotinsky and I were free presented some difficulties, but eventually I entertained him at my home. Inwardly, Michael was not greatly changed. He had become very gray. He was serious, almost to the point of being somber, certainly not much given to humor. But this had always been typical of him. In this instance, it was his humility that bothered me. In his quiet, dignified way he seemed to place me above himself, whereas I had always thought of him as my General.

Early the following morning I was summoned to the palace by a very curt note from Ivan, scratched out in his own hand. For the first time in many years, I received a tongue–lashing from the Czar. He expressed his extreme displeasure over my association with a man who was not to be of the inner circle. "But you could not know," he finished, his tone more conciliatory. "We will soon go to the Abby at Alexandrov, and everything will be explained to you there."

I had not been asked for any explanation, so I didn't offer any. In fact, I had hardly uttered a word. I left the palace in a state of confusion, unable to understand the reasons for Ivan's vehemence. It was right that he should know anything he wished about my private affairs, but I was also disturbed to realize he felt it necessary to plant spies within my household. Worst of all, he had commanded my presence at Alexandrov, a trip I really did not wish to make. More than the ominous circumstances, themselves, I was concerned about Nina. She was very close to her time. Yet I dared not offend the Czar, who had apparently made elaborate plans to install me with some degree of ceremony into the *Opritchina*. Our departure was to have been two days after my conversation with him, but a falling star appeared in the sky that same night. For a moment, it looked as though it were going to fall into the Kremlin. The Czar happened to see it, because he was returning from his devotions in the new church and had just passed through the Savior's Gate when the heavenly sign appeared. He advanced our departure to the next morning.

Alexandrov was the same little village to which the Czar had fled when he announced he was putting aside the crown. It had previously been a place of minor consequence, boasting only a popular hunting lodge. I think Basil had taken his court there a few times. The town was located in a heavily forested region, about half way between Moscow and Rostov. Wild and forbidding to those who did not appreciate God's wilderness, the setting was beautiful enough to inspire a man's devotion. Bordering the dense stands of pine and birch trees, there were many hectares of virgin land, still covered with natural wild plants and flowers. A few streams crisscrossed the plains, most flowing eventually into the Oka via the Klyaz'ma River. At the Czar's orders, a large ornate palace had been built on the spot where he had received the homage of his people. It was this structure that he referred to as "the Abby." The interior was furnished with the finest fabrics and highly polished woods; the service was all of gold, and it had a large staff of servants.

Attached to the palace, or Abby, was a magnificently appointed chapel, rivaling the grandeur of those in the Kremlin. A number of other houses and barracks were still being built, only the Czar's house having been completed. In contrast to its elegant trappings elsewhere, the bedrooms of the Abby reflected its monastic status. Each was furnished like the cell of a hermit monk, with a hard–surfaced cot, prayer stool, and a large wooden crucifix over the bed. We were supposed to sleep in humility, remembering how our Lord and Savior had suffered in the flesh for our salvation. I must admit that the rigid horse–hair mattresses served that purpose very well.

The monastic ritual was followed very closely, at least in these early days. We all wore black monk's cassocks, and our heads were tonsured. Ivan would personally ring the bell for early matins, at which all the brothers were expected to assemble at once, ready to begin their devotions. This was usually long before dawn. Services lasted for two or three hours, while consecrated priests performed the full rituals before a golden altar, heavily inlaid with rubies. After this early service came matins proper, lasting another hour. Then we went to breakfast; but Ivan did not partake of the meal. Instead, he took his place behind a lectern, where he read to us from Holy Scripture. He explained this as his additional penance, for he felt his sins to be heavier than other men's.

After each meal the remains were taken out and given to the beggars, who soon began to congregate from all over Russia. The Czar would take his luncheon alone, as it came too soon after breakfast for the rest of us. In the afternoon he would sometimes visit the chambers beneath his palace, but this was not yet a regular practice.

I did not have an opportunity for much conversation with Ivan on this first visit to Alexandrov. Except for the ritual of my installation as a member of the brotherhood, I hardly exchanged a word with him. Nor did anyone else, for the Czar spent nearly every waking hour in prayer and meditation. The only break in this routine was a brief, daily conference with his architects.

While we were in residence, the finishing touches were applied to the Czar's palace, or his *Freedom,* as it came to be called. I watched as the final digging was completed to channel water into the moat. This was an extremely deep fosse, with sides so steep no demon could possibly cross it. Foundations were also being laid for other buildings.

Outside Alexandrov, on the only road leading into it—this off the main Moscow–Rostov highway—was a heavily manned guardpost centered about a kiosk called the *Unfreedom.* Here, all visitors were questioned before being allowed to enter. Only members of the Czar's company, or the poor beggars who brought with them the mercy of God, were permitted to pass. Other visitors were required to have the Czar's specific permission. To assure compliance with his orders, Ivan had placed Ivor in charge of the guards. This was the first I had seen of my old friend since returning from England; but we had several long talks and visits during the month or so I was in residence. These provided my only breaks from the dreary monastic schedule.

My stay at Alexandrov was interrupted when a messenger arrived from Doctor Bomel, informing me that Nina was about to give birth. I immediately asked the Czar's permission to leave. He severely chastised me, reminding me that my oath to the brotherhood took precedence over my wife and family, before he finally consented. Then, before I could depart, a second courier arrived from the Kremlin, also from Doctor Bomel. On the Czar's order, Elysius had been trying to ease Yuri's final hours, and this message informed the Czar his brother had only a few hours to left to live. Thus I returned to Moscow with the entire group.

My son was born a few hours before I could reach the capital, but I was there when Nina opened her eyes from sleep following the delivery. The child lay in a cradle beside our great bed, already a handsome boy, with eyes as blue as the mountain lakes and boasting a few tufts of blondish hair. I spent as much time with Nina as I could, leaving only to pay my last respects to Yuri, and to help the Czar in arranging for the funeral. I think Nina understood my absences; at least she made no protest. Lily attended most closely upon her mistress, while Anne Bomel also bustled about the room. Elysius had stayed close by all the while, though he informed me I need have no concern. "She is a natural mother," he remarked. "She will give you many fine, healthy children."

The state funeral for Yuri was attended by nearly everyone in Moscow, with huge crowds standing in sorrowful silence outside the cathedral. Inside were all the ranking members of both the *Opritchina* and *Zemschina,* each group remaining on its own side of the church. A great many tears were shed, I think most of them sincerely, as the columns of chanting monks filed into the cathedral and around the bier. Yuri had been greatly loved. He had never been unkind to anyone, and had frequently interceded for those who incurred his brother's disfavor.

I stood with Ulyana during most public portions of the service. I would have done this anyway, but the Czar had specifically asked me to fill in as a member of the family. Of all Yuri's friends I had been the closest, and Ivan recognized this.

At the end of the forty days of mourning, when the final service had been read, Ulyana announced she would retire to a convent. This was a fitting gesture, one almost to be expected, and customary for a widow of her rank. But Ulyana was sincere in her desire to become a simple sister, and she informed the Czar of this. He granted his permission, after which she immediately retired to the nunnery near Sergey–Troitsky. This led to one of the most distressing experiences of my life – one I am loath to speak of, even now.

After Ulyana left the court, Ivan brooded heavily on having lost both his brother and his brother's wife. He had loved both of them greatly, and their absence left a terrible void. The empty wing of the palace seemed to exude an oppressive gloom. In an attempt to express the devotion he felt for his sister–in–law, despite her being in holy orders, Ivan dispatched several carts loaded with expensive gifts. Among these were such things as a golden table service, many fine linens, casks of good wine, comfortable furniture and a small staff of slaves. The Czar made a great point of personally selecting an unusually handsome bedstead, all hand carved and with the best goose–down mattress. Watching the carts depart after he had supervised their loading, Ivan expressed his satisfaction at being able to add such pleasure to the remaining years of a woman who had been ever loyal and considerate to his beloved brother.

Two days later the carts returned, still laden with their precious goods. The senior servant bore a note from Ulyana to the Czar, thanking him for his thoughtfulness, but declining the rich gifts. She truly wanted to live out her life as a sister of mercy, she explained, and her vows required that she abjure the world and all its material things.

In all fairness, I must explain that the Czar was already in a very foul state of mind. Justifiably so. He had just demanded a thousand rubles from the treasury of the *Zemschina* to help pay some of the construction costs at Alexandrov. He had finally received the money, but there had been a most unpleasant discussion with Vorotinsky, as Michael protested a shortage of funds. He had gone on to complain about excursions by members of the *Opritchina*, whom he claimed had pillaged the homes of several *Zemschina* members.

After that, there had been word from Peter Shuisky, commanding our forces in Livonia. The Polish general, Radziwell, had launched a new attack through Lithuania and from Kazan came word of a riot by Tartar malcontents. On top of all the rest, Ulyana's note was more than Ivan could sustain.

Without warning, the Czar emitted a horrible shriek, contorting his face, tearing at his beard and clothing. He smashed his *kisten* against the servant's head, and when the man turned to flee, Ivan stabbed him through the center of his back with the pointed end. Allowing the staff to fall from his hands, still embedded in the servant's body, Ivan tore his hat from his head and rent it into shreds, screaming all the while about the lack of consideration shown him by everyone. He ripped his fine robe to tatters and plucked several handfuls of hair from his beard, shouting all the while for the commander of the palace guard.

Quaking, the man appeared before the Czar almost as soon as he had been summoned. Ivan still roared and shouted at him for being slow. Had the *kisten* remained in his hands, he might well have done the fellow some harm. As it was, the Czar threw a sliver bowl at his head and ordered him to lead a company of men to the convent. He was to execute Ulyana!

I had been standing behind the Czar, between Mikhailof and Basmanov. I took a step toward Ivan, about to try dissuading him. Both my friends grabbed at my arms, pulling me back. "Keep your mouth shut!" Mikhailof whispered harshly. "There is nothing you can do!"

The guard commander was staring at the Czar in disbelief. Then he tried to stammer a question. "How?" he finally managed to ask.

Again the Czar's temper flared. He screamed at the man, kicking out with his foot, barely missing the fellow's groin. "I don't care how you do it! I want her dead this very night! Go, you gaping ass, go!"

The man spun about, never losing his military bearing. Calling to his men outside the chamber, he raced to the stables. They were out the Kremlin gates within seconds.

The Czar collapsed at his writing table, sobbing into his folded arms. "The weight of the world is too much," he moaned. "How can one man be expected to bear such burdens as I?"

At length he retired to his chapel, where he remained until morning. Several of us kept a silent vigil in the hall outside the door, fearful lest he harm himself when the captain returned to report. But the Czar never spoke to him, nor to my knowledge did he ever discuss the order with another person. Alexi Basmanov and I intercepted the guards captain outside the chapel door, long before Ivan came out. In reply to our questions, and the frightened looks of others who stood about with us, the man nodded sadly. It was difficult for him to speak, as he was choked with guilt and horror at the act he had been required to commit. He had accomplished the Czar's orders mercifully, he said, having strangled Ulyana with his own hands. She had prayed for his soul with her final breath, he sobbed.

I tried to keep word of this from reaching Nina, as I knew she would be unable to understand the reasons behind the Czar's actions. However, I could not cope with the gossip of servants. The next day she found out, becoming nearly hysterical with fear. "He must be mad!" she cried out. "No sane man would behave like this!"

I tried to silence her, finally having to slap her firmly across the face to bring back a semblance of calm. I was still troubled by her illogical outburst, when I received the first harbinger of danger. Barely two hours after my scene with Nina, a note arrived from Mikhailof, summoning me in all urgency. I went at once, not knowing whether it was he or the Czar who called.

The message had been from the Czar's secretary, personally. "I speak as your friend, Dmitri," he told me, "but I can warn you just this once. I must not keep information from his Majesty. It's my sworn duty to serve him, even as you do."

"I understand that," I said, bewildered, "but what has this to do with me?"

"I have a report that your wife is critical of our Czar," he replied, watching me sharply. "Although we know a woman counts for little, it is also truly said that what a man hears upon his conjugal couch may well influence his future behavior."

"You beady–eyed little rabbit!" I shouted angrily. "I thought it was Ivan's spy in my household! Now I can see it's yours!"

"Hold, my friend," he said calmly, although his eyes bulged a bit when he thought I was going to seize him. "I do only my duty, *as ordered by the Czar.*"

"You mean the Czar has ordered spies in my home, working through you?"

"Not specifically in *your* home," he replied. "I am ordered to place them in the house of every important man. I even have them in my own house, although they do not report to me, naturally."

I was about to leave, still very angry. I did not wish to speak with him further, for fear I would completely lose control of myself and beat him. "Wait a moment, my friend," he said again. "Please believe that I *am* your friend, Dmitri. I would like to suggest something."

I sat down, my temper cooling as I realized he intended no harm. Quite the contrary, he had done me a service, possibly at some risk to himself. A less scrupulous man might have made use of my wife's ill–timed ravings.

"I should not tell you this," he said, "but I trust your discretion, and you will soon be informed anyway. The Czar is unhappy with the conduct of the Livonian War. Peter Shuisky is not doing well, commanding the foreign levies, especially the barbarians. Ivan has decided to put Kurbsky back in command, and to send you along as assurance that he not – well, that he doesn't do anything foolish."

"What is that supposed to mean?" I snapped. "Do you also doubt Andrew's loyalty? Has his wife farted at the wrong time?"

"Now Dmitri, there is no need for such animosity," he tried to soothe me. "No, the Czar does not distrust Prince Kurbsky, else he wouldn't place him in command. But again, I have not passed on all my suspicions. I hesitate to tell the Czar, lest I . . . overburden his . . . soul. On the other hand, as his sworn servant, it is my duty to assure against any of these suspicions becoming an act of open treachery. I must have a man with Kurbsky whom I know is completely reliable."

"I am to spy on him," I noted with disgust.

"I do not ask you to spy," he replied, "and if your beliefs are justified there will be nothing to spy about. But, if you see something to require your reporting it, then I should expect your loyalty to overcome whatever reluctance you might have. Do you understand me?" he asked firmly.

I thought a moment before answering. I wanted to serve with Andrew, and I was certain there would never be anything to report. However, Mikhailof was right. If there were something to be observed, then Andrew would be guilty of mortal sin and treason. Only in such circumstances would I be required to act as spy. I was Andrew's friend, I reasoned, and would react fairly to whatever I saw. Better I than someone else, who might harm him by false or exaggerated tales.

"Very well," I said finally. "I shall be your spy. Is this the suggestion you wish to make?"

"No," he replied, "no. These things I have mentioned will be your orders. My suggestion concerns your personal problems. I wonder if you have forgotten the grant of land you were given in Livonia?"

"Not at all," I told him. "I have one of my servants running the farms, and have been receiving a regular profit from them. Why do you ask?"

He leaned back in his chair, clasping his fingers, pressing them up under his chin. "It is such lovely country, especially during the autumn season," he mused. "I am sure your wife and family would enjoy the . . . climate. It would remove the lady from the rigid confines of Moscow, as well."

"Are you implying she is in danger?" I asked, keeping a tone of malice in my voice.

"Dmitri, you are behaving like a damned fool!" he exploded, speaking as loudly as I had ever heard him. "I'm not trying to threaten you. I *am* trying to tell you how I foresee the future, and to allow you to guard against it."

I eased back in my chair and apologized.

"That's better," he said. "Now let me explain a little more to you, lest there be any further misunderstanding. You and I, Dmitri, are of the same group. We are the 'old order,' so to speak. We are men who were brought up to serve the Czar within his court. We behave as gentry, and we acknowledge the proper rules of behavior. These newcomers – Skuratof, Chibotovy – you know who they are – they are mostly men of low birth and no breeding. But they are in favor." As he spoke, I thought of Simon's remarks and wondered briefly if the two men had exchanged ideas. Not likely, I realized – two perceptive observers, both arriving at the same conclusions. "But they are in favor," Mikhailof repeated, ". . . for how long I have no way to tell. They are greedy, always seeking greater wealth and power. Beware of them, my friend, because they will destroy you if they can, just as they will probably destroy me."

"You're not seriously afraid of them, are you?" I asked, now honestly concerned for him.

"Yes, I am," he said flatly, "and there is nothing I can do. If I try to resign, they will surely accuse me of desertion. If I remain they will seek other means to destroy me, until they finally succeed. But you are different. You can move about the realm, and you are still a young man who can best any of them with a sword or lance. Take your family to Livonia, Dmitri, and keep them on your estates. You will have the perfect excuse to do it when you are ordered to the front. When you are told to return, leave them there. I fear what may happen in Moscow before much more time has passed."

I thanked him and left soon after, troubled by all he had said. I reminded myself that he was a man to be easily frightened, and I tried not to share his anxiety. Yet, in his own way, Mikhailof had always been a good friend. His clerkly attitudes had frequently annoyed me, but I knew he intended only good. In the end, I followed his advice and organized my household for departure as soon as I received official word from the new Bureau of Military Affairs.

Before we left, my son was baptized "John," the English equivalent of "Ivan." That greatly pleased the Czar, who became his Godfather, although the service was by proxy, with Simon standing in for him. The new Czarina – whom I had never met, for Ivan married her while my party was traveling south from Kholmagora – was the Godmother. The Czar would have come to the service, except it was performed by the Metropolitan, whom Ivan refused to meet face to face. Watching Phillip perform the sacred rites, it was hard for me to reconcile the Czar's feelings with the holy demeanor I was able to observe. I had never had that talk with Phillip, as suggested by Vanya. Fortunately, both he and the Czar seemed to have forgotten about it, and my orders would now preclude a meeting.

CHAPTER III

Andrew Kurbsky and I departed for Livonia at the head of a large army. We rode side–by–side, followed by the other senior commanders. All of us were resplendent in highly polished armor, mounted on impeccably groomed warhorses. There had been an unusually grand ceremony in the Square of Executions, with the Czar making an eloquent speech to the people about God's willing our success. However, the blessing had been given by a simple priest. The Metropolitan had not made an appearance. Gabriel pranced about like a colt, this being the first real trip for him since my return from Alexandrov, almost four months before.

A formation of cavalry rode behind the commanders, all very fine and proud in their new uniforms, wearing the short fur *barmas* to indicate their status as elite troops from the Czar's personal corps. Nina's carriage was just behind these men and ahead of the peasant soldiers on their shaggy hill ponies. At the end of the column were the various foot soldiers, supply wagons and heavy artillery pieces. Nina had recently developed such an attachment for the Tartar girls she had insisted on bringing both of them with her. More for this reason, I think, their closed carriage caused considerable curiosity among the men. The stories of my adventures in Kazan were still told, embellished more than ever by time. Knowing that two ladies, reputedly from the Khan's harem, were riding in the center of our line created far more interest than Nina – herself a foreigner, and hence a curiosity.

Autumn had burst upon us with all its glory and color. Birch trees blazed in yellow clusters along the roadside, contrasting against the deeper reds and oranges of oak and sycamore. In the early morning, a heavy hoarfrost lay over the ground. This dissolved into a steamy mist as the sun climbed heavenward, casting the last warm rays of waning summer upon us. As yet, the chill north winds had not begun to lash us with the bitter cold we would soon experience. Still, it was nippy enough at night to limit my casual strolls with Nina.

On the evening of our first day, Nina informed me she was again with child. She had not mentioned it before, for fear I would insist she remain in Moscow. Of all the suggestions I had made since coming to Russia, none had pleased her more than the prospect of living on the Marienburg estates. Once removed from the fearful atmosphere of the capital, she seemed more as I remembered her in England. She played with the baby, and chattered with Lily as the latter attended to the infant's needs.

Because the physical problems of travel made observance of the usual decorum impossible, Andrew dined with us in our tent. From the first, Nina was permitted to sit with us, and the commander did not object – not even a subtle grimace of disapproval. After our first meal together, I think he rather came to enjoy my wife's company. She did not speak Russian very well – in fact, she never learned it well enough to speak with ease. Still, they were able to understand each other, and Andrew was pleased to find her well versed in art and literature, subjects he greatly enjoyed discussing. Except for a few days' rain after leaving Novgorod, our entire trip was blessed with mild weather.

Nina had been especially pleased by the old, Hanseatic city, as it looked more like her homeland than any other place she had visited in Russia. For one thing, the streets were mostly cobblestone, and those that were not at least had logs pounded in to make them solid. In Moscow, none of the streets were paved outside the Kremlin and Kitaigorod, except for the main carriage roads. She also found the shops more like those in the west; she had never enjoyed the confusion of the Moscow bazaars.

Unfortunately, our group could not escape notice, and my wife's open appearance in the city was quickly reported to Archbishop Pimen. When I called to pay my respects, he was ready for me. Like Sylvester of old, he harangued me for permitting such lack of propriety within my household, promised the tortures of hell if I did not more closely observe the ways of God. He was as terrible as I ever remembered him, making me extremely grateful to escape the city. Our tents were cold and leaky when the rains came, but because of Pimen I was glad the weather had not broken until we were two days travel from Novgorod.

I took a short leave from the army once we were in Livonia, and escorted my family to the estates. I had personally seen the land only once, and that had been at night. The previous owners had allowed the place to become terribly run down, so it was a pleasant surprise to see the changes Jacob had brought about. I had assigned him the task of overseeing the farms, although he could not remain for long periods; he was too important to our trade. But Heinrich had assigned him to some of the Czar's work, which kept him in the area for extended stays. As a converted Christian, he was attempting to enlighten some of his Jewish brethren. Ivan had ordered all Livonian Jews to be baptized, by force if necessary, hoping this would satisfy the Church and give his western campaign the aura of a second "holy war." Jacob had spoken to many of his race, convincing large numbers of them to submit voluntarily and accept the true faith.

Nina was thrilled with the huge stone house and the long curved drive leading up to it. The wooden facade and fences were all freshly whitewashed, and the grass had been cut very close to the ground, in imitation of a western green. All around the *dacha* were stands of stately, colorful trees: sycamore, birch, and elm. Well-trimmed hedges and shrubs ringed the park, while beyond were the cultivated fields. We were south of the nearest swamps, and these were distant enough that insects were less of a problem than in most parts of Livonia.

I stayed two or three days with Nina, during which we were like carefree children, roaming the fields, inspecting the well-filled barns and silos. When I departed, I left Serge with her. Toby – now eleven, I guess, or twelve – came with me.

The campaigns that fall, and into the winter, were not very glorious. The Polish–Lithuanian armies fought halfheartedly, and while we should have beaten them soundly there were problems with our own troops, many of whom had been forced into the Czar's service. The war had lasted too long, until our men had lost the spirit of conquest. In the late winter, we actually began to lose ground, although we outnumbered the enemy – sometimes by three to one. The only major battle took place near Wolmar, and it lasted several days. We were doing very badly, being slowly pushed back by a much smaller force. I knew Andrew was becoming concerned, because the Czar had punished several other commanders for failing to achieve victory in similar circumstances.

Finally, the day came when Andrew made his fateful decision. The fighting had continued since dawn, against Livonian troops under the personal command of Grand Master von Ketler. Their army was not especially large or well equipped, but they fought with a determination we had not seen since just after the Polish intervention. As before, we outnumbered them by two or three to one; yet we continued to lose even the small skirmishes. When the armies retired into their respective strongholds for the night, Kurbsky was very tired, not only from his physical exertions during the battle, but within his soul and mind. Nothing had gone right, and his heart was heavy with concern and despair. When I entered his room, he was slumped despondently in a tattered leather chair. His legs were stretched out in front of him, still clad in their mud–covered boots.

"I brought you something to drink," I said cheerfully. I had a large wooden cask of German liquor on my shoulder. I heaved this onto the table and started to tap it.

"No amount of spirits is going to cure my ills, tonight," he said, groaning as he struggled to sit up. He started to shove the boots off his feet. "It is about over for me, Dmitri."

"What do you mean, 'over'? You're the best commander in the Czar's whole army!"

"No more," he said sadly. "It's all left me. I can't seem to give a proper command any more. Worse, the men know it. Desertions are increasing and my best soldiers are failing me."

"The Czar will understand," I assured him "Perhaps if you took a rest."

"A rest? Do you know what that madman would say if I asked him for time to take a rest? He'd call me a traitor and slit my guts for the amusement of that gang of perverted vultures –"

I stared at him as if he were a spirit suddenly risen from the grave. I could not believe it was Andrew Kurbsky who had uttered these words. "Andrew," I said slowly, "it must be your illness. I can't believe. . . ."

"Believe?" he shouted. "Dmitri, how can you be such a blind fool? You're as intelligent as anyone I've ever known. You've traveled farther and seen more than almost anyone else in Russia. Yet you persist in this stupid, unseeing loyalty to a man who is no longer a man. Ivan has turned into a beast! There isn't a sin he hasn't committed! Even now, he grovels in the muck of perversions that have never been equaled since God destroyed the cities of evil. It has all been paraded before you, played out in every disgusting detail. And you still refuse to see it. You speak of him as if he were actually the Hand of God. How can you? How can you go on serving a man without ever considering that he has destroyed every principal for which you ever fought – almost every friend you ever had?"

Andrew's vehemence was horrible. I wanted to turn from him and flee, holding my hands against my ears that I not be forced to listen. But I couldn't leave. I thought of Mikhailof and his fears for Andrew's loyalty – all the suggestions I had previously refused to believe. I was angry with Kurbsky for speaking as he had, though in my heart I knew some of it to be true. But I could not acknowledge these feelings. To agree with him would be a monumental sin. To turn against one's Czar was more odious in the eyes of God than any act committed at his command. At the moment I feared for my own salvation, torn between the loyalty I knew I owed the Czar and the obedience I must give this man who was my superior officer. If I were to admit the Czar was less than sacred, what of the things I had done myself in response to Ivan's orders? No, I told myself, Andrew was upset; in the morning he would come to his senses. But above it all, Mikhailof's words continued to echo in my mind. Somehow, he had foreseen this moment.

"Please don't say any more," I begged. "You may be right, and yet you can't be right. I've seen the sacred oil poured upon Ivan's head, and I've stood by his side in times of trial. Some horrible fire of hell has always burned in his soul. I know this; I've always known it. But the Czar is the Czar, guided by the Grace of God. I could never accept any other conception of his status."

Andrew had dropped his first boot onto the floor. The second was still in his hand. He threw it with all his strength against the wall, where it splattered mud in every direction.

"The Czar is a man, Dmitri! A man! Can't you understand that? Regardless what rituals have been performed over him, or what mumbled phrases have been spoken by the priests, he is still a man – nothing more than that! And he's an evil man. He pounds his head upon the floor in front of the holy icons in the morning, and commits the sins of Sodom all night."

This accusation startled me, for it was one I never expected. This unnamed sin was common enough among soldiers and others who were deprived of a woman's company, and many men committed it. But no decent man would ever mention it, nor use it as the basis for a condemnation of his fellow, certainly not in reference to his Czar! "He would never commit such an act!" I said heavily. "How could you accuse him of such a thing?" I expected Andrew to let it go at that.

"Then what is young Basmanov doing in his room every night? What entertainment does the Czar have in his chambers before he goes into the basement to torture the wretched souls who hang in chains about the walls? Why, he is nothing but a disgusting, Godless degenerate – buggering a young boy! And when they also have a woman with them, God alone knows what vile sins they may commit!"

His pompous attitude inflamed me. In a blind rage, I leaped at him across the table, landing hard against his chest and smashing into his neck with my shoulder. I was beyond any rational control, and bitter tears streamed from my eyes. Through this diffusing curtain, I could barely make out the form of Andrew's face and head. I beat him with my fists and plunged my knees against his body as we both fell onto the floor. At first I do not think he resisted me, for his own guilt must have been very heavy. His despair had left him with little reserve of strength to continue living. Eventually, he began to return my blows, finally striking me with something hard and heavy – a metal mug, perhaps, or a candlestick. The noise of our struggle attracted Andrew's personal guard from outside, for I, at least, was screaming oaths at him. Whether Andrew ever answered me I cannot say for sure.

It took several pairs of hands to drag me off. I was still gasping and hurling insults at him, the man I could no longer see, the man I had admired as the greatest strength within the forces of the Czar.

"What shall we do with him, sir?" asked one of the men who held me.

"I don't care," said Andrew wearily. "Take him to his quarters. Don't imprison him; he will be needed in the morning. Keep guard on him until daylight, and then let him resume his duties." Almost as an afterthought, he added, "It would be better if no one were told of this." His breathing was heavy, heavier than it should have been as a result of our struggle, and his tone reflected his misery.

I made no move to resist as I felt myself being led away. The men took me to my room with proper courtesy and respect. If someone stood guard at my door that night I did not know it, for I made no attempt to leave. I flopped onto my cot and lay staring into the blackness for a long time, my mind tormented by a great many woes. Finally, I fell asleep. I was very tired, almost as weary as Andrew, so my slumber was deep as death. If I dreamed I do not remember it.

In the morning, Toby awakened me at the usual hour, but from the expression on his face I knew something was terribly wrong. I bolted up from my bed. "What's happened?" I demanded before he had time to speak.

"General Kurbsky is gone," he said. "He left camp late last night, and it is said he went through the lines to the enemy camp."

"Andrew? Deserted?" I gasped.

"It looks that way, sir," Toby said. "The other commanders are awaiting your orders."

My first act was to send a messenger to the Czar. I was still debating whether to contact the enemy and try to arrange a truce when a courier arrived from them. Kurbsky, who must have completely lost his reason, sent to ask that I join him! It was a terrible letter, full of accusations against the Czar and blasphemous assertions concerning Ivan's activities since assuming the throne. In a rage, I hurled his filthy insults into the fire – I wished later that I had kept the letter – and ordered a massive assault against the Livonian forces outside the city of Wolmar.

Ruthlessly, I led the army myself and stayed in the front ranks all day. I killed more men in those few hours than I had in all the previous time I spent in the field. I saw Kurbsky's face on every enemy soldier, and I struck at him with my sword until my arms grew stiff and heavy from the exertion. I sustained a number of small wounds; my coat of mail was ripped and dented from the many blows that fell upon it. I was numb to everything but the need to kill. Shouting at the men to follow me, I led them into a frantic series of engagements until the enemy force was routed. Cut off from the sanctuary of Wolmar, they fled beyond Lemsa, into the mists along the coast. When night fell, I returned to camp, ordered a hasty head count and retired to my quarters, where I quickly drank myself to sleep.

That night, I was not spared my dreams. Not since my delirium after the fall of Kazan, had I experienced such terrifying nightmares. Again I saw the Czar on his great black stallion, rearing up from the yellow flames of the underworld. But this time it was clearly Andrew's arms I saw raised against him. In the Czar's hand was an enormous scimitar, with which he severed Andrew's head. Tipping up the gleaming skull, he held it like a goblet as he drained the blood. All the while, the souls of the damned wailed about us, and in their torment they called out to Ivan that he had destroyed them with his evil. Like Pimen and Sylvester in chorus, they moaned an eerie warning of his own judgment to come, when he himself must kneel before the throne of God. Then the devil's imps began to pelt us with clumps of slime and greenish globs of obscenity. I must have cried out, for Toby came in to awaken me. I drank another bumper of Vodka, and went back to sleep, mercifully to no more dreams.

The next day it began to rain, a violent, howling torrent. The old farmhouse where I had been sleeping leaked worse than a tent. This gloomy atmosphere, combined with the response of my body to the dreams and the liquor of the previous night, sapped all my desire to fight. Fortunately, none of the enemy was left to face us. I remained in my quarters, ordering the junior officers to conduct a full inspection. There was nothing else to do until the rains stopped. I was the senior general remaining on the line, so the whole army must reflect my mood, my lethargy. I decided not to move our forces until word came from Moscow.

Surprisingly, the Czar's reply to my message was very slow in arriving. I later discovered that the delay had been due to his receiving a letter from Kurbsky, only a few hours after my message reached him. Andrew's harangue was so long and articulate, he must have spent days composing it before his departure, dispatching it immediately after he crossed the lines. In essence it accused the Czar of the same crimes Andrew had enumerated in his discourse, and in his letter to me.

Because Ivan already had my report when Kurbsky's letter came, he knew what to expect. The messenger, apparently a surly German from the Grand Master's own guard, attempted to deliver the scroll into the Czar's hands. Instead, Ivan impaled the brute's foot to the floor with his *kisten* and ordered the man to read the letter aloud. I saw the message later, and it was most insulting. It ended with a comment to the effect that, "Because it enumerated the greatest sins of the Czar, it should be kept and buried with him!" Such audacity! As Ivan remarked, himself, it reflected how poorly Andrew understood the teachings of Christ. A man is supposed to be buried in a state of grace and forgiveness. To place such a letter in his grave, with its bitter animosity, would be to mock the very God to whom we pray for salvation.

Kurbsky's messenger was subsequently questioned under torture, but he apparently knew nothing of any further conspiracy – nothing beyond the earlier negotiations that led to Andrew's unholy desertion. Eventually, the Czar ordered my return to Moscow in all honor, for he had heard of my violent argument with Andrew on the eve of his heinous treachery. He knew of my night's confinement and of my furious charge into battle the following day. From this, he assumed that I had struggled in vain to recover Andrew's body from the enemy. The body, he said, I might have taken; the soul was gone forever, fled into the very depths of hell, where it would burn in fire and misery.

Heinrich joined me shortly before I received the Czar's order to return. My stepfather had finally been able to leave his post, and had journeyed to my *dacha*, not knowing whether I was there or not. He had spent a few days with Nina and the rest of the household, and it was there he learned of Kurbsky's desertion. Cautioning Nina to make no ill–guarded remarks, he came at once to my camp and we left for the capital together. Shig Ali took over my command.

I now began a period of my life to be looked back upon with a strange mixture of pride and revulsion. Although at the time I felt I could understand the reasons for most of my own actions and the behavior of those about me, I am now ashamed to tell of much that I did. Worse, I personally committed some of the most dreadful acts on my own volition. The forces of hell, ever sustaining their evil fires in Ivan's heart, no longer banked their coals. When his beloved Anastasia died, those flames had been fanned by his grief until they grew into a terrible plague – a great pestilence inside his soul. In the end, the horrible corruption burst forth, infecting all of us. As I describe these times, I shall try to put myself back into them, to feel again the energies which compelled my actions, and the twisted reasoning which allowed me to do as I did. I can only pray that God, in His Divine Benevolence and Wisdom, may look upon my spirit and read within it the sincerity of my own despair. The crimes I committed were done in service to His Anointed Shepherd, or so I convinced myself at the time. Even now, I can feel some justification because of this, and during the period of which I speak my devotion to the Czar blinded me even more completely. Yet some of this was commanded by the demons who strove to consume my own soul, for much as I wish I could claim otherwise, I did derive pleasure from my own depravity.

For years afterward, my answer to any who questioned me might be summed up in the words I once used in a letter to Nina, attempting to ease my conscience and assuage her terror. *What does it benefit a man,* I wrote, *if he serves God only within himself, or when he bows his head and bends his knee in church? Is he not still mean and neglectful of his duty if he permits the soul of the ordained leader of many men to starve? Can there be heavenly grace within a man who would not encourage the sacrifice of a few useless, or less valuable underlings, that the being of his Czar be thereby granted peace? I am no Kurbsky to condemn him; my understanding of the world and of the heavens beyond our reach is not so great that I would presume to these pretentious judgments. I know my moods and my actions frighten you, but remember that my love is always constant.* How empty and foolish these words sound today! Yet when I wrote them, they expressed my single excuse, and at the time I believed them to be sincere.

CHAPTER IV

It was a somber, mirthless court to which I returned – an attitude that seemed to pervade the entire city. I was glad that Nina was not in Moscow to see it. Although I was already a member of the Czar's new priesthood, Ivan asked me to renew my vows. I did so without question. Not all members of the brotherhood were publicly known, and my own membership had never been announced or proclaimed. Still, everyone in Moscow either knew or assumed I was of the *Opritchina*. When I rode through the streets men bowed their heads, not daring to look at me. Women hastened to pull their children back from my path. I took to wearing the black cassock and cowl like all the others, and when I went forth with my comrades at night I covered my face with the dog's head mask. This device denoted our servitude to the Czar, as well as our being the instruments whereby he slew his enemies, as his hounds had slain the Shuisky. I carried a broom on my saddlebow, to sweep the realm clean of foes and traitors. By my oath to serve the Czar, I had sworn to place his interests above those of family, wife, or friends. My very soul was his, and in return I became one of his limbs. What I did, I did in the name of the Czar. I and all the other *Opritchniki* might go where we liked, take what we wished, and none could question us. We had been assured in advance of God's Grace and Pardon. Our beings were now spiritually merged with the Czar's; we were sacrosanct, and in us the people should see their Anointed Lord. There were three hundred men within this inner circle, but the entire *Oprichina* was growing from the originally projected thousand. It would eventually total six times that number.

Kurbsky's desertion had accelerated the *Oprichina's* growth, for it added substance to the Czar's suspicions. Ivan was certain a conspiracy was fermenting, and his closest scrutiny fell upon the boyars who were nearest to him. I cannot honestly say how much truth there was to his beliefs. I knew nothing of any actual conspiracy, but a number of *dyaks* and other officials had fled from Russia soon after Andrew. Others tried to leave and were caught. Yet, when even the mousy little Mikhailof continued to make light of these being a serious nest of plotters, it caused me to doubt it, too. Heinrich agreed with the secretary, and was a good deal more pointed with his remarks.

"Like an old woman looking under the bed for evil gnomes," he said, "the Czar sees an assassin in every window."

Ivan's immediate action was to close the Kremlin palace, and to order a new house built in the city, between the Bielgorod and the Arbat. To make room for this, many existing residences had to be destroyed and removed, putting a number of citizens into the street. But so great was the love of the common people for their Czar, we heard hardly a word of protest. How different would have been the whining of the boyars!

Along with the Czar's decision to remove himself to different quarters, he also ordered the houses left standing around his new palace – and for some distance in every direction – confiscated for the use of the *Opritchniki*. This included the land on which our house stood; but as both Heinrich and I were members of the inner group, it had no effect on us. During the period of construction the Czar ordered us all to Alexandrov.

I wrote Nina before I left, hoping she would understand the necessity of my continued absence. The Bomels were to remain in our Moscow house, where they had continued to reside. Elysius, particularly, seemed quite comfortable there. With a number of new faces added to the foreign community, neither he nor Anne would lack for company. He had also established a very profitable business, casting horoscopes for the court and preparing various medicines and love potions for any who could afford his services.

Before the Czar's party left, however, there was some business to be completed. Fortunately, my own background of service and close association with the royal family had placed me above suspicion. With Kurbsky's actually confining me on the eve of his own treason, none dared point a finger at me. Some others of the highest rank could not display so unsoiled a record. One of these was Gorbatof–Shuisky, the former governor of Svyazhsk. He had made remarks in the past, criticizing the Czar's war in the West. It was also rumored that he had been in communication with Sigismund's agents. Ivan summarily ordered his execution; with him, his son Peter was to die as well. There were others, mostly men of lesser note: Dmitri Sheviref and some other traitors caught fleeing toward the Polish border. Ivan believed all of them had been allied with the Kurbsky faction, though again I must deny knowledge of these facts. I assumed the Czar possessed information obtained during my absence from the capital.

On the appointed day, I went to the Square of Executions with Ivan's personal group of friends. Heinrich, Simon and Alexi Basmanov were with us, in addition to Fedka, Malyuta Skuratof, and both of Ivan's sons. Vanya sat just below his father's chair, and beside him was little Fedya. I had not seen the younger Prince since returning from England, and was surprised, as one always is, to see how he had grown. Yet I wondered at his being there at all, for he must have been less than ten.

"The lad must learn the truth of life's evils," Ivan told me. "The sight of a little blood will steel his soul for what he is going to face as a man."

I looked at the boy, and could see little of either parent in his features. He was a simple, kindly child, much like Yuri had been. Already, people were commenting on his limitations, as he seemed to have inherited his uncle's spiritual affliction.

I sat in the upper row, near the Czar. Skuratof was below us with his group of cronies. I still did not know most of these others very well: John Chibotovy, Alfansy Viazemsky, Michael Saltikoff; yet all were high in the Czar's favor. We reclined in a most elegant pavilion, which Ivan had ordered set up for the occasion. There were red velvet draperies and deep cushions on the chairs. Gilded poles supported the red and white striped canopy above us. A mass of household servants and guards were employed to assure our comfort and safety.

"You have gone to a lot of trouble," I commented to the Czar.

Ivan's face was gray, as it always was when he had to observe a public execution. The lines about his eyes and chin were thin and intense, firmly set to avoid any show of emotion. He hardly looked at me when he replied. "It may be a long session," he mumbled softly.

I tried to match the Czar's decorum, as did Heinrich and the others of us who had been brought up with the manners of gentlemen. Some of the newer additions to the Czar's entourage had no idea at all how they should behave in public. Skuratof, especially, was very coarse, and looked upon this sacred ritual as a sport. He laughed and joked with the others, completely ignoring the Czar's solemnity. He was not in the least concerned over Ivan's obvious strain at having to execute men who had served him. In his benevolence, the Czar ignored their poor manners.

The executioners soon had a block in place on the *lobonoyo mesto,* and then started to work implanting a stake off to one side. Only then did I realize why the Czar had made preparations to remain all day. Someone was going to be impaled. Whose crime was deemed serious enough to deserve this severe punishment, I did not yet know.

The first to be executed were the Shuiskys, as befitted their rank. The few days in prison had drained the pompous arrogance from both father and son. Peter, only eighteen or so, had been as vain and overbearing as all his breed. They were led out in chains, wearing only their shifts, for the Czar did not wish to emphasize their rank by allowing them the trappings of wealth. He felt they should die in humility, that they might face their creator with a more acceptable attitude.

The speech was made by Gorbatof–Shuisky. As one might expect, it was properly phrased and affirmed his last wish that the Czar's reign continue as gloriously as it had started. Whatever other faults they had, the Shuiskys at least observed the proper forms at public rituals. Peter did not wish to speak, so the executioners pulled him to the block as soon as his father had finished speaking. As they forced his head down onto the wood, he must suddenly have realized how near death hovered. He struggled a bit, though not badly enough to disgrace himself. It was his father who created a terrible scene. He could not bear to see his son die, he whined. He fell on his knees, facing the Czar, beseeching him with open palms, clanking the chains which fastened them to his waist. Please, he must go first, he begged, all the while gesturing with those manacled hands. He strained until small trickles of blood began to show about his wrists.

All of this was unpleasant enough, but the spectacle was made worse by Skuratof and his friends. They had been drinking heavily, and were already incoherent, though it was hardly past mid–morning. They began shouting insults at Shuisky, and some of their remarks were extremely obscene. A huge crowd had gathered to watch, mostly, I suppose, because word had gotten out about the impaling. When it was learned that the Czar would be there in person, the Square became packed with curious spectators. While executions had been frequent of late, and the Square was virtually ringed with severed heads mounted on pikes, this type of punishment was rare. To have a display such as Shuisky put on before this crowd of commoners was very insulting to the Czar's dignity.

In all, Ivan took it well. He silenced Skuratof's company with a few softly spoken words, and called to the executioners to carry out the sentence of the father first. They did so, separating his head with a single blow. Before the crowd's cheer had faded, however, Peter shook loose from the guard who stood with him and bounded to where his father's head had fallen upon the stones. He bent his body into a tight knot, for his hands were manacled in front of him and attached to a belt about his waist by a very short chain. He managed to grasp the severed head in both hands. Raising it to his own face, he kissed the dead lips, crying and moaning all the while.

The guards grabbed him, and a priest gently took the head from his hands. The boy continued to sob and quiver, whether for the fate of his father or for himself we cannot know. His failure to maintain proper composure to the end was unfortunate, and I knew it displeased the Czar. Covered with his father's blood, Peter was finally returned to the block. The headsman was good this day, and the boy's head also fell with just one blow.

Several more were beheaded after that. The only one whom I knew very well was Prince Peter Gorensky, who had been a casual friend during the Kazan campaign. He had served under Morozof, if my memory does not fail me, and also had been an officer in Shig Ali's first Livonian offensive. He was a more dignified person than any of the others, even the Shuiskys. His family was no longer as powerful or as wealthy, but they came from a very exalted lineage. Unfortunately, his speech was much too long, and near the end it was interrupted by derisive remarks from the Skuratof–Chibotovy–Viazemsky group. The Czar said nothing to silence them this time, and seemed to accept their spoliation of his dignity as just another penance for his own sins. For the sake of the crowd, he kept his lips set in the grim semblance of a smile.

With these other executions finally completed, everyone became quiet. It was now obvious who was to be impaled. Sheviref was led up to the stake by two guards, who held him firmly by both arms. Showing no sign of fear, the prisoner made a short speech – more a prayer, really – speaking so softly it was difficult to hear him. When he finished no one realized it, as it seemed he had hardly started.

"I have no more to say," he told the guards.

At the Czar's nod, they took him to the stake. Like the Shuisky's, he was dressed only in a shift, but his hands were bound behind his back with rope. Because he was a small man, it required only two of them to lift him up, while a third man stood by to hold the prisoner's garment out of the way and to help guide him onto the stake. It was all done very skillfully, with Sheviref being lifted onto the pointed stake, his lower body exposed only briefly. From the expression on the executioners' faces, the penetration must have been exactly right. No scream escaped the prisoner, just a grimace of pain and a rasping intake of breath.

As soon as his feet touched the ground, his arms were freed and Sheviref began to pray, which he continued to do until he was dead. He was a young man, perhaps twenty–five years old, and possessed the strength of youth. He did not die until after the torches had been lighted at dusk. Many in the crowd had grown bored by then, and left, for the condemned man made no effort to lift himself from the pole. He allowed his pain to show only in the contorted lines of his face, as if his prayers were indeed sustaining his dignity. Custom required the Czar to remain, if he once came to attend an execution. Naturally, Ivan did this and all the court remained with him. The noisy group around Skuratof played at dice most of the afternoon, with the betting heavy as to the exact time of Sheviref's death. I think the reason for the pointed stake – rather than a smoother round – was to make the prisoner's death come sooner. Otherwise, he might have lasted a day or more. As it was, the sun had been gone for two or three hours, when the guards examined the slumped, kneeling figure and called to the Czar that he had expired.

That night, Ivan remained at prayer in his private chapel until very late. Without any rest, he went from there to the chambers beneath the Kremlin prison, where he remained until dawn. I had long since gone home to bed, but I was told the Czar returned again to his devotions, remaining on his knees most of the morning. Nor did he partake of food or drink until dinner that evening.

Up to the moment of the brotherhood's departure for Alexandrov, I harbored the hope of being sent back to Livonia. I doubted an actual request would bear much weight with the Czar, however, so I did not ask him. I was afraid it might seem to evidence resistance to his plans. I therefore remained with the *Opritchina,* and during the next few months I made several trips with the Czar, back and forth between Alexandrov and Moscow. At the Abby, we engaged in activities I would prefer now not to remember, for this was the beginning of the time when a terrible blood–lust took possession of my soul. The chambers beneath the Alexandrov palace were, if anything, more extensive than those in the Kremlin. I was well informed of their structure, for I acted as Ivan's aide, maintaining a close check on the building activities – also the installation and testing of new equipment.

Somehow, only blood seemed to assuage the tortures of Ivan's soul. Public executions became more frequent, and were terrible, gory purges. Roman Kurbsky was caught, trying to flee across the Polish border to join his brother. He was publicly beheaded. Many others fell, some of them men who had been friends and companions of mine on past campaigns.

The activities of the *Opritchina* continued, with raids by bands of brothers upon the homes of the people a commonplace occurrence. None were secure save those who lived within the Kremlin walls. Merchants, farmers, poor people, even princes and boyars who were members of the *Zemschina* had their homes broken into. Valuables were looted and women raped. Any who refused to submit or who raised a hand against the black–robed servants of the Czar were either slaughtered on the spot, else taken to the dungeons where they fared far worse. I tried not to enjoy these activities, telling myself I took no pleasure in killing except in battle, but as time passed I found my attitudes changing. Though I might not participate with the others, I would watch, and the lust would rise within me – needing an outlet I was loath to let the others see. With my wife in Livonia, I began to seek other women. My only escape from the horrors of reality, and the equally frightening experiences of my dreams, came with sex and vodka. In truth, I was afraid to sleep alone at night. Equally fearful lest I catch the pox, I took only young virgins into my chamber, where I used them cruelly in my horrible lust and drunkenness.

Like the Czar, I began to feel the need for extra prayers to expiate my sins. I frequently joined him in the morning, even when he hadn't ordered me to come. I knew he was pleased by this, as he had lately chided me for my lack of piety. While he maintained my soul was less in need of prayer than most, he feared that my dislike of the clergy might prejudice God's judgment. That may have been true in years now gone, but as spring turned to summer I knew my spiritual being was decayed, putrid as any carrion. I was lower even than Skuratof, for I understood the sins I committed. But the Czar was my master, and to obey him was my duty as ordained by God.

The issue with the Metropolitan was fast coming to a head, as well. Phillip had openly stated his discontent with the Czar's behavior, and condemned the actions of the *Opritchina*. He was ignored by all save the Czar, who as yet had only cursed him, making no move to curtail the Metropolitan's freedom to speak. And speak he did, pointing out the sins and crimes of the leading brothers.

Despite my stated loyalty, I could not help feeling that the actions of Viazemsky, Skuratof, and some of the others had become excessive. They began extorting taxes from their neighbors, especially from noble families who belonged to the *Zemschina*. When they were drunk they would sometimes roam the streets with their gangs of bullies, stealing from the shops and raping any women who crossed their path. Not to condemn them further than their behavior would merit, not all of these women were poor deflowered virgins. Many females purposely placed themselves where they might be found. Still, the public actions of these men brought angry denunciations from Phillip and from the higher clergy around him. This, in turn, widened the schism within the Church itself. Many priests voiced support of the Czar. The Metropolitan was regarded as a saint by the common people, however, and they listened in dumb silence to his words. In nearly every sermon he delivered from the pulpit of the Great Cathedral in the Kremlin, he thundered the threats of heavenly vengeance against the Czar and the brotherhood.

Even such *Opritchniki* as Morozof, Alexi Basmanov, and I began to feel the venom of those attacks, for we were regarded as silent participants. True, we would sometimes commit a public act, but always in company of others. I never discussed it with Alexi or Michael, but I am certain they acted as I did – largely because it was felt necessary to display a continued loyalty. Yet some of these things I enjoyed, may God forgive me, and I continued to derive an unholy pleasure from the torture of men I disliked.

With all of this, I gradually overcame my revulsion at having to watch the technicians. I no longer hated going to the chambers, either in Alexandrov or beneath the Czar's new house in Moscow. Admittedly, they were miserable places – cold and clammy in winter, oppressively hot in summer. Smoke and stench from the fires would not rise properly during warm weather, which caused the underground rooms to become fetid and stinking. Of course, the odors were terrible enough in any season, for Ivan went through a period of taking solace from seeing a man burned or roasted alive. With Skuratof's help, he designed a giant skillet, like the pans used to fry meat, but much larger. In this a man could be broiled in shallow grease until his skin would crackle, peeling off the flesh. It left the victim flayed, but still alive to kick at his bonds and scream for mercy.

All of these things were somehow reported to the Metropolitan. We never learned by whom. From the sanctuary of the church he would tell of our "sins," and rant about the condemnation of our spirits. Hearing these accusations, those of us who still possessed enough of our original souls to care, would fall upon our knees and beg the Lord's forgiveness. Despite the stand taken by the head of the Church, there was always a priest willing to grant us absolution.

Word of the *Opritchina* had begun to spread abroad, especially in Poland, where our ambassadors were questioned by the King. They had been ordered to deny such an organization existed, for it was supposed to be secret. But Kurbsky was always there, and he would repeat what he knew of our activities. Frequently, he was armed with amazingly detailed information, supplied from God–knew–what source. I was in such a state of confusion during these months, I hardly knew – and now have trouble remembering – where my dreams left off and reality began.

I did not break out of this trancelike state until I was summoned again to my wife's bedside, to be with her when our second son was born. He was a good, sturdy boy, whom we named Demetrius. I spent a few weeks with Nina, and was beginning to recover the essence of my being, when a summons arrived from the Czar, commanding me to return at once.

The time I spent with my wife had been during the warm season, and this last evening was Midsummer's Eve. I had almost forgotten the old traditions and customs followed by the peasants, even by many of the gentry on this night. It was so different here from the fear and tension of the capital I thought. As darkness fell, the people of this land, where battles could occur at any time between powerful, opposing armies, began wandering innocently across the fields and into the forests. They were in search of the illusive fern blossoms. These flowers were supposed to bloom twice each year – on Midsummer's Eve and on the eve of the Feast of the Assumption. On these nights a man might hope to find the flower, and once possessing it he would be wealthy forever. Of course, the old legends tell us the woods fairies are especially vigilant, alert to divert the seeker, or to throw dust into his eyes if he got too close.

There was also the belief that if a young maiden went into the woods on this eve, and collected pollen from seven different wildflowers, she could place them beneath her pillow and would dream a vision of her future husband. Such were the concerns of these simple country folk on this last night before my return. They were only my serfs and servants, but I envied them their clean, unhaunted existences. On the morrow I knew I must return to the great city, to my fine, elegant home – and to the further damnation of my soul.

When I made ready to depart the next morning, Nina insisted she would come with me. She could leave the children with the girls, she said, where they would be out of danger. She feared I might be returning to my death. I ordered her to remain, and left just after first light. Convinced at last that I would not weaken in my resolve to leave her behind, she sent me away with such a memory of love I could think of nothing else all the way back to Moscow. I could not look at another woman for a long, long time.

I arrived in Moscow at night, on the eve of another massive schedule of executions. Among the most notable was Prince John Sheremetief, who had led our armies against the Tartar hordes. He had been sorely wounded in battle, and was now a cripple, able to hobble about only with the aid of crutches. He had been held in a dungeon since a few days after my departure, and was slated to be the prime victim on the morrow.

The Czar had left instructions that I was to come to him at once, the moment I arrived. At this hour I was sure he would be in the chambers, so I would be picking up the threads of my life exactly where I had left them. Because Ivan had ordered it, I had to attend him. I went, wishing all the while I could return to Livonia.

With the fall of darkness, a warm, sultry breeze began a subtle stirring, causing black, almost invisible clouds to glide across the inky sky. Stars and moon appeared only furtively, alternately obscured and revealed by the restless movement of the heavens. Very few lights showed in the Kremlin, for the palace was dark and shuttered. From the city, the pink walls were completely lost in the night, except for an occasional silvery ridge along the top, when the moon broke through the gloom. Approaching the Czar's house, I thought of the oath I had taken at the foot of that wall. As a boy, kneeling in the snow, with tears swelling in my eyes, I had made a promise which still compelled my obedience. Was I the same person, I wondered. It was hard to realize how the world had changed since then. It was with lagging steps that I covered the distance on foot, Toby following behind me, leading the horses which I had declined to use. I wanted this extra delay to fortify my mind against the impact of conflicting emotions – of horror and of lust – that I knew I was going to experience.

Reaching the royal *dacha*, I experienced an overwhelmingly painful craving for the warmth of Nina's body. I needed her being to surround me, to engulf me in her spirit, and to shield me from the madness of reality. The feeling of freedom I had experienced for the past few days was gone. The old fetters once more shackled my soul, settling none too comfortably into their well–worn ruts. Guards saluted me courteously as I mounted the steps into the main reception hall. I was quickly taken in tow by a chamberlain, the fellow going before me, bearing a large, golden candelabra. I was still deep in my own thoughts, and had automatically returned the servant's greeting. At first, the reason for the candelabra failed to penetrate my mind. With relief, I had noticed lights in the upstairs apartments as I approached the house, and now expected to be received there by the Czar.

I was jarred from my reverie, however, when my guide took a certain turn along the way. Instead of proceeding up the stairway to Ivan's rooms, we began the long descent into the bowels of the earth. As we continued on our way, the walls ceased to be hung with rich, heavy tapestries; the thick carpets gave way to flimsy, threadbare remnants. Finally, the unmistakably sour mustiness of dungeons replaced the scented air of the upper levels.

Although I had supervised much of the construction at Alexandrov, I had been indifferent to these areas while the Moscow palace was being built, and thus did not know my way through the maze of tunnels. Blindly, I followed the flickering light and the shadowy back of the servant. A gnawing fear, never far from my consciousness since returning to the city, now swelled into an almost compelling pressure within my gut. Irrespective of the cool, almost chilly atmosphere, a cold sweat stood out on my brow, and I wondered how I would feel if I were being arrested – seized and dragged here in chains. For a moment I harbored the irrational thought that I might be being led into a trap. The fear became so strong I started to reach out for the chamberlain's shoulder. "Foolish," I muttered half aloud, and let my hand drop to my side. But the burning anxiety persisted, and I knew the reason I hadn't asked was the possibility of his confirming my fears, depriving me of those final moments when I might console myself with doubts.

We walked for a seeming eternity, first through one long corridor, then down a short flight of stairs, through more twisting passageways until I was completely turned about. I knew I could never find my own way out. The only illumination came from the candles held by my guide, though many short, squat tapers were set, unlighted, into niches at the intersections of each tunnel. In my state of tense expectation, I stumbled on the rough stones, and my guide turned to me, offering his hand.

After this more or less friendly act, I found my voice. It rasped at first, but by an enormous effort of will I managed to swallow my dread. "Good God, man," I demanded, "where is the Czar? If we go down much further, we'll find ourselves at the gates of hell!"

The faintest trace of an ironic smile played briefly on the servant's lips. In the cool tones of officious authority, he replied, "We are almost there, Highness," but whether "there" referred to Ivan or to hell, I could not tell. As it happened, the difference was very slight.

We continued on our way, suddenly encountering a bright glow as we turned an unexpected corner. Then we passed through the open doorway of a large, stone chamber. The servant halted just inside. Here was another flight of steps, leading down into a massive vault. Holding his light aloft, he intoned, loudly enough to cause an echo to rattle along the walls behind me: "General Prince Dmitri Simeonevitch Marensky, your Imperial Majesty!"

The servant bowed deeply, still holding the candelabra perfectly level, although it was above his lowered head. He took two steps backward, and disappeared into the corridor, leaving me to blink in awe at the scene before me. A great hearth blazed at the far end of the room. The whole area was easily as large as the formal reception hall in the Kremlin palace. Metal rings and chains were set into the stones of the walls, forming the principal decor. Interspersed with these were a variety of instruments hanging from wooden pegs, most of which I recognized; but a few were incomprehensible to me. The functional properties of several machines were not left to my imagination, however, as attendants were busily engaged in demonstrating their effects on a variety of prisoners.

I had only a few seconds to absorb the sight, as my attention was quickly diverted after the chamberlain's announcement. A loud guttural roar emanated from the center of the room, where a large velvet-covered settee rested on a low dais. From where I stood I could see only the back of it, which curved up to about the height of a man, forming an arched canopy over the top. The couch skidded backward a few inches as its occupant pushed himself upright, and Ivan staggered around the obstructing wall of cloth.

A thunderous voice – "Dmitri! At last!" Like an enormous, shaggy bear, Ivan lumbered toward me. He was wearing an old robe, brown in its earlier state, now stained and tattered. He was drunk, though not excessively so – just enough that his voice had taken on a deep, throaty quality. He seemed so genuinely happy to see me my previous fears departed like so much morning mist, and I suddenly felt guilty for the disloyal thoughts I had permitted to infiltrate my heart. When I reached the foot of the stairs, he embraced me as if I had been away for months, or years. He made a series of sticky, slobbering sounds, and enfolded me in an overpowering hug, half dragging me with him as he started back toward the settee. Overriding my previous doubts and anxieties, the guilt I had felt over my part in his past activities, I was now struck with the crushing impact of realization. When all else was said and done, this man was my friend – not only my Czar, but the companion of my youth and of my childhood. To each other, we were nearly all that remained of those early days. The bonds that held me to him were more than superficial loyalties. My feelings transcended any requirement of law or custom. I loved him as a man must love father or brother, whether or not we shared a kindred blood.

When Ivan finally released me, my face and neck were wet with a mixture of his tears and saliva. With our arms about one another's shoulders, we mounted the dais together. I was oblivious to our surroundings, feeling only the warmth of our regenerated love, our mutual sense of companionship.

"My dear brother," he muttered, his tone so low that no one else could hear. "I have such need of you!" he added with a sigh. "You cannot imagine the burdens I have been compelled to bear these last few days – the extent of the treachery around me!"

I sat beside him, dumbfounded. It was almost as if he'd looked into my thoughts. Never, not in all his life, had Ivan ever addressed me as his brother. This was the one and only time he ever would. Later, thinking back upon it, I wondered if he might have referred to our figurative brotherhood within the *Opritchina*. But I think it most likely he meant exactly what his words bespoke, that he referred to our common blood and the many experiences we had shared since the beginnings of our lives.

We sat silently, side by side on the filthy cushions of the settee, each absorbed in his own thoughts. Our closeness communicated itself without need of words. It was only gradually that my mind began to catalogue the material world around us. The once fine velvet on which we sat was stained and spotted with such a variety of substances it was impossible to imagine the sources of contributing fluids. At length, a servant appeared with a salver, filling a silver, jewel–encrusted goblet for me, as Ivan poured the dregs of his own drink down his throat and ex- tended the vessel for more.

"You see these miserable swine decorating my walls?" he asked, swinging his arm to indicate the several naked figures suspended in various painful positions along the stone facade. A fat old man, with the flowing gray beard of a priest, hung directly in front of us. His sagging, unprotected flesh vibrated with every gasping breath. He was suspended from one of the iron rings, held by wire ropes about his wrists. These had cut deeply into the skin, causing blood to trickle down his arms and along the sides of his body. A small bed of coals glowed on the floor beneath him. His unfettered feet executed a weird dance, as he struggled to keep them out of the roasting heat. I recognized him as the abbot of a small monastery near Yaroslavl. Most of the other victims seemed younger, all with the shaven heads of monks. I took them to be common priests, or church servitors of some lower order.

"It looks like an ecclesiastical assembly," I noted sardonically, keeping my tone light and reflecting an indifference the liquor was beginning to make me feel.

Ivan turned toward me, laughing suddenly at my wit. Flecks of sallow moisture oozed from the corners of his mouth. "I know you do not fully approve of my nightly diversions, Dmitri; but I shall try not to offend your delicate sensitivities. You needn't fear for what you'll be forced to see, and you needn't force yourself to appear in agreement, either." He walloped my back with several good–natured blows. "You are loyal, and you are my friend. You defend whatever I do, whether you like it or not. You never need pretend to do more!"

He took another sizable gulp of vodka and swilled it about his mouth, slavering some of the liquid into his bedraggled beard. Several small droplets found their way onto the crusted surface of the couch. "But you are right about our guests. They are, indeed, the self–styled, earthly representatives of Almighty God. Fat thieves, rather!" he roared. "Gorging themselves like cannibals on the very soul of Russia!"

His eyes, reflecting the fierce flames on the hearth, glowed a deep scarlet. But the fires seemed to come from the very depths of his being. His staff, never far from his hand, lay propped obliquely against the seat on his other side. He seized it, and in an unexpected burst of anger slammed it down against the surface of our serving table.

"If need be, I shall destroy every last vestige of this cult which seeks to prevent my carrying out God's holy mission! Russia! Russia!" he bellowed, and all eyes turned toward him. Even the helpless prisoners, in their varied stages of graceless agony, responded to the commanding thunder. "The gathering in of the Russian lands – that is why I was placed upon the earth! That is why no one – *no one* – shall interfere with me. I cannot wage a proper war unless I have the control God meant for me to have over my domain. And these *are* holy wars! But I cannot have that proper, necessary control with a flock of sniveling churchmen preaching against me – turning my people against me – uttering treason within the very cathedrals my fathers and I have built for them!"

His voice dropped to a more conversational tone, and after a moment the others returned to their diverse occupations. Two of the priests were praying in unison to our right, and Ivan glanced at them contemptuously. "Hypocrites!" he grumbled, pausing to suck noisily at the contents of his goblet. "Prattling to a God who knows them not! Only I, Dmitri! Only I stand as bridge between God and the peoples of Russia. And not just the peoples of Moscow, or the old lands of Muscovy! I mean all the lands our fathers and I have brought into the fold of grace, into the arms of the true Church of God." He hugged a great column of air, crushing his invisible children to his breast. His eyes focused on the blank wall, between two of his struggling prisoners. "All the lands of Russia!" His voice was almost a whisper.

"But treachery!" he shouted again. His blazing eyes turned once more in my direction. He seemed almost to beg for my understanding.

"I know, Ivashka," I said, using the name I had not dared to utter since Ivan became Czar. "I know," I repeated, patting his arm.

"Dmitri," he cried abruptly, pressing his forehead against my shoulder, "help me. I don't wish to harm the Metropolitan of Moscow, but what am I to do? He mocks me, condemns me before the masses. I *must* do something about him, but I fear lest this be more than God would tolerate. What harm would I do my soul if I struck him down? Could there ever be absolution for such an act?"

"I have failed you, you know," I said softly, and in response to his questioning glance I continued: "You asked me – or perhaps it was the Czarevitch who asked in your name – that I go to Phillip and try to reason with him. I never have, for it was a task I never felt capable of undertaking. If you like. . . ."

"Yes!" he shouted. "Yes, Dmitri! Go now. Go to him now, if you must drag him from his bed. Make him listen to you! If you fail – if you fail, you may cost me all that remains of my soul. Do you understand? Do you realize the importance of the mission I entrust to you? This is more vital than what you have done in England, or Astrakhan, or Livonia. You deal now with my very. . . ."

His frenzied speech was interrupted by a horrible scream from the far side of the room. We both looked up in time to see a tremendous spurt of blood cascade from the throat of the farthest man. The prisoner's struggles palpitated in ever decreasing motion, finally ending altogether. The body hung limp against the wall.

"You stupid clumsy fool!" shrieked the Czar. He leaped to his feet. Grabbing his *kisten,* he charged the attendant, beating the man violently with the staff until the other fell onto his knees, holding his arms above his head to ward off the blows. Then the Czar remembered me. Abruptly, he broke off his attack and turned back to face me. "Go, Dmitri!" he shouted.

I stood helplessly. "I . . . I don't think I can find the way," I told him.

"Oh!" Ivan started to laugh again, and kicked the man who knelt before him. "Up, you oaf," he shouted. "Show Prince Marensky the way out."

CHAPTER V

Still fired by Ivan's zeal, I entered the Cathedral of the Assumption, again leaving Toby outside with the horses. I was fully prepared to deliver a stern injunction to the Metropolitan. Afterward, I planned simply to withdraw, leaving him to dwell upon my words. On the way up, I had worked out the phrases I would use – trying as I did so to suppress the paradox – my own assent from the underworld. I needed only to confront Phillip, I reasoned, and my wisdom would flow into a classic statement of his failures. Unfortunately, as soon as I entered the great, somber structure, its hallowed walls deflated my mood.

At night, the cathedral's interior seemed to house the spirits of darkness. The high arches rose into shadows about the ceiling, even when the lower portions were illuminated. On this particular evening, the huge vault was dim, with only an occasional taper; and these were being systematically extinguished by a young *ponomar* – or church watchman. The hushed atmosphere overwhelmed me – jarred my composure and brought back childhood fears. I pictured the many ghosts of long dead leaders who were said to haunt the enormous crypt. I remembered my own experiences as an altarboy, and how fearful I had always been on entering the church after sundown.

Softly, I approached the young servitor before he had completed his tasks. I had seen him about the cathedral before, and he must certainly have known who I was. I know I frightened him. His eyes reflected his terror, and I knew he wished to run away. How base had I become, I thought, that my very presence inside God's house should so horrify His servants?

"I mean you no harm, son," I said by way of greeting. I meant for my tone to reassure him, though I doubt it did. "It is important that I speak with the Holy Father. Can you inform him I am here?"

Again the look of anguished fear, and again I declared my intention not to harm anyone. But it was important I speak to the Metropolitan, I insisted. The boy finally found his voice. Swallowing hard, he whispered hoarsely, "If Your Highness will be so kind," motioning to a seat in a small alcove. "I shall fetch someone right away."

I remained on my feet, trying to reformulate my speech. A few moments later a priest came out of the vestry – a tall, gaunt man, with full gray beard. He approached me with a stiff, cold dignity, and demanded to know my business with the Metropolitan. It was on the tip of my tongue to put him in his place at once, but I controlled the impulse. "It is important that I speak with the Holy Father this evening," I said softly. "I have just come from His Imperial Majesty."

The man's eyebrows shot up, and his right hand started involuntarily to make the sign of the cross. Still he stood there, and this time I allowed my ire to show. "Since when does a Russian priest cross himself at mention of the Czar?" I snapped. "I told you I came on important business; now take me to your master."

"There are no 'masters' here," he responded with the same cool dignity, "save Our Lord God, Himself." He looked up piously at the screen of icons, and before I could speak again he had turned away. "If you will come with me, My Lord," he said without looking back.

The priest led me through a passage used by the clergy to enter and leave the church. It came out only a short distance from the Metropolitan's house, where I probably should have gone in the first place. But it was better this way, I thought. My appearing on Phillip's doorstep at this time of night would surely have frightened them into refusing to admit me. Surprisingly enough, the priest walked up to the door and opened it. It was not even locked! Inside, he led me to the same room where I had sat with Phillip's predecessors – Joseph, and after him Makari. Many of the furnishings were the same; but all semblance of grandeur was gone. There were no cushions on the seats and only rushes on the floor instead of the fine carpets Ivan had given Makari. Hard wooden benches, rough–hewn chests, and a few matching tables comprised the only furniture. The whole place smelled of straw, like a stable. I looked questioningly at the priest, and he indicated I should sit on one of the benches.

Phillip must already have retired, for when he entered the room a few moments later I could see he had just thrown water in his face, and his silky white beard was freshly combed. He wore a house robe over his shift, and a skull cap on his head. Even without the clerical trappings, his piety and priestly state were manifest. In seeming disregard of the danger in which he placed himself by his constant harassment of the Czar, a saintly calm had etched itself into the lines of his face. His deep brown eyes regarded me with compassion.

I had not intended to place myself in a subservient position to this man. I was going to speak to him as a friendly harbinger of impending disaster, should he fail to heed me. Still, I yielded to the atmosphere of the house and to the Metropolitan's holy presence. My first words were to request his blessing. Surprisingly, he gave it without hesitation, capping the ceremonial phrases with a few words intended to put me at my ease. They did not. Instead, I sensed the fingers of uncertainty steal about my heart. When he finished speaking he watched silently, obviously waiting for me to state the purpose of my untimely visit.

I allowed my eyes to rove the room. A great many books – at least forty or fifty – were lined neatly along the shelves of one wall. Scrolls, rolled around their intricately carved cores, reposed in niches beneath the bookshelves. In a corner, a modest tile–faced stove stared uselessly into the room. It was warm, I realized, and slightly muggy. The heat of the day had been trapped inside. The odor of the dead grass rushes was overpowering. Several more minutes passed, and I wiped a trickle of sweat from the back of my neck. But Phillip must have conducted many other interviews where the person had trouble saying what he wished. At length, he motioned me to a straight backed chair beside his writing table, and eased himself into a similar seat behind it. He smiled at me, encouragingly. "Now, my son, what brings you to an old man's study on such a beautiful evening?" he asked. I had forgotten how ethereal his voice could sound.

It was hard to look directly into the eyes of such holy innocence. His simplicity and his serene expression were disconcerting. I was unable to begin. Then Phillip, who had not gained his high position through lack of acuity, broached the subject himself.

"I am told you come from the Czar," he said quietly, never changing his expression.

"That is true," I replied. Involuntarily, my hands twitched, and I paused before continuing. "Although my coming was not exactly ordered, I did not really wish —"

"You are here to convince me I wrong the Czar," he said evenly. "But you know I have spoken only as God would wish me to."

"That may be," I said tentatively, "but as Your Holiness is aware, this breach between yourself and the Czar cannot be allowed to continue."

The Metropolitan nodded, saying nothing, and never taking his eyes from my face. He was not a large man, smaller than the average, really; yet he possessed an inner power. He seemed a formidable foe, although he was clearly no man's enemy. I went on, finally, gaining the confidence I needed from the sound of my own voice.

"Because we must achieve some understanding, and because we deal with two strong willed men of rank – all other circumstances aside – it occurred to me the first move might be most easily made by someone other than either Your Holiness or the Czar."

"I see," he said thoughtfully, "and how would this . . . reconciliation be brought about?"

"His Majesty would expect certain considerations," I began, "specifically your fulfillment of the covenant made in Alexandrov by your predecessor."

"Surely, the Czar does not seek to place himself above his God – the Lord of us all?" said the Metropolitan abruptly. As he continued to speak, explaining the holy scripture which dictated his behavior, I watched carefully for some sign of guile or irony. There was none. This skillful churchman was the sincerest man of God I had ever known.

"Father," I said, when he had finished. "Please heed me. I cannot hope to combat the logic of your goodness, or the basic directives of our faith. I speak in the most simple, secular pragmatism. Unless you expect a divine miracle to intervene, you cannot stand against the Czar much longer."

"Nor can I, with any honor to my faith or my God, pretend to condone what I know is wrong," he replied simply. "The Lord has seen fit to place this burden of responsibility upon me, regardless of the fact that He worked through these same Imperial hands which I must now oppose." He spoke softly, without hesitation. With a slight gesture of his fingers, he continued. "As Metropolitan of Moscow, I can speak only as the Lord commands me."

"Do you realize what you're saying?" I asked. "Do you know what Ivan is capable of doing to you?"

"If an earthly king would destroy my flesh, that, too, must be the Will of God."

What could I say? Always, the answer was the "Will of God." Ivan said this to explain his excesses; I said it as my reason for obeying him; Kurbsky used it to excuse his betrayal. And now Phillip. Yet all of us were sincere in our beliefs, I no less than the rest.

I allowed my head to sag forward on my chest, and I motioned helplessly. "I do not know what to say to you, Father. I have placed my own soul in jeopardy by following the example and the orders of my Czar. In doing so I have violated the Commandments I learned in this very room. If the Czar is wrong and evil, I am already damned for all eternity. But how much greater might have been my crimes in the eyes of God, had I failed to obey the Czar, the anointed leader of us all?

"Now I come to you, the most holy of men, and the only argument I have is the threat of your physical destruction if you fail to follow my path of . . . of what? Am I a great sinner, Father? Or am I a righteous man, as I would like to believe?"

I looked at him and he sighed deeply. "My son, the confusion of your spirit shows your soul still lives. More than this I cannot tell you. You must obey the dictates of your own conscience. But this I can say with certainty: The sins which the Czar – and possibly you, yourself – observe within your own beings, and the sins you pray most loudly to have forgiven, are not the heaviest blots upon your accounts with God. Your immoderate drinking, your excesses of the flesh, your avarice in accumulating wealth: all of these are sins of a lower order. They are common failings of most men in these times. I am sure they are errors Our Heavenly Father can understand and in many instances forgive. Were these the only sins we had to consider, I would not speak so harshly against the Czar.

"But the terrible, immoral crimes committed by him and by you of his minions – the murder and torture of hundreds of people! It is against these things I speak, and yet the Czar fails even to recognize these acts as wrong! To punish his people for their crimes, and their imagined crimes – he considers this to be his duty, or his right. How can God forgive these acts when there is no remorse, no recognition of any wrong?"

His words were defeating me, and my position seemed momentarily helpless. Yet as he continued to speak, I perceived an opening. When he paused, I took it. "Holy Father," I said, "while I know you speak from your heart, and as an earthly voice of the Lord, I seem to observe an error in your reasoning. Or perhaps 'omission' might be a more proper term."

He blinked at me in surprise, taking no apparent offense at my directness. He was genuinely puzzled that there could be an error in his own thoughts. "I would be interested in your opinion," he said quietly.

"Your opposition to the Czar," I began slowly, "is causing a greater breach between the Church and the secular authority than has ever existed before."

He nodded his agreement, and I continued: "Because of this breach, this great distance between the secular head of state and the holy See of the Metropolitan, there is no proper guidance available to the Czar. It would seem to be your duty, your *compelling* duty, to convince the Czar that he has sinned and that he must not stray farther from the righteous paths of God's directives. All of the sincere, truly holy men of Russia have sided with you, leaving the Czar to rely upon the questionable advice of less skilled, less well–intentioned clerics. Instead of making the effort which would seem proper to your holy office, and trying to mend this difference, you increase it by condemning a man who cannot understand why you revile him. By taking the first step toward reconciliation, Father, you could return yourself to a position within the secular hierarchy where your guidance could have some meaning, where gradually you could regain the confidence of the Czar. By care and unhurried effort, you might divert him from his present course toward eternal damnation."

"I cannot compromise my faith," he replied guardedly.

"I do not mean to imply you should, Father," I said. "But how much more beneficial would be your influence upon the immortal souls of all Russia – to say nothing of the Czar's – if you could offer some spiritual guidance to the court, not guiding us so completely as you would like in the early stages, perhaps, but gradually, as your influence becomes reestablished, you will surely be able to bring the Czar – and all of us – back into the life of goodness and true faith."

When I finished speaking, the silence of the room crowded in about me, and I again became aware of the closeness. With the ever–present odor of the rushes, the atmosphere was mildly unpleasant.

Phillip sighed again, very deeply this time. Wearily, with a great effort, he rose from his chair. "Tell the Czar," he said, "that the Metropolitan will await his coming, whenever it is convenient. I will bestow the blessings I have previously withheld, and I offer my services as it is proper I should."

He stepped around from behind the table, laying his hand gently on my arm. "It is not that I want this conflict, Prince Marensky. Please assure His Majesty I desire only peace upon his house and within his realm."

Once outside, I stood gazing up at the crosses atop their golden copulas, barely visible against the blackness of the sky. I hoped I had succeeded with Phillip; yet somehow I felt I had not. He had made a tenuous concession, at best. Toby came up from the shadows and asked if I wished to ride home. It was now nearly dawn.

"No," I told him. "I would prefer to walk home." I wanted time to think before I entered the house and was confronted by whatever problems would await me there. We left the Kremlin through one of the smaller gates.

The guards were surprised to see me on foot, but they passed us immediately. One man offered a lantern, which I declined. Our route lay just along the edge of the Square of Executions, dominated now by Ivan's new church. At night, its gleaming white columns seemed to rise in regal splendor against the blue–black sky. Oil lights had been planted in various spots around the base of the building, where they cast a soft glow over the entire structure.

The visit with Phillip had done nothing to ease my own confusion. Now I could only wait, hoping some good would result. The probability did not seem great. The Metropolitan was a most holy man, and I do not exaggerate when I imply that the people already considered him a saint. He had been born into a wealthy family, coming from noble, respected lineage. He had not chosen the Church as a path to wealth or greatness; these he already had.

Phillip had been Abbot of the Solovetsky Monastery, far in the north, on an island in the White Sea. The area was so remote, considered so barren and desolate it was best known as a place of exile for men who had fallen into disfavor. Sylvester had been sent there when the Czar ordered him from court. I did not doubt there had been conversations between Ivan's former confessor and the Abbot, until everything known to Sylvester was known to Phillip. In many ways the two thought alike, although their methods of expressing these beliefs were quite dissimilar – so much so, one tended to look on Phillip as an embodiment of holiness, while regarding Sylvester as a madman.

When the former Metropolitan Alfanasy had died, and the bishops had sought a replacement, the two major contenders had been Pimen of Novgorod and Herman of Kazan. The Czar, as was his prerogative, had intervened. Through his influence over the clergy, Phillip was elected. And here was another example of the Czar's strange mixture of attitudes. He *knew* how Phillip stood on moral issues. He should have foreseen the new Metropolitan's reaction to the *Opritchina*. Still, Ivan selected him. Nor could the Czar have anticipated a weak leader, for Phillip's reputation was well established. As Abbot of Solovetsky, he had brought enlightenment to the northern wilderness. His administration of the monastery had gone beyond the exceptional. He had started a reindeer farm and a salt factory; he had caused part of the swamps to be drained, permitting the monks to farm during the few warm months of summer. The roads had been improved until the island could easily be transversed by the heavy carts used to carry blocks of salt. In all, he was an amazing man of unbounded energy. I knew he would never give in to Ivan. The only possible compromise would be for the Czar to reform his ways.

As we approached my street we began to hear riotous sounds, these from several houses where members of the brotherhood were carrying on their usual, nightly bacchanals. Staying in the shadows, lest we be seen by someone wandering outside to urinate in the street, Toby and I reached my own house. I had to knock for several minutes before Teshata, my stepfather's personal servant, cautiously peeped out the grill in the front door. Recognizing us, he opened it and began to recount the events of the last few days. What he said was not encouraging to my hopes of reuniting the Czar with the Metropolitan, and his words made me impatient. Teshata had never been a man whose company I could enjoy. He looked like a weasel, and his mind fit well with the body. A Tartar turncoat whom Heinrich had befriended long before Kazan, the man seemed to worship my stepfather, and Heinrich refused to get rid of him. When I had heard enough I sent the servant off to bed. I then retired myself, exhausted and more than ready for sleep.

In the morning I had a short breakfast with Heinrich and the Bomels. Elysius was exuberant, bubbling with enthusiastic accounts of court developments. Heinrich sat silently for most of the meal, but I caught him glancing distastefully at the doctor several times. Elysius began questioning my feelings on this and that, friendly chatter for the most part, all apparently quite innocent. Again, I noted the expression on Heinrich's face and realized he was warning me.

"Your Doctor Bomel has his fingers in too many plots," Heinrich told me afterwards. We had walked to the stables together, and stood chatting while the grooms were putting a saddle on Gabriel. "The astrological predictions he is making are too flavored with innuendoes, hinting at results favorable to his own friends. I would be careful of him, Demetrius."

I thanked him and mulled over his suggestions as I rode the short distance to the Czar's *dacha*. Was no one above suspicion? It made one question the concepts of man's basic goodness. Ivan had just returned from his prayers, and received me immediately. I recounted my conversation with Phillip, and spoke as encouragingly as I could of my hope that they might reach an understanding. I am not sure how convincing I was, but Ivan seemed to be pleased. I hardly finished, though, when he abruptly announced some unhappy news.

Mikhailof was no longer his secretary, nor was he head of the Bureau of Secret Affairs. Before I could ask what had happened to him, Ivan waved me silent. Triumphantly, he walked to his table and opened a drawer. "I should have told you last night," he said, "but I wanted you to see for yourself." He handed be a letter. "You have been trying to tell me there is no conspiracy. Take a look at this!"

The letter had been addressed to "M" – I discovered this referred to Michael Vorotinsky. It was a promise of very great honors from the King of Poland, if the Prince would forsake his Czar and lead the *Zemschina* in revolt against him.

"Sigismund seeks to turn our supposed weaknesses to his own advantage," Ivan chuckled, "but the final service performed by our former head of the third bureau was to unmask the others who were supposed to receive these treasonable communications."

"There really was a plot, then," I said, without meaning to express my surprise quite so decisively.

"Yes, there *really* was!" Ivan boomed. "I was not so mad as you though me, was I?" he crowed.

"I never though you mad," I replied softly.

"But you did not think there was a plot, either," he retorted, "and now you see there was."

"I see only that the King of Poland would like to foment a conspiracy," I said. "Who else received these?"

"No one else *received* them," he told me pointedly. "But they were being sent to the most prominent men in the *Zemschina:* Mstislavsky, John Bielsky . . . a few others."

"What have you done about it?" I asked.

Ivan started to laugh. "The first thing I have done is to prepare this certificate," he said, handing me an ornate parchment scroll. I started to open it, but he stopped me. "Read it later," he said. "It names you to head the Bureau of Secret Affairs," he added casually.

Before I could react to this, he went on. "Vorotinsky brought this letter to me as soon as he received it, and by his quick action I was able to apprehend the messenger. His name is Kozlov – a Russian, not a Pole. He is being questioned now." Ivan leered meaningfully. "He had the letters for the others in his possession." He handed me several other messages.

"Have you allowed anyone else to learn of this?" I asked.

"Not yet," he said, "but I intend it shall be known by every man in Russia. The perfidy of the Polish King shall be doubted by none – not even the Metropolitan."

I had been thinking as quickly as I could, listening to Ivan and trying to foresee what he was likely to do. To me, the King's actions seemed aimed at creating whatever dissension they could. If he could capture the loyalty of just one leader within the *Zemschina* he would have achieved an immediate advantage. But he must have foreseen the possibility of exactly what had happened. If Ivan struck down these leading men, as a result of the King's unsolicited communications, it would also favor the cause of Poland. Besides, all three of these principal boyars were friends, not only to me, but to the Czar. Mstislavsky, of course, was Simon's father–in–law. I did not wish to see any of them destroyed. "I might make a suggestion," I said at length.

The Czar stopped short and waited for me to continue.

"Why don't you answer the letters in the names of the supposed recipients?" I asked. I awaited his reaction, hoping he would formulate the rest of the idea without my having to present it. He regarded me silently for a few moments, obviously intrigued by the suggestion and its many possibilities. "It might be amusing at that," he mused.

"As a condition of their cooperation, they ask for the whole of Lithuania – or the King's domains in Prussia or White Russia," I urged. "If Sigismund ever committed himself to give these up, think what chaos it would create in his own realm, when the present holders of those lands discovered his plans."

Ivan laughed as if someone were tickling him. He held his sides and whooped, making such a racket it brought Fedka Basmanov to the door, two guardsmen close behind him. Ivan waved them away. "Dmitri is not trying to murder me," he squeaked, "unless by making me laugh myself to death. All right, all right – get out!" he shouted at them.

He turned back to me once the others had withdrawn. "I see I was right in choosing you for your new post," he said, more seriously. "I hope you have no – er, reservations in accepting it."

This would have been my chance, but I knew better than to take it. "The responsibilities are heavy," I replied. "Are you sure I am the one to do it?"

"You have just proven it," he chuckled, starting to laugh again. "Oh, what a trick to play on that Polish ass!"

"I shall caution the three gentlemen to keep it secret, then," I said, "and we will have to find some excuse for the messenger's having been taken." That I had also placed Ivan in a position where he must allow all three *Zemschina* boyars to live did not seem to have entered into his considerations.

"Once we have all the information we can get from the messenger," I shall order him terminated," Ivan said easily. "Later, we shall let it be known we have taken a Polish spy, but everyone will believe he was captured empty–handed and died without giving us any information."

"Best if he were said to have died while being captured," I added, and the Czar agreed.

I left the palace a short while later, and spoke to the three men concerned. Each was in a state of high anxiety, for Vorotinsky had informed the others of their danger. Seeing me on their doorsteps, they must have been certain the Czar's minions were close behind. When Mstislavsky realized I was not there to arrest him, he fairly wept for joy and relief. Vorotinsky greatly embarrassed me by falling onto his knees and kissing my hand. Horrified, I pulled him to his feet, begging him never to do such a thing again. His jaw trembled a little when I reminded him of our year's campaign together, when I had been a very junior officer and he the Czar's imperial general. It was unseemly, I told him, for a man of his dignity to so humiliate himself.

"The day may come when the world stands right side up again," he said as I was leaving. "I pray we may all live to see it."

The third call I made was to John Bielsky, the son of Johannes. He was a few years younger than I, and since the death of his Uncle Dmitri he had come into all the family lands and wealth. However, he had been badly stripped by the Czar's grants to the *Opritchniki,* and I think he was in poor financial shape at the time. I am also certain he was in the process of gathering together the things he wished to take, in preparation for flight. I pretended not to see any of this, and simply gave him the Czar's message.

"I am certain your conduct has been above reproach," I assured him, "and you may rely on the Czar's continued favor."

He looked at me disbelievingly, but I think he understood what I was trying to tell him. When I left he thanked me, his gratitude best expressed by his refraining from the histrionic displays of the others.

That night the Czar was in high spirits, and told many obscene stories at the table. He had ordered all three hundred of his inner circle to attend him, as well as the usual court hangers–on. To this point, I have refrained from describing some of the more dreadful acts I saw committed, for they would add little to my narrative. To this very day some of them still haunt me. But I must tell of the events this evening, for they bear heavily on all that came to pass the next day.

Among the letters intercepted by the Czar had been one intended for old Prince Federof, a poor dottering ancient, who had already been elderly when all of us were children. He was a distant cousin of the Czar's, having been related to his grandmother. That Sigismund had written the old man denoted how poorly informed he was – else that he intended his messages to be intercepted. I could not imagine the King doing this without Kurbsky's advice, and Andrew certainly knew Federof would be unable to help anyone in any conspiracy. His only position was as it had been for as long as I could remember – a fixture about the court. As a courtesy, he was invited to every large banquet. Unfortunately, this reverence for age and a venerated record was not shared by the newcomers of the *Opritchina*. They looked upon the old man with scorn and referred to him as the "Old Fool."

After dinner this evening, the Czar became extremely drunk. The more he drank, the less humor he saw in the attempted conspiracy by the King of Poland. Near the end of the meal, he got up and called to Federof. By then, the old Prince had fallen asleep in his chair, snoring softly and dreaming, no doubt, of his youthful glories. He came awake with a snort, much to the amusement of everyone. Ivan ordered him to sit in the imperial chair.

Once Federof was on the throne, Ivan removed his crown and his ermine robe. He placed them on the old man, who stared at him in consternation, not knowing exactly what to do. Turning to the rest of the company, Ivan began telling them of a suspected conspiracy, instigated by the Polish King. As he spoke he continued to excite his own emotion, though he was clever enough not to reveal knowing about the letters. Soon, he had rambled on to his old complaints against the Church and boyars, who now denied him the rights he felt he had won on his first flight to Alexandrov.

"In taking back my crown, which you all know I once before tried to give up," he said, "I was assured there would be no further treachery. Now, I find it more rampant than ever before. Therefore, I give my crown and my high office to this loyal, venerable Prince, the friend of my father and grandfather."

The Czar began bowing before Federof, and making all the courtly obeisances required by Byzantine lore. Everyone was laughing, and seemed to accept Ivan's behavior as genuine humor. But I knew him too well. I could hear the malice underlying his words. He bellowed suddenly to silence the company, demanding to know why they did not also bow before their Czar. Soon all of us, the full three hundred, were on our knees before Old Federof, bowing and touching our foreheads to the floor. Ivan continued to rave about the treachery of his boyars and others close to him in his court.

I wanted to step forward and somehow end the farce; but there was no possibility. Glancing across at Heinrich, I could tell he shared my feelings. I do not think Ivan had any plan to his actions, and when he started I am sure he did not know how he would finish. Neither did anyone else. Suddenly, without warning, Ivan drew his dagger and turned on the old man.

"As I have placed you on the throne," he shouted, "so can I remove you!"

With that, he stabbed the aged Prince through the heart. Federof's eyes bulged almost from their sockets. His mouth hung open in disbelief as he tumbled from the throne and sprawled onto the floor at Ivan's feet. Without wiping the old man's gore from his blade, Ivan stuck it back in its sheath. He pulled the robe from the dead man and shrugged it back onto his own shoulders, still wet and discolored by the Prince's blood. He motioned Skuratof and a couple of others, ordering them to remove the body. With that, the Czar retired.

I left a few moments later, knowing I was going to be sick and not wanting anyone to see me. Unfortunately, in taking the shortest way out of the house I found myself in the courtyard where the old man's body had been taken. Skuratof and his fellow fiends were attacking it with their knives, cutting loose the head and the private parts. Seeing me come out they called merrily that I should join them. I muttered something about being on an errand for the Czar, then stepped around the corner where I could vomit without their seeing me.

I knew it would take less than an hour for this story to reach Phillip, whom the Czar intended to approach the next day. How he would react to such behavior I was almost afraid to think. When I finally finished heaving, I whistled for the stable boy, mounted Gabriel and went directly home. I had left Toby to look after the house, for the servants had reported someone prowling about the night before. I trusted the boy's judgment better than the older servants, should it prove to be someone other than a common thief. Because of my position with the Czar, many people tried to reach me, asking that I intercede for them. I never knew who might be lurking around my home.

When I reached the door, I knew something had happened. Lights were burning in nearly every room. The shutters were still closed on the lower floors, but they had been opened upstairs. The front door swung inward before I could knock, and Serge stood there grinning at me. Nina was right behind him!

I froze, dumfounded. Jacob walked out of the salon, and I knew what had happened. He had been due to arrive at my Marienburg *dacha* later on the same day I had left. He was coming to Moscow to pick up another shipment of horses for the army. Nina must have persuaded him to bring her. I went inside quickly, and slammed the door shut behind me.

My composure exploded into a flood of angry words – expressing the frustrations and fear my wife's presence evoked. "What do you think you're doing?" I shouted. "I told you to stay in Livonia I *ordered* you to stay! I turned on Serge. "And you!" I continued, grabbing him by the collar. "You little ferret! I specifically ordered you to remain in the house with your mistress, didn't I?"

The little man grinned innocently. "The mistress said she wished to return," he said, still with that silly smirk on his face. He infuriated me. Because he was really the only person I could do anything to, I ripped off his belt with my free hand and thrashed him soundly – right in front of everyone. I then had some especially well–chosen words for Jacob. I ended by ordering him to take care of his business as fast as he could, and to make arrangements for my wife to return to Livonia with him. I can not adequately describe the deadly fear that gripped me, having Nina in the city at that specific moment.

After finishing with Jacob, I started to calm down. Once the others were gone I turned to Nina. She stood stock still, her face drained of all color. She had said nothing as I harangued the servants. I took her in my arms and kissed her, and told her how sorry I was to have acted as I did. I tried to explain the danger if she should remain, but she refused to understand.

Passionate, as all Italians, she would not accept my explanation. She had already been upstairs, she said, and she was sure she saw evidence of another woman's having been there. That this had happened before I went to Marienburg to visit her made no difference. Her ideas of proper marital conduct were much different from ours, and she refused to hear me. Finally, however, I was able to convince her of my love, and I proved it many times that night. It was a continuation of our Midsummer's Eve on the country estates.

But very early the next morning, while we were still in bed, I made it clear I still intended she should go. We began to argue again. Speaking softly, so we would not be overheard, I tried to tell her what had happened, and how the responsibilities of my new office were going to place me in an especially dangerous position. Nothing convinced her, and in desperation I described the happenings of the previous night.

This so shocked her, she began to revile the Czar, calling him a monster and a perverted demon – all manner of terrible things. Her voice was completely uncontrolled, speaking half in English, half in Russian. I was sure we must be overheard, and whoever was assigned to spy on my household would certainly report this to the Czar. I tried to stop her, and finally shoved her down on the bed, pushing my arm into her mouth to quiet her. I explained, as carefully as I could, the peril in which she was placing us. Then I let her go, and she started screaming all over again, repeating the same, terrible things about the Czar.

My eyes fell upon the whip hanging above our bed. I could think of nothing else to do. Out of fear for both her safety and mine, and I must admit in anger as well, I seized the handle of the leather weapon and I beat her. I curled the cruel, braided surface across her naked body, time and time again, until at last she fell weeping upon the bed, moaning that I was the monster and she did not know why she had ever married me. I threw the whip into a corner and left the room, colliding with two servants who had been listening at the door. I boxed the ears of one, as the other scurried away. But at least I could now be sure that the only report made would reflect no dishonor on me. As long as I remained in favor with the Czar, all of us were safe.

Jacob was unable to leave that day, because we were short of men to drive the horses. The Czar had ordered seven hundred animals, and a transport this size required at least a hundred men to act both as drivers and guards. I was tempted to send Nina off without waiting for the shipment to be ready, but other factors intervened to forestall any immediate action. Not far from our door, Skuratof and his gang – followed by their motley crowd of ruffians and vagabonds – were rampaging through the streets. I issued a stern admonition to the entire household, insisting they remain inside with the downstairs shutters closed. They were to open the door to no one but Heinrich or me, should my stepfather decide to return. He had spent the night in the Czar's *dacha,* as he had learned from servants' gossip of Nina's coming and did not wish to intrude.

Before leaving the house, I went back to Nina's room, tapped softly and walked in. My wife was still in bed, for it was barely dawn, and she had apparently cried herself back to sleep after our dreadful argument. She drew herself into a ball, cowering under the covers when she saw me. I sat down beside her and tried to comfort her, but she cringed at my touch, trembling like a trapped animal who expected death. I spoke to her as soothingly as I could. I stroked her body, moving my hands back and forth beneath the quilt until she responded, tentatively touching my hand with her own.

Before we were finished it had become a scene of tears, forgiveness, and passion – such passion that we became oblivious to the screams and shrieks of terror and death outside. Mingled with the other sounds were shouted obscenities and loud, coarse laughter. But our lovemaking was able to overcome these distractions. Symbolically, it marked another achievement in our marriage. We never again allowed such misunderstandings to come between us. Nina knew my decision had been correct. Regardless of my deep, abiding love, I had been willing to deprive myself of her company to better assure her safety. Perhaps the old maxim was right: Beat your *shuba* and it makes a warmer coat; beat your wife and she will be sweeter. Of course, I had never treated Nina as a proper Russian husband should have done. She was from another land, where women were not trained as ours were; it was not easy for her to accept these differences in our ways of life. In Russia there was no law of redress for women. But, as Nina observed that morning, there currently seemed to be few laws for men, either.

I had dallied much longer than I should have. I rolled off the bed, pulling on my clothes as quickly as I could while the noises outside drew closer. Before I had finished, Toby was knocking on the door. "Master," he called. "Master, they're heading this way!"

I pulled on a pair of felt boots, leaned over Nina and kissed her once more. "Stay in the house," I reminded her. She nodded silently as I dashed out the door and down the stairs, Toby right at my heels.

"How many men have we in the house and stables?" I asked.

"About twenty, counting the house servants," Toby said.

"Then get them all inside," I told him, "and have them meet me in the front hall. Now move!"

I went into the room off the salon which served as my office, picking up my new commission from the Czar. I had tossed it onto my writing table, unread, where it lay amidst the usual confusion of shipping lists, orders and account books. I unrolled the scroll, and quickly scanned the lines. As I had hoped, it contained a clause authorizing me to command the services of any Russian citizen below the rank of prince or boyar, to assist me in my activities. In the next line it placed an injunction upon those of higher rank "to cooperate in all things." Poking the scroll under my arm, I returned to the front hall, where my servants and Heinrich's German retainers were gathering.

Once all of them were there I made a short speech, commanding them to remain on the grounds until I instructed them differently. They were to safeguard my wife above all else, I told them; and then, as if to add official sanction to my orders, I emphasized that the contents of my office must not fall into anyone else's hands. The room was locked, I said, and it was to remain that way. I read a portion of the scroll to them, for no public announcement had yet been made of my appointment to head The Third Bureau. If nothing else, I intended they should fear me enough to assure their obedience. When I finished we could hear the rampaging mob near our front door. They had no business here, for the entire area was *Opritchina* territory. But they were drunk, and probably cared little for rules.

"Are we really in danger, Dmitri?" came a voice from the back of the group.

I had been about to go out the door, and turned sharply at this familiar form of address, ready to chastise the speaker. But it was Elysius, who now spoke Russian so well his accent was not even noticeable.

"Where have you been?" I asked in surprise.

"I was with my – our friends for a while last night," he said, "until their activities became a little too athletic for a man of my years."

"You mean to tell me you've been in the house all this time, and I didn't know it?" I didn't know whether to be annoyed or amused. A couple of men chuckled, but I silenced them with a glance.

"My wife and I have continued to avail ourselves of your most gracious hospitality," he reminded me, adding, "but we have always endeavored to remain in that portion of the house assigned to us, and not interfere with your familial . . . er . . . adjustments."

"Doctor, I fear you are a great fake," I said in English, amused in spite of myself. "Since you are so well liked by my comrades, suppose you come with me."

"It is said in my country, my *former* country," he replied smoothly, "that discretion is the better part of valor. In this case I prefer to follow the advice of our Western sages."

"Just remember what I've told the others, then," I said, and started again for the door. Toby clutched my arm.

"I'm coming, too," he said.

I was about to tell him to stay, but seeing his earnest face and determined stance, I agreed. I might need someone with me, if only to run a message or perform some other task requiring more than one set of eyes or hands. Toby was steady, and fast becoming a man – a brave man, at that. I clapped him on the back, and we went outside together. The mob was gathered in front of John Chibotovy's house, just one down from mine.

"Go get us two horses," I told Toby.

"Shall I bring Gabriel?" he asked.

"No; he's too conspicuous," I said. "But get two good mounts."

As I waited for him, I watched from the steps. Men were milling about, swilling down mead from a barrel which John had set up in the street before his portals. Someone was standing on top of the cask, speaking to the crowd; but he had his back turned and I could not see who it was. Toby arrived with the horses and, clasping the scroll tightly under my arm, I mounted. Together, we rode into the group, who stepped back to let us through.

As I should have guessed, the speaker was Skuratof. He was obviously as drunk as any other, and appeared to be sustained by liquor rather than sleep. His eyes were bloodshot, almost dazed. They peered out from two black sewers in his sallow face. I was fast growing to hate this man, but for the moment I knew better than to challenge him. We were both of the brotherhood, so it behooved us to pretend a friendship in public. I have little doubt, though, that his feelings toward me were much the same as mine toward him. I also sensed that he was afraid of me, which was my greatest advantage.

"What merry adventures have you planned for today, Malyuta?" I called.

"We may have some bishops' robes before the day is done," he shouted back drunkenly. "Are you going to join us?"

"I'd like to speak to you first," I said.

"Speak," he replied. "These men are all of the brotherhood." He spoke haughtily, knowing the crowd was made up of his own men, many of whom were certainly not of the brotherhood.

"I see a few faces here I do not know," I replied cautiously.

"They're all good fellows," he insisted, at which there was an almost menacing growl from the group surrounding me.

"Still," I insisted, "I have some tasks to perform for the Czar. These concern you and me, not these other – gentlemen."

He did not answer me at once, and I think he actually contemplated setting the mob on me. It was one of the few times in our relationship where he had the advantage. But he was too clever for that; I was mounted and might well have escaped. It would be one thing to explain my corpse to the Czar, quite another to stand before my accusing finger. With a great show of joviality, he leaped off the barrel, hollering for his men to drink their fill as he came to me.

Once I was sure the men were sufficiently occupied, pushing and shoving like so many hogs to get at the barrel tap, I slid off my saddle and stood with Skuratof. The man reeked of spirits, although his stance seemed surprisingly steady. In a feigned camaraderie, he started telling me of his adventures during the night. They had found Federof's wife, he said, and dispatched her after "inducing" her to entertain them for an hour or so. He would have gone on to describe the robbery and looting of several merchants' homes, but I stopped him. The murder of poor Federof's widow was enough. The woman had been several years younger than her husband, but still quite elderly. However, she had lived a virgin, despite her marriage. She had been a young girl when she wed the Prince, and the marriage had been only a protection lest another claim her hand. She had been a true ascetic, doing all the things that had been improperly attributed to Maria Maddelana. While she had lived her life in a virginal state, Skuratof had apparently changed that just before her death. The man revolted me! The old woman must have been close to seventy.

Trying not to display my anger, I pulled the Czar's scroll from under my sleeve and started to show it to Skuratof, suddenly remembering he did not know how to read. I was about to read it to him myself, when Toby's horse shifted its weight and happened to nudge my back. Looking up, I noticed several of the men around us. They had filled their bumpers and were standing about watching. Taking advantage of Toby's position, above us on his horse, I handed him the scroll and told him to read it aloud. "Just the important passages, the ones I read to the staff this morning," I said loudly. "No need to burden these good fellows with all the details."

Toby cleared his throat and began shouting the Czar's commission, but not exactly the way the Czar had worded it. The differences were so subtle no one realized he was not actually reading them. Clever lad, I thought. In my excitement, I had forgotten Toby did not know Russian script, although he could do very well with the Western alphabet. He proved his quick wit by recalling the text, almost exactly, from just having heard me read it once. When he finished he rolled the parchment and placed it on his saddlebow.

Skuratof and his men were silent. The Czar's commission had surprised them. I am sure it also frightened Malyuta.

"Now," I said, getting back onto my horse, "I am going to tell this to you fellows just once. I have gone to a great deal of trouble to negotiate some delicate business for His Imperial Majesty." In this, I referred to the pending reconciliation with Phillip. "And this nonsense is not helping me at all. I want every one of you to go home and get some sleep. You are not to assemble on the streets again until either the Czar or I give you permission. I shall leave Captain Skuratof to see my orders are carried out."

That placed the responsibility squarely on his head, and I knew he would not dare cross me. However, I also knew I had deepened the hatred Malyuta bore me. I rode away without further comment, without allowing anyone time to protest. Actually, I had exceeded my authority, for I was sure the Czar would not have ordered his *Opritchniki* to desist.

I went directly to the Kremlin, where the government bureaus still operated, and walked into Mikhailof's old office. The clerks, busy clearing out his things, bowed and scraped when I entered. I ordered the flock of them out of the room and went through what papers I could find by myself. After an hour or so I called the head clerk and told him to send a message to the Czar, requesting an audience.

"That is never necessary, sir," he replied. "As head of the Third Bureau, you may always attend unannounced."

His officiousness irritated me, but I decided not to make an issue of it. I ordered him to continue packing Mikhailof's possessions, adding that I expected him to complete the job with care. I thought he regarded me with some surprise, but the cause for this was something I was only to discover later. Mikhailof, his wife, his children, his servants – even his dogs and cats – all had been obliterated during the night's orgy by Malyuta Skuratof and his pack of raging madmen. Such was the way it could happen, more than ample justification for my domestic arrangements. My life was the Czar's, but I could not bear to think of Nina or my own children being in the hands of such a monster as Malyuta.

When I found Ivan he was in the dining hall of his *dacha*, and had been drinking vodka since coming from morning prayers. He was dressed in his black abbot's cassock, but I could see the gold of his robe beneath it.

"I was wondering when you would get here," he shouted. "Are you ready to attend upon the Metropolitan?"

"Right now?" I asked.

"Certainly, right now! Why not right now?" he bellowed.

"I think he is conducting services in the Cathedral," I said.

"All the better," shouted the Czar. "The multitudes shall see him bless me. Get your robes, Dmitri, and come with us."

Most of the Three Hundred were quickly assembled outside, as couriers were dispatched to collect them: Basmanov, Viazemsky, Saltikoff, even Fedka, who had just been initiated. They all wore their black habits, and several had donned the dog–faced masks. I called a servant to bring a cassock for me, and a few minutes later I joined them. It took Ivan a little longer to come out, during which time I called Toby aside and sent him home to assure Nina I was all right. He was also to instruct Jacob that I wanted the shipment of horses on the highway first thing in the morning. I did not want my wife in the capital for one night more than was absolutely necessary.

Ivan came out, and the company rode to the Cathedral, a mass of black–robed monks, nearly three hundred strong. To those who saw us we must have appeared like the demons of death and pestilence. I think I was the only sober member of the group, for the others had consumed vast quantities of spirits, and were shouting and singing as we rode. Most of these men were very young, many being second or third sons of wealthy families. Some of their fathers were members of the *Zemschina;* but this did not spare them. The brothers of the *Opritchina* were true to their oaths; the Czar came before all else.

At the Cathedral, we dismounted and flocked inside. We could hear the service in progress, for the chorus was chanting and Phillip was speaking the liturgy very loudly, endeavoring to be heard above our voices. The inner doors were thrown open with a crash, and our group swept in. While nearly the entire congregation turned to look at us, the Metropolitan hardly paused in his recitation, going on as if there had been no disturbance at all.

Ivan walked directly to the front of the church and knelt before Phillip. The Metropolitan ignored him, simply continuing with his service. After a few moments the Czar stood up and moved a few feet closer. Still, the Metropolitan ignored him. Again, the Czar moved closer, this time being so much in the way, the Metropolitan had to move around him as he continued with the liturgy. When Phillip still refused to recognize the presence of the Czar, one of the fellows behind me – Viazemsky, I believe – shouted loudly: "Holy Father! The Czar Ivan, son of Basil, asks thy blessing!"

At this, the Metropolitan stopped the service, gesturing the chorus into silence. A deathly hush fell over the entire vault, for until this moment the people had continued to whisper among themselves, wondering what was going to happen next. Standing directly above the Czar, Phillip looked down upon him with a scornful expression.

"Who do you think you are imitating?" he demanded. "You are falsifying your faith behind a costume you have no right to wear."

The Czar bowed his head, contritely, and by this motion made clear his request for absolution and blessing. I believe, had Phillip said the proper words right then, the whole future might have been very different. But the Metropolitan was also a mortal man, and he failed to seize the opportunity. Instead, he began the most vicious denunciation he had ever made of Ivan, calling him a dishonorable sovereign, who had offended against his people. He accused the Czar of having shed more Christian blood than all the princes of Islam, and ended by threatening him with the judgment of Heaven.

Ivan allowed him to finish, remaining all the time with his head bowed. If even then, after saying all these harsh things, the Metropolitan had granted a mere suggestion of grace or blessing for the humbled Czar, it might still have been well. Again he withheld it.

Ivan stood up slowly, and though I was behind him I could tell he was in a towering rage. He lifted his *kisten*, and for a moment I feared he would thrust it through the priest's frail body. Instead, he pounded the steel tip against the agate floor. "Monk," he shouted, "it shall be as you have spoken. I have come to you for your blessing and for God's forgiveness, and I have humbled myself before you, and before His holy alter. But you have seen fit to reject my humility. I have spared you rebels too long! Henceforth, I shall behave with the character you have given me!"

With that, the Czar strode from the Cathedral, leading us back to the horses. He mounted, and his gaze darted back and forth among the masked, black–robed figures until he recognized me. "You see, Dmitri?" he called. "Even you could not persuade him!" He then led us, at full gallop, out of the city

It was now late afternoon, but still warm. We were in the early days of September, when the sun expends its last, sudden spurt of warmth before the cold winds descend from the north. The Czar ordered a whole cow roasted on a spit to feed us, and a large pavilion with tables was set up in a meadow outside the city walls. It was a pleasant site, far enough from Moscow that we could roister about without attracting a crowd of curious onlookers. We ate and drank very heavily for the next few hours, until nightfall found many of the brothers beyond any reason or sensibility. Skuratof had joined us by then, and much to my surprise Heinrich appeared as well. In fact, my stepfather, Malyuta, and Fedka Basmanov were drinking together when I first noticed him. I was sitting with Michael Morozof and Fedka's father, Alexi.

I called to my stepfather, asking all three to join us. The hostilities of the morning seemed to have dissipated, at least temporarily, as in our drunken states Malyuta and I were able to be friendly – or civil – to one another. Heinrich had recently returned from some joint trading venture, involving our own merchandise as well as the Czar's. I had heard it rumored that he was dealing in slaves, selling Livonian prisoners to the infidels; but I did not wish to believe it, and lest my fears be confirmed I did not ask. The others had been discussing Heinrich's experiences when they came to our table, and I heard my stepfather remark on this being his first opportunity to relax for several days. The Tartars were beginning to threaten trouble again, he said, and he further surprised me by launching into a vehement denunciation of all barbarians. Prejudice against the Tartar race had always been common to our class, but I had never heard Heinrich speak out so strongly. As we had gathered in Tartar lands, and added the former infidel nobles to our court, it had been necessary to change some of these old feelings. My stepfather had been one of the first to recognize this.

I glanced at Malyuta, whose features reflected agreement with Heinrich's words. "Lowly swine," he growled, "black, base–born curs, the lot of them." His aging child's face was contorted with hate and contempt. Of late, Skuratof had made much of his being related to the Bielskys, even hinting at some illegitimate descent from old Johannes. While I doubted it, I never made mention of my feelings, as I was not one to speak against this sort or inheritance. Yet, his use of the term "base born" amused me.

I was more than ready for home and bed, looking forward to my last night with Nina, when Ivan suddenly leaped to his feet, commanding us all to mount. The disorder that night was led by the Czar in person for he wished to impress the Metropolitan with the sincerity of his promise. A great many *Zemschina* houses were broken into, the occupants killed and their valuables taken. The women were raped whenever they were found, usually by ten to fifteen men. Nor were the younger sons always spared. It dismayed me to see not only the Czar, but my stepfather engaging in some of these acts.

I prayed that God would read my thoughts, for I did not do any of this with my whole heart. However, especially after having brought the morning's rampage to a halt, I was being watched by more than one pair of eyes. I had no choice but to join with the others. While I tried to tell myself that I experienced no joy, my flesh was weak and the pleasurable sensations flooded my being. This was surely a sign of my hardened consciousness, and the depraved state of my soul. When I finally did go home, well after dawn had broken, I went into a back bedroom and bolted the door. I was ashamed for Nina to see me with the blood of slain men on my clothing, and with my body still reeking of rape and pillage.

Several *Zemschina* boyars had been killed during the course of the evening, among them Vorontsof's old friend, Vassily Pronsky, the Prince of Riazan. At least I did not add to my own shame by having a personal part on this; but I saw it happen. Vassily was an elderly man who had been advisor to Ivan's father and a great *hetman* in the old days, before the conquest of Kazan. This night he was flogged to death, being dragged to his place of execution from the chapel where he had been at prayers. He had long taken the tonsure, though he remained at home instead of entering a monastery. From the Pronsky house we also took the son of Turanty–Pronsky, who was drowned in the river after several of the brotherhood had stripped him naked and thrown him down in the street, using him as a woman. But this younger man had always been of questionable loyalty and had been closely allied with the Shuiskys; while I regretted the manner of his death, I had little sympathy for him.

With all these images in my mind, it was some time before I was able to fall asleep, even behind the securely bolted door. When I did drift off, my body collapsed into a deathlike slumber, my senses so numbed I had no dreams. Thus I was not on hand to see my wife depart. But I do not think she knew I had returned. I later wrote her a long letter, begging her forgiveness and her love. The answer expressed her understanding and her deep concern.

With the strife between the Czar and Metropolitan, the increasing blood lust of the court, and general disorder within the capital, I suddenly found a great many duties thrust into my unwilling hands. Before me, Mikhailof had inherited many responsibilities as a result of Adashev's removal. Now, despite my being commissioned to head only The Third Bureau, I discovered many people looking to me for other decisions and assistance. Among these were some of the foreign delegations, most especially the English. All but one of the men who had returned from London with me were still in Russia. Sir Jerome Horsey headed the party, as Commissioner of the Muscovite Company, although I believe Thomas Randolf was the Queen's accredited Ambassador at this time. In the more than two years they had been in Russia, Randolf had been granted only two personal interviews with the

Czar; Horsey had but one. They now came to me, prevailing upon our past friendship, and asking that I use my influence to gain the concessions they wished from Ivan.

I made an appointment to interview both men in my office. I knew very well why Ivan had not been friendly, and so did they. The Czar was offended on the same two counts: The Queen's failure ever to give a proper answer to his proposal of marriage; and secondly, her failure to send Jenkinson back to Moscow. Casting all diplomatic nonsense aside, I told them exactly what their problems were, probably offending Horsey, because he was there in Jenkinson's stead. By being honest with them, I made a lifelong friend of Randolf, who at the conclusion of our exchange made a peculiar statement – a warning, really – about Doctor Bomel.

"I see the old dog is performing his old tricks," he quipped.

Unfortunately, right at this point in our conversation, I had been speaking to Horsey, and I did not pick up quickly enough on Thomas's comment. When I thought of it again, they had left. Afterward, the whole incident became lost amidst a deluge of other worries, thoughts, and labors. It was some time before Doctor Bomel or the English delegation – or anything else – came close to distracting my attention from my duties imposed by the Czar. Immediately after my conversation with the English, Ivan sent word for me to attend upon him at once.

"I am going to do something about that priest!" he shouted by way of greeting. "As my head of Secret Affairs what are you going to do to assist me?"

"The first thing I am going to do is ask you to fill the vacant post of Your Majesty's personal secretary," I said. "Then, I'm going to ask that you appoint a new man to head the Bureau for Entertainment of Foreign Ambassadors. If I am to be effective in the special operations of my office, you must take these others off my shoulders." No one else spoke to Ivan like this anymore, and I did not do it often. It always surprised and amused him when I did. But his mirth was restrained this time. "Consider it done," he said with surprising ease. "Now answer my question and don't try to evade the issue!"

Now really "on the spot" as the English would say, I was momentarily without an answer. The tale of Thomas 'a Becket was not unknown to me, and the two situations bore several frightening similarities. Perhaps I was doing the devil's handiwork, but I suggested old King Henry's solution, neglecting to add that the process had also gained sainthood for the Archbishop of Canterbury. Or course, I never expected our contest with Phillip to go beyond simply deposing him and sending him into exile.

"Has there been an audit of the Solovetsky accounts?" I asked.

"You don't believe Phillip would –" The Czar's face broke into an evil grin, and he started to laugh like a strangling crow. "Ha, ha, ha, ho, ho, he, he, he!" He ended in a violent choking, coughing fit. He spat several times onto the heavy Persian carpet. "I am assigning Malyuta to assist you," he said, suddenly taking on a benevolent tone. "You can send him to Solovetsky to look over the ledgers."

"Malyuta cannot read," I answered coldly.

"Who would you suggest we send?"

"Any clerk would do. Mikhailof had several who –"

"Do not mention the name of that traitor in my presence!" snapped the Czar.

I cleared my throat. "Well, one of the clerks can go. Perhaps Skuratof could act as protector, and question the monks while the clerk goes over the accounts."

I was speaking very boldly, with an uncontrollable tone of disrespect. Inwardly, I cursed myself for plotting Phillip's downfall, wondering if anything could ever excuse my complicity. But the Czar did not notice my coldness, nor did he seem aware of my distraction at any time during the conversation. Distraught as I was, the prospect of getting Skuratof out of Moscow for several weeks was a boon I could not fail to seize upon.

As for Ivan's assigning Malyuta to assist me, I could not have been less pleased. The only happy aspect to the relationship was that it now forced Skuratof to be my subordinate. He would surely resent the status, having always been jealous of my position with the Czar, but he would be clever enough not to allow anyone else to see it. Before he left for the north country I had a long conference with him, and made it clear I expected more than mere suspicion if he returned with any charges to be leveled against the Metropolitan. In talking to him alone, I was surprised to find a fairly penetrating mind, albeit evil and sinister. Watching him depart, I considered myself fortunate not to be the one he sought to destroy.

While Malyuta was gone, there continued to be angry words between the Czar and Phillip, but nothing more than this. Ivan was biding his time, waiting for the results of our investigation. Overwhelmed by my own guilt, I took it upon myself to speak once again with the Metropolitan. But now everyone knew of my position, and even this holy man was afraid of me. He refused a private interview and met me in the presence of several other clerics. He repeated some well-known maxims, quoting long passages from the scriptures to justify his own position. My most pointed impression was of a frail, very mortal man – somehow a strange contrast to the saintly figure I had previously carried in my mind. Phillip was human, and he was afraid. But fear, as it so often does, served only to make him appear braver in his stance against the might of the Czar and the *Opritchina*. Slyly, as if anticipating Malyuta's find, Ivan's tactics turned toward the material possessions of the Church.

Because our war in the West had continued, spasmodic as it was, it never ceased to be a drain on the Czar's treasury. Fearful lest he be beggared by such expenses, Ivan began to tap the greatest source of wealth in the realm – the churches and monasteries. He also demanded adherence to the laws made during the time of Adashev. The Church was called upon to give back the lands left to it by the patrimonial estates of deceased boyars and other wealthy landholders. His first move in this direction was to enforce the laws regarding forfeiture of estates when a man was executed. Until now, if a prisoner had left a portion of his properties to the Church, the Czar had allowed these to pass as bequeathed, taking only the remainder for himself. Over a violent protest from the Metropolitan, Ivan announced that henceforth the royal treasury would receive it all.

Then we began taking a closer look at the properties belonging to the individual parishes and abbeys. Many parcels of land had passed to these surrogates of the Church since the formulation of laws to the contrary. The Czar demanded these acquisitions also be immediately ceded back to the crown. When protests were made by the fat priests and other clergy, the Czar ordered them arrested. I was responsible for a number of these apprehensions, and I must admit that I did not perform the tasks with any great feelings of shame or guilt. As a result, I became the recipient of a personal denunciation by Phillip, who condemned me by name along with the Czar.

This only reaffirmed the opinion of many people who had secretly accused me of being ungodly, because of my life–long attitude toward the clergy. I did not feel such charges were justified, for while I had come to despise most churchmen, I dearly loved the Church and the Holy Beings it represented. My resentment was directed at the greedy priests, whose avarice was unbounded. Their justification for existence was some alleged relationship to Almighty God, whom they actually mocked by their own luxurious manner of living. At this time the wealth of the monasteries and cathedrals was so vast no man could estimate it. The Czar was right to restrict their growth, even to confiscate. Naturally, we did not take it all. As a gardener trims the excess growth from a plant to make it bloom more fully, so we sheared the bloat from the Church. But, with all my well–founded reasons for opposing the churchmen, I tremble to think of my responsibility in bringing about Phillip's indictment. I consider this the greatest blot upon my account with God, and I pray I may be forgiven.

Skuratof's absence from the city did not, in any way, restrain the *Opritchina*. The constant raiding and harassment of the *Zemschina* boyars continued. When the Czar himself was not with the raiders, Alfansy Viazemsky and Fedka Basmanov generally took the lead. Because of an increasing threat from the Tartars to the south, and the prospect of future battles with the Pollacks, I prevailed upon the Czar to place our greatest generals under his personal protection: John Mstislavsky, Michael Vorontsof, and John Bielsky. My original list had been considerably longer, but Ivan pared it down. As a result, a great many others perished – some of whom we sorely missed in the days to come.

The Rostovsky brothers and their families were completely obliterated. Two were already dead, for they had been executed while trying to flee into Lithuania after Kurbsky's desertion. The third commanded our army in the east. Fedka led some thirty men to Nizhny Novgorod, arriving before the news of his coming, so the soldiers did not know to defend their general. Wearing masks to terrorize the troops, Fedka's company rode through the camp, dashed into the commander's tent, and beheaded him without further ceremony. Leaving his body to be disposed of by the soldiers, Fedka rode back to the Czar, carrying Rostovsky's head in a game bag.

We were at dinner when he brought it in, and kneeling before Ivan he bared the trophy at his feet. I am sure Fedka meant this as a grim joke; he was always full of mischief, and was one of the few who could play tricks on the Czar and get away with it. With a roar of horror, Ivan kicked the head away from him, shielding his eyes with his arms, as if to ward off some evil emanating from the skull. It upset him so badly he was unable to finish his dinner, and he retired to the chapel to pray. We did not see him again that night.

But Ivan's reactions were never consistent. The next evening he suddenly bolted up from the table and ordered Temgryuk, brother of the former Czarina Maria, to seize Tiutin, who was then the treasurer – the second since Fumikov. While Tiutin was apparently honest, I think Ivan was especially annoyed with him for failing to confiscate some gold from the monastery in Pskov before the monks were able to hide it. Of course, Tiutin had been too young for the office to begin with. A dark, prettily handsome youth, he had been a childhood playmate of Fedka's and undoubtedly received his appointment because of this. When the evil, grinning barbarian had dragged the boy into the middle of the room, inside the horseshoe arrangement of the tables, Ivan casually ordered that his treasurer be severed.

Several brothers left off their meal and leaped upon the prisoner, ripping away his robe and immediately carried out the sentence on his naked, thrashing body. First, they removed the nails from his fingers and toes, then the digits themselves. After this, they cut away the hands and feet and private parts, finally separating the limbs at knee and elbow. Ivan watched them, calling out advice from time to time, berating them for being drunk and clumsy. Through it all: the rivers of blood, the hideous shrieks of agony, he never missed a bite. He continued eating until he had his fill, washing down each mouthful with a heavy draught of wine. I suppose I was becoming hardened to all of this, because I sat and watched, unable to eat, but drinking small sips of wine while my mind seemed to drop a curtain between the struggle on the floor and my place at the table. I saw it all as if gazing at a distance painting which had miraculously achieved the ability to move. Before it was over a message arrived for me, which could have provided an excuse to leave. One of my spies had just returned from Tiutin's house where others of the brotherhood were disporting themselves with his wife and servants, before subjecting the entire household to the treasurer's fate. A few months before, I would probably have excused myself from the table, but on this night I did not. My soul had decayed to such a degree that I did not even wish to leave. Even more surprising to me was the Czar's failure to enter his chapel afterward. And the next morning he spent only a short time at his devotions.

No doubt my heart was becoming hardened to all this bloodshed. While often avoiding direct participation, I frequently watched in fascination – and, yes, sometimes in lust. I carried a terrible burden of guilt deep inside me, allowing the world no glimpse of the torments that rose to haunt my dreams. But I never turned away to be sick anymore, and I no longer felt the desperate compulsion to flee when some particularly gory scene was to be enacted. In fact, some acts were done on my orders, although some definite purpose was supposed to be served by each instance. Essentially, there are three reasons for subjecting a man to torture: to abstract information from him, to punish him and make an example of him for others to see, and finally – as was the case for most of the assaults by the brotherhood – for the amusement of the torturer. It was this third reason that had no justification, in the eyes of the Metropolitan, although we continued to maintain that the lives of the victims were being sacrificed to gain peace of mind for the Czar. The bodies of his subjects were his property, anyway, to be used as he saw fit. The *Opritchniki*, as figurative extensions of the Czar's being were also supposed to be acting in his stead, and for his benefit.

An overall result of the terror, of course, was to stamp out every vestige of revolt. Each man feared his neighbor. My spies were so active that men who had been lifelong friends no longer dared speak a word to one another if it could be construed as treason. On the Czar's instructions I prepared a daily list of men who might be suspect. From this, he selected the ones to be removed, and while the names taken from my list were always arrested and executed, they were certainly not the only victims.

Shortly before Malyuta returned from the north country, an incident took place which was given great attention in foreign lands; much more notoriety than it deserved or would have received had Heberstein, the Austrian Ambassador – and a notorious gossip – not happened to be present. This was particularly unfortunate, as some of our delicate foreign negotiations were disturbed by the rumors he carried home with him.

On the Czar's orders, I had dispatched a pair of brothers to perform the routine execution of a former clerk and his family. My instructions were standard under the circumstances: the entire household was to be eliminated. Instead of doing their job properly, the fools returned that evening when we were sitting about after dinner, entertaining the Ambassador with drink and stories. (Heberstein was quite elderly at this time, having originally been sent as ambassador to Basil's court.) One of my men carried in a baby boy in his arms!

Before I could stop him, he and his brother had approached the Czar, probably hoping their behavior would attract his attention and hence his favor. Bowing before him, they explained that they had found the child in the house and taken pity on it. Ivan looked at me with annoyance, but I could only shrug and hope his anger would not extend beyond the two dolts who stood before him. Impulsively, the Czar held out his arms, and the man gave him the baby. For a moment Ivan peered into the infant's face, and I heaved a sigh of relief, assuming he was about to have one of his strange swellings of remorse and would spare the child.

Ivan cast his gaze on the Ambassador, as if to say: "See how merciful I can be?" I motioned for the men to take the child back from the Czar, but they did not act quickly enough. Suddenly, the naked infant began to shriek, and without warning urinated all over Ivan's robe. In a blind rage, and now completely oblivious to the Austrian's presence, Ivan stood up and pitched the child through the nearest window. The Ambassador sat with his mouth open, and later embellished his tale by stating the bear pits had been beneath. That was simply not true. Bears were never kept in that part of the palace yard.

The two stupid wretches who had disobeyed my orders were quite properly strung up and punished – sliced by swords, as I recall. I can no longer remember for sure. But their executions were carried out by my orders, not the Czar's. As the Austrian later told it, Ivan had taken personal pleasure in having the men tortured for showing pity to an infant victim. How easily words can be twisted from the truth!

The Austrian Ambassador was only one source of diplomatic problems. As always, the various bureaus were going about their business, functioning in the calmer waters beneath the troubled surface. The English were the first to make efficient use of this circumstance, working through the appropriate offices to obtain concessions to use our newly acquired Baltic ports. I knew what they were doing, and I watched with some interest, never letting them know I was aware. Inevitably, they reached a point in their own intrigues where the clerks were afraid to make a decision. I received a note from Horsey, just after Ivan had announced his intentions to leave again for Alexandrov with the entire court. The Englishman was about to start his trip north, to Kholmagora, although the weather was already turning cold. I had previously done all I could for him with the Czar; now, as a result of the good will I had helped establish, the petitions coming to Ivan through the Bureau of Trade were being approved!

I made some inquiries, and realized that Horsey had made a bold move, and a dangerous one. He had promised to try persuading the Queen to reconsider Ivan's proposal of marriage, leaving the impression that he expected to be successful. As a result, the Czar had sent his third Czarina off to a convent, proclaiming himself free to marry and expressing his intention to await the Great Queen's decision. In anticipation of this, he granted the English permission to use the Baltic seaports. After listening to Horsey's lengthy description of plans to reach Kholmagora before the heavy snows, I made some remark about the greater ease they could enjoy in the future, landing at Ivangorod and coming to Moscow over the western trade routes. To my surprise, he indicated that the English intended no immediate use of any western facilities, expecting we would lose them at any time. Questioning him further, I discovered that the concessions we had given the English had created a more serious problem with the Danes than we had realized. Horsey, who had spent the last month in Pskov, related several pieces of concrete evidence to the effect that the King of Denmark was preparing to launch an attack against us in the spring. Even now, Horsey insisted, the Danish army was being assembled. Coming upon such information in this manner did not speak well for the efficiency of my western agents, but I was very grateful to get the story at all. I made haste to inform the Czar, and we immediately began formulating plans for defense. Ivan ordered me to Livonia to investigate.

I was overjoyed to be heading west, while the rest of the *Opritchina* galloped like a great black cloud across the early snows toward Alexandrov. By a little care and manipulation, I was certain I could prolong my stay through Christmas and Epiphany – a season that was most important to Nina, as it was to most Westerners. I still remembered how sentimental the English would become on the anniversary of our Savior's birth.

Inevitably, my route led through Novgorod. As I approached the walls, I could see a mass of dark storm clouds gathered on the horizon, to hang menacingly above the gray stones of the city. I cursed silently under my breath, for I would have no alternative but to remain until the storm passed.

Darkness brought an unexpectedly heavy snowfall, which lasted all the following day and ended only when the bitter north winds began to howl that night. I had traveled with only Toby and a lightly armed group of men for escort, as I wanted to make the best time I could. I had not ridden Gabriel, as he was getting too old to face such extreme weather. My present mount was not nearly as good. All things considered, I was afraid to set out for Pskov until the skies promised at least a full day of good weather. This dalliance in Novgorod brought the predictable discomfort of an invitation to dine with the Archbishop.

If the Pimen I remembered had been unpleasant, the Pimen who now sat at head of the table was completely unbearable. With every mouthful I took I was made to feel guilty for my own survival. As much as he must have hated Phillip, Pimen maintained the Metropolitan's right in all things. Once he had thoroughly taken me to task for my sins in supporting the Czar, he started on Ivan himself. Did I know, he demanded, that the heavens would open and swallow us if the Czar did not cease his flirtations with the Lutheran rites? Did I expect the Czar to allow himself to be converted? He ranted on for a good hour about this, referring to

Ivan's conversations with old Ebervelt, who had been Martin Luther's student. If the Archbishop had been as well informed as he should have been, he would have known Ivan always enjoyed conversing with foreigners, especially religious men. His talks with Ebervelt had been no more than this. But Pimen built his case on the English Queen's Protestantism. Knowing Ivan desired her hand, the Archbishop was certain of his conclusions. After parrying his original onslaught, I tried to explain the difference between Lutheran heresy and the Anglican beliefs. I comletely failed to penetrate his pre–formed opinions; but at least the discussion took his mind off further condemnations of the *Opritchina*.

The source for much of this blasphemy against the Czar had been another letter from Kurbsky, delivered in Moscow just before I left. Its contents were well known in Novgorod, as Andrew had seen to its printing and distribution before he had the courtesy to send the original copy to Ivan. As always, I left Novgorod with a feeling of tremendous relief and wished I never need visit it again.

In Livonia, I was received with such overwhelming joy it almost made the intervening absence worthwhile. Nina, lovely as ever, ran out to greet me before I dismounted. The children had sprouted like weeds, and young John was developing into a sturdy lad, giving the appearance of being much more than his three years. Demetrius was also large for his age, but of a much quieter disposition. I was very proud of both my sons, and I spent as much time with them as I could, taking them for long rides on my saddlebow, playing soldier with them, and generally assuming my proper role as father.

While I disported myself with my family, several agents from The Third Bureau were at work. It did not take long to uncover the poorly devised plans of Sigismund and the King of Denmark. The threat was not nearly as serious as we had feared, but circumstances required my making a hasty trip to Riga. I did this just after Christmas, and for my own pleasure as well as cover for my true purpose, I took the family with me. We spent Epiphany in a lovely castle, atop some cliffs which marked the edge of Pruss. While chill north winds came in strongly off the sea, it was not nearly as cold as it had been inland.

The boys and I played in the snow, enjoying the freedom and the different landscape. Even Nina joined us, and we borrowed some of the small sleds used by the children of the region, on which we took turns sliding down the shallow hills. It was a wonderful time of peace and relaxation. My love for Nina had mellowed into a relationship of warmth and greater depth than one can experience in the early stages of marriage.

Being so far from the horrors of the capital, my wife had ceased to start at every sound, and no longer looked over her shoulder when we walked outside. A few minor skirmishes had been fought within earshot of the Marienburg estates, but we had a large force of retainers nearby, and there was not the terrible fear one experienced in Moscow. Lately, our armies seemed to have gained a greater advantage than they had the year before, or the year before that. Victory, even a small victory, always tended to raise their spirits. After concluding my business in Riga, I was convinced the family could safely remain in Livonia, for which I was extremely grateful. Before leaving for Moscow, I remembered to render thanks to God. At the same time I prayed He might find some way to permit my quick return. The life of a simple country squire seemed ever more attractive.

CHAPTER VI

I reached the capital in late February, to discover the city enjoying a tentative peace and quiet. The court was still in Alexandrov. After spending an uneventful night in my own house – also strangely quiet with neither friends nor family about – I was pleasantly surprised to be joined by Heinrich. He had been in Kazan, and was on his way to the Czar - coming to Moscow, because he thought the court would be there. My stepfather had aged badly in the last few months, and now looked his full fifty years. The gnarled muscles of his powerful arms were still hard as stones, his back was straight and proud as ever. But crisscross lines around his eyes and on his neck cut heavy paths through the leathery skin. His eyes, themselves, looked very tired, and his once–blond hair was mostly white.

Perhaps it was anxiety that made him appear as he did. When we left together for Alexandrov, he told me of his problems, which were disturbingly similar to my own. He was vehement in expressing his dislike for the very things he now found himself enjoying. He especially detested Skuratof, too, with a passion nearly equal to mine. As he did not share my strong religious convictions, he said, he despaired of being beyond redemption. Nor was he able to find consolation in calling his behavior a service or obedience to the Czar. It was his own lust and depravity, he insisted, that led him to act as if he were demented. I suggested that his being forced into the company of men like Viazemsky and Malyuta might be the cause, but Heinrich only shook his head and continued to blame himself. In this, he made me question whether my own excuse – that of following the Czar – would spare me the scourge of heaven.

". . . and if the Czar destroys the Metropolitan, as it now seems likely he will," Heinrich continued, "all who take part in such sacrilege will forever forsake hope of forgiveness."

Heinrich had been present when Skuratof returned from Solovetsky, and was most disturbed by his observations. Malyuta had brought the new Abbot with him, a poor excuse for a churchman named Paisy. I knew I should not condemn, as it had been my idea to examine the accounts; but I had not fully anticipated the results. By making the suggestion I had postponed having to face the issue, thus avoiding it for the moment. Now, all the frightful evil I had sidestepped a few weeks previously was coming into full bloom – bearing much fuller fruit, for Paisy was a factor I had been unable to foresee. The exact opposite of Phillip, the Abbot was fat, indolent, and sly – a classic example of the most objectionable form of clergyman. When I first saw him at Alexandrov, I could easily have mistaken him for a Tartar merchant had it not been for his clerical garb. If he had been a Persian, he would have been selling carpets. I knew his projected testimony against the Metropolitan could only be sheer perjury. But, I did not learn the full extent of this evil man's accusations until I had spoken to the Czar.

Our sleigh paused only a few minutes at the kiosk of the *Unfreedom*, while I talked with Ivor and his guards went through our baggage. My friend still remained in his office, here, as he had since the founding of the abbey. He was badly frightened by all he had seen, even more so by the tales brought back by soldiers who attended the Czar. Other than superficial hearsay, however, he had little information to give me. The most difficult aspect for Ivor to believe, I think, was that so many of our brave commanders from past campaigns could have been traitors, and executed as such. He was most upset over Sheremetief, whom he had personally served. While he did not openly chastise me, I knew he felt that I shared the blame for some of this; but he was afraid to express his thoughts. With his typical humility, he did not consider himself competent to pass judgment. We broke off our guarded exchange when his men announced they had completed their inspection of our baggage sleigh. Heinrich heard the soldiers laughing with Toby and Teshata, who were riding in the second conveyance, and remarked on its being the last sounds of mirth we would hear.

We progressed from the *Unfreedom* into the strange grandeur of Ivan's wilderness retreat. The natural beauty surrounding Alexandrov was completely lost, once one passed the kiosk. All I could see were wooden walls, gradually being replaced by stone. Ugly, rough–hewn buildings surrounded the Czar's palace, most of them large barracks to house the brotherhood and their servants. There were also a few separate houses for men like myself, holders of important government posts. Here, at least, I could maintain an office and have a degree of privacy. As we entered the first of several inner courtyards, I noted a number of visitors among the crowds of black–robed brothers. Nearly the entire *Opritchina* was in residence, as well as many priests and high clergy. Strangely enough, with a crowd that choked the narrow passages between the buildings, and all the motion of their seemingly pointless wanderings, there was hardly a sound. Heavy layers of snow lay over everything, except where ragged footpaths cut through the waist–deep cover. Snow always creates a singular quiet, yet the silence of Alexandrov reflected more than this. The atmosphere was muted, like the universal mood of the place. Even with the sun reflecting brightly off snow–covered roofs and ground, the enclosure seemed gloomy and foreboding.

The Czar had summoned the foremost authorities on canon law, I found, as well as other leading churchmen. He intended to gain their support in his coming contest with Phillip. I doubt if any bishop had been pleased to be invited, but all of them came. They would have been afraid not to accept. A good example was Cyril, Archimandrite of Sergey–Troitsky, with whom I spoke at length that afternoon. He frankly admitted to coming only because he feared for his life were he to refuse the Czar's invitation. He obviously wanted to say more, but did not dare – at least not until later in the evening.

I remained with Cyril through dinner, which was attended by a good three thousand of the brotherhood, all in full clerical costume. I had not been present for matins, breakfast or lunch; but I presumed the routine of these had been the same as before. Such mockeries of church rituals must have appalled Cyril, as his eyes – if not his voice – made clear. At the end of the meal, as the brothers began their accustomed heavy drinking, the Abbot drew me aside. "Could you spare me a few more moments?" he asked.

"Certainly, Father," I told him. "I must attend the Czar for an hour or so, but would very much enjoy talking with you afterward."

We arranged to meet in the chapel, which I was sure would be deserted. The brothers made certain they were present at any service ordered by the Czar, but they were seldom seen to enter the place of prayer on their own.

Leaving the Archimandrite, I went to join the Czar in his private apartments. In jarring contrast to the cells of the brothers, Ivan's rooms were dazzling in their magnificence. The furnishings were all of the richest brocades and damasks, mostly from Cathay and India. The carpets were the thickest, finest examples from beyond the Inland Sea. Brilliant blues and reds clashed with equally vivid yellows and greens. The tables were covered in velvet, and cloth of gold hung from the walls. In the midst of all this vibrant color, the Czar sat upon a low dais, dressed in his somber black habit. The air was heavy with perfume and incense. Drapes had been drawn across the doorway leading to the *terem* rooms, where I knew Ivan had at least a dozen women.

Fedka let me in, and quickly withdrew when the Czar and I began to converse. Our conference consisted mostly of reviewing the information brought by Paisy. The accusations were so gross I was appalled the Czar had accepted them. If he merely intended to discredit the Metropolitan, he had no need to mount such a vicious prosecution. In my opinion, it would have been better to accuse Phillip of lesser crimes, acts the average person might believe him capable of committing. As Paisy told it, Phillip had virtually looted Solovetsky of its entire treasury and had lived the life of an unmitigated profligate. During our discussion, I hinted at some of these thoughts, but I could see Ivan tense when I had barely started to speak. Acting in shameful cowardice, I pressed no further and ended by lavishing praise on Skuratof's labors. This weak, half–hearted beginning of a protest that never materialized had been the only voice lifted in any semblance of defense for the Metropolitan. His fate, sealed during these days at Alexandrov, was nearing its final, unholy implementation.

I met with Cyril as I had promised, and soon discovered the source of his agitation. The Czar had offered him the See of Moscow – a bribe to assure his cooperation in the removal of Phillip. Being absent from the capital, I had not learned of this until my conversation with the Czar a few moments before. The Archimandrite was another very sincere holy man. He was tall and slender with a dignified bearing, though I think he did not possess either the enormous energy or the penetrating intellect of Phillip. His eyes continued to drift toward the holy icons as we spoke, and he constantly lowered his voice as if afraid the Lord would overhear him. "I have heaped irrevocable shame upon my soul," he moaned, "for I have been too afraid to refuse. Each day I have beseeched Our Lord to show me some way of dissuading the Czar."

"I am certain it has gone too far for that," I told him.

"Then may God have mercy on us all," he said sadly.

I watched his face as he spoke, able to note hardly a line or wrinkle. Because his habit covered his head, save just the face itself, only his beard protruded to proclaim his lack of gray. Cyril must be younger than I realized, I remember thinking. His coloring was such a gentle blond that at a distance, dressed in the white robe he generally wore, he appeared to be much older. Like Phillip, Cyril was of noble birth, and had chosen to serve the Lord because of his strong faith and conviction. The present conflict lay so heavily upon his conscience I could almost see his soul grappling to find an honorable solution.

"I have discussed all of this with your friend Joseph," he told me, referring to the former Metropolitan, who still lived at Sergey–Troitsky. "It was at his suggestion I sought you out. He felt you might offer some means. . . ."

"Phillip will be brought before an ecclesiastical court and charged with the crimes as outlined by Paisy," I told him. "Will you have the courage to go against the Czar when you're a member of the court?"

He regarded me thoughtfully before he answered. "Do you believe I could change the course of events if I were to do so?" he asked simply.

"Probably not," I said.

"And I might also find myself in the Czar's ill favor?"

I nodded. "Which would only result in the loss of two reputable churchmen," I added.

He did not fully understand me. "First you speak almost as if you would have me defy the Czar," he said, "and yet you tell me how hopeless it would be if I tried."

"I only present both sides of the dilemma," I told him. "In many ways, your problem is not so different from mine. I would obey the Lord if He would tell me what to do, but without hearing His voice I can only follow the dictates of my own conscience. I obey the Czar."

"But you do not agree with all he does?" Cyril watched me appraisingly, almost in dejection, for Joseph had no doubt led him to expect a nobler spirit in me.. "I see in Ivan the embodiment of a sacred cause," I explained. "He will lead our nation to a greatness it has never known before, and along with this he will implement the spread of our Orthodox faith. In doing this he will serve the Lord. If a few men – or a few thousand men – must die in order that it all be accomplished, it can be no more than fulfillment of the ancient prophesies. The scriptures warn us that the Lord may take strange means to work his will on us."

"In general, that is what I have tried to tell myself," he replied, "but when I kneel before the icons and speak only to God, I wonder if He does not see through such verbal travesty and condemn me for the coward I really am."

"We are all cowards at times," I said simply. I might have spoken more honestly, but Cyril was not a man I knew enough to trust with a full confession of my doubts. He would support the Czar's will, and this was really what I wanted him to do. It was clear that Phillip had already been marked as the sacrificial lamb, something neither the Abbot nor I could do anything about.

Following from the decisions at Alexandrov, there now came a continuous harassment of the Metropolitan and his staff. Hostile words were exchanged between the monks of the brotherhood and the priests of the Kremlin cathedrals. Because Phillip had been approached by a delegation of Novgorodski when he was on the way to Moscow from Solovetsky, Ivan harbored suspicions they might now support the Metropolitan. He decided on measures to assure the continued loyalty of this area. For a number of years there had been talk of a possible insurrection, and at Ivan's request my bureau maintained a close surveillance on the people. Because the fears were largely imaginary, my men turned up very little, which only served to convince the Czar of the deep and secret nature of the conspiracy.

The more he thought about it, the more convinced Ivan became that the Novgorodski had to be gathering strength in opposition to him. In a sudden gesture of annoyance, he dispatched Basmanov with a large force of *Streltsi* and *Opritchniki* to collect five hundred families from Novgorod, another hundred and fifty from Pskov. This was two months after his initial instructions to me. The hostages were returned to Moscow, where they were held to assure the continued good behavior of their neighbors. Only after this flock was secured within guarded residences inside the capital, did Ivan order the ecclesiastical court to convene.

At first, Phillip refused to come. The Czar informed him he would either attend on his own, or in chains; he would be allowed no other choice. The next day Phillip appeared before the court. I knew I should have been there, but every fiber of my being rebelled against it. For the first few sessions I managed to find excuses to remain away, attending to urgent business in my office. Ivan suspected how I felt, and possibly as an act of grace, he contrived an excuse to send me to Livonia. I left the next day, and did not return until the trial was long since over. Naturally, Phillip was found guilty, his conviction based largely on the falsified accounts produced by Paisy. I understand the Metropolitan had been very firm in his answers to the court and his accusers, telling the Czar he would rather die a martyr's death than see the terrible crimes of the brotherhood continue, without some voice being lifted against them. For a time, it must have seemed questionable as to who was really on trial.

Shortly before it was over, Skuratof journeyed to Marienburg to confer with me. Away from the capital and the rest of his friends, he assumed a rather pleasant demeanor. Had I not known the man as I did, I could almost have found myself liking him. Nina's reaction was also accepting, but she always seemed to find the good in a person. Malyuta's purpose in coming was to discuss some further investigations we were to conduct in Novgorod. The Czar continued to hear rumors of conspiracy and insurrection. He had been especially angered by the report of a sermon, delivered by Pimen in the Novgorod Cathedral, openly accusing him of persecuting Phillip.

Unable to avoid it, I made the trip to Novgorod, where I personally conducted the investigation, questioned dozens of people. Whereas I found widespread fear and confusion, there did not appear to be anything of a subversive nature. By early summer, I was convinced the Czar's anxieties were groundless, and I sent Malyuta back to make a full report. Using the excuse of further inquiries to be made in Pskov, I was able to prolong my stay into September. Having no plausible reason for additional delay, I returned to Moscow.

Although Phillip had been convicted several weeks prior to my arrival, he had not yet been removed from his See. Nor had he been restricted from conducting services. During the period following his trial he had apparently made no further statements against the Czar; at least I was not able to learn of any. Ivan seemed satisfied that he had frightened the Metropolitan into keeping still in the future – another serious underestimation of the man.

Shortly after my return, the open animosity began again. The Czar, with Skuratof and Viazemsky, became disgracefully drunk one afternoon, and just for sport ordered a half dozen bears turned loose in the *gostiny dvor*, the main bazaar. Soldiers had brought the cages up from all sides of the square. At a signal from the Czar, who was watching from the wall of a nearby *dacha*, the animals were all released at once. Before it was over, a number of people were killed, some by the teeth and claws of the rampaging beasts, others trampled in the ensuing panic. Bears, especially when starved as these had been, can be the most ferocious of animals and will readily eat human flesh. A number of children were devoured that day, and many of the people who lived through the attacks were maimed or disfigured for life.

As a result of this debacle, the Metropolitan unleashed his most violent attack against the Czar, the *Opritchina,* and all who served the "Anti Christ." This last accusation was the final stone; the Czar sent for me, as well as issuing summons for all his major officers and a large part of the brotherhood.

A meeting was held on about the fifth of November. I no longer remember for sure, but I know it was a few days before the feast of the Archangel Michael, which fell on the eighth. As he took the raised seat of authority, the Czar presented the most horrible appearance I had yet observed. In his fury and rage he had had pulled out nearly all the hair in his beard. What remained was a tattered few strands of reddish gray wool. He had been drinking for days, even taking spirits with him into his chapel. But these prayer sessions were shorter, now, and he did not beg God for forgiveness. Instead the Czar questioned Him, and beseeched the Lord to grant a sign of His Will, to offer some guidance in solving the dilemma of the Metropolitan.

The words Ivan had used in speaking to God were the same he repeated to us that evening. "It is the right of the Czar to do as he will with his people," he shouted. "Their flesh belongs to me; their souls are the only concern of the Church!"

I am certain that Ivan had contemplated some immediate action, but when it actually came to issuing the orders he trembled before the possibility of God's vengeance. He raged and shrieked about the Metropolitan's perfidious conduct, but ended without publishing the order for his arrest. Between then and the Feast of the Archangel, he had no formal banquets. Ivan's soul was in such turmoil he could not sit still long enough to go through the required rituals. Instead, he spent hour after hour in the chambers, attended by Skuratof, Fedka, and a few others. I had been casually invited to attend them, but it had not been a command and the odors coming from the air shafts were enough to keep me away. I shuddered to think what they were doing.

By this time I had been in the chambers with nearly all these men: Ivan, Skuratof, Viazemsky, Chibotovy – several others. Each of them had rooms beneath their homes where they could practice the skills at which they had become so adept. I alone, among the senior members of the brotherhood, had not installed any extensive amounts of equipment in the subterranean portions of my house. Mayluta chided me for this, but I had unlimited access to the facilities in the Kremlin. Except for the chambers beneath Ivan's *dacha,* those of the Third Bureau were the most extensive of any. But as Skuratof knew, I seldom used these, either. When I did, it was always for some specific purpose – extracting information, punishment for some offense that was politically unsuitable for public trial, or perhaps to give a recalcitrant man a taste of the alternatives, should he continue to disobey. On the surface, these all seemed innocent enough; although in the secret recesses of my own soul I knew that my motives were not always so pure. Especially as time passed, and my reputation – deserved or not – became so frightening, most men gladly told me anything I wanted to know, or performed any deed I demanded without my having to take them below.

Despite whatever gratification I received in situations where I could control the action of the technicians, I eventually found it difficult to accompany any of the others into their beloved pits. In the very beginning I had expressed a simple horror, tinged with fascination. Later, these attitudes had given way to a hardening of my soul, in which I really did not much care what happened to the victims, convinced as I was that they were no more than pawns whose sacrifice was of minimal importance. But at the time which I now seek to describe, each of my *Opritchina* brothers had come to find a specialty in which he had honed some particular skill or set of conditions into a routine that more precisely matched his own perverse desires, and these went beyond anything I could accept or condone.

The Czar, who was the only one with the power to command my attendance, very seldom did so. In fact, he seemed reluctant to have anyone except Fedka or occasionally the Czarevich attend him. Thus I really do not know exactly what went on in his private chambers during this later period, although the rumors hinted at some truly monstrous activities including blood rituals and even cannibalism. His relationship with young Fedka remained suspect, as well, but I preferred not to think on this. I do know that, by and large, Ivan had always preferred to leave the actual performance of the various activities to his technicians, merely directing it all from the comfort of his chair. This may – or may not – have remained the case later on. There was also a story circulated to the effect that Ivan had a small amount of equipment in a room off his own chambers, where he and Fedka were said to perform certain rituals together – sometimes by themselves, else with the addition of a woman or a young boy.

As to the others, there was no longer any pretense of justification in what they did. Driven by a terrible blood lust, they sought to kill their victims in as painful a manner as they could. But each devised methods which were as individually gratifying as possible. Malyuta, for instance, took pleasure in prolonging the agony for days – weeks, if the prisoner was young and strong enough to withstand it. He delighted in having perfected more subtle methods of rendering pain than any of the others – doing it without causing the victim's immediate death. He used long needles, which he would personally press deeply into the large muscles of the chest or legs. With the patience of a woman weaving a piece of tapestry, he would insert hundreds of these, each bringing a shriek or groan as it entered, sometimes penetrating clear to the bone. As long as the victim remained absolutely still, the pain would subside. If he moved – or if she moved, for Malyuta particularly enjoyed females subjects – he caused himself to feel the agony anew. And Malyuta saw to it that his victim was always positioned so that his growing fatigue would eventually force him to move. He would also use smaller needles on the most delicate parts of the body – under the nails of fingers or toes, through the testicles or into the female organs, even into the eyes. He would cause liquids containing harsh caustics to be introduced via long tubes into the fundament, where they caused excruciating pain, as if the victims' bowels were being consumed. He would sometimes nail flaps of flesh to a board, eventually suspending his victim by several of these junctions. He might make a hole in the tongue or through the penis, and from these he would suspend a series of gradually increasing weights. While all of these methods caused dreadful pain, they did not immediately bring death.

Chibotovy, who was a great brute of a man with a big belly and cleanly shaved head, was much more gross in his behavior. He preferred the lash, and had a huge collection of scourges. It was said he once flayed a prisoner alive with a wire whip, starting at the ankles and working upward to the neck. He was also fond of boiling his victims in water or oil, but having them removed before the searing liquid brought death or unconsciousness – then leaving the wretch spreadeagle against a wall, manacled so he was unable move as various irritants were sprinkled on his wounds. As he always drank heavily during his sessions, he would eventually become irritable and impatient, usually assuring his subjects were dead before he left the chamber to stagger off to bed.

To me, Viazemsky was easily the most disgusting, although he was also the most interesting personality. A minor princeling, he had received some instruction in history and church lore. He could read and write, and always dressed well. Handsome in an indolent swarthy way, he was quick witted, and could be quite charming in a normal social situation. He was also totally fearless. He seemed to know that his present status and the power it gave him was eventually going to end, and he was determined to squeeze out every drop of pleasure before it was all taken from him. Nor did the prospect of his own demise seem to weigh upon him. He always gave the impression of being careless and lighthearted. And his passion was for children.

It made no difference to Viazemsky whether his subject was a boy or a girl, as long as he or she was young. He preferred pre–pubescent youngsters, but I know he had some quite extensive sessions with boys who had entered into the early stages of manhood. Except during the periodic rampages of the brotherhood, where even noble homes might be broken into and during which terem doors formed no barrier, it was easier to acquire young men or boys than it was girls. Regardless of the victim's gender, his sessions usually started in the same way, with his subject forced to perform a variety of sexual activities – always in his dungeon room, with the horrible, frightening equipment all about and a group of his flunkies looking on. The youngster would be bound and instructed as to what was expected of him. The child would rarely refuse to comply, but was often unskilled or so terrified as to be unable to obey. This would form the excuse for a progressively severe series of punishments and mutilations, eventually resulting in death.

I was only in his chambers twice, and my own sexual responses to the initial parts of his activities so frightened me that I refused ever to go again. Viazemsky, of course, perceived my unadmitted lust and made a point of teasing me about my own fear of damnation, and – whenever the occasion permitted – took great delight in describing his latest adventure in all its sordid details. At this stage of my life I still retained sufficient grace to be totally repelled by this evil man, and my skin would crawl as if covered with vermin whenever he came near. On the few occasions when he touched me it was all I could do not to cry out in sheer revulsion, for I knew – as he did – that I could easily fall prey to many of the vices I tried so desperately to condemn.

On the day of the Feast of the Archangel, Ivan sent for several of us. It was late morning, and while the Czar's eyes were very red, I could see he had only recently awakened – which meant he must finally have gotten some sleep. He was also reasonably sober. Custom required us to have a proper meal that evening, for this was one of the great feast days. It commemorated the festival of the harvest, among other things. The crops had been sparse, however, for the *Opritchina* had destroyed many fields of grain. Few of the peasants living near the capital dared venture outside to properly tend their farms. God had also sent an unusual amount of rain, which had ruined much of the wheat and rye before there had been time to bring it in. Nonetheless, the feast was traditional and there would be great crowds in the cathedrals. Ivan spoke to us for a long time, working himself into a terrible rage, and finally ordered us to seize the Metropolitan.

"He has been convicted of horrendous crimes," screamed the Czar, "and through my mercy he has been allowed to continue in his office. Now he blatantly betrays my trust and condemns me for nothing. Nothing!"

I held my breath until Basmanov was named to head the company, but I was never given time to heave the sigh of relief. Alexi immediately asked me to accompany him. I could see that he was disturbed by his assignment – perhaps frightened – so I did not feel I could refuse him. Only those members specified by Basmanov were to ride with us – some thirty in all. Each man wore his black cassock and cowl; and I wore my mask, as did most of the others. But I wore mine because I did not wish to be identified, should some violence be done the Metropolitan. Strange as it may seem, my own depravity never reached so low a point that I ceased to care what people thought of me. Yet to most honest men, like Vorotinsky and Mstislavsky, even my overtly admitted actions must have been revolting.

When our group arrived at the Cathedral of the Assumption, Phillip was in the middle of conducting service. I nudged Alexi's arm. "Better wait till he finishes, Father Bear," I whispered.

"Wait nothing!" bellowed Basmanov. Gesturing for his men to follow him, he banged open the inner doors of the church and led the black–robed company down the center aisle, shoving the crowds aside to reach the iconostasis. There were mostly common people at the service, all freshly scrubbed and wearing their best rags for the occasion. Dumbly, they stood staring at us, unable to believe we would commit such a sacrilege. At the far end of the church, the Metropolitan had tried to ignore us and was continuing with the service. By now no one was paying any attention to him. The attitude of the group advancing across the gleaming agate floor was too menacing to be ignored; even Phillip was human enough to be afraid. He broke off the liturgy and stood waiting for us. He was dressed in the full glory of his office, in his magnificent robes of golden cloth, heavily stitched with pearls and gem stones. A huge tiara crowned his head, and his fingers were heavy with the sacred rings. As we approached he spread his arms, allowing the full sleeves to hang like a jeweled replica of the icons which depicted Christ in the act of blessing the people. Phillip's eyes were sad, and the only words he spoke were to ask God's forgiveness for those whom he thought were about to slaughter him.

Instead, Alexi and two or three others bounded onto the raised area in front of the altar. Before anyone realized what they were going to do, they ripped the rich vestments from the Metropolitan's body. Their movements were so violent they tore his shift, as well, leaving the Metropolitan of Moscow standing naked before his congregation. Someone grabbed a cloth – one of the sheets used to cover the tables beside the altar – and Basmanov draped this around Phillip's shoulders.

With no further formality, they dragged the Metropolitan from the church. I had been standing toward the rear and stepped aside as they passed me, falling in behind them. There were several more of the brotherhood in back of me. Trailing our group, like a huge flock of multicolored sheep, the entire congregation followed.

Phillip was brought directly before the Czar, who hardly deigned to speak to him. Ivan had been drinking vodka while we were gone, and was barely coherent. "Put him in the Monastery of the Annunciation," he shouted. "Lock him up, and don't let anyone talk to him!"

There now followed a strange contest between the Czar and the people of Moscow. Once Phillip was placed in his cell, a great crowd gathered outside. They were not hostile, and no voices were raised to demand his release. They simply stood there, some with heads bowed in prayer, others merely staring at the windows they thought belonged to Phillip's cell, hoping to catch a glimpse of him. Ivan made no move to disperse the crowds, but several times during the next few days he had Phillip moved in the dead of night to another prison – there were several in or near the capital. Each time, the people seemed to know. Every morning found a new crowd outside the prison wall. They always looked the same – quiet, sad–faced peasants – people who could only stand and wait.

The day following Phillip's arrest, Ivan reconvened the court which had convicted the Metropolitan in the first place. This time he was charged with practicing sorcery. It took just one day for Phillip to be charged, tried, and convicted – all *in absentia*. Hearing of this, the Metropolitan sent word he would forgive the Czar, if Ivan would repent his sins. In a frothing rage, Ivan ordered irons placed on the Metropolitan's body and moved him to another prison. As the crowds continued to follow, the Czar became increasingly annoyed, referring to his people as "stupid cattle" – which they were. Finally, Ivan sent the prisoner north to Tver. This was far enough away to prevent the people of Moscow from standing to gape. Whatever crowds might still gather would no longer offend the Czar, for he would not see them.

At Ivan's insistence, Cyril came to Moscow and assumed the duties of Metropolitan. But while Phillip lived he refused to go through the ceremony of consecration. As the people more than ever considered Phillip a saint, Cyril had no desire to be remembered in history as the Russian Judas.

All these maneuvers had taken enough time for the tale of the Metropolitan's arrest to reach Novgorod and Pskov, from which areas my men began to report on the people's reaction. Along with these accounts – none of them especially disturbing – came a flood of rumors about another conspiracy. Try as I would, I could not discover the source, and every time my men followed down a lead it proved to be groundless. Several rumors implied that the plots were generated by followers of Phillip, indicating plans to march on the prison and set him free. Others blamed the unrest on activities by Sigismund's agents. But no one seemed to know anything definite, nor could I discover any facts behind the conflicting stories. Naturally, Ivan responded to every tale, being more agitated as the year wore on. I was convinced he expected a full–scale insurrection.

Because of Ivan's state of mind, I did not think it advisable to leave him. Thus I had to forego any plans for being in Marienburg over the holy days. I made only one short trip – in secret – to Novgorod. Into the new year, I had still been unable to uncover any plot. The only certain information I could report was that Archbishop Pimen was increasingly vehement in his attacks upon the Czar. These were never made in public, however, certainly not to the general populace, or from the pulpit. Pimen unleashed his venom in private, speaking to other officials or supposed friends, a number of whom were actually working for me. I had little else to tell the Czar until near the end of January, when a curious situation began to develop.

Two men, known to be personal henchmen of Skuratof's, were seen in Novgorod. My senior agent there sent me daily reports about them, these arriving regularly for about a week. Then they suddenly stopped without further explanation. For another week I received no word at all from Novgorod, and since I relied on my sources in that city to receive and pass on the reports from Pskov, I was getting nothing from there, either. Naturally, all of this was relayed to the Czar as soon as I knew it myself.

On the third day of silence from my agents, I requested permission to go in person to ascertain what had happened. Ivan told me to use my own judgment, but indicated he would prefer I delayed my departure; so I did. It happened, therefore, that I was still in Moscow when a dirty little beggar man, named Peter, hobbled into the Square of Executions. He mounted the *lobonoyo mesto,* and hammering the stones with his staff, called out to all who would listen: "Treachery in Novgorod! Beware, good people of Muscovy! You are betrayed. The Bishop of Novgorod would humble himself before the King of Poland!"

Without taking time to request instructions from me, two of my men seized Peter and brought him to my offices in the Kremlin. After questioning him for a few minutes, I sent word to Ivan. To my surprise, the Czar did not order me to bring the prisoner to him; instead, he came in person. It was the first time Ivan had set foot within the palace since his house had been completed in the city.

With the Czar came Skuratof, for the two had been together in the cellars when I sent my message. These sessions, incidentally, were now starting earlier in the day, and I was happy to supply the Czar with the able talents of my assistant – for whatever the Czar now did in his private cellars, he seemed willing to share the secrets with Malyuta. But I didn't care. It kept my assistant away, and allowed me to operate the Bureau without his constantly nagging for an explanation of everything I did.

As Skuratof entered the room behind the Czar, it seemed to me that a quick exchange of glances took place between Peter and my erstwhile associate. I was never able to prove any connection between them, though, despite Peter's story being peculiar and hardly credible. Regardless of my own doubts and suspicions, our meeting marked the beginning of a dreadful series of events, leading to such an avalanche of destruction as had not been seen since the hordes of Genghis Khan.

"Behind the Icon of the Virgin Mary, in the Cathedral of Saint Sofia," Peter wheezed, "there is a hidden letter, written by the Archbishop of Novgorod to the King of Poland."

"What is such a document doing there?" I asked skeptically.

"It has been hidden until it can be picked up by a messenger," Peter replied.

"What guarantee have we that the messenger has not already come and gone?" I asked, trying to hammer at him hard enough to shake his aplomb. He remained unruffled.

"The last messenger sent by the Polish King is dead," he replied flatly. "He was the only other man who knew the letter was there; he was a man called Quintus."

The Czar and I exchanged glances. Quintus had been my agent, but I was sure Ivan did not know that. "Who killed this fellow?" I demanded.

Peter grinned. "The men sent by Your Lordship to protect me," he whined slyly.

"I sent no men to protect you, as you damned well know," I barked.

Malyuta spoke up softly, modulating his tone as if he did not wish Peter, standing several feet away, to hear him. "I sent two men in your name," he whispered. In response to a flicker of annoyance across my brow, he added: "I am your assistant, am I not?"

I sensed the possibility of a trap, or at least a ploy on Malyuta's part to discredit me. I was not quite ready for a full confrontation with him, and he knew it. When I struck Skuratof down, I wanted enough evidence to destroy him completely. "You had no business interfering without advising me!"

I let it go at that, because Ivan had been watching us and I could see him nodding agreement. The situation was still potentially dangerous; the Czar had become so unpredictable I did not know what his reaction would be if he realized it had been my agent whom Peter accused of being Sigismund's messenger. If Ivan believed Peter, it was possible for suspicion to fall on me. It was not likely, I felt, but in these times one took no chances. It was out of this very situation that I was first forced to start thinking seriously of eliminating Skuratof, whom I was certain had similar plans for me.

"Is there any possibility of someone else removing the letter?" I asked at length.

"There would not have been time for word of the Polish agent's death to reach the King, and for him to have sent someone else," Peter wheezed. "Your Lordship can still get there first."

Ivan had been listening to us without comment. Now he spoke softly, but with a note of excitement in his tone. "You and Malyuta should leave at once, Dmitri," he said. "I must have that letter!"

"As Your Majesty wishes," I told him, "Get yourself ready," I ordered Skuratof. "I want to be underway in an hour."

Masking his usual surly response to my orders, Malyuta rose, bowed deeply to the Czar, and withdrew. Once he was gone, I turned to Ivan. "I don't know what you wish to do," I said, motioning for a couple of men to take Peter into the next room. "I know Malyuta's agents have been in Novgorod for several days, as I've already told you. I suspect this letter may not be genuine."

"That will make little difference," he replied harshly. "There is enough open treason in that city to more than merit punishment."

"Then we shall presume the letter is what it purports to be," I said simply. "But for the sake of our own knowledge and guidance in planning any future moves, I would suggest our friend, here," indicating Peter, who watched us apprehensively from the doorway, "be questioned in a manner to assure we have the full truth from him."

The Czar and I took a couple of steps toward the cowering beggar, moving close enough to detect the sour odor of his filthy clothing. "You always give me excellent advice," said the Czar with a chilling seriousness. "You may be sure I will personally see to it while you're gone."

"I can supply you with a clerk, if you like," I added. "It might be well to take down his exact words."

We had been speaking as if Peter were a dumb animal, unable to understand us. Whereas he may not at first have understood exactly what I intended, Ivan's words made him realize his danger. Forgetting his crippling injuries, he suddenly bolted for the door. Ivan made an involuntary move as if to stop him, but I motioned the Czar to leave it to me. The tramp flung open the portal, at which point two of my men fell on him in the hall. He struggled violently until his arms were securely bound, after which he sat dejectedly on the floor.

"I doubt he will have much to tell us," I said, "but he should still prove an interesting subject. A healthy man is always more of a challenge."

The Czar laughed harshly. "You are still closest to my heart," he muttered.

I returned the smile, but I felt a heavy lump in my stomach, as if someone had cut me open and inserted a cannonball. It was obvious to me that Skuratof had caused the letter to be planted, assuming it existed at all. If Malyuta were manipulating the situation, the truth might just slip out when the Czar questioned Peter. At least I could hope it might – unless, of course, Ivan had contrived the whole thing, himself.

I had given myself so little time, I was barely able to get home and speak a few words to Heinrich. The servants were still packing my saddlebags when Malyuta arrived with the rest of our men – my men, not his. As we planned a fast trip, we would use the Czar's post horses, which eliminated my having to take mounts from my own stable. Skuratof did not come into the house; in fact, I never invited him inside my home, except when I entertained and he was with the Czar. His absence gave Heinrich a chance to speak his final words to me alone. He had been drinking, and at first had seemed ashamed to have me see him. But he had come out when I knocked on his door, calling to him that I had to leave for the west. Though his voice was slurred, his mind seemed keen and alert. "For the good of your own salvation," he said laboriously, "do not allow a further fraud to be perpetrated against the holy men of Russia." He placed his hand on my shoulder, leaning heavily, regarding me with that unhappy seriousness one can manifest only with drink.

It annoyed me to see him this way, for I felt he should have been above such vice. I acknowledged his remark with a nod, otherwise not answering him. Drunk or sober, by stepfather was the one man to whom I could not lie. I did not know if he foresaw the sin I was about to commit, but I was certain he suspected its nature. "May God be merciful," he murmured as I opened the door to leave.

I looked up sharply at his uncharacteristic words. "I hope He will," I replied evenly. "Pray for me," I added, wondering why, even as I said it. No amount of prayer could ever cleanse my soul.

When I joined him, Skuratof was in a jocular mood, obviously very pleased with himself. He must have seen this trip as a culmination of the most devious plot his mind was capable of formulating. That the deceit he sought to foster was transparently clumsy, did not trouble him at all. He was oblivious to it. The Czar seemed to be in agreement, and what more could he ask? I was in exactly the opposite frame of mind as I mounted, taking my place at the head of the column.

Malyuta sidled up beside me, clapping his hand against my thigh. "We have a marvelous adventure ahead of us!" he said exuberantly.

I smacked his arm away and turned on him fiercely. "Put your paw on me again," I told him, "and I'll slit your guts!"

Even with frequent changes of horses, our trip to Novgorod was dreadfully slow. God did not seem to favor our mission. Two men were killed when their mounts slipped and fell on the ice – this when we traveled along the frozen surface of the river. For nearly the entire distance we had nothing but foul weather. A fierce snow storm held us up our second day out of Moscow, as howling winds forced us to seek shelter. This holocaust continued into the night, after which it started to rain. A soggy snow mixed with water continued to fall well into the next evening, and when it finally let up the violent winds resumed. To gain time we left the winding river bed and tried to follow the highway. The freezing air had left a crust soft enough for the horses' hooves to penetrate. Beneath this was two or three feet of soft, powdery snow. We floundered through as best we could, but several of the horses' legs were badly cut by the sharp edges of ice. It became so cold, our huge fur *shubas* were not enough to protect us from the fingers of frigid air, and we dared not leave our mounts outside at night, for fear they would freeze where they stood.

I had brought Toby, as I always did, lately. The lad had shot up like a river reed, and his head now came a little above my shoulder. A soft, fuzzy beard was beginning to cover his chin, and his voice was settling into the deeper tones of manhood. On our final overnight stop, I took him aside and explained all I could of the situation I expected to find in Novgorod. We were staying in a large farmhouse, about two hours' ride from the city, so we were able to get away from Malyuta for a few moments. I quickly expressed my concern that my assistant was up to something. I pressed one of my English pistols into Toby's hand, telling him to "guard my back." The boy was intelligent, and he understood with a minimum of instruction. He passed my weapon back to me, however, and hitched up the side of his tunic to display a pistol of his own. It was one of those I had bought for Vladya during that far away time in England. "You told me I might carry it when my beard began to sprout," he said simply.

I called a halt when we came in sight of Novgorod the next morning. Since leaving the capital there had been little conversation between Malyuta and myself, for I had made no effort to speak to him and my threat had made him wary of me. Now it was necessary to plan our first moves within the city.

"Despite our delays," I said, "we have traveled fast enough that I doubt Pimen will be expecting us. He will assume the storms have prevented anyone leaving Moscow. Have you any information to make you believe otherwise?" I asked meaningfully. It was an assumption on my part, of course, that the Archbishop would have any inkling of the original conspiracy, or any reason to expect us to be reacting to it.

Malyuta shook his head in response to my question. "No," he said, "but there are many people within the walls who fear us. Our arrival will be reported immediately." His tone implied relief that I should deign to consult him, and it reassured me to realize how sensitive he was to my hostility.

"It matters little what Pimen thinks or knows," I said. "As soon as we have our hands on that letter, I intend to turn and leave."

"If we're allowed to leave," he added.

"I just asked you –"

"But – what if those who are watching us should decide to interfere?" he interrupted anxiously.

"Are you afraid?" I asked coldly.

"I am never afraid!" Skuratof blustered.

"Malyuta," I said, "let's not deceive ourselves. I know as well as you that Pimen never wrote the letter. I'm certain it was your men who placed it where it is. This doesn't matter to me, because I know the Czar is aware of it. He wants the letter, for what purpose I can only guess. But the fact that he wants it is enough reason for me to risk my life in getting it for him." I locked my gaze onto his eyes until he had to look away.

"Then we shall have nothing to fear from Pimen, will we?" he muttered sarcastically.

"Not unless your men have been clumsy enough to let some hint of your plot get through to him. If Pimen thinks we've come after evidence which may endanger him – forged or otherwise – he will try to stop us. If, as I suspect, the material *is* forged, Pimen will not know where to find it until we lead the way. This means we shall be in no danger until *after* we have the letter in our possession. If we can obtain it without Pimen's knowledge, he won't move against us. If we're careful, we may be able to leave before he realizes what we've done."

Malyuta looked back at me, like a cur who tries to acknowledge an unaccustomed kindness. His mouth twisted into a poor attempt at a smile, and he started to place his hand on my arm, stopping a few inches short as he remembered my previous threat. "This day," he said significantly, "you are the master."

"Then obey me, and we shall see what happens," I told him.

We entered the city at a good pace, as fast as we could without attracting undue attention. Unfortunately, I was known to many, nor could the size of our party pass unnoticed. I led our group directly to the cathedral and posted men outside to guard every entrance. Malyuta and I went in alone. The vault was hushed and bitterly cold, deserted except for a few poorly dressed women who knelt at prayer about halfway between the door and the iconostasis. They looked up as we passed them, responding to the click of our boots upon the stones. The echo had a certain tone of authority, unlike the padded feet of a priest. Because the Icon of the Virgin was on the altar, it would require our treading on a portion of the sacred floor, where laymen were not supposed to go. I paused to make a proper genuflection, in which Skuratof imitated me. Without my example, he would have blundered through, never stopping to beg the Lord's indulgence.

Behind the icon, exactly as Peter had stated, we found a small, tightly wound scroll. It was sealed with wax, but no device had been imprinted. I cracked the seal with my thumbnail and unrolled the parchment. The letter was an offer to surrender the cities of Novgorod and Pskov to Sigismund if the King of Poland would guarantee to protect them from the Czar's wrath. I was unfamiliar with the Archbishop's handwriting, but I had seen his signature enough times to recognize the forgery beneath the text. Such wobbly lines could only have come from an unskilled hand, tracing the name from another document. Pimen was old, but his hand was steady.

Shrugging my shoulders, I rewound the scroll and shoved it under my coat. As we turned to leave, I noticed all the women were gone. I had no time to reflect on their absence, however, as there came the immediate sounds of a scuffle outside, then loud shouting and angry voices. I ran to the main entrance with Malyuta right behind me, and flung open the portals. Our attendants were standing with drawn swords, facing about twice their number of uniformed town guardsmen. Unlike most Russian cities, Novgorod maintained the ancient, Western tradition of mount- ng a city watch. Apparently, these men had been summoned to investigate us.

"Why do soldiers of Novgorod draw swords on the Czar's servants?" I demanded.

Their commander did not know me, or at least he pretended not to. "If you are the leader of this group, sir," he replied firmly, "we have been ordered to bring you to the Archbishop."

"Are you going to be foolish enough to follow those orders?" I asked.

"A soldier must obey his superiors," he said evenly.

"Or die in the attempt," I countered. Skuratof made a snickering sound in support of me. Whatever other faults he possessed, he was not afraid of a fight.

"I hope it will not come to that," said the commander, almost pleading. His men had all retreated a step or two, as they must have realized we were *Opritchniki*. Pressing my advantage, I said coolly: "Must we put on our robes and tie brooms to our saddles before you get out of our way?"

"We would rather not have an open conflict with you," the fellow replied. His speech made him a gentleman, though his present station denied it.

"Exactly what do you want us to do?" I asked.

"The Archbishop would like to speak with you," he told me.

"Wait a moment," I said. I turned back to Malyuta and drew him into the church. Once out of their sight, I pulled the scroll from my *shuba*. "Take this," I said, "and if I'm held, get it to the Czar."

"I should come with you," he growled.

"You should obey!" I snapped. "If I go with them, they'll probably leave you unguarded. If they do, get outside the wall and wait for me by the main gate."

He started to argue again, but reconsidered. We rejoined the others.

"All right, Captain," I said. "I'll go with you, but there's no need to detain my men, is there?"

"My orders concern only you, sir," he replied, obviously relieved.

I glanced at Skuratof and stepped forward to join the soldiers. Toby would have stayed with me, but I waved him off as the Novgorodski formed a circle around me. I was, indeed, a prisoner, although my captors seemed afraid to ap- roach too close to me. Well, no matter, I thought. It seemed unlikely I should be in any real danger.

We were only a short distance from Pimen's house, which had purposely been situated close to the cathedral. I made no protest over the guards' surrounding me, being more concerned that my own party be allowed to mount and leave the city. I saw them do just that as we rounded a corner and passed from their sight.

Once inside the Archbishop's *dacha*, the captain and six of his men remained with me. Pimen came into the room and seated himself behind his writing table, while I remained standing.

"You'd better explain yourself!" I said sharply, before the Archbishop had a chance to speak.

"It is you who has the explaining to do, sir," he countered. "By what right do you trespass into the sacred portions of my church?"

I was startled until I remembered the women. One of them must have worked for Pimen. "I was not aware that religious laxity was an offense for which a senior officer in the Czar's army might be arrested," I replied coldly.

"Please, General, you are not under arrest." he protested.

"It appears that way to me," I said sternly. Do you realize the jeopardy. . ?"

"I would like to know what you were doing in my cathedral!" he insisted, his tone rising with his anger.

"*Your* cathedral!" I shouted back. "I suppose this is also *your* city! I wonder what the Czar would say about that!"

"The Czar is several hundred leagues away," he replied, in better control of himself, "and I might remind you that we have equipment in our cellars, similar to yours beneath the Kremlin."

"I am surprised to hear such words from a servant of God."

"The Lord God may be served in many ways," he answered, "as you should certainly be well aware."

Without waiting any longer for permission, I shoved one of the soldiers out of the way and seated myself in a chair beside the writing table. By this move I ruined the effect of my seeming to stand a prisoner before him. Leaning an elbow on his desk, I stretched my legs in front of me. Pimen watched, anger flooding across his face in florid waves. But he was not quite sure enough of his own position to order me back into my former posture. His beady eyes flicked across my face, and the loose dewlaps beneath his chin vibrated like the wattles of a frightened chicken.

"By now, my own men are outside the city," I said, pursuing my seeming advantage. "I would hate to be a Novgorodski if the Czar's favorite general were not with the group when it returned to Moscow."

"You are free to join them as soon as you answer my question," Pimen insisted.

I could foresee an impasse if I continued to defy him. While I doubted he would dare subject me to torture, the possibility did exist. At the moment, though, he was uncertain and he had to be afraid . . . not of me so much as the eventual reaction of the Czar to whatever I might carry back to him. Better to appease him, I thought. "Very well," I said. "Get rid of the others, and I'll tell you."

He waved the soldiers away.

"We will be right outside," said the captain, as much to me as to the Archbishop.

When they were gone, I said, "Are you aware of the murder of a man called Quintus?"

Pimen nodded. "He worked for you?"

"He had a duty to perform for the Czar, through my office," I replied, without elaborating on the functions of that office. But Pimen knew. He did not question anything, just waited for me to continue.

"To assure his information's getting to me if something happened to him, we arranged for Quintus to leave his messages in a certain place within the Cathedral. They would normally remain there until he could dispatch them to me."

I said no more, and Pimen sat for a minute or so, apparently expecting me to continue. When I did not, he asked, "Well?"

"When Quintus stopped transmitting messages, I came to find anything he might have left in the Cathedral. There was nothing."

"Such a simple mission took both you and that other fiend of the devil, plus a full company of the Czar's *Opritchina?*"

"Had we found something, there might have been need for the men. And . . . travel is uncertain these days," I added coolly. "I do not like to boast, but the Czar would be extremely unhappy if anything were to happen to me."

The Archbishop picked up a small silver bell from his table and rang it. The soldiers were back almost instantly. "Search him," he said.

I was immediately subjected to an embarrassingly thorough search; but, of course, they found nothing. When I was dressed again, Pimen rose and left the room without further comment. I also started to leave, but the captain took a step forward to block me. At this point he had not been given any orders, one way or the other.

"Unless you want to go down fighting, sir," I said, "get out of my way."

I could tell the man was as fearful and uncertain as his master, for even Pimen had not been ready to authorize my detention. The search of my person had been done without forethought, and the possible consequences must then have been flooding the captain's imagination. He stepped back, just far enough that I was able to pass through the door. Once out of his sight, I broke into a run. Skuratof, at Toby's suggestion, had left two men on the street between the cathedral and Pimen's house with an extra horse for me. Within the space of a few heartbeats I was on his back and gone. The troop of guardsmen came pelting out after us, as the Archbishop must have belatedly decided to hold me. By the time they reached the street it was already too late. Moments later we were out the city gates and a league or two down the road. It would have been useless to chase us.

CHAPTER VII

Skuratof made sure to return the scroll into my keeping. It seemed almost as if the document were searing his flesh, and he was obviously anxious that I should hand it to the Czar. His attitude confirmed my previous conviction. The letter had been planted by his agents – at the Czar's orders? Or with the Czar's consent? The turmoil within my own conscience, the dreadful weight with which I had been forced to live for many months, was given an additional twist by the combination of knowledge on the one hand, uncertainty on the other. I could not know what would follow from my act of carrying the scroll. If I had, the prospect might well have driven me over the brink of madness. As we thundered through the city gates of Moscow, I had no inkling as to my degree of infamy.

We reported to the Czar at once, where I delivered the document. He took it and glanced at the message, making such a cursory examination of the contents I might almost have thought he knew them beforehand. Laying the scroll on a table, he looked at us with a sad and drawn expression. Like a father who has just heard of his favorite son's misdeeds, his face reflected disappointment mingled with anger. With it all, his wrath did not seem completely real.

"It is now my unpleasant duty," he said softly, "to administer a proper punishment. The *Opritchina* will be ready to ride in two days!"

In an effort to impugn the document's legitimacy, I asked Skuratof some pointed questions before we left the Czar's presence. How had Peter the tramp known the contents of the letter? Why had Pimen not seized the whole troop of us? If he had really written it, he would have known how damning the contents would appear. Why should Novgorod turn to Sigismund for protection, anyway? The King of Poland could not protect his own cities or those in Livonia. Most of the latter had been occupied by our forces for almost six years. Mention of the tramp reminded me of his interrogation. "Was any information obtained from Peter?" I asked of Ivan.

"Unfortunately, he expired during the first night of questioning," the Czar replied casually. With a tone of solemn finality, he added: "I doubt he had much to tell us anyway."

At this, I decided I had better keep quiet. The decision had been made. The *Opritchniki* began preparations for our heinous assault, an act that caused the Czar to be remembered ever after as *Grozny* – "the Terrible." Messengers were dispatched to Alexandrov, where over a thousand of the brotherhood were in quarters. The Czar summoned other members from the eastern towns, where the *Opritchina* had been stationed to supervise certain caravan routes – Rostov, Nizhni Novgorod, Kazan. All of this took time – much more time than Ivan's projected two days. It would obviously be more than a fortnight before we would be able to leave. That was too long for Ivan, who had grown restless and left for Alexandrov before half the brotherhood was assembled, dragging everyone back with him. At the last moment, he ordered me to remain in Moscow to receive the various groups of men as they arrived from their widely scattered posts. I was to send them on to the abbey.

With the Czar and the rest of the brotherhood out of the city, I was able to visit a few friends whom I had lately been forced to neglect. Ivan's assignments – investigations, arrests, interrogations – all these had left me little opportunity for social exchanges. I suddenly found myself feeling very much alone, and without these old friends I would have gone into a terrible state of melancholy. Few people aside from my family would speak to me in more than monosyllabic answers. Everyone else was afraid.

I spent a day with Simon, hunting upriver where the farmers had been suffering from a sudden influx of wolves. The former Khan was growing fat and lazy in his Kremlin mansion, but his anxieties persisted. "I fear to leave the safety of my home," he said, "and now I'm beginning to worry on another score. There have been several men of my race invited to join the brotherhood, but the Czar has not expressed any desire to see me a part of it. Worse yet, I'm lonely – no one to visit . . . ."

"There are others you could see," I suggested. "What about your father–in–law?" I referred, of course, to Mstislavsky.

"He is of the *Zemschina*," Simon replied. "I fear to express sympathy for those whom the Czar would destroy."

I was disappointed by his lack of faith, or courage. "Simon," I remon–strated, "how can you be so forgetful of the Czar's benevolence? He isn't going to destroy these men. He only wished to demonstrate the truth of his beliefs. The *Zemschina* leaders are typical of the old aristocracy – the whole boyar class. Without the Czar's leadership they can't begin to achieve the greatness he's seeking. Once the point is proven, I'm sure the court will once again be united."

"I have every intention of remaining loyal to him," my friend replied, "but because it's still difficult for me to understand the Russian soul, I must tread softly. Being of a different origin, I'm naturally subject to suspicion, anyway, so I don't want to bring still more of it upon myself."

I realized he shared my own dilemma, though for very different reasons. "Would you like to visit my Livonian estates?" I asked him suddenly. "I hope to be there myself in another month or so."

He looked at me in surprise, grinned uncertainly as if doubtful I really meant it. "That would be most gracious of you," he replied slowly.

"Why not leave now," I urged, "while the brotherhood's away and no one's about to – disturb your tranquillity. You could travel under protection of my next caravan. I expect old Abraham up from Astrakhan almost any day."

He finally agreed to accept my invitation, especially when I assured him his wife and children would also be welcome. Our hunting was good for the rest of the day. Using my good English musket, I brought down three huge gray wolves. Simon accounted for two more with his bow. When I noted that his aim was considerably improved, he explained it was due to the many hours of practice in his own courtyard, when he had nothing else to do. It was after dark before I arrived home. Toby told me Doctor Bomel had asked to see me, and said he had seemed very agitated. I sent the lad to get him. He and Anne still lived in a wing of my house.

Elysius appeared very anxious, indeed, as he entered my office. His hands trembled and he could hardly wait to tell me his troubles. He rushed through the proper forms of greeting, his wit and levity having vanished without a trace. "Demetrius," he told me, "I fear the Czar's wrath when Thomas returns from England."

"What have you done this time?" I asked, amused at his concern.

"I am very serious," he assured me. "I have made a grave error, and the more I think about it the more certain I am of the Czar's extreme displeasure. I will confess to you, because I trust to our friendship that you will not cause Ivan's hand to be raised against me."

He was so serious – and so badly frightened – I could not help laughing at him. As fond as the Czar was of Elysius, it was inconceivable that he could have done anything serious enough to justify such terror.

"Please, Demetrius," he begged, "don't laugh at me. I am in dire straits. I have sinned, as you would say, and I desperately fear the punishment I shall receive."

"All right," I told him. "Tell me the details of your terrible crime."

"You are aware, naturally, of the ill treatment and scorn shown the English representatives on their last visit?"

"Of course," I said. "I also helped them recapture a modicum of the Czar's favor."

He smiled over my remark for a moment. "Well," he began hesitatingly, "you may also be aware of something more than just your help, involved in the Czar's drastic change of attitude."

"I was quite busy during that time," I said slowly, "but I saw to their being received, and what happened afterward was a matter between them and the Czar. It was shortly after Mikhailof's removal, if you'll recall. I didn't have time to involve myself further."

"Yes, yes – well, you see, the Czar had restricted certain privileges he had previously granted to the Muscovite Company, and Horsey was especially concerned lest these be reassigned to the Dutch or Flemish, as it seemed at the time they might."

"I know all this," I said impatiently. "Get on with it."

"... er, well , you know, the subject dearest to the Czar's heart has always been the hand of the Great Queen. . . ."

"Haven't Randolf and Horsey returned to England with the idea of arranging this?" I asked, still having no idea what to expect he would name as his crime.

"That is just the point," he said sadly. "You see, Randolf knows full well that the Queen will never marry Ivan."

"I implied as much when I returned from London," I said. "I doubt Ivan seriously expects. . . ."

"But he does! Don't you understand? With my help and . . . should I say somewhat . . . eloquent persuasion, Randolf convinced the Czar of the Great Queen's favorable attitude toward the marriage. He explained her delay as stemming from a fear of other international complications if it became known too soon. I, well, there was a little astrological prediction, you see, and – when such a marriage fails to materialize. . . . And I did it all for a few pieces of gold!" he moaned.

I watched him writhe in his agony of fear and remorse for several minutes before I said any more to him. "You're an ass!" I said at length. "You have misused the trust the Czar placed in you, and the trifling amount you received for your deceit has probably already gone, hasn't it?"

He hung his head in shame. "It is all true, Demetrius," he wailed. "What shall I do?"

"If you have any sense at all, you will go to the Czar before Randolf returns, and beg his forgiveness."

"But he will execute me for sure," he continued to cry. "Oh, I'm lost, and to think I have brought this not only on myself, but upon my poor wife as well. Oh woe!"

He was beginning to annoy me. "I think Master Shakespeare might have used your talents, had you not practiced your perfidy in England to an extent where you had to flee," I told him. "If you go to the Czar and make a clean breast of your crimes I will try to intercede for you."

"Oh, Demetrius," he moaned, sinking to his knees and slobbering over my hand, which I tried unsuccessfully to pull away from him. "You have saved my life! I am forever in your debt!"

"I think we'd better wait until after this trip to Novgorod," I said. "I imagine the Czar is going to string up that wild–eyed priest and a few of his minions as an example to the citizens. After that, he may be in a mood to hear you. In the meanwhile, you'd better send Anne to Livonia, where she'll be safe until I can get you out of this mess."

"Oh, thank you; thank you." he continued.

"Stop wallowing about on the floor," I told him, "and tell Anne to get herself ready. She can leave with Simon and his family on the next caravan."

He almost ran back to his own quarters. The man was a fool, I thought. That glib tongue was no more than a facade to cover up his basic stupidity. I was not very impressed with Randolf at this point, either, for he had based the entire future of English trade in Russia on the impossible promise of a marriage with Queen Elizabeth. I was sure they must also have convinced the Czar of her uncommon beauty. The last time I remembered Ivan's mentioning her, he had made joking reference to my poor taste in evaluating the charms of a regal lady.

"You always did like them too skinny," he had laughed, then turned to Viazemsky and added: "Dmitri is always too bashful to look upon the face of a great lady; though he'll pinch the ass of a harem girl every time!" He had roared with laughter at his own wit.

So I now had the problem of trying to extricate Elysius from the bed of nails he had made for himself. In addition to his difficulties, my stepfather was again in a state of depression. He had remained in the house after Nina's departure; he had now given the property to me as a wedding gift. He liked it better here, he said, than his new *dacha* which the Czar had given to him. For one thing, he was too close to a number of boisterous neighbors – other members of the brotherhood. As it was, he spent most of the time in his own room, drinking con-stantly and bemoaning the Czar's refusal to give him a command in Lithuania.

"I am a trader, it is true," he told me, "but our operations are so well established I no longer need to watch them every moment. My hands long for the heft of a weapon."

"I am sure you will not be overlooked forever," I assured him, and made a mental note to request the Czar's indulgence at the first opportunity. The next day, we rode out together through the glittering snow–covered countryside, accompanying the last few stragglers to Alexandrov.

Just before I left, however, a letter arrived from Nina, brought in by one of our traders. Her tone was reasonably happy, or at least resigned; though she questioned how long it would be before we could all live together as God intended married people should. The boys were fine, she wrote, and casually added that there would be another arriving soon. She had been looking forward to telling me when I was home for the holy days. As I had not come, she could not delay much longer, lest she inform me by pressing the child into my unsuspecting arms.

I wrote back at once, telling her I expected to be in Novgorod and Pskov on the Czar's business, and would try to spend some time at home afterward. I expressed the hope that our third child would be a girl, for she would provide companionship for Nina, should the present political situation continue beyond the immediate future. I also wrote of my love, expressing these feelings more strongly in writing than I was ever able to in spoken words. Embarrassed lest the letter be seen by my comrades or servants, I wrote in English, noting that Anne Bomel and Simon were soon to arrive.

As it had prior to Phillip's arrest, the full *Oprichina* was assembled in Alexandrov. It was such a group as one might doubt could exist were he not able to see it for himself. Very few of us were over thirty; still fewer were less than the age of twenty. We were thus a hardened core of men in the prime of physical prowess – all fanatically loyal to our vows. On the morning following Heinrich's and my arrival, the whole force moved out toward the west – a full six thousand men, all robed in black, and many wearing the fearsome, dog–faced masks.

The very earth thundered to our advance, and hardly a man dared look upon us. The houses we passed were closed, the windows tightly shuttered. We rode at a steady canter most of the day, occasionally breaking into a faster lunge down a hill or across a plain. We must have presented a dreadful aspect – our massive force, black cassocks streaming behind us, cascading in surging waves across the shimmering, icy crust of snow. At our head rode the Czar on his huge black stallion, holy banners of the *Oprichina* fluttering about him, held aloft by the men of his personal guard.

The first night we stopped at the small town of Klin, having passed north of Moscow without coming in sight of the city walls. Because our mission was secret, no preparations had been made for lodgings along the way, nor had there been advance knowledge of our arrival. At first, townspeople did not know who we were. Many ran outside before they saw our robes; after that, very few remained on the streets. Once these curiosity seekers heard the sneers and laughter of the brothers, they also disappeared very quickly. We dismounted before a tavern, this being the property of the Czar – as were all taverns – and about fifty of us went in with Ivan. The rest were to set up tents or requisition what housing they could for the night. This detail was left to Viazemsky.

Now, Alfansy Viazemsky – as I have previously described – was a base, villainous embodiment of evil, whom I now assiduously avoided. Despite his princely rank, he had lived his life as such an unmitigated profligate, associating with the lowest orders, one tended to think of him as belonging to this class. While physically handsome, his mind was badly twisted, and when overcome with drink and lust, his face reflected his soul, appearing as if badly scarred, frozen into a perpetual glare of hatred. In such a state he was surely the most cruel of any within the *Opritchina* – worse, even, than Skuratof – sullen, sluggish, laughing only to express his pleasure at another's suffering. His sexual appetites were insatiable, and no act of depravity was beneath him. The rank or gender of his partner – or victim – seldom mattered, and, as I have noted, his sessions in the chambers were revolting exhibitions of unbridled lust. It was lately rumored that some of his sessions involved animals. I cannot testify to this; but on two recent occasions I had personally observed him perform acts of revolting perversion upon newly dead corpses. A more vile and disgusting man has never lived, for he somehow seemed capable of arousing the same, terrible passions in those around him. He even cast his evil influence over the Czar and my stepfather; I feared lest he do the same to me.

As soon as Viazemsky took charge, he ordered the men to break in the door of every house and to drive the inhabitants outside. He had an elegant, velvet chair brought from one of the better homes. This was placed in the street, were Viazemsky sat to pass judgment on those who were dragged forth and cast into the slushy snow at his feet. We could hear the shouts and screams from outside the tavern, but none of us was much concerned. Like the others, I assumed our brothers were amusing themselves with a few peasant girls. Finally, the noise became so great I went to the door to see what was happening.

Hard and depraved as my heart and my soul had become, the sight brought a gasp to my lips. The snow outside, white when we had entered the town, was now mostly red. Puddles of blood lay congealing in the street and dead men lay everywhere. Ghastly wounds yawned up at me. Corpses stared blankly at the sky, mouths agape, hands still clutching. In several places, naked bodies were stacked one atop the other; but most had been simply cast aside and allowed to remain where they fell – a feast for the rats and scavengers that would come with the night. Quietly, I closed the door and went back inside.

The old, heavy conflict immediately began to tear at my inner being. Such rapine went beyond my personal limits to accept or understand. Yet these very thoughts were laden with guilt, were disloyal to the Czar I was sworn to serve. Adding a still more brutal weight upon my sanity, I knew it would be taken as weakness were I to express any of these emotions; and the appearance of weakness was something I could not afford to give. The mere indication of doubt or dissatisfaction could be misinterpreted, seen as opposition to the will of the Czar. When all was said and done, the desires and acts of the brotherhood were always supposed to be his.

By the time I returned to my seat I had steeled myself to retain a normal composure, and simply remarked in a casual tone. "Alfansy's tearing the town up a bit – a little too much peasant flesh for my liking, though."

Ivan grunted, having already downed enough mead to stupefy an ordinary man. "Dmitri," he said, waving his arm at me, "take Malyuta and Heinrich –

anyone else you want. Go out there and tell Alfansy to stop making so much noise. I'm going to rest a bit before dinner."

The three of us stepped outside, into the late afternoon chill. Long shadows already stretched across the snow, gradually darkening toward their final, deep purple. What had earlier been a light breeze from the north was fast becoming a hard, steady gale, already casting the first white pellets of hail into our faces. But neither the cold nor the impending fall of stormy darkness had dampened the spirits of Viazemsky and his cronies. Everyone was engaged in some form of mischief or vandalism: robbery, rape, destruction of homes and other property. Brutal as these activities may have been, they were things I could endure. To a large extent such hazards were the peasants' lot. But a small group stood about the prince's chair, committing such crimes as defy description. They were forcibly stripping the clothes from several dozen children, boys and girls alike, requiring them to go naked in the bitter cold and snow. These youngsters – some as young as six or seven, others in their teens – were ordered to perform acts of lewdness and perversity upon each other or with the men, being slaughtered on the spot if they refused. When a child seemed not to understand, one of the men would demonstrate upon another of the shivering captives. The face of God, Himself, must have blushed that day, for shame over these beasts He had created.

My own revulsion was stronger than I had ever felt before, so great that I wanted to turn away and ride out of Klin, maybe out of Russia. As I came up to Alfansy, one of the children looked at me, holding out her hands as if imploring me to protect her. Another actually reached for my coat as I passed. Without voicing any implication of criticism, I bluntly relayed Ivan's command, ordering Alfansy to help us get the others quieted down. Because my instructions came from the Czar, there was nothing he could do but obey. Still, there was a hostile gleam in his eyes when he answered me, marking him as another man to consider my sworn enemy. Standing at my side, Skuratof had to support me, thus forcing a further small wedge between my two strongest foes, men who already competed silently against each other for the Czar's special favor. As long as I can keep them enemies, I thought, neither will be strong enough to harm me. United, they could prove my undoing.

In a short while, the town had become quiet. The scattered sounds of revelry were lost in the howl of the wind and the staccato beat of hailstones against the buildings. Those brothers of lower rank, who had to sleep in tents or on the ground, must have spent a miserable, sleepless night. In addition to the foul weather, the dead bodies in the streets attracted a band of wolves. I awoke several times myself, and I could hear them snapping and snarling at one another, fighting over the human flesh. In the morning there were many reddened eyes among our companions, and tempers were unusually short. But the storm had subsided, allowing us to depart.

Leaving the frozen death and desolation of Klin, we continued on our way, making two more overnight stops before reaching the town of Tver. At the Czar's order, no one was left alive along our path, for he had now become obsessed with the need for our mission to be kept secret. While I might normally have deplored the necessity, I could find no adequate counter to his reasoning. The countryside through this region was not heavily populated in any event, as migrations into the lower Volga had drawn most of the people away. Many farms and homesteads stood empty and abandoned. Despite these precautions, however, word somehow spread ahead of us. We found a number of deserted cabins, which had obviously been in use only a day or two before. The Czar ordered these to be burned.

Our fearsome black thunderhead continued to sweep across the snowy fields, generally traveling the frozen waterways, but sometimes on solid ground. We seldom saw a living creature, and left none after we had passed. Each night we stopped at a small town, selecting those with clusters of buildings that were large enough to shelter the Czar and his inner circle. But even those of us who enjoyed the best these villages had to offer still looked forward to the comforts of a larger city. There was no denying that Russian country life was hard. On the evening of the third day, when we rode into Tver, the leading citizens and the bishop met us at the city gate, bowing to express their welcome. Ivan, though unhappy they had known we were coming, graciously acknowledged their greetings before assigning Heinrich to make arrangements for quartering all the men in regular buildings.

The Czar expressly forbade any vandalism within the city walls, for this was the place where Phillip was lodged in the prison. As soon as we were settled into our quarters, Ivan ordered his principal officers to assemble in the dining hall of the bishop's palace. This was the finest building in town, and therefore the temporary residence of the Czar, as well as those of us who acted as his advisors. As best I recall that evening, there were nine who attended Ivan. In addition to myself, these were: The Czarevitch Vanya, Fedka Basmanov and his father Alexi, Heinrich, Skuratof, Viazemsky, Chibotovy, and Johnny Vorontsof, son of Feodor – the latest brother to join our group. Fedka, Vanya, and Johnny, all being younger fellows, formed their own close clique, sitting together giggling and playing dice. The rest of us joined in a discussion of how best to obtain Ivan's desired blessing from Phillip.

It had now been several months since the Metropolitan's final arrest and confinement. While he had officially been set aside, many people would consider him head of the Church for the rest of his life. I am sure the Czar had no intention of harming him; but he was determined to receive Phillip's blessing, especially as our present mission was supposed to be a form of holy crusade. Ivan's stated intent was to purge the Church of its traitors, thus relieving it of questionable involvements. Because he sought to spare the higher clergy the disastrous consequences of further treason, the Czar felt justified in what he asked. After we had spoken at some length and still reached no miraculous conclusion, Ivan looked from one to the other of us, trying to decide whom he should send to persuade the Metropolitan. Each time I saw the Czar's gaze making its way toward me, I cast my eyes downward, for I did not wish to be chosen. I prayed silently that he would remember my previous failure to make any sense out of Phillip. In the end, it was Malyuta whom Ivan selected. His instructions were to demand and obtain the blessing for the Czar and his entire company. There was no alternative to the order; the blessing was to be obtained!

The decision having been made, Ivan ordered meat and drink to be brought for us. We fell to it at once, hungry and thirsty from the day's long hard ride. I noticed that Skuratof delayed his departure, hanging about at the fringe of our group until he was able to pluck my sleeve without the others seeing him. When I looked up, he jerked his head toward the door, asking me to walk out with him. I shrugged and followed him into the hallway.

"Please, Dmitri," he begged. "I know we have never been proper brothers, but I beseech you to come with me."

"I do not wish to see the Metropolitan," I told him coldly. "We have talked in the past without its having done any good."

"Just wait outside the door," he pleaded. "If you do this for me, I will never refuse anything you ask," he promised. "Please!"

I could see he was genuinely afraid, which puzzled me. He had certainly never displayed a belief in anything sacred. I finally agreed, not from any feeling of sympathy for him, but simply because it might provide a further weapon when we had our next confrontation. His begging for my help had placed me in a position of strength. The only reason I could imagine for his wanting me with him was his tendency to be superstitious. He was probably afraid Phillip would place a curse upon him; Malyuta was one of the few people who seriously accepted the Metropolitan's conviction for sorcery.

It was late in the evening when Malyuta and I arrived at the prison. We went alone, entering through the main gate, unnoticed in the darkness by the people who maintained vigil outside. Even with the full body of *Opritchniki* in town, a large group stood about in the gloomy cold, always beneath the Metropolitan's window. Phillip was being held in a tower cell, overlooking the main square of Tver. Occasionally, he would appear, from what I had heard, gazing through the bars at the fields and forests beyond the town. He would sometimes bless those who waited silently below. Because he had been here for a number of weeks, many pilgrims had come, some of them from as far as Pskov in the west and Yaroslavl in the east.

Skuratof was let into Phillip's cell without question. He wanted me to come with him, but I went only as far as the outer door, refusing to go farther. I thank God for giving me this guidance, for it spared my having to watch the most heinous crime in all the history of Russia. Or perhaps God hid His face, as I might have prevented it had I been there. I have no way to know, and who can guess the reasons for Our Lord's direction?

Malyuta actually trembled at having to face Phillip by himself. In company with others he would have been brave enough; nor did I think he would greatly fear death in battle. Even an assassin's blade would probably hold little terror for him. But to venture alone – into the presence of a living saint – that was enough to totally unnerve him.

I could hear their voices fairly well through the door, but the portal had no window and I could not see into the cell. I heard Malyuta attempt a properly respectful address to the Metropolitan, speaking as he might if he had been standing before the cathedral altar. Phillip barely answered him, mumbling something I could not make out.

I heard Skuratof say, "I beg your blessing, Father."

"You are a very evil man," replied Phillip sternly. "When did you last make your confession?" The Metropolitan's voice was hard, far firmer than Malyuta's despite the difference in their present situations.

Phillip's tone and attitude must have grated on Skuratof's sensibilities. He had been one of the Czar's favorites for so long he was unaccustomed to justifying himself except to Ivan – occasionally to me. Had he maintained his original, humble approach, he might have achieved at least a partial success. Instead, he leaped to his feet in anger – I could hear the sudden scrape of a chair across the floor – and shouted, "What right have you to question me? You are only a discredited priest! You *must* bless a man when he asks it of you!"

"Are you really a man?" asked Phillip softly. "Have you not lived so long as an animal as to have lost all resemblance to a man?"

They argued then, for a long while. Phillip always spoke in a softly modulated voice, while Skuratof went into a rage, his attitude more violent each time he spoke. Finally, he shrieked in a frenzy of anger, screaming at Phillip: "It's the Czar who commands you! The Czar of all Russia! You dare not defy him!"

"I shall never bless such heresy," said Phillip calmly. "The Czar, and you, and all your cursed brotherhood – you are all abominations to the Holy Name of God! That you dare to tramp about in those travesties of religious vestments only compounds your sin. Were I to bless you . . . any of you, it would make me party to the height of blasphemy, and the Gates of Heaven would be slammed against me forever."

I heard Skuratof try to answer, sputtering, nearly strangling in his fury – animal sounds, growling, snarling, his breath coming like a bellows making iron. I had been grinning to myself, amused at the ease with which the priest had taken command of the exchange, when it suddenly occurred to me that the sounds were all being made by Skuratof. Phillip had not been speaking emotionally enough to have lapsed into such guttural noises, nor had he actually said anything for too long a time! With a dreadful, mounting fear, I heaved on the door. It stuck, resisting me as I pulled again. Finally, it creaked open, grudgingly giving way to an opening large enough for me to squeeze inside.

It was dark in the cell, with only a pallid shaft of moonlight filtering through the bars. Neither man had lit a lantern. Yet even in the shadowy darkness it took but a glance to see what had happened. Malyuta stood hovered against the far wall, shoving against it with his back, his hands pressed tightly onto the stones. I could not see his face, but the stark horror at his own act was manifest in his stance and from his labored breathing. On the floor, feebly silhouetted by the moonlight, lay the slender body of the Metropolitan. At first glance one might have thought him asleep, although his head lay at an awkward angle and a tiny trickle of blood showed at the corner of his mouth. I dropped down beside him and tried to lift his shoulders. His head fell loosely at the end of a broken spine. I started to listen for his heart, but I already knew he was dead. I knelt beside his body and prayed God to forgive my complicity. When I touched him, I had somehow gotten a drop of his holy blood upon my finger. I carefully wiped it off, onto a bit of cloth I had torn from my robe. I shoved this relic into my waistband after first pressing it to my lips.

Skuratof continued to stand, trembling, against the wall. At length I looked up at him, his form almost completely lost in the deepening darkness of the room. "You had better pray for your own soul," I said softly.

"I do not fear for my soul," he growled. "I fear only the Czar."

In disbelief, I gazed into the blackness around him, wondering if he could truly be untouched by the magnitude of his crime.

"You'd better stop groveling around on the ground, yourself," he continued, "and help me think of some answers for Ivan."

"I am not going to lie to the Czar, not for you or anyone else," I told him. I got up from the straw–covered floor and stood facing him across the pallid, broken body. "Your sin is too gross to be concealed." I added.

"Since you were with me," he answered slyly, "who is to know the sin wasn't yours as well as mine?"

"Are you ready to place your word against mine and allow the Czar to decide – to punish the one he does not believe?" I asked harshly.

He didn't answer me.

"Well?" I demanded.

"Please," he whispered hoarsely. "I'm afraid. For the first time in my life, I'm really afraid!"

"But not of God's vengeance?" I asked again.

"Maybe that, too," he admitted, "but God has never helped or hurt me. It is the Czar whom I must convince that I didn't intend to do it."

I still found his attitude amazing, but my own mind had started working as the shock wore off. After another few moments I commented: "I was outside the door, Malyuta. I did not see what happened. As long as you make this clear to the Czar, there is no way I can dispute your story."

Before we were back in Ivan's presence, the body had been discovered by the guards and a terrible cry went up from the people gathered outside the prison. When Malyuta stood before Ivan, he hung his head as if ashamed of his terrible crime. He told his master that he had shaken the old man, trying to convince him to bless the *Opritchina*.

"I didn't realize how weak he'd become," he wailed. "His poor old head just snapped loose at the neck." Then Skuratof the murderer, Skuratof the torturer of women and children, fell on his knees before the Czar and conjured up a flood of tears. But through the length of his lamentations he had made it apparent that I had been outside, that I had no way to see anything that happened. In this, I suppose, I received God's Grace, for the monstrous crime was never laid to me. Later, hardly anyone remembered I had been there. Whatever punishment may await me in heaven I cannot know; among my fellow men, at least, I am blameless.

Ivan listened in silence to the words of his servant. As Malyuta groveled before him, the Czar looked at me as if to question the truth of what he heard. I shrugged and opened my palms in expression of my being unable to affirm or contradict. In the end, Ivan placed his hands upon Malyuta's head and comforted him.

"You could not have known," he said. "Your soul is clean," he said. *His soul was clean!* Rage and indignation were swelling up inside me. I was about to break my coward's vow and shout my thoughts without consideration of the consequences. Then the groaning of the crowd outside ebbed slowly into a menacing growl. Someone had opened the door, allowing the sound to thunder about us until it seemed to echo against the walls. Ivan looked up, startled. Skuratof, his eyes still wet from weeping, gaped in fear at the unearthly wailing from the street. Had I been an artist about to portray the face of Judas after his betrayal of Our Blessed Lord and Savior I could not have chosen a better model than Malyuta at that particular moment.

Yet a greater fear showed on the Czar's face. He bellowed for Viazemsky, who commanded the guard, and for Heinrich. "Go out there and silence them!" he shouted. "Silence them forever, if you must; but no further sound must reach my ears tonight!"

I think the full horror of Skuratof's act was finally penetrating the Czar's awareness, and he was terrified – not so much of the mob, perhaps, as of the punishment awaiting him from the Judge of Heaven. Without another word, Ivan rose from his seat. Half limping, his face twitching and twisted by terrible contortions, he went into the Bishop's private chapel.

For a full five days, the Czar did not appear. He knelt before the holy icons, begging God to forgive his sins, beating his forehead against the stones. Finally, he fell exhausted and lapsed into a restless slumber. Still, he found no peace. When I looked in on him, I could see his body shake and tremble in sleep. Muttered words escaped his mouth, mingled with a bubbling foam and some greenish slime he vomited from the depths of his empty guts.

During Ivan's five days of prayer and fasting, his repentant mood had not been reflected by the brotherhood. While he remained on his knees, begging forgiveness for past sins, a continuous storm of sound must have beat upon his brain. Six thousand *Opritchniki* were systematically destroying the entire city of Tver! Every house was sacked and every living creature was dragged out into the streets. Because it had started to snow again, the reddened ground continued to be cleansed by successive layers of white, until finally the deluge of blood came faster than the snow. Men were flogged and burned alive in the streets; women were raped by so many men they expired on the ground, and still their bodies were allowed no peace. Children were herded into groups to be shot with muskets or arrows, sometimes being forced to flee in order to make a more sporting target. Babes were torn from their mothers' arms, their heads smashed against stone walls.

While all this had started on the Czar's orders, I am certain he never intended it to go so far. At first, I tried to stop it, and I call upon God to witness my honesty when I say this. I went to Viazemsky, begging him to reconsider before he condemned us all to such wretchedness that Satan would devise new torments in hell to properly reward our infamy. He and his henchmen laughed at me. Finally, I could not make myself heard above the boisterous hilarity of the brotherhood – or through the screams of their terrified victims. All about me, the snow was defiled with gore and the organs of human bodies: hearts and lungs and guts, and other parts I could not name. The streets became so filled with bits of human flesh it was impossible to walk without stepping on them.

The third night – I think it was the third night – there was an especially heavy snowfall, over two feet above the previous layers. It covered all signs of the previous day's slaughter, the outlines of all the bodies being buried and hidden. But only a few hours after daybreak, the scene was the same as before. In the end, I doubt a single resident was left alive within the city.

Somehow, through all the killing and torture and bloodshed, a few pilgrims had gathered to bury the Metropolitan behind the cathedral altar. It was said they laid him to rest with a martyr's crown upon his head; but I think that was probably a later embellishment. After the day of heavy snows I remained within my room in the Bishop's palace. I lay upon my bed, with the drapes drawn tightly across the windows, trying not to hear the sounds from outside.

I could not sleep until I had consumed so much vodka I did not remember where I was. Even then I could not fully escape. Terrible dreams descended upon me again, and I saw the horrors of hell awaiting me. I was weak and shaken when Toby forced me awake. It was the morning of the sixth day. We were to depart, he said.

"Where were you all this time?" I asked. I could not remember seeing him since we arrived.

He grinned. "I was never far away from you," he assured me, and I noted he was wearing my sword. "We had better hurry," he added. "I've ordered a sleigh for you, and it's right behind the Czar's in the column. I thought you'd rather not try to ride a horse."

I retain only a few, vivid impressions of the ride from Tver to Great Novgorod. One of these was the continuing butchery all along the way. Where we had passed, no living thing remained. We were like the horde of Attila the barbarian who once boasted no grass would grow where his horse had trod, or Ghengis Khan, who left only smoldering earth behind him. It depressed me to see Heinrich taking part in much of this; but he seemed to do it sullenly, without the others' display of lust.

I think of all the scourges we set loose upon the countryside, none compared with the three boys: Vanya, Fedka, and young John Vorontsof. Like three killer hawks among a flock of eagles, they would spin away from our column, dashing headlong across the snowy plains to reach some distant farmhouse, which might otherwise have gone unnoticed. Far in the distance, above the pounding of hoofs and heavy breathing of the horses, seeming to ride upon the constant moan of the wind, terrified shrieks and screams drifted back to us. Several times the boys chased women across the snow, from the distance appearing almost comical – like a farmer chasing a goose before butchering it for the table. Fedka carried a lance, and frequently returned with a head to decorate the tip.

When we drew near our destination, and the city walls of Novgorod could be seen in gray miniature outline against the far horizon, Ivan ordered the column to halt. He had regained his composure during the days of travel, and climbing atop his sleigh he addressed us in firm, ringing tones. No one was to enter the city until ordered, and when we did enter there were to be no acts committed without the Czar's specific permission. Anything that was to take place was to be supervised by officers. When he finished, the brotherhood was silent. Everyone understood, and some were surprised, for they realized they had been told: "To disobey is death."

The Czar stood down, then, calling Heinrich, Basmanov, and myself to join him in his sleigh. We rode together for the rest of the way. The bulk of the brotherhood was strangely silent, and for the first time since its formation I sensed a surliness among the men – hostile anger directed toward the Czar and his officers. I may have imagined it, for I had few real friends among the *Opritchniki,* and even those whom I liked – and who knew I liked them – would never have dared express any hostile feeling in my presence. But they were a spoiled, indolent lot, men with the souls of evil children. I said nothing about these feelings, and the Czar seemed not to notice.

"You are my strongest commanders," he said, once we were settled in his sleigh. "I want you to take charge and see that everything is done according to my instructions. First, I want a strong palisade erected around the town. No one is to escape!" He spoke quickly, the old fire seeming to flash from his eyes. We were inside the sleigh where the others could neither see nor hear us – in the semidarkness with a pair of lanterns suspended from the ceiling, swaying to the motion of the runners over uneven ground where the rutted snow had frozen to preserve the tracks of previous travelers. Watching Ivan as he instructed us, I seemed to see him once again as he had been at Kazan, and in other moments when his true greatness had emerged. Yet his words were so ominous I felt my heart grow cold. "No one is to escape," he had said. But Novgorod was no Klin or Tver. This city was over half the size of Moscow; I could not believe the brotherhood would be permitted to destroy it!

As he continued to speak, the image of Ivan the conqueror began to fade. It was the later man – the man of haunted features and hell's possession who spoke to us. He ordered us to secure every public building within the city. One of us was to take a select body of men and see to the sealing off of every church, preventing anyone from taking sanctuary within. Every monk and priest was to be driven from the monasteries, after which the buildings were to be locked. It was well known that these ancient structures contained all sorts of hiding places, secret tunnels and rooms where a man could disappear. Homes of the wealthy and influential were also to be sealed, but the occupants were to remain inside. His orders were so concise and exact, I was sure the Czar had carefully planned every detail for his projected punishment of Great Novgorod.

Our column moved on, arriving before the walls while there was still daylight. The black–robed *Opritchina* spread out to surround the city, and to set to work without delay, building the timber palisade. Trees were felled in the nearby forests, and other materials were provided by demolishing the houses and cottages, scattered about the countryside. From atop the city wall, the inhabitants anxiously watched our activities. Our patrols captured several groups who were attempting to flee from the western gates; they were driven back inside. Heinrich took a company of men into the city, and saw to the implementation of Ivan's orders. Pimen made no move to interfere. There was no company of town watchmen guarding any of the buildings.

The Czar's pavilion was set up outside the new wall, making it obvious that he had no immediate intention to enter the city. At dusk, Pimen appeared at the gate with a delegation of clergymen and a few wealthy citizens who had avoided being locked within their homes. The Czar refused to see them, instructing us to drive them back inside. I took personal pleasure in that, and swung my broom so close to Pimen's craggy face that the bristles scratched the end of his nose.

It took only two days to complete the palisade, as a full six hundred had been assigned to help. On the third day Heinrich and I were sent into the city with a hundred men apiece. We were to arrest and bind every man of means we could find. We were also to take the higher clergy, except for the Archbishop himself. These prisoners were divided into two groups, the larger being laymen, who were placed in cells beneath the civic buildings. Guards were set to watch them, while the second group – the clerics – were taken before the Czar.

There were several orders of priests and monks in Novgorod, creating a hodgepodge of habits – gray, white, black, brown – as they were tossed into the muddy snow before the Czar's pavilion. Ivan came outside, dressed in his black cassock as Abbot of the Alexandrov Monastery – Archimandrite of the *Opritchina*. "You will carry my message back to your master, the Archbishop," he shouted, "and he will know We do not give orders without expecting absolute obedience." He looked sternly at the frightened cluster of men, each priest and monk with his hands bound behind him, some trying to rise from the ground, others merely surrendering to circumstance and lying where they had fallen. I was certain that most of them expected a blade to pass between their ribs at any moment.

"You may inform your archbishop," continued the Czar, "that I shall expect each and every clergyman: priest, monk, or bishop, to assemble in the great square tomorrow. Failure to appear will constitute gross disobedience to your Czar, and will be punished with death. With him, each priest, monk, and bishop will bring a fine in the sum of twenty rubles. This is to help defray the cost of Our expedition, for the pay of soldiers is expensive," – laughter from the troops at this – "and since it was the treasonous activities of churchmen that necessitated these measures, it shall be the Church that pays."

When he had finished speaking there was dead silence, until a single monk took courage and crawled a little forward of this companions. "We are poor monks, who have forsaken the world and all its material goods. Where are we to get such a sum?" he cried.

The Czar, who had already turned his back on the captives, spun abruptly back to face them. "Who dared to ask that question?" he demanded.

Again there was a long silence. "Well?" shouted Ivan. "How many wish to die right here?"

The little monk, already a foot or two closer than the others, wriggled up to Ivan's boots, bowing his head before the Czar, but now too frightened to speak. Ivan shifted his *kisten* to his right hand, as if he meant to use it. Then he stopped short and started to laugh. "How you find the money is your business!" he said. "But if I were you, I should find it somewhere!" He turned, still laughing, and entered his pavilion.

We hauled the clergymen to their feet and marched them back to the main gate, where we turned them loose. There was no place for them to run, and each knew he faced certain death if he failed to return on the morrow. That night saw a great orgy of laughter and singing within our company outside the walls. We drank heavily from the fine stocks of wine and liquors brought to us by the anxious townspeople. In some ways, it was similar to being in the field again with an army of good companions – singing many of the old songs I remembered from our marches to Kazan and Astrakhan. But noisy and merry as we were outside the walls, there was not a sound from within the darkened city. No living creature dared show itself upon the streets; not even a cat was heard to screech its amour that night.

In the morning, as dawn cast long gray fingers across the icy crust of snow, the bell in the Cathedral of Saint Sofia began a mournful tolling. The tocsin was sounded at our orders to tell the monks and priests it was time to gather in the central marketplace. The bell was huge and of heavy brass; within its shell the clapper swung slowly, making a natural funeral sound.

I entered the city after breakfast with the other senior officers – this being an hour or so after the mournful tolling had ceased. When we finally appeared in the square the huge crowd of quivering priests and monks stood facing us, bunched together for warmth, watching our every move with fearful awe. I carried the scroll bearing the Czar's orders for those who failed to pay, and Heinrich carried the accounts book to record the fines we expected to receive.

We mounted the dais in the square and Heinrich gave his book to a clerk, calling in a loud voice that all who wished to pay should line up before us. Of the nearly fifteen hundred clergymen, only a scant thirty or forty stepped forward. These were mostly the fattest ones, the bishops and abbots of the city's monasteries. Like pigs shoving at the trough, they fought to surrender their rubles and have their names inscribed in the accounts book. The whole process took only a few minutes, resulting in a small pile of coins upon the clerk's table. It was obvious that neither Pimen nor any other high clergyman had stripped his treasury for the benefit of his fellow priests.

During the short interval while the wealthy churchmen were paying their fines I tried not to see the mass of faces upturned to watch us. Their fear was so overwhelming it pained me to gaze upon it. For a large part these were poor priests and honest servants of God, the ones for whom I felt the least distaste. My contempt fell upon the fat, over-fed wretches who were the very ones about to escape by paying the price of freedom – or so I believed. I had not read the words inscribed by Ivan's clerks, for as yet I had not cut the waxen seal to glance at the orders I carried on the parchment scroll.

At the last moment I seemed to lose courage, feeling a sudden revulsion at what I knew must be about to come. I experienced the familiar tightening in my bowels, this time accompanied by a pain in my upper stomach that almost made me double over. As Malyuta was beside me, still acting as my assistant, I handed him the scroll and mumbled some nonsense about having a bit of a cold that morning, would he mind. . .?

"Mind? Certainly not!" He leered happily at the crowd of priests and almost tore the scroll from my hands, gesturing for one of his more literate henchmen to accompany him. Standing on the highest part of the dais, he watched in hungry anticipation as his man read: "To the treasonous clergy of Great Novgorod, from Ivan, son of Basil, Czar of Russia, Grand Duke of Moscow, Kazan, etc., etc." Those who had paid their fines were to be bound and lodged in the city prison until the Czar decided their further disposition. So they were not to escape as easily, after all, I thought – not without some sense of satisfaction. Those who had not paid their fines were to be stripped of all their clothing, tied to posts, walls or any other convenient surface. They were to be flogged with whips or knouts until they remembered where their stores of gold were hidden.

A hissing moan went up from the huddled group of men, with a few – very few – protesting voices. Most of them had expected their punishment to be harsh. Alexi Basmanov, standing at the foot of the dais, barked orders to the company of brothers who sat on their mounts between the square and the city gates. They galloped in and immediately implemented the Czar's orders. I busied myself supervising the men who bound those who had paid, and went with the group escorting them to prison. Once inside, I decided to remain, thus hoping to avoid most of the first day's sights. Even with the bright sun blazing down from a clear sky, it was wretchedly cold. Some of the older priests did not survive past noon. The few who had been stupid enough to hold back when they actually had the money, confessed before an hour had passed. They were escorted by *Opritchniki* to wherever they claimed the gold was hidden. Generally, the hiding place would contain more than twenty rubles, which the brothers would seize before bringing the bedraggled prisoner to me.

Twenty rubles, under the Czar's new system of coinage – one of the innovations started by Adashev and brought to fruition by Fumikov while I was in England – was a great sum of money for the common man. By Ivan's order, the gold was strictly weighed, so the value never fluctuated. Twenty rubles was the price of a small farm, or a very fine team of horses. Few men of less than noble rank ever saw such an amount at one time in all their lives. It was understandable that very few priests could produce it. Pimen, of course, and some of the other higher clergy, could easily have paid the fines for all. Their failure to do so proved exactly how little they cared about the welfare of their subordinates.

I remained in the prison for as long as I could, but the place was extremely uncomfortable, almost as unpleasant outside the cells as within. The frigid temperature was intensified by the bare stone walls. There was no place to sit, much less to lie down, without becoming infested with vermin. The men on guard duty were thirsting to go outside and they talked of nothing else, watching greedily from the windows. They made me so edgy I finally left, wrapping my fur coat more tightly about me against the bitter cold.

Most of the priests were very brave, else so frozen they could not speak or cry out. Toby, who had disappeared just after I entered the prison, now joined me and pressed a bumper of brandy into my hands. I gulped this down, then tossed the empty container into the snow. The warmth of the liquor helped to dispel the chill, although what I was feeling was less a result of the weather than the responses of my own conscience. I started back to the Czar's pavilion as quickly as I could, looking down to avoid the withered blue bodies, the red flecks of blood and skin upon the trampled snow. But I could not close my ears to the groans and whimpered sounds of pain – audible only as I passed through the central square, weaving my way past the hundreds of naked, suffering captives. A group of brothers were gathered about a post, where three young monks were chained together. The *Opritchniki* had paused in their beating of the captives and were passing about a small cask of liquor. One of them called to me, offering me a drink. I stopped and took a long pull from the container, downing so much of the fiery fluid that the youngsters chided me, laughing about my hollow interior. I passed the cask back to them, forcing myself to laugh and making some remark about "having to catch up with my brothers." I moved away from them, feeling the additional warmth begin to spread through my body, growing out of the pit of searing pain Toby's brandy had ignited in my gut. As I mounted and rode out of the city, the fumes reached my brain and made the scenes of death less real and clear. There was no point to any of this, I thought, no reason. There had been no plot. The letter had been forged. There was no danger to the realm, and the Czar knew it. My place was not to question, I consoled myself. I had not personally been ordered to kill, so I had not. Yet if I *am* ordered – well, I can worry about that when it happens, I told myself. Perhaps tomorrow will see the end of it.

Ivan and I played chess for the rest of the day, sitting within the warmth of his pavilion. The huge tent was made of many layers of cloth, heated by several large stoves. Heaps of furs helped to keep the chill outside. The Czar beat me badly, almost every game. At first I played poorly because my mind was not on the board. Later, it was due to vodka; Ivan was drinking only wine.

By nightfall, fully half the clergymen of Novgorod were dead, and still the meager pile of coins had not grown much larger. Those who lived through the day were left outside that night to freeze. The ones who were already dead were cut down by the brothers. In a sudden act of grace, Ivan ordered them returned to the monasteries for burial, though none were left to receive the bodies. The following morning, the frigid corpses of the remainder were merely removed from their posts and walls by the brotherhood, no one bothering to cart them back to the monasteries. They were simply stacked in the square, like cords of firewood.

"They'll keep till summer," I heard one man laugh.

"They'd make a good, long wall," commented another.

Stacking the dead did not seem to trouble any of them, and they laughed as they worked. They joked about the physiques and physical endowments of the various monks, noting which must have been most popular within the abbey. I remember one sad–faced acolyte, whom I had noticed the day before. When he had been unable to pay his fine, he had stood helplessly near the front of the group, wanting to weep, but forcing back the tears and fighting to keep his chin from trembling. His blond hair had been wispy, blowing slightly in the breeze, except for the tonsure at the back of his head. He must have been little more than fifteen – the same age as the Czarevitch. Now his slender body lay atop a dozen others, tossed carelessly to one side in the town square, frozen hard and covered by a thin layer of frost as evening fell on this second day. The night promised to be still colder than the one before.

Again, the Archbishop tried to see the Czar, and again Ivan ordered him driven back inside the walls. I had continued drinking heavily since the previous afternoon, and I remember thinking through my drunken haze that if more men must be killed, I wished Pimen to be among them. He was one, I thought, whom I might take some pleasure in dispatching myself.

In the morning, the Czar ordered us to sack the churches and monasteries. "What they will not give graciously, we must take as taxes," he declared. "Our expedition was necessitated by the churchmen of Novgorod; it is they who must pay for it," he repeated.

Thus the day was spent ransacking the houses of God. We found many items to bring back to the royal pavilion: golden vessels and candlesticks, chains and incense burners of gold and silver. There were crosses of precious metals, inlaid with gems, and the wonder–working icons of Novgorod's patron saint. All these things we brought to the Czar. In one monastery we found some gold coins, hidden beneath the altar in the large chapel. I wondered if the foolish owner had refused to pay his fine and died to preserve his horde. Or had he been one of those who paid, but hid the balance of his wealth rather than save his comrades? I thought about this for quite a while.

How very fleeting our material possessions are! A man might work a lifetime to amass a vast store of gold, and yet have it taken from him in one swoop of an army, or by a single, determined tax collector. After all his work and saving, how much of his wealth would a man give to sustain his life? When you close your eyes at night, what difference does it really make whether you lie within a gilded mansion or in a peasant hut? Yet, who would give away his wealth? Who would wish to be poor?

Thoughts and strange imaginings! Drink, drink and dreams – terrible dreams again, mixed with the reasonings of my conscious thoughts and the darker fears of my old deliriums. Whips and hell's fire, black stallions and imps – dead men staring up at me, frozen in the flames of Satan's pits. I cried out again in my sleep, so loud as nearly to waken the dead. Toby shook my shoulders during the black of night, cautioning me to be still. I was saying things I should better keep to myself, he said. When I was quiet again, he slipped away to his blanket–roll and shoved his body against the entrance. I heard the clink of a dagger as he resettled himself, and I went back to sleep.

Coming awake, it seemed as if my entire being were trying to force itself from a long dark tunnel, with light showing only at the distant end. There was a sustained hammering, beating against the passage, assailing my senses and threatening to pitch me back into oblivion – clanging bells, the bells of Novgorod – tolling, tolling, every bell in every church, slowly sounding matins. Each stroke reverberated within my brain as if I were bound to the tongue of the largest clapper, striking against the brass with my skull.

I sat up, groaning. Toby rolled out of his blankets and approached my bed. It was still half dark. "Do you want to get up?" he asked.

"Yes; I think I may lead a raid on the city *ponomari*," I told him. "Oh, God; what pain! Why don't they stop?"

"They are tolling for the dead," said Toby seriously.

"They would do better to toll for those who are still alive," I replied.

"Will it be bad today?" he asked.

"The Czar may announce his decision this morning. He will have to pronounce sentence on Novgorod either today or tomorrow."

"Do you want armor?"

"Just the mail shirt," I told him. I would be uncomfortable enough in that, I thought. Wearing full armor beneath the *Opritchina* cassock was too restrictive to my movements. Our armor was old–fashioned, anyway, at least by Western standards. The English, for instance, never wore more than breast plates and leg guards. Strange, lately I found myself thinking more and more of England.

"Will you exercise this morning?" Toby asked me.

I nodded. A small circle of fat had been forming about my waist, and there was a suspiciously soft spot on either hip, all the result of too much drink and too infrequent exercise. Despite my aching head, I was determined to maintain the routine I had started a few days before beginning our present journey. I had been lodged within the city because the men who guarded the prison were under my command. I went downstairs to the courtyard where Alexi was already waiting for me. We went a few rounds with wooden swords. Afterward, we galloped out to the Czar's pavilion, where we spent an hour in the portable bathhouse behind his tent. Then, rolling in the snow until my skin turned a healthy red, I felt much better. We joined the Czar for breakfast, shortly after he had finished his morning prayers.

While we were eating, Ivan announced his intention to enter the city personally that morning. I was to go ahead of his party, with Skuratof, and make sure the populace was informed, that they might offer proper respect to their Czar.

Not wishing to speak with the Archbishop myself, and afraid to send Malyuta after his experience with Phillip, I selected a junior officer to carry the message. This was a pleasant young fellow, distantly related to Ivan, by the name of Boris Godunof. I had been impressed with his bearing on previous occasions, and I suspected he shared my lack of enthusiasm for the excesses of the brotherhood. A stout enough fellow, I felt he could handle himself in the present situation. As assurance of his safe return, I sent a fifty–man escort.

In the city, I divided the remainder of our force into groups of ten, having them go from street to street, informing the inhabitants of the Czar's pending arrival. As I had half expected, the people were afraid to come out of their houses. We had been ordered not to break in – not yet, which placed me in an awkward situation. But, as an additional act of grace, the Czar had ordered all surviving churchmen released. I went to the prison and personally gave the orders, instructing each priest as he left that we expected them to bring their people out to welcome the Czar.

Ivan was in no rush to enter the city, continuing with his leisurely breakfast until well after I had left him, then returning for another session of prayer before ordering the *Opritchina* assembled. It had been announced that he would enter in a carriage, but at the last minute he decided to come on horseback. Just prior to leaving his pavilion, the Czar sent a second message, informing the Archbishop of his desire to dine with him that evening. Prior to this, Ivan expected to attend service in the Cathedral of Saint Sofia, where Pimen was to officiate.

It was close to midday when the Czar finally passed through the main gate and proceeded directly toward the center of town. He was attended by most of the brotherhood, which followed him four or five abreast. In a few places, where the streets narrowed, they had to pass in pairs. The Czar remained at the head of the procession, fearless of any danger. He would have been an easy target for any assassin, as he was mounted on one of his usual black stallions, always in the open and frequently ahead of the others by some distance. I was quite concerned when I first saw this, for the Czar's security was my responsibility. However, I need not have worried. Despite a desperate effort by the priests, the streets were as deserted as if a great pestilence had depopulated the entire city. No man stood along the way to greet his Czar; no windows were open, with young maidens dangling garlands to throw in Ivan's path. Instead, the tall stone buildings were silent and dead; the only sound was the slosh of horses' hoofs as the company trotted slowly toward the center of town.

Novgorod, like Moscow, was divided by its river, except in this city the stream was much smaller and in most places the banks were steeper than ours. Only one bridge of any size crossed the water, and it was here I awaited the Czar. Pimen, surrounded by his surviving priests and servitors, stood upon the other end of the bridge, behind me. I glanced across the stone surface at the Archbishop, dressed in his full paraphernalia, huddled in a huge sable coat. Surrounded by his fearful cluster of priests, he waited humbly in the slushy snow. Boris Godunof commanded the group of men who stood a few feet from the gaggle of churchmen.

I waved to Boris, indicating he should hold the priests on the far side until I told him otherwise. A few moments later, the imperial procession came into view. The black figures of the brothers, all in monks' habits over heavy, sheep's wool liners, were mounted mostly on black or gray horses. They trotted proudly forward, between the ancient stones. Clouds of steam billowed from the mouths of both men and animals, giving the procession an appearance of some long, puffing dragon.

The visage of the Czar, as head of this legendary beast, was more than stern. His mouth was set in a hard, straight line above his scraggly beard. On his head he wore a tall abbot's hat; in his hands he held the *kisten*, resting this symbol of secular power across the saddlebow.

As they approached the bridge, I slowly rode forward to meet them, coming up to the Czar from the side and allowing my mount to fall into step beside him.

"Pimen is waiting across the bridge," I whispered.

"No one else?" he asked.

"Just the usual clergy – all the riffraff we turned loose this morning," I told him.

"This displeases me greatly!" he growled, spurring his horse forward. I knew how badly he wanted the people to stand forth and greet him. Their failure to do so would now bring a terrible retribution.

I fell back with the rest of the officers, allowing the Czar to move well ahead and to start across the bridge alone. He stopped abruptly, about the length of two horses from the center. We came up behind him as Pimen approached on foot from the other side, followed by his flock of trembling priests. The Archbishop was dressed in a magnificently brocaded robe, beneath his coat of tawny sable. Twice, I noticed, he resisted the impulse to lift his hem above the watery mess underfoot. He bowed respectfully, and as he raised his head I had the fleeting impression of Sylvester – so much so it gave me a start. Behind Pimen, the priests carried all sorts of crosses, icons, and *khorugvi* – holy pictures and flags on their long, slender poles. They seemed to crowd about the Archbishop as if to make him their shield, warding off the evil which might be expected to emanate from the Czar.

Pimen stopped a few feet in front of Ivan, raising his arms to bestow a holy greeting.

"We do not wish thy tainted blessing!" shouted the Czar.

"My purpose was only to offer proper respect," replied Pimen, greatly taken back.

"Your purpose has been all too clear for many months!" shouted Ivan, "yours and that of your revolting flock!"

"We come only with the life–giving cross, that we may dedicate it to Your Majesty's spiritual well–being," replied Pimen. His voice was naturally harsh and crackling, hardly suited to soothing an angry man.

"In *your* hands, no cross is capable of holy acts," Ivan roared. "You are no pastor of this flock; you are a rapacious wolf, a hater of God, the Church, and my crown. Proof of your perfidy is your determination to desert your homeland and turn this city over to the King of Poland!"

Pimen tried to answer again, but Ivan shouted him down, finally ordering the Archbishop to lead his procession to the Cathedral. Once inside, the Czar's mood seemed to change. He prostrated himself and listened with great patience and intensity to the service conducted by Pimen. After this, we retired to the Archbishop's house. I had come here under such different circumstances the last time, I thought, I had hardly noticed how splendidly the old man feathered his nest. Where had all this sudden wealth come from, I wondered. While the letter I had brought back to Moscow was surely a forgery, was it possible there could be some truth in the Czar's suspicions? Where could Pimen have gotten such richly carved vessels of gold and silver? Many such items decorated his walls and table – things he had not displayed when I had dined here last, less than a year before. I mentioned this to the Czar, who nodded, his lips pressed tightly together as his eyes took in the grandeur.

The meal was served in a large hall, capacious enough to hold several hundred of the brotherhood. After receiving the Czar's instructions, Pimen must have whipped his cooks into a frenzy of preparation, for the meal they brought out was sumptuous. Pimen seemed more at ease once the Czar had been seated at the head of his table. But I could tell Ivan was not at all calm. His facial muscles worked, and he made a point of submitting every morsel of food to be tasted before he partook of it himself.

Through all of this travel and activity, and though I was far from my offices in the Kremlin, it must be remembered that the functions of my Bureau did not cease. As in all the government offices, my clerks kept the routine going whether I was there or not. I was also in constant communication with a vast network of spies and agents all over Russia and in many parts of the world where we had specific interests. While sitting at dinner in the Archbishop's palace, Toby brought me a letter from one of these men. I excused myself to read it. I knew it had to be important, else Toby would not have allowed it to be delivered while I was in the Czar's presence.

Ivan watched me curiously, so I dropped onto one knee beside his chair and whispered to him the contents of the report. My men at the Polish border had intercepted a courier bearing a coded message. Under intensive questioning, the fellow had admitted bringing the paper from Novgorod, but he could not name the man who had sent it. He had been ordered to deliver the message to Andrew Kurbsky in Kovel, in town just southwest of the Pripyat marshes! Ivan's eyes flicked up from their thoughtful concentration when I finished, his gaze traveling across the room. He stared for a moment at the far wall, his breath lapsing into a series of short puffs, his face darkening until it finally became a mask of unrestrained fury. He leaped from his seat with a shriek of rage, snatched at a joint of meat from the board and slammed it against the table. The whole company fell silent, watching the Czar and awaiting his orders. He finally regained enough composure to speak. Pointing a long, crooked finger at Pimen, the Czar shouted: Seize him! Bind him and place him in his own dungeon!"

Ivan now began to tear at his clothing and to pull the few hairs remaining in his beard. He beat against his head with his fists and leaped about the room, hammering the floor with his feet and his *kisten*. "Ransack this house!" he shouted. "Such wealth is not for a man of God! Take it all; destroy what you cannot carry!"

Pimen was hurried away, while most of the men left the table to carry out Ivan's orders. As the room emptied, the Czar slumped into his chair and I handed him a goblet of wine. Almost as fast as the rage had come, it passed. We continued our dinner as the men began hauling the rich, heavy furnishings out of the house, loading them into sleighs and carts to be taken to the Czar's pavilion. Only the day before I had held serious doubts that any sort of plot existed and had rejected the idea of its being anything more than a few random hopes in the minds of a handful of evil men. Now, I had to believe as Ivan did; and once again I had to admit the incontrovertible depth of his intuition. I was ashamed for having doubted his judgment. The letter from my agents was definite proof of a link between the citizens of Novgorod and the traitor Kurbsky. As Alexi and Skuratof led the brotherhood in completely stripping the Archbishop's *dacha*, Ivan and I discussed an appropriate punishment for the city.

I drank very heavily again, and I fear I was not very articulate in my feeble efforts to dissuade the Czar from the harsh retribution he had in mind for the common citizens. Foremost in my thoughts was the guilty knowledge of how completely wrong I had been, and my second strong conviction was that the heaviest punishment should fall on Pimen. But for the moment, I seriously questioned my own judgment and ability to advise.

Ivan's plans were proclaimed the next morning. Each day, a full thousand citizens, chosen at random from the population, were to be brought before him. The exact punishment they were to receive would be announced after they were assembled. No sooner had the echoes of the Czar's voice died away, than the brotherhood began gathering the first day's quota. These came mostly from the wealthier classes, people who resided in large houses near the square. Later, the brothers would take people from the other districts, and even from farms around the city. The regimen begun that day was to last a full five weeks. To prevent total chaos, a few of us suggested dividing the city into sections and setting some pattern for the selection of hostages.

Ivan refused to hear us. Instead, he removed all the restrictions he had previously placed on the brotherhood. He was angry over the Novgorodskis' failure to greet his arrival, and furious at their attempted communication with Kurbsky. That the message had been coded convinced him we had intercepted only one of many, and I had to agree. Although the investigation following this incident required my leaving the city several times on the Czar's business, I was there long enough, and often enough, to observe how dreadfully Ivan's fury was vented through the *Opritchina*.

Once their restraints were removed, the men ran completely amok. No one had control, and no one made any attempt to maintain a semblance of order. Ivan's sole command was for a specific number of men to attend him each day, these to implement his instructions regarding the thousand prisoners. Although these people were subjected to a wide variety of punishments, it took Skuratof to devise the most imaginative method. He ordered a large hole cut in the ice of the river, close to the shore beneath one of the steepest banks. He then ordered ten or twelve people bound to a sled. This was shoved down the slope, causing it to fall through the hole, after which its forward motion carried it beneath the frozen surface. From the shore, especially if one were standing at the top of the bank, it was possible to see the people quite clearly as they struggled against their bonds. Generally, the sled would be tumbled by the current, while those who had been able to free their hands beat futilely upon the frozen underside of ice before drowning.

This method of execution seemed to fascinate the Czar, and as the days went by, its implementations were greatly refined. First, the occupants of the sled would be stripped and deliberately bound in a manner that allowed them to work free at about the moment they entered the water. The upper surface of ice was carefully scraped, then covered with small amounts of boiling water to make it extremely clear. This transparent passage was extended for some distance downstream. By placing the Czar's dais along the route, it was possible for him to watch the drowning prisoners for quite a long time. I was with him twice – first out of curiosity, the second time because I had urgent business to discuss. Those faces came to haunt me, soon becoming the dominant elements of my dreams. Struggling figures, desperately pressing their faces into the narrow pocket of air beneath the surface of ice, they beat against the transparent barrier.

Whole families were sent to their deaths this way, with the brothers wagering on the exact distance or direction the sleigh would travel, how long different members of the family would persist in their struggles. Circles and lines were marked on the ice, to indicate the various records. Intrigued by these executions, the Czar paid hardly any attention to the others for better than a week. Even the continuous noise from the city did not distract him. Screams, cries and laughter – loud crashes as timbers shattered or doors were broken down, the clatter of breaking glass and pottery – all the usual sounds of rape and pillage continued unabated. The accumulated loot and booty was enormous.

During the entire period of Novgorod's punishment, the Czar entered the city only during the day, returning to sleep in his pavilion outside the palisade at night. There, he was not disturbed by the shouts and other noises. Because I was in charge of a large area of town, I had to sleep within the walls. I took quarters in the Archbishop's palace, for its regular occupant was still being held in the downstairs dungeons.

I made some interesting observations here, for I inspected the cellars more than once. This holy man of God had not been making idle threats the previous month when he had told me he had the means of abstracting information. His chambers contained the most modern and efficient equipment I had ever seen, some of it more finely made than the Czar's. I was sorely tempted to try some of the machines on Pimen, but was afraid Ivan would not approve. Malyuta used several of the engines, however, and he had two of the larger pieces removed to be set up in the street, utilizing them in the daily executions.

My work being the excuse to stay inside during the day, I continued in close contact with The Third Bureau in the Kremlin. Near the end of our five weeks in Novgorod, I began to receive some disturbing reports from the south. There was an ominous and unusual restlessness among the Tartar tribes, especially the Crimean Horde. I tried to pass the information to Ivan, but he refused to pay attention.

"Nonsense!" he told me. "The Tartars are too weak to offer a threat, especially in the winter."

Regardless of the Czar's disinterest, I made certain that Vorotinsky was informed. He, of course, still headed the *Zemschina* in Moscow. I had also made sure during all the confusion and looting to maintain a guard on my own and Heinrich's warehouses in Novgorod. By the end of the Czar's sentence of destruction, there was very little left except for these stores belonging to us. Assuming that neither Heinrich nor I would be able to remain, I sent word to Marienburg for Jacob – whom I had ordered to remain on my estates as a safety precaution for both himself and my family – to come at once. When the *Opritchina* had gone, our stocks of grain and pickled meat would be the source of tremendous profit. There would be little coin left in the city, so I wanted a man in charge who would know the proper means of securing notes and sureties against land or other possessions, particularly those located outside the city itself.

I have been told I violated the commandments against greed and usury by these acts, but I do not feel especially guilty. Heinrich and I were, after all, merchants; and adversity can destroy men such as we in less time than it takes to count the losses. When an opportunity for profit presented itself, I saw no reason not to seize it. By supplying food at all, we performed a service. It was only right we be paid for it.

At the end of the fifth week, the Czar ordered all survivors to be brought before him in the central square. Fearful and with great dread, they came, many having to be dragged or otherwise forced along by the brothers. Ivan mounted the dais after everyone had assembled, and looking upon his people like a stern, but kindly father, he spoke to them:

"Living citizens of Novgorod," he said softly, "know you that your Czar has completed his punishment of your city. Tomorrow, We shall leave you. You must also know that this harsh retribution was brought upon your lands by the treacherous conduct of your Archbishop and his subordinate clergy. These men, and the other citizens of Novgorod whom We suspect of being involved, will be taken with Us to be questioned at Our leisure in Moscow. The rest of you will be left to continue your lives and to follow God's holy laws. Pray for your Christ–loving army that it may crush the forces of evil. And pray for me, your Czar. Let the Judges of Heaven render their verdict upon that arch traitor, your former bishop, Pimen. I leave in charge your new governor, Prince Peter Pronsky, the son of Daniel. Return now to your homes, and live in peace."

While the rest of us were busy getting ready to move on, the Czarevitch and a few of his young friends rode through the countryside, destroying the farm buildings and cattle. These lands also belonged to Novgorod, and were held equally guilty in the Bishop's conspiracy. I personally attended to sending the prisoners to Moscow, Pimen among them. The next day we decamped for Pskov. Behind us, we left near sixty thousand dead.

I knew in my own mind that the Czar had been within his rights, and the lesson had been necessary. Yet every night my dreams grew worse, finally becoming unbearably horrible. They were filled with visions of gasping faces, contorted beyond one's wildest imaginings as they struggled to escape their icy bonds. The mouths of these specters worked in frantic, erratic movements. Fists struck soundlessly against the glass–like surface. And this remained the strangest sensation of all. We heard no noise from the drowning victims, though their lips had formed the screams of fear and torment.

Every night, I awoke in quaking terror, the nightshift plastered to my body. On the coldest night, I would sweat as if it were summer. Finally, my fears became so intense I couldn't rest at all, unless I drank myself unconscious. Even then, my dreams were so frightful I struggled not to sleep. Before we reached Pskov, my whole body began to tremble so badly I seemed to have the ague.

It was during this period that I first experienced a particularly terrible dream, one I was destined to have over and over again, for a very long time. It was not as violent as some of the others, and it incorporated a certain quality of beauty. Still, it was more frightening than any I had previously sustained. First, I would see the young acolyte who had stared up at me from the crowd of clergymen – the same I had later seen stacked in frozen death with his many brothers. The poor emaciated face, distorted by fear, and now in my imagination by the decay of death, with its glazed, dead eyes would stare up from beneath the layer of ice; but the mouth was alive. It moved, working to scream in pain or fear. I could never hear the sound, but I seemed compelled to hear it, and I strained to catch some whisper. Until I could note the words from that dead boy's mouth, I knew I would forever be haunted by his specter. I tried to drink enough to obliterate this ghost of the acolyte, but it still came to haunt me. The more I tried to assure against his coming, the more certain it was he would appear. I was in mortal terror of sleep, itself.

Toby did all he could to lessen my torment, wakening me when I began to thrash about, sometimes before I actually screamed in my dread possession. Thus my internal holocaust was wearing on him, as well. Our relationship had always been close, rather like father and son – as I had been to Heinrich. I know that Skuratof and some of the others enjoyed pretending that I slept with my young servant, and they joked about his being my "second wife." But this was not true. Nothing improper ever passed between us – unlike the situation in some of the other officers' quarters. I would later learn just how perfidious Malyuta really was in all this, for he was laying his own sins at my feet and accusing me of the perversions he practiced with Illya, his own body servant.

On the trip to Pskov I had continued to travel by sleigh. This was a large covered conveyance, similar to the one Ivan had previously used. At the end of each day's journey I generally waited inside until my tent was set up, then went directly into it. On the few occasions when I came outside at night, I found others of the brotherhood shying away from me. They were afraid, for my appearance had assumed an unhallowed aspect, and many claimed I possessed the evil eye. Only Malyuta seemed not to be affected, and much as I distrusted him, I tried to explain my dream. He only laughed; but the next time I dreamt he was there! Now, as the face of the acolyte drifted beneath the ice, Malyuta began to pound upon the surface with a heavy mallet. But he, too, made no sound. The dead mouth kept forming the words I couldn't hear. Sometimes, Malyuta was able to crack the ice with his hammer, and then I felt I could almost hear the boy's voice. I would strain and try to move closer, but something always held me back. I would struggle, and the nameless force would grip me tighter until I screamed and tossed about, and Toby would have to waken me.

I was glad the Czar did not observe much of my condition. He avoided my company, for I had been telling him things he did not want to hear – more reports on the Tartar activities. When I did not approach him during the journey, I am sure he was relieved at not being forced to listen to me. Afterward, he became very busy, involved in the removal of treasure from Pskov. I think Heinrich supervised most of this, and he was the one person with whom I wanted most to talk. Unfortunately, he had gone ahead of us and was now in the city for most of the day, returning to his tent at night after I was either drunk or asleep.

At the last moment, the Czar decide to spare Pskov. When we arrived, he ordered our camp set up outside the walls, planning to enter the city the next day. But the bells of every church tolled all night long. In the morning, the entire population met him before the walls. They fell on their knees, wailing for him to be merciful, begging him to forgive them. I think he might still have led us into the city, except for a tattered wretch of a man who hobbled forward on a rustic crutch. He called out a terrible curse upon the Czar if he did not heed and spare the city. As always, the influence of the *yurodivy* was much greater than anything said by the higher clergy. Ivan could see the majesty of their madness, and he was afraid of them.

The Czar could still change his mind, but there was no immediate sack of the city. Although it was spared, Ivan sent a selected group of brothers to collect the valuables he demanded from the citizens. I was excused from this, because Toby let it be known I was ill. It was at this point that the Czar appointed Heinrich to collect his tribute. The eventual fate of Pskov was still in doubt all this while, with the inhabitants trembling inside their homes, uncertain as to the Czar's intentions. The brotherhood was restless as well. Most of them expected to be turned loose once Ivan had taken all he could without sending them in to search for the hidden remainder.

Then the holy man came again – Nikola, I think he was called. It had been rumored that the Czar would take a great bell from the Church of the Holy Trinity. "If thou touchest that bell, thy horse will fall dead beneath thee!" threatened the cripple.

But Ivan had already given the order. Even then, men were starting to work on the ropes and rigging pulleys to lower the massive piece of bronze. Just as Nikola predicted, the Czar's mount collapsed beneath him and died. This frightened Ivan, and he immediately repaired to a chapel in the nearby Monastery of Saint Nicholas, where he remained at prayer all day and through most of the night. The *Opritchina* took the bell, but otherwise the city was spared.

In the morning – having prayed without consuming any spirits – the Czar sent for me, suddenly realizing he had not seen me for several days. Heinrich was with him, having finally completed the systematic collection of Pskov's city treasury, as well as the hoarded wealth of every leading family. I must have appeared as if the very wrath of God had fallen upon me. The Czar crossed himself when I entered, and Heinrich took a step forward as if to catch me. I managed not to fall until a servant had brought a chair, and I was able to drop into it. My head felt very light and the room tended to spin about me. Nothing was quite level; the world itself seemed tilted.

"Dmitri? What's wrong with you?" demanded the Czar. "Are you sick or are you drunk?"

I shook my head. "Both, perhaps," I mumbled. "Perhaps I'm going mad."

Heinrich came up to me and felt my forehead, speaking softly as he tried to ascertain my condition. "Toby tells me you are suffering from bad dreams again," he said.

"I don't know if they are dreams or omens from heaven," I told him. "I think if I could rest. . . ."

"Would you like to stay with Nina for a while?" he asked.

"If the Czar would permit," I said, "maybe it would help."

"Our mission is completed," Ivan commented. "Dmitri has done his work well, and may now be spared. You may accompany him if you like, *Freiherr,*" he added to Heinrich. By his expression he told my stepfather to take me; I think the Czar doubted my ability to get home on my own. Even in my befuddled condition I knew I could not allow this to happen.

"No!" I protested. "No! One of us must remain with you!"

Both Ivan and Heinrich looked at me in surprise, as did the Czarevitch and Fedka, who were sitting together a few feet away."

"That is a strange statement," remarked the Czar.

"I can't explain it," I told him. "I only know that I have this terrible dread. If one of us is not with you, some horrible catastrophe will befall us all! Maybe the Tartars – I don't know –"

Ivan looked at me seriously, no longer ready to laugh at my wild ravings. Somehow he must have seen in me some suggestion of madness, akin to that of the holy men he feared. He listened, and for the first time tried to question me about the messages I had received from the south. Did I really think the Tartars were massing for an attack? When? How many? Who was the leader? Did Sigismund have anything to do with it? Might it be coordinated with an attack from Poland?

I tried to answer him, but I did not have all the facts. There were messages in my tent I had not even read. Fortunately, Toby was standing behind me. He had looked over each note as it arrived. Speaking for me, he answered many of the Czar's questions. Listening to them, I knew in my own soul that my greatest fear was not of the Tartars, though they might attack us at any time. My heaviest concern was not to leave the Czar with only Skuratof and Viazemsky to advise him. I considered both these men my enemies. If neither Heinrich nor I were present to speak for ourselves and for each other, I did not know what evil the others might whisper into the Czar's ear.

In the end, Heinrich remained with Ivan, while I left for Marienburg in the care of a small detachment of Imperial household guards. Toby, of course, was with me, and at my request Boris Godunof commanded the guard unit. Because the spring thaws had begun, the ground was too wet and muddy for a sleigh. I traveled by coach – also a difficult vehicle to haul through the slippery quagmires. But the earth was still frozen beneath the immediate surface. In a few weeks this, too, would melt, after which no coaches would travel the roads until a warm June sun had dried the muck into hard, crusty ruts.

Once I crossed the border out of Russia, I stopped drinking. I no longer felt the need. The farther I went from the scenes of Novgorod, the less trouble I had sleeping. In fact, I dozed peacefully for almost the entire afternoon before reaching my estates.

CHAPTER VIII

Marienburg – a fresh ascent from hell, into the arms of my wife and the company of friends. Simon and his family had arrived with Anne Bomel, shortly before the Czar's force reached Novgorod. I had brought Toby and Boris – the latter fast achieving a special place in my affections. The only person missing from the circle was Heinrich, but I felt better knowing he was with the Czar. As my mind began to clear, I found myself increasingly concerned over the Tartar threat. The more I thought about it, the more ominous the situation became. I knew the leeches who clung most closely to the Czar were unable – or unwilling – to perceive the danger. Few of them had ever faced the Horde. While I had made a point of commanding Skuratof to bring all messages from the Crimea to Ivan's immediate attention, I had no assurance he would. With my stepfather among the group closest to the Czar, I was hopeful he would not be allowed to forget the danger. That being the case, I felt compensated for his lack of company.

In my own mind, I had no doubt that the Crimean Khan would mount a devastating attack on Russia if he thought he could get away with it. We could easily defeat him, but we had to know his movements and we had to prepare ourselves. I was sure Sigismund encouraged the infidels, possibly promising to attack from the west at the time of the southern assault. I also knew the King of Poland was ailing. He was old, and it was possible he could die in the near future. Were that to happen, a tremendous power struggle was sure to follow, and it could end with a Dane or a Swede on the throne – another serious threat. I hoped we could settle the Tartars before having to fight again for our western possessions.

These were the problems I discussed with my friends during the otherwise restful days at Marienburg. For the time being a truce was in effect, which neither side had violated for almost a year. The quiet countryside, green with spring growth – the meadows interspersed by well–tilled fields – all allowed me to forget the horror only a few leagues to the east.

I was surprised – and pleased – to hear Boris speak out, expressing his opinion that Ivan should discontinue the *Oprichina*. He was an unwilling member, like myself – a condition, we decided, which we shared with a number of others, especially among the men of better background and above the average age. It was a matter never to be mentioned, and the very fact of our discussing it between ourselves marked a degree of mutual trust that had become extremely rare. Unlike myself, of course, Boris had not been pushed into a position of prominence. Only recently had he begun to attract the Czar's attention, with the result that ambition now conflicted with conscience. By cooperating with men like me, he seemed to hope we could persuade Ivan to consider reorganization. He saw the Czar's miserliness as a major potential weapon.

"The *Opritchina* is very costly," he maintained. "This is the greatest argument to press in persuading Ivan to abandon it. The whole country is going to experience famine before this year is over; already the poor of Moscow are boiling grass and tree bark because there isn't any grain. While the common people starve, the *Opritchniki* have food and plenty to drink. Feeling is strong against them, and they are not powerful enough to stand against the entire population of Moscow."

"Do you think the people would ever revolt?" asked Nina doubtfully.

"Hungry people can do some very strange things," he told her.

"And it will get worse next year," I added, "because many farmers have been killed or driven out. Those who remain do not tend their fields for fear of being caught in the open when a gang of brothers decides to make a raid. But I don't know, Boris," I said, turning to my friend. "I really doubt Ivan will disband the brotherhood until he gets weary of it. And, frankly, I don't care as long as he puts some restraints on it. That is the real problem. We're a powerful army without discipline."

"And without an effective leader," added the young man. "The Czar has never been a great field commander – not like the Emperor or one of the Germanic Kings. And in the *Opritchina* no one else has the authority. Oh, I've seen you try to bring some order into the mob, but I've also seen the signs they make at you when your back is turned."

"The greatest leadership is actually in the *Zemschina*," I remarked. "I'd like to see our army organized to include all this wasted ability. Someone like Vorotinsky should be put in charge. That would be an army! We'd never have to fear the Tartars or anybody else!"

But all this talk did us little good, and we dared not stay away very long. Ivan would probably listen to Heinrich, but my stepfather was not able to exercise the influence that I could. If I guessed correctly, Malyuta would more than take over during my absence. If any messages arrived that he didn't like, the Czar would never see them. In addition to his jealous rivalry with me, Skuratof was driven by base avarice. And if he could find some way to hang a crime on me, he would assume the office closest to the Czar. I knew how badly he wanted this.

Before we left, Anne managed to catch me alone and question me about her husband's problems. I had almost forgotten, for they seemed so trivial in comparison to all that had happened since. I assured her I would do everything I could. She also suggested I might get Elysius to help me if the bad dreams started to bother me again. He had treated people for this sort of problem before, she said.

It was harder than ever before to part from Nina. Our third child was nearly due; yet I dared not delay to see it born. The peaceful calm evoked a heavy longing not to have the warmth and love of my family so far away from Moscow. But more than ever I feared to have them in the capital. In the manner of my own feelings, I suppose our marriage was very "Western." It was far different, certainly, from those of any Russian friends.

Shortly before I left I made a seemingly unimportant discovery, but something I should have taken as a warning of trouble to come. Nina made a remark about being "so surprised and pleased" when Simon and Anne arrived. She had never received my letter, telling her they were on the way. Nor did I happen to think about the long delay there had been in her last letter getting to me. She had written it in December, and it had not come into my hands until late January. But, I quickly forgot about it. Transport during the winter months was always uncertain.

During those final days, I engaged in vigorous physical activity to get my body back into condition. I rode hard every morning, and put in long practice sessions with wooden swords each afternoon. Boris, dark and powerfully muscled, was a good match -- better than Simon, who did not have the physique to handle our heavier weapons. The matter of Nina's and my lost, or delayed, communications was buried by these other activities. In all, I remained a month, during which time I lost the bloat about my face and waist. I would return to Moscow in the best condition I had enjoyed since Ivan's formation of the brotherhood.

Simon decided he had better return with me, lest the Czar wonder at his motives if he stayed away much longer. As it would be impossible to haul a carriage during this season of thaws, his wife and children would remain. Anne was also to stay with Nina. Thus, with the Tartar girls she would be well attended. Nor was Serge ever far away. I promised to return as soon as I could, grieving at being forced to leave so soon. My wife's terror, though well concealed from others, was plain – and painful – to me.

Our return route took us into both the cities of Pskov and Novgorod. There was no way to avoid them, for the only highway to Moscow lay through these two victims of the Czar's wrath. The first, Pskov, was not badly ravaged. The people suffered only from hunger, due to the farms and storage sheds all over the area having been burned by Fedka and the Czarevitch. All of this was particularly disturbing to Boris, who was involved with the Kremlin bureau dealing with food supply and taxes. He had already been frustrated in his attempts to cope with famine in the area around the capital. Now a similar situation would exist in the western lands. To further complicate their own misery, hungry peasants had eaten most of the grain set aside for seed in the spring plantings.

However unhappy we found the people of Pskov, they could not approach the abject despair of Novgorod. The city projected an aura of death and mourning. The Czar's new governor was no kinder than his father had been, and thus far had only expressed concern over clearing the dead bodies – and parts of bodies – from the streets. Even in the winter's cold the stench had attracted every type of vermin. Rats invaded the stone walls in droves; starving dogs, many of them frothing with the wolves' disease, made it dangerous to venture outside. Already, pestilence had come upon the city.

Holding kerchiefs tightly against our faces, we rode through as quickly as we could, not pausing to refresh ourselves at the watering places. We traveled until long after dark, camping some thirty miles beyond Novgorod. Other towns along the way had also descended into a state of ghostly lethargy. People stood about dumbly, staring at nothing, moving only if ordered to. They were unable to set their own tasks, or to fend for themselves. Stark skeletons of burned–out buildings stood like black gravestones against the fields of slowly melting snow. At night, wolves roamed about the sites of former towns, sometimes being the only inhabitants left alive for mile after mile of desolate, snowy waste.

Still, in some of the villages devastated by the brotherhood there were a few who retained their senses, and it was these men who began organizing the remainder of the population. Upon such leaders, the remaining wealth – mostly in land – began to devolve. An entirely new aristocracy was being formed across the countryside, with many of these emerging headmen as rapacious as the wolves they drove from their settlements. Always, they were harder masters than the former, decadent landlords.

Boris, Simon and I had some long discussions about this, for the dreadful plague of fire and sword had struck down the old established order, acting at the same time as a purge. In the end, the strongest were gaining ascendancy over the weak. Hopefully, the spring would blossom forth in a new spirit of determination. If it did not, few would survive the following winter.

In all, it took us a month to reach Moscow, and the closer we came the more tightly my former depression began to grip me. The spasms within my gut recommenced, while the old fears started to gnaw once more at my entrails. The capital, when we entered it, was very quiet, reflecting the same mood as the towns through which we had passed. However, I was certain no wholesale destruction or punishment had taken place in Moscow.

Entering the *Kitaigorod* we noted the absence of lights in most of the houses, and took this to indicate the absence of the Czar and the brotherhood. I groaned inwardly, for the prospect of an additional two days' travel to Alexandrov was an unhappy thought. The thaws had turned the roads into strips of muck, until it was impossible to travel in any comfort. One had to go on horseback, which meant riding through a constant barrage of mud, kicked up by the animals' hoofs. Neither did I relish the prospect of following the routine at Alexandrov: the hours of prayer; listening to Ivan drone on for hours more, reading obscure passages from the scriptures. I hoped it might somehow be avoided.

I found enough work in my office to keep me busy for an additional few days, so I sent word to the Czar that I had returned and had started to resume my duties. On the night of my arrival Elysius met me at the door of the house. He was still afraid that the Czar would punish his stupidity. He had learned of a large English expedition arriving at Kholmagora, apparently led by Randolf and Horsey – again without Jenkinson. But Randolf's presence brought the doctor closer to his fate. I ordered an escort north to meet the English party, then sent Doctor Bomel to Livonia. At least he would be on hand when Nina's time came.

During my absence from the capital there had been a few more messages from the south, describing the Tartar activities. It was apparent we should be making preparations to defend ourselves. Even old Abraham, writing from Kazan, told of the unrest he sensed among the infidels with whom he dealt every day. I forwarded all of this information to Ivan, but I never received a reply.

Finally, when I could find no further excuse to delay, I resigned myself to visiting the Abby. Besides, I felt a certain urgency to reach the Czar and persuade him to make the necessary military preparations. I was about to set off with Toby, and our mounts were already saddled, when a short note arrived from Skuratof. Surprisingly, he was warning me of danger! Undoubtedly written by one of his clerks, the message read: "Tread lightly in Alexandrov. Beware of Viazemsky."

At first I thought it strange he should take the trouble to warn me; but he had mentioned Viazemsky as the culprit, and I knew Malyuta was more afraid of him than of me. Besides, I had done him several favors. Not only could this be his way of repaying me, there was also the possibility of our forced association in the Third Bureau placing him in a position to survive or fall with me. Although

Skuratof's message did not especially worry me, it did add some weight to the blackness of my mood. More trouble, I thought as I mounted up, and my solemnity dampened even Toby's usual chatter. Boris had already left, so there was just the two of us, attended by a half–dozen soldiers.

We arrived on the second day, covered with mud, stiff and cold from the hard ride. The wretched trip had done nothing to brighten my mood. We passed into the *Freedom* compound without encountering anyone I numbered among my friends. Ivor had not been at the kiosk, nor were there any brothers whom I knew. Mostly I saw junior men, newcomers to the order, or servitors who remained permanently in Alexandrov. I sent word to the Czar, but he did not respond to my arrival.

I had been in the compound for over an hour, when the bells sounded for dinner. I still had not spoken to anyone other than servants. I had finished bathing, and quickly donning my robes, I went directly to the dinning hall in Ivan's palace. Toby came with me, as it was customary for the senior brothers to have their own servants. These stood in a row along the wall behind our chairs and attended to us during the meal. This may have been a little menial for Toby, but I did not think he objected. Having him there was also an expression of my trust.

We entered the hall just ahead of the Czar. I took my place at the long table, and Toby squeezed into the row of retainers along the wall. I spoke to a few of the brothers, but generally the atmosphere was cold. There seemed to be fear in the ranks, and several prominent men were missing. Skuratof arrived after I did, but other than a nod of greeting he hardly acknowledged my presence. He took his place at the far end of the head table, on what would be the other side of the Czar from me.

Ivan entered the room and everyone rose, bowing their heads in respect. The Czar had not tied his cassock shut, so revealed the splendor of a cloth of gold robe he wore beneath it. He glittered with jewels from head to toe. The black habit was tossed carelessly over his shoulders, covering only the back of his richly appointed costume. He would have been majestic and imposing, except for the condition of his beard and the scraggly gray hairs peaking out from beneath his tall, abbot's headpiece. The residual signs of a recent rage were apparent in his pallid face and in the twitching muscles of his jaw.

Because I had averted my head in proper obeisance, as had everyone else, I was unable to see what Ivan was doing. My eyes were focused on the square of floor at my feet. Suddenly, the Czar's golden robe and wine colored boots came into my field of vision. I glanced up quickly, unexpectedly face–to–face with the blazing red eyes. A cruel smile came across his features, and I stood before him dumbfounded. I could hardly believe his wrath was being directed at me, but I felt the point of his *kisten* come to rest on top of my right foot. I froze. However, my very fear and its resulting paralysis gave me the appearance of being extremely cool – at least that is what others told me later. I could smell only mead on Ivan's breath, which suggested he was probably not very drunk. He continued to stare at me before he spoke; then the words came clearly, not slurred as when he drank heavy wine or vodka. I think it was this semisobriety that saved me – that, and his own doubts of my accusers.

"So, Dmitri," he began, almost in triumph, "so you, too, have betrayed me!" His voice mounted slowly in volume, but that was the last thing I observed for several moments. I was suddenly racked in horrible pain, as the Czar shoved down on his staff with both hands. The steel point penetrated my felt boot with ease, fastening my foot firmly to the floor.

I was so shaken at this juncture, I might well have knelt before him, or backed away and begged for mercy. But with my foot pinioned in place, I could only stand where I was. Though almost faint with agony, fingers of pain now reaching clear up my leg, I retained enough control not to cry out.

This lack of response, or at least apparent lack of response, seemed to curtail Ivan's rising anger. He eyed me coldly before he continued. "You have been in correspondence with that traitor, Kurbsky, have you not?"

Already white with pain and surprise, I must not have blanched further at this remark, and so continued to appear serene.

"If it would not ruin the appetites of these noble guests, I would disembowel you on the spot!" continued the Czar. And after this unlikely statement, he burst into an evil laugh, which was tentatively echoed along the tables, finally spreading the full length of the hall. From the corner of my eye I could see Heinrich struggle half–way to his feet; then slump down again in his chair. He must have come in late, for he had not been there when I arrived.

My mind, recovering from its original debilitating fear, now began to function. I knew I had only a few moments if I was to save myself. Tears of pain were flowing down my cheeks, as I fought to keep from giving way to complete hysteria. "I have never communicated with Kurbsky," I gasped. I continued to look straight into Ivan's eyes – into those twin, glowing pits of hell. The Czar pressed down again on his stick, sending a fresh flood of agony through my body. But I could see my words had penetrated – my words or my apparent calm. He allowed me another few seconds to speak.

"Of all Your Majesty's true friends and servants," I began, forcing my voice to be steady, "I alone know the depths of Your Majesty's spirit – Your Russian soul, a soul more profound than any other. I have never written to Prince Kurbsky, other than in the names of Your *Zemschina* boyars, and then only at Your Majesty's instructions. But if – *if* someone else has accused me of this, beware!" I paused to let the word ring throughout the hall. "Whoever accuses me," I continued, "does so only to weaken the forces about the Throne, and in so doing to serve his own, selfish ends."

Ivan stared at me another moment, and I was sure his indecision was clear to everyone present, because there was complete silence. No one wished to commit himself – either to my defense or my destruction – until they were certain of the Czar's next move. Without removing his hands from the staff, Ivan motioned with his head for Viazemsky to step up. "Show him the letter," growled the Czar.

With a sly grin on his face, Alfansy pulled a folded sheet of parchment from his waistband and opened it so the Czar could see it. Ivan looked sharply into my eyes. "Well?" he asked.

Grudgingly, the swine turned his paper in my direction. I recognized the letter I had sent to Nina, informing her that Simon and Anne were coming to stay with her. Alfansy must have planned this for a long time, I thought, and I tried to remember which of my men I had entrusted with this message.

"I am accused of treason on the basis of this?" I laughed, ". . . because I wrote to my wife in English? This makes me guilty of betraying my Czar and my country?"

Viazemsky looked uncomfortable, and the Czar eyed both of us sharply.

"Who accuses me?" I shouted. "Alfansy Viazemsky? Can you read English, Alfansy? Would you care to translate a love letter to my wife? It hardly contains the sentiments *I* would write to another man!" I emphasized the "I," which brought a soft, quickly terminated rumble of mirth from the onlookers.

Ivan pulled part of the weight up from his staff, but he kept it in position. He growled deep in his throat, glancing first at me, then at Alfansy. If I get out of this, I thought, I would be one of the very few who ever had.

"With Your Majesty's permission," I said. Taking advantage of this further moment of indecision, I gestured for Toby. He came at once, and I pulled the letter from Viazemsky's hand, giving it to my servant. "Be so kind as to translate this for His Majesty," I said.

His hands shaking, Toby began to read the letter, translating it smoothly into Russian. From the first, it brought chuckles from the company, as it began with a somewhat flowery statement of my devotion – hardly the beginning of a communication between two men. After that, it went into a rather matter –of– fact statement of household business, then the part where I informed my wife of the impending arrival of her guests. It concluded with my hoping to be with her soon, after finishing my part in the Czar's business at Novgorod and Pskov. Toby's face became a little red, for he had come to the words intended for none but my loving wife. Before he had to decide whether to read them aloud, Ivan stopped him.

"Even a Czar must indulge his servants by allowing some privacy between them and their wives. Those words were obviously not intended for Prince Kurbsky." He looked angrily at Viazemsky, who seemed to shrink away. The fiend had cast his best throw and lost. He had counted on working the Czar into a frenzy, where he would strike me down without giving me a chance to defend myself. Ivan's reference to Kurbsky's not being the recipient of such devotion had brought another spasm of laughter from the brotherhood. Even the Czar had permitted a fleeting grin to cross his features. My foot was now numb, but the pain was still traveling up my leg and an icy hand gripped my loins. Still, I kept my stance and bland expression, forcing my voice to hold steady, though my entire right side was beginning to tremble.

Fortunately, the Czar picked this moment to relinquish his own posture. I doubt if I could have maintained my composure much longer. Tears had continued to cascade down my face from the effort of holding back a cry of pain. Ivan must have taken this as an indication of sincerity. I know I spoke again, but I do not remember what else I said – some fairly lengthy expression of devotion to the Czar and to the brotherhood. I must have been eloquent, for when I finished everyone applauded me, and the Czar wielded his stick to swat Viazemsky smartly across the backside. "Get out of my sight!" he shouted. Alfansy fled from the room, the laughter of his former supporters ringing in his ears.

The Czar turned back to me and threw his arms about my shoulders. As always, he embraced me like a bear trying to crush his victim. Ivan's tears mingled with mine, and I was nearly smothered in the folds of his robe, my nose bent double as he drove my face against his chest. I could hardly breathe, but I feared to pull away, praying silently that his expression of friendship would not succeed where Viazemsky's intentions had failed. Finally, he stepped back, leaving one massive arm draped about my neck. He held his stick up high, my blood still glowing on its tip. "See you all!" he bellowed. "This one true friend of the Czar! Only this man, who knows my soul, can understand the misery in which I must live, surrounded by traitors and greedy scavengers – ready to suck the very essence of my being!"

Ivan's speech was long and very incoherent, as he quaffed several goblets while he spoke. I struggled successfully to maintain my standing posture until it ended. At last, the Czar pounded me firmly on the back and retired to his seat at the head of the table. Gratefully, I sank into my own chair, half fainting in a mixture of relief and pain. My foot began to throb, but I did not wish to withdraw. Instead, I proposed a toast to the everlasting glory of the Czar. Ivan downed a huge goblet to himself, then turned his attention to a wild, barbarian girl who had been brought in to dance for us.

Food continued to arrive in the usual, enormous quantities. While this was being consumed, the girl finished her lewd exhibition and everyone's attention turned toward the next event. A powerful naked giant, glistening with grease, hair braided down his back in the manner of Cathay, was about to wrestle a small brown bear. Unlike most such matches, I noticed this beast had been deprived of neither teeth nor claws. At this point, Toby slipped up behind me and crawled under the table. I do not think anyone noticed him except Boris, who had taken the seat beside mine. The circumstances only added to my reputation. I was later credited with having sat there all evening, with my wound unattended, oblivious to the pain. Actually, Toby gently pulled off the boot and slipped my foot into a bowl of warm water. I sighed with relief, praying I would not be called upon to do more than sit for the rest of the evening.

After subjecting me to such a severe and unwarranted expression of his displeasure, the Czar spent several days making up to me – a unique honor in these chaotic times. I was called into his presence after matins the next morning. Instead of lecturing to the brotherhood during breakfast, Ivan had a quiet meal with me. I had to walk with a cane, and had been unable to get the injured foot into even my largest boot. Although the wound caused me to walk with a limp for the rest of my life, no words ever passed between the Czar and myself regarding the incident. Instead, he inquired about my family, and expressed an interest over my personal life in a variety of ways that had not concerned him for years. While he remained in such a solicitous mood, I tried to press him on the Tartar issue. He listened, but continued to put me off. His mind seemed to churn with other thoughts. A great turning point was about to be reached, he told me.

Many of the prisoners brought back from Novgorod had been subjected to extensive questioning in the chambers of the Alexandrov Abby. As if suddenly doubting the righteousness of his actions, Ivan had started an entire re–examination of the evidence against Novgorod. I think he had convinced himself that the full blame did not lie with Pimen. Or perhaps the death of Phillip made him unwilling to execute another high churchman. Whatever the reason, the Archbishop was eventually spared, but exiled to the monastery at Riazan.

Near the end of our breakfast, the Czar expounded on his displeasure at certain discoveries he had been making. Under torture, it seemed the Novgorod captives were working a strange form of revenge. They began accusing certain members of the brotherhood, claiming these men were guilty of conspiring with them to turn over our lands to the King of Poland. Already, the Czar's wrath had fallen on several – hence the absence of some familiar faces the previous evening. Most perplexing to me was Ivan's condemnation of the Basmanovs – both father and son. They had been among the first to suffer. I had noted Alexi was missing the night before, and I had missed Fedka when I entered the Czar's chambers that morning. I was shocked to discover that both were already imprisoned, but I knew enough to keep these feelings to myself. The accusation against them had been leveled by Feodor Lovchikof, a Novgorodski whom I had listed as suspect many months before. It seemed strange that the Czar should take the word of this man, but it soon became apparent how terrible a conspiracy existed among the prisoners. They had agreed, I was sure, that since they must die in any event, they would take as many of their tormentors with them as they could. When one man implicated a certain *Opritchnik,* he was always supported by several others.

With the injury to my foot, it was several days before I could take over the duties of inquisitor, and until then I was forced to leave most of this supervision to Skuratof. As quickly as I was able, however, I put a stop to the Novgorod trickery. I ordered the prisoners separated, and set up elaborate restrictions to prevent their communicating with one another. I am sure this saved a number of innocent men; but the damage already done to certain of the brothers was beyond my power to repair.

There had also been some change in Skuratof, I thought – a sudden sobering of attitude and a tendency to support me instead of going behind my back to curry favor with the Czar. His warning against Viazemsky bore testimony to that, although his actions were most likely based on fear. For the moment, his greatest advantage lay in cooperating with me, for I had devised the only certain means to assure against our being accused by the prisoners. Just then, my status was higher than ever. Not many men could have survived my ordeal in the dining hall, and the fact of my still being free after having been impaled by Ivan's *kisten* made me a man to be reckoned with. Malyuta was shrewd enough to see this.

Between us, we made sure to utilize the Czar's displeasure with Viazemsky. After being ordered from the royal presence, Alfansy had gone to his own house, where he had remained all the following day. I am sure he must have expected Ivan to call him, at which time he would no doubt have presented a properly contrite explanation of his "mistake" and begged forgiveness. He was so spoiled by Ivan's indulgences, I am sure he expected no ill to befall him. He did not realize how determined his folly had made my desire to destroy him. Working with Malyuta, I assured Viazemsky's accusations by two of the highest ranking prisoners.

Within a week after my brush with the *kisten,* our subtle campaign began to have its effect. Without explaining the reason, Ivan ordered me to ready a team of men for a special mission. I obeyed without questioning the Czar, for I had learned through my own sources that Ivan had finally permitted Alfansy an audience. I expected we would be called to arrest him. Instead, a note arrived from

Ivan while he was actually in conference with Viazemsky, ordering me to have his *dacha* in Moscow sacked. All the servants were to be killed. In this, the orders were most specific. Alfansy's wife was to be hanged over the front door, and none of the bodies was to be removed from the premises. I was to arrange for a group of guards around the house, and this was to remain until the Prince had entered the city walls; they were to be removed in that interim before he actually reached the house.

I sent a number of my most trusted men to carry out Ivan's orders, impressing on them the need for promptness. I expected the Czar would immediately dispatch Viazemsky back to Moscow, ostensibly to begin arrangements for a grand execution of traitors. In this I was wrong, for he was not ordered to leave until the morning. I am certain he never suspected his own peril. After his conference with Alfansy, Ivan invited the Prince to sit beside him at dinner, smiling benevolently whenever he spoke, even toasting him during the meal. Just once, the Czar looked over at me and grinned slyly. I shuddered within myself at the ease with which so powerful a man could fall!

The next morning, after Viazemsky had departed and Ivan had finished his usual reading of the scriptures, he called all of us to attention, announcing that we would leave for Moscow on the morrow. We would have a grand display for the people, he said, for it was now clear who the traitors had been. He finished by asking Malyuta and myself to attend him later in the afternoon. I was apprehensive, although there was no reason why I should have been. My danger was surely past. The only prisoner I knew of who had tried to accuse me had been eliminated by my men. Actually, I had been fortunate in this respect, for being absent during most of the interrogations, the Novgorodski seemed to have forgotten about me. I later discovered that two minor officials had tried to implicate me, but they had been foolish enough to name Malyuta as well. Since it had always been either his men or mine who conducted the interrogations, no words from their lips ever reached the Czar. As reward for their stupidity, their bodies had been devoured by wolves in the forests behind the abbey.

Our conversation with Ivan that afternoon was merely to plan the transport of prisoners and to arrange for the removal of certain equipment from the Alexandrov chambers. The Czar wanted these to supplement the machines already in the capital. There were a few refinements in the instruments we had here, not yet duplicated in Moscow.

Because of all this, our departure the next day was a rather bizarre procession. We transported both the prisoners and the machines on which many of them were to die. The brotherhood, as always, traveled in black gowns and hoods. Most of the prisoners were loaded into lightweight, covered carriages, bound and chained. A few, however, were forced to walk. None of them was allowed to communicate with anyone except Malyuta or myself. Such a dreadful fear permeated the entire group it even seemed to affect the men of the brotherhood. Some of those who had been closest to the Czar were now going to their deaths. Could any man be certain of his own future? Even I, who had been closest of all, had brushed very near disaster, and still nursed a badly injured foot.

As we neared Moscow, the tense gloom began to lessen. We had good weather, and the roads had dried enough to permit easy passage for the light carts. In the capital, I ordered the prisoners placed in their cells while Malyuta took charge of storing the equipment. Our arrival had been a signal for people to withdraw from the streets, so we found hardly a man out of his house. The Czar ignored this, going directly to his *dacha* and calling for an assemblage of the brotherhood that night.

After addressing us in front of his palace, Ivan ordered Malyuta to take a team of men and start setting up the machines and other engines of death in the *gostiny dvor*. He obeyed eagerly. The sound of hammers soon filled the air, adding further to the people's fears. I purposely passed Viazemsky's house on my way home from the prison. The wretched swine had been in Moscow for two full days; yet the body of his wife still dangled above the front door. Such was the character of this man. While he must have passed beneath it many times, he had not cut it down. I supposed he hoped to impress the Czar with his indifference. The bodies of the servants had at least been removed from the house, though my men reported they still lay tossed about in the rear courtyard.

Alfansy's pretense of unconcern didn't save him. The Czar instructed me to arrest him that evening, and it was one of the few times I did this chore with unmitigated pleasure. I personally held the rope about his neck as we conducted this devil's servant to prison. I kept Gabriel at just a fast enough pace to make Viazemsky run all the way. Ivan arrived shortly after we did and looked in through the peep hole of the cell where I had placed his former friend – a cramped, stinking crawl hole on the lowest level.

"Good," muttered the Czar. "Tomorrow, he will make a prize spectacle."

Ivan now led the way through the corridors, pausing at various doors to look at the prisoners. Some were in very poor condition, for they had been subjected to all manner of experimental questioning at Alexandrov. Finally, the Czar ordered the guards to open the cell where Alexi and Fedka Basmanov were chained. He seemed to have some fearful compulsion about them, something I wished never fully to understand. This night, he did an unholy thing, and because he commanded me to be present I am forced to share his guilt.

The Basmanov cell was a little larger than most. It was square, perhaps three times the height of a man in each dimension. There was no window, for it was a dungeon room below the cellars of the prison. One of the guards who accompanied us carried a taper, which he set into a wall niche. Until then, the cell had been in total darkness. Except for a thin layer of moldy straw scattered about the floor, the area was completely devoid of any furnishing. Several sets of irons were attached to the damp stones of wall and floor. It was from these that the Basmanovs were suspended. Alexi's wrists were pinioned above his head, at a height just sufficient to prevent his being able to sit. Fedka was fettered to the opposite wall by a long iron chain and collar. The younger Basmanov responded immediately to our opening the door, regarding us tearfully as his eyes adjusted to the light. Alexi, who had obviously suffered harsher treatment, could barely move his body. He simply watched us through half–closed lids. Both men were covered with filth and grime, Alexi still wearing the tattered remains of a shift to cover his bloated body. Fedka was completely naked.

Entering the cell, Ivan remained by the door, leaning on his staff. He spoke softly, soothingly, first directing his words to the father, then to Fedka. Alexi was very weak, for he had been stretched, among other things, and several of his ribs were broken. Still an enormous man, his huge frame seemed shrunken; his head hung as if he no longer possessed the strength to lift it. I wished I might spare him, somehow, for he had always been a good friend. But I knew how violent the Czar would become if I were even to suggest it. Then, much to my surprise, Ivan ordered me to turn Fedka loose.

The boy was badly frightened, of course, but this could not excuse his failure to maintain some semblance of dignity. I was embarrassed for his father, forced to watch his son's disgraceful behavior. With the chains removed, Fedka flopped about the floor, wailing and begging the Czar to forgive him. He mumbled some strange phrases, but they were so inappropriate I tried not to understand them – tried not to remember my conversation with Kurbsky the night before he deserted.

Ivan seemed unperturbed. He continued to speak softly to Fedka, cooing words of compassion, slyly planting a flame of hope in his heart. Finally, the Czar pulled a jewel–handled dagger from his belt and tossed it to the boy. Involuntarily, I gripped my sword, but Fedka only stared at the weapon lying in the straw before his knees.

"It is possible," whispered the Czar, "that one of the Basmanovs may leave this cell alive."

Fedka stared at him dumbly, slowly reaching out his hands to finger the blade. His long blond hair was a matted tangle on his forehead, and it tumbled forward in a mixture of straw and filth. Through this unkempt curtain, the bright blue eyes suddenly came to life. His mind, previously paralyzed by fear and despair, now responded to Ivan's words. He gripped the dagger in his right hand. Getting to his feet with some effort, he leaned against the wall, as if momentarily overcome with dizziness. He raised the knife, took the single step necessary to bring him to his father, and without further warning – without apology to God, the Czar, Alexi, or any other man – he plunged the blade deeply into the heaving breast. Alexi groaned, but made no other move. His body sagged against the stones, and his breathing came in heavy gasps. Fedka stabbed him again, and again. Alexi's entire chest and belly were red with gore; still the boy did not stop. I turned away and went into the corridor, motioning one of my men to attend the Czar.

Ivan must also have been amazed at the viciousness of the young man's attack upon his father. At last he shouted for Fedka to stop. I was in the hall, with my back to the cell when the Czar called out. Fearful that Fedka might have turned on him, I bolted back inside. How vile a creature existed beneath that exquisite exterior! With the blood of his father still covering his hands and splashed in globs all over his face and body, he again went onto his knees before his mentor. "Can I go home now, Ivashka?" he whined.

Ivan laughed, but made no other answer. Even this sound seemed forced. I wished he would come away, but he lingered in the cell for several minutes before he spoke again. "You have tempted me into the depths of sin and degradation," he muttered at length. Then he started to leave.

Fedka grasped his boot, leaving a smear of blood across the felt. "But you said one of us could leave here alive!" he cried.

"And so you shall," answered the Czar, with an evil sneer. "You will leave here tomorrow morning, and you will be alive. You will also be bound and naked, and how long you stay alive will depend upon your stamina."

We could hear Fedka's scrams of rage and fear all the way to the outside entrance. What a dreadful terror must have filled his heart! We had left him alone in the dark, unbound, with the knowledge of his heinous crime and the certainty of his own impending fate. He was free to move about in the total darkness, with only the corpse of his father hanging on the wall for company – that and whatever malevolent spirits might visit him during the night. As we were about to leave the building, I remembered that Ivan had left his dagger in the cell.

"Aren't you afraid he'll kill himself before morning?" I asked.

Sadly, Ivan shook his head, seeming suddenly on the verge of tears. "He is much too much in love with life to take his own." he said.

"And Alexi's body?" I asked. "Shall I have it removed?"

Ivan looked at me, his face a strange mixture of sorrow and scorn, the semblance of a smile on his lips. "No," he said simply.

Then, it was as if an unexpected bolt of thought had struck the Czar. He stood frozen on the steps of the prison, his right hand clutching idly at my sleeve to halt my progress. Several retainers had come up with horses and with Ivan's carriage. He waved them off and pulled me gently back inside the doorway. No one else was within hearing distance.

You observed the English methods of execution, didn't you?" he asked abruptly.

I nodded. "Several times," I replied cautiously, wondering what strange idea was forming in his mind.

"And for the highest crimes?" he continued. His eyes were now focused on my face, "the punishment for treason, the method they call 'drawing and quartering'?"

I nodded again, almost afraid to answer, because in the gloom of the entryway I could not define the finer workings of his features, and could not guess the direction of his thoughts.

"There is one man in this building who has sought to undo you," he said, "a man whose evil is so perfidious I do not think he deserves to survive the night." He paused, then, regarding me closely. I knew that the light from the doorway illuminated my own face, while leaving his in darkness. Was he testing me? I have never been sure, but in that moment I had no choice but to serve as his instrument in whatever it was he wished to do – and I was beginning to understand his intent.

"I assume you mean Viazemsky," I replied evenly, and despite my own fatigue and the fear which lurked around the edges of my thoughts, I also felt a tug of satisfaction – excitement. Then, when Ivan simply maintained his silence, I continued: "Do I understand that Your Majesty would like to see the English punishment administered to Alfansy?" I asked.

"Have you the stamina to do it with your own hands?" he asked. His voice was louder, now, and his pensive moment appeared to have passed. When I looked up sharply in response to his question, he suddenly grinned and slapped one hand heavily on my shoulder. "I'm not testing you, my friend," he continued in a softer tone. "But no one else has ever seen it done." He licked his lips and I could hear the dryness in his mouth. "Do it for me," he urged. "Do it for yourself."

As we turned back into the prison, Ivan started toward the passage leading to Viazemsky's cell, but I plucked at his sleeve. "I think this would be better done in the courtyard," I said, to which the Czar nodded solemn agreement.

I had seen two men conducted to their deaths in London, arriving late for the second execution. In neither instance had I been close enough to see exactly how the finer processes were done. I explained this to Ivan as we sauntered toward the courtyard. I did not relish the idea of actually subjecting Viazemsky's flesh to this miserable punishment, but I can not deny the satisfaction it gave me. Nor could I suppress the undesired excitement which stirred within my bowels. Ivan wanted a show, it seemed, and I had been selected. So be it.

We were seated in comfortable chairs, drinking a rather good French wine which had been taken from Viazemsky's cellar when the prisoner was brought out. He was already in poor shape, for he had been subjected to the scrourge. He was dressed in only a tattered shift, his hands manacled behind his back. The two men who held him were long–time servitors at the prison and I knew them by name.

"Mikhail," I said, addressing the senior man, "we will need a stout rope, a hammer and some heavy spikes, and a very sharp dagger." He motioned for his assistant to fetch the materials, then added: "And an apron for you, Sir?" There was the barest semblance of a smile on his lips, for he had somehow fathomed that I would be physically involved. In the past I had seldom touched a prisoner myself, leaving it to various functionaries to carry out my instructions.

"Yes," I told him. "This will be a very special execution." I glanced at the prisoner as I said this, but Viazemsky refused to look at me. He showed no fear, although I had as much as told him he was about to die, and to die painfully. I got up from my chair and approached my victim, thinking as I did so that he seemed suddenly very small. I ripped the rags from his body, leaving him to stand in naked humility as he awaited the guard's return. The marks of the whip were clearly etched on his milky flesh, but he still gazed in defiance at the wall.

The guard returned with the materials I had requested, and held out a large leather apron for me. I was wearing a cassock, which I removed, leaving only a woolen shift as I stepped into the apron. Mikhail tied it around me, covering the front and sides of my body. From the periphery of my vision I could see the Czar sipping at his goblet, watching me, making no move to interfere or direct the action. He had expressed his desires; it was now my duty to obey despite any reservations I might have.

I took the rope and tied it into an English hangman's noose – thirteen loops around the central sliding core. I motioned for Mikhail to toss the loose end over a beam, then approached Viazemsky, who stoically awaited his fate. He hardly moved as I slipped the noose around his neck, positioning it as I had seen the London executioner do, so that the knot pressed against the prisoner's left ear. The guards watched me expectantly, unsure of my intention, since death by hanging would terminate the exchange, when obviously more was expected.

I could feel the increased speed of my own heart as I instructed them to haul on the rope, to lift Viazemsky off the ground, but to be ready to lower him at my command. They tugged; the rope tightened and the beam creaked above our heads. Viazemsky's body tensed as he felt himself being lifted, and just as his feet left the ground his gaze flicked across my face. His lips curled into a cruel smile. He tried to speak, but the weight of his body tightened the noose and he was unable to form the words. Choking, he hung suspended, his bare feet inscribing a strange pattern, a dance of death as his features gradually darkened.

I watched this miserable man in his suffering, knowing it was only the beginning, but still gratified to realize he was on the road to hell, and that I was the instrument to send him there. In those few minutes while his body swayed and jerked at the end of the rope, I felt my own reserve melt away. My hatred seemed to blossom, and a blood–lust gradually took possession of me. "Lower him," I said, when it seemed that another moment would see him pass from this life, and thus escape the rest of his fate. He sagged as his feet touched the earth, but when I loosened the rope about his neck I could see the blackness drain from his features, and after a moment's struggle he was able to stand without assistance.

Night had descended by then, and servitors had ignited several torches set into wall niches about the courtyard. The Czar remained in his place, quietly drinking his wine, saying nothing, but watching intently. My hands trembled as I approached the prisoner, limping and feeling the pain in my foot that was the result of his perfidy. It was the moment when I must perform the ultimate defilement of his body, as I had seen it done to those two men in London, and not sure I could carry it through. Yet I knew I must – and deep within my own soul I knew I wished to do it. Keeping slightly to one side so that Ivan could observe my motions in the shadowy, ruddy light, I motioned for the guards to support the prisoner, whose hands were still bound tightly behind his back. I took the sharpened dirk, tested it tentatively with my finger, then reached down and grasped Viazemsky's testicles with my left hand.

He knew then my intent, and for the first time he permitted his pretense of unconcern to shatter. "In the name of God, Dmitri!" he cried. "*In the name of God!*" His desperate shriek resounded off the walls, but this in itself would not have stayed my hand, except that Ivan suddenly spoke up behind me. "Better that you cry out to Satan," he shouted. "God will not hear you! Go on, Dmitri; go on!"

My hands were shaking badly, now, and for a moment I felt unsteady, as if I might swoon. I had never touched a man in this manner before, and despite its making me feel degraded it also gave me a sense of power to know that at last I had my most deadly enemy so completely within my control. I made one abrupt stroke with the knife, then stepped back quickly as a cascade of blood poured from Alfansy's body, and his terrible shrieks rent the air. He struggled against the grip of the guards, looking down at his mutilated body. I still held his severed parts in my hand, and I cast them down at his feet. I staggered back to Ivan and seized my goblet from the servant who stood beside the Czar.

As I drained the contents, struggling for control of my own body, seeking sanity in the cool fluid now coursing down my throat, I heard the Czar beside me. "Good, Dmitri, good," he muttered. "This English method is interesting, most satisfactory."

The servant held out a napkin, and I wiped the blood from my hands, forcing myself to keep control of my voice. "The next part is the most difficult," I said in a casual tone. "I hope I can do it properly."

"If you kill him, it makes no difference," said the Czar. "His flesh is as worthless as his soul. But I would like to see it done as in the West," he added softly. "Try, Dmitri, see if you can emulate the English technicians." I thought I heard him chuckle, but when I looked down at his face it was set into lines of intense concentration, no other emotion apparent – no sadness, no levity. It was as if he were watching a troop of his soldiers on maneuver, or a new piece of artillery being tested.

I ordered the guards to position their captive facing a scarred, vertical pole, set into the ground several feet from Ivan's chair. It was a post to which any number of men had been bound when they felt the scrourge. Viazemsky had used it himself, as had Skuratof and many others. "Pull him back a bit," I told them. "I need a little more room to move." Then, realizing how close it was to the Czar I warned him, "If I don't do this exactly right, it may be messy. Perhaps Your Majesty should move back a few. . . ."

"No need," replied the Czar. "Go on, Dmitri. Go on," he urged me, and I could hear the expectancy in his tone.

The servant had refilled my goblet and handed it to me. I downed about half the contents, gave it back to him, and held out my hand for the dirk. Viazemsky had ceased his howling, and now made only a gasping, rumbling sound in his chest. He watched me apprehensively, not sure of my intent. I felt a moment along the muscles of his belly, as I had seen the hangman do in London. Then I made a cut across his gut. Blood gushed from the wound, but I plunged my fingers in and after a moment I grasped something, hooked one digit around the slimy mass and drew it out. Viazemsky howled again – deep, guttural groans. "Tack this to the post," I told Mikhail.

I staggered back, trying to wipe the blood from my hands onto the leather apron. But it was already so coated with gore I could not clean them. Ivan's servants were experienced in this sort of situation, however. One of them hurried up with a bowl of warm water, another with a stack of napkins, and between them they washed my hands and arms. The two guards were now supporting Viazemsky's faltering body, as he stood transfixed, gazing in disbelief at his ebbing existence. I had them back him up to another post and bind him to it. I then told the servants to untie my apron, and I dropped onto the chair beside the Czar. "It should take him several minutes, now," I said, "Maybe more, before his strength fails."

At a gesture from Ivan, the men stepped back from the prisoner, who struggled briefly to maintain his upright posture. then sagged against his bonds. Intermitantly, he seemed to regain some strength and twisted about violently. Each motion caused more of his entrails to pull free of his body, but it must not have caused him as much pain as I had expected, as it seemed to have caused the miscreant in London.

After another few pulls at my goblet, I felt my head reeling and whispered to the Czar, "That is really all that I can do," I told him. "Once he expires, his body should be cut into four pieces – 'quartered,' as they call it. In England the head would be placed on a spike – either on London Bridge or above the battlements of the Tower."

Ivan grunted, repositioned himself, never breaking his gaze as he watched Viazemsky begin his final struggles. He motioned for the guards to cut the prisoner free, humming contentedly as Viazemsky staggered to his feet, stumbling into the pole upon which his entrails were secured, sliding off it, dropping to his knees, crying out as he felt still more of his guts pull free. Each movement brought another groan or cry of despair, until he finally regained enough control to steady himself on his knees. He looked at Ivan, then at me, and he forced a sardonic grin. "You won, Dmitri," he gasped. "You won in this world, but I'll await you in hell." He muttered something else that I couldn't understand, then collapsed face down on the earth.

That night I wept for Alexi and sincerely prayed for his soul. He had been one of the last friends left from my childhood, and I deeply felt his loss. Even Fedka's impending fate distressed me, for I also remembered him from earlier days and knew within the depths of my soul that his destruction was not entirely the result of his own perfidy. In his way, he had merely sought to serve the Czar, even into the very depths of depravity. For Viazemsky, I felt very little, though I could not suppress a shudder as I recalled his final words and as my mind's eye recreated that moment when his last evil smirk had smote me. I had soaked in a tub of warm water for an hour before going to bed, trying to assure that no part of him still adhered to my body. I had that day sunk to the nadir of my spiritual existence. Thus, to this extent, Alfansy had bested me.

I was awakened before dawn the next morning by the thunderous tolling of the Kremlin cathedral bells. Compelled by their clamorous demand, I dragged my protesting body out of bed. It seemed I had just laid down. Still struggling against a drug–like daze, I was soon riding through the crisp spring air, listening to the chatter of birds in the trees and on the rooftops, wondering what was real and what was not. Abruptly, jarring me back to harsh reality, I rounded a corner and stared into the yawning arms of one of Malyuta's terrible machines. Others were lined up behind the first, all on rollers, ready to be towed into the bazaar. As I continued on I wondered how God was going to look upon our work this day. As ever, the time–worn justifications rose up to form a protective wall about my mind, as always seeking to protect me from guilt. The will of the Czar was law, I told myself; a stern Czar was an earthly reflection of the stern God of Israel. Yet, so many to die; so many already dead. It was not for me to understand, not for any man to question the means by which the Lord of Heaven worked His will. I prayed more fervently that morning than I ever had before. Sitting astride my mount, I begged God for some assurance. If He granted a sign, I was not clever enough to perceive it.

The brotherhood assembled in the Square of Executions. It was after matins, with dawn breaking in pink streams across the gray, misty sky. We followed the last of the machines, watching as it was towed by a pair of plodding oxen into the *gostiny dvor*. The other instruments of death had already been set up facing Ivan's huge green and white pavilion which dominated the far end of the square. Several tiers of seats had been ranged on graduated platforms with the Czar's throne in the center providing ample seating for all the members of his immediate entourage about him. The rest of the brotherhood were provided with as many platforms and perches as possible, but many would still have to stand. Malyuta had done his work efficiently, and all had been put in readiness except for the most important element, the audience. There was no mass of people; not a single citizen had come forth to watch the spectacle.

Sitting stock still on his great black stallion, Ivan surveyed the setting in silence, his eyes traveling from one machine to the next. He had just turned toward me as if to speak when that horrible cripple, Basil the beggar, hobbled out of a doorway and placed himself directly in the Czar's path.

"You dare not commit this further sin!" he shrieked. "God's wrath shall fall upon you if you so forget His commandments and ignore the teachings of His Beloved Son!"

Ivan's face went ashen white and even his horse took a backward step. The appearance of this Fool for Christ had been so sudden it took us all by surprise. Ivan tried to edge his mount around the tattered form, but Basil managed enough agility to keep in front of the animal's head. He reviled the Czar in the strongest terms I had ever heard, and I could see he was making Ivan very angry. Yet the Czar was also afraid, and would neither order or permit any of us to harm the *yurodivy*. I finally motioned a few guards into position so they blocked Basil in his weaving movements. When the distance between Czar and beggar became wide enough, I wedged my own horse into the breech, calling for a couple of men to pick Basil up and carry him away.

"Lock him in one of the stables," I told them, "and keep him there 'til we finish. But don't hurt him!"

Recovering from his encounter with the holy man, Ivan looked about the square again. "Where are my people?" he asked in surprise. "I have planned a marvelous entertainment for them. Are they aware of it?" He continued to canter about the open area for another few moments. "Where are they?" he asked again, his voice rising in anger.

In the end, all of us – including the Czar – had to go from street to street commanding the occupants to come out. It took hours to assemble a few thousand trembling people. Thus it was close to midday before the executions began.

The prisoners, tightly bound, and stripped of all their finery, were led out in groups of fifteen to twenty. Some were extremely depleted from their weeks of imprisonment and questioning, but even the weakest strove to bear himself as he knew the Czar would expect. Except for Fedka, a few other members of the brotherhood, and a handful of local dissidents, the prisoners were entirely Novgorodski. Some were from the original group of hostages, brought to Moscow before our punishment of the city; but the bulk were people taken by us during our five weeks in Novgorod. Pimen was among those led out, as Ivan had decided to let him tremble until the last possible moment. The Archbishop, clad only in a tattered shift, was escorted to a rack set directly in front of the Czar's dais. There he was informed, along with several others, that he had been pardoned.

Once Pimen had been taken off to await transportation to his place of exile, the small group of political prisoners was brought out. The Czar had decided to clear the prisons as much as he could, feeling it foolish to keep incorrigibles in cells, feeding them and paying men to guard them. In all, there must have been close to five hundred people awaiting execution. There were two *dyaks,* as I recall – Stepanof and Vasilief – several members of the old boyar council, and John Viskovaty, who had briefly taken over some of Mikhailof's duties. There was a Fumikov among the prisoners – a brother, I think, of the former treasurer. There were several other men of rank, but I can no longer recall their names. We had considered adding some foreigners to the list, but Ivan decided against it at the last minute. Otherwise, we might well have executed a few members of the English colony, simply as a lesson to the Queen.

A dense pall soon hung over the bazaar, for the wind had lessened and the many fires contributed to a heavy cloud of smoke. Groups of black–robed *Oprit-chniki* stood or sat on their mounts, completely surrounding the square. They seemed bored with the preparations, impatient for the executions to begin. Banners and pennants hung limply from their staffs above Ivan's gaily colored pavilion. I thought for a while that it might be going to rain; then the sun, which had been appearing for only brief periods all morning, suddenly burst through the mist. As the afternoon progressed, it became quite warm.

With so many men to be executed, it was necessary to operate several machines at once. Thus it made little difference where one stood to watch; he was always close to at least part of the activities. As a result of our continued assurances to the population, and especially after the original group of spectators saw the huge crowd of prisoners, word began to spread through the city. People started trickling into the square, finally arriving in droves, crowding into every passageway and gathering in tightly packed masses on all the rooftops. Watching them, I had the feeling that these were not the same people who had once stormed Ivan's palace to threaten the Glinskis. Nor were they the stout peasants who had marched behind us to fight the infidels. There was an air of watchfulness about them – an aura of suspicion – not only of us, but of each other. Most of all, I knew, they feared the Czar, and many did not dare to look upon him. It was rumored that his very glance could turn a man to stone, and many people believed it.

The Czar provided barrels of mead for the people, and many casks of wine or vodka for us. As these liquors were consumed, it was natural that many of the earlier tensions should melt away. When the executions began, and the screams of the dying caused a forward surge among the crowds, an almost voluptuous air possessed the people and their former restraint began to disappear. They cheered the executioners, offering suggestions and making wagers on different men's endurance. A few even spoke to men of the brotherhood.

At the height of the activities that afternoon men were being hanged one after the other on a gallows to the left of the royal pavilion. Others were stripped, bound hand and foot, and thrown into a huge caldron of boiling water directly in front of us where a younger man might last three or four minutes, screaming and struggling against his bonds. The couple of elderly victims died almost instantly. Fumikov, who had been singled out for special attention, was dropped into the massive brass container after a dozen or so others had proceeded him. But Malyuta had him hauled out immediately, ordering his reddened, naked body pitched into a second vat of cold water. He was then shifted back and forth between the two caldrons, several of the brothers forming a line like a bucket brigade. After five or six trips, while he was still conscious and shrieking as if possessed, I noticed his skin began to peel. In the end, it came off in almost solid sheets, but by this time he had swooned, passing from this world a few moments later.

Two of Ivan's huge frying pans had been brought up from Alexandrov. These were filled with oil, about a hand's width deep. Prisoners to be executed by this method were stripped, bound and thrown in, two at a time. Because the odors from the pans could be offensive, the equipment was situated some distance away from the Czar.

Fedka and a few others who were to die more slowly, were placed, one at a time, into a special machine set to the right of the royal pavilion. They were bound in an upright position, devoid of any protective clothing, arms extended above their heads, feet attached to the base. Ropes were stretched vertically inside the wooden framework, pulled taut so their centers lay against the flesh of the victim, while the ends were secured to pegs attached to levers. Several brothers sat with their feet upon a series of pedals, beneath the platforms. As these were worked up and down, the ropes rubbed irregularly against the skin, eventually stripping it away. Because of the small area covered by each rope, it could take many hours to kill, while at the same time being excruciatingly painful. There was some irony to this in Fedka's case, for he had helped Viazemsky design the engine on which he died.

Nor did he depart with any dignity. From the very first, he begged the Czar to spare him. I watched Ivan's face, wondering if he might relent, but his features were set in hard, stern lines. Only about the eyes could I detect his sorrow – whether for grief over the loss of a friend or distress at the display of cowardice I could not tell. Next to his father, the Czarevitch also strove to remain expressionless, for Fedka had been more than his bosom friend and companion. Like an older brother, he had guided and taught the heir to the throne a good many of life's early lessons. I was close enough to note the trembling of his jaw, however, and to see the trickle of tears down his cheeks. He kept trying to glance away, but his gaze was continuously drawn back to Fedka's naked, twisting form. It took his former friend several hours to expire.

In the very center of the bazaar was a cage of bears – nasty, snarling brutes, which had been starved for several weeks to intensify their natural ferocity. A number of prisoners were given to them, one or two at a time. This particularly delighted the citizen spectators, for bears were always a favorite spectacle with the people – as long they, themselves, were not in danger.

The most chilling display, I suppose – certainly the most gory – was the death of Mikhailof's successor, Viskovaty. A young, careless fellow, he had particularly antagonized the Czar by imitating him for the amusement of his friends. He was strung up by his feet, within a rectangular framework, and sliced to death. The brothers who did this stood to either side, taking careful measurement as they swung their keenly honed swords to cut line after line down the length of the writhing, blood–slick body. Because Ivan personally supervised Viskovaty's execution, there was never a lapse in the utmost exercise of skill. It lasted nearly two full hours, with just tiny bits of flesh being removed by each cut near the end. The victim's screams were so unearthly he attracted almost everyone's attention.

Ivan had come down from his place to instruct Viskovaty's executioners, and now he returned to the pavilion. He grunted in satisfaction as he took his seat, and I half caught some remark about having equaled the best of the Roman circuses. I had stayed in my assigned place, fascinated, yet trying to drink myself into a state of numbness where the perceptions of my eyes and ears took on a misty, almost ethereal quality. I had been successful in doing this before, and in such a state I could find the bloodiest execution to be, if not enjoyable, at least entertaining. On this day, I was not able to reach the trance–like condition I desired. I drank, but nothing happened. I might have gotten up, but my foot was still not healed and it was painful to stand on it. My senses remained as clear as they had been at the moment I entered the square, and the memories of the day remain in my mind as vividly as any other experience of my life. While I never became ill, the lump in my stomach swelled until it pressed against my sides. The fear of God's punishment was uppermost in my mind, for I had suddenly begun to wonder if the appearance of the crippled beggar might, indeed, have been the sign for which I had begged in my prayers. And this fear of God's punishment would remain uppermost in my mind; while I would continue to defend the Czar for years to come, the doubts of Judas began to prey upon my soul.

At the end of the day, the Czar was heartily cheered by his people. The crowd had grown enthusiastic over the fine show he had given them, and there were many cries of "Long live Your Majesty!" and "Death to dogs and traitors!"

That night, the brotherhood was instructed to cut up the bodies and strew the pieces throughout the streets and alleyways of the city. This was to be a reminder for any who might betray the Czar. Afterward, the brothers visited the homes of the few victims who had resided in Moscow, stripping the houses and making what use they would of the women and servants. Ivan insisted I accompany him and the Czarevitch when they went to Viskovaty's house. The dead man was reported to have had an especially attractive widow, and several lovely stepdaughters. I was physically tired by then, this being the only reaction I seemed to have sustained from my heavy consumption of vodka. I would have like to decline, but it was apparent the Czar intended to be obeyed. The Czarevitch Vanya had already made some remarks about wishing to watch me work my charms on the ladies. I had lived too long on reputation, he said, and it was time I gave a demonstration of my abilities. In the hope of avoiding this, I pretended to be drunker than I really was.

While the execution of prisoners in the Czar's name should entail no burden of sin, I had my doubts about the aftermath – the ravaging of widows and children. I followed Ivan and Vanya into Viskovaty's house, unwillingly within my heart, but openly as bold as any – and secretly, deep within me, experiencing a certain degree of lust. Yet I really did not want this additional crime upon my conscience, and I prayed for some miraculous force to intervene. I had not violated my marriage vows for a long time, looking upon this self–denial as a general might regard his fresh reserve of troops. When all the other evidence of my good and evil was weighed before the Judge of Heaven – the great weight of my sins balanced against the good I had done in the furtherance of Russia's holy cause and Christianizing of the infidels – if the scale should still be in doubt, perhaps this single item might tip it all toward the good. It was a silly theory, I suppose, but during these difficult years I did not always think clearly.

Viskovaty's *dacha* had already been ransacked by the brotherhood when we entered. The removable goods had all been taken, and everything else destroyed. Chunks of broken furniture lay cast about the entrance halls, and downstairs the house was in shambles. The fine carpets were gone, but the paddings remained. Lewd symbols and pictures had been drawn on the walls, and the single word "traitor" had been scratched in letters as tall as a man along the side next to the stairs. In this house, the *svyetlitsa* was upstairs, as it was in many of the newer homes. Followed by a dozen brothers, I mounted the steps in company with Ivan and his son.

Here we found the same state of wreckage, and I began to wonder if the *Opritchina* might not already have found the women and carried them off. But no, the Czar's seal had been etched upon the door of the *terem*, thus placing it under his personal protection. Ivan tried the door and found it bolted from within. Without trying to knock or call to the occupants, he signaled the men behind us to break it down. The door yielded on their second rush, collapsing in a crash of splinters, which tumbled half a dozen men into the room. At the far side, a handsome matronly woman sat on the edge of a big four–poster bed. She shielded a female child under each arm. Viskovaty's widow remained as if frozen, staring at us in abject terror, making no move to flee or otherwise defend herself.

"Show proper respect for your Czar!" shouted one of the brothers behind us.

Her eyes flickered into life, and pulling the girls along with her, she sank to her knees in front of Ivan. She touched the floor with her forehead and kissing the toe of his boot, mumbled, "God will bless you for your mercy."

"He will also bless you for serving your Czar," shouted Ivan. He grabbed the widow by the back of her dress, and – half dragging, half carrying – threw her onto the bed. This left Vanya standing alone, before two cowering girls. The eldest must have been sixteen, the other a year or two younger.

"Which one do you want, Dmitri?" he asked in a matter–of– fact tone. "I shall give you your choice." With that, he grabbed both girls by their hair and forced them out of their crouched positions, though they remained on their knees. "The younger one is the prettiest," he said lightly, "but the other's got bigger tits!"

I looked at the pair of sorrowful faces, each quaking with fear, eyes bloated and wet from weeping. They made me think of wounded birds flopping about helplessly because the hunter's aim had been poor. The younger girl reminded me of another, many years before. I reached down and seized her shoulder, just as an ear–splitting shriek sounded from the bed. The mother was putting up a struggle, as Ivan ripped away her clothes. I turned in time to see him sink his teeth into the flesh of her neck. Two of the brothers stepped forward, shoving the woman back upon the bed. With one sweep of his hand, the Czar ripped the remaining clothes from the front of her body, exposing her white, blue–veined flesh. Though buxom, she was very firm, and the little extra weight about her hips and thighs seemed to excite the Czar, until his assault fell not only upon her womanhood. He seized her flesh between his lips, working down from the neck to the ample breasts, applying the full force of his jaws. He left huge welts upon her skin, and the eerie screams were no longer a simple expression of fear or revulsion. Her agony was manifest. Had the two brothers not continued to hold her, sheer terror and pain must have given her strength to pull away from Ivan's unwelcome form of lovemaking.

The two daughters were now so badly frightened they also began to wail, and Vanya became impatient to emulate his father. "You want the younger one, then?" he asked me.

I nodded, although in truth my loins were bursting with lust, and I would have liked nothing better than to have cast myself upon the well fleshed body of the elder. "I like them a little on the skinny side," I said, forcing my tone to remain steady.

At this, the Czarevitch heaved the older daughter to her feet and shoved her onto the bed beside their respective parents. I waited until neither Ivan nor

Vanya was paying any further attention to me, then seized the younger girl and tossed her over my shoulder. As I bore her out the door I had to limp past a pair of brothers who stood guard in the hallway. As they were already intent upon watching the Czar and his son, I made only a passing comment about there being no room for me. One of the men laughed, saying I just wanted privacy. Further down the hall, a couple of others made some vulgar suggestions. Beyond this, there was no comment. I don't believe anyone ever questioned my making proper use of the girl. My injured foot sent bolts of searing pain up my side, and I trembled badly as I struggled forward.

Distractedly terrified, the child hardly struggled as I carried her. Instead she gripped my waistband for fear of falling. Once outside the house, I pitched her across Gabriel's withers and mounted up behind her. "Just keep still," I whispered, "and you'll be all right."

Toby had returned home, as I had told him to. I wanted someone in the house when the revels began, following the executions. As I had surmised, most of my servants had slipped away to join in the excitement. Other than an elderly woman in the kitchen, Toby was the only one home. He greeted me at the door, a look of surprise on his face when I entered with the girl across my shoulder.

I tried to set the child on her feet, but her knees buckled and she swooned. I explained to Toby what had happened, telling him I wanted her kept out of sight if anyone called at the house. We took her upstairs to the women's quarters, where we placed her on a bed. She was beginning to come awake, and as I watched I realized she really was a pretty little thing. Her features were very fine and her body, though not fully developed, already showed signs of the voluptuous woman she would be. And in that moment – may God forgive me – I wanted her, longed to strip her naked and force myself upon her. Had I been alone with her – I don't know, but the boy's presence saved me from this further sin.

Toby seemed perfectly capable of taking care of her, so I started back downstairs.

"Make sure she understands we mean her no harm," I told him, "and don't let her escape. I dare not ruin my reputation by having it thought I failed to rape her."

I decided it would be a good idea if I returned to the Czar, so I went to the kitchen and had the old woman cut me a slice of brown bread. I ate it with a piece of cheese, as this practice usually helped to curtail the pain in my stomach, and also helped to sober me. I was finally beginning to feel groggy from the spirits I had consumed earlier in the day. Now, with the worst behind us, I wanted my wits about me. On the morrow it could also be beneficial to remember the happenings of the moment – especially when others might not. I was still dawdling about the house, not wanting to reappear too soon, when one of Jacob's men arrived from the south.

The fellow came the back way, entering through the kitchen. He was nearly spent, face and clothing caked with grime and dirt. His robe was badly ripped and tattered with numerous scratches and abrasions showing through the rents. "The Tartars," he gasped. "There is very little time!"

It did not take much questioning to obtain a good picture of the happenings. As I had tried to advise the Czar, the Crimean Horde had been slowly rebuilding its fighting strength for years. The Khan had been biding his time, preparing for the day when he could launch a full offensive against us. This had been obvious in the many reports I had already received. The power of the Turkish Sultan already posed a threat to the Christian kingdoms along the Danube. The Crimean Horde would become the long arm of Islam, carrying the Crescent into the Northland. From Jacob's message, their immediate aim seemed to be the recapture of all they had lost along the Volga. Because it would be too costly for them to try retaking Astrakhan and work north toward Kazan, I expected their attack elsewhere. According to Jacob's intelligence, this should be toward the center of our defensive chain – Tula, perhaps, or even across the Oka toward Moscow. In any event, the Horde was definitely on the move. The commanders of every outpost had to be told, and proper reserve forces had to be assembled in the capital.

I set out at once through the confusion of milling crowds and laughing, drunken men, trying to find the Czar. He had left Viskovaty's *dacha* and apparently joined some one of the roving bands of brothers, carousing the city. I rode frantically from street to street, desperately trying to locate him. It was no use. I did find Malyuta, but he was too drunk to be of any help. Finally, I went to Boris Godunof's house, and he, at least, was home. Sharing my feelings on many subjects, he had slipped away as soon as the executions had ended.

Boris, incidentally, had recently married Malyuta Skuratof's daughter, this being arranged by the Czar and intended as an expression of his great favor. The girl, what little I knew of her, seemed to be fairly innocent, perhaps even a little stupid. She was reputed to be extremely attractive, and must have been quite young; Malyuta was not much older than I. When Boris had returned home that evening, it had been to enjoy the company of his new bride and to assure her safety during the uproar outside. He was having a quiet dinner with her in the terem when I arrived. He responded at once to my summons.

I explained to him what news I had received from my agents and emphasized that I considered the situation desperate enough to require some immediate action. At this point, I had no way of knowing whether the Tartars might be right on the heels of my messenger. The man had been so frightened he had ridden two horses to death on the way, anxious not to be overtaken by the infidels and cut to pieces for their amusement.

Somehow, speaking to Boris had a quieting effect on me. In the cool and calm of his tastefully furnished home, I began to regain my own aplomb. For the Horde to appear this quickly was, indeed, unlikely. Any army, with all its supply problems and masses of necessary equipment, could never move as rapidly as a single messenger. I had allowed my agent's hysteria to grip my own heart. Whether or not preparations to meet them were started this night or the next day would make no difference. We arranged to meet in the morning and to approach the Czar together.

I drank a goblet of wine with Boris and returned home, knowing I could not possibly be missed by the brothers. I found Toby sitting beside the girl's bed, in the women's quarters. She had awakened, and drew herself into a ball, trembling with fear when she saw me. I noted that Toby had been holding her hand when I came in.

"Didn't you explain she has nothing to fear?" I asked.

"Yes, but she has had a terrible fright," he replied sagely.

"Sir? My mother . . . ?" she began.

"You are safe here," I assured her. My tone was stern, now that drunken passions had subsided, and I felt a genuine compassion for her. "You must forget about the rest," I added more softly.

She turned her head into the pillow, weeping inconsolably. I never detailed her father's fate to her, but she knew how both her mother and sister must have died. I doubt if the older woman survived Ivan's love–making. I had seen him start before as he had with this one, and his biting frenzy could easily end in the death of his partner. Out of curiosity, I later verified that both women had been thrown into the river. If they had not died before from the attentions of the brothers who took their pleasure after the Czar, they were surely drowned – they and many others. That night, some eighty widows of discredited *Oprichniki* and other men of the *voivode* class – all executed as traitors – met a similar fate. Both Romanovs – Anastasia's brothers – perished in the frenzy of rape and pillage, as did several other men from the "old court" – that which existed prior to the formation of the *Oprichina*.

The girl eventually learned the full details of her father's fate from others. During the course of Viskovaty's death by slicing, Skuratof had cut off his left ear, presenting it to the Czar just before the victim died. This trophy had somehow survived, and one of the brothers had nailed it to a post in front of its owner's house. It remained there for several days, long enough for his daughter to see it, when – against my instructions – she crept back a night or two later, vainly hoping to find some member of her household alive. With it all, however, the girl – Anna by name – was quite sensible. Once she had recovered from her ordeal and was able to speak rationally, I found her rather charming. Resigned to whatever Fate had in store for her, she obeyed me without question – except for the one incident of returning to her home. As it happened, Toby was already captivated by her and in the days to come he became her virtual slave. I retained her in my household, as there was no alternative other than to cast her out into the street.

CHAPTER IX

Ivan's reaction to the mass of executions was akin to a man's holding his head in pain after a drunken orgy. When Boris and I went to the royal *dacha* the next morning, we learned that the Czar had never gone to bed. He was still in his chapel with the door bolted, refusing to see anyone except his chaplain and the treasurer. To expiate his sins, he had sent a large sum to Sergey–Troitsky for the construction of two new cathedrals – one dedicated to the Assumption, the other to the Descent of the Holy Ghost.

A short time later, the Czar ordered money sent to the Monastery of his patron, Saint Cyril. This was to pay for masses and continuous prayers for his soul, as if he were already dead. Each time the door opened and the chapel priest carried out Ivan's notes, Boris and I sent back word, urgently requesting an audience. Ivan finally called us to him in the early afternoon.

Looking more dead than alive, the Czar personally opened the door to his private chambers. He escorted us in, an arm about each of us, and seemed almost to beg our understanding. The flesh of his face had sagged into a mass of wrinkles. There were deep pouches beneath his eyes, and the sockets were two black pits, where the glowing coals had turned to cinders. The Czar dropped onto a bench, inviting us to sit on either side of him. He seemed exhausted until, in a sudden explosion of energy, he looked about him, his face holding the expression of an old man just awakened from a deep slumber. He shouted at the servants, commanding them to leave us.

When they were gone and the door was closed again, I tried to explain the reason for our urgent insistence on an audience, but the Czar was not ready to listen. Instead, he heaved himself wearily to his feet and dragged us to his writing table. He showed us some sketchy notes he had made for the extra fortifications to be built about the Monastery at Beelozersk. Helplessly, Boris and I exchanged glances. Beelozersk, far to the north, had long been a repository for some of Ivan's gold. But the Czar was not so lost in his own depression as to miss our interchange.

"I know what you two are doing," he said, "and I know you both seek to serve me. Dmitri fears the Tartar, and Boris – you would have me end the brotherhood. Both of you are wrong, and yet neither of you would betray me." He worked his way around the table to his big chair. Once seated, he gathered his robe close about him, as if to keep out a draft.

I told him what I knew of the Crimean movements and urged him to organize the army. He listened, too tired to argue, his face a lifeless mask. His only reaction was an occasional shake of his head.

"We shall send an ambassador to the Sultan," he said, at last. "We shall flatter him, and We shall win an armistice. You will see, Dmitri; the Khan will not attack Us. He has been so humbled by the power of Muscovy, he knows better than to attempt invasion."

Both of us remonstrated with him, but Ivan held firmly to his original conviction. He never lost his temper, although we challenged his reasoning and cajoled him all afternoon. The final decision, of course, was his. An ambassador was sent off the next morning. While this eventually proved a mistake, confirming the Saracen's perception of our weakness, it did delay the impending attack. Word reached us a few weeks later that the Horde had gone into its usual summer pasturage. Ivan laughed at us, calling us alarmists and old women. He still ordered a large portion of the loot from Pskov and Novgorod sent to the newly fortified Beelozersk Monastery. Our greatest accomplishment in forcing these problems on the Czar was to return his attention to governing the realm.

There had been few executions since Ivan's great circus, but he never rescinded the original order to the *Opritchina* that the bodies be dismembered and scattered throughout the city. Boris and I tried to persuade him to reconsider, but Malyuta agreed with him. As a result of this division among his advisors, the Czar stubbornly refused to budge. When warm weather came upon us, the result was inevitable. Moscow was beset with a pestilence similar to Novgorod, for heavy rains in April and May only made the flesh putrify faster. Swarms of rats invaded the city, sometimes racing down the alleyways in broad daylight, their packs several hundred strong. People became so used to seeing parts of human bodies in the streets, they simply kicked them aside. Dogs chewed the bones of men, while those residents who were inclined to remove the source of stench and revulsion were afraid to touch what the brotherhood had left.

In early June I received the anxiously awaited letter from Nina. She had borne a daughter in March, and asked when I might be home again. Desperately as I wanted to go, I dared not leave. The Third Bureau had become the center of tremendous activity, for I had activated every possible agent in every area of interest to us. None of the information was encouraging. Sigismund was failing badly, and would surely die within the year. Without a strong king to restrain them, some of the Lithuanian nobles were causing trouble along our border. I persuaded the Czar to send an ambassador to renegotiate the truce. I knew Ivan was beginning to toy with the idea of a new offensive in the west, but by recruiting Simon and Boris to support me, I was able to convince him otherwise. In the end, we signed a three-year extension of the peace with Poland.

From the south, I never ceased to receive disturbing reports. The Sultan had assembled a large number of Russian defectors, treating them well instead of placing them in prison as he had done in former years. He was now using them to organize a military force, promising rich rewards if the traitors helped his Islamic armies destroy the Christian Empire of the Czar.

"Let this be a lesson to you," Ivan said, when I brought him the reports. "It only goes to prove the necessity of executing all these traitors before they have a chance to become vassals of some infidel king and turn upon their own God and country."

I had no appropriate answer for him; perhaps there was none. But these particular men were safely over the border. It was a situation we could do nothing about. Our immediate problem was to assure a defense against them, an effort in which our prospects of success continued to worsen.

Following on the heels of disease and pestilence came famine. We had no appreciable supply of foodstuffs remaining from the previous year. With heavy rains in the spring and early summer, most of our grain crops were destroyed in the fields. By autumn, many people were forced to survive on roots and bark, facing the coming, terrible winter. The shortage of food eventually became so acute, especially in the outlying areas, that people turned to cannibalism. Small children were slaughtered and roasted like suckling pigs; old people were driven out into the snow and left to freeze, thus conserving the meager hordes of cabbages and sweet roots. Later, when these supplies were exhausted, the frozen bodies were recovered and butchered to sustain the lives of the family. But this was still to come.

By midsummer, the odors within the city became unbearable, and the Czar withdrew to Alexandrov. There he remained, living in the Abbey until well into winter. Though the brotherhood occasionally raided the capital, sweeping down upon the citizens like an invading war party, Ivan did not accompany them. He was said to have fifty women in the *terem* above the monastery. While the number was undoubtedly exaggerated, I knew he had ample diversions. I was too busy in the Kremlin to concern myself with the brotherhood's mischief. Being absent from Ivan's side no longer posed a threat to my continued favor, I felt, for the example of Viazemsky had discouraged those who might have worked against me. Even Skuratof would move with caution. I was more concerned at not being able to take the time for a visit with my family, but I had become a slave to my office, afraid to surrender this potential weapon to Malyuta.

The Czar came to Moscow only once, just after the first October snows. Dreadfully drunk, he ordered bears turned loose in the city streets and remained until dark to enjoy the spectacle. He slept in his Moscow residence, but returned to the Abbey early the next morning, instructing me to send him all the remaining prisoners from the Kremlin cells. From this, I assumed he meant to recommence his activities in the Alexandrov chambers.

I was too preoccupied after Ivan's departure to personally supervise the loading of these prisoners – not that I should have been expected to concern myself with such routine matters. But an error occurred, and I was later unable to say whether the fault lay with my people in Moscow, or with Ivan's in Alexandrov; but somewhere the guards were careless. Within the group we sent was a Lithuanian nobleman, taken in battle some time before. I no longer remember his name. But somehow, the fellow had hidden a knife on his person, and he attempted to use it on the Czar when brought before him. Fortunately, Vanya was beside his father, and intercepted the blow on his arm. The resulting wound to the Czarevitch was deep and painful. Ivan was furious! I had to send a number of replacements for guardsmen who were eliminated as a result of the incident, and in the end I had to visit Alexandrov myself.

For a prisoner to obtain a knife could imply an accomplice among the *Opritchina*. The Lithuanian was subjected to extensive questioning, and we might have obtained the information we needed, had Ivan left me alone to conduct the interrogation. As anyone experienced in this kind of work is aware, the *threat* of pain and injury is the key to making the prisoner talk. He should know what awaits him if he fails to comply with the interrogator's demands – perhaps even to the extent of receiving a sample of the alternative should he continue to resist. Unfortunately, Ivan personally supervised the questioning, and ordered the fellow stripped and beaten with wire whips. When I tried to intervene, he told me to keep out of the way. Then, when the prisoner still refused to answer – although I felt he might have been on the verge of giving in – Ivan ordered the intensity of the whipping increased, and the prisoner collapsed. He died without regaining consciousness.

Despite our questioning a few other prisoners, we were unable to uncover a connection between the assailant and anyone else. Still, the incident caused a new purge within the brotherhood, and extended to a few outside the ranks. Johnny Vorontsof, the son of Feodor, was the first to be executed – beheaded as his father had been. I was sorry to see him removed, for he had been developing into a good officer, and I still anticipated our need for a strong defensive army. As I recall, no other boyars fell during this time; but a number of *voivodes* were accused and executed. The last of these was a fellow named Golokhvastov, who had been in charge of our garrison south of Moscow. As an *Opritchnik*, he had friends within the Alexandrov councils, and learned he was in trouble before I had actually sent anyone to arrest him. He fled to a monastery by the Oka River.

We found him right away, for his movements were known to every peasant in the region, and they all hated him. When I sent Golokhvastov to the abbey, I submitted a note to explain the delay. "Hiding in a monastery, was he?" shouted the Czar – this account being told me later by Boris – "Well, he must be in a hurry to get to heaven. We shall help him along his way!" Golokhvastov was packed into a cask of gunpowder and exploded – all of which seemed to satisfy Ivan's immediate craving for blood. There were no more requests for prisoners until much later.

We had very heavy snows, starting early that winter. The Czar decided to remain at his abbey rather than suffer the inconveniences of travel. With the storms so frequent and severe, my agents were having trouble getting messages through to me. At the end of November, I called Skuratof in from Alexandrov, leaving him to look after the Bureau. I battled the elements to spend the holy days in Marienburg.

I asked Heinrich to come with me, but he declined, remaining in Alexandrov with the Czar. I think my stepfather had continued to become concerned with his salvation, for I had heard that he spent a great many hours at prayer every day. He had also continued to drink very heavily, especially since his return from Pskov. Simon, who had lost his wife and both children during the summer's epidemic of fever, also declined my invitation. He was suffering from a bad cold and aching teeth, he said. As he advanced in years, Simon took each snow a little harder than the last. Boris, of course, had his own wife and family in Moscow. He made a great show of pleasure when I called Skuratof to the capital, for his bride had always been her father's favorite and wished to be with him over Epiphany. In truth, while Boris was very devoted to his wife and treated her with almost Western liberality, I doubt he ever really cared much for his father–in– law. I do not think Malyuta realized this, for he seemed to idolize Boris.

Elysius Bomel was still in Livonia with the women, and I was somewhat troubled to be carrying the Czar's order for his return after the holy days. I was confident I could save him from any serious punishment, but he would be forced to face the Czar and answer for his trickery of nearly two years before. I did not tell Elysius of Ivan's order until it was nearly time for us to leave, thus allowing him to enjoy the traditions of the season.

When I arrived, the interior of the *dacha* had already been decorated with boughs cut from pine trees, tied all over with ribbons and bits of colored cloth. The boys had been eagerly awaiting me, certain I would come. Both were sturdy lads, and handsome. I was a little disturbed that they spoke Russian with the same heavy accent as their mother, but they could also speak German, English, and Italian – sounding more native in any of these than in the tongue of their mother country. They had helped Elysius with the decorations, and in fashioning the large, multi-colored candles which he said were customary in his native Germany. We placed a number of smaller candles on shelves and tables all over the house, these to be lighted on the eve of the anniversary of Our Lord's birth. Nina took over the kitchen and made many loaves of bread and cake, traditional to her home in Florence. Anne Bomel spent hours in the woods with the boys, gathering mistletoe and holly, which they hung above the doorways and over the fireplaces.

Small gifts were exchanged among us, also after the Western fashion. I had brought some sweets from the last caravan to arrive in Moscow before the snows, and the children presented me with a new fur hat they had helped their mother make from the skins of the native weasels. My little daughter, whom we named Christina, gurgled with delight when I held her up to see Doctor Bomel's candles. We allowed her to eat one of the honey cakes Anne Bomel had made.

I had arrived this time in a much better frame of mind than on some earlier visits. I had been too busy with my work to fall into the pits of black despair and helplessness which had contributed to my near madness of the previous years. Still, the contrast of peaceful countryside to the life one was forced to lead in the capital evoked the same desire to remain. As evening fell on the day of Epiphany, it seemed to spread its darkness over our spirits, as well. My sojourn was almost over, and as always we talked wistfully of finding some way for me to serve the Czar in Livonia. I toyed with the idea of asking for a command, as the present generals – a pair of Germans, Kruze and Taube – were miserable officers. If Sigismund or the Danes should launch an attack in earnest, the whole western front could collapse overnight.

But I knew these ideas were sheer fantasy. Ivan needed me in Moscow. My private life would have to take second place to the needs of Russia and the Czar. On the following day, I broke the news to Elysius, telling him the Czar required him to return with me. I was to leave two days hence. The doctor's eyes widened with fear, and his whole body trembled violently.

"Is there no other way?" he begged. "Could you not tell the Czar I am too ill to travel, and will come along later?"

I eyed him with annoyance, and my seeming sternness only added to his apprehensions. "I will not lie to the Czar," I said.

"What if I refuse to come?"

"You can't refuse," I told him simply.

"You would force me?"

"I have been told to bring you back. If I must, I will return you in chains," I assured him.

He wept, then, in bitter fear and frustration. That night he told Anne, and in the morning his wife informed Nina. I was subjected to such a barrage of female opposition I wished I might have given in. But I had no choice. Elysius had to return with me, whatever fate lay in store for him. I tried to reassure him, certain I could salve the wounds in Moscow. But the doctor's dread infected all the others, with the effect that my parting was seriously marred. Both women considered me unnecessarily cruel, and nothing I could say would placate them.

Our trip back was slow and very difficult. We experienced several heavy falls of snow, and one of these caught us on the road between Pskov and Novgorod. We were delayed a full two days, as the drifts piled clear to the roof of the monastery where we had taken refuge. When the storm finally ended, we floundered through banks of snow piled higher than my head. Two horses died along the way, and three others were unfit to pull the sleighs by the time we struggled into Novgorod. Fortunately, we had left little Anna Viskovaty with the women in Livonia, rather than trying to bring her back with us. Toby had requested my permission to marry her, but I told him to wait a little. They were both still very young, and I needed the boy with me. I trusted no other servant as I did Toby, and he certainly proved his mettle during these few trying days.

For once, I was thankful to reach the sheltering gray walls of Novgorod, which we achieved just as another storm was breaking. With Pimen gone, there was no need to dread the previously inevitable invitation. Leonide had been named to succeed him; but he was a cautious old man, afraid to invite me without my indicating I desired it. This I did not do. Instead, I made sure the governor, Peter Pronsky, was aware of my arrival. He had been a casual friend to Heinrich in years past, and we currently had some commercial dealings with him. A heavy–set fellow, about my own age, he had once been on campaign with me and we had always been friendly. His brother John had been very close to Vladimir at one time, and had actually been executed as a result of this association. Peter was also a cousin of poor Vassily Pronsky, an ascetic who had been eliminated by the *Opritchina*. A member of the brotherhood himself, he held no malice toward any of us. Following the proper form, he invited me to dine with him.

The meal was nothing unusual, and would hardly be worth mentioning except for Elysius, who had naturally been included. He drank much more than he should have, and committed a serious error in judgment. Being basically gregarious, Elysius had the ability to make most people feel they knew him well, on what was actually a very brief acquaintance. He succeeded in doing this with Prince Peter, whom he had only met briefly at one or two receptions in Moscow. But Pronsky was a rather withdrawn, phlegmatic personality, easily overwhelmed by the doctor's social graces. In the busier, rowdy atmosphere of Ivan's court, he had usually been overlooked. Thus I am certain that Elysius did not remember who he was until they were introduced that evening. Nonetheless, Peter was so flattered by Doctor Bomel's pretense of recognizing him, he gave the doctor a very fine piece of local silver work and sat conversing with him after dinner. I was talking with some other people, and did not hear much of their conversation. In trying to piece it together later, I could only assume that Bomel, having heard some remarks concerning my fears of a Tartar invasion, had innocently made a statement that sounded critical of the Czar. As it was later repeated, he seemed to have implied that Ivan was touched with madness.

Now, this placed Pronsky in a difficult position. Several prominent members of his family had already been executed for disloyalty to the Czar. If Elysius, traveling with me, were actually one of my agents, saying these things to test the Governor, his failure to report it could go hard with him. On the other hand, he obviously liked the doctor and admired him. He knew Elysius was drunk, and might well have overlooked the entire incident, except I was sitting close enough to have heard. He had no way to know whether I had missed it. Fearing to do otherwise, he reported the exchange in his next routine communication to Moscow.

As a matter of course, this report was channeled through my office, where I should still have had a chance to withhold it. I imagine that was Pronsky's expectation. Unfortunately, the document arrived on a day when I was busy with some *Streltsi* maneuvers on the far side of the Sparrow Hills, and Malyuta was in the office. My assistant had now achieved a fair skill in reading, although he never learned to write very well.

Skuratof had recently come to dislike Doctor Bomel, largely because he could never compete with the doctor's wit. Elysius had foolishly exercised his cleverness in front of others, making Malyuta the butt of his humor. Taking advantage of my absence, Skuratof brought Pronsky's message to the Czar's attention. All this happened ten days or so after we had returned to the capital, and immediately on the heels of my having interceded for Elysius with the Czar. I had persuaded Ivan that the predictions about Queen Elizabeth had been caused by Doctor Bomel's natural enthusiasm, rather than any desire to deceive. I had thereby gotten him through his first scrape, though the Czar retained a certain suspicion of the doctor's motives.

When Malyuta dropped Pronsky's report on Ivan's writing table, it should really not have produced the anger that it did, and I think the Czar's reaction was as much to display his annoyance with me as for any other reason. I had been pestering him constantly, again urging extensive preparations against an assault by Devlet Gerei, Khan of the Crimean Horde.

"You had Us scared half to death last year, with this same nonsense!" he bellowed at me. "Now you're at it again!"

"My agents are not getting paid for making up stories to frighten little children," I told him. "When I continue getting messages like these –" and I threw a stack of papers on his table "– then I know it is time to organize the army and establish a defense!"

In the end, he had grumbled and muttered about my being a nuisance and an alarmist, but he had turned command of the Moscow garrison over to me. This was my occupation on the day Malyuta brought the report on Elysius to the Czar. I was struggling to get a poorly trained, uninspired group of loafers whipped into some kind of fighting shape. I was handicapped by many problems. First, the best and most able officers were of the *Zemschina,* and I had been ordered not to employ them. Secondly, the *Streltsi* had largely been absorbed by the *Opritchina,* which meant they were used to an indolent existence. The only action they expected or desired was the looting of houses, and other orgies of destruction and murder. The idea of facing a horde of hostile Tartars was decidedly unappealing to them. In addition to this, they only half believed in the danger.

Thus, on this fatal day, I returned to the city late, well after dark. I was in a black, foul mood, and dead tired. I did not stop by my Kremlin office, intending to go straight home, bathe, and fall into bed. To my consternation, I found a small contingent of white–uniformed men on the doorstep.

"What brings you fellows to my house?" I asked the captain casually. I expected to be informed of some social function, or possibly a military ceremony, as Ivan was again entertaining a houseful of Pollacks.

"We are seeking Doctor Elysius Bomel," said the officer. "We bear the Czar's warrant for his arrest."

"Arrest?" I cried. "Let me see!"

He handed me a paper bearing the seal of the two headed eagle. The charge was conspiracy to commit treason, and the ink was barely dry. Ivan had signed the order personally, so I could not simply countermand it. I hammered on the door, calling at the same time for Toby. I could hear some conversation on the other side – the doctor trying to persuade Toby not to open.

"Come on, Doctor," I called. "I don't want these fellows breaking down my door. Open up!"

It was a quaking, squealing man the soldiers took away. The doctor exhibited every possible response to his terror. He actually wet himself when the guards clamped irons on his wrists. I felt compelled to follow along after them, to discover what had happened.

Ivan received me without any difficulty, but he absolutely refused to hear any arguments in Elysius's behalf. "He has offended me too deeply," Ivan insisted. "I forgave him once, but this time he has gone too far. I will not tolerate these things being said behind my back by a man who takes such pains to please me when we stand face to face."

Nothing was going to make the Czar change his mind. He was convinced Doctor Bomel had been playing with him, mocking his dignity. Elysius was placed in a cell, scheduled for exile to Beelozersk. I was too tired to think, and had to admit to myself that Elysius had more than stretched his luck. Perhaps a few months in prison would make him less prone to involve himself in foolhardy plots and ill–considered derisions. I went home to bed. As I lay waiting for sleep, I continued to mull over the doctor's plight, struck again by the ease with which a man can plummet from the heights of favor. While I had thought these same things many times before, having the Czar's displeasure strike this close to me rocked my own self–confidence.

In the morning, I still found myself worrying about Elysius, so I took a final chance on his behalf. I sent a note to the Englishman, Sir Jerome Horsey, asking if I might stop by to see him. Naturally, I was extended an immediate invitation, for the English were still in borderline circumstances. Any attention from a Russian of my rank was welcome. Without going to my office first, I went to Horsey's residence. While not actually suggesting it, I implied that his request for clemency might bear some weight with the Czar, as Ivan looked upon Elysius as an English subject. At this particular time, the Englishmen's previous disfavor was lessening, and to make this display of concern might impress Ivan with their determination and unity. The Czar, of course, continued to be passionately fond of anything Western, especially the English.

When I finally went to my office, I was dumbfounded to discover what had transpired during the night. My manipulating was all to no avail, for I had failed to reckon on Skuratof. When Bomel was placed in his cell, the door had hardly closed before Malyuta arrived to question him. He did this quietly, using only his own men, to assure no one's coming to me. By midmorning, when I discovered the circumstances, nothing could save the doctor. And in the meantime, also unaware of Malyuta's activities, Horsey presented himself at the Czar's residence. He was never granted an interview. Instead, Ivan's secretary received him, after allowing the Queen's Ambassador to cool his heels in an antechamber for over an hour. When I think back on it, I cannot imagine a single happenstance being worse than it was!

Malyuta, who had some information to start with, knew more about Doctor Bomel's activities than I did. By frightening him into making a partial statement in his cell, he had obtained enough additional evidence to gain Ivan's permission for more extensive questioning. He had stretched Elysius on a rack, and eventually beat him with a knout, all the while producing a flood of damning confessions. The doctor had shoved his fingers into a great many more pots than I had ever suspected. After abstracting the information, Skuratof had it written out for Elysius to sign, eventually sending the whole sordid story to the Czar.

While Horsey was being detained in the secretary's antechamber, Ivan authorized his executioners to start on Elysius; and it was a terrible death they dealt. Following his experiences in the dungeons, he was taken out to the courtyard, tied naked to a spit, and roasted alive over a slow fire. When they thought he was dead, the body was dumped onto a sledge and dragged out to be thrown into the river.

Just as Elysius was brought out the gates at the side of the Czar's palace, Horsey exited through the front. He looked in horror at the half cremated body, gasping in further shock when it opened its eyes and tried to speak. The guards, seeing Elysius was not yet dead, laughed and began dragging him back to the spit. That was when I arrived, and ordered him returned to his cell. Horsey, of course, spread the tale throughout the foreign colony.

I knew it was too late, for the Czar would not have tolerated our saving him, even if there had been a magician capable of restoring his flesh. Elysius died that night, after hours of writhing in horrible agony. I stayed with him, at the risk of the Czar's displeasure, and it was I who administered the *coup d' grace*. It was apparent the doctor could not survive, and his pain was monumental. I shoved a knife into his heart, ending it for him, and he thanked me with his final breath.

My friend's death prodded my soul in a number of ways. In addition to convincing me of the danger Malyuta could one day present to me, I suffered a terrible guilt over my failure to provide the security I had so blithely promised. Had he been open and honest with me, of course, I could have been prepared to defend him. But this did not enter seriously into my considerations, nor did it serve to soothe my distress. I had loved Elysius, despite the stern tone I had so frequently taken to him. He had been a trickster and full of mischief, anxious to gain his own ends. Yet I knew he had been fond of me, and had looked upon me as his protector. The knowledge of my having failed him was a deep wound within my being, making his death as appalling as any circumstance I had faced in my months of membership in the *Opritchina*. I slipped into a state of melancholic depression, much as I had after witnessing the destruction of Novgorod. Several times my stomach pains became so great I could not eat at all, and if I drank strong spirits I suffered terrible, burning agony, as if a knife had been thrust into my guts and twisted. Then my nightmares started again, and there was no Doctor Bomel to treat them. For some strange reason, my dreams offered some relief from the stomach pains, though I did not know which was worse. I lost weight until my waist was like a boy's. Loose skin replaced the fat about my neck and face; I looked like a sick, tired old man. I had finally decided to ask Ivan for a command in Livonia when affairs in the west made the request unnecessary. A series of seemingly unconnected events combined to cause my being posted there without my having to ask for it.

While we still enjoyed a truce with Poland, and the Livonian Grand Master was supposed to have become a vassal of the King, the old man refused to be bound by Sigismund's agreements. He did not precipitate any major battle, but several clashes and skirmishes took place at various points along our western line. Those two great bumblers, Taube and Kruze, had continued to mismanage our defenses until we were in danger of losing the entire Baltic coast. Whenever the Livonians attacked them, giving them an excuse to advance, they either lost ground or ended up exactly where they started. A new truce had been hastily negotiated, and Sigismund brought pressure to bear on his Livonian allies to honor it. Our commanders should have had no further trouble, but their incompetence was now obvious to their troops. A flood of disturbing reports came into my office, telling of rebellions against officers, assaults on the local populace by bands of our soldiers – many of whom were Tartars or Cossacks, and admittedly difficult to manage. There was sinful conduct among the men, and pilferage of supplies, resulting in short rations for the armies.

These problems might not have been sufficient to send me, had it not been for the circumstance of Magnus, brother to the Danish King. Whether by skill or plain good fortune, one of my agents had made successful contact with Magnus, who indicated he would like to discuss coming over to us. Preliminary negotiations had been underway for several months by coded message, and Magnus had agreed to most of the Czar's desires. He was to be granted the hand of Euphemia, Vladya's eldest daughter, who was still the Czar's ward, and living in his household. She would go to Magnus with a handsome dowry – five barrels of gold.

In addition to acting as inspector general and straightening out our military command, I was to confer secretly with Magnus, and discuss some arrangements for his coming to Moscow. Before leaving, I had a long conference with Ivan, and was authorized to offer Magnus the entire kingdom of Livonia, to be held in vassalage to Muscovy. The Dane would also be given command of all our armies within his new realm, except for the native Russian troops. In exchange for this, he was to guarantee complete expulsion of the Swedes from the northern areas and maintain his own defenses against Poland.

I departed before the end of the thaws, leading a large troop of *Streltsi* and a regiment of Cossack replacements. I seemed to be escaping madness. Adding sorely to my own mental state, the Czar had become extremely morose, frequently shutting himself in his rooms for several days at a time. He often refused to make decisions or receive any visitors. While the Kremlin bureaus handled everything of a routine nature, important matters had to await the Czar's change of mood, else be made by his subordinates. Later, if these decisions were not to Ivan's liking, the man who made them was likely to make no more. It was a relief to turn the Third

Bureau over to Skuratof, for I had already been forced to justify myself more than once. Only because I knew the Czar so well, and could anticipate his reactions, had I come away unscathed.

I was concerned about Malyuta, however, as he had become increasingly greedy and insolent. His suppressed hatred of me, along with his pretended loyalty, were no longer any mystery. He had been conniving to obtain my post, and now it had been given to him. Boris told me how he boasted of his achievement.

I tried to caution Malyuta not to neglect the southern network of agents. I told him to keep in close contact, and immediately replace any who were discovered and eliminated by the Khan. But he did not share my anxiety. It had been largely due to his opposition that I had failed in my attempt to persuade the Czar to move our basic defense line farther south. As it stood now, an enemy advancing from the Crimea would not be met by any sizable force until it reached the Oka. In my opinion, that was far too close to Moscow.

But Ivan was not inclined to listen, and Malyuta curried favor by joining him when he laughed at my fears. I had tried to enlist Heinrich's help in arguing the point, but my stepfather had sunk into such a state of drunkenness and sin he had no interest in anything. There was no one else to whom I could turn. Because Vorotinsky was not of the brotherhood, the Czar would not listen to him. Simon was so afraid of Skuratof he refused to voice a contrary opinion. In fact, Simon had become so timid he never left the Kremlin enclosure, for he was sure Malyuta intended him harm. As the Czar never came to the old palace any more, never entered the Kremlin except to attend services in the Cathedral on holy days, there was no way to bring them together.

These, and a great many other concerns, weighted my mind as I led the troops into the west. I was sure the Tartars would come this year, but the only men who seemed in agreement with me were the discredited *Zemschina* generals. The farther I traveled from Moscow, however, the lighter my burdens seemed to be. Merely being in the saddle again leading an army gave me a feeling of usefulness and pleasant fulfillment – until I came face to face with the problems in Livonia. This chaos did little to further my recovery from gloom. That part of our western provinces where my own estates were located was in imminent danger of falling into the Grand Master's hands. My men also informed me of our German generals' secret communications with Sigismund – this, through agents under Kurbsky's sponsorship. My first concern was to evacuate my family. I sent them under heavy guard to Novgorod.

Due to the urgency of the situation, I had only one night with Nina and the children. I had scheduled them off the next day with a contingent of returning troops. The emergency eliminated much of the coldness that might otherwise have resulted from my failure to save Elysius. Later, Nina realized how sincerely sorry I was. She forgave me, and eventually Anne did, too. It was obvious I could not have done otherwise, and Elysius had brought about his own downfall.

When they left, I told Nina to continue through to Moscow if she was not too fatigued by the journey. Otherwise, she could remain in Novgorod. I was sure of her safety either way. Pronsky would make her comfortable if she chose to remain; otherwise she would be traveling to the capital under the protection of a large escort. The situation being as nebulous as it was in Livonia, I had no idea how long I would have to stay, nor could I foresee the likelihood of another sizable group of soldiers heading east until everything was settled.

I was momentarily out of touch with Magnus, for one of our go–betweens had been lost. I therefore spent the time trying to bring some order out of the mess in which I found our army. It was all but in shambles! The disorganization was worse than any report had led me to believe. Generals Taube and Kruze were merely soldiers of fortune, who had seen an opportunity to enrich themselves by joining us. Now that we seemed involved in serious internal difficulties, I knew they were more than willing to transfer their loyalties.

I met Taube in Reval, and was not in the least impressed. He was a little squinty–eyed rat of a man, with a long pointed beard. Extremely vain, I am sure he blackened the hair of his head and face with boot polish, for he was long past the age when he should have been gray. When he tried to convince me of his loyalty and devotion to the Czar, I made the pretense of believing him. That night I sent off a detailed report to Moscow, outlining my suspicions and strongly recommending both Germans be replaced – by *Zemschina* personnel if necessary, even by former Tartars. I never received a reply, and Skuratof later denied receiving the message. I did not know if he lied, as Taube could have intercepted my courier.

Unaware that my report was not safely on its way to the Czar, I managed to arrange a secret meeting with Magnus a few days later. He came ashore near Narva from a small renegade Danish vessel. We conferred in a fisherman's hut, during the dark of night. If Taube had been an unpleasant surprise, this man was enough to turn one's stomach. He had only one eye, the other being filmed over by an ugly white web, which he made no effort to cover. He had a clubfoot, a hunched back, a voice like sled runners over gravel, and the personality of a starving weasel.

We sat on either side of a small table, with a flickering candle stuck onto the wood between us. Through a mouthful of rotten teeth, he outlined his grandiose plans for subjugating the Baltic coast. Despite his repulsive appearance, he seemed to possess a nimble mind, and I tried to respect him for this. He was extremely flattered by the Czar's offer of such a close kinswoman in marriage, though he tried to wheedle a larger dowry from the "wealthy and generous Czar." I told him he could broach that subject with Ivan in person, and arranged for his going to Moscow later in the year.

So far, Magnus's intentions were supposedly a secret from his brother, the King of Denmark. It seemed that the disfigured Prince expected a certain amount of support from Danish deserters, whom he was certain would flock to his banner in opposition to the King. It would simply be a matter of making public his intentions, he told me.

I had concluded this business satisfactorily, I thought; and after watching Magnus rowed back to his ship, I intended to start south. I wanted to meet the second of our German commanders, Kruze. I was formulating a plan, whereby I hoped to turn one against the other and eventually ease both of them into a position where I could arrest them for treason. I was hardly out of Ivangorod when a report was brought to me by one of my best agents, making all these problems pale to insignificance.

While the spies who were employed by the State now reported to Skuratof, I had used many of my own people scattered through the areas where Heinrich and I had trade interests. Thus I continued to be well informed, unless I got myself into a location where my men could not reach me. Once out of the coastal area, where our troops restricted travel by anyone not on official business, I was contacted at once.

Jacob sent word of a large Tartar force under the Krim (Crimean) Khan, moving north through the Volga basin. I lost no more time in Livonia, not even trying to relay a message to the capital. Heinrich should have gotten the same warning as I; he would surely inform the Czar, even if Skuratof did not. I selected the fifty best mounted men in my present command and left at once for Moscow.

No sooner had I departed, than our treacherous Germans defected to the Poles and swore loyalty to Sigismund. They returned large areas of land to the King, including the region where my estates were located. But reclaiming these territories would have to wait; the very heart of Russia was now in danger.

In Moscow, we found that the Czar had taken the *Opritchina,* and whatever *Streltsi* forces had been in the city, and gone to man our defenses along the Oka River, establishing a line of defense less than a hundred miles from Moscow. I spent about half an hour with Nina before continuing on my way. As yet there was no real fear within the city, for no one believed the Tartars could possibly get close. There had never been a foreign threat to the capital within the memory of living man.

At the river I found a discouraging lack of preparedness. Despite my efforts to bring some degree of discipline into the ranks of the brotherhood, it was a very sloppy army that stood between the enemy and Moscow. The lesser part of our forces was strung out over five or six miles of river bank, to either side of the main ford. Mstislavsky was in command. This, at least, gave us a general with some experience, though I would have preferred Vorotinsky. The Czar and Czarevitch, with the main body of men – including the entire *Opritchina* – was encamped at Serpukhof. This was a small dusty town, about three miles from the ford.

Despite the huge forces we still had in Livonia, and the sizable garrisons at Kazan, Nizhni Novgorod and Astrakhan, we stood to face the Tartars with less than thirty thousand men. There had been no time to summon more. When I conferred with the Czar in his field tent, he sat dejectedly on the edge of his bed and behaved like a man who had already been defeated.

"God is punishing me," he wailed, "for my sins are very heavy."

"We're not beaten yet," I told him. "Why don't you call in the *Zemschina?* With their added strength, the Tartars could. . . ."

"No!" he howled. "I would rather lose all of Russia to the infidels than go on my knees to the *Zemschina* boyars!" For a moment the fire returned to his gaze, and I hoped I might have stimulated him into personally assuming command. At least he might speak to the men and inspire them with the zeal he had shown at Kazan and in Livonia. But his ferocity didn't last. The flames of his spirit died as quickly as they'd come, and he resumed his gloomy pose upon the bed.

Two days later, the Khan's army began to spread its might along the far side of the river. If anything, the reports of my observers had been conservative in estimating the enemy strength. I am sure that Devlet Gerei must have commanded at least two hundred thousand men. He had the entire Crimean Horde, reinforced by other local tribes. There were several barbarian groups from along the lower

Volga, and thousands of Turkish Janissaries. They had followed the *szlak*, the old paths utilized by renegades and bandits, which had permitted them to slip past our guard posts along the Tula–Nizhni Novgorod Line.

It was clear that the infidel force would attempt a crossing the next morning, for we could see their commanders organizing teams of men to guide the army along the high ground to the ford. I sent Toby into Moscow to warn my family, instructing them to leave at once. I told him to be sure Nina took only what she needed to pay for passage. She was not to encumber herself with goods or treasure, and was to embark the household for Vologda. Once Toby was on his way, I returned to Serpukhof for further conferences with the Czar.

When I arrived he was preparing to withdraw! He was in a terrible rage, as well, for a message had just arrived from Devlet Gerei, challenging him to personal combat. The Khan had boasted he would cut off both Ivan's ears and send them to the Sultan. "We shall go to Alexandrov," said Ivan, between heavy wheezing breaths.

"The brotherhood will see to your safety," I said. But by my tone I asked if he intended to take the whole force with him.

"I shall leave the *Opritchina* to defend the capital," he said. There was almost a touch of pride in his remark. He intended taking only a hundred men to guard his person. I agreed he should leave, for the life of the Czar was more important than any city – even Moscow. Yet without his personal guidance, I was certain the brotherhood would collapse. Because I did not answer immediately, Ivan must have thought I felt him wrong. "Do you suggest I should not leave, then?" he asked harshly.

I shook my head. "The person of the Czar must be protected." I answered dutifully. "But I fear the men lack training."

It was a genuine fear I felt gnawing at my insides, for if they broke nothing would stand between the capital and the infidels. The glory we had achieved in former years was about to be dashed to nothing. I spoke no condemnation, but within my heart I blamed Malyuta. If he had supported me, instead of contributing to the Czar's complacency, this would never have happened. We would be taking the field with an army of proper strength, and we would be meeting the invaders at some point far south of Moscow. Now, he departed in the Czar's company, casting a sheepish glance in my direction as I watched the group depart for Alexandrov.

Shortly after the Czar left, a second message came from the Khan, which I took directly to Mstislavsky. The Tartars demanded we immediately surrender Kazan, Astrakhan, and all lands east of the Volga. If we would agree to this, he would spare Moscow. In an attempt to delay the impending assault, we returned a message explaining that the Czar was in the capital, and it would take time to obtain his approval. We still held the desperate hope of reinforcements from Nizhni Novgorod.

It was a mistake to inform Devlet Gerei of the Czar's absence. He immediately assumed Ivan had fled the field. Until that moment, the Tartars may have suspected we held a heavy reserve in hidden readiness. They now realized how meager our defenses really were, and there was no further communication. At daybreak the enemy force began to ford the river.

For an hour or so, our men along the banks put up a gallant but useless defense. Our archers did terrible damage to the infidels in the water, and at one point we almost caused a panic. Men in front attempted to retreat, but were unable to flee because of the pressure from behind. I honestly believe we might have saved the day, if we could have relied on the forces of the *Opritchina*. Unfortunately, when Mstislavsky sent for them, they advanced only far enough to see the enemy before they turned and ran.

This had been an opportunity for the brotherhood to expiate much of its shame and sinful guilt, but such was not the case. Before midday, the remains of our little army was also in full retreat toward Moscow. Mstislavsky was wounded, and almost fell captive to the onrushing Tartars. I was barely able to keep enough of a guard about us to fend off the enemy's advance units. The main body of infidels was busy setting fire to everything they could not carry away. They also captured every person they could find, below the age of forty. Had it not been for their greed in taking slaves, none of us would have escaped. Prisoners always slow an advance, and guarding them takes a large number of men out of action.

We entered Moscow amidst complete chaos and panic. The distant glow of burning fields and villages lighted the sunset sky, and the whole horizon was black with smoke. Most roads to the south were now in infidel hands, while frenzied mobs of people rushed for the northern exits. I had long since become inured to the appearance of a Tartar, and I had forgotten how frightening his visage can be the first time one sees him in battle. There is no doubt they are the ugliest people on earth, and their screeching war cry is a sound like no other this side of hell. The refugees who had fled before the oncoming horde told such terrifying stories the local people had been driven into an impossible frenzy of disorder. In the city, a final message awaited us from the Czar. His safety was assured, for at the last minute he had decided to sail for Yaroslavl.

With the capital surely lost, my one concern was my family. Frantically, I tried to force my way through the tangle of bodies in the narrow alleys of the outer city. I feared Nina might have refused to obey Toby's command until it was too late to get a boat. If she had not left immediately upon receiving my warning, the entire household might well be trapped in *Kitaigorod*, the inner part of the city. I was sure the Kremlin gates would long since have been locked.

So now the prophecies of the Apocalypse had come to pass in the City of Moscow! We had already suffered for our sins: pestilence, famine and death. Now we were to be visited by still more death, and with it the final penance – fire. As is true of all large cities, the lands around Moscow became more densely settled with farms and houses the closer one came to the walls. As I fought my way through the screaming, terrified masses, trying to reach my home, the Tartars had already cut off any escape to the south and east. They were still advancing on us, but the increase in the density of habitations outside the city was slowing them down. They persisted in setting fire to everything, and the closer they came the more structures they found to loot and burn. The wall of flames set up by the forward units now tended to slow the bulk of their force. Soon, the conflagration was spreading from building to building without having to be rekindled by the advancing horde. Long before the main body of infidel troops reached the outer gates, the *Arbat* and lower end of the *Bielgorod* were ablaze.

The terror inspired by the heat and smoke and crackle of burning timbers reached a pitch I would never have believed possible. The entire population of the city was struggling through the streets, over buildings, and in many places over the crushed bodies of other people. The dead lay two or three deep in many of the narrow alleys. Had I not been well mounted and wearing armor I would probably never have reached my house. As it was, I had to draw my sword and force my way through several of the minor bazaars in the middle city.

A brisk wind was billowing smoke across the buildings and into the fields to the north, carrying with it sparks and embers which ignited the dry roofs and even some of the meadows beyond the northern walls of the Kremlin. Screams of terror, anguish, and pain formed a continuous, deafening drone. Men raced to escape the flames, frequently forsaking wife and child in their fear. Children separated from their mothers were quickly trampled by the mob. The stink of burning wood and moss soon mingled with the acrid stench of seared flesh. Many animals were running loose on the streets – horses, dogs, swine, cattle. Their fire–driven fear having no logical goal other than blind escape added seriously to the confusion and injuries.

I passed close to the river at one point, and saw that hundreds of people had already leaped in, hoping to find refuge from the flames. However, many could not swim, and as more bodies forced their way into the water, those already in the stream were shoved into the deeper part of the channel. Many more were so weighted down with possessions and treasure they could not remain afloat. Even in this time of fear and flight, there were men who sought to enrich themselves by robbery and pillage. But God quickly punished their avarice. They had no place to run with their ill–gotten wealth, except into the river. If they tried to cross so laden with gold and silver, they were surely drowned.

At last I reached my house and ran in through the half–open door. I noticed a wisp of smoke coming from the roof as I entered, and knew it would not take long for the entire place to be ablaze. Quickly, I raced through the lower floor and up the servants' staircase in the rear – then through the women's quarters and into my own rooms. I ran down the main stairs, back into the front hall. There was no one in the house. I should have known; it had been foolish to come, and yet I could not have done otherwise

I could smell a heavier odor of smoke, now, and I heard a crackling sound above me. I could not see the flames, but I knew the roof had caught. I glanced about, realizing there was nothing in the house I treasured enough to risk trying to save. I was about to leave, when I thought of the stables. I wondered if Gabriel could still be there. I had left him home, and if the family had gone by boat they might not have taken him. I ran back through the kitchen and into the service yard. The stables lay directly across from me; but already the pile of hay stacked between the house and the barn were in flames. I could probably not get through, and once back there I would never have gotten out. I was turning to go when I heard a whinny. Then I saw Gabriel, rearing up beside an open window. There was no mistaking his silvery coat and flying mane.

I started forward, but was stopped by a solid wall of flame. There was no way back, and I was wasting valuable time if I ever hoped to save myself. God alone knew where my family was, yet I could not leave my faithful mount to such a fate. Wildly, I ran back into the house, where the flames had now burned through onto the upper floors. I bolted into my study. On the wall was a bow and a quiver of arrows, given me by one of the Tartar emirs who had served under me at

Astrakhan. I grabbed them and ran back to the rear of the house. I could not get out the back door, because of the heat and licking flames; but I could see Gabriel in the stable, and I could hear him squealing in pain and fear.

I fitted a shaft to the bow and took careful aim. I would only get one shot, I thought, for if I took more time the whole house would be crashing down behind me. I let fly the bolt, and saw it pierce Gabriel's eye. His head fell from sight, and I could not hear any more from him. I hoped I had killed him, or at least rendered him senseless so he would never feel the flames as they destroyed his body. Still gripping my weapons, I ran back through the house and out the front door. I had left my mount tied to a post in the entry yard; he was gone.

I was now on foot, encumbered by a suit of heavy armor, and having no idea where to go. The streets were still jammed with people: pushing, shoving, climbing over each other to move away from the flames. Nowhere was there an open place, and over all the black, choking smoke seared one's very lungs.

I stepped quickly back into the yard and hastily as I could I shucked my breastplate and coat of mail. I tried to get my shin guards off, but the straps on one of them tangled. I left it, as the heat from my house was now too intense to bear. I picked up my sword from the pile of metal accouterments, and tossed the quiver of arrows over my shoulder, taking the bow in my free hand. I paused a moment in the street, looking up at the high pink walls of the Kremlin. They towered above me, several blocks away. The gates were closed, and I knew the men inside would admit no one else. To open the gates for one would invite a sea of others. Then, if there should be a siege, all would starve. There had to be a way to get inside, I thought. It was the only place of refuge left. I doubted that much would burn within the enclosure. Since the great fires of my youth, the Czar had ordered most of the Kremlin buildings to be roofed in slate or tile. Unless the Tartars were able to crash the gates, the fortress would probably remain untouched.

I must reach the river, I thought. That was my one chance. Holding a cloth over my face to filter out some of the smoke, I dogtrotted toward the Square of Executions. As it always did when I ran, my damaged foot pained me and forced me to go more slowly. I hoped by getting to the square, I would find a large enough open area that I could get past the milling crowd, and into the water. I reckoned not on the huge number of people. I found myself enmeshed in the mob, crushed on all sides by terrified human bodies. Like the others, I tore at those in front, and in turn was pushed and shoved by those behind. My leather shift was ripped from my back, and I lost the quiver of arrows. I still had my sword.

At length I could move no farther forward, and after being held immobile for several minutes I feared I might never be able to move again. There was a roof to my left, and without taking time to think about it, I leaped upon the shoulders of a man in front of me. From his back I tossed my sword onto the roof, grabbing the eaves with my free hand. The people were squeezed so tightly together, the fellow could do no more than swivel his head to look at me. Certainly, he could not move away or fall. However, he could step backward into the space left free by my removal. This he did, but by then I was safely on the roof. From there, I leaped to another, and then onto a wall which bordered the square. People completely filled the entire area, and the noise was so great I could not shout to anyone to get out of my way in order to jump down. I hesitated a moment, finally leaping onto the heads and backs of those below.

Without the buildings so close on either side, it was easier to get through the mob. By sheer, brute force, I pushed and rammed until I came near the river, where I faced another closely packed mass of people. All I could see was a field of heads, almost completely obscuring the water. The people in the river were not screaming, as were those on land. This made it possible for me to shout and have someone nearby hear it. Holding my sword in the air, I let out a terrible scream, as if I were amok. Swinging the huge blade in an arc above my head, I raced toward the water. Somehow, enough people heard or saw me that I had a clear passage beyond the bank. I dropped my weapon and leaped far into the stream, striking out for the center of the channel.

It was a hard pull, for I had not done any heavy swimming for a long time, and the one piece of armor still dragged at my leg. I finally came opposite the Kremlin, where I tried to line myself up with the old landmarks, hoping I could find the place where I used to pass under the wall as a child. I paddled back toward the bank, again coming against the crush of humanity. I was weaker by then, and out of breath. Somehow I managed a fresh spurt of energy and worked my way past the outer fringe of people. In front of these the bodies were so tightly packed I knew that once I went underwater I would never be able to come up again. If I missed the tunnel entrance I was finished. I also remembered how it had used to take all the wind I could hold to swim the distance. Well, I could either try it or die like a dog with the rest, I thought. Taking in all the air my lungs would hold, I went under the water.

It took me a few seconds to locate the outcropping of rock. But I found it! Gripping the edge, I forced my body through the opening and pushed myself along the slimy walls, gliding quickly up the tunnel. Just when I despaired of making it, I broke through into the underground chamber. Gratefully, I inhaled the stale air, resting my head against the stones while my heart settled back where it belonged. I felt my way through the absolute blackness, up the slippery stone stairs. I came up under the pavingstones in the courtyard, and pushed against the surface. It would not budge. I struggled for several more minutes before I remembered that a *Streltsi* guard box had been placed in the general area, possibly on top of the stone I was trying to move. I felt around in the dark until I found a loose rock, and began beating it against the surface.

After a long time, I heard voices shouting above me, and I began to call back. I could hear someone probing with a piece of metal. There was one unsuccessful try, the stone being lifted a finger's width, then falling back into place. Suddenly, it was removed. Smoke–filled air cascaded down on me, while I looked up into several pairs of startled eyes. All that had been holding the stone was the wheel of a cart. There were certainly some confused, comical expressions as a score of men watched General Prince Marensky crawl out of the hole, naked except for a metal shin guard. The secret tunnel was no longer secret; but hopefully, I would never have to use it again.

One of the soldiers threw his cloak over my shoulders. With this to maintain some degree of dignity, I hurried up the stone steps to look over the top of the wall. I hope never to see such a sight again! Out of the blackness of night flames soared upwards in pillars of gold and crimson. Scarlet cinders twinkled like floating gems upon the twisting currents of air. Every few minutes a building would seem to explode sending showers of sparks in all directions. There was only fire and death and terror as far as the eye could see.

Beyond the flames rode the Tartars, occasionally visible between the clouds of smoke. The air was so heavy with soot, and so hot from the fires, one could breath only by holding a wet cloth over his mouth. The heat still singed the eyes, hair, and clothing. I squinted, shielding my face in an attempt to see what was happening to the south; but my fleeting glimpse into the darkness beyond the flames could tell me very little. The sounds and smells were frightful, and the scorching waves drove me back after only a few moments.

There was still no fire inside the Kremlin, except for the wooden roof on the Bell Tower of Ivan the Great. Bucket lines worked here and there to soak the stores of straw by the stables and firewood stacked behind the houses. Had these caught fire, they might have carried the blaze into all the wooden structures beyond the government buildings. After experiencing the crush outside, the relatively smaller crowd of people in the Kremlin seemed few, indeed. Back on the ground, I stood uncertainly for several moments, not knowing exactly where to go. I had no official position in any Kremlin ministry, so there was no office to which I could retire. The only place I could think of was Simon's house.

I hammered several times on my friend's door before it finally opened – by Toby! "Sir!" he screamed. "Mistress Nina! Nina! Dmitri is safe! He's here!"

Nina came out of the *svyetlitsa*, followed by Lilly, Lotus Flower, Ann Bomel, Anna – my entire household. And behind them came Simon's dark face, smiling in relief and welcome. We all stood as if seeing ghosts. Then Nina was in my arms, sobbing, and there was a chorus of gleeful shouts as the boys came running down the stairs. My whole family was united through all the chaos, and for the moment we were safe in each other's embrace.

The door of Simon's *dacha* closed behind me, cutting off the sounds of death and agony. The rooms and halls were full of smoke, but otherwise the house seemed an island of muted peace. While fear remained, it was pushed into the background. We all knew it was unlikely the Kremlin would fall, which is not to deny our lingering anxiety. Both Simon and I would be prime captives – he, because his former brothers considered him a traitor; I, because I had led more successful campaigns against the Tartar hordes than any other Russian officer. A few glances between the former Khan and me were the only expressions of our dread. To mention the punishments awaiting us would have further upset Nina and the other women.

The reason for my household's being here was that my message had simply arrived too late; no boats were to be had at any price, and none of our own were in the city. Toby had decided to set out with the family by carriage, when one of Simon's servants arrived to offer the protection of his house. I was extremely grateful for this, as the roads quickly became open ground for robbery and murder. Hungry peasants beyond the city walls were just as deadly as the Tartars, who on their part were more interested in taking slaves.

"As you once offered me the sanctuary of your home," said Simon, "so I now extend the refuge of mine."

By morning, it was obvious that the Kremlin would stand. The Tartars, in setting fire to the buildings, had defeated their own purpose. The city became such an inferno they were unable to enter. Flames destroyed much of the booty they might otherwise have obtained. In this sense, the fire had become our most effective line of defense. Simon and I climbed the wall at dawn, and looked upon the destruction below us. From the southern rampart we could see nearly all the city. The *Arbat* was completely gone – a smoking, blackened heap of rubble. In the *Bielgorod*, a few gutted buildings were still standing, but they were too badly damaged ever to be reclaimed. A number of larger structures were still in flames, and while the fury of the blaze could not compare with the previous night's holocaust, the fires in *Kitaigorod* boiled upward in a frightful, tumbling display. It was difficult to breathe, even this far from the actual fires. We could not assess the fate of the populace, for a heavy pall lay over the entire city, obliterating the streets and other open areas. It seemed doubtful that any human or animal might have survived beneath the suffocating blanket.

Beyond the outer walls, we caught an occasional glimpse of the enormous infidel bands, galloping through the shifting masses of misty black. They were riding back and forth along the periphery of the city, shouting and screaming their terrible curses. Other enemy units had worked their way around to the north, and for a time they completely encircled Moscow. Within the city, our people faced the deadly flames and smoke; if they tried to flee, bands of half–naked savages waited on horseback at every gate, ready to run down and capture whoever fled the beleaguered confines. Already, long columns of prisoners had started their dreary march to the slave markets of Kaffa.

All day, Simon and I continued to climb the wall, watching for a short while, then returning to the courtyard when we could no longer stand the heat and smoke. We never saw much more than we had on first view, as most of the city remained obscured. From the direction of the river, we could hear people shouting, and many voices were lifted in lamentation for the dead. Others were moaning prayers for their own salvation.

Shortly after midday, the Tartar forces seemed to begin a withdrawal! We could hardly believe what we saw. All Moscow would have been theirs for the taking had they waited for the fires to die and the smoke to clear. They could have occupied the capital of Muscovy, and Devlet Gerei could have sat in victory upon the throne of Russia. But they could not believe how defenseless we really were. For all his threats and boasting, the Khan was certain that Ivan would take the field with a huge army, and rumors to this effect were already circulating among the infidels. The Czar was on the march, they said. *Ivan Grozny* was coming! Rather than risk defeat after such a stunning success, Devlet Gerei withdrew. With him, he took fifty thousand slaves.

By nightfall, when it was apparent the Tartars had gone, there was laughter and celebration in the Kremlin. Men slapped each other on the back, and many flagons of wine were passed around among the soldiers. They were grateful to be alive. Those of us who knew the enemy well were equally relieved not to be marching with iron collars about our necks and feeling the lash of an infidel slave driver across our naked backs. I watched my companions and joined them by taking a few sips as the flagons were passed around. For me, it was the very holiest of celebrations.

The devastation of Moscow was nearly total. The fires we had previously sustained had burned out large sections of the city, but never had there been the like of this. Smoke hung over the landscape for miles around and it was late in the afternoon before one could see clearly for any distance. The vista was stark and depressing. Nothing but ashes, the burned skeletons of buildings, and blackened rubble remained for miles around the city. Fires still raged in several sections to the north, while below us there was nothing left to burn. A light wind continued all night and into this second day, carrying the flames to every possible scrap of wood and timber. Almost the only remaining structure was Ivan's great church in the Square of Executions. It stood with fire–blackened sides; its brick and stone had withstood the holocaust.

I do not know how many people died, and I am guessing at fifty times a thousand being the number of captives taken by the Tartars. There had been a fierce rush of refugees into Moscow from the south and east, just before the Khan came across the Oka. No one had been able to keep count of these people. The Moscow River was literally choked with bodies, and in the weeks to follow its waters reflected the terrible aftermath of destruction. Decaying flesh made the stream a hell hole, a plague pit of stench and disease. Yet among the horrors of human remains there was also a vast treasure. Over half the people who drowned had carried some form of wealth – golden ornaments, coins, candle sticks, jewels, bracelets. With this to stimulate their greed, men worked from almost the first day, dredging up corpses and stripping them of valuables. I believe the English estimated our losses at eight hundred thousand souls, but it probably came closer to half that number. Perhaps a little less.

It would still be several days before the Kremlin gates were opened, as bands of roving Tartars rampaged through the countryside, and the remainder of Moscow's population had become a ragged, hunger–driven mob. Mstislavsky had retreated north with the remnants of the army, and with the pressure of Devlet Gerei's huge force removed, he was able to stand his ground – being stronger than any of the robber bands, either Russian or Tartar.

I knew the Czar would need me, and I was frustrated at not being able to leave the Kremlin. It was impossible to exit by any of the gates, as large crowds gathered outside every day, begging to be admitted or at least thrown some scraps of food. I could not use my tunnel, due to the sickening sewer the river had become; nor could I have myself lowered over the walls at some point away from the gates. I would then have found myself on foot with miles of brigand–infested countryside to travel. Nina, whose emotions were already near the breaking point, became almost hysterical when I suggested it.

Finally, a detachment of our *Streltsi* rode into the Square of Executions several days after the Tartar withdrawal. Mstislavsky had sent a scouting party to reconnoiter the area. It was my first news of the commander since we had parted at the city gates only heartbeats ahead of the advancing enemy. I was happy to learn he had survived his wounds.

I called to the captain of the detachment, who seemed surprised to see me alive. My death had already been reported to the Czar, he told me. Before dark, I was well on my way – to Vologda, rather than Yaroslavl, for the Czar had changed his mind again. He had retreated to this more northerly town, where he had a comfortable summer palace. I paused briefly in Mstislavsky's camp to confer with him before continuing on my way with a sizable escort of men.

By now, the Tartars were streaming south, carrying with them every ounce of booty they could find. They drove their slaves before them and set fire to anything they left behind. Naturally, accounts of all this had been brought to the Czar, who wept openly for his people. He divided his time between receiving dispatches, sending orders, and prayer. I do not think he had slept since arriving at his present headquarters.

"It's really me," I said merrily. "I'm not a ghost come back to haunt you!"

Ivan crossed himself and staggered to his feet. His fine robe was filthy with grime. He wore no hat, and his head was scratched nearly bald, probably from his having pulled at the hair during his lamentations. He almost fell in getting to me. "Thank God, Dmitri," he gasped. "At least you have been spared to stand beside me! Oh, God's wrath is a terrible thing!"

He dragged me back to the couch where he had been sitting, and bellowed in a raspy voice for the servants to bring refreshments. We spoke together in low tones for several minutes, telling each other of our respective experiences since parting in Serpukhof. Whatever horrors I had survived, it was nothing to the torture done the spirit of the Czar.

At length he looked about him, where several clerks and other officials had gathered close to hear us. "Get out!" he shouted. "Get out, all of you! Our words are not for the likes of you!"

In a moment the room was empty save for Ivan and myself. He sat silently for a few moments more staring at me, obviously deep in his own thoughts. "I do not think I would say this to any other man," he began at last, "but you have never lied to me, nor have you sought to gain your own ends by flattery or by agreeing with me when you thought I was wrong. From the days we were children and you brought food to keep my poor orphaned brother and me from starving, you have always served me well. Now I must ask you – and I shall not vent my anger upon you, no matter what you tell me. . . ." He stopped, for the words came very hard. "Have I been wrong, Dmitri?" he asked finally, his tone almost pleading. "Have my sins been so great that God should punish me in this manner?"

Now it was my turn for silence. I did not fear the Czar, at least not as other men feared him. Except for that fleeting moment in Alexandrov, when he had pinioned my foot with his *kisten*, I never had cause to be afraid of him. Although it was true I had never really lied or deceived him, I had sometimes tempered my remarks with consideration for his feelings, thereby trying not to add unduly to his heavy burdens. And at this particular moment, his burdens were heavier than they had ever been before. If I had expressed the most basic doubt, I would have injured him and caused him further pain. That was something I could not do, despite this being my singular opportunity to plant the seeds of thought I wanted desperately to sow.

"In the first and second Romes," I said finally, "the Caesars were looked upon as Gods. Their words were holy edicts, and their decisions were divine. Because no one – not even they, themselves – could admit their errors, their empires fell in ruins about their feet. In this, The Third Rome, we have a Caesar who is no less divinely endowed than the emperors of Rome and Byzantium. But we are more fortunate, because *our* Czar knows himself to be a man—"

"Then, you see errors in my judgment?" he replied calmly.

"I think you have sought to create something beyond the ability of your people," I said. "At least, you have tried to create perfection too quickly. The men of the *Opritchina* have failed you. Although they were the best you could obtain, they were not staunch enough –"

"The *Opritchina* is no more!" he growled. "As I would pluck out an offending eye, so I have brought an end to this pack of corruption! The very word shall be abolished from our language!"

I had no answer for him; his decision was more than I would have dared advise.

"Well?" he demanded. "Isn't that what you and Boris Godunof have been telling each other, but didn't have the guts to tell me? The *Opritchina* was a failure! It was a mistake from the beginning! It was mad! I am mad!" He shouted the last, and the old fire returned to his eyes. "Do you think me mad, Dmitri?" He grabbed my shoulders, and stared into my eyes with such intensity I was sure he could see my soul.

"I don't think you're mad, Ivashka," I said softly. "But even if you were, it would only be God's way of setting aside your own will that he could speak through you."

There was the trace of a grin about his lips, now. "Do you really believe that?" he asked.

"I must believe it," I said firmly, speaking with all the sincerity of my being. "I have obeyed you, because I believed it God's will that I should obey. If this weren't true, if you are only a mortal sinner wearing the mantle of Caesar, then my own soul is doomed with yours. I pray to our merciful God that His plan was greater than I can envisage, and in fulfilling it we have both done His Will."

He let go of me and leaned forward, his elbows on his knees, his head sunk below his shoulders. Finally, he reached a fumbling hand in my direction, not looking up to guide it. Finding my knee, he patted me gently for several minutes. "I have always said your spirit was more pure and simple than mine," he sighed. "If my sins have brought eternal damnation upon you. . . . But I wasn't wrong!" he declared suddenly, the strength returning to his tone. "The burning of Moscow has been no more than God's warning, the momentary exhibition of His displeasure over the sins I have committed while trying to further His ends. You will see! His face shall smile upon us again, and I shall fulfill my earthly mission!"

We spoke on like this until far into the night. Ivan's mood seemed to change as readily as the winds of early spring. He spoke of the glories still to be won, and the Christianizing of people who still lived in the blackness of infidel ignorance. He spoke of his sins of the flesh: drunkenness, gluttony, debauchery, the nameless sins I had refused to ascribe to him. All these he confessed to me. But of the executions in Novgorod and later in Moscow, he never said a word. These had been his duty, for the lesson had needed to be taught. Ivan was the Czar, and the bodies of his subjects were his to do with as he pleased. If some of those he ordered to their deaths were blameless, God would surely know of this. The innocent would find their reward in heaven. When I finally departed from the

Czar, I carried away a peculiar mixture of inspiration and confusion. Well as I had thought I understood him before, I certainly did not comprehend his arguments that night.

I had to search the halls before I found a chamberlain, for I did not know where I was to sleep. The fellow directed me to a small room, not far from the Czar's apartments. "Boris Godunof is across the hall from you, sir," he told me, "and Malyuta Skuratof is in the next room."

The three of us, I thought. The three men most closely trusted by the Czar. How strangely aligned we were! Boris and I would like to see a return to the greatness of Ivan's early years, when the people called him "the Good," and when we lived within a State of progress, law, and conquest. Malyuta favored the anarchy of the brotherhood, ruled by the fear and power of *Grozny* – The Terrible or The Dread. Yet with Boris married to Malyuta's daughter, what bonds might there be between them? It came to me more clearly than ever before as I lay waiting for sleep. Malyuta and I were naturally on opposite sides, born to be one another's antagonist. Now that the brotherhood was no more, we were destined to engage in a constant struggle for the Czar's affection and confidence. In the end, one of us would have to destroy the other. At that moment, I saw the balance to lie with Boris, for his natural alliances must be divided. To be faithful in his beliefs, he must side with me. Blood and marriage demanded he support his father–in–law. The lines were clearly drawn, I thought. Or were they?

CHAPTER X

Late the following afternoon, a guard detachment reported capturing a small band of Tartars, which had been making its way toward the Czar's temporary residence. Earlier in the day Ivan, Skuratof, Boris, and I had been discussing the possibility of the Khan's sending a delegation. In the meantime, Ivan had retired to the chapel and I called to him through the door. Offhandedly, he told me to "take care of it for him."

I rode out to meet the soldiers who were to bring the Musselmen in. At first glance, I was sure the men could not be ambassadors. They were dressed in smelly sheepskins, like the poorest shepherds – certainly an unimposing group. However, the captain of our patrol handed me some scrolls he had taken from their leader, and even my scanty knowledge of the Tartar language permitted me to recognize the message for what it was. These men were, indeed, the Khan's representatives. I was about to order their release, when I realized how subtle this insult was intended to be. Instead of finely garbed ambassadors, the Khan had sent his envoys dressed more poorly than they would be if going out to administer his laws to some infidel herdsmen.

I told the captain to continue on his way. The Tartars remained bound, mounted upon pack horses and asses instead of the fine steeds our men had taken from them. There were six infidels in all. As soon as the column started up again, the Tartar leader set up a howl, demanding he be accorded the respect due his rank. "Your lord, the Khan, will flay you alive for this insult!" he shouted.

I laughed at him, as did the other soldiers. "You look more like swine-herds to me," I told him. "You probably stole these papers from your own am-bassador." I refused to hear any more, taking my place at the head of the column. The prisoners were kept in the rear, where they could eat our dust. In Vologda, I ordered them to be lodged all together in the smallest, most miserable cell beneath the summer palace.

Ivan was highly amused when he heard of the way I had treated them, but the Khan's insult still rankled. He would have liked to depart for Moscow on the morrow, but decided to remain an extra day to put on a proper show for the envoys. Accordingly, we allowed the Tartars to remain in their cell until the next afternoon. They received only tepid water and the toughest horseflesh to eat. At the dinner hour they were brought out, given back their materials, and escorted under heavy guard before the Czar.

Ivan sat on an elegant throne atop an especially elevated dais. Before him reposed the crowns of Muscovy, Kazan, and Astrakhan; and he wore an extremely fine robe of gold, covered with so many jewels it was difficult to see the cloth. All the court and attendants were also in glittering finery, most of which had been borrowed from the Bishop of Vologda.

Four elegantly uniformed officers escorted the Tartars into the hall. Before they could speak, the Czar turned to Skuratof. Talking in a whisper, but loudly enough to be heard by everyone, he said sadly, "Malyuta, these poor barbarians have no proper clothing to wear in Our presence. At least throw a decent robe about their leader."

With that, Skuratof stepped down from beside the Czar, took a magnificent golden robe from the arms of a waiting retainer, and cast it about the Tartar's shoulders.

"The fellow should have something better than that dirty hair to cover his head, as well," added the Czar, at which I jumped up and took a really fine, gold–embroidered cap from another servant, placing this upon the ambassador's head.

The man was so surprised he made no protest. In fact, he was probably greedy enough to desire these gifts, even with the insulting implication that accompanied them. When Malyuta and I were back in our places, Ivan raised his hands and gave the ambassador his permission to speak.

Insolently, the little brown man stood before our mighty Czar and, in a nasal whine, pronounced the words of his master's communication: "The powerful Khan, Devlet Gerei, Lord of all lords and khanates, demands of his vassal Ivan – still by grace of the Khan, Grand Duke of Russia – how he has enjoyed the display of his master's displeasure. The fire, sword, and famine which the Khan has brought upon his offending people have been but an example of his wrath. Yet, in his goodness my master would not let the matter rest here." At this, the fellow produced an ancient, rusty knife – at least he produced the sheath; I had removed the blade lest he do some harm with it. "Your master, the Khan, has graciously sent you this dagger," he said, "that you may find consolation by cutting your own throat."

Ivan's already gray complexion turned a deathly white, and I could see his anger begin to rise. Malyuta and I, standing on either side of the throne, exchanged glances over the Czar's head. "Better get them out," I mumbled.

Malyuta nodded, and calling a half–dozen guardsmen to help us, we hustled the Tartars from the room. "Take them back to their cell," I told the men. I hurried back to the Czar, for I could already hear his furious shrieking. By the time I returned, Ivan had torn his robe to shreds, and his scalp was bleeding where he had pulled out a patch of hair. His cap was on the floor, and the Czar was leaping up and down upon it. "I'll have them impaled!" he screamed. "And I'll send their heads back to that camel's turd in a box!"

With Boris and myself on either side, Malyuta going before us, we were able to escort the Czar into another room. We sent for his confessor, and more or less forced Ivan to lie down. It was the first time anyone had taken such liberties with his person, but it was a spontaneous and unanimous act among the three of us. Regardless of anything else, it was essential we gain time. If the Khan should strike again this summer, it would surely spell disaster. We needed at least a month to organize an effective defense.

It took a full two days for the Czar to become calm enough that we dared readmit the Tartars to his presence. This time, I had a short session with the leader beforehand, and told him I would personally remove his tongue if it was used to provoke the Czar again. The men were brought before Ivan, who immediately made his pronouncement: "Tell this heathen, your unbelieving master," he said, "that it is not he who has conquered me. It was God, who by reason of my sins and those of my people, has granted the Khan, the son of Satan, the power and opportunity to become the instrument of my punishment. Still, I do not doubt for a moment that with God's grace and assistance I shall be able to avenge myself and make your master my vassal. Inform him how great my desire is to do so."

There was a deadly silence when the Czar had finished speaking, and the wizened little Tartar looked at me cautiously before he answered. I am sure he was tempted to make some caustic remark. I ran my hand along the hilt of my sword, edging a step closer to the Musselmen.

"I would not dare carry such a message to my master," replied the ambassador at length. "As a loyal servant of the Khan, I must decline any such commission from the Czar of Russia."

I think Ivan was about to reinstate his demand, when Malyuta leaned over him and whispered something in his ear. Ivan looked at him, then at me, then at the Tartars. "You may leave Us," he said.

The Tartars were allowed to depart the next day, their leader keeping a tight hold on the finery presented to him by the Czar. Our own ambassadors were dispatched at the same time; and they arrived in the Crimea shortly after the Khan returned to celebrate his victory – a cruel reverse of fortunes, when contrasted to the Czar's homecoming.

Ivan returned to Moscow, and wept bitter tears when he saw the havoc left by the invaders. He prayed for many hours in the Great Cathedral, berating himself for the tragedy. "It is God's punishment for my sins," he repeated over and over. "He has visited His wrath upon my people."

Nor could we offer much hope to those who survived. There had been some effort to replenish food supplies before the infidels came, but the fire destroyed it all. The people would have to feed, clothe, and house themselves as best they could. Even for the better classes there was a shortage of many foods, and for several weeks we had very little to eat. Fortunately, Simon had laid in a heavy stock of onions and sweet tubers in his cellar, as well as a large bin of flour. We supplemented this by slaughtering a couple of young mares and living off their flesh until some other meats became available.

It was not long before messages began arriving from our ambassadors to the Khan. At Malyuta's suggestion, Ivan had cleverly sent clerks, who had no authority to act without his specific approval. Each question put to them by the Khan had to be referred to Moscow. Because we had never previously undertaken a prolonged negotiation with these infidels, they did not know the procedure was other than our usual custom. The ploy gained us time to reorganize the army.

At my urging, supported by Boris and opposed by Skuratof, the Czar recalled the *Zemschina* officers. He placed the distinguished, dignified Vorotinsky in supreme command. The very best of our surviving leaders were assigned to serve under him, and I had the honor of being among those chosen. Quickly and efficiently, we began collecting a powerful Russian army.

While deeply involved in these military operations, I discovered a terrible, personal misfortune. Heinrich, who had been so depressed for many months past, had left the bulk of our business transactions in the hands of underlings. I had been too involved in military and governmental work to help much, and in fact had cost us some extremely heavy expenses by diverting our people to the Czar's service. When our Moscow homes were destroyed by the fire, I naturally assumed we would rebuild immediately. But there was no money. Heinrich had invested heavily in western lands, particularly in the conquered territories of Livonia. Now, with our perfidious commanders turning these possessions back to Sigismund – and with my own estates also in enemy hands – our losses were staggering. We still had goods in southern warehouses, and in transit from the bazaars of Bukhara and Samarkand – all too far away, and available only if we could transport them through areas infested by Tartar bandits. Their total value would still be insufficient to maintain the business and to permit the rebuilding of our *dachas* at the same time.

For the moment we were nearly penniless, surviving solely on Simon's bounty. Yet the situation was not quite as desperate as it might have been. Simon was very rich, and his house was one of the finest – and largest – in the Kremlin. He had become not only a devoted friend, but he had lived such a lonely existence since the loss of his own family he sincerely enjoyed having mine about him. The boys were very fond of "Uncle Simon," especially as he had time to play with them and to instruct them in the use of his native weapons. My eldest son, Johnny, was now a strongly built boy of six. Demetrius was nearly as big, and would eventually grow into the larger man. Christina was a lovely child of only a year, with a face much like her mother's. But her hair was blonde, like mine, and her skin was very fair. Her eyes were green and deep, awaiting the day when they would flash with the fire of spirited womanhood.

Heinrich, suddenly sobered by the tragedy, took a post on Vorotinsky's staff. His hands were shaky at first, but he gradually began to recover from the degeneration into which he had allowed himself to fall. The terrible crimes he had committed with the brotherhood – crimes that had haunted him worse than mine did me, haunted him at the very moment of their commission – all seemed to have become vague shadows in his past. He said to me he felt like a whole man again. I suggested he might find a wife, but he shook his head. He would never marry again, he told me.

Both my stepfather and I were confident we could eventually rebuild our fortunes, and because of our friends we had little to fear in the immediate future. At the moment, I had a greater threat looming large in my path: Malyuta Skuratof. Being assigned to the army, I was kept constantly busy and away from the Kremlin. So was Heinrich. Not only did Malyuta have easy access to the Czar, he had been left in charge of my former office. The old hostilities he had previously kept hidden, now surfaced and threatened to destroy me. I was the greatest barrier to his goal of prime favor and control.

Despite the huge losses all the rest of us had sustained, Skuratof was rich. He had plundered the *Zemschina,* and because he retained his position in Ivan's affections, he had not been forced to return his ill–gotten wealth as many others had. He had hidden his treasure where it escaped destruction – some in vaults beneath the Kremlin, the rest in the northern monasteries. He also knew I could no longer afford a network of private agents. While Jacob was loyal, and continued to serve as he always had, he was hamstrung by the limited funds available to him. Abraham was now very old, and no longer as alert as he once had been. Many of our servants had been killed or carried off by the Tartars. There had also been a raid on one of our large caravans during the time we had been in retreat before the onrushing horde. There was no escaping reality: I was in a position of weakness, while Skuratof was assuming powers he had previously only dreamed of possessing.

My single strongest asset was the Czar's good will. Ivan would never admit it, but he knew I had advised him correctly and he trusted me. Most important, his trust was communicated to the Czarevitch, thus assuring my continued favor in the succession – if Malyuta didn't succeed in destroying me first. By clever, insidious means, he began a campaign to usurp my place in Ivan's heart and to discredit me before the boyars.

His first move was to start a small, nasty rumor, implying that I had poked fun at the Czar's second son, Fedya. Of course, I had never maligned him in any way. I felt toward this lad as I had toward his uncle Yuri, for the similarity in their handicaps seemed to have increased through the years. His mind refused to develop as it should have, nor did his body possess the manliness of his brother. Like Yuri, he was pleasant and simple, never offending anyone. He was frequently neglected, even by his father, for he was unable to participate in many activities. Still, I would have been the last to make fun of him. He reminded me too much of a man for whom I had always borne a deep, brotherly affection.

I do not think Ivan believed the stories, but he asked me about them when I was in the palace one evening. I convinced him of my innocence over a game of chess, and that ended the matter. Neither of us realized at the time just how the story had started. But the fact that Ivan would question me at all proved a point; I was vulnerable, and Skuratof continued his efforts.

He bribed one of my subordinates to misinterpret an order I had given for troop distributions along the new defense lines south of Tula. I discovered what was happening only because the man Malyuta hired was not very clever. He sent a message to the Kremlin reporting his success. I intercepted this, and immediately corrected the error. Although I did not report the incident to the Czar, I knew there was no longer any alternative but to destroy my enemy before he destroyed me.

A form of unspoken war existed between us. Yet when we met, especially in the Czar's presence, we behaved like the best of friends. No harsh words or open hostility characterized our conflict, but each took every opportunity to subtly point up the other's failures – to place stumbling blocks in his path.

The Czar had ordered the immediate rebuilding of his city, with the work well underway by the end of summer. There was never a shortage of laborers, for the tremendous loss of life had not seriously reduced Moscow's population. The dead were replaced by refugees from areas which had been devastated by either the Tartars or the *Opritchina,* with the result that there seemed to be as many people living in the capital as ever. Before the first snows, a great many houses had been rebuilt, a new city growing once again upon the ashes of the old. The river alone remained a source of annoyance. The stink of rotting flesh refused to subside. Even in the coldest winter months there was an odor of death about it.

Ivan had been in a miserable state of depression during much of the summer, and retired to Alexandrov for several extended periods. He spent hours by himself, locked in his apartments or in his chapel. He had ample diversion, as there were still forty or fifty girls in his *terem.* Despite all of this womanhood being available to him, he still went through an extensive harangue with the Church, finally obtaining its sanction for another marriage. This would be his fourth.

I have not fully described Ivan's peculiar domestic arrangements because I never completely understood them myself. He had taken his third wife while I was in England, and she had been so closely sequestered I had never really seen her – certainly did not know her. The Czarevitch had also married, this during the time of the *Opritchina*, but because of all the chaos there had been only a small ceremony. I had been in Livonia and had not been summoned back to attend. Then, apparently, things did not work out well. It was something neither Ivan nor Vanya wished to discuss, but I was certainly aware of the rumors about the goings–on in the *terem*, where father and son were said to be disporting themselves with each other's concubines, and even with one another's wives! I do not know how much of this was true, and it was clearly not a subject I could question them about.

Vanya spent much of the summer with his father, and to the best of my knowledge, there were days at a time when he was the only man permitted to see him. Boris Godunof was in Moscow, where he served as steward to the household of Ivan's second son. Negotiations were already underway for Boris's sister, Irene, to marry this younger prince. I was sure Malyuta had been instrumental in the arrangements.

By utilizing my official travels, I was able to reestablish some business interests in Kazan, and in the Pskov–Novgorod area. For the most part, I managed to straighten out the havoc Heinrich had allowed our business to become. I was fortunate enough to make a fine buy in horsehides south of Kazan, and I sent these to Pskov with Jacob. Through some personal contacts in Livonia, I arranged for their transshipment all the way to Luebeck. This greatly improved our fortunes, although we were far from attaining the powerful position we had formerly held in the world of trade. Shortly after this, a Persian merchant came to me – in Novgorod, actually – desperately seeking jade to sell in Cathay. Through one of the Stroganov agents, I was able to obtain a large consignment in exchange for interceding on their behalf with the Czar. Finally, I left Jacob in charge of our posts in Kazan, giving him unlimited authority and granting him a tithe of the profits.

Abraham died during the summer, and this greatly limited our ability to tap the Astrakhan markets – for a time it hampered our trade throughout the entire Volga region. It was necessary for Jacob to trace down a good many of his father's personal associates, and to ingratiate himself without the benefit of a proper father–to–son transition. As a result of all this work, we continued to turn a profit, benefiting from the heavy Russian migrations into these southern areas. I would have preferred going to Astrakhan myself, but the Czar's business required my return to court when he again took up residence in Moscow.

Because my family and I remained with Simon through the winter, the former Khan had frequent occasion to host the Czar. This annoyed Skuratof, as he generally felt compelled to stay away, apprehensive to confront me on my home ground. Having Ivan more or less to myself on these occasions, I was able to press for some of my own ideas without Malyuta's immediate interference. Vorotinsky, who had never expressed any hostility or resentment over my part in the activities of the brotherhood, now began using me as his best avenue of approach to the Czar. The advice Ivan received from his commander – either directly, or through me – greatly affected his decisions during this period. Malyuta must have been furious! The disbanding of the *Opritchina* had not been finalized, and Skuratof was doing everything he could to delay it. The brotherhood was his strength. Without it, he felt like Antaeus removed from the earth. He was impotent, dependent solely on the Czar's whims for his power. Each inroad made by Vorotinsky or myself must have cut deeply into his sense of security.

Another result of the Czar's visits to Simon's house was the development of a closer friendship between them. Over the years, Ivan had gradually forgotten about his former enemy. Now, he renewed his acquaintance and his interest. Because of Simon's penetrating mind, and extensive knowledge of Tartar, Ivan listened closely to his suggestions for dealing with the infidels – another loss for Malyuta, and one he could do nothing about.

It was spring before the Tartars realized how we had duped them with our ambassadors. Enraged, the Khan moved against us again, this time striking north, not bothering to slip into our territory by the back trails and secret paths used by other thieves and highwaymen. As before, Devlet Gerei led his army in person, making the same boasts and threats. Moscow had been reborn from the wreckage he had left, and from this new city a tremendous army went forth under Vorotinsky. We numbered close to three–hundred–thousand men when we engaged a Tartar force south of Tula, routing them in a single skirmish. Actually, we never met the main part of the horde. We sent their advance units fleeing in such terror, their entire command took flight before *Grozny's* advancing army. They did not stop until they were all the way into the high meadows of the Crimea. For Devlet Gerei, the moment of glory had come and gone. We were once again masters of the steppe.

We returned to Moscow in triumph. Because we had again established the Czar in his proper position of power and prestige, he was more willing to listen as Vorotinsky and I pressed for ambassadors to be sent into the border areas, and to the lowlands about the Don River. As soon as Ivan did this, we had many barbarian tribes swearing fealty to him. We even made an alliance with the Cossacks in the region.

With our southern borders secure, we could return our attention to the west. Magnus came to Moscow that summer, his trip having been delayed a year by the Tartar invasion. He was met at the city gates by a delegation of boyars, all of them *Zemschina*. And this was the turning point, for Ivan formally ended the *Opritchina* two days later. Only a few of us, like Malyuta and myself, retained the Czar's favor. Most of the others had been of less than noble birth, so without the brotherhood to give them status they sank into the obscurity from which they had come. A few former *Opritchniki* were murdered by the sons of men whom they had killed, but in general there was no great purge. The *Opritchina* simply ceased to exist. The houses given to the brothers by the Czar had been largely destroyed by the fire. Now the land was deeded back to the former owners – or to the heirs if the man was dead. The very word *Opritchina* was forbidden, for Ivan kept his promise and ordered it stricken from the language. It would never again be used in his presence.

Magnus was still in Moscow when we received some news we had long awaited. Sigismund August, King of Poland and Grand Duke of Lithuania, was dead! There was considerable rejoicing at this, and a great banquet that night – not officially to celebrate Sigismund's demise, but the King's death became a principal subject for our toasts. Ostensibly, we celebrated Ivan's proclamation of Magnus as King of Livonia.

The wedding of the new King to Vladya's daughter Euphemia was supposed to have taken place as quickly as the various religious and social requirements could be satisfied. Unfortunately, the girl died quite suddenly, and from no apparent cause. I was certain she had been poisoned, and I strongly suspected it was done by one of Skuratof's people. He opposed reopening the war in Livonia, possibly afraid I might become wealthy enough to oppose him more strongly. Our unproclaimed struggle had become that desperate, for he knew I meant to destroy him. He did everything he could to thwart Ivan's plans, short of openly committing himself as being against them. This might have been my opportunity to ruin him had I been able to bring sufficient proof before the Czar. I would no longer have hesitated as I had on previous occasions. In the end I had to let it drop. But he knew I had tried and he actually acknowledged it by several knowing smiles when we passed in the palace corridors.

Following Euphemia's death Magnus returned to Livonia, still unwed, and assumed command of his armies. He had been betrothed to Vladya's younger daughter, Maria. As she was a child of only thirteen, it was decided to let matters stand as they were for a year or so. One of the most unpleasant duties I ever performed was to inform that poor little girl of the Czar's decision. The child became hysterical, for she had seen Magnus from behind a screen at the Alexandrov palace. She wept for days, refusing to eat or to leave her rooms until I feared she might follow her sister to the grave. Magnus's appearance was enough to make a brave man grow pale; Maria's response was more than understandable.

From the beginning the new King had difficulty handling his troops. Although Ivan had originally decided otherwise, he now agreed to the Dane's commanding our Russian levies as well as the other soldiers. In an attempt to help Magnus regain control, the Czar unwittingly granted me the opportunity I had been awaiting. He sent Mstislavsky, Skuratof, and myself to Livonia as advisors.

We fought a number of battles in and around Reval, one of the cities given back to Poland by our turncoat German commanders. None of these campaigns was especially decisive, nor glorious enough to merit special note. Summer ended and fall weather set in, with dense banks of storm clouds blowing inland from the restless Finnish Gulf.

I was constantly in the thick of battle, and within a single week I had two very close calls. In both instances, bullets came very near ending my career. I thought little about it the first time, assuming it to be a lucky shot by some enemy soldier. The ball glanced off my shoulder plate, having struck at too great an angle to penetrate. But the second shot did not come from the front, where our cannon had momentarily routed the enemy. It had definitely been fired from somewhere on the right. Again my armor protected me, but the impact left a jagged rent through the edge of my breastplate – only a finger's width from ending my life. I held no doubt as to the instigator of both attempts.

Only the love Ivan bore him prevented my having Malyuta murdered. By the strange logic that governed my life, his attempts to have me killed could not justify my responsibility for the pain his death would surely cause the Czar. I prayed he might fall, or somehow be struck down by heaven – anything to avoid my hand having to be turned against him. Knowing the futility of such wishful thinking, I was stymied until the matter was suddenly settled for me.

Ivan had come to Novgorod several weeks before, and had made two inspections of our battle lines. His appearance always bolstered the spirit of the troops, although he never exposed himself to the enemy. He now made a third trip, to be with us when we attacked the town of Paide. It was a typical gray morning, with heavy ground mist and dark clouds floating on the horizon. It never actually rained, but the air was so moist it dampened one's clothes.

The fighting that day was as it had been on a great many others, unspectacular, but characterized by a stubborn determination on either side. The town we fought for was small, and would have been unimportant had it not dominated a hill. We needed it to curtail overland supply convoys into Reval. Because the Czar was present, Skuratof made a great show of leading his contingent. Usually, he was too lazy to exert this much energy. As he always drank heavily at night, he frequently suffered the usual consequences. He had also developed that malady of the fundament, so common to many horsemen, making it uncomfortable for him to sit in his saddle for long periods.

With the Czar on a hillock overlooking the battleground, Malyuta donned his finest battle garb. Servants had polished his armor until it gleamed like silver. Mounted on a heavy red stallion, and riding atop a deeply padded saddle, he galloped onto the field with his troop of *Streltsi* cavalry. Some of our larger guns had been moved into new positions during the night, and they now opened fire on the town. The enemy force met us at the base of the hill, and the battle was joined.

Toby, who now acted as my squire, made a remark I only half heard and thought little about at the time. We were on another hill, a little south of the Czar's position. We had seen Malyuta's charge down the far slope, and Toby said something to the effect that leading such an assault would be a glorious way to end one's career.

I hardly answered him, mumbling some obscene retort before calling to my own men, preparatory to taking up Malyuta's flank. Lithuanian footsoldiers were rushing in with pikes, and bowmen had suddenly popped up from hidden redoubts. I did not pay any further attention to Toby, other than to note the longbow slung over his shoulder. He usually carried only a broadsword and the brace of pistols I had originally bought for Vladya. I casually wondered about this change of weapons, but for some time I had seen him practicing in the evenings. I knew he had become a very skilled archer. The longbow was an English weapon given to him by Horsey. The Englishman had taken a liking to Toby, instructing him while the Muscovite Company officers were living in the Kremlin following the great fire.

I soon forgot everything except the battle, for I found myself in a desperate struggle almost as soon as we reached the field. It turned into a very bloody engagement, with men falling on all sides of me. Even a few of our knights found themselves in trouble, as the enemy was using a new musket, capable of firing a heavier shot that could pierce armor. I had ridden at the head of my heavy horseman, through the lines of enemy archers to the left of Skuratof's unit. I was still whacking heads when I heard sounds of a great confusion behind me, followed by several trumpet calls. We made short work of the Lithuanian bowmen because their cavalry had been pushed back and could no longer protect them. Those who survived our assault surrendered. It was only then I could turn my attention to the excitement behind our own lines.

I went at a gallop, crossing laterally through our freshly acquired fields where dead and wounded men still lay unattended to where Malyuta's men had been engaged, and saw a large number of them clustered about something on the ground. Several of the officers looked up at the sound of my approach, stepping back to reveal Malyuta lying on the ground. An arrow protruded from the side of his neck, colored with Lithuanian markings. To my highly trained eye, it appeared a bit too long to have come from an enemy crossbow, but I did not think anyone else noticed. There was utter confusion among the men, including the officers who did nothing but stand about whispering among themselves, glancing helplessly at their leader's body. Because none of them seemed to know what to do, I shoved my way through and knelt down beside Skuratof.

"Malyuta," I said, "can you hear me?"

His eyes flickered, but he did not open them. With the shaft penetrating his throat, he couldn't speak. It would only be a matter of minutes before he died. I looked up at those about me, shaking my head sadly, telling them by this gesture that their commander was as good as gone. I noticed Toby standing behind the others, fingering his bow where it rested on his shoulder. He pushed through the crowd and squatted down beside me.

"A long arrow," I mumbled, speaking softly so the others couldn't hear me.

"A Lithuanian arrow, from the look of it," he replied in the same tone.

We both had our faces averted, but looking sideways we could see each other without the men standing above us being able to note our expressions. When I glanced at Toby, he winked. A second later, Skuratof breathed his last.

"He's gone," I said sadly. Casually, I broke off the arrow and dropped the end onto the ground, where I stepped on it and shattered it completely. I lifted the body and carried it in my arms, all the way to the Czar's pavilion. With a great show of grief, I placed him on the ground before Ivan. "Our friend is gone," I said.

I do not think the Czar ever recognized the true situation between Malyuta and me. We had been careful to keep our differences from his notice and no one else would have dared mention it to him. The only possible exception would have been Boris, but for his own reasons I am sure he never said anything. Because of this, Ivan spoke to me at some length, trying to console me. He was crying bitterly, himself, and I wondered that I should feel so little when the Czar was this distressed. I had little time to dwell on it, however, as his sorrow turned abruptly to violent anger. Just a moment before he had been standing over the body, weeping silently. Now he emitted a horrible shriek of rage. He called to heaven, demanding that God lay a curse upon the enemy, and bellowed for the guards to bring forth every prisoner we had taken during the day.

Ivan's pavilion had been set near the crest of a steep hill some distance from the point where our lines had been that morning. He stepped outside as the trembling captives were assembled into a group about halfway down the slope. The Czar ordered them bound, which most of them already were, then had them roped together in groups of three or four. Other men were stacking up a huge heap of dried wood and branches. Ivan ordered the captives interspersed with the logs, near the top of the enormous pile. Heavy cable was thrown across the entire mound of men and tinder, with the ends staked tautly into the ground. The terrified prisoners could see the inevitable result; it was impossible for any of them to wriggle free. With his own hands the Czar ignited the brush beneath them, ignoring the cries and pleas of his victims. Only then did his rage seem to subside. He stood back transfixed, watching the red and yellow flames begin to leap and the black curls of smoke that twisted about the pile of men – a scene of fearsome horror, with no break in the frantic sounds of pain and abject terror. Some of the men deep inside the pile of bodies remained alive for hours, feet or legs consumed while the rest was shielded by the dead flesh of those about them. As darkness fell, the Czar kept half my command busy carrying brush and logs to feed the flames. The stink of burning carrion drove the living men – those on top or within the pile – into renewed paroxysms of demented fear. The fire did not burn well, and needed constant attention. The heavy smoke and attendant odors made me think of the dreadful conflagrations in Moscow. The victims numbered close to a hundred by my count, so the agonized cries resounded until close to dawn then the last of them finally died, consumed in the swirls of vile, choking smoke.

His act of vengeance eventually worked its soothing balm upon the spirit of the Czar, while I sought solace in drink – something I seldom did anymore, especially when I commanded troops. In my drunken haze, I remember thinking how fitting a tribute that pyre made to Malyuta Skuratof. Fire, death, misery – horribly mingled in the darkness of a misty night. It marked a proper, symbolic end . . . an appropriate memorial for a completely evil man.

CHAPTER XI

The next day, the Czar gave Malyuta a fine funeral and contributed a huge sum to the monastery at Pskov to assure eternal prayers for his soul. As I stood listening to the chant of the monks, my head throbbing from the night's excessive drinking, a strange, unholy doubt gave way to the repetitious rhythm within my mind. "The Czar is mad! The Czar is mad! The Czar is mad!" The unwanted thought continued to beat against my senses. It seemed to spin about itself, to take innumerable other forms and disguises. Why it had required the burning of those hundred prisoners to awaken the belief I could not later understand. But it had, and in years to come when I tried to discuss my thoughts with others – especially foreigners – they were astonished I had taken so long to reach this conclusion. I suppose the seed had been planted by Kurbsky when we argued on the night before his defection. Perhaps I had known it all along. In looking back on my controversies with so many people, I realized they had been trying to say this to me, but most had been afraid to form the words, knowing I would refuse to believe them, and dreading the consequences I might cause to fall upon them.

I hardly slept on the night following Malyuta's funeral. I lay in bed staring at the roof of my tent pondering the ramifications of this thought. I remembered the childhood discussions with the former Metropolitan Joseph about souls and madness. I had spoken to many other learned men since then, and I knew that no man understood the essence of madness; I doubt that any ever will. I questioned whether the Czar could be an earthly representative directed by the Hand of God as our beliefs indicated. Some believed him possessed by the forces of darkness – a possibility I still could not accept. The more desperately I tried to understand, the more confused I became. There was no one to whom I could turn for advice, nor any kindred fool who might discuss my disordered wanderings. In the end I convinced myself that however mad the Czar might be, his very affliction made it ever more incumbent upon me to render whatever support and comfort I could. The evil had been generated by forces outside his being.

In the morning, while I was still exhausted from my sleepless night and looking forward with no great pleasure to the day's activities, I had an unexpected caller. With the body of his patron hardly cold within its grave, Malyuta's servant came to offer me his services. The man's name was Illya, a rather handsome, dark–complexioned youth who had been his master's virtual shadow for a number of years.

"Now that my lord is dead," he told me, kneeling to emphasize his supplicating respect, "I would gladly enter into your service. I will be faithful to you as I was to my old master. I am strong and I am familiar with the intrigue of the court. I could be of great value to you, my lord." He glanced up sharply at the last, giving a secondary meaning to his statement.

"This is an unseemly hour," I replied coldly. "Besides, you have been involved in more than one plot to murder me." I added this second remark harshly. It was a guess, but it proved a good one.

The lad's face burned crimson. He dropped his gaze to the floor, and answered in a muttered undertone. "I have served my master in *every* way. But he is dead. I offer my body, and the same loyalty to you that I have given him."

"You are not a slave?" I asked.

"No, my lord. I was born a free man and I have always lived as such. My mother was of gentle birth."

"Your father?" I returned without thinking.

Again the blush of red, and I knew what he would have liked to reply. He smiled grimly. "So I've been told," he said simply.

"I must think about this," I told him, speaking more kindly now. "I must limit my staff as you probably already know."

"I have brought you something," he said, "and I hope it may convince you of my sincerity." He handed me a packet of several papers. I unfolded them and glanced quickly from one to the other. At first I was shocked to immobility. Then I flared in anger. Two were letters I had received from Toby's uncle, Henry Fowler, the overseer of my properties in England. The others were letters from Ridolfi to Nina. They had been brought to us, over a period of years, by the English traders. For them to be stolen from our home was an intolerable affront, and an act that must have required some extensive planning – to say nothing of treachery within my own household.

"You dare to admit such perfidy, and yet ask for my protection?" I demanded. I was on the verge of swinging my foot to kick him out through the open tent flap.

He edged backward a bit, anticipating me. "Please, sir," he said. He spoke quickly, in a soft, harried tone. "I have taken these from the chest of my former master, and I bring them to you as a token of good will. I would never have done such a thing while Malyuta lived. Now he is dead, they can be of no value to anyone but yourself."

"Do you know what these are?" I asked.

"No," Illya replied simply. "I cannot read the Western languages."

"What did your master, your *former* master intend doing with these?" I demanded sharply.

"I cannot say," he replied. "They were in his possession for a long while."

"Do you know how he acquired them?"

"He employed several skilled thieves, especially during the days of the Brotherhood when it was possible to slip into a man's house during the times of chaos. But I do not know which of his agents performed the actual theft."

"Are there other items in your former master's effects that I should know about?" I demanded harshly.

The young man looked at me helplessly. "I can not be sure."

"But if I employ you, they will come into my hands," I suggested coldly.

Illya remained silent, slowly getting to his feet, his eyes downcast.

In the end I told him to go, but gave him permission to return in a day or two, after I had time to think. I promised to give him my answer then. I really did not want Illya in my service, but I was afraid to have him in someone else's employ.

I was particularly concerned that he might seek service with a Shuisky, or some other boyar who could turn his knowledge against me. The Buturlins, my former in–laws, had also rebuilt their fortunes, and they still disliked me. In time they could also become a threat. I knew they had recently hired several new servants. When Illya returned, I reluctantly took him on, though it was a long time before I allowed him a place of trust. For the moment, I assigned him to assist Toby, and from the first they seemed to get along with no problems.

From this servant of Malyuta's and from the assortment of materials he brought with him I garnered several bits of information, and was able to confirm several of my suspicions. The plots my enemy had concocted were marvels of an evil, disordered mind. Some were so devious I could never have anticipated them. Fortunately, they had failed. In one singular instance I learned he had been in-nocent of a crime I had always attributed to him. He had not murdered Euphemia, Vladya's daughter and Magnus's prospective bride. The poor child had apparently taken her own life rather than marry such a disgusting creature. Whereas Malyuta had supplied the poison – and Illya had taken it to her – it had been more an act of grace than murder. My futile attempts to gather proof of Malyuta's guilt must have amused them at the time.

For days, whenever he spoke of Malyuta, tears streamed down Ivan's cheeks; and those awoke my old compassion. I cursed myself for thinking as I had, and for allowing myself to doubt the Czar. He had never seemed more rational, nor had his mind ever been more penetrating. There were moments of anger and other emotions that went beyond the average man, but they were few and they happened less often. Yet they could still be frightening. It became a period of terrible conflict for me; in the final resolution I had been awakened to the truth, however much I tried to deny it.

Several evenings after the funeral I dined with the Czar and Boris, who had come immediately after word of Malyuta's death reached Moscow. We had returned to the original camp following the ceremonies in Pskov. While overcome with grief, Ivan was not neglecting his duties. He was determined to win the campaign in Livonia, and felt that the empty throne of Poland offered an unprecedented opportunity. It created such an uncertain state among our enemies, he reasoned, we should easily achieve our purposes. I tended to agree until Boris, who never ceased to surprise me by his quickness of mind, expressed some contrary ideas. Through his ready wit and cleverness in sidestepping the guilt of his former membership in the brotherhood, Boris had established himself solidly within the court, even among the haughty boyars who were now being returned to power. Untitled himself, his forebears were of the Saburov–Godunofs, who had been boyars since the days of Basil the Blind and Ivan Moneybags. He also had a few kinsmen in key court positions who passed him information or friendly warnings. One of these was Gregory, Ivan's Lord Steward. The other was a lesser person named Feodor or Alexander – I no longer remember which – a taster of fifth or sixth rank.

Therefore, despite his being Malyuta's son–in–law, Boris's minimal involvement in all the evil of the brotherhood had left him with very few enemies within the new power structure. On this particular night he spoke at great length, trying to persuade the Czar to attack in the northwest, against the areas held by Sweden.

"Leave the Poles alone for a few months," he advised. "You could even grant them the extended truce they want. With proper guile, you might be elected King of Poland. Don't you agree, Dmitri?"

"With enough gold in the right places," I replied thoughtfully, "anything can happen." I did not really believe it possible, but Boris had opened a new train of thought – both for the Czar and myself. Finally, I shrugged. "An interesting possibility," I added, laughing.

Ivan laughed with me. "We have been enemies too long," he remarked, but his answer bore no tone of finality. Boris had prodded him into an entirely fresh series of considerations.

With hardly a glance at me, Boris went on to relate all he had learned of Polish politics. He was surprisingly well informed, and I remember wondering if he might also have taken some of Malyuta's servants. Otherwise, I could not account for his knowing so many intimate details. In the past, Boris had never employed agents of his own. In the future, he would. As I subsequently discovered, he had fallen heir to his father–in–law's existing network of spies. Watching as he spoke, I could see the Czar's changing response, first incredulous, then hopeful. As he listened, he gradually began to nod in agreement, almost as if he were falling under some peculiar spell.

Nor was I immune to Boris's persuasive words. Eventually, I also found myself agreeing with him. Before this exchange, I had not seriously thought of Ivan as a candidate for the Polish Throne; now the possibility seemed less remote. Although we spoke of several other things later on, the conversation kept returning to the same subject: the next King of Poland. Subtly, with each new opportunity, Boris continued to weave his web. The new tranquillity of the court, he noted, should impress the Poles and permit a competent spokesman to persuade them by pointing up Ivan's recent kindness and magnanimity. He followed the observation by a strongly stated suggestion that we maintain a rigid adherence to the laws of Adashev's council. This might have been dangerous ground, but Boris never faltered in his logic, nor in his apparent conviction that Ivan had been responsible for every desirable aspect of these rules.

Thus, out of this extraordinary conversation, the need for a greater degree of order was established. In the weeks to follow, there were few executions, and these were seldom of a political nature. Whenever a Pollack representative was in Ivan's presence he was treated with the greatest honor, all of us having been ordered to extend the maximum respect and friendship.

"It is a sad thing," Ivan told the Polish Ambassador, "when such a noble King must die without any children to pray for his soul."

Also following from Boris's persuasive arguments the Czar ordered us to move against the northern territories held by Sweden. I accompanied Magnus, ostensibly as the King's advisor. Actually, my orders were to assure his loyalty. At the first sign of treachery I was to take whatever action I deemed necessary to protect the interests of the Czar. Boris and I had laughed about Magnus's regal airs. Even a child should have been able to see that the Czar would never permit a foreigner to rule independently – especially in a newly won border area. But Magnus, shrewd and conniving as he might otherwise have been, was eager to believe everything Ivan told him. Backed by Boris's soft assurances, he even took the Czar's subtle implications as promises.

Our campaign was extremely successful from the first. The Swedes fled before our cannon, and as winter came on we took any area we were able to reach. Into November, the snows became heavy even for this region, and the Swedes never have fought as well as we under these conditions. Finally, though, the weather became so dreadful we had to go into winter quarters. This was around the middle of December. Feeling sentimental, I foolishly decided to brave the elements in an attempt to reach Moscow by Epiphany. There would clearly be no further fighting before the spring thaws. Not only did I long to see Nina, but within the close confines of our snowbound camp I had reached a point where I simply could not face Magnus any more. His personal habits were as revolting as his appearance.

The trip proved nearly fatal, and I doubt I would have lived through it had Toby and Illya not been with me. As it was, we did not reach Moscow until the middle of January, well past the holy season. The Czar seemed extremely pleased I had come, for he had been under great pressure in assigning precedence within the court and the army. Many of the old families could not understand why a grandfather's position in command of men did not qualify the grandson for the same. But it was an ancient tradition we fought, and many feathers were ruffled before positions were finally established within the new court. When I stood by the Czar as he announced his decisions, my very presence served as mute testimony to his wisdom. Whereas some of the various contenders disliked me – some even feared me, still – none could deny my competence as either a military commander or a courtier. The fact of my being alive to stand before them was ample proof.

All of this allowed me to stay in Moscow, which delighted Nina and the children. When the Czar still hesitated to order my return to the front after the roads opened in the spring, we spent the most pleasant days we had ever enjoyed in the capital. The building activities were resumed and the entire city was alive with trade and a new, expectant vigor. Both boys were old enough to accompany me on short hunting trips; Nina sometimes coming along as well. The Bureau of Hawk Tenders loaned us some excellent birds, and the whole family enjoyed a few days on the edge of the swamps along the Novgorod highway. We returned dirty and covered with mud, but with our game bags full of fat swan and geese.

Unfortunately, the Swedes appointed a new general to command their units – a fellow by the name of Akeson. When he defeated a very large force of our troops outside Lode, Magnus arranged a truce. Ivan was displeased, but he affirmed the agreement and finally extended it for a year. Soon after this we had to send another force into Kazan to quell an uprising. At first I thought the Czar was going to entrust the command of this expedition to me. I was so sure, in fact, I had promised my son Johnny to take him with me. Then fate intervened, dashing Johnny's hopes and my future peace of mind into a thousand, tinkling bits.

A small group of Polish nobles arrived in June as soon as the roads were dry enough for them to travel by carriage. They did not constitute an official delegation as there really was no proper government in Poland at the time. However, they did represent a powerful faction within the establishment of Princes. They entered Moscow with little fanfare and requested an audience with Boris Godunof, unaware that he was in Alexandrov with the Czar and most of the court. Boris's sister Irene was about to wed Fedya, following a season of royal marriages. Both the Czar and Czarevitch had remarried during the winter. Ivan had solved the problem of the Church's injunction against a man taking four wives, when Leonide – Pimen's successor as Archbishop of Novgorod – finally granted the dispensation. I know that Vanya had succeeded in placing his first wife in a nunnery, but do not recall the details – mere palace intrigue, in any event.

As the Pollacks had arrived unannounced, no one remained in the capital to receive them. The only reason for my still being there was the involved series of preparations to assume command of the southern army. When they discovered the absence of practically the whole court, the Pollacks bypassed the Czar's secretariat and came directly to me.

I received them in my home – or rather Simon's home – and heard them out, knowing the Czar would be interested in whatever they had to say. Wily as Pollacks always are, they told me little, but implied a great deal. I felt they were up to something, and for this reason I took them with me when I joined the court, unaware as I did so that I was about to involve myself in a most unpleasant adventure. What the Pollacks had been reticent to tell me was that they represented a group of nobles who were seeking Ivan's permission to submit Fedya's name as candidate for the King of Poland! While the Czar's consent would not necessarily assure his son's election, they explained, his chances would be greatly enhanced if the Czar's Majesty were willing to supply the necessary funds. Pretending a complete ignorance of Ivan's maneuverings to have himself elected, the Pollacks went on to explain how it had been arranged for the entire Polish nobility to cast votes in the election – not just members of the Diet as it had been in the past. Polish nobles, being traditionally poor, were always open to bribes the fellows suggested. And who was wealthier than Ivan?

The Czar was greatly surprised by their proposal, as was I. At first, I thought he was uncertain whether to be amused or angry. He had always been critical of this stupid electoral system, and such an offer only proved how ridiculous it really was. Allowing no emotion to show in his manner, the Czar listened to everything his visitors had to say, finally announcing that he would retire to consider their suggestions. Poor Fedya was never invited to attend our meeting, although it was supposed to be his future we discussed. Instead, the Czar, Czarevitch Vanya, Boris Godunof, and I went into Ivan's private chambers. Once out of sight and hearing, with the doors bolted behind us, we howled with laughter. Fedya . . . Feodor I, King of Poland!

"Why, the fools have no idea what they're suggesting!" Ivan bellowed. "Fedya can't even rule his own household!"

I kept still through this, remembering the incident with Malyuta and his contrived accusation. But there had been no malice in Ivan's remark, and he was not seeking to trap anyone. Fedya, whatever his other attributes, was a simpleton. Everyone knew it, and much as we might love him, our affection could not alter the facts. Of course, the Pollacks must have known it, too. This may have been their reason for seeking him. A weak King easily controlled by his nobles – this was probably what they wanted.

"Well, what shall we tell them?" I asked at length.

"Tell them?" roared the Czar. "Why I shall tell them that if they want the House of Rurik to rule in Poland, it must be in the person of the Head of that House!"

We all started to laugh again, for it seemed the Pollacks had blundered into a perfect position to forward our plans. "Ivan I, King of Poland!" I shouted.

"Sigismund must lie very uneasy in his grave," added Boris.

"Could it really happen this simply?" Ivan squealed, trying to speak through his paroxysms of mirth. "After all these years of war; what a positively simple solution!"

When we confronted the Polish delegation the following afternoon, and expressed the Czar's decision, they seemed as shocked as we had been by their original proposal. To elect the feeble–minded second son of Ivan IV would be one thing to unite their nation under the Czar of Russia was quite another!

After the formal conference in Ivan's salon, he invited the Pollacks to join us for a few flagons of wine in the sunny garden behind the royal residence. With some further discussion, a fair amount of spirits, and a small display of the Czar's fabled wealth, our suggestions became less appalling. In the end, the visitors agreed to support our proposal. Unfortunately, they made a final request just before departing. The Czar should send a Russian advocate to speak for him, they suggested, and their spokesman's gaze fell on me! Impulsively, Ivan appointed me his personal representative. I was to leave at once – a Russian Prince, traveling in enemy country with no official standing or immunity, because there was no proper government to grant it.

CHAPTER XII

My entire life had been devoted to the Czar's service, and in the course of that service I had been in many circumstances I did not enjoy. I had been in physical danger any number of times; I had endured hardships of every sort; and I had traveled halfway around the world at his request. But I had never been on a more distasteful mission than this – made still worse, because I traveled without my usual retinue. I had given Toby permission to marry Anna just before the Czar ordered me to go. When the lad asked if he might remain in Moscow, I agreed to let him do so. Then Illya came down with a fever on the eve of my departure. Ivan suggested a clerk from his secretariat, but I declined the offer, as I knew the man he intended to give me and I didn't trust him. As a result, I left the capital in the company of four Pollacks, with a small escort of soldiers to see us to the border.

Try as I would to find some good in these men, it was an impossible undertaking. There are many disgusting, inferior breeds of people on the face of this earth: Tartars, Livonians, Danes, Jews, Swedes – I have known them all, and at times I have found a man in each class who is worthy of friendship. But of all the creatures who walk upon two legs, there is none so vile as a Pollack! They are not proper Slavs, nor are they German; they have no land properly to call their own. By stealth and crafty political maneuvers they gleaned vast territories after the Mongol invasions, much from the barbarian princes to the west of Russia. In the process, their polyglot nation ingested the seeds of its own demise, the most obvious being the preposterous autonomy of their provincial nobles. The very concessions which had united these bickering scoundrels behind their royal buffoon now projected them into a state of absolute anarchy. With the death of Sigismund, all semblance of unity had disappeared. The result should rightly have marked an end to the unholy union called "Poland." They had no one amongst themselves fit to rule. Only a powerful foreign sovereign had any hope of salvaging the remains.

All of this became more obvious to me once we crossed the frontier. I could see that gold would provide the key to unlock the door to the Polish throne. Although Ivan had been unusually generous in allotting my "expenses," we had traveled in a single, lightweight coach, which limited my ability to carry funds. So did the problem of brigandage. I knew that a shipment of the Czar's trade goods would be ready to leave for Warsaw within a few days – one economic benefit of the latest truce. As it would be necessary for me to pass through Warsaw enroute to Krakow, I planned to make arrangements for one of our agents in that city to get the additional gold to me in the capital. From Vileyka, I sent a dispatch to Ivan, requesting the goodly sum I expected to need.

We were forced to abandon our coach near the border and continue on horseback because the Polish roads were even worse than ours. We continued through rivers of mud to Lida, then on to Grodno, encountering foul weather all the way. It rained almost constantly, a hard pelting downpour that kept us soaked to the skin. On the few occasions when the rain let up, we were immediately devoured by insects. The one advantage we gained from the weather was a degree of secrecy, as no one stood about in the open to gape at us. We now traveled without escort, and I doubted any of my companions would be much use in a scrape with highwaymen. One was an old man named Paul; the second was a middle–aged merchant; the others were a pair of simpering youths, more concerned with the appearance of their clothing than with more manly practices. All of them used perfume to mask their Pollack stench.

At Grodno the weather broke, and Paul persuaded me to buy another coach. The roads were better from here, he said, and he was already suffering from a constriction in his chest as a result of our rigorous journey. I finally agreed, but regretted my decision the first day. Crowded into the swaying, jouncing vehicle, I had no way to escape either the sickly sweet smell of my companions' scent, nor their endless chatter. As none of them spoke Russian very well, I was forced to converse with them in Polish.

Under a clear sky, word of our coming seemed to spread ahead of us. Groups of dour peasants stood along the roadside, staring stupidly as we rumbled past. At night we had to stay in the filthy hovels of the lower nobility, for we were not welcome in the homes of those who did not favor the Russian cause. Most of the major landowners in those eastern sections of Poland were afraid to have Ivan for their King – unlike the Lithuanians, who wanted him. Twice, it was necessary to share a bed with one of my companions – once with Paul, who kept me awake with his snoring, the other with one of the youths who snuggled against me in his sleep like a suckling pig to a sow. I could hardly wait to reach Warsaw, where I would finally be able to bathe and enjoy a few hours of freedom.

We were eight days inside of Poland, making good time as we headed toward a town called Zambrow. Our light, poorly designed coach was jouncing through a wooded area, and for once my companions were quiet. I had dozed in my corner of the seat, half dreaming of home and generally feeling better than I had since leaving Moscow, when abruptly – with no warning whatever – we pitched sideways off the road! For a moment, the coach balanced precariously on its left wheels, then slowly rolled onto its side, throwing us into a pile against the lower door.

Before I had recovered enough to react, the other door was wrenched open and a head appeared in the aperture. Several others crowded about the first – dark faces, heavily shadowed against the brilliant blue of the sky. "The Russian's still alive, all right," shouted one of them.

"Haul him out of there, then!" called a harsh voice from behind the others. "I want to see what the bastard looks like."

A moment more and a rope dangled through the opening. My traveling companions began to chatter anxiously among themselves, and Paul groaned in pain as I think he had broken a leg.

"Come on, Russky!" called one of the Pollacks from above. "Use this rope to climb out of there, or we'll have to tie it around your neck!"

There was laughter at this, while the men about me stared upward in silence. Fear was clearly inscribed on their faces, but they offered me no explanation. We had obviously been captured by men of some other faction, and my companions knew they were good as dead.

"All right, Russian!" came the call again. "This is your last chance to get out of there on your own."

Resigned to my fate, I seized the dangling end and hauled myself through the open door. I made the mistake of retaining a grip on the rope, and the men standing below gave it a hard yank, pulling me over the edge of the upended coach. I landed on my back, in the middle of a clustered troop of guardsmen. When I tried to question them, their leader snapped: "You'll find out all you need to know when you need to know it, General!"

Quickly, my hands were tied behind me while a couple of men made a hasty search of my person, removing the dagger I had concealed in my left boot. One asked me which of the bags tied to the back end of the coach were mine. Once I pointed them out, they were also hastily searched and any papers removed along with the gold coins I had concealed in one case. They then tossed the rest of my baggage into the coach, and poured lamp oil all over the wooden vehicle. Another struck a spark to ignite it. That was the last I knew of the four men with whom I had traveled, for one of the guardsmen grabbed the reins of a riderless horse while two others helped me into the saddle. As soon as my feet were in the stirrups, I was led away from the burning coach at a hard gallop. At least half of the men who surrounded me were clad in a distinctive blue livery, but I knew so little of Polish society I was unable to recognize it. Nor did it seem important, for I assumed I was also good as dead.

We traveled all day, stopping only twice to rest the horses. No one would tell me anything; in fact, none but the leader would speak to me at all. I wondered, at first, if we might be going to Koval, the fief which had been given to Kurbsky. But no, we were definitely headed north. We spent the night in a heavy forest, sleeping on the ground, then proceeded the next day to a small village facing a very wide lake. Here, I was transferred to an ancient, battered coach. One leg was chained to the floor, while I was otherwise freed of my bonds. As yet, no one had offered any explanation. I rode for several days, alone in the vehicle, having no idea what the future held for me. I even slept in the coach at night, being allowed to alight only in the morning, and again when we stopped at dusk. Although I was not given much to eat, and was forced to attune my natural functions to these two brief rest periods, I was not otherwise abused.

My trip ended, after eight or nine days' travel, in the center of a very large city on the North Sea. I only suspected, at first, where I was. It was nearly a full day before anyone spoke to me and confirmed it. I was being held in the city prison at Danzig. It was some time before I discovered exactly what had happened, and a far longer time before I was able to leave my miserable cell.

The entry of Ivan into the list of candidates for the Polish throne had caused some serious realignment among the competing factions. The supporters of Ernst, son of Emperor Maximillan, included nearly all the powerful and influential men of Danzig. When faced with the possibility of Ivan's election, they had united with those supporting the Frenchman, Henri, Duc d'Anjou. They agreed to cooperate in eliminating the Czar from any serious contention. John Zamoisky, leader of the Polish nobles who supported the Frenchman, had arranged my kidnapping. They had sent me to the Austrian faction in Danzig for safekeeping, thus effectively removing me from any area where I might be freed by sympathetic Polish supporters of Ivan. A seething hostility currently existed between the Czar and the French, incidentally, because France maintained friendly relations with the Sultan. Nor do I mean to imply any lack of division among these other factions. It was only in this single cause of opposing the Czar that the operatives of Austria and France had united.

In Moscow, none of us had realized how completely at odds these Pollack groups were over the election of their King. There were several contenders, each with a good number of powerful supporters. The Swedes proposed to place their King's son, Sigismund, on the throne. Another faction wanted Stephen Batory, Prince of Hungary. It was a terribly confused political turmoil I had entered, without half knowing the dangers and pitfalls I would face.

The administrator of the prison, one Helmut von Mulke, was an elderly German knight whose family had been prominent in regional politics for several generations. Because he knew my background and had known Heinrich in earlier times, he treated me with some consideration. After a few days I was moved into a tower cell, where I was away from the dripping moisture of the lower dungeons. He told me I could correspond with anyone I wished, though only a few of my letters were ever delivered to Moscow. Strangely enough, I found it easier to get messages through to Ridolfi in England – this due to his close ties with the Medici regime in Paris.

After receiving my first letter, Ridolfi made contact with Montluc, the French ambassador to Krakow. He tried to arrange my parole, at least, if not an outright release. At first, he was unable to accomplish anything, and I languished in prison for over six months. When Ivan discovered what had happened to me he was furious; but there was nothing he could do, either. Finally in proper tribute to Pollack stupidity, the least likely candidate was elected to the throne of Poland. The brother of Charles IX, King of France, became Henri I, King of Poland. When the news reached Danzig, von Mulke came up to my cell with a flask of German whiskey. We drank every drop together, jointly cursing the perfidy of Polish nobles.

Eventually, the selection of a king led to my parole – though it still took many months. Henri swore his first oath as King in Paris, then dallied almost into the next year before finally coming to Krakow with a large flock of chattering French and Italian advisors. Among these was Cavalcanti, the agent of the Medicis whom I had met in the Castle of Leicester a number of years before. Ridolfi apparently had been in close communication with his friend, because I was released almost as soon as Henri arrived to take his throne. I was not allowed to return to Russia; instead, I was taken to Warsaw; and placed in the care of Andrew Kurbsky!

I remained a political prisoner, hated by a large number of Polish nobles. Had it not been for the good offices of my friends in England, I would probably never have left Danzig alive. As it was, I found myself in debt to the French, the very faction most distasteful to Ivan. I had never wanted anything so much as a safe–conduct back to Moscow. I hated Warsaw; I despised the Pollacks; and I scorned the French. I was furious at being suddenly placed in virtual slavery to Andrew, for whom I had only the greatest contempt. But most of all, I grew to detest the miserable excuse for a man who now sat upon the Throne of Poland.

I was taken to Warsaw under guard, but free of bonds because I had given my word not to attempt escape. I was delivered to Kurbsky, who gave me the choice of accompanying him to Krakow as his guest, or remaining in Warsaw in a cell. My alternatives being rather limited, I accepted the lesser evil. We arrived in the capital about a week before the coronation ceremony.

From the first, Andrew seemed delighted to see me, although he was stern and demanded a promise of good behavior. Once I gave him my word, we continued on as friendly a basis as we had enjoyed when on campaign together. He had aged, of course, but his new life seemed to agree with him. He was still tall and slender, unbowed by the years, and appeared to be in excellent condition. His hair was gray, clipped short in the Western style. When I was first brought into his Warsaw mansion he greeted me like a long lost friend.

"Dmitri!" he said, rising to greet me. "I have wished for this moment for years!"

"I'm afraid I can't equal your enthusiasm," I replied coldly.

He looked surprised, then smiled encouragingly. "I did not mean your captivity, my friend," he said pleasantly. "But I have always wished you could join me. I miss many of my old companions."

"Again, I cannot share your feelings," I told him.

"You always were a stubborn fool." he sighed. "Why not make the best of your present circumstances? I shall make you as comfortable as I can, and perhaps if we speak together you will understand what compelled me."

I shrugged. "I have no choice," I told him. "I am completely at your mercy."

It was then he demanded my pledge, after which he offered me wine, and we at together talking until far into the night. I had to despise him for his treachery, but it was difficult to hate him. Andrew had become a man of captivating personality. Beside this, I think he really held me in high regard. However, some of the news he gave me was extremely distressing – almost unbelievable.

"Who is acting as the Czar's ambassador?" I asked him.

"Your old friend, Pissemsky," he replied evenly, although an almost mischievous grin appeared on his lips. "But I think you might better ask, 'Who is acting as Czar?'"

I looked at him blankly, I suppose, because I could not understand what he meant. Andrew laughed lightly, and poured some more wine. "*Your* Czar," he said, "has taken off his crown and placed it on the head of another friend of yours – old Ediger, or Simon as you now call him. It is even rumored that Ivan has sent large quantities of his treasure to Solovetsky, in preparation for a trip to England."

I did not know whether to believe him or not. My expression obviously showed this, and Andrew shook his head. "I shall arrange for you to speak with Pissemsky when we get to Krakow," he continued. "He can confirm what I tell you. In the meanwhile, I hope you will come to appreciate the refinements of a more civilized nation."

"I doubt that," I replied coldly.

"The Poles are not all that bad when you come to know them, Dmitri," he argued. "Some of them are quite pleasant people. At least the court is ordered, and life here is based on law – not the whims of a madman!"

"The last time you said things like this to me, I came close to killing you!" I replied. I forced my voice to remain at a conversational level, but there was anger in my tone.

Andrew raised his hands placatingly. "There is no need for harsh words between us, my friend," he continued. "I say – and I firmly believe – that your Czar is mad. That is why I left Russia, and allowed myself to be branded a traitor; all future generations of Russians will spit upon my memory. But what I have done was an honest act. I could not support the actions of the Czar within my own soul and conscience. His subsequent behavior following the time of my departure, has done nothing to prove me wrong."

He paused, awaiting some comment from me. I watched him in silence. "Go on," I said at length. "I have wondered how you would justify your treachery."

"You are needlessly bitter," he said evenly, "and yet you are an intelligent man. An honest man in most respects, you are unable to be honest with yourself. Can you look into my eyes, Dmitri, and tell me it has never crossed your mind that the Czar is mad?"

Again he paused, and though I wanted to look away, I forced myself to stare into his face. The steely gray eyes returned my gaze. There was complacency there, and sincerity. But there was also doubt, and I knew Andrew was fighting a battle within his own soul, much as I must struggle within myself. He had taken a path opposite from mine and wished to convince himself, by convincing me of its propriety. When I still made no response, he went on.

"The horror that Ivan has visited upon his own people is an abomination in the eyes of God," he said. "The formation of the *Opritchina* could only have been the act of a raging madman. True, he's abolished it, but do you think that has stopped the insanity? Why do you suppose he failed to be elected King of Poland, even with all of Lithuania supporting him? It was not because we took you out of action. The Czar sent others behind you, and sent more gold than his miserly soul has ever parted with before. But while his agents cooed, and tried to persuade the nobles of Poland to support the merciful and benevolent Czar, what was he doing in Russia?"

"I have had little news of my homeland during the last ten months," I replied.

Andrew gestured broadly. "He has done nothing new," he said, "nothing he had not done many times before. He wanted to divorce the present Czarina in order to marry another. . . ."

"You mean Anna?" I asked in surprise. Ivan had barely consummated that marriage when I had left.

"Yes, Anna. It was only by the connivance of Leonide he was able to take her. Failing to get dispensation to marry a fifth, when the Church forbids a fourth, he had old Leonide arrested. The Archbishop of Novgorod was brought to Moscow in chains. In front of the entire court, the Czar stripped him naked with his own hands and had him sewn up inside a bearskin. Then he was thrown to the hounds! Blood! All that will ever appease that man is blood! That is what cost him the throne of Poland!"

"That and the speeches of people like yourself," I added softly.

"Yes, people like myself! Men who had seen enough of cruelty and violence, and left before they condemned their own souls to everlasting hell by becoming a part of it!"

"And you consider me eternally condemned?" I asked.

"I don't know, Dmitri," he sighed. "Your reputation, even here in Poland, is as a fearsome opponent in battle, but a man of fairness. I know that men have walked many miles knowing they were going to be captured anyway, seeking to be taken by soldiers of your regiments rather than some other commander. If even simple men can see the spark of goodness within you, surely God can do no less."

"What of your own soul, Andrew?" I asked. "Do you not believe God must reserve a special place in hell for a man who betrays his earthly Czar? How can such a man expect mercy from the Czar of Heaven?"

Again he shrugged. "I have no proper answer for you," he said simply. "I have wondered the same thing many times, myself. Yet I did what I felt was right; what I had to do. It would have been far less honorable for me to remain with Ivan, obeying his commands when I felt they were wrong. It was better simply to leave than to place myself in a position where I might one day refuse an order – or worse. In this, at least, I've been honest. Right or wrong, I have done what my conscience told me to do."

"Even as I have done," I answered.

Andrew nodded. "I do not dispute you," he sighed. "Nor should we argue it further. Each of us understands the other. Our final judgment must be made in heaven."

"Or in hell," I added, my mind involuntarily conjuring up the image of Viazemsky in his final expression of malevolence.

Once my parole was given, Andrew placed no restraints on my movements. In Krakow, I was able to visit or speak with whomever I wished. I had an opportunity to visit with Feodor Pissemsky a day or two after our arrival, and I found that Andrew had told me the truth. The Czar had put off his crown, and placed it on Simon's head. Nor had he made any move to take it back. My first thought was to wonder if Simon was in danger of meeting old Federof's fate, but Pissemsky assured me otherwise.

". . . but it's creating a great deal of confusion," he added, "especially among the foreign embassies. Some report to Czar Simon; while others, like the English, refuse to deal with any but Czar Ivan."

"Do you think he means to give up the throne forever?" I asked.

Feodor shook his head, smiling. "As Ivan told the English, 'Simon wears my crown, but I have nine others.' In the end, he will take it back."

"What of all this marriage business?" I asked.

"Ivan cast off his crown when he heard of Henri's election," explained Pissemsky. "By then, he had already sent Anna to a convent and taken another – Anna Vasilchikof – as mistress, although he had previously declared his intention to enter a monastery. Now, as I understand it, the second Anna is displeasing him, for she is also barren. He has taken another into his house as well."

"And the Church?" I asked.

"The Church has refused to bless either union. Cyril would never give in, as you know, not even on the earlier marriage, which was Ivan's reason for going to Leonide in the first place. With him gone – I guess you heard about that! – well, with him out of the picture, the Church refuses to say anything. Both women are accorded the respect of wives by the court." He abruptly halted his swift flow of words, shook his head and looked directly into my eyes. "I find myself confused, Dmitri," he admitted softly. "We have been taught to accept the behavior of the Czar as divinely inspired. Now, Ivan is no longer Czar. Are his actions still sanctioned by God? It is hard enough to explain this to you; imagine what I must go through when I am questioned by foreigners – especially foreigners of rank whom I cannot ignore or refuse to answer."

"You, too?" I remarked.

"Eh?"

"I have been listening to the doubts and arguments of Kurbsky," I explained. "Now I suspect I hear the same from you."

Feodor looked surprised, almost horrified. "No, I've never given in to these adverse impulses – at least not in front of strangers. To you –" He regarded me seriously for several moments. "You are like family, a kinsman. To you I can confess that I am sometimes disturbed. I've experienced doubts and confessed them to God, asking Him to absolve me. Surely, you have experienced the same, have you not? You have never acted to oppose the will of the Czar, but you must assuredly have had your own doubts from time to time."

"I consider such thoughts to be unworthy," I replied pompously.

"Yet you do not deny their existence," he countered.

"We all have doubts at times," I replied, dropping the rigidity from my voice. "But some thoughts . . . I will not admit to God, nor to myself. I cannot admit them to another man."

"Even the saints have doubted," he muttered. "They have doubted God Himself, and have still been forgiven," he continued more stridently. "It is the manner in which a man resolves his doubts that counts . . . in the end."

"Do you believe the Czar is mad?" I asked directly.

The question so surprised him he seemed unable to speak, merely gawked at me. Then, wily ambassador that he was, he forced a broad grin. "Which Czar?" he said.

The question of Ivan's madness was not accorded the grace of doubt by members of the Polish court. I discovered this in the weeks that followed, and in time came to accept the Pollacks' attitude without surprise or anger. The tumbled uncertainties of my own mind were further disturbed by this, and while I still refused to acknowledge it – to myself or anyone else – my own attitudes were gradually changing. Reports of Ivan's conduct were continuously related to me – never as simple statements of fact, but always tainted and embellished by the person who carried the tale. And in every instance, these remarks reflected the speaker's assumption that he was voicing further proof of Ivan's demented condition.

In all, I spent over six months as the unwilling guest of Andrew Kurbsky. In spite of myself, the effects of this association were profound. Viewing events within the Russian court from such a distance made each appear as an act of horror, senseless, sins committed without reason, punishments rendered without cause. The letters I eventually began receiving from Nina only emphasized the attitudes of those around me. My wife was deathly afraid of Ivan. She had always distrusted him; now, her terror seemed close to hysteria. My family had continued to reside in Simon's house when the new "Czar" moved into the Kremlin palace. With Ivan maintaining his status as a simple gentleman of noble birth, he was enjoying a greater freedom of movement than had been possible as Czar. He had visited Simon's home several times, Nina wrote, and had remained longer than she considered seemly – on one occasion insisting on a "Western style" banquet, with the women of the household invited to sit with the men. My wife had learned to express herself in guarded terms, mingling her message with both English and Italian words, but I understood her message quite clearly.

This knowledge only added to my desperation. I could have left, it was true; but I had given a knightly oath not to escape. Having few assets other than my honor, I could not violate such a promise.

As to the situation in the Polish court, I can only describe it as scandalous! What I saw put me in mind of the remarks made by Cavalcanti when I first met him in England. His implication in those days had been so understated, I was ill–prepared to face the revolting conditions I found in the Krakow palace. Henri's unmanly conduct would have repelled even Elizabeth.

The Frenchman had been crowned as King in the traditional ceremony, but his crafty Italian advisors had contrived to omit some clauses from the oath, whereby Henri would have relinquished several important prerogatives to his council of nobles. As the Bishop of Warsaw was about to place the crown upon Henri's head, two members of the Polish Diet rushed forward. They snatched the diadem from the Bishop's hands, refusing to allow the coronation to proceed until the proper assurances had been included. Meekly, Henri agreed. He swore to such conditions as no king should have to accept. He promised not to marry without permission of the Diet, nor would he condemn any man for his religious beliefs. He must govern the land through the Council of Fourteen, and these men would be elected by the nobility! The King could not even appoint his own advisors. The terms were impossible. Yet Henri agreed, and he became the King.

But what a King he was! I was invited to attend at court when Andrew Kurbsky had a petition to present. This was about two weeks after the coronation. I was dressed like the rest of the courtiers, for I had borrowed clothes from Andrew. My own Russian robes had long since fallen into tatters. I did not attract much notice, therefore, as most people did not know who I was. Lines of age and worry and sin had etched away the perfection of features which used to call attention to me. I stood to one side in the grand salon, jammed against the wall amidst a crowd of highly perfumed gentlemen and ladies. The court was comprised of nearly as many women as men – a condition I had not seen since leaving England. I must admit to being impressed by the grandeur and glitter, for the Poles had been quick to adopt the customs of their monarch's land. Everyone was dressed in elegant, brightly colored costumes; an orchestra played softly in the next room. There was laughter and chatter, as the ladies and gentlemen exchanged pleasantries while awaiting the arrival of their King.

There was a fanfare of trumpets, at which the court fell silent. A chamberlain announced the entrance of Henri I, by the Grace of God, King of Poland, Grand Duke of Lithuania, etc., etc. But the figure who entered the room could hardly qualify as a man. Whereas I had considered Robin and his friends effeminate, I could see no manhood in this fellow at all. With a mincing gait, like a vulgar prostitute walking the streets of the *Arbat*, he waddled the distance to the dais. Behind him came a flock of voluptuaries with painted faces, in garish tunics and enormous collars. Ringlets of artificially colored hair cascaded about their heads, and none of them wore a beard.

When the King was seated and began to speak – in French, of course – one might have closed his eyes and thought he heard the high–pitched voice of a woman. Because I could not understand the words, as was the case with most of the people about me, the quality of his voice assumed a special significance. With fluttering hands and the graceful gestures of a very great lady, he spoke for several minutes. Then another creature, one of His Polish Majesty's weirdly costumed flock, translated the King's pronouncements.

Nor was this appearance of degeneracy merely a surface trapping. The chubby little King, with his powdered face and colored lips, was already committing such acts of immorality as to shock even the depraved nobles of Poland. When I tried to discuss this with Andrew later that evening, he could offer no arguments to counter my derision.

"Henri is the King," he said simply. "Whatever his personal conduct may be, the nobles of Poland maintain control of his government. He can do no harm, and coming from a great line of kings, he may yet prove a wise and gifted ruler in the years to come."

"You will follow him, then," I replied sarcastically, "although he flaunts the very sins you found so distasteful in your rightful Czar?"

"What I personally approve is not important," he insisted. "I serve a King whom I may not respect as a man, but whose sins do not include the murder of his subjects, nor the torture of innocent men. In Poland, a man is even free to practice whatever Christian faith he chooses. I still worship after the Orthodox rites."

"I understand that the Roman followers of the Medici Queen in France recently displayed something less than open tolerance – and on a saint's day, at that," I taunted him.

"You would lay that crime at the feet of Henri?" he asked, surprised that I should even know of the mass killing in Paris. Von Mulke had told me the story, although I am certain his orders had been to withhold all news from Russia. The old Queen, mother to both Henri, and his brother of France, had arranged the massacre of a thousand men on the holy day of Saint Bartholomew. If Andrew could condone this, I found it difficult to reconcile his attitude toward the Czar.

We argued for some time, neither of us giving ground. Yet each could see the merit of the other's words. Andrew had never been able to overcome his heavy guilt, and I am sure it was our discussion that generated his need to write another insulting letter to the Czar. He tried to justify in writing, what he could not express in words to me. Although I always seemed able to counter his attacks upon Ivan, and to find the proper defenses against Andrew's charges, our discussions perpetuated the continuing changes in my heart. It was this, added on top of the doubts I had experienced after Malyuta's death, that eventually led to my own acts of infidelity.

The months passed and seasons changed without my being able to arrange a release. Ivan, through Czar Simon, tried several ploys to affect my return, while Pissemsky did what he could in Krakow – always without results. I would remain until the King deemed otherwise. I was a hostage, of sorts, and it pleased my enemies to have me in their power. The elderly Radziwell, who had so often commanded the Polish armies, and who probably hated me more than any of the others, was the loudest in opposing my release.

In June, when I had been away from my homeland for over a year, word reached Krakow that Charles IX, King of France was dead. Though a very young man – not yet in his twenty–fifth year – he had died of some unknown malady. Some claimed his own mother had poisoned him. Regardless, Henri was now King of France, as his brother had died without issue. And what a storm that created in the Polish court! Henri made plans to leave for Paris, as he had probably wished to do from the day he first set foot on Polish soil. But the Pollacks would not let him go!

It was during this turmoil that I obtained my release. Andrew had never been pleased at the selection of the French candidate. He favored the Hungarian, Stephen Batory, and as second choice would have taken Ernst of Austria, who was fiercely opposed by the clergy. With the loss of their present King inevitable, the Poles would have to hold a new election.

"You are paroled to me," he said, "and as such I can personally release you from your vow. Would you be willing to do me a simple service in exchange?"

I regarded him doubtfully. "I will not be a part of your treachery," I replied.

"I will not ask you to do anything to the detriment of the Czar, nor in opposition to your own conscience."

"Tell me what it is you wish," I said, "and I will make that decision." I hoped fervently he was going to ask something I would feel able to do. I was frantic, by now, to return. I was afraid for Nina, as I knew the acts of which Ivan was capable should he truly desire her. I also feared for Simon. When the day came for Ivan to end the farce of his Czardom, I wanted to be present to exert what influence I could to assure his safety. I had lately come to realize how few friends I had left in this world; and of these, I numbered Simon among the best.

"It is rumored that Ivan is about to take back his crown," said Andrew, cutting into my reverie. "When he does, he may again attempt to take the throne of Poland."

"That would be his prerogative," I replied.

"Yet he cannot be elected," said Andrew. "You have heard the remarks of the nobles to whom I have presented you. You have seen my lists of men, and you know how the alliances are joined. If Ivan should try again he can only fail, which would add further injury to his pride. You must try to dissuade him."

"If his chances were really so remote, why do you bother yourself about it?" I asked. "At this late date, I can't believe you're that concerned with his peace of mind."

Andrew looked at me in exasperation. "I will not explain my motives any further," he snapped. "That is my proposal. You may accept the terms or not."

"How do you know I will be true to my promise once I am back in Russia?"

"You have remained here in my parole for seven months," he said. "I have no fear of your ever violating an oath made in the presence of God."

"I must think about it," I replied.

Andrew agreed, and I told him I would give my answer the next morning. I already knew what it would be, for I *had* to get home. Yet I would be promising something I should not. Kurbsky knew very well that Ivan could get himself elected if he were willing to spend the gold to do it. With my knowledge of current Polish politics I could be invaluable to him. Possibly, that was it! Andrew was clever. In extracting a promise from me to dissuade the Czar from trying, he may have really sought something else. Whereas I might find an excuse to do a poor job in persuading Ivan not to try for election, my conscience would keep me from offering the assistance I could give. It would certainly prevent my returning to Poland as the

Czar's agent. I also thought Andrew wanted me out of the country, which may have been the real reason behind this offer. I had already been contacted by several Russian agents, but I had turned them away because of my oath of parole.

In the end I agreed to Andrew's terms and he let me go. At this time there was no higher authority from whom he might seek approval. The King was in virtual custody to prevent his flight. I crossed the Russian border in late July.

CHAPTER XIII

My return to Russia – then Moscow – and finally through the yawning gates of the Kremlin was such a joyful experience I nearly wept. I'm getting to be an old fool, I thought, wiping my eyes with the back of my hand. My arrival had already attracted attention because I had been given a squadron of *Streltsi* as escort from the border. I did not pause until I had entered the capital, although a number of the junior officers at the gate called out to me. It was a little past midday on a bright, sunny afternoon as I rode up to Simon's house and entered through the rear, after leaving my mount in the stables. Illya was the first to greet me when I came through the kitchen, and he ran to inform the other servants.

"I have blamed myself ever since your were taken," Toby said by way of greeting. "If I'd been with you, I'm sure it would have been different. Thank God you're back safely!"

I returned his embrace without really breaking my stride, and continued up the stairs to Nina's apartments. My wife nearly swooned when I suddenly appeared at her bedroom door, almost the entire household clustered behind me in the hall. Anne Richards was with her, as well as little Anna – now Toby's wife. All of them stared in disbelief, until the shock wore off. Although I would have preferred to be alone with Nina, I was forced to tell the story of my capture and imprisonment to the whole group. It was well after dark before we were able to clear the others from the room.

Nina wept for a long time, as she told me all that had happened while I was away. Ivan had given her such a fright, she said, that she was almost to the point of gathering up our children and trying to flee the country. Fortunately, he had become involved with his two mistresses and finally went off with them to Alexandrov. Simon had been partially responsible for this, she thought, though she did not know exactly what he had done.

"All I know is that I finally went to Czar Simon," she said, "and he told me it would be all right. Not long after that, the Czar – I mean Ivan – left Moscow."

I stayed with Nina until late the following morning, when we were joined by Christiana and the boys, who came in with Lotus Flower when she brought us breakfast. We clustered together on the great bed, all talking at once, renewing the bonds of familial love. Johnny had begun to develop the carriage, as well as the stature of a man. Demetrius had lengthened out, becoming so tall and slender he stood half a head above his brother. I was very proud of them both, especially as they now spoke Russian without the accents that had jarred me when I heard them in Livonia.

It seems I had returned just in time to see my friend Simon on the Throne. He sent for me on the afternoon of this first full day home, and we visited in the private apartments of the Czar. The year of responsibility had weighed heavily upon him, leaving deeply rutted lines beneath his eyes. His hair and beard were silver gray, and he took no pains to hide his anxiety.

"I have sat upon the Throne, and worn the robes of office as if I were really the Czar," he said. "Yet I have never dared to make an important decision without consulting Ivan. He bows before me and bumps his forehead against the carpets as if I were the incarnation of God, Himself. But I can see the fire in his eyes, and I must be careful to take no action that I am not sure he wants. What frightens me most, is the certainty that he will eventually take back the crown. After that, after all my years of carefully avoiding notoriety, what is to become of me?"

He was badly shaken – justifiably so, for he knew his days as Czar were numbered. Ivan had already ordered him to recall the royal grants to churches and monasteries. The clergy were furious with Simon, blaming him for depriving them of their possessions. Ivan might well be mad, but he still had no peer when it came to the acquisition of wealth.

Within less than a month, Ivan returned from Alexandrov. He spent two days at the palace, in close conference with Simon. After this, he quietly announced that he had "been prevailed upon to once again take up the duties God had ordained as his." There followed a period of general rejoicing throughout the city, with public feasts and bonfires at night. There was a great deal of drunkenness and revelry, but through it all I detected a certain hollowness – the air of forced celebration.

Despite his fears, Simon did not fare badly, though Ivan left him to sweat for several days before announcing his intentions. The former Czar was deeded all the lands of Tver, the fief formerly held by the Mikulinsky family. He was also granted title of Grand Duke. Almost immediately, Czar Ivan began returning the properties of the churches and abbeys, though it cost each of them a princely sum to reclaim their lands. All government debts, resulting from the Tartar invasion three years before, were canceled in a general moratorium.

As to my own position, I am still not sure how much of my perceptions were valid. The Czar had expressed delight at my return, and had embraced me as warmly as ever at our first meeting. Still, I sensed a certain distance in our relationship. Boris told me it was nothing, that the Czar seemed generally less able to express his emotions of late. But I could feel the difference and it bothered me. I had always maintained that Ivan could see into other men's souls. Perhaps he read the doubts in mine, though I was treated well and had no genuine basis for these reactions. When Simon was granted the lands of Tver, he returned his Kremlin properties to the crown. Ivan then gave the house to me. This was a reward for my service, he said, and to compensate me for my months of misery in the Pollack court.

With all this display of favor, however, my uncertainties and my fear of the Czar continued to grow. Rather than waning with our continued association – as they had in the past – these feelings now became paramount, mostly because I seemed to have lost the ability to anticipate Ivan's reactions. Several times, I found myself the recipient of his angry retorts – always over minor issues, of course, so I never felt the full thrust of his anger. At other times, he would call me to him and we would sit together for hours, playing chess and drinking wine, discussing the future of Muscovy. Yet even here, his friendship seemed brittle and inconsistent.

The years lay heavily upon Ivan's face and body, but his features could still assume a dreamy expression as his eyes focused upon some distant point beyond the walls of our room when he spoke of the final gathering in of our lands. In these moments he became young again, little changed from my memory of the youthful monarch who had subdued the infidels along the Voga. But the Czar was not the same. Approaching his fiftieth year, Ivan had grown so heavy he sighed and puffed from the effort of standing up. His face was deeply furrowed, with lines of worry and anxiety deeply etched into his puffy flesh. He no longer rode a horse, traveling only by carriage, sled, or boat.

The more I spoke with him, the more I came to accept his malady – his madness – as fact. Madness! I dreaded to use the term, even in my private thoughts. But there was no way to avoid it. One day, Ivan summoned me and outlined his plans to give the crown back to Simon and depart by ship for England. He went so far as to have me draft a letter to Ridolfi, instructing him to procure a suitable residence for the retired Czar. Then, before the letter could be sent he called me in again and announced his plans to become a simple monk. He would retire to Solovetsky, he said, and spend his remaining years in prayer and meditation. He never did either.

Nina had told me of Ivan's brief fourth marriage, beginning and ending while I was still away. The girl had died mysteriously, she said, although previously in perfect health. I thought back to the terrible night in Viskovaty's when I had watched the Czar ravage the widow. He had quite literally torn the flesh from her body with his teeth. Foolishly, I told Nina about it, causing her to tremble for hours.

"One day, you will be forced to flee," she said simply. "Either that, or perish at the hands of a madman."

We were together in our bedroom. The door was closed, and we had spoken softly. I knew I could not be overheard, for Toby and Illya took turns to assure no one listened at our door. Thus I could have answered her honestly. I could have expressed all the doubts and fears that welled up in my own heart. But this would only have added to her burdens and increased the dread she already held within her. Instead, I said nothing, my lack of chastisement a sufficient omission to express agreement.

Winter came late that year. While not especially severe, it curtailed activity, as it always did; and as usual, the Czar became restless when he could not leave his palace. He had reopened his chambers beneath the Kremlin, and I knew he spent hour after hour in the cold, subterranean vaults. He had continued to respect my feelings, never insisting that I join him. He extended the same courtesy to Boris, who was known to feel as I did. It was the Czarevitch who attended his father most of the time, thus strengthening the bond between them. But even the company of his son failed to stave off Ivan's fresh set of irrational fits of depression.

The Czar also resumed the longer sessions in his chapel, sometimes staying on his knees for an entire morning, and by midwinter he had embarked upon a fierce, new series of self recriminations. He would take vodka with him when he prayed; by noon he would be sobbing and incoherent, calling for Boris or myself, sometimes for both. He would cringe upon the floor and wail in quaking terror, asking us if we thought God condemned him for all the executions he had ordered. He had never before expressed doubt that these had been within his right. Now, he behaved as if he saw the spirits of his victims crowding behind us to demand his soul. Naturally, we tried to reassure him, affirming that it had been his duty to punish those who conspired against him. He would still collapse into long periods of weeping despair, crying out that he had sinned so grossly he feared he could never be absolved. One moment he would pray to be forgiven for his cruelties, the next he was bemoaning his sins of the flesh. He had violated God's commandments, he said, for he had taken more women than the Lord allowed. He had taken pleasure in the agony of others when he should have felt only pity. He should have prayed for the souls of those he executed. Instead, he had sought their eternal damnation.

For me, it was a wretched, miserable season. As the layers of snow grew deeper upon the ground, the Czar shivered and wept over the ravages of age. He refused to venture outside, which certainly ruled out any trip to Alexandrov. Nearly every day I was called to attend him, and every meeting seemed to sap some of my own vigor. As a result, I again had trouble sleeping. I dreamed strange and disturbing visions, in which I saw the Czar in death. The white maggots of the grave wriggled about his pallid features, swarming by the thousands through his putrefying flesh. My groans would waken Nina, who would shake me as I seemed to emerge through the clinging essence of death.

My own body also reflected the weight of years. Only by constant exercise and practice was I able to keep away the flab and excessive flesh. Even so, the face that stared back at me from Nina's silver mirror was old and haggard. Tiny lines crisscrossed about my eyes and mouth. My hair and beard were more gray than blond, and the top of my head was nearly bald. In some ways I was fortunate, I suppose, for I never experienced the maladies suffered by many of my old companions. My limbs moved freely, without that stiffness in the joints than many soldiers acquire. My wind was good, and I could still take a full turn in the exercise pen. Within my belly, though, I carried a heavy weight. As winter neared its end, I found it difficult to eat a large meal without hours of discomfort afterward. I had to give up vodka, and even Heinrich's German whiskey made my stomach retch. I might drink only a small amount of wine without feeling the pain, finding it best to eat some bread and cheese beforehand.

I anxiously awaited the spring thaws, for I was sure they would bring a new assault upon the west and result in my being given a command. Our armies were in firm control of many Livonian cities. Magnus, now wed to Vladya's youngest daughter, had been fobbed off with a small estate. When he was suddenly summoned to the capital, I expected Ivan was about to announce his plans.

One morning, shortly after Magnus had arrived in Moscow, I went to the palace early while the Czar was still at his prayers. I had hoped for a moment to speak with Boris. On the way to his rooms, I was intercepted by the Czarevitch who met me in the upper hall. Vanya had just come from the *terem,* still laughing at some story his servant had told him. When I stepped back to allow him passage, he invited me to join him at breakfast, throwing an arm across my shoulders and repeating the tale for my benefit. The Czarevitch was a fine figure of a man, I thought. Now in his prime, he seemed very like his father had been, though blessed with Anastasia's gentler features. Nonetheless, it was disturbingly like speaking to the old Ivan as I sat beside him, listening to his lighthearted chatter.

Magnus was in the audience chamber, he told me, eagerly awaiting the Czar. "I don't know what poor little Maria is going to do without her husband to attend her needs," he laughed. "Old Crunchback used to go out every morning to buy her sweets, and they say she's still a virgin because that creeping horror isn't fast enough to catch her!" He laughed and launched into some obscene descriptions, repeating stories he had heard from servants. It was no secret that Vanya and his father had been exchanging bridal couches, and I was surprised that the Czarevitch also made several passing references to this. He passed it off with humor, and seemed especially amused that some of the more conservative courtiers were so horrified by these sins.

I knew Vanya did not speak this way to everyone, so I should have been honored at being taken into his confidence. Far less serious than his father, the Czarevitch refused to be weighted down by the heavy cares of government. Nor did the Czar permit his son much freedom in this respect. There were times when Vanya would chafe impatiently over the bumbling mistakes of clerks and lesser officials.

"You must speak to the Czar," he told me, finally, "and see if you can persuade him to give me the command of Livonia. I could certainly do as well as that Danish gas bag, and if you help me I'll make you my chief of staff."

"The idea is appealing," I admitted, "but I do not seem able to approach your father as easily as once I did."

"He still pays more attention to you than he does to me," Vanya replied. "He respects your judgment as a commander."

I agreed to do what I could, although I knew his idea had little chance of fruition. We spoke for a while longer, before the Czarevitch broached the subject he had probably wanted to discuss all along. "When you were in England," he said, "you performed a secret mission for my father, didn't you?" His question had been quite sudden, and it surprised me.

"Yes," I stammered, uncertainly. "I . . . well, has your father discussed this with you?"

He shook his head. "I know only what I have been able to learn from others," he said. He seemed to be waiting for me to tell him more. It was an uncomfortable moment. I felt it the Czar's prerogative to inform his son and heir, if he wished Vanya to know. Yet, I spoke to the man who could become my Czar at any time. He was still watching me intently.

"I would hesitate to violate the Czar's confidence, even to his son," I replied at length.

He closed his eyes, nodding slightly. "It is your right," he said softly. "But the secret now lies with just two men, with the Czar and with you. If fate should take a hand. . . . Should I not also be aware?"

"Yes, you should," I agreed, "but it must be your father who tells you."

"Can you give me no more than this?" he asked, not really pressing me, but with a certain urgency in his tone.

"If the Czar should die," I said, openly expressing the possibility, "it would be my place to inform the heir."

"And if you are also . . . gone?"

I thought a moment, and finally replied: "My wife could tell you," I said, "or you could contact her father, the banker Ridolfi in London. Either of them could supply the information you sought."

Again he nodded. "Will you one day be as loyal to me as you have been to my father?" he asked seriously.

I smiled. "You may be assured of my loyalty," I replied, "though God alone must determine whom I shall live to serve."

We finished our meal, and joined the Czar soon after. Ivan was in exceptionally good spirits this morning, and amused himself by mischievously abetting Magnus's anxiety. He forced the King of Livonia to wait an extra hour before receiving him, but the interval allowed me opportunity to suggest Vanya's appointment as commander. The Czar had already made up his mind, and he told us he intended to announce Magnus's appointment, affirming his title as King. No sooner had he told us this, then he continued outlining his other plans.

"We have decided," said the Czar, "that the nobles of Poland impose an unworthy status upon their King. For this reason, We shall make no attempt to gain election at this time. We understand the Diet is now in session, and at any time We expect to hear they have deposed the French Lady."

A number of people had been permitted into the audience chamber by now, and Ivan's remarks evoked a raucous laughter, followed by the murmur of some vulgar witticisms.

"Because We deem it beneath Our dignity to accept the restrictions of the Pollack nobility, it will be necessary to take what is rightfully Ours by force of arms," added the Czar. He then enumerated the army command, with major posts going to Grand Duke Simon of Tver, to Mstislavsky, to Vorotinsky, and to me. I was assigned the military governorship of the territory in which my old estates were located, most of these areas now having been won back by our troops. The Czar had provided for a massive force, so all of us expected a quick and easy victory.

My single reservation was in having to leave Nina in the Kremlin; yet I hesitated to move the household back to Marienburg. I felt my wife was safer in Moscow for the moment, although Nina was so terrified of the Czar she became fretful and anxious if I had to be away just overnight. I finally discussed it with Boris.

"She looks too much like Anastasia," he said. "That's your problem." But he proposed a partial solution, arranging to have my stepfather recalled from his post in Ivangorod. With Heinrich living in the house, I could be reasonably assured of my wife's safety. The Czar would be unlikely to commit any act of impropriety while a man who held his favor resided under the same roof.

I had to leave before my stepfather returned, and only encountered him by chance, when we passed on the western highway. Heinrich was quite elderly now, close to sixty years of age. But he had recovered so completely from his former decline, he looked younger. His extended service in Livonia had returned a healthy glow to his cheeks, and he sat as straight as ever in the saddle. He had been perplexed by his recall, and was apprehensive until I explained the circumstances.

"It was a proper decision, then," he told me. "You can be sure I will look after your family."

We spoke briefly of some business matters, and I was able to report a considerable advance in our fortunes. During my absence in Poland, our affairs had continued to prosper under Jacob's stewardship. The Tartar raids into Lithuania had also helped, for they drove some of our most persistent competitors to the verge of bankruptcy.

Teshata still served my stepfather, and when we separated the rangy little weasel pressed a small chamois pouch into my hand. "Carry this with you," he said solemnly. "Your father never went into battle without it."

When they had gone, I looked inside. It contained the scrap of cloth I had torn from my robe on the night of Phillip's murder. The brownish spots of blood were still upon it. I shoved the sacred relic into my waistband, surprised it should have been Teshata who passed it to me. He had laughed when I gave it to Heinrich several years before.

CHAPTER XIV

I spent slightly over a year in Livonia, commanding an area that saw hardly any action. Little glory was mine, as the most serious enemies I confronted were the peasants and country folk of the region. In recent years past we had been looked upon by the native people as little more than a change of overlords, no better or worse than those who had ruled before. Now, we became objects of hatred, demons to be feared and exorcised from the land. During the thirteen months I served as military governor, I must have hanged a hundred men. Even so, there were at least twice that number I pardoned, men who would have been swinging beside their brothers had a sterner man than I been in charge.

It required nearly the entire length of my tenure for the Pollacks to decide upon their next King, or I should say "Kings." When their election was finally completed, the fools had decided on two men to rule them; the opposing factions had not been able to resolve their differences intelligently. The First King was Maximillian, the old Emperor of Austria. Somehow, they decided on him instead of his son Ernst. The other King was Stephen Batory, Prince of Hungary. Then, God must have taken pity on them in their simplicity. He spared them civil war by taking Maximillian's soul before the old man could learn of his election.

Stephen Batory came at once to Krakow, where he married Anna, the younger sister of Sigismund August. We had to laugh a bit over this; for despite his virility and youth, King Stephen would gain no heir from the union. While the marriage would likely assure his crown, the old crone was far past the age of rearing children. They were crowned as King and Queen in the spring, almost a year to the day after I had been posted to Livonia.

The Pollacks had been trying to negotiate a truce with us ever since Henri fled their land. Just before Stephen was crowned, the Czar agreed – by which time my fellow commanders had reclaimed nearly all the lands handed back to the Poles by Taube and Kruze. Unfortunately, this Russian supremacy was not to continue, and I have always been thankful that my own apprehensions kept me from moving my family back onto the Livonian estates.

As I had feared might happen, King Stephen soon proved himself a dangerous opponent. Not only a skillful soldier, he quickly displayed a certain guile in politics. As a younger man, from a poor and grasping nation, he seemed possessed by the need to conquer vast territories for his new kingdom. He subtly announced these intentions in his first communication to the Czar, carefully omitting a great number of Ivan's titles – most especially those pertaining to cities along the border: Smolensk and Podolsk among others. We took this as a declaration, almost a challenge.

Soon after this letter had been received in Moscow, I was recalled along with most of my men. Ostensibly, we were to take part in a display of arms when Ivan greeted the Polish ambassadors. I had not been able to return even for a brief visit during the last year. Thus my arrival became a grand homecoming, with a great display of affection on all sides. As much pleasure as I still took in commanding the Czar's forces, a soldier's greatest joy is returning home.

Nina had supervised the preparations for a magnificent feast at which the senior servants were permitted to dine with us. Serge served me, while the Tartar women – no longer girls by any stretch of the imagination – attended their mistress. Lotus Flower was easily as plump as Jasmine had been, and her shape occasioned a number of joking remarks. Heinrich sat beside me, preoccupied, but participating in the festivities the best he was able. I could see he was troubled, not by anything in his immediate surroundings, but by something more deep and basic. I knew he wanted to talk with me alone, but the time was inappropriate.

It is difficult to describe the Czar's behavior during these years, and to relate the peculiar effect it had on all his subjects. Age had definitely slowed him down, and especially during the months of snow he seemed to be almost dormant, like a great, fierce bear in its winter sleep. Occasionally, he would seem to waken – as the sun might break through a bank of silent clouds – and his unexpected fury would strike someone down. The attitude of the people was one of resignation, or acceptance. Among those of higher rank, this became apprehension – for some, an endless, uncertain fear. When the Czar rejoiced, it was a forced joviality that echoed his display of pleasure. For the time, he appeared to have forsaken his fearsome habits of the past. His use of the chambers became only rumors. Few men knew what actually transpired in the vaults beneath the Kremlin palace. Yet the memory of all that had gone before could never be forgotten, and an air of ominous expectation remained in its wake.

Because our house was located inside the Kremlin, facing toward the royal palace, members of my household were able to observe the movements of Ivan and his servants more directly than almost anyone else in the city. Nina continued to be deeply disturbed by all that she heard and by the few instances where she had actually been able to see the result of Ivan's periodic flares of anger. Our own servants, of course, kept her informed of everything they knew or heard, with the result of its leaving her with an inner core of seething fear. She never allowed our friends or anyone else to suspect her feelings, however, for over the years she had developed an outer calm to effectively cover these deeper anxieties. I teased her about it, calling it her "Medici bequest." Even I would never have guessed how afraid she really was, for her fear expressed itself only when she lay with me in our great bed, and her trembling body clung to mine. Only then was I able to perceive how desperately she distrusted the Czar. In these moments I was often tempted to confess my own misgivings, and to assure her of my understanding. But it would have been a futile exercise, only serving to lend substance and further credence to disturb her. Instead, I would stroke her brow and mutter soothing words, assuring her all would be well. And in doing this, I took upon myself a still heavier burden of responsibility. "There is one key to the welfare of us all," I whispered. "I must retain the Czar's affection. As long as I can do this, there is no need to fear."

With the Czar's official reception of the Pollacks still several weeks away, I was as-signed to help Michael Vorotinsky in making preparations and setting up quarters for the continuing influx of troops. My duties frequently took me into the royal palace, sometimes several times a day; and all I saw there distressed me. The Czar was in a strange state of mind, drifting between periods of joviality and boisterous enjoyment of various physical pleasures, to grim moments of black, silent depression. Before the end of the first week, the old gnawing dread began to churn inside my belly. Away from Moscow, my mind had sought other channels, and other cares had occupied my attention. As before, I now seemed unable to think of anything but the Czar's unstable disposition. Like a clanging hammer inside my skull, the thought continued: Ivan is mad! Ivan is mad! Ivan is mad!

Then, as if to confirm my most dreadful fears, Ivan summoned me to the palace late one evening. He sent a servant with a note in his own hand, so I left the house with no apprehensions either on my part or on Nina's. But when I reached the palace I was immediately taken in hand by a steward and guided down into the chambers. I followed the flickering light from the man's candelabra with the familiar mixture of revulsion and lust, and entered the old, stone–faced crypt with a heavy weight in my gut.

Ivan, not as drunk as I had expected, was standing on the edge of a shallow pit, where a hideously distorted figure writhed on the straw–covered floor. "Ah, Dmitri, I wanted you to see this – the last of my evil memories."

It took me a moment to recognize the filthy, naked creature – almost skeletal from starvation. "John Chibotovy?" I asked uncertainly.

"He has received some special treatment," Ivan explained.

I stared in shocked disbelief, for Chibotovy had initially disappeared during the great circus in the Square of Executions, prior to the Tartar sack of Moscow. I had assumed he died with all the others. I cared nothing for him, and had been so torn by my own conflicting emotions on so many other scores I had never even thought to ask about him. Later I heard – from Skuratof, I think – that the man was alive and assigned to the permanent staff at Alexandrov. Then, on one occasion, I saw him in company with the men who were responsible for converting the "abbey" into a proper royal palace.

He had served Ivan for all this time, working in the chambers in Alexandrov, until the renovations were completed. Now, the Czar had decided to dispense with this final reminder of the brotherhood, and had brought him to Moscow. The previously heavyset, well–muscled man had been starved to his present, pitiable condition; then the bones had been broken in all four extremities, so that he could only gasp in agony, unable to move any muscle in his body except the neck and midriff. Even this caused him such pain he chose to lie still, panting like a dog and staring helplessly at the Czar.

Ivan went down the three steps and stood directly over his victim. "You are last," he muttered, delivering a hard kick to the twisted legs. Chibotovy screamed, begging Ivan to kill him and end his pain.

Ivan laughed at him, mumbling something about the end of unholy temptation. He kicked the distorted mass of bones again, and came back up the steps to drag me into a side chamber, where he had several comfortable chairs. There were wall–hangings and carpets which made the area seem warmer and which also tended to deaden the sounds from without.

We sat drinking for several hours, discussing the inevitable campaigns against King Stephen, the probability of the Czar's having to deal harshly with Magnus – whom he did not trust. In the course of this conversation Ivan admitted a number of his concerns and feelings – seeming to confide in me as he had in years past. Yet, I retained a sense of wariness, bordering on fear. The sight of the last

Opritchnik writhing in his ultimate agony only a few feet away had deprived me of any sense of quietude. I left, much the worse for drink, just before dawn and staggered the short distance to my own front door. A palace servant lighted my way, holding his lantern on a long pole, so that he walked behind, but his light hung slightly ahead of me. In my own mind, I pondered the idea that Chibotovy had not been the last of Ivan's inner circle among the _Opritchniki_. I was the last. Was it possible that the Czar – my friend, my confidant. . . my brother – might one day turn on me? It was a thought I had harbored before, but never in such stark immediacy. I trembled inwardly as I bid the servant good night, and entered the security of my home.

Nina was asleep when I entered our room, and I slipped into bed beside her. But I could not sleep. My mind was in a worse turmoil than ever before. I thought of the things the Czar had just told me – still horrified to imagine how he must have toyed with Chibotovy for all this time – keeping him employed in the chambers at Alexandrov for over three years – then accused him of polluting his soul, had him starved and beaten, finally subjected to such abject pain and certain death. And he had kept his intentions a secret – if such they had been. I wondered how much of this the Czar might have planned, how long some twisted logic might have dominated his scheming mind. It was frightening, and it exemplified a hitherto unsuspected degree of deviousness on Ivan's part. It terrified me, and it added greatly to my anxiety – to my concern for my family's welfare.

The next day, following my previous pattern of indecision, I fell victim to an overwhelming guilt because of my disloyal ideas. The greatest difference in my own current attitude was the strength of these negative feelings. Even when I faced Ivan, my certainty of his madness did not dissipate as before. Deep within me, I knew I had perceived the truth, emphasized by his treatment of Chibotovy. And because this truth represented such a severe, monstrous departure from all I had ever forced myself to believe, a dreadful melancholy began to weigh upon me, to deprive me of every solace, and to deaden any pleasure I might otherwise have experienced. My mind and body responded with all the usual maladies – with horrifying dreams, with crippling pains throughout my gut, and by a heavy, continuous depression. I was not a pleasant man to serve during these days, for my temper grew exceedingly short. I struck several of my servants in irrational flashes of anger. I had again been given command of the Moscow garrison, and I also vented my frustrations on them. When the troops displeased me one afternoon, I ordered the entire company to march in circles about the city from dusk until first light of dawn. I ordered men flogged with the knout for infractions I would normally have ignored, and so terrified my subordinates they would come to me only on matters of greatest urgency.

Nina became concerned about all this. She knew it was unlike me to mistreat a servant or the men whom I commanded. It was all the more frightening for her, because I dared not explain my feelings, nor the source of my troubled emotions. She tried to talk to me about the sternness I displayed, but I always found an excuse to evade a full discussion.

Heinrich was still living with us, although he had offered to leave after my return. I think he was uncomfortable, feeling he trespassed upon our privacy. But the house was huge – the very finest _dacha_ in the Kremlin, and I prevailed upon him to stay. He was a stable force, and I wanted him near us. One day, when my stubborn reticence had driven Nina to the verge of tears, she went to my stepfather and poured out her troubles to him. At the first opportunity, Heinrich took me aside and we talked. It was the first real discussion I had with him since long before my detention in Poland.

Initially, I think both of us were uneasy, overly aware of the reversal in our present positions. I was the man of greater rank, and I stood as head of the family. My position at court still placed me within the inner circle, although the boyar council had begun to function again and I had no place in this. But I could approach the Czar as few others dared to do, and a great many powerful men still came to me with requests that I intercede for them. While no blood bound us together, I regarded Heinrich as my parent, as the only father I had ever known. His mind was still keen, and he had perceived a good deal more of my condition than I would have thought possible.

"You seem increasingly distressed, son," he began. "Do you realize how it's frightening your lovely wife?" He paused, and continued more gently. "I think you may be experiencing a similar dilemma to the one I went through a few years back."

His light blue eyes were watery and lacked their former clarity, but they now returned my gaze with unflinching firmness. Heinrich's tone was kindly, and his manner so disarming I made no effort to hide the truth from him. "Let's go outside," I suggested, getting up from my chair. "If we are to discuss my soul, I would prefer to be overheard by none but the Almighty."

We walked together through the Kremlin courtyards, keeping a good distance from any buildings or other structures, while Heinrich told me of his own strange, but fulfilling experience.

"While I rode with the *Opritchina*," he said, "I did things I shudder even to remember. I know you remained aloof from many of the activities, and you were able to get by without much comment because you had official duties that gave you the excuse to be busy elsewhere. Because I had no other occupation, I consorted more closely with Skuratof and Viazemsky; I committed the same crimes they did. I cannot seek to excuse myself, claiming I did it to make a show of loyalty or for any reason other than my own lust and greed – and cruel desire. Whatever extraneous urgings may have motivated me, God alone will have to judge. I have sinned, purely and simply. While it's true I've repented, I am sure a terrible retribution awaits me in heaven. Because I've experienced these dreadful realizations, and because I'm aware of my own soul's distractions, I think I can understand your present condition,"

"You credit me with too light a crime," I replied, assuming he ascribed my behavior only to guilt over my own part in these same sins.

He stopped, and we stood facing each other. "No, I do not think so," he said. "You are disturbed, even as I was, with your own thoughts about the Czar. In your heart you condemn him, and you think you should not." He watched my face carefully. "Am I right?"

I nodded uncomfortably. "Yes. But even more. . . ."

"You think him . . . possessed," he whispered.

I looked directly into Heinrich's eyes as I replied. "I am convinced the Czar is mad," I said softly.

My stepfather nodded slightly. "It was an accumulation of these same thoughts that drove me to become a drunkard and an unrestrained profligate," he replied. "I drank and I sinned until I had committed such unspeakable acts of depravity I thought I could fall no deeper. By some evil, ill–conceived logic I sought to bury my guilt in ever blacker crimes. Even then, I knew it was not the answer; yet I could find no other way. Then one night – it was shortly after the grand executions in the bazaar – I fell in the street, so drunk I could no longer walk. I was carrion, lying in the dust beside the mutilated remains of Ivan's victims with my face pressed against the filth and offal of the gutter. Sometime during the darkness, a band of thieves came upon me and stole my purse and nearly all my clothes. They would have killed me, I suppose, except that I lay like lead and they must have taken me for another corpse.

"Shortly before dawn, while the darkness of night could still conceal his movements, a hermit priest came upon my naked body. He did not know who I was, and from my condition he probably took me to be some poor slave or peasant who had been robbed by his fellows and left for dead upon the street. I guess I groaned or made some movement that told him I was alive. Not caring who I was, nor stopping to consider the harm I might do to him when I awakened, this holy man carried me into his wretched hut, just outside the walls of the *Arbat*.

"In the morning he shared his food with me – a dry crust of black bread and some roots he had boiled with herbs gathered from the forest. I was too weak and too sick to leave, else I would never have stayed to hear him. But I had reached a point in my life where I no longer cared if I lived or died, so I made no effort to go. Instead, I lay upon his tattered pile of rags and listened as he spoke of God's forgiveness and mercy. Thinking I might have left a hungry wife and family, he tried to persuade me I should return to my responsibilities.

"I asked if he was a priest, and he told me he was. But he had forsaken the luxuries of the monastery for a more humble life, he said, and because of this he experienced the daily joy of knowing his God. I cannot explain why even to this day, but I asked him to hear my confession. I had not done this, you know, for many, many years – not since the death of your mother, may God grant her rest. So I unburdened all the guilt and all the bitter corruption of my soul onto this poor priest. I told him who I was, and what I had done. I held back no sin that weighed upon me, not even the vilest and most secret depravities.

"When I had finished, this humble, innocent man still sat beside me, his face as complacent as when I had begun. I think this may have been why I was so unrestrained in all I said, for he never once looked at me in dismay, or indicated by the slightest sign that I had shocked or horrified him. Maybe I wanted to shake that air of peace and composure – I don't know. I can think of no other reason for going into the horrible detail that I did. But in doing it, I removed such a burden of wretchedness it made my entire body feel lighter.

"I looked up after I had finished speaking, and the whole room suddenly seemed to brighten, as if dawn had just broken, although it was easily midday and the sun had been out for hours. Then the holy man spoke to me again, telling me how Our Lord had already suffered the pain and humiliation of death and crucifixion to expiate the sins of all mankind. 'If a man truly repent, no matter how black his sins may be, he shall find forgiveness,' he told me. 'You have been sent to me in the moment of your darkest despair, naked and unarmed. You have this day confessed and repented your crimes. I can give you no more fitting guidance than the words of Our Lord when He spoke to another sinner: *Go now, and sin no more. He who truly repents shall be saved.'"*

There was no reply I could make to Heinrich after this, for he had spoken in tones of sincerity, telling me of this most intimate moment of his life. Hearing him, it was as if my own sins were also being granted an expiation by the very act of listening.

"You think you have found your salvation, then, within the Church?" I asked at length.

Heinrich shook his head sadly. "No, I did not mean to imply that," he said. "I do not really expect to be forgiven. How can I express it to you? My sins are so heavy and of such foulness I doubt I can expiate them without suffering a good deal more than I have. Nor can I claim to feel sheltered by the Church. Like you, I find little consolation from my contacts with the clergy. Just this one, poor beggar priest . . . he alone has been able to point the way. I feel a certainty within me, a very strong conviction that I can live the few years I have left in a state of semigrace. But to do this, I must not indulge in the vices that nearly destroyed me. The longer I am able to exist in this state, the greater mercy I may expect after death. Can you understand what I am trying to tell you?"

"I'm not really sure," I admitted. "But regardless of the peace you've found for yourself, I don't think it can be the same for me. You have been able to name the sins of which you are guilty. You can differentiate between acts that amount to a crime, and those that were merely duty. So far, I cannot do this. I have deluded myself into believing that I could never commit a sin when I obeyed the orders of the Czar, or when I acted to shield him from pain. But if I am right, and the Czar is truly mad, then my sins must be heavier than I had imagined. I, too, must be condemned beyond redemption."

"And I suspect you believe your greatest sin to be the doubt which makes you question it?"

"My only choice is to serve as I have always done," I said, "because I believe it is my duty to obey the Czar, even in his madness; this *must* be my continuing duty."

"Then, for you it is right," Heinrich murmured.

"And it is not right for you?" I asked.

My stepfather looked disturbed. "How can I explain what I know God's Will to be?" he asked me. "I think the rightness or the wrongness of a man's actions must be determined by the man himself – who he is, and whom he serves. I wonder, too, if God might not take into consideration the manner in which a man regards his sins. Surely, it must be a greater crime in the eyes of Our Lord if a man commits an act he believes is wrong than if the sinner acts in the honest belief that what he does is right."

"Then you are telling me I am correct, and should continue to serve?" I asked him. While puzzled, I suspected he spoke God's own wisdom.

"Do you still love the Czar, even believing him mad?"

"Yes," I replied honestly.

"Then you must obey him," said Heinrich.

"And you?" I asked. "Will these new convictions permit you to continue serving him?"

"Again, like you," he responded solemnly, "I have given my life to his cause. I shall carry on as best I can."

I did not question him further, because I knew it would make the subject more painful for him. Although my stepfather seemed to have found a way to reconcile his conflicting allegiances, I doubted that his philosophies could point the way for the remission of my own sins.

Then came the day of Ivan's reception for the Poles. I was in the Square at dawn, attended by a large staff of junior officers. As the units of troops and horsemen began to arrive, we assigned them their places and made sure each man understood what his position should be. This was the greatest display of Russian might I had ever seen within the capital. Regiments, legions – whole armies had been summoned and were assembled at dawn in the Square of Executions, directly in front of the Kremlin main gates. Vorotinsky took charge, for he commanded all forces within the borders of the State. He was a grand figure that day, resplendent in gleaming armor, with a shimmering coat of mail and the finest fabrics laminated to the steel plates of his chest and shoulders. He wore the white cloak and golden insignia of the household guard, as he commanded them as well.

In the Square he assembled several thousand mounted troops, many of whom were Cossacks on their half–wild steeds, snorting and difficult to maintain in formation. *Streltsi* and other mounted levies were set on the far side facing the fortress wall, while hundreds of pikemen and other foot soldiers ringed the entire enclosure. A passage had been left from the river, where the ambassadors would arrive. They would ride in an open coach, between the tightly packed ranks of soldiers, allowing them a full view of our power.

Inside the palace the court had been decked in the accustomed imposing majesty, all wearing the heavy brocaded robes laden with festoons of jewels and pearls. I could not see much of this for I was stationed with the army of the West, facing the Savior's Gate. From the place where I sat my mount I could see into the Kremlin main court, however, and I watched as the full household guard was marched out. They were set in two ranks of gleaming white, their lines leading from the gate to the palace portals on either side of the ambassadors' route.

At last the Pollacks arrived, disembarking from their boat with the usual ostentation in a flurry of plumes and gaudy colors. They were dressed in the tight fitting, foppish costumes of the West; though to give them their due, they did not display the same degree of poor taste I had observed among the French followers of Henri. The procession passed us quickly – so quickly it seemed hardly worth the effort and hours of preparation to assemble the display. Nor did the palace reception last much longer. These ministers of Batory greatly displeased the Czar. King Stephen held himself in much too high regard, Ivan told us later. In the end, he dismissed the ambassadors without inviting them to dine.

I was not privy to much of the guile and intrigue after this, and I did not observe all that transpired within the Czar's council. I was at the head of an army, riding south only two days after the grand reception. Word had come of another Tartar sweep into our territory. Only because I rode in the forefront of our advance units did I catch a glimpse of the invading infidels. Neither I nor anyone else saw much more than this. The Khan's scouts reported the size of our force, at which the entire horde wheeled about, fleeing much more quickly out of our lands than they had entered them. We took some heavy booty from the slower moving baggage wagons, and even captured the elegant yurt of the Khan, with its hundred yak tails flying from mastheads all about the roof. Other than this, there was no contest. We could not catch the fleet–footed Tartar hill ponies, although we chased them deep into the steppes. All of this took time, of course, and it was winter when I was finally free to return home.

Cold winds and snow had cast a veil of depression, with its undercurrent of restlessness, upon the court – most especially upon the Czar. The Pollacks had long since departed; our truce still prevailed in the west. There was little activity outside the capital to require the Czar's attention, and nothing to occupy him at home. All of this seemed to drive Ivan into a deeper state of gloom. Again, he took to heavy drink, and divided his time between chapel and the chambers. By December he had become so morose he frightened even the Czarevitch, who spoke to me several times, expressing his concern.

"My father has become possessed by some terrible demon," said Vanya, "and he moans continually about my mother's death."

"I'd like to ease his pain," I replied, "but there is little I can do. He is apt to strike out at me as quickly as anyone else."

And this was true. I would sometimes breakfast with the Czar, or spend an afternoon with him playing chess or discussing some new manuscript he had acquired. But these were limited moments of lucidity. They were sunny islands in his black, stormy ocean of despair and dread. Even during the holy days, Ivan never slackened his consumption of liquor. The more he drank the more depressed and fearful he became. Vanya had spoken of his father's principal mania when he mentioned Anastasia's death. Somehow, all the other women he had possessed in marriage or otherwise were now forgotten. Anastasia's memory dominated everything else in his mind.

"My little heifer," Ivan would cry. "They have taken my life from me; they have taken my only love, my very essence!"

He would moan and bump his head against the wall, weeping floods of tears and foaming with a soapy scum about his mouth. Moments later his sorrow would turn to anger – to a blind, raging fury. He would shout and scream, tearing at his clothes and beard, stabbing the furniture and floors with his *kisten*. When these moods came upon him, no one could salve his pain; none dared come near enough to speak soothing words to him. It was useless to try distracting his mind into areas where it might find peace or the fulfillment of basking in past glories and accomplishments.

I think Ivan also frightened Boris, who was usually the calmest of us all, and generally the most successful in placating the royal outbursts. Seeing even Boris' helplessness, the Czarevitch gave up any attempt to interfere. Catching his father in a sober mood one day, he asked permission to withdraw to Alexandrov. Ivan agreed, then found cause for further sorrow after his son had gone.

"He has left me," cried the Czar. "Like all the others he has gone away and left me to wallow in my misery without a word of kindness or understanding. His mother wouldn't have done this! Her soul was good and pure. But she's been taken away – gone. When I was a child I lived as an orphan, and as a man I finally found the love I could never possess as a boy. Then it was stolen from me and I'm alone again . . . alone. . . ."

There was no way to keep all of this from reaching Nina's ears, especially as she had many friends among the English, who are notorious gossips. Their colony now numbered some forty–five or fifty people, all living in the area set aside for them just outside the Kremlin. They visited frequently, as did several other foreigners – Italians, mostly, who still designed some of our new buildings or planned the remodeling of old.

Nina was afraid for me, imagining that the Czar might kill me in one of his rages, or order me thrown into a dungeon for some supposed offense. I assured her I was perfectly safe, although I must confess there were times when I did not feel as confident as I pretended to be. Naturally, the fluctuating moods of the Czar could not be as terrible and deep as they were without some tragedy resulting from them. Ivan's belief that Anastasia had been taken from him by his nobles eventually became an obsession. He again directed his anger upon the boyars, convincing himself that he had been compelled to reinstate them to power. "They have poisoned her!" he screamed one day. "They have taken her life, and they shall not go unpunished!"

We were in the large *svyetlitsa* of the Czar's apartments – Boris, the younger son Fedya, and I. As Ivan raved on he became more furious and violent in his accusations against the boyars. Boris and I could only remain there in silence, sitting on a long divan at the far side of the room from the Czar. Fedya, who was easily frightened by his father's outbursts, tried to slip out of the chamber; but Ivan saw him.

"You would leave me, too, you ingrate!" he shouted. "While I seek to revenge the death of your own dear mother, you wish to desert me – leave me to suffer in solitude!"

Fedya began to weep and Boris went to him, placing his arm about his brother–in–law's slender shoulders. Together, they approached the Czar. Boris tried to console Ivan, and after a few moments I joined them. At first the Czar listened to us, but he had bolted down a heavy quantity of liquor, which continued to take greater effect even as we spoke. Ivan began to weep, reaching out to drag all three of us down, onto the floor around his chair. He embraced each of us in turn, soaking our faces with his tears and moaning that we were the only men in the world who cared about him.

His mood had seemed to soften until I expected he would sleep for a while, although his dreadful compulsions would probably only have been postponed. As it happened, a page tapped on the door and told Ivan that Nikita Odoevesky requested an audience. Now, Nikita had never been a man of great power, nor was he exceptionally close to the Czar, although his family ranked most senior behind the Staritskys in direct descent from Rurik. He had always stayed in favor and had been highly honored on a few occasions. He was the younger brother of Evdokia, the woman who had been Vladya's wife. Not realizing the jeopardy into which he placed himself, he strode into the room in full battle dress. A member of the household guard, he still wore his weapons, as was his right. To the best of my recollections, he had just come from supervising some training maneuvers.

Nikita must have been close to forty years at this time, a stout, bandy-legged little man, with a gray–black beard and light, penetrating eyes. He did not normally appear imposing or especially threatening, even when dressed for battle. But on this afternoon, as he walked toward us, he seemed large and suddenly more powerful – probably because he stood, while the rest of us sat on the floor. Whatever the reason, the Czar suddenly let out a terrified scream that brought guards running from both ends of the hall.

"This man is trying to murder me!" he shrieked. "He has killed my beloved wife, and he wants to destroy me as well!"

Both Boris and I started to protest, but the Czar had already staggered to his feet. He was screaming for the soldiers to arrest Nikita and throw him into a dungeon cell. His denunciation became so violent, both Boris and I were afraid to interfere. Fedya had hidden himself on the floor, behind some draperies.

This was the strange beginning of a frightful, sickening purge. By the standards of some previous executions, not many men were involved. But the selection of victims made it the worst I had ever witnessed. Men who were nearly as close as I, myself, were made to suffer for Ivan's sudden, obsessive madness.

Odoevesky was impaled in the Square of Executions the next morning. Several criminals were also beheaded, but Nikita was the only noble prisoner. The Czar did not attend the rites, which spared my having to witness them. Despite my sorrow, I knew my safest place was at Ivan's side, where I could not be accused of deserting him. Thus, while Nikita suffered the pain and humiliation of impalement, I sat with the Czar and listened to him wail about his loss and the murder of his "little heifer." But Odoevesky's death did not suffice to quell his blood lust, though Boris thought it would. I knew better, and we actually wagered on it. Unfortunately, I won.

A day or two later the weather cleared, and the Czar decided to go into the city, saying he would visit the *gostiny dvor* – the main bazaar. Most of the household accompanied him, except that Boris was not among us. Fedya rode beside his father in the open coach, and I was directly behind them at the head of a dozen or more mounted officers. Just as we came to the entrance of the bazaar, we happened to pass a heavily veiled lady on the street – obviously a woman of rank, as she was attended by several guards and female servants. The Czar shouted for his driver to halt the coach. The lady had also stopped when she realized it was the Czar who passed her. After a moment I recognized the livery on the retainers; it was Michael Vorotinsky's wife.

Ivan ordered his entire procession to back up, until his coach came even with the woman, who now looked up at him in some alarm. Ivan sat staring at her for another moment, then calmly commanded that she remove her clothing. The order surprised everyone, for Vorotinsky's wife was no longer young. She was a dignified, matronly woman of nearly her husband's years. "I shall not repeat my order, Madam," shouted the Czar. "You will either obey, or I shall have my men carry out the instructions for you." With that, he signaled for all of us to back up again, thus making it necessary for the whole procession, even the guards who rode ahead of the royal coach, to pass the spot where Vorotinsky's wife would stand.

Mortified, her face white with terror, the poor woman had no alternative. Slowly, with the help of an attendant, she began to remove her clothing. A warm day for this time of year, the air was still brisk enough that one's breath would mist before his face. The remains of the last snowfall lay about us, and in some places it was still knee deep.

When she had removed her clothing as far as the shift and final petticoat, she looked up at Ivan, pleading with her eyes that he not force her to continue.

"Everything!" he shouted. "And make it faster! You have already detained your Czar too long!"

When the woman was completely naked, standing like a rigid, white marble statue, the Czar gestured for the procession to move on. Slowly, we rode past her as she fumbled helplessly with her hands, not knowing what part of her body to cover. Tears welled in her eyes, while the drooping flesh of her breasts and hips quivered with shame and from the cold.

That night the Czar ordered Vorotinsky arrested, and the following morning the warrant went out for Michael Morozof. All of this frightened me badly, especially Morozof's arrest, for he had been a member of the Czar's inner circle since the days of Adashev. I had known him as long or longer than I had Vorotinsky. I was depressed beyond description, and Heinrich was more disturbed than I, though he expressed his displeasure only once, in a few harsh words spoken to me outside the house. After that, we did not mention it between us and my stepfather maintained a stony silence for days.

I prayed to God that I not be required to take part in the executions which I knew were bound to come. I was not; at least, not immediately. Morozof was condemned without a trial. For Vorotinsky there was a long, wretched farce to be played out before a tribunal of boyars. The Czar did not attend these sessions, as he convinced himself that Vorotinsky had cast an evil spell upon him. He feared lest the prisoner do so again, thus avoiding a just sentence for his crimes. The men who sat in judgment on this great general were all men of lesser stature, toadies who feared to make any pretense of independent thought. The Czar had obviously told them he expected Vorotinsky to be condemned.

Testimony was taken from a wretched serf, a fellow who had fled several months before from one of the Vorotinsky estates. I saw the man as he was being taken into the hall to give evidence before the tribunal. He was trembling with fear, and I could tell he had been harshly treated in prison. I do not know all that he claimed to have observed, but from the stories of men who were in the room I gathered that he swore to having seen his master perform strange rites about a fire in the dark of night. Weird chants had been sung, which caused the wolves to howl. On the night of Anastasia's death, he claimed to have seen Vorotinsky throw a female doll into the flames.

The general was condemned, and only after this was he brought before Ivan in the great hall of the palace. I was present this time, as was nearly the entire court. After the Czar had pronounced sentence, Vorotinsky, always straight and dignified, tried to remonstrate with him. "Even as my father and my grandfather," he began, speaking in a clear, firm voice, "I have served my Czar in good faith with a never–faltering zeal. I have never served a demon. I am a man of good Christian faith who has never resorted to sorcery or witchcraft. Nor would I ever have harmed the Czarina, whom I loved as I love my Czar. The witness who was heard against me was a runaway thief. How can the word of this miscreant be taken against mine?"

The Czar ordered him to be silent. Vorotinsky's words, and his tone of sincerity had effected everyone in the room. Ivan did not allow him time to curry more sympathy from other members of the court. "You seek to work your spell upon Us, even here," replied the Czar. "But you will never again have the opportunity to do Us harm!"

Vorotinsky was removed to his cell. As he left the hall, he walked with the same poise in his tread, holding himself as rigidly proud as ever. He looked neither right nor left, and even in captivity he seemed to be leading, rather than following the soldiers who guarded him.

The Czar had pronounced Vorotinsky's sentence of death; but it was not carried out in Moscow. Instead, Ivan ordered Morozof beheaded the next morning in the Square of Executions, along with his two sons and a number of their servants. It was all done very quickly, as if it were hardly more important than the death of a common highwaymen. Again, the Czar did not attend, and an hour or so later the court was en route to Alexandrov with Vorotinsky. I went, because it was expected I would. Heinrich remained behind, claiming he suffered from swollen joints and a severe cold.

Because the Czar no longer rode horseback, except for brief periods on ceremonial occasions, we were forced to move at a slower pace and to make two overnight stops. In order to provide the necessary comforts, the royal coach was easily twice the size of the wagons which had transported my entourage from Kholmagora. I thought of this as I rode, trying to reconcile the span of time – so many years, so many men who had lived and died and were now no more than memories. In my youth the days had seemed much longer – somehow brighter, as if a different sun had shone upon them. Now, my very life seemed to rush toward its inevitable climax and I found myself no longer able to placate my cravings by promising their fulfillment in some obscure, distant future.

For some reason my inner mind dwelt upon distorted images of men who had been close to me, all of whom were gone: Adashev, Vladya, Malyuta, Elysius – so many, all dead because fate or the Czar's whim had required them to die. As my mount loped slowly along at the head of the column, with the creaking and bumping of Ivan's carriage forming an irregular background of sound, I realized I had been equating myself to these others, wondering not so much about the possibility of joining them as pondering the manner in which it was going to happen. I was seeing myself as one of them. I was musing over the manner of my own death!

The thought brought me back to a chilling reality, so much so that I actually reined my horse to a stop, caught myself just in time to prevent the entire column from being called to a halt. Thoughtfully, I spurred my mount forward. My own fate would come as it would, I reasoned. If I must die for the Czar, well, I had always maintained my willingness to do that. But Nina, my family, my children. . .

No! I could not permit them to endure some public circus for the populace. I knew how the common people assuaged their own envy by gazing upon the finely dressed families of the nobility, mumbling to themselves that bright fires burned more quickly, speculating on how one or another would face the specter of death when his moment came upon the Place of Skulls. How I might assure against such a fate was momentarily beyond my ability to foresee. I knew only that when the moment came – as it eventually would have to come – I would do my utmost to prevent it.

As we neared Alexandrov the sky began to darken and heavy rain clouds loomed across the horizon behind us. We were within the heavy forests which the Czar had insisted remain untouched about his residence. The few farmhouses which once had stood along the highway were gone, and native brush had sprung up to obscure the former tiny patches of peasant gardens. Only here and there could one see the remains of buildings, a few stones to mark the place where a family hearth had been battered to ruins by the brotherhood.

The storm broke at dusk, and we arrived at the *Unfreedom* in a pelting downpour. The guards in the kiosk tumbled out in poor semblance of military order, standing uncomfortably in the lashing rain until Ivan's sloshing, groaning coach had passed them. Thoroughly soaked, my teeth chattering from the cold, I trailed the procession into Ivan's sequestered retreat.

With the brotherhood disbanded, the Czar's *dacha* was no longer draped as an abbey. It was brightly lighted by huge candelabra and smoky oil lamps. The rooms had been furnished with elegant, highly polished woods; expensive tapestries had been hung in nearly every room. In many respects, the Czar's home in the wilderness was grander than his Kremlin palace, as most of the appointments were new and unscarred by heavy usage.

Outside, however, the wooden barracks and storage sheds had turned a sickly gray, while most of the other houses had begun to fall into ruin. Many of the former owners were dead, victims of the evil they had helped to spread across the land. No new occupants had been chosen. Without the huge body of guardsmen, monks, and servants who had once attended the *Opritchniki*, there was ample room for everyone in the Czar's *dacha*.

Vorotinsky, who had been brought to Alexandrov in a closed wagon, was lodged in one of the cells beneath the house. In the morning, the rain having stopped, the Czar led all of us into the woods. The prisoner was brought along in chains, forced to walk with a halter about his neck, while the rest of us rode. Vorotinsky maintained his bearing, although the chains that joined his ankles were snagged several times by roots and other impediments. Twice, he was pulled off his feet by the rope about his throat. I think many were as depressed by the circumstances as I was, for there was no spontaneity in the forced laughter over Ivan's comments. Neither was any derision heaped upon the prisoner.

Water still dripped from the trees and underbrush. Rain had washed away the last of the winter's snow, leaving a cold, soggy gloom over the forest. The Czar ordered two fires started, a few feet apart, near the base of a large pine tree. Vorotinsky was suspended by his wrists between them. Because of the moisture, they were smoky and difficult to maintain. But gradually one fire, then the other, would be built up, forcing the victim to struggle, pulling his body away from one side until the heat from the other became too great. He had been dressed in only his shift, but this soon began to blaze. The flames badly seared his body, and the cloth carried wisps of fire into his face, burning the hairs of his beard. I remember feeling very cold, trembling from the moist chill which seemed to seep through the fur of my coat. My breath frosted before my eyes, but I found myself stepping back several paces, away from the fires' heat.

A number of us openly displayed our sorrow, but there was nothing to be done. Once Vorotinsky's clothing had been burned from his body, the general still hung silently with his eyes open and his breath coming in short, labored gasps. He never cried out – never emitted more than a groan or a sigh. After some time, Ivan came forward with his *kisten*. He heated the steel tip in the fire and tried to evoke a scream from the general by poking the glowing metal into the flesh of his belly and genitals. Vorotinsky tightened his jaw, looking to the side, refusing to see the Czar. He stifled any outcry, though his body twisted involuntarily against the pain. I had moved around the group by then, and I stood a few feet from the Czar. "God has granted him the grace of sleep," I whispered. "He can no longer feel anything."

Ivan turned toward me, and I was surprised to see tears streaming from his eyes. "Take him down!" he said. His voice was deep and hollow, breathy, as if suddenly horrified by his own actions. Without saying any more, he started back toward the palace on foot, sobbing and muttering to himself. Most of the court went with him.

I signaled a couple of guards to help me lower the General's body. I assumed he was dead, as nearly all the skin had been blistered off large areas of his body. But he groaned as we placed him on the litter, and I ordered him carried carefully back to the *dacha*. Ivan had gone into his chapel, where he remained for the rest of the day.

Vorotinsky was still alive the following morning, but his body was wracked by a high fever. He cried out in his delirium, responding to the pain only now, when he was no longer in control of his voice. Ivan refused to look upon him, though he called me to him after matins.

"Take him to Beelozersk," he told me. "If God has spared him, I can do no less."

I started off with my general's body soon after that. I had him placed with all care into a large carriage, and I found an old woman to attend him. She was famous for her ability to cure the local peasants. But nothing could help Vorotinsky; his mind never returned to him, and he never knew he had been pardoned. He died before we made camp that night.

I returned to Moscow with the body and saw to its proper burial, rushing the rituals to completion before the court returned a few days later. I did not want the Czar to arrive and countermand my orders. But I could not anticipate how deep an impression this dreadful act would make upon the Czar. He had stopped drinking altogether, and his first command on entering the city was to call the Metropolitan to him for a special blessing. He began spending entire days at prayer, and made several trips to Sergey–Troitsky, where he would remain for a week at a time, lying on his face before the sacred relics. It was the end of June before he seemed himself again.

While the Czar was going through this ordeal of guilt and recrimination, both Boris and I made frequent attempts to bring his attention back to governing the land. With the spring thaws almost over, it was time to formulate plans to consolidate our Livonian gains. The truce with Poland having nearly run its course, we should have been preparing to defend what we already held and to seize those areas which were vital to our defense. We also wanted a regional government established, either civil or military, headed by a skillful administrator. Magnus was worse than useless, for he left every decision to his dishonest, incompetent subordinates. The result was extreme unrest among his subject populations. Peasant heroes, like the brigand who called himself "Hannibal," were appearing in several parts of the conquered territories and raiding our garrisons. Through stealth and clever maneuvering by their ambassador, the Swedes had taken possession of Reval. We should at least have recaptured this area, for we were bound by no truce with Sweden.

At first, Ivan refused to do anything. The King of Sweden had written him a very courteous letter, he said, asking us not to attack the city and implying that we could acquire it by negotiation. Only after Boris and I had wheedled for days, did the Czar agree to allow our forces to try taking it. He also granted permission for Magnus to take Wenden, which did not violate the truce with Poland. But Boris had convinced the Czar and his other advisors that the unrest among the peasants was due to agitation by Polish agents. This also constituted a violation of the truce, he maintained.

Heinrich was sent to advise Magnus, and to act as Ivan's personal representative. Our armies moved into Wenden without a struggle for Magnus promised the inhabitants his personal protection against the excesses of Russian tyranny. I was with the Czar when he received Heinrich's report of this. His only immediate response was an angry growl, but a few days later he ordered me to ready the entire army.

A flood of reports now began to arrive from agents working out of the Bureau of Secret Affairs. Magnus had followed his initial success by marching beyond Wenden, sweeping into village after village, always making the same promises to the people. He, Magnus, King of Livonia, would rule them with justice and mercy. He would personally protect them from the Czar!

Ivan went into a frothing rage. His age, his weight, the season – all notwithstanding, he would lead the army himself. In less then three weeks we were on the move. The truce with Poland had now been shattered, but King Stephen was having too many problems within his new realm to do much about our activities in Livonia. Danzig and a few other regions had refused to accept Batory's election, and it was necessary for the King to take these areas by force. Arriving in Pskov, the Czar received a full report on the Polish dilemma.

As for our own King Magnus, a message was awaiting the Czar from him, asking Ivan to "respect the rights of his (Magnus's) subjects." If the Czar ever had any intention of holding back, or granting Magnus the opportunity to explain himself, that letter was enough to extinguish his resolve. Flying into another terrible fury, Ivan ordered the messengers flogged. The next morning we entered the Kingdom of Magnus the Crunchback.

The Dane had listed which towns were under his protection, and of these the first on our route was Kokenhusen. The forces under Ivan's immediate command numbered close to a hundred thousand men, many of them Cossacks and Tartars. We struck a fearsome picture as we advanced across the lush green meadows toward the ancient township. Like so many German settlements, Kokenhusen comprised a large cluster of white–walled houses, with wooden beams showing through the plaster. Most of the roofs were thatch or wood; only a few were tile. The *Rathaus*, the mansion of the Burgomeister, and a few other stone structures stood in the center of town.

Magnus had left a garrison of German troops in the village, and assuming us to be a friendly force these men made no move to oppose our entry. It would have been a useless defense, anyway, as they were barely a hundred men. In typical German style, they lined up to form an honor guard, intending to escort the Czar into Kokenhusen. Instead, Ivan called a halt just short of the city, where the Russian army stood like a solid wall of flesh and steel. The front of our line was nearly as wide as the town, and the column stretched beyond the horizon.

I had charge of our forward units, and had received my orders before we broke camp that morning. I sent several hundred Cossacks in, having them sweep around the edge of our halted formation. Before the Germans realized what was happening the horsemen were upon them, swinging their terrible scimitars. The soldiers panicked and tried to flee, only a few managing to draw their swords before being struck to the ground by our fiercesome warriors. No civilians were touched, but most of the townspeople fled into their homes before Ivan ordered our men to make camp for the night.

Pickets were dispatched immediately to assure that none of the population would leave the city. The *Burgomeister,* a rotund, elderly gentleman, came to us on foot, followed by most of the leading citizens. Ivan refused to receive him, but his presence hastened the fate of his citizenry. The Czar ordered the entire population routed from the their homes and bound.

"We shall show them how Magnus is able to protect them!" he growled. "King of Livonia, indeed! Without me, he would be less than a scavenger!"

The Czar was in a foul, black mood all evening, annoyed by the screams and crashing sounds from the city. A number of houses were already on fire, giving up a heavy, oily smoke that blew directly into camp, where it created a dense pall inside the royal pavilion. Eventually, Ivan heaved himself up from his chair and told me to attend him. I motioned for a group of guardsmen to follow us, as we set off toward the city. It was only a short walk, but the exertion tired the Czar. He leaned heavily on his *kisten*, but huffily pushed me away when I tried to offer him my arm.

Ivan was in little danger within the village, for the population had mostly been taken into custody. No one attempted to fight us, although a number tried to escape. Hundreds of our soldiers were still in the streets, searching the houses for valuables, swilling down beer and liquor from the cellars and taverns. Recognizing the Czar, several men staggered up to offer him a swallow from their cups. As they intended no insult, being in a jovial state of drunkenness, Ivan accepted several bumpers along the way.

We wandered into the center of town, where a supervised unit of our men was busy stripping the city hall and treasury. We paused in the square to watch them. Behind us was a fairly good sized church, obviously Protestant by the austerity of its adornments. One could see the scars where older, Romanesque devices had been removed. After a while I saw a priest, or pastor, emerge from the door of this building and walk slowly in our direction. As a matter of course I motioned for some of the men to keep the fellow back, but Ivan called out and commanded him to approach.

The pastor immediately began trying to dissuade the Czar from his sack of the city. The fool was quite typical of these Lutheran ministers, a man of middle age who allowed his graying locks to drape like a woman's on either side of his head. His body was slender, skinny really, topped by a crafty, pointed face. He spoke pompously to the Czar, expressing an assurance of his righteousness as if he had the personal acquaintance of God. Using the scriptures to justify his arguments he strode along with Ivan, lecturing him on the heavenly salvation awaiting a man of mercy.

For quite some time – much longer than I thought seemly – the Czar allowed this heretic pastor to argue with him, even permitting the fellow to interrupt his own discourses. Eventually, the discussion became heated and in the end the Czar's leniency encouraged his antagonist to compare Martin Luther to the Apostle Paul! This exceeded the limits of Ivan's tolerance. Lifting his *kisten,* he drove the heavy steel tip through the pastor's chest, using such force that I had to help him pull it free. "Now he can join his hero in the devil's own chamber," said the Czar.

This exchange with the priest had made Ivan angry, left him muttering about the fellow's presumption upon his tolerance. We returned to camp, the incident having ruined the Czar's formerly complacent mood. Still seething over his encounter with the Lutheran, the Czar dictated a letter to Magnus, calling him, among other things, "the Beggar King of Livonia." Thus, the Danish upstart was given fair warning of his fate, should he continue to give himself airs and turn against the very power to which he owed his existence. Ivan insisted on writing that letter himself and refused to allow his clerk to copy it. He said it would impress Magnus with his determination if he received a letter written personally by the Czar.

Unfortunately, Ivan's penmanship had become so poor – especially when he was angry – it was nearly impossible to read. As a result of this, there followed a series of mistakes, misunderstandings, and blunders. Magnus stupidly doubted the Czar's resolve to enforce his demands. Instead of sending a letter of apology and supplication as he should have done, he failed to answer at all. We remained in our camp outside Kokenhusen for nearly two weeks, waiting for a reply that never came. Finally, in a fury of vengeful, determined anger, Ivan ordered the entire population of the village – men , women, and children – to be sold as slaves in Novgorod and Moscow.

The incidents occurring here, while of little consequence on the great face of history, were like the end of life itself for me. During all the months when Magnus had been advancing through the Livonian countryside, Heinrich had continued to act as advisor. My stepfather was still with him at Wenden when forces of the Czar appeared outside the city walls. Magnus came out at once, being too much of a coward to assert his beliefs in the face of such power. Although the Dane was followed by a number of his principle officers, I noted that Heinrich had remained inside.

King Magnus approached the Czar on foot, dressed in a flamboyant scarlet robe, wearing a golden diadem upon his misshapen brow. For this occasion, Ivan ordered a black stallion saddled for himself, and went forward at the head of his officers. He halted several feet from Magnus, glaring down at him contemptuously. The rest of us formed a circle around him. I noticed that a number of the other Russian officers had drawn their swords, as I had, to guard against any treachery on the part of the Germans and Danes who groveled with their master. Seeing the entire group were Magnus's men, I thought I understood why Heinrich had not come with them.

Magnus stared up at Ivan for several minutes, the fear plainly etched upon his gruesome features. His white–filmed eye seemed to bulge worse than usual, while the other hardly dared to look into his master's face. At my distance I could see the throbbing at Magnus's neck and temples. Ivan said nothing, which only added to the King's terror.

At last, Magnus threw himself full length upon the ground before Ivan's mount. He pressed his face into the moist earth, and in this position crawled forward a few inches at a time.

"Get up, you blockhead!" shouted the Czar. "How can you imagine yourself King of Livonia when you lack the courage to stand before me like a man? You are nothing but an adventurer, a beggar whom I've foolishly taken into my family and given in marriage to my beloved niece! I have clothed you, fed you, set you up in a station far beyond your most fanciful imaginings. And after all this, you dare turn your back on me and flaunt my authority? Answer me!"

Magnus struggled slowly to his feet, still hesitant to look Ivan in the eye. "I have sinned against you," he whined. "I cannot deny it. But I have been misguided by those you sent to advise me, else I would never have betrayed Your Majesty's grace. I beg to be forgiven!"

He fell on his knees again and kissed the edge of Ivan's saddle trappings. In an effort to control his anger, the Czar reined back, pulling the cloth from Magnus's fingers. Then he launched into a long harangue, naming the crimes committed by the King and condemning him in very harsh language. In the end, he ordered Magnus and his entire entourage tossed into a nearby cattle barn, where they were kept under guard for several days.

Our men entered Wenden, setting up posts in the center of town and in the main market place. As usual, we met with no resistance, although a number of townspeople and soldiers took refuge in the old castle above the city. I had expected to find Heinrich among those who came forth to greet us, but he wasn't there. I inquired after him, and was informed that he had gone into the stronghold with those who still wished to oppose the Czar!

I could hardly credit the truth of such a story, and at first assumed he must be a prisoner. I rode back to our camp, where men were busy setting up Ivan's pavilion. I found the Czar in conference with the city elders, and prevailed upon him to send them away long enough for me to speak with him. Annoyed, he responded to my urgency, and listened in amazement when I told him what I had discovered. He also assumed that Heinrich must be a prisoner, and immediately authorized me to go to the castle as his representative. I was to negotiate both for its surrender and for the release of my stepfather.

From the beginning, an inner sense warned me that something was wrong. I wanted it to be otherwise, but I already suspected the truth. Thoughtfully, I rode back into Wenden, which was a large town, with a great many people living within its walls. At the moment, its population was considerably swelled by an influx of refugees, people who had swarmed into the protected enclosure in fear of our army. Now reasonably certain of their safety, many of these were coming out of the houses. Some of the more aggressive shopkeepers had opened their stalls, and the wine merchants, especially, were doing a thriving business, as were the taverns.

I was only vaguely aware of all this activity about me. I was concerned for Heinrich's safety, knowing within my own soul that he had not been simply kidnapped as a hostage. I looked up at the towering walls of the old castle, where many faces lined the battlements, gazing down in silence upon their city. As I approached, the steep slope caused my mount to strain, and several times his hooves slipped on the gravel surface. Then suddenly, they were shooting at me! From several places along the wall, arquebusks flashed in my direction, each burst followed by a sharp, growling report.

I jumped down from my horse, and kept him between me and the fools who were shooting from the fortress as I eased my way back to the bottom of the hill. I stood there for several minutes, wondering what to do. Finally, I bought a piece of white cloth from a stall and fastened this to the tip of my sword blade. Holding this above my head, I again began to climb the hill. This time, I was allowed to approach the gate. Looking up from the edge of the dry moat, I stared into the muzzles of a dozen arquebusks, aimed at me by men on the battlements above the drawbridge.

"What do you want, Russian?" called a voice in German.

"I want to speak to your commander," I hollered back in the same language. "I am authorized to speak for the Czar!"

There was some motion on the parapet, and a man with a round, moon–like face – his bald head fringed by a shaggy ring of gray – leaned through one of the openings. "I am Henry Boismann," he shouted. "I am in charge here."

"I am authorized to guarantee your safety, and that of all of the citizens inside, if you surrender immediately," I called back. "This means the surrendering of your hostages, as well."

"We have no hostages," he returned. "And what of the officers who served the King?"

"The men who served King Magnus are subjects of the Czar," I replied. "It is he who shall determine their fate. But you say you have no hostages? What of *Freiherr* von Staden?"

Boismann pulled himself back onto the walk, and I could see his shoulders as he spoke to someone standing farther in from the wall. Then he leaned through again, and behind him I saw Heinrich's face.

"Go back, Demetrius," called my stepfather. "We shall not surrender."

"It means your death!" I cried.

"Sometimes death holds less horror than – other things," shouted Heinrich in reply.

"Tell your Czar we will fight to the last breath," added Boismann.

"You are fools! Heinrich, let me in to talk to you!"

"No use!" he replied.

"No use, no use," mocked a number of voices down the wall.

"Better get going before one of my men splits your breastplate, General," added Boismann.

I let my gaze travel the length of the parapet, and all along it I could see determined faces above ugly snouts of the guns being poked out at me. "Go, General, while you still have a chance!" came the order once again.

I turned my mount and cantered down the slope into town. I was completely disconcerted, though I knew well enough what Heinrich meant, why he was taking this foolish stand – all the others, too. They must have realized their position was hopeless, and their bravery was worse than mad; it was suicidal. But strangely enough, I recognized the soulfulness in what they did. They would die, but not with any spirit of foolhardiness or ostentation. Not a single voice had derided me with laughter when I turned to leave, nor had any man boasted of his bravery.

I did not know whether to be angry or sad. In the end I was simply bewildered, and in this state I returned to the Czar. I made no attempt to hide the truth, or to soften Heinrich's part in it. "They defy you," I told him. "Heinrich is one of the leaders."

"Your father leads these scum against me?" bellowed the Czar.

"He has joined the rebels," I replied unhappily. "However, he is not first among them."

The Czar stood up and paced about his pavilion for several moments. "How do you feel about all this?" he asked at length, stopping directly in front of me.

"It saddens me greatly," I replied.

"And your loyalty to me remains unshaken?" he demanded. He leaned close to me, and I could smell the German beer upon his breath.

Without permitting my gaze to waver, I answered him firmly. "It makes no difference who else may turn against you," I said. "I am not only your servant; I am your friend."

"Good, good," he clucked, rubbing his palms together. He turned away and laughed harshly, almost evilly. Abruptly, he spun back to face me, closer than before. "You will command the force that takes the keep," he snarled.

I dropped my gaze to the floor. "If I must do this to prove my loyalty, then so be it," I replied. "Shall I order the assault at once?"

He did not reply immediately. I think he was sorry for placing me in such a position; but he would not back down. Still, he knew he had hurt me, more perhaps than Heinrich had. Finally, he turned away. "No," he said. "Do not attack them tonight. Let me try to arrange a surrender, first."

On the Czar's orders, I sent a large force of men to ring the fortress. Before they were all in position, a few men from the peasant levies became careless, going a bit too close to the walls. They were promptly shot by the defenders.

This angered the Czar, although I do not think it determined his next action; I am certain the decision had already been made. Without explaining his intentions, he ordered me to send for a certain Georg Wilke, a young officer who had been in command at Wolmar. He had been taken by us several days before, to be held as hostage for the good behavior of his followers. Despite his youth, he was already a distinguished commander and a highly respected officer. Tall and blond, he seemed an almost heroic figure as they led him from his cell to the base of the hill. A team of Tartars were working on a stake, not yet planted in the earth.

I do not believe Wilke spoke Russian, so failed to understand the Czar's order. He thus had no idea of his fate until a pair of Tartar officers in soiled white robes and turbans approached him with drawn daggers. Without cutting loose his hands, the Tartars slit his shirt and doublet in the necessary places, stripping him completely. He was not to be permitted even the grace of a shift to hide his nakedness. Wilke was then thrown onto his back, held down by seven or eight little brown men, while his legs were thrust apart and the blunt knob was rammed inside him. Until that moment, he was probably not certain of his captors' intentions. He had been silent all this while, and had offered no resistance. Now he began to scream and struggle against his guards, but his fate was sealed. The lower end of the post was braced against the hole, and the young man was lifted, stake and all, forced to stand while rocks were hammered in about the base of his post. Once certain he was securely impaled, the Tartars withdrew, leaving their victim in full view of the castle defenders.

Wilke's stake had been set just outside the range of the enemy arquebusks. Bonfires were kindled behind him and to either side, assuring the defenders would have a clear view of his miseries. The flickering red brilliance added an eerie quality to the tableau, as the young man struggled in frantic, naked hysteria. His hands had been cut free after the stake was firmly implanted, and he flayed the air about him – violently, bending down to grasp the slippery shaft, where his own blood now mingled with the grease. The men who placed him were not professional executioners, and they had skewered him badly, tearing him up before leaving him to his sufferings. His agony must have been frightful. Though notably a brave soldier, he screamed for the entire two hours it took him to die. It was a dreadful, sickening spectacle: the strong, muscular body covered with its own gore as Wilke's hands touched the flesh of his chest and belly, streaking himself with blood and the slimy black oil that had been used to coat the wood. He twisted and writhed as his frenzied mind drifted between terror and anger, finally despair.

I stood in the background, just beyond the circle of heat from one of the fires. I was paralyzed by conflicting thoughts and emotions: distressed by the Czar's failure to understand the effect his orders would have on the defenders – Heinrich in particular, appalled by the spectacle of a young officer's disgraceful mistreatment, yet compelled by my own inner compulsions to watch, totally unable to tear my gaze away. Toby brought me a flagon of wine, and stayed with me until fatigue and drunkenness forced me to withdraw – this about the time Wilke expired. With Illya assisting, he got me into bed shortly before dawn, but I once I was lying on my back, I came fully awake, and eventually staggered back outside.

Hundreds of faces had lined the walls to watch; yet no sound was heard from within the fortress. When the young officer finally sagged limply on the stake, the Czar ordered his body left where it was. More fires were lighted, these at intervals all around the citadel. They were kept blazing all night by the Tartar soldiers who guarded against anyone's escaping from the ancient fortress.

In the morning I moved as if in a trance. I had not slept at all, and I wanted nothing to do with the action about take place. But I had no choice. I was in command. When the defenders again refused to surrender, we moved up artillery and I ordered a bombardment of the walls. Unlike the situation we had faced in Kazan, these defenses were stone and mortar. The guns were much closer, and our more modern weapons were far more powerful than the older cannon which Kurbsky had commanded. It was not long before great sections of wall began to collapse. Huge clouds of dust billowed skyward, while the odor of expended gunpowder became thick and biting.

I was about to halt my fire and give the rebels another opportunity to surrender, when they took the situation completely out of my hands. In a foolish, glorious display of bravery, they collected all the powder inside the fortress and piled it into vaults beneath the main tower. While everyone knelt in prayer, Henry Boismann took a lighted torch and threw it into the enclosure. There was no warning whatever, and before I knew it was happening, I was thrown to the ground by the force of an enormous explosion. Stunned, I retained just enough sense to pull myself under a nearby cannon, while stone and brick, and obscenely mangled bits of human bodies began falling all around.

A few moments later, I was leading a group of men into the ruined keep. Frantically, I sought my stepfather, though I knew it was useless before I started. I am thankful I found no trace of him, for I feared to come upon his head or half of his torn body. It was better this way. He was simply gone, without a trace.

Strangely enough, the only person found alive was Boismann. I had his battered body carried out of the shattered building and sent to the Czar. Ivan, of course, was in an uncontrollable rage, ordering the man impaled, although Boismann was dead before his fire–blackened body could be lifted onto the stake.

Afterward, the Czar's anger knew no bounds. He turned the army upon the population of Wenden, and never since the days of the brotherhood had there been such rapine and destruction. The blood lust of the Tartar and Cossack squadrons was equal to the worst of Viazemsky or Skuratof. Men were hacked to bits in the streets, still beating hearts were plucked from their chests and thrown to the swine. Strongly locked houses were set afire, with the occupants still inside – escapees shot to death with arrows if they later sought to flee. Woman were thrown down in the street and used so brutally it was painful to watch. Thoroughly sickened, not only by the aftermath, but by Heinrich's terrible decision, I must have become completely mad . . . or possessed. I took a fresh mount, turned his head eastward, and rode away.

I galloped at full tilt along the dusty roads, racing through forests and meadows, with no idea where I was or where I was going. I recall branches tearing at my face and clothing, while mud and clumps of turf splattered me from head to toe. My horse grew tired, the foam thick and heavy over his entire body. Froth streamed from his mouth and nostrils, flying back into my face. I continued to spur him on, until the froth became pink with his blood.

Finally, I stopped, dropping from his back onto the ground. I lay deep inside a forest, on my back, staring into a dark tangle of branches above my head, feeling the coolness of woodland moss beneath me. I must have slept, because it was suddenly morning. Birds hopped about in the boughs and a squirrel sat inquisitively on his haunches a few paces away.

It was several days before I returned to my command. I lived like a wildman, eating only a few berries and avoiding contact with other people. On the third or fourth day of my madness, a pair of lovers passed close to me while I hid in a thicket of prickly brush. I listened jealously as they made love, promising each other eternal fidelity. I could not see them for the bushes, but they were too close for me to slip away unseen, and at first I feared to have them observe my presence. I stood stock still, leaning against a tree trunk and allowing my mind to drift back to my own loves – to Nina, and beyond her to Suunbeka and Anastasia. None of the others had counted, really, just these three. But of them all, it was Nina – Nina – Nina, in danger because of my foolish actions! How I longed for her at that moment! My impulse was to rush from my hiding place, to begin the long trip home, to forsake everything to be with her.

As I thought these things I started becoming myself again, and I realized how stupidly I was acting. Such a flight would gain me nothing, and it would certainly not benefit the woman I professed to love so deeply. For her, if for nothing else, I must force myself to return. Without thinking further, I burst from my hiding place, straight into the glade where the lovers lay naked in one another's arms. They must have taken me for a woods demon about to punish them for their sin. Both cried out in fright, but I laughed at them and told the lad to finish what he had started. Hysterical with mirth, I continued to chortle as I walked away from them. They surely thought I was mad, and for the moment I suppose I really was.

With Toby's help, I had not been missed. He had stayed at the door of my tent, guarding against anyone's entry. If someone asked for me, he told him I was drunk, or too sick for visitors. In the meanwhile, Illya had scoured the countryside in search of me. I was already trudging back along the road – on foot, for my horse had died – when he came upon me.

The final throes of Wenden's destruction were still in progress as we re–entered the city. There were the smoldering remains of a few houses, and several small bands of barbarians continued to poke about in the ruins, gleaning what treasures they could from the ashes. I washed myself and reported to Simon, who was currently acting as aide to the Czar. My friend seemed relieved to see me. "I was afraid you were dead," he told me, "and I was also afraid to make inquiries, because I did not know where you might have gone."

"I was ill," I replied flatly.

"So it shall be told," he said grimly.

Soon the army moved on, and the cruelty of the Czar spread terror before us. Fear became our most powerful weapon, and few dared to resist, lest the wrath of *Grozny* fall upon them. That summer we swept through all the German lands, and we took far more than we had previously expected. Riga and Reval were the single exceptions, and they held out only because we deemed their conquest too costly in time. With the rest of Livonia lying open before us, we could afford to starve out these strongholds at our leisure. Everywhere, victory was ours, as the Czar led his armies in person, his name enough to make the people tremble.

Magnus, still in disgrace, had been brought along behind us, riding in chains within a wooden cart. At Dorpat, he was brought before the Czar, and must have expected his end had come. But Ivan had seen enough of battle. He longed for the peace and solitude of his own apartments in the Kremlin and Alexandrov. In an impressive ceremony before the entire army, he granted the King his blessing and caused the irons to be struck from his wrists. Magnus agreed to rule as a vassal of the Czar, and to pay a high yearly tribute.

Ivan left for Russia a day or two later, writing a final letter to Kurbsky before he went, boasting of his victories and asking again why Andrew did not return. "If your reasons for deserting Us were really just," he wrote, "then surely God will grant you the highest rewards of Heaven when I have sent you to Him."

I asked the Czar to take me with him when he returned. I longed for my family, though I did not give this as my reason for wishing to go home. Instead, I stressed my anxiety over the management of our business affairs. Unexpectedly, the Czar refused. "We have need of you here," he told me bluntly. It unnerved me a bit that he gave no other reason, and his gaze seemed to cut through my skin. I had the dreadful feeling that he was examining my soul and sifting out the doubts.

When Ivan departed – shortly before the first snows – the spirit of conquest seemed to go with him. The men ceased to sing at night, always a sign of their discontent. We would remain secure enough during the winter, I reasoned, with snow to inhibit the movement of enemy troops. But I feared the advent of warmer weather. Inactivity was draining what little remained of their prouder mood, that spirit possessed by an advancing army. Hostile subject populations also contributed to our woes. While the brigand, Hannibal, had been captured and publicly hanged, it had not served as a sufficiently forceful example. The dread which the peasants had felt when the Czar was personally on hand to punish them now dissolved into bitter hatred. This seemed to manifest itself into a compelling desire for revenge. Any man who wandered away from his fellows and was caught alone by the rebels was doomed. Frequently, the Russian victims were subjected to punishments more severe than Ivan, himself, had meted out. Men were suspended from trees by their wrists or ankles, and scourged with wire whips until they died. Others were stripped and beaten, left bleeding and naked in the woods to freeze or to become helpless prey for the roaming packs of wolves.

By spring, the insurgent bands of brigands had become so bold it was necessary to mount double and triple guards at night, even in our larger encampments. Smaller garrisons were in constant danger. Much of this bravado stemmed from the persistent rumors of King Stephen's growing strength. During our campaigns of the previous year he had been too weak and too involved with the internal problems of Poland to come to Livonia's aid. Now, his forces were said to rival ours.

Extensive political maneuverings were underway, both in Krakow and in the Kremlin. At first, I was not able to obtain much information regarding these negotiations, and knew only that Stephen had somehow retained the Swedes as his allies. What promises he had made them, I could only guess. But in Moscow, ambassadors from both Denmark and Austria arrived, having traveled through the heaviest storms of winter. I was pleased to receive this much news in several letters from Boris Godunof, who also assured me of my family's welfare, while describing some of the politics within the Kremlin.

At Boris's urging, the Czar proposed an alliance with Rudolf of Austria, recently crowned Holy Roman Emperor. Together, they would crush Poland, Hungary, and Lithuania. Talks had been in progress for several months, and the Czar was greatly enthused. In the end they came to naught, however, because of Rudolf's greed. Hungary was not enough for him; he wanted most of Poland as well. And because Ivan awaited the expected agreement with Austria we missed our chance to join with Denmark. With their help we could easily have driven the Swedes from Livonia, and from our own northwest territories. By spring it was too late.

King Stephen had not been idle in sending his share of messages and envoys to Moscow. He beguiled the Czar with a continuous stream of friendly, conciliatory letters, assuring him that Poland desired only peace. He proposed a new truce to last for three full years, and in doing this he was as wily as any Slav. I knew he had agents in contact with Magnus.

At this time I was encamped at Duneberg, with a full staff and a large garrison of about ten thousand men – mostly *Streltsi* and peasant volunteers. Magnus was with his German army some hundred miles northwest of me. At this distance it was difficult to keep close watch on him, and it took my spies several days to get a report into my hands. Still, I had a good idea what was going on. King Stephen had spared no expense to flatter Magnus, and had made him all sorts of wild promises. I wrote of this to Ivan, but I received no reply. While I still hoped to hear from the Czar, I sent a second, more urgent report to Boris Godunof. For once, Boris was remiss. Instead of goading the Czar into taking action, or persuading him to authorize my seizing the Dane as I had suggested, Boris wrote asking for more detailed information. Ivan's only comment was to forbid my taking any action without his prior approval.

Before my reply to this could possibly have reached the Kremlin, Magnus signed a treaty with Poland and escaped across our lines. Too late for any action regarding Magnus, I felt it imperative to confer with Simon. He commanded our entire sector, and personally headed the forces in Wenden. Accordingly, I left my second in charge and departed with a strong escort for this city of painful memory. Before I arrived at my destination, the supporters of Magnus went into action. Our garrisons, spread widely apart in all the major towns and villages, became the targets for heavy raids by local brigands.

No sooner had I arrived in Wenden, than we learned of our having lost two small settlements south of Riga. Then the Germans sent a dozen barrels of heady wine as gift to my stupid subordinates in Duneberg. Instead of realizing it must be a ploy, they drank themselves into a state of helplessness. Then the local peasants, enforced by a squadron of Magnus's soldiers, fell upon them, destroying nearly half the garrison. The rest fled in disorder, leaving the post in enemy hands.

Only a few days after this, John Mstislavsky, in command of our army at Dorpat, sent an urgent message. He was under siege by a Swedish army. Simon and I set out to relieve him. In Wenden, we left a strong, well entrenched force behind the city walls. Even so, the city fell before we reached Dorpat, which seemed a signal for the Polish army to begin its move.

CHAPTER XV

It had been a truly terrible year! Worse for me, because I was granted only one short respite to visit Moscow – this being in June or July. I cannot remember exactly, for one month faded into the next very quickly. All along our crumbling front, everywhere, the Pollacks pushed us back. They took so much territory they threatened to enter the very heartland of Russia, territories Ivan had inherited from his father. Frantically, Simon and I dispatched message after message to the Kremlin beseeching the Czar to come and show himself to his troops, to lead his armies in person. Only his presence could inspire the men to the effort we needed to win. Grudgingly, Ivan came to Novgorod, sending his new favorite, Daniel Nogtief, to command the northern sector.

Finally, the men seemed to take heart once more, and we halted the Polish advance outside Polotsk. I commanded the region, with my headquarters in the fortress of Sokol. For the moment, we seemed to have recovered our balance – and rightly so. Our army outnumbered the Pollacks by two, sometimes three to one, and I was already formulating plans to start a fresh advance. I would strike toward Vilna, perhaps even march on Warsaw. Such an offensive would at least have gained us a truce and prevented the loss of any additional territory. The Polish Diet had been squeamish from the first, and I suspected that if Batory began to lose they would force him to desist. But my plans were destined to melt like so much snow in the warmth of spring. Without explanation or warning, the Czar returned to Moscow.

Again, the spirit seemed to desert our troops. The Polish forces continued to besiege us, holding a line to the south and east of Polotsk, engaging us in a continuous series of short, bitter exchanges. The cold weather set in early and continued to grow worse, until there seemed hardly a breathing space between the violent storms. By November, the snow was deeper than the height of a man and we should have gone into winter quarters. But King Stephen was resolved to take the city.

Eventually, I had to admit to myself that I was getting too old for the kind of fighting I was being called upon to do. The King was a masterful commander and despite his troubles with the nobility of his own country he always seemed able to take the field with enough troops to give us a desperate battle. Our Russian losses had been so heavy over the past two years that my own troops were either inexperienced youngsters, else regiments from the Southern steppes – Cossacks and other barbarians. I could not complain of their abilities as fighting men, but they demanded a commander who would personally conduct them into the fray. My Russian troops would turn and run if they did not see me there. The Cossacks would simply not follow a general who did not lead them in person. As a result, my body was a mass of small wounds, bruises and lumps where I had been struck, or where my armor had rubbed me raw. It was difficult even to remember the joy I once felt at the prospect of battle.

On a particularly cold day in late November the fighting had not ended at sundown, but had continued well into the night. When both armies had finally flopped exhausted behind their own lines, cannon on either side continued to belch forth the terrible fires of death. The constant roar made sleep impossible, unless one were so dead tired he could ignore the noise. I was alone in my quarters, nursing my aches and pains, coughing badly from a cold in my chest. Lately, I found that I choked up if I stayed near the cannon for any length of time. I supposed it was caused by irritating bits within the smoke and debris. This night, I was very lonely. I had few enough friends left alive, and none of them were on campaign with me except for Toby. Simon commanded to the north, between my forces and those of Nogtief. Mstislavsky was with the Czar in Moscow, as were Boris and the members of my household. Everyone else I loved was dead. It was hard to realize.

Being in command meant that everyone was either afraid of me or wary lest he be accused of currying favor by associating too closely. Nor was I in any condition to attract men to me. I had become very stern, and I maintained as rigid a discipline among my troops as Kurbsky ever had. To achieve this I made harsh demands, sometimes out of hand. I gave orders – cruel orders – things I would have hesitated to contemplate a few years before. Certain infractions meant flogging; others brought death. There were no exceptions. Yet, since I instituted these rules, there had been fewer instances to require their being put into practice. It was their very existence, though, and the knowledge that I would enforce my edicts, which caused the junior officers to remain aloof from me.

On this night, loneliness compelled me to seek the company of others, so I dined in the officers' pavilion with my staff. I drank heavily, but it only increased my fatigue until I returned to my room, too tired to think of anything but sleep. I shoved the door open, chucking my helmet and breastplate as I entered. Toby followed me in and started to unbuckle the rest of my trappings. Then Illya wriggled up from his pile of blankets.

"Sleeping again?" I asked.

"Yes sir," he admitted guiltily. He staggered to his feet and went to my cot returning with a tightly tied lump of cloth.

I took it from him and turned it several times in my hand. He stood watching me, saying nothing. "Well, what is it?" I demanded sharply.

"I don't know, sir. It was sent to you by the guest, Jacob."

"Jacob?" I exclaimed. "Where is he now?"

"He awaits you in town. *The Sign of the Golden Hart*," the man told me.

I groaned, but I knew I must go. Jacob would not have come unless it were important, and the fact of his awaiting me in town instead of coming to my quarters indicated some need for secrecy. He had probably risked his life in getting to me. The lands about us were full of roving bands of thieves and peasant insurgents. Without my telling him, Toby began to lay out a heavy robe. He held up the mail shirt I had taken off earlier, and looked at me questioningly.

It took a moment to decide. "No," I said at length. "If an assassin seeks me tonight, I don't think I really care."

My fingers plucked at the cloth package. I could feel something hard inside, like a piece of jewelry, and I already suspected what it contained. Finally, I took the point of my dagger and cut the material. It was the broach Ivan had given me as a wedding gift for my wife. In the back of the piece, folded tightly and pressed into the recess behind the stones was a tiny scrap of paper. I unfolded it carefully and had to hold it close to the light to make out the letters: "In the name of God, come at once. Nina."

I was on my horse and out of camp within the time it took me to call the groom. Toby followed some distance behind, still wearing his battle gear, trying to reset the straps as he rode. I found the tavern without any trouble, scattering farmers and townspeople as I galloped through the slushy streets. I reined up in a flurry of mud, straw, and dirty snow. The whole town stank, even in the cold of winter. Nothing could obliterate the stench of foul hay, and the offal from pigs and peasants. By the time I dismounted, Toby was beside me. I tossed the reins to him and strode briskly inside. The room was half filled with local men, all of whom stopped talking and turned to watch me. I did not see Jacob, and walked to the serving bar where an old man was busily carving a joint of meat.

"The traveler from the east?" I demanded. "Where is he?"

The man was surly, or perhaps just stupid. He stared at me without answering. "Did you hear me, old man?" I asked sharply.

He replied in some farmers' dialect I did not understand and went back to cutting the meat. Without another word I drew my sword; swinging it with one hand I brought it down with great force against the joint, slicing it neatly in two. Everyone was still watching me, and my act brought a murmur from the others. The old man simply stepped back and continued to stare.

"Your friend is upstairs," said one of the men behind me.

I turned, feeling the waves of hatred and resentment. Toby stood in the doorway at the far side, fingering the hilt of his own weapon. "Keep an eye on them," I called in English, and took the stairs two at a time. Jacob's door stood open, as he lay half asleep on the narrow, grimy bed. He seemed wary, even in repose, resting with his shoulders against the frame. He jumped up when I came in, a pistol appearing suddenly in his hand. As he recognized me, his face relaxed and the flesh fell into lines of sallow exhaustion. He looked totally depleted, and I guessed he must have traveled the distance from Moscow in utmost haste.

I tried to make my voice sound normal as we greeted each other, but Jacob shrugged off the customary pleasantries and drew me into a corner, where a flask of wine stood on a table. "I brought this from Novgorod," he said. "Thought you might enjoy it. That swill downstairs isn't fit for pigs."

"Is Nina in trouble?" I asked.

"I don't know what may have happened since I left," he replied carefully, "but I don't think it was quite as bad as she may have made it sound."

"What is that supposed to mean?" I snapped.

He swallowed hard, as if afraid to answer me. "It is difficult for me to explain –" he murmured. He stared at his feet and fidgeted nervously.

"Well, you've damned well come a long way to tell me," I reminded him. "What kind of trouble is she in?"

"The Czar –" he began. "The Czar is – not the way you may remember him." He watched me carefully, fearful that I would react angrily at his implied criticism.

"Would it help you to speak openly," I asked softly, "if I tell you I believe the Czar . . . possessed?"

He cleared his throat and nodded. "Well, the Czar has been acting – strangely. Last month he canceled our agreement to carry his goods in our caravans. Now he has posted guards about your house in the Kremlin. I don't like to suggest this," he continued, "but both your wife and I feel the Czar may – desire her."

"That was settled ages ago!" I said in surprise. "I can't imagine he is rekindling the old interest."

"Your wife was reticent to explain everything to me, as you may understand," he replied, "and I do not know all the people who are your friends. But it seems that during the time when the Czar was not the Czar, he came frequently to your house. During this period he became acquainted with your wife?"

"That's right," I nodded.

"And your wife still lives in that same house, the one that used to belong to Simon of Tver."

"Of course she lives there!" I replied impatiently. "You know that!"

"I wanted to make sure you understand she has not departed, or been taken away. But there are men about the house at all hours, and she is followed whenever she leaves. These are the Czar's men as best I have been able to ascertain. She feels there would be no reason for this, except that which I have suggested. It has happened this way with other men's wives."

"I know," I said quietly. "I know the rest. How many days did it take you to find me?"

"Twelve," he replied.

"Can you leave tonight?" I asked.

"If you need me," he said. He seemed surprised I should ask.

I stopped to think a moment. In a fight, or any contest of strength, he would be of little value. But if it should come to flight, he would be invaluable. I told him to rest a day, and then go to Novgorod. He was to remain there, pending my further orders.

"I will send men to guard you," I told him. "You must not expose yourself to further danger." I turned to go downstairs, so concerned with my own thoughts and problems I almost neglected to express my gratitude for his faithfulness. At the last moment, I paused by the door. "You know I am most grateful to you, my friend," I said sincerely.

He nodded and I continued down. Toby had gone into the public room while I was with Jacob. He stood at the counter, drinking a tankard of local beer. A menacing group of men had crowded around him, asking sarcastic questions and poking fun at him because he was a foreigner.

I slammed my fist on the board, causing mugs and dishes to jump from the impact. "If I must draw sword again," I said in a very loud voice, "it will be heads it severs!"

Most of them pulled back, but a few still hovered, glowering at me. I added a few comments about leveling the tavern if they displeased me further. After this, they all moved back from me, and I left with the knowledge that Jacob would be safe until I could get a guard back for him. We returned to camp, and I sent Illya for my two junior commanders. They were both on the far side of the compound, still lingering at the officers' mess. But I had counted on its taking a while for them to attend me. Before they arrived I busied myself, establishing an excuse to leave the front without the Czar's permission. If all that Jacob had said was true – and there was no reason to doubt him – I would likely walk into a hornets' nest when I entered the Kremlin. If the Czar should lust after Nina, I would be the last man he wanted to see. I still doubted this as the real cause, but his act of placing men about my house could only mean trouble. It would be a treasonous offense for me to leave without some sort of excuse.

Quickly, I pulled out some letters from my chest, including several from the Czar's secretariat. These were usually sent in scrolls, written on good quality parchment. The material for them was purchased by the secretary in large rolls, then cut to proper length after the message had been inscribed. If the letter was to travel a great distance, the clerks usually left an extra portion at the upper end to serve as additional wrapping and protection for the text. I found one of these and, imitating the handwriting of the Czar's secretary, I wrote a short message. The secretary was informing me that the Czar was very ill. It ordered my return to Moscow at once and in all secrecy. I signed it with the secretary's name. The scroll already bore the proper seals at the upper end, so I severed the wax remaining from the other half and sliced off the old message with my knife.

My hands trembled as I hurriedly unrolled the rest of the unwanted paper, pulling it loose from the center roller and stuffing it into the fire. Fumbling badly, I worked the end of my new message into the slit in the center roller just as I heard my deputies arriving outside. Toby detained them for an extra few moments, long enough for me to heat my knife blade and to apply it against the rest of the broken seal I had taken from the old message. I set this onto the proper spot on my forgery, and was then ready to receive them. I composed my face into a mask of tragic gloom, and speaking softly I gave them the unhappy tidings. I also cautioned them, under penalty of death, not to let anyone know.

I showed them the message then, and I could tell they were not the least suspicious. Despite his display of concern for the Czar, I could see the greedy reaction of Dmitri Shuisky, the younger of my two officers. His mind was already considering the possibilities of his own advancement now that I must leave them. He was by far the most able commander, and the workings of his mind were apparent in the subtle play of facial muscles. He waited anxiously for me to appoint my temporary successor.

I knew it should have been he, but I had never liked him. I did not think it would matter much which man commanded, as they would soon have to retreat inside the walls of Polotsk, driven there by the weather if not by Batory's army. From within that fortified position and with the snow too deep for the enemy to maneuver, the defense should have been simple enough to maintain. A relieving force was due to arrive at any time, after which the commander of that army would take over.

My second man, Alexi, was also competent and the troops liked him better. They would follow him to the death. Looking at them sternly, I went through a short tirade, telling them both how poorly they had done, and demanding a better showing while I was gone. When I named my replacement, they were both too shaken to argue. I was certain I had frightened Dmitri enough that he would obey Alexi's commands.

When they had left, I shoved the forged letter inside my robe. It was important I not forget to keep it with me. I would travel lightly, taking no more than I needed. Hurriedly, I pulled out the papers I wanted and left them on the bed. The rest of the packing, the actual stuffing of material into saddlebags, I left to Toby and Illya. There would be the two of them, plus our groom, traveling with me. At the last moment I decided it would be best to take a small guard, as well. I called my scribe and had him take the chest with the rest of my papers to Alexi; he was to request a dozen man escort at the same time, as well as the guard for Jacob.

Before midnight I was on my way. As an afterthought, I had given the forged scroll to Toby, telling him to carry it so it would be scuffed and damaged during the trip. I hoped to make it more difficult for anyone to ascertain how it came to be sent. We did not pause in our travel for any reason, except to rest at night, and once to take shelter during a severe storm. By using the Czar's post horses we reached Moscow in thirteen days, entering the gates in the very early, predawn hours.

I went directly to the Kremlin, and by the fawning respect I received from the guards I knew Nina was still all right. Had the Czar made any overt moves against my family, I would have received some indication of insolence or derision. I sent Illya to the palace to inform the Czar's secretary I had come, and to inquire after Ivan's health. Then I went directly home.

It took a long while to bring a servant to the door, and when one did come the fellow seemed terrified as he looked through the peephole. I am sure everyone must have thought that the Czar had come for his prize. When I finally convinced him who I was, despite my disheveled appearance, the door was opened and Nina ran to me in her nightclothes.

Playing the role I must continue to assume, I greeted her saying: "Is the Czar still alive?"

She looked at me as if I were insane, but I began speaking to her in English and explained as we went upstairs. I am sure any agent of the Czar – and there was surely more than one working in my household – would have thought we spoke only of our concern for Ivan's health.

From Nina's account, her situation seemed unchanged from the time of Jacob's departure, and this was almost frightening. If it were Ivan's desire to posses my wife, he would certainly have acted before now. He was never one to delay the yearnings of his loins for such a length of time.

"I have somehow fallen into disfavor," I told her. "There can be no other explanation. Perhaps because of Heinrich. I don't know. I have not received a letter from Boris in months. Has he been in touch with you?"

Nina shook her head. "We have been like an island," she said. "Other than the English, no one has dared visit us. Everyone knows the Czar's men are outside and no one can be sure what he intends. I tried to find out through Thomas Randolf, but they wouldn't tell him anything."

"I'm going to the palace as soon as I clean up," I said.

She looked at me with fear evident in her expression. "Will you be safe?"

"Until I make my move none of us is safe," I told her. "But I came back because the Czar was supposed to be ill. I must act as if I believed this, and be surprised when they tell me I was not sent for. After this, we shall see."

I had spoken lightly, almost casually, as if I were confident my deception was going to succeed. But I knew my family's future depended on my actions during the next few hours. I had decided to place the welfare of my wife and children above everything else, even above my duty to the Czar. If that be sin, God would have to punish me. If I could delay any move against me for a few days I would have my loved ones beyond Ivan's reach. How long they would remain so, however, would depend on many circumstances.

It was still a difficult move I was about to make, and I knew how heavily the guilt would lay upon me later. I thought of all the unkind things I had said about Andrew Kurbsky. Now I was in the act of preparing to follow his example. Yet Andrew had been unable to save his family. His wife, his brother Roman, all his kin and all their households had fallen victim to Ivan's vengeance. If I were to escape with my wife and children I would be one of the first men of rank to do it. But the others had always waited too long, I thought. I hoped not to make that mistake. What this would mean when I stood for my final judgment I could not stop to consider. How the high sounding arguments I had used to convince myself and others of the righteousness of my past activities could stand, confronted with the fact of my ultimate desertion, I did not care to think about.

I looked at Nina, sitting demurely on the bed, looking so tiny and defenseless. I felt a surge of love and passion – inconvenient as the moment was for that. But I knew her life was more important than mine, more important than my soul's journey after death. Perhaps this very love would weigh somewhere on the Lord's scales of justice.

After a while I went into the bathing room, where Lilly had already prepared a tub of water.

I gave Nina very specific instructions, then called Toby and outlined what I wanted him to do. I had my best mount saddled and rode the short distance to the palace. I wore the full insignia of my rank, lest there be any who did not know me. This allowed me to stride through the portals without being questioned. I went directly to the secretary's office where, as I'd expected there was only a clerk on duty.

"General Prince Marensky reporting as ordered," I said curtly.

The man looked up, befuddled; but clerks do not argue with generals. "Please have a seat, sir," he said uncertainly. "I will try to find the Secretary for you."

"I have no intention of resting my backside in some clerk's waiting room!" I barked. "I have come to see the Czar before he dies!"

"Dies?" squeaked the man. He looked at me like a trapped mouse, unable to decide whether I was mad or possibly a conspirator in some plot to assassinate the Czar.

"You know full well I was ordered to return in all haste, because the Czar is deathly ill," I said, never breaking my rigid bearing. I was very convincing, I thought, for I had frightened the poor little man to distraction.

"Pl . . . please, s–sir," he stammered. "I . . . I, I don't know anything about it. I – Let me try to find the Secretary, please," he begged.

"Where is my man – Illya, the one I sent ahead to inform the Secretary of my arrival?"

"I, I did not know what to make of him, but I sent him to the Secretary's apartments. He has not returned. Let me go myself. The guard's may not have let your man. . . ."

"You may inform the Secretary he will find me in the Czar's apartments," I interrupted coldly. "I intend to find out for myself what kind of chicanery is going on here!" With that I strode out and clumped off toward Ivan's rooms. I did not look back, but I heard the clerk scurry off in the other direction, beginning a desperate search for his master. I bullied my way through several guard points, being questioned at only one. At the anteroom I encountered the Chamberlain who had been with Ivan and was on his way out. "Prince Dmitri!" he gasped in surprise. "What. . . ?"

"How is the Czar?" I whispered.

"The Czar is fine, a little irritable, but otherwise. . . . What do you mean, 'How is the Czar?' Is something supposed to be wrong with him?"

"I was ordered to return because he was ill," I said evenly. "I expected to find him on his death bed." I watched the Chamberlain, my brow wrinkled in perplexity.

"Wait here a moment," he said. "I shall find out what happened." He turned back into Ivan's chambers, and I knew my time of confrontation was very near. My palms suddenly began to sweat and I felt an icy finger along the back of my neck. It took but a short while for the Chamberlain to return, by which time the Czar's Secretary had come up behind me. He puffed an apology for not being on hand to receive me, indicating that Illya had not found him until a moment before the clerk to whom I had spoken. In the same breath he also tried to express his surprise at my return.

Ignoring him, and not waiting for anyone's permission, I entered Ivan's rooms, purposely closing the door behind me before any of the others could follow. The Czar said nothing for several seconds, and his face remained completely expressionless as if incapable of surprise or recognition. His buttocks pressed hard against the edge of a large writing table. Obviously half stupefied by drink, he might well have fallen without the extra support. Gradually, a crafty smile crept onto his lips, until he was facing me with an expression which seemed to reflect a combination of surprise and suspicion, anger merged in concern. His body had become a heavy mass of fat, bulging in fleshy rolls unhidden by the fine drape of his brocaded robe. His face was sallow, almost ochre in hue, and his beard was completely gone. Only the barest few wisps of stubble remained. His eyes were sunken and red, ringed about with purple. When he finally opened his mouth to speak, a heavy foam coated his lips and his toothless gums.

"Dmitri, you treacherous cur!" he bellowed, weaving drunkenly against the table, "What are you doing here without my permission?"

"Thank God you're alive and well!" I exclaimed. "Your Secretary wrote . . . ."

"My Secretary wrote nothing!" he roared.

I pulled the scroll from my waistband and held it out to him. He snatched it away and, swaying from side to side, he held it almost against his nose to read. I could see his lips move, as his eyes strained to scan the lines. At length he dropped the document on his table and leered at me. Suspicion was plain on his face.

"Would even you conspire against me?" he asked. His terrible eyes traveled the front of my body, but his gaze was dull. I realized he could not see me clearly. His left eyelid drooped as it always had in time of stress. He looked at the floor and his mountainous body shuddered as he was suddenly convulsed with weeping.

I approached him cautiously and placed my hand on his arm, half expecting he would strike me away. Instead, he let me lead him to a chair, where he dropped listlessly onto the cushions. "I am accursed forever," he moaned. "Every night, I hear the voices of dead men wailing for me to join them." He gripped his head, moaning, rocking back and forth.

Then, as suddenly as the spasms of weeping had begun, they were gone. Ivan sat looking up at me, blinking, as if to free his eyes of tears. "What are you doing here?" he asked. I might just have walked into the room, to judge by his tone. "You are supposed to be commanding my armies in the south! Have you been defeated?" He leaped to his feet, grabbing my arms; terror spread across his face. "Are the Tartars pursuing you? Are they right on your heels?"

"No. No, my command was in the west," I reminded him. "But the letter . . . ." I paused. "That damnable Secretary of yours!" I shouted. "What does he mean, ordering me back here when there's nothing wrong with you?"

Ivan started to speak, but he was surprised by my sudden display of anger. He hesitated and I continued. "His stupidity could have cost us the entire campaign! It's fortunate I had good seconds to leave in charge."

Fate played into my hands at this point, for the door behind him opened and a young woman came in. I did not know her, though I soon realized she was Vanya's wife. She had entered unannounced from the *terem* passage, and I expected Ivan would chastise her for exposing herself to me. But apparently I was close enough, still, to be accounted family. Ivan permitted the girl to come up beside him – quite an attractive, dark–complexioned creature with gleaming brown hair and gray–green eyes. She whispered something into the Czar's ear, and a smile spread across his lips as he listened.

Abruptly, Ivan grabbed his daughter–in–law about the waist in a most familiar manner. He pulled her down against him as he sat back in his chair, pressing her backside tightly into his crotch. I supposed the stories I had heard from time to time must have been true for she made no protest and seemed to accept these attentions as commonplace. It had been whispered that the Czar and his son had shared their respective brides for years, and while I had known this, the sight was still disconcerting.

I heard the door open behind me and I turned to face Boris, who had entered without any other invitation. He left the door ajar and I could see several people outside, the Secretary and a few others. Boris seemed unchanged, except he might have been a little heavier. His dark beard was untinged with gray, and his deep brown eyes seemed to examine me appraisingly.

Still holding the girl against him, Ivan reached back with his free hand to pick up a flagon of spirits – vodka, I thought. I spoke a few words to Boris, who was also surprised that I had returned. It was apparently my presence which had brought him into the Czar's apartments. That he should have entered without permission spoke well for the favor he enjoyed. We spoke the usual greetings between ourselves, as Ivan continued to fondle the girl, chuckling and smacking his lips between massive gulps of liquor.

"The court is leaving for Alexandrov this afternoon," said Boris casually. "Has the Czar asked you to come with us?"

I looked at Ivan, who stared blankly at us both.

"We have been trying to ascertain who sent this to me," I replied to his questioning expression. I picked up the scroll and handed it to Boris.

He barely glanced at it before placing it back on the table, then made a depreciating gesture with his hands. "See me before you leave the palace," he muttered. He turned toward the Czar, smiling broadly and speaking in a loud, pleasant voice. "Is His Imperial Majesty ready to begin the trip?"

Ivan grunted, shoving the girl away. He nodded agreement. "My servants should have everything loaded by now," he said. "What about him?" he added, looking in my direction.

"Why not ask Dmitri to accompany us?" Boris suggested again. This time the Czar seemed to hear him and agreed. A moment later I was outside with my friend.

"I hope you know what you're doing," said Boris, as soon as we were alone. We had walked down the hall from the Czar's apartments and stepped into an unused suite of rooms. "That message is obviously forged, and I suspect you know it."

Deciding to put my full trust in him, I replied, "Of course I know it. I forged it myself."

"But why?"

"Why are the Czar's men surrounding my house?" I asked.

He seemed puzzled. "There are no men on guard about. . . ."

"Boris, I am being honest with you. I am placing my life in your hands. Why am I suspected?" I insisted. "Or is it Nina?"

He sighed. "No, it isn't your wife. But when your stepfather betrayed the Czar it damaged your position with him. Lately, he goes through moods of fear and suspicion. That is why the guards were placed – one day in a moment of despair. I doubt he's even thought about it since, but the order was never rescinded." Boris paused, shook his head sadly and shrugged. "The reason we are going to Alexandrov," he continued softly, "is because the Czar feels safer there."

"You do not think my family is in any danger, then?" I asked.

"I shall be honest with you, my friend, as you ask me to be. The Czar's moods have become completely unpredictable. Yes, I would say both you and your family are in danger. There were moments when Simon was Czar and Ivan visited your home that he actually confused your wife with Anastasia. Who is to say the thought will not suddenly strike him again? I have done all I could to prevent his harming you or your household, and I have done this because we have always been friends. But he may act sometime when I am not around to dissuade him." Again he hesitated, gazing deeply into my eyes with a sad, almost pained expression. "I will not deny my own perfidy," he whispered. "I did seek to usurp your position with the Czar and to garner his affection for myself. But, I never wished to see you destroyed."

I ignored his unspoken plea for forgiveness. "Will you help me?" I asked coldly.

Boris nodded, his face averted like a child being chastised for his misbehavior. "I will order the guards removed from your house. What more do you want of me?"

"If I and my family were no longer in Moscow, no longer in Russia, I could never again compete with you," I suggested gently.

"You wish to escape, and you ask for my help?" He looked me in the eye again, staring as if I had shocked him.

"I ask only for your silence, and that you do not seek to learn more than I shall tell you," I assured him.

His accustomed mask slipped completely, then, and he glanced behind us to make sure no one was listening in the hallway. "You know the Czar is completely mad, do you not? If you are caught in this wild venture, you will receive no mercy." He spoke in tones of concern, and I believed he was truly afraid for me.

"That is a risk I must take," I replied.

"Then to this extent I will help you," he said firmly.

"I shall not ask for more," I promised, thinking as I spoke the words that this was almost exactly the conversation I had held with Vladya on that night so many years ago when he had come to beg my help in concealing Euphrosyne's crime.

I hurried back to my house and ordered Toby to get together the clothes I would need in Alexandrov. The court's departure came as a fortunate happenstance, for it would allow my family time to leave without the Czar being in the city where he might issue orders to stop them. I let it be known among the servants that I was sending the household to my estate in Dorogobuzh, these being the farms I had received as part of my first wife's dowry. I had no idea what condition the house was in as I had badly neglected the estate for all the time I had owned it. But it made no difference, for the family would never go near them. Toby would be in charge, and was to guide them to Novgorod. I planned to join them there.

It was necessary to procure three large sleighs to hold the entire group. I would have preferred sending only Nina, the children, Toby and his wife. However, it would seem strange if they did not leave with the usual, proper attendants. Therefore, the group must include the Tartar girls, as well as Serge, for he always attended Nina on her travels. Fortunately, Anne Richards had found favor in the eyes of an officer in the English company, and had left our household. Four women and a little girl were enough to worry about. I had Nina use the chest Ivan had given me for my trip to England, and in the secret bottom compartment I hid what valuables I could scrape together without attracting undue attention.

All this was done in the space of less than an hour. I would take Illya to Alexandrov with me, although I would have preferred leaving this additional pair of arms to safeguard my wife. But my own sons were now large enough to offer some protection and I had half a dozen German retainers left to escort them as well. Though getting on in years, these old servants of Heinrich's were still fearsome opponents. I told Toby to wait only an hour after I had left with the Czar. I gambled on Boris being able to intercept the report that was sure to come from Ivan's spies, thus giving my family the maximum time for their difficult trip to Novgorod. Nina wept when I departed, expressing her fears that we would never see each other again. I struggled to maintain my composure, assuring her it was going to be well.

She stood in the doorway when I left, one son on either side, Christiana standing in front of her. Toby held the heads of my team as I mounted the *troika* and took my place beside Illya. "We'll meet again in Novgorod," he whispered.

"With God's blessing," I replied.

I nudged Illya and we were off, gliding smoothly across the icy cover. I glanced upward at the clear, blue sky, praying within my soul that the weather was going to hold. A heavy storm could ruin my timing and result in disaster.

The Czar's party was just loading into their sleighs outside the palace as we came up. A chamberlain waved us into our position, about the middle of the column. Not too many months ago, I thought, I would have been in the second sleigh, if not in the first with Ivan. The trip was mercifully fast, but cold. My fur hat and *shuba* were not enough, for the chill did not come only from outside. Every few minutes I found myself calculating the spot my family would be passing along the Novgorod highway.

Nor did my anxiety decrease at Alexandrov. The Czar was as morose as before leaving Moscow. The change seemed to have done him no good. He went from moods of racking laughter to fits of violent weeping, all in the space of a few moments. Several times a day he cried out to answer the voices of those he had killed and whom he was convinced were coming back to haunt him. Night held a special terror, when the howling of the wind never failed to make him tremble. Boris told me in confidence how the Czar had drawn up a list of the men he had executed and had sent money to several monasteries, assuring eternal prayers for their souls.

We had been in Alexandrov four days when Boris called me aside. For the first time in our acquaintance he seemed so tense and his face was set in such anxious lines I imagined I could ascertain his Tartar blood . . . *descent from Mirza Chet,* I thought to myself. "The guards reported your family's departure two days ago," he said. "I can keep it from the Czar a little longer, but there are others who know and he is going to find out."

"They were sent to Dorogobuzh," I told him. "I have property there."

He smiled grimly. "A healthier climate than the capital?"

I nodded, returning his smile.

"You can delude yourself, Dmitri," he told me, "but that story is not going to satisfy the Czar." I realized the moment for my own break had come, and if I intended to do it there was no time for further delay. I made plans to slip away the next evening and alerted Illya to have our equipment in order. We would also want provisions, because I did not intend to stop in Moscow.

It was still morning on the same day I had spoken with Boris, and I went to Ivan's apartment as usual. For the moment my status had improved to a point where the Czar expected me each day along with Boris and his two sons. I arrived ahead of the others and found Ivan with his arm about his daughter–in–law in much the same situation as when I had first observed her in Moscow.

Neither of them seemed the least embarrassed that I should intrude upon their moment of intimacy, and this time neither had been drinking very heavily. I was bothered by this total lack of moral restraint, and I suppose some of these feelings showed on my face. Rather than responding as I would have wished, the Czar seemed to enjoy my discomfort and whatever distress he could provoke me into showing. He deliberately stroked the girl's body, running his fingertips across her bodice, patting her belly in slow, sensuous motions.

"Lovely thing, isn't she?" he gloated. "She has the figure of a full, ripe pear."

He poked his hand inside her blouse and fondled one breast through the tight lacings of her underclothes. The girl giggled and was being coquettish. She had surely been brought up to behave properly, I thought, but she did nothing to restrain the improprieties of her husband and father–in–law – no single word of protest, though I did seem to note the trace of a blush on her cheeks.

Ivan continued to enumerate her charms, describing things no man should ever tell of his own wife, much less his son's. His hands alternated between the girl's belly, breasts, and thighs until, suddenly, to illustrate some point he was trying to make, Ivan leaned forward and grabbed the bottom of her skirts.

"She has lovely plump legs, too," he said, dribbling foam from his mouth onto her shoulder as he stretched to pull up her dress. She shrieked with laughter, and I wanted to turn away. I was humiliated and my face burned with shame, as I am sure Ivan intended it should. He was playing with me as much as with her, enjoying this form of torment. But this was no tavern girl, no peasant. She was supposedly going to be the next Czarina of Russia. I was looking at the floor, trying to spare her my stare when the Czar emitted an unexpected howl of rage.

"Two petticoats!" he bellowed. "How dare you enter my presence wearing only two petticoats!"

The girl pulled away from him, and at first I though he had been playing with her. He had not. His jovial mood had shattered in that single instant, leaving the visage of a rampaging beast in its place. Picking up a heavy scroll roller from his table, Ivan began beating the girl about her head and shoulders, screaming in rage and indignation. In terror, she bolted back through the *terem* door and into the hall beyond. The Czar followed right behind her, although his corpulence prevented his moving as quickly as she. Blind with fear, and screaming at the top of her lungs, she raced down the hall, tripping on a carpet at the far end and falling in a heap against the wall. Ivan continued to bear down on her, until the Czarevitch bolted out from a side door and blocked his way.

"What do you think you're doing?" shouted Vanya at his father.

"I am going to chastise that whore you call a wife!" returned the Czar.

Vanya shoved him backward, making him strike the wall with a hard, resounding "Crack!"

"You're not going to touch her!" he roared, sounding for all the world like his father. "She is three months with child. You ruined my first marriage and you're not going to do it again."

Their argument was awesome! Raging like two wild animals, they screamed and shouted at one another, waving their arms and bellowing the vilest names I had ever heard used between them. Boris, who had entered as I stood watching down the *terem* corridor, stepped past me and quietly shut the door.

"They will argue themselves out," he said calmly.

"Does this happen often?" I asked.

"They have frequent disagreements," he replied, "but their devotion is no less for it."

We had both sat down to await the Czar's return, when the *terem* door burst open, crashing back against the wall. The Czar strode into the room first, still choking with fury. Vanya, just as angry, followed right behind him. They were both still shouting as Ivan approached his writing table and turned to face his son. Abruptly, the Czar reached behind him and seized his *kisten*. He began to scream in ever–mounting rage, waving the stick in the air, then pounding its point against the floor.

Seeing me, he broke off his tirade against the Czarevitch and shouted in my direction. "And you, you bastard, you deserter! Did you know we lost Polotsk because of you? It fell less than a week after you quit your post!"

"If you weren't so stupid and fat and lazy," shouted the Czarevitch at his father, "and led your armies like a proper Czar, these things wouldn't happen!"

"Ingrate!" screamed Ivan.

"Then why don't you let me lead your armies? he shouted back. "If you're afraid, let me do it."

I was forgotten again, as they went back to screeching at one another. I was more embarrassed at having to hear this than I had been over Ivan's earlier behavior with the girl. I was also deeply distressed, already ashamed of the act of treachery I was about to commit. I had looked away from them when Boris suddenly shouted and I glanced up into a blur of motion, struggling bodies and a veritable explosion of red. Blood! In his fury, the Czar had struck his son in the chest and he now delivered several more blows with the point of that terrible *kisten*! Vanya was already on the floor, lying very still, his face against the carpet.

Boris grabbed the Czar from behind, while I snatched the stick from his hands. It took another moment or two for Ivan to realize what he had done. The room was completely silent, except for the harsh labored gasps from the Czarevitch. Then, with an agonized roar, Ivan threw himself upon his son. "Vanya!" he screamed. "Vanya! Oh God, Oh . . . oh, God, I've killed you! No, no! God, give him back! Give him back!"

I sent a servant running for a doctor, and tried to pull the Czar off his son's body. The Czarevitch seemed still alive, and I was shouting in Ivan's ear, trying to make him hear me over his own sounds of grief. But the Czar was deaf to anything outside himself and the still, prone figure on the floor. When the doctor finally arrived, all of us were slippery with blood, trying to keep the Czar from crushing what life remained in Vanya's breast. A good dozen people milled about the room, several women screaming and sobbing, guards and court officials – I do not remember who half of them were. Finally, I was able to get two guardsmen to help restrain the Czar long enough for the doctor to start working on his son.

The Czarevitch was still breathing when the doctor eased him over, onto his back. We could hear his rasping intake of breath, but a thick trickle of blood kept oozing from his mouth with every gasp. There was not a finger's width of his chest not covered with red, and one huge puncture in his chest seemed to churn with each faltering beat of his heart.

Ivan continued to howl, making sounds such as I had once heard from a mortally wounded wolf. These eventually became deep, guttural groans. His eyes were wide, staring at nothing as his body heaved and he struggled to draw breath between the sobs that threatened to choke him. Abruptly, he shook free of my grasp and rushed wildly into the outer corridor. There was an unused wing on the upper floor, beyond the royal apartments and connected to them through the *terem*. The Czar rushed into this area, moving blindly along the cold, bare rooms, down the empty, echoing hallways. His bestial cries reverberated against the frigid stones through the deserted, unheated passages.

I started after him, but Boris gripped my arm. "There is nothing you can do for him," he said sternly. "This would be the time for you to leave."

His suggestion horrified me. "I can't run away and leave him, now," I said sharply.

Boris did not relax his grip. "Are you going to sacrifice your wife and sons? You can't help the Czar. Probably no one can help him. The Czarevitch won't last the night, so there's nothing you can do for anyone. When the Czar recovers his wits he may blame you. He just learned of the defeat of Polotsk this morning, and was going to throw it in your face in front of the entire court. The tragedy has spared you that, and probably saved your life. Perhaps it was God's hand; I don't know. But if you want to get yourself and those you love out of Russia, now is the time to do it."

I stared at him thoughtfully for a few moments more. I knew he was right, and yet it seemed I was deserting the Czar in his hour of greatest need. In the end, I followed Boris's advice. Hurrying back to my rooms, I called to Illya that we must leave immediately. Taking what we could carry in our arms, we fled down a back staircase to the stables. My servant had already stored provisions in the *troika*. We hitched the horses ourselves, for the confusion on the upper floor had penetrated to the stable yard. Men stood about in small groups, repeating the unbelievable news: "The Czar just killed his son. *Grozny* has murdered the Czarevitch!"

We traveled without stopping, except to rest the horses or change them at the Czar's post stations. Always, one of us drove while the other tried to sleep. Because we moved ahead of the terrible story, no one suspected that I was other than one of the Czar's commanders, in a hurry to rejoin my unit. The weather was good nearly all the way, with only a light fall of snow the day before we arrived in Novgorod.

It was after dark when we reached the city, and we had to summon the watch to open the gates for us. I went directly to my warehouse in the southern part of town. It was closed and tightly bolted, but I saw a light in the rear, shining dimly through a crack beneath the heavy doors. I hammered until Jacob finally understood who it was and opened. My household was staying with friends of his, he told me, in a farmhouse a few miles west of the city. He did not believe anyone knew who they were.

I explained what had happened at Alexandrov, and Jacob shuddered at the grisly details. We estimated I would have two days at the very most before the news caught up with us. After that, it would be only a matter of time before an order was issued for my arrest as a deserter – or worse. We had to keep ahead of the Czar's couriers. Any of them might bear his warrant, although it was unlikely that the men who carried this would be the same who brought the news of Vanya's death.

Jacob had kept close watch on developments along the battle front. He knew exactly who commanded which sector on either side of the line. I had planned to cross in an area where Simon was in charge, which meant we had to go east, then south again toward Ostrov. This town was our main garrison south of Pskov, and was Simon's last reported position.

"And fortune has smiled upon you again," said Jacob. "Your friend Kurbsky commands the Polish forces advancing on the Velikaya River. The northern hand of his army should engage the southern flank of Simon's any time now, if they are not already joined."

"Have you any means of getting a message across?" I asked.

Jacob grinned, proud and self satisfied. "I took the liberty of sending a message several days ago," he replied. "I have no confirmation that my man got through, but he has crossed the lines many times before. There is no reason to suppose he would fail."

"Then Kurbsky knows I am going to try it," I mused bitterly. "How the idea must amuse him!"

"At least he'll be laughing at a live man, not a gravestone," observed Jacob dryly. "Do you want to leave tonight?"

"I want to write a few contracts first," I said. "I still own a good deal of property, and there is no reason why you shouldn't have it."

"If you ever decide to return," he told me, "it will always be yours."

I quickly wrote out several deeds and backdated two contracts, whereby Jacob would inherit if anything happened to me. The Czar would probably seize everything I owned after my escape, but I knew Jacob would be clever enough to hide the movable goods and to come out of it a very wealthy man. My lands and other real properties would surely devolve upon the crown, and trying to pass them on could well cost Jacob's head. Still, I deeded a couple of the smaller ones to him, making them appear as sales.

It was dawn before I finished, and the city gates were open. We started for the farmhouse without attracting much attention. Jacob had kept two fresh teams of horses in readiness, one of which pulled our *troika,* while we led the others behind. After a quick breakfast with Jacob's friends, I departed with my family and household in four sleighs, plus the small retinue of mounted retainers. Jacob stood in front of the building, watching us go. He had given me careful instructions on whom to contact, and how to make use of all his preparations. As his figure grew smaller in the distance, the full impact of my momentous decision seemed to strike me. Until this moment I had been so involved with formulating plans and rushing into them with such speed and stealth I had not had the time to appreciate the finality they represented. Already, I had seen Moscow and Novgorod for the last time. Now I was departing from a faithful friend and servant, a man to whom I owed a great deal. But the most important people were coming with me.

I rode in the sleigh with Nina, Anna, and Christiana. Toby was driving. Behind us, Illya handled the second team. Johnny sat beside him, with Demetrius and three retainers behind. Serge drove the third *troika,* with two more of my men and the two Tartar girls as passengers. The baggage was mostly in the fourth, except for the Czar's chest, which rode with us in the first vehicle. We found the river firm enough that we could travel most of the way on its surface. But we had to return to the highway beyond Porkhov, where the river turned south.

Here we encountered our first real trouble, for the snow was well over the horses' heads in some places, and we had to take several detours off the main road. The backtracking and other maneuverings took us miles out of our way before we finally reached the smaller Velikaya (Pskov) River, after which it was an easier passage. But in all, we had lost a good day's advantage. By the time we sighted the city walls, I feared we had narrowed our lead over Ivan's less– encumbered couriers by only a scant few hours.

Because the women were cold and tired, I decided to enter Pskov. They had to have a few hours in warm shelter and a decent meal before we continued. Here again, God favored us. We arrived at dawn to find Simon in command! A besieging army with Andrew Kurbsky as one of its commanders, was less than a day's march away. If the Pollacks surrounded the city before any messages arrived from the Czar, we could be safe indefinitely.

One of my major warehouses was situated in Pskov and it was here I directed our party. Entering the gates as early as we had, very few people saw us, and I doubted that anyone recognized me except for the guards who passed us through. As for Simon, he would have no reason to suspect my plight. Even so, I assumed he would help me, although I did not wish to compromise him. That was a question I would have to resolve immediately. Once my household was settled into living quarters behind our complex of buildings, I set out to talk with Simon.

When I entered his headquarters, my friend was involved in an argument with Daniel Nogtief. The younger general wanted to take a large part of our forces into the field, and to engage the Polish army south of Pskov. Simon, who was senior, would not permit it. He was preparing for a siege. The city's defenses were strong, he explained, and he had already dispatched an urgent demand for reinforcements. He foresaw no difficulty in holding out, well into spring if need be. Besides, his method would cost far fewer lives. I had been greeted warmly by both men, though Daniel and I no longer knew each other very well. We had served together once – a long time before. As he had not been of the brotherhood, I had not spoken to him in years. •

Once I was seated, they returned to their argument, and as it continued I became edgy. I wished Daniel would give up and leave so I could speak with Simon. Several plans were forming in my mind, and I wanted to discuss them with him. If I could get out of Pskov onto the western highway, it would be an easy matter to simply await the advancing army under a white flag. Assuming that Andrew knew we were coming, he would personally see to our safety.

Finally, close to midday Daniel stormed out slamming the door behind him. Then, as I was about to tell my tale to Simon, we were interrupted again – this time by a messenger who reported Polish forces less than thirty miles away. They could be outside the gates by nightfall, or at least by the following day. That made my time very short. When the messenger left, I hurriedly spoke to Simon, explaining everything that had happened and begging him to help me.

He was surprised, of course, and distressed to the point of weeping when I told him of Vanya's death. Nor did he hesitate to offer whatever help he could give, and he confirmed Jacob's report of Kurbsky's being with the advancing Poles. However, he emphasized Andrew was not in command. King Stephen led the forces himself, with Kurbsky as advisor – all of which should make little difference. With Andrew there, I knew we had nothing to fear from the King.

Simon's principal concern was Daniel Nogtief. The latter had seen me and knew I spent the day with Simon. If it should later become known that I had taken my family through into the enemy camp, it could go hard with him. We discussed the best way to work it, and in the end we decided that I should personally wait a day or two before departing. I would thus avoid placing my friend in jeopardy by making it appear I had arrived, reported to him, and promptly deserted. For my family to go ahead of me, however, would probably make little difference. We doubted if Daniel knew they were in Pskov, as my sleighs had looked no different from the usual conveyances used to transport goods. Their movement through the city had not created any interest, being in no way uncommon. My people could leave in the same manner, and once outside the city no one would see them. Even now, every person living near the walls was flocking inside for safety.

With the plan more or less settled, I hurried back to the warehouse and instructed everyone on this final move – all except Illya. He had wandered off, against my orders, and we had no time to look for him. I wrote a short, explicit note to Andrew Kurbsky, telling of the happenings at Alexandrov. I gave this to Toby. Then I guided the group, reassembled into three cargo sledges, out of the city by the eastern gate. I accompanied them on horseback, leading them down the road until we were out of sight from the city. We circled around Pskov to the south, passing far enough from the walls that no one should have seen us. As far as anyone in Simon's headquarters knew, I was escorting a shipment of goods and personal property through the guard posts, seeing it off on the road to Novgorod. Instead, of course, I turned onto the southern highway, where King Stephen's army would find them. I prayed they would be safe; but it was too late to turn back. I could only depend on Andrew's good will and past assurances. After kissing Nina good–bye, I hugged each child in turn, praying it was not for the last time. I turned and rode away, not looking back all the way to Pskov. Instead, I prayed for God to continue favoring us with His Grace.

It had been foolish of me to return. I knew it, almost as soon as I re–entered the walls. I had been so concerned that I might compromise Simon, I had missed my only easy opportunity to escape. Returning to army headquarters, I again found Nogtief having an argument with Simon. He looked up, annoyed, when I came in, but Simon greeted me cordially and I joined their discussion. Daniel had finally prevailed, to some extent. He forced Simon to concede the value of keeping the Novgorod road open. It would mean running a line of defense between Pskov and Duo, near the southern tip of the large lake below Novgorod. The defense should not be difficult, as there would be little chance of a flanking attack by the Poles. They could not circle Pskov to fall upon the defenders from the rear, as the Peipus Lake blocked their line of march for some fifty miles north. Any attacking force would have to travel clear around the water, with its unsafe layer of ice, then fight past the garrison at Gdov.

I bit my tongue to keep from trying to influence them. While Daniel's plan would mean easier access for the Czar's couriers, and hence additional danger for me, his perception was correct. Strategically, it was the only proper decision. When Nogtief finally accepted Simon's alterations to his plans, the latter casually asked if I would accept an assignment. Naturally, I had to agree, and he placed me in charge of garrison supply. This was a job for a man of lesser rank, but he had no other excuse to assign me a duty which would give me freedom to move about the city and through the gates.

I stayed with Simon until quite late, then went to the quarters assigned me. So far, the Poles had not arrived. I was terribly tired, not having slept for two days. Still, I could not afford the time to rest, as it would now be necessary to use Jacob's contacts within the city. I would need a place to hide once I got outside the walls, for with enemy troops moving through the countryside I needed a safe conduct from Andrew before I dared to move beyond our own lines. My future status in Krakow depended strongly on the manner in which I placed myself into Polish hands. If it even appeared I was taken captive, I would probably find myself in prison – even sent to the Sultan for his entertainment. At the time, King Stephen seemed to have made some sort of peace with the infidels. Simon had already told me of his agents' reporting a regiment of Tartars marching with the Polish army. This added greatly to my anxiety over Nina's safety and I prayed it would not be this barbarian element which came upon our three sleighs waiting helplessly for Andrew on the snowy, open plain.

I had just finished throwing cold water on my face to keep awake, when Illya knocked on my door. He had gone to the walls, he told me, to look over the countryside and ascertain how far the sentries would be able to see. He had been detained by the guard, for they were questioning any able–bodied man who was not in uniform. As it was, they had come close to impressing him into the army until he convinced them he was my servant. I offhandedly denounced his stupidity, but I was too tired to say more than a few sharp words to him – or to consider the ramifications of his story. His intentions seemed to have been good enough, and I later had him accompany me while I tried to find Jacob's friend in the merchants' quarter. We were on the street walking in the direction of the bazaars when the long–dreaded couriers arrived from the east. The Czarevitch was dying, they announced, injured in an accident at the Czar's palace in Alexandrov. Prayers were to be said in every church for his recovery. They did not announce Vanya's death, nor the circumstances of the "accident." Nor was any mention made of a renegade prince. The messengers must have been dispatched before I was missed, I thought with relief. They apparently carried no warrant from the Czar, although at this moment I had no way of knowing what secret communications they might bear for Simon. I heard only the public announcement made in the main square. The fact of their reporting only Vanya's injury most likely meant they would soon be followed by the men who would herald his death.

I searched for several hours trying to locate Jacob's contact. But the city was in a frenzy of fear and chaos. The man was nowhere to be found. Even our local representative seemed to have disappeared and the warehouses were securely locked. Two of my guards patrolled outside, but they did not have access to the buildings, only the small guard shack against the wall of the main repository. Finally, I gave up and returned to my quarters. I had to get some sleep. Illya knew who Jacob's contact was, and he went out again to seek him. I slept until dawn.

One of the sentries awakened me as I had requested when our army was assembled the next morning. I dragged myself from bed still feeling heavy with fatigue, hurriedly donned my armor and went up onto the walls. Far across the snowy countryside the first elements of the advancing army could be seen as tiny black forms against the horizon. They moved like so many ants, seeming to emerge from some hidden burrow and spread across the stark white plains. Through the crisp, freezing air of early morning their commanders' shouts carried faintly across to us. We could also hear a distant sound of trumpets as the Polish army was organized into its final order of march. Hopefully, my family was now safe beyond its lines.

Illya returned to me at noon, by which time the Poles had established their basic siege lines all across the southern periphery of Pskov. Our own forces had taken up their defensive positions to guard the Novgorod road, with the smaller gates in the east wall still open to facilitate the movement of troops. Otherwise, the city was completely sealed, presenting a formidable barrier to the attackers. No shots had yet been exchanged, as the Pollacks remained several miles away. Our cannon were in position all along the wall, but with the enemy forces scattered as they were we could have done little damage. Actually, their attempt to take the city did not frighten our commanders very badly. The walls were easily defensible; the garrison was large, and the weather was on our side. Watching from my vantage point it seemed like the early moves in a game of chess with the opposing players maneuvering their forces into the best position for attack or defense. I was still drawing these mental comparisons when Illya found me.

He had contacted Jacob's man, he whispered, and arrangements had been made for me to leave the city just after dark. Illya knew the route we were to follow. I would be met at a farmhouse not far from the outer ring of Russian defenses. From there I would slip across to the Polish lines, guided by one of their agents. Word would be sent back to Pskov that I had been captured, which would relieve Simon of any suspicion. It sounded almost too easy, but I had no reason to doubt Illya's intentions. Besides, he would be with me and his fate would be the same as mine.

I did not see Simon again, other than to observe him when he ascended the wall some distance from where I stood. He acknowledged me with a casual wave, before moving down the line in the opposite direction, inspecting his cannon emplacements. Soon after this I returned to my quarters and made ready to depart. Less than an hour before dark I left Pskov by the east gate. Attended by Illya, I had walked through as if seeing to my duties. The guards saluted, but other than this no one seemed the least interested in my movements as we went on foot along the row of trenches. These were cut into the snow, extending east from the city wall. Garrison posts had been set up in farmhouses and barns, with our nearest large defense force outside the walls of Pskov some two or three miles distant.

With the fall of darkness it began to snow heavily. Huge, weightless clumps whispered down through the black, motionless air. They drifted silently before us, brushing wetly against our faces as we made our way along the line of guard posts. These were set in a wavy, irregular pattern, as Daniel had placed his men where they could use the existing structures for shelter. Still, the men we passed were already cold and grumbling, complaining as soldiers always will. As most of them were peasants they had lived through worse, and I remember thinking that the cold should not have bothered them any more than it would a sleigh horse.

We finally reached the building were Illya said I was to meet the Polish agent and we went inside. The farmhouse was dark and cold, deserted by its owners and not yet put in use by our guards. This, alone, should have made me wonder, because it was directly on our defense perimeter and should have been in use as a command post. I was still too tired to think clearly, I suppose, and too anxious over my family's welfare to concentrate on anything else. After a time, there was a gentle tapping on the door and a short, muffled figure slipped inside. His name was Gregor, he told me. He had been sent by Prince Kurbsky. When I asked him about my family, he hesitated a moment before replying. I looked at him, wondering, but I could not see his face in the darkness; everything was fine he finally assured me.

We left the farmhouse and started across the snow, heading in a generally southern direction. A large barn loomed ahead of us and beyond this was a wide expanse of open field, indistinct in the darkness and drifting masses of white. We had reached the barn and just started to feel our way around it, when a voice shouted for us to halt. My companions broke into a run, and without thinking I followed them. A moment later we were fallen upon by twenty–five to thirty men who had been hidden behind the far wall of the barn. There was less than a moment's struggle, for I was quickly borne to the ground, my face pressed roughly into the snow while my arms were yanked together behind me, and ropes were hastily tied about my wrists.

"Traitor!" said someone in back of me. Several blows were struck against my back and sides. I could not see who hit me, for it was very dark and all the men appeared as shapeless forms of blackness in their heavy fur coats.

I was forced to march, dragged along at a fast trot, back to Pskov. There, I was taken to the city prison, where Daniel Nogtief sat in the commandant's office waiting for me. His dark features leered cruelly as he lounged in his chair, his feet propped up on a writing table.

"I knew you were going to try it," he said triumphantly. "I have suspected your loyalty for a long time."

"My loyalty has never been a matter of question," I replied sharply. "It's your head will be on the block!"

"Would you like to explain your actions this evening?" he demanded coldly.

"I have nothing to explain to you!" I bluffed. "Simon will have you flogged for this!"

"If Simon interferes he will be lucky to keep his own head," said Daniel. He grinned again, as the door behind me opened to admit Illya and my supposed Polish guide.

"These are both my men," explained the general. "Your *former* servant has betrayed you. Have you anything else you would like to tell me?"

I glared at Illya, who hung his head, unable to look at me. The other man was a nondescript soldier whom I had never seen until that night. The trap had been neatly set, but as yet it reflected only the treachery of my servant. Daniel's greed and his anxiety to capture a prominent man in an act of treason might have been his undoing if I did not have to fear the retribution from Alexandrov. He said nothing about a warrant from the Czar, however, and I hoped Illya had not thought to include the telling of this tale in his betrayal. Apparently, so far, he had not.

Daniel amused himself, taunting me with his questions for a short while longer. He had no doubt of my guilt, so I was unable to bully him. In the end, I was cast into a cold, wretched cell on the ground floor of the prison. A pair of guards was posted outside, and I was left alone in total darkness, shivering inside my frigid prison. I dared not call for Simon. There was nothing he could do to help me, for if he tried he would play into Daniel's hands. I knelt on the cold stones, praying that my family had come to no harm. As for myself, I saw no possibility for salvation or escape. All the people who might have rendered aid were far away. Simon, alone, would know where I was, and I hoped he would have the good sense to forget about me. I had finally destroyed myself, I thought. Let no one else suffer for my stupidity. In a way, it was a fitting reward for having turned my back on a lifetime of loyalty and duty.

I finally fell asleep sometime before dawn. My body had become so numb I could no longer feel the cold. The cell was completely unfurnished except for a straw pallet on the floor. But none of my clothing had been taken from me, and I still wore a heavy sable *shuba*. My deep slumber was shattered abruptly by a cascade of sunlight streaming through the bars of my single window – or so I thought in those first moments of consciousness. After a few seconds I realized it had not been the light that jarred me to my senses; our cannon on the wall directly above the cell had begun to fire. The enemy must have moved closer to the city, I thought, and I could visualize our forces to the east as they must have been engaging the forward units of the Polish army. In the distant background I could hear flurries of sharp, staccato reports from firearms.

Sometime after midday, a guard brought me some bread and a bowl of watery soup. He refused to speak to me, probably in compliance with orders issued by Daniel Nogtief. With the Poles attacking, there was little chance of anyone bothering with me. They would all be too busy on the walls. It was a long day – longer, I think, than any I had ever lived before. I could hear the reverberations of battle and all about the prison enclosure there were sounds of bustling activity. I could also hear people moving through the corridors, but no one so much as opened the peephole in my door. I was left alone with my bitter thoughts, cursing myself for a fool. To think I should expect to succeed in escaping with my entire family! How many men of rank and notoriety had been able to get across by themselves? Then, I had passed up my best – my only chance, and returned, to be destroyed by Illya! Skuratof's servant whom I had been such a fool to trust! It was almost as if Malyuta's evil hand were clutching at me from the grave where Toby had sent him. My single consolation was the firm resolve not to add a further blot upon my soul. I would say nothing to aid Nogtief in pulling Simon down with me.

Darkness fell again, and with it came a wave of really bitter cold. My stomach contracted with hunger, while my body trembled in violent spasms of – fear? Cold? Probably both. A strong wind began to howl, blowing in frigid gusts through the open window above my head. There was no way to close it, nor was there any straw or other material to stuff into the opening, unless I wanted to give up my bed. I sat on the pallet, shivering, wondering how long I might survive.

Several hours later I heard some murmured voices – the guards, I thought, speaking together at the end of the corridor. There was a moment of silence, then a man laughed softly as if at some subtle joke. After that, it was quiet except for the continuous rise and fall of the moaning wind. I huddled more tightly into the corner as the freezing gusts seemed to reach for the marrow of my bones. Again, I must have fallen asleep, or at least reached a condition of semiconsciousness. I do not think I had been aware of anything for quite some time.

Then I bolted awake! There was a muffled clink at the door, followed by a shrill creak as it swung inward on its rusty hinges. As it slowly opened, I saw a man peering in, unable to see me as he gestured blindly for silence. He slipped inside, leaving the door half open. He came up to me when I made a sound, my body shifting to an upright position. I could not imagine he had come to help me, and expected he had been sent as an assassin, dressed in the red uniform of a *Streltsi* junior officer – a handsome, blond man, of about thirty or thirty–five years, as best I could make out.

"Keep still and follow me," he whispered. He shoved a pistol into my hand. "Don't use this unless you have to."

Quickly, he led me from the cell and down the corridor, away from the main prison entrance. The building was in almost total darkness, only a lamp in the front, where the guards officer kept his watch. We passed several rows of cells along the passage, but there was no sound from any of them. At the rear of the building was a small door, heavily bound in iron and blocked by two heavy beams. Together, we lifted the bars and pulled the door inward. It had apparently not been opened for a long time, as a cascade of snow fell onto the floor from the drifts outside. Then we were through, running quickly along the shadow of a wall, across into another large structure.

This appeared to be an army supply building of some sort. Unused at the present time, it was empty and unguarded. We crossed the open floor and exited on the far side. We quickly made our way across the city, coming at last to the west wall. This faced the water, where a wide eddy backed up from the lake and had been dug into a moat beneath the parapet. Now, of course, it was frozen.

"We must wait here a few minutes," said my guide. "I have arranged for horses, but they will not be in position until after the next change of guard."

"Who sent you?" I asked. I was sure it must have been Simon, and grateful as I was for the rescue I did not wish him to risk his life.

The fellow smiled at me, a warm and knowing expression – what I could see of it. There was a soft reflection of light off several buildings across from us, although we were concealed in shadows at the base of the city wall. "Don't I look familiar to you?" he suggested.

"There is something. . . ." I whispered. I could not place it, but the man did seem to be someone I knew.

"I have waited a long time for an opportunity to speak with you, but I could never find the way," he said. "I have served under you several times, and on more than one occasion you have said something to me, given me an order or made a remark in passing. But you never realized who I was."

"Then you acted on your own?" I asked in surprise.

He nodded.

"Just because you served under me?"

"Not that alone," he replied, still with that mysterious smile.

"I am confused," I admitted.

"Would it help to explain if I told you my mother's name was Sonya?" he asked. His eyes fastened on my face, and he seemed almost to plead for my recognition. "All my life," he continued, "until she died, my mother told me I should take pride in your achievements, and in your blood. When I was a child, she would take me to see you as you passed at the head of your troops, or when you attended the Czar at public ceremonies. I have always hoped to speak to you," he repeated, "– to have you acknowledge me."

I stared at him, still completely at a loss to understand what he was talking about. Sonya, Sonya – who?"

"What was your father's name?" I asked at length.

Now he looked startled. "I bear the name Furstenberg," he replied.

"Richard Furstenberg," I whispered. I had not thought of these people in years – all the years of this man's life. Richard had been Heinrich's servant, the man whom my stepfather had driven from the house when he was caught making love to my mother's maid, the same Sonya who had crept into my room at night, who had given me my first lessons in the art of love.

I was unable to speak for several moments. So this man was the result of our childhood affair! And Sonya had carried that memory with her to her grave, bringing her son to yearn for the day he would greet his father. "My God!" I groaned. "All these years! Why didn't you ever come to me before?"

He swallowed hard, shuffling his feet uncomfortably. "There never seemed an . . . opportune moment," he said. "I never knew how you might react. You were always so proper and so stern, I was afraid you'd have me flogged if I presumed . . . ."

I threw my arms about him and embraced him warmly. "A son I never knew I had!" I whispered. "God has been kinder than I ever deserved, nor could He have chosen a better time to send you to me!"

The young man cleared his throat before he spoke. "It was not exactly God's decision," he replied, "unless we acknowledge the Lord's guidance in everything we do. I went to your friend Prince Simon and I explained who I was and what I wished to do. He seemed suspicious at first, but I finally convinced him – probably because he saw how much I look like you, or so he told me. He arranged to have me replace the regular officer of the guard tonight, working through two or three others, to protect himself. After some exchange of money, it was done. Then, when my second shift came on duty, I drugged them – not too skillfully, I'm afraid. One looked like he was dead." He watched me unhappily, his eyes brimming with emotion.

"Then you will be punished if they catch you," I replied.

"I had not meant to return," he whispered.

"Have you a family?" I asked.

He shook his head. "They perished when the Tartars raided Moscow."

"Then there isn't any reason for you not to come with me, is there?"

He drew back into the shadows so I could not see his face. "No, there is no reason," he replied softly, "if you will take me."

"If I. . . . To find a son and have him save my life, all in one day, then refuse to take him when I escape? Do you really think me so harsh?"

He embarrassed me by his thanks as we continued to whisper together in the shadows by the wall. Both of us had been so affected we failed to keep track of the hour. Unexpectedly, we heard the tread of guards above us, and quickly flattened ourselves against the stones. We could hear them exchanging sentries down the wall, then fading footsteps as the officer escorted his men to the next post.

We waited another few moments before mounting the wooden ladder to the parapet. A lone sentry stood some distance away, gazing out at the lake. "We have to silence him," I whispered, then stifled a nervous laugh as I gripped my new found son by the arm. "Your name," I rasped. "I don't even know your name."

"Demetrius," he replied simply.

That will present one more complication, I thought, wondering briefly what Nina's reaction would be when she met this child of love. He was nearly her age. "Stay here," I said. "I can probably get close enough to handle the man before he recognizes me."

I walked boldly toward the sentry, cursing my limp lest it cause him to identify me. He turned as he heard my approach. The night was very dark just then, as a bank of clouds moved across the moon. The snow had stopped, though the wind continued to howl, making it difficult to hear sounds at a very great distance. I gripped my pistol, pressing it into the folds of my coat, holding the barrel.

"There is something moving down there, soldier," I said sharply.

He could see I was an officer, but it was too dark to tell much more. He leaned against the battlement, looking down into the frozen moat. "I don't see. . . ."

I left him lying there, unconscious. I did not think I had killed him. I ran back to Demetrius, who had already unfurled a knotted rope and was busy tying it to an abutment. Below, several shadowy forms awaited us, hidden by the narrow lips of darkness beyond the ice of the moat. My son descended first, pulling the rope taut when I swung myself over to follow him.

As we galloped swiftly across the snowy plain, I gazed back at the receding walls of Pskov and knew I was looking at my homeland for the last time. In a matter of moments, I would be crossing forever into the lands of the West. I was an exile, a man with no country. It was thus I would stand before God, and I was very much afraid.

DMITRI'S FOURTH JOURNAL ENDS HERE

EPILOGUE

The following is taken from one of the notes found with Prince Marensky's journals in the hidden compartment of his chest, now in the possession of the Royal Academy:

This morning, I stood on the crest of a grassy hill, gazing across peaceful countryside and wondering if God's curse still lies upon me. This concern grows heavier, for one can never leave such fears behind. Now, with so few days separating me from my inevitable judgment, the past reaches out with cruel, ugly fingers. The old icy fear still casts itself about my heart and I am tormented by a question I am unable to resolve. I can only ask myself what my Czar would wish for me to do.

I have lived here on my estates in Leicester for almost twenty years. I had thought all such problems were long since resolved by the grave if not by someone else's action. Time alone should have lifted these concerns, as it has taken nearly all my friends. It has been so many years since I committed any act of cruelty or even harshness, it seems strange that God should now torture my final hours with dilemma.

The advice I receive is all well intentioned, coming only from those I love. My three sons are all men of substance and dignity and I am a grandfather many times over. My daughter is married to another proper man, who serves his King much as I served the Czar. My blessings on this earth have truly been very great, and God has granted me a long, unmerited period of grace.

When I took my family from Poland and traveled through Luebeck, I expected the Wrath of Heaven to fall upon me before I ever led them to these shores. Yet God saw fit to spare us. Through Ridolfi's German agents we booked passage on a coastal trader which took us into the lowlands where the Earl of Leicester commanded the Queen's forces against the Spanish. Once we contacted Robin, he arranged our passage into England. Later, when he returned, we spent many happy hours together prior to his unfortunate death in the Year of the Armada.

My spirits, so at peace these many years, seem to foretell an everlasting happiness. My Czar is dead – may God rest his tortured soul – and all his progeny have gone to join him. Never again will the House of Rurik sit upon the Throne of Russia. His earthly penance was a death of sadness and unfulfilled desires, but he was spared the full knowledge of his failures. The very madness that robbed him of his proper greatness also shielded him from this. I am told he lived a waking death for two years after my departure, never recovering from his terrible crime, never able to wash Vanya's blood from his body. He begged God's forgiveness in his moments of lucidity, but lived mostly in the despair of madness, wandering the empty corridors of Alexandrov. Boris Godunof acted for him then, and later continued his regency through Feodor's short reign. Now, of course, he has destroyed the other usurpers and sits on the throne himself. I wonder what tortures his mind must endure! He is also mad, if I can believe the reports of English traders to my homeland. So, after him. . . ?

My one great sorrow is in seeing the glorious plans made by Ivan during our youth come to such indecisive failure. Yet the lands of the Volga and others to the east still mark his greatness. No other man has gathered in such territories to swell the realm. For ever after, whoever rules in Russia, he shall be called by Ivan's title. These things mark his greatness, and none can take them from his memory.

My own quandary stems from the request of Nina and my sons, John and Demetrius, who have inherited the House of Ridolfi in England. Wise and skillful bankers, they insist I should avail myself of the fortune I deposited with their grandfather for the Czar. Ivan and both his sons are gone, they argue, and I am the only man alive who can activate the contract. Besides, am I not the rightful heir? Who else of Ivan's blood still lives to claim his estate, they ask me. Thus I must still ponder the Czar's desires. What words will he speak to me when I confront him beside the final Throne of Judgment? Can he forgive me these twenty years of bliss, I wonder. How loud will be his protest to God if I take his gold and end my days as one of the wealthiest men in England?

So even now, my life is not my own. As I have so many times before, I wonder what my God and my Czar would have me do.

GLOSSARY OF NAMES, TERMS AND PLACES

ARBAT – The outer portion of Moscow, generally the slums, or poorer section.

ARCHIMANDRITE – An abbot.

ARQUEBUSK (or ARQUEBUS) – Ancient form of flintlock firearm with an unrifled barrel.

BARMA – A short cape, frequently of sable or other fine fur; although in ceremonials it was often of fabric, such as cloth–of–gold.

BIELGOROD – The middle portion of Moscow, containing most merchant homes, tradespeople's shops and secondary bazaars.

BULSHA DWOANEY (or DVOANEY) – Literally "chief horseman," the medieval Russian equivalent of a sergeant.

BYLINY – A popular song, frequently telling an epic tale.

CHAMBERS – As used in our text, these are the subterranean vaults, or dungeons, where prisoners were subjected to torture and other abuse.

CHEREMISIANS – Any of several tribes of barbarians, inhabiting the areas mostly northeast of Kazan. Generally of lighter skin than most Tartars or Mongols. Probably descended from Finnish stock - kin to the Komi, Mordva, Suomi and Estoniane.

CZAREVITCH – The eldest son of the Czar, the Crown Prince.

DACHA – A large house or mansion, generally owned by a boyar or wealthy noble. It would inevitably have a *terem,* or women's quarters, separate from the rest; a large stable, or possibly a barn behind; and one or more large salons for the entertainment of guests.

DVORYANSTVO – Young warriors of noble birth, frequently the elder sons of secondary nobles, or the younger sons of the boyars.

DYAK – An official of lesser noble rank, literally "servant." They frequently held chancellery posts (or in our simplified depiction of the Russian court, under the Council of Boyars – the Duma.)

EPIPHANY – Twelfth Night, or the twelfth day of Christmas (currently January 6th, although the Russians of our period used an older form of the Julian calendar.)

FREIHERR – A German noble rank, roughly equivalent to baron or knight.

GOSTINY DVOR – The main bazaar of Moscow, located in the Kitaigorod.

GROZNY – The name given Ivan IV by his enemies, and eventually by his own people. It has no exact English equivalent, being most closely translated as "the Terrible," or "the Dread."

GUEST – A literal translation of the Russian word for merchants who traveled from one city to another in the course of their trading activities.

HALL OF FACETS – The great hall in the Czar's Kremlin palace, so called because of the pillars which supported the ceiling, sloping outward at the top, forming four-sided, arched divisions within the greater hall.

ICON – A painted wooden surface, usually not more than 16" by 20", and generally smaller, depicting one or more saints or holy figures. Displayed in churches and homes of the Russian Orthodox, much as a crucifix and effigy of Christ are used in Roman Catholic chapels and houses. Some of these works were deemed to possess miraculous powers to heal or overcome various other forms of adversity.

ICONOSTASIS – A filigree screen, usually in the forepart of the church or cathedral, separating the congregation from the alter. The collections of icons belonging to the particular parish were attached and thus displayed for the laity.

KHAN – A senior Tartar rank, often denoting an independent ruler, roughly equivalent to a King in western nations.

KISTEN – The staff carried by Ivan IV, of which he probably had several. The upper portion was of heavily carved wood with a knob; at the base was a steel sword, or javelin-like point. A potent weapon in the hands of an angry man, it could kill by either a hard blow from its upper end or a jab from the point.

KITAIGOROD – The inner portion of Moscow immediately surrounding the Kremlin. Most of the higher nobility, boyars, and foreign ambassadors who did not reside within the Kremlin had their homes in this section.

KHOLMAGORA (or KHOLMAGORY) – A port on the White Sea, where the British set up their first trading posts. The area was administered from the nearby Monastery of Saint Nicholas. Archangel eventually replaced Kholmagora as the principal port, but the city had not been founded during the reign of Ivan IV.

KHORUGVI – A staff supporting a holy image, usually on a cloth banner.

KLOBUK – A monk's cowl.

KNOUT – A hard, knotted crop of leather or sometimes of fibrous material like parchment, soaked and pressed together, thus forming a heavy cudgel when dried. Popular as an alternate for a whip in questioning or torturing prisoners.

KRESTANI – Peasants; generic derivation seems to be from the Mongol word for Christians, which to them meant lesser beings.

LOBNOYO MESTO (or LOBNOE MESTO) – The place of skulls (literally "brow.") A raised, stone dais, in the Square of Executions (now Red Square) where prisoners were beheaded or otherwise executed in public displays. Also the "town square" often used for reading government announcements.

MESTNICHESTVO – The Russian seniority system, already ancient in the time of Ivan IV. Ivan tried to do away with it, particularly in the army, and during his reign it fell into lesser use and some disrepute.

METROPOLITAN – The office and title held by the Archbishop of Moscow, and a few other cities (e.g., Kiev.) The Metropolitan of Moscow was recognized as the senior prelate of the Orthodox Church in Russia. In rank and power he was second only to the Czar. Shortly after the death of Ivan IV, the Metropolitan of Moscow was raised to the rank of Patriarch, there being only four prior to this time: Constantinople (Byzantium), Alexandria, Antioch, Jerusalem.

MUEZZIN –The Muslem priest who calls morning and evening prayer from the minaret, or holy tower.

MUSSULMAN – The vernacular, old English word for a Muslem.

OKOLNICH – One considered "close to the throne"; originally a boyar rank of second degree, Ivan IV had a number of favorites who held the title without the rank of boyar.

PONOMAR – A church servant, or sexton – one who lights candles, rings the bells, etc.

POSTELNIK – A gentleman of the bedchamber; quite similar to that found in the French or English court. Usually a man of lesser noble rank who is a favorite of the ruler and attends to his various needs during the night, be this to procure the Czar a fresh young virgin or to carry the royal chamber pot.

PRIEST – MONK – The reader may note that priest and monk are sometimes used interchangeably in the text. In the old Orthodox Church a man was frequently both. A priest was permitted to marry; however, this meant giving up his status as monk. As no churchman above the rank of priest could have a wife, all bishops, archbishops, abbots, etc., were monks.

SHUBA – A heavy fur coat worn by boyars and other nobles in winter. Frequently of sable; those of lesser purses had to settle for rabbit or other pelts.

SKOMOROKH – A traveling juggler who earned his living by singing, telling jokes or stories, prestidigitation, etc. Sometimes a spy for the government.

STRELTSI – The soldiers who comprised Russia's first standing army under central command from the Kremlin; founded by Ivan IV.

SULTAN – The Muslem ruler in Bzyantium. The richest and most powerful of the "infidel" kings.

SVYETLITSA – Literally "the large room with windows." A salon for the entertainment of guests.

SZLAK – A network of backwoods trails and paths used generally by smugglers and other brigands.

TAFYI – The skull cap worn by priests and monks.

VLASYANITSY – The hair shirt worn by a true ascetic as an act of bodily mortification. Usually of horse hair.

VOIVODE – A noble of less than boyar rank, but generally higher than a dyak. These men were frequently army commanders or large landholders – "squires," as opposed to "barons," might roughly place the relationship in terms of English nobility.

YURODIVY – "Holy Idiot" or "Fool for Christ's Sake." These were generally looked upon as priests by the Russian people, though many of them had no training as such. They were frequently wild hermits who lived in the woods or caves, and suffered the rigors of such an existence as their method of achieving heavenly grace. Some of these men were reputed to have miraculous powers of prophecy or healing. Some, of course, were simply madmen.